A
DIFFERENT VIEW

Also in the Series

A
DIFFERENT
VIEW

Jane Hatton

About the author

Jane Hatton was a child during World War II, and grew up in the unpermissive fifties, when career options for women were largely confined to Secretary, Nurse, Teacher, Physiotherapist. She opted for the first, thinking the skills required would be useful in her preferred career as a writer, but has also worked in hotels, as a sailing instructor, in a craft workshop and as a cookery demonstrator – a remarkably unstructured career – while continuing to write whenever there was a spare moment: sometimes there were not many! She has had two children's books published in the mainstream (a while ago now), followed by three novels in the genre of "literary fiction", plus The One Too Awful to Mention – which

we don't mention – and has also independently published a long series about the Nankervis family and their friends and relations, all set in various areas of the West Country. Apart from writing, her interests include sailing, painting – including at one time scenery for the local pantomime – archaeology, photography and cooking. She lives in Cornwall, on her own these days, with a small black cat for company and a background of family and friends.

This one is for ELMA, who wished she could be a fly on the wall at the party.

I

Dot watched the departing car until the last flash of the brake lights blinked out onto the road and was gone. Such a vulgar colour, that little car of Deborah's, she thought absently, but her mind wasn't really on this perennial grouse, she had far more than that to think about.

Something had happened over the past hour, and she wasn't quite sure what it had been. If it was meant for an olive branch, it had borne more resemblance to the whole tree, uprooted and flung at her head; it had been flagrant defiance on the part of her two daughters, with distinct overtones of blackmail – and she knew who could have taught them all about that! She should have felt resentful, furious and justifiably hurt at their behaviour, instead, she felt strangely relieved, as if a heavy weight had fallen from her shoulders. A wall of intransigence had grown between herself and Deborah and Susan lately through which there had seemed to be no door, but today they had simply blown the whole construction apart. What happened now, as they had made quite clear, was up to her, and that, she reasoned, had given her back the upper hand.

Or had it?

She had thought that they had made their choices and walked out of her life to join the two highly unsuitable young men that they had chosen over their mother and against her pleading and advice. She had grieved over it, not understanding where she had gone wrong, for surely any reasonable mother would wish to protect her daughter from a working class ex-convict with a conviction for violence and a penchant for blackmail, or, come to that, from exploitation by a vagrant fortune-hunter who lived by his pen on a boat, particularly when her precious grandchildren were involved. But by trying to protect them, she had lost them, or so she had believed.

Except that it now appeared that she hadn't lost them. They were ready to put up a fight, but they were also prepared to discuss making peace. All she had to do was to accept the terms of surrender they offered.

Terms of whose surrender? She suddenly wasn't sure.

The whole business with Deborah and that criminal from a council estate had raised issues that Dot really didn't wish to think about.

1

He had appeared on her doorstep, she remembered with a shudder, after she had offered him more than generous terms to remove himself from the scene. He hadn't been at all what she had expected: she had imagined a small-time crook who managed a public house in a Cornish backwater and served microwaved fast food for his clients so that he could call himself a chef, and had envisaged him as flashily good-looking and on the whole, despicable, specious and blatantly on the make. What she had brought down upon herself had been a full-blown menace that had terrified the wits out of her. Threatening. Solid, pugnacious, and rougher than she had ever dreamed, a big-time yahoo with no scruples, who had turned her one weapon – money – on herself and used it to force her hand. She had found it horribly easy to believe that he had killed his brother-in-law and had, at his brutally expressed instigation, gone to her best-beloved daughter's wedding against her proclaimed intentions.

But not to the reception. In spite of the wonderful smile that had appeared on Deborah's face when she saw her mother in the back of the church, she wouldn't cross that man's threshold, even had she been welcome there, which he had made quite clear she was not. Defeated, she had returned home to Embridge and this big, beautiful, lonely house that had never been the home she had longed for it to be, in spite of the presence of a husband and three children.

Something else that she didn't understand.

They were all gone now: the first husband who had inconsiderately died, leaving her to bring up his child alone, the second husband who had returned finally to his first love, the stepson who had defied her all his life, the dutiful daughter of her first marriage, the joy of her heart that was the daughter of her second. Her grandchildren. She was a lonely woman, legally separated from her husband, whose children had gone off into the world and never once looked back to the mother who had reared, nursed and cared for all three of them, whatever their parentage. Her life had become empty, her friends proved false.

And that last had been that thug's fault, too.

For a minute, Dot had an awful feeling of things slipping out of her control. For her son-in-law, the reviled and feared Mawgan Angwin, had unexpectedly hit the small screen that autumn and metamorphosed into the latest celebrity chef. The public loved him, loved his cheeky grin and rich, creamy Cornish accent, his friendly approach and his obvious talent and warm charm. And he had won his appeal against his conviction for manslaughter and emerged whiter than white, and only she seemed to know that he really was that thug from the wrong side of the tracks that she had correctly taken him for. Worse, all the sympathy her friends had felt for her over Deborah's headstrong behaviour and disastrous marriage had evaporated like snow in a sudden thaw. She had become a laughing stock overnight. She could only feel relief that none of them had ever seen the historic old Cornish inn that she now knew he actually owned, not just managed: that would have put the tin lid on her humiliation. There was no guarantee that none of them ever would, and contemplating this possibility, Dot suddenly found her legs giving under her, and she sat down. It had been a bad morning.

They had appeared unexpectedly, her errant daughters, sweeping up the drive in Deborah's showy, bright-yellow, foreign car: unmistakable, unexpected, and wholly welcome, when she had begun to wonder if she was ever going to see either of them again. But she should have known, she told herself as she hastened to the front door. They had come to apologise, to ask her advice and beg for her forgiveness, as she had always made herself believe that they would.

Only it seemed that they hadn't, not exactly.

'Why, what a lovely surprise!' she had cried. 'Why didn't you let me know that you were coming? I would have prepared a special lunch!' The hug she gave them came from her heart, but she couldn't help thinking that they looked shifty. As well they might, she considered, but nevertheless a very slight cloud of uneasiness crossed the shining sun of her pleasure. 'Come in, sit down, let me look at you both.' Deborah was more than six months pregnant with that thug's child, she looked radiant, lovelier than ever. Dot tried not to think about the father, and continued, 'Oh my darlings, how nice this is! I'll just go and ask the girl to make us some coffee and then we can have a lovely chat!'

She had hurried from the room, and was halfway across the hall before she recognised a *frisson* of ... no, surely not *uneasiness*? Their own greeting, she realised, had been less than warm, but surely they didn't think she would turn them away? She gave instructions about the coffee more thoughtfully and returned to the drawing room, her pleasure in their arrival, inexplicably, very slightly dampened. They were sitting there in separate armchairs, silent; beautiful blonde Deborah, and pretty brunette Susan who, sadly, took after her father's family and had always been overshadowed both by her half-sister and her good-looking stepbrother, Oliver, but a good, sensible girl nonetheless – until recently, that is.

'Now then,' she had said, seating herself where she could see them both. 'What brought you here so unexpectedly? How are you, Deborah darling?' It was impossible to ignore her daughter's condition, even though it stuck in her throat considering who was responsible. 'Are you keeping well?'

'Yes thanks, Mum.'

'I hope you've given up sailing those boats of yours, it won't be good for Baby you know,' Dot said, warningly, for Deborah and her friends ran a sailing school down in Cornwall. Deborah had muttered something that Dot didn't quite catch. She smiled at her and turned to Susan.

'And you, Susan dear? Is everything all right at home? The children aren't too upset?'

Susan had divorced her husband and almost straight away invited her new boyfriend to share the new home she had created down in Cornwall for herself and her two children, Annabel and Sebastian. Another thoroughly unsuitable young man, although not actually criminal so far as Dot knew. He lived on a boat and worked for Deborah as an instructor at her sailing school on the Helford River, and had ambitions to write a book, although Dot had little faith in this ever happening. Susan's money, however, would doubtless enable him to waste time on the attempt.

Getting no real response from either of them, for Susan didn't even bother to reply, she smiled at them instead. 'Well I never, what's the matter with the two of you? Usually, I can't get a word in edgewise and here you are, hardly a syllable between you!'

And so they had told her. What they had said had amounted to blackmail – no doubt in Dot's mind as to who would have taught them that! They were prepared to come to her house and organise a pre-Christmas party for her friends, dinner or a buffet would be her choice. Mawgan would do the catering with help from Susan, Carl would see to the wine, Debbie would do whatever unskilled jobs needed doing. The prestige of having the latest celebrity chef cooking for her party would go a long way to silencing her enemies. The downside, of course, was that she would have to welcome those two young men to the house and thereafter continue to do so. That last was made perfectly clear.

Something else had been made clear, too. Susan knew exactly what her mother had done in the run-up to Deborah's wedding, and presumably also how her brother-in-law had retaliated.

That made Dot feel slightly sick. She hoped that Deborah didn't know too. To cover her shock, she had asked confrontationally, 'And the other young man?'

'He has no idea you ever banned him from the house, I haven't told him,' Susan had replied. She hadn't sounded conciliating.

Nonetheless, the offer was a lifeline. She would have to accept it, but there was not, Dot decided, any need to grovel. She said, 'Will you bring the children, too?' in the voice of one who didn't expect to be refused.

'If it's not in school time, of course we will.'

'But not the dog,' said Dot, taking a firmer stand. Susan's dog was a large black labrador, and in Dot's opinion, he smelt of dog even after a bath and was always underfoot: she couldn't understand what Susan and the children could possibly see in him. Susan laughed.

'No, not the dog. We'll leave him with Chel, or Gosia and Roger maybe. I know he's not your favourite.'

Gosia, or Maria as Dot preferred to think of her, was another sore point. She had been Susan's au pair and had precipitated a frightening family crisis by her negligence, and the man she still thought of as her son-in-law, Tom Casson, had dismissed her out of hand, quite rightly in Dot's view. She had turned up in Cornwall along with the rest of the hangers-on that took advantage of her wealthy daughters, and unfortunately seemed set to stay.

'Well,' said Dot, because she had no options, 'we'll call that settled then, shall we?'

She didn't say thank you, and she didn't press them to stay for lunch. They had made their point, but just for a while, she really didn't want to look at them any more.

Now, in the aftermath of their brief, cataclysmic visit, she found herself wondering how Susan knew, and assuring herself that Deborah couldn't, and on balance, neither feeling very proud of herself nor savouring the taste of defeat.

Defeat, however, wasn't something that Dot felt she deserved, and neither was she going to admit to it outside the privacy of her own head. It was necessary to confront it, yes, but only in order to turn it into a victory. With this in mind, she got decisively to her feet and went to pick up the phone. Time to start restoring her social position, they wouldn't be laughing now, those fair-weather friends!

Alex Hetherington returned from his office at the end of the day, his mind still more than half on a problem that was beginning to go critical, to be greeted, as he came through his front door, by a wonderful smell of beef casserole and a smiling wife with a glass of his favourite whisky in her hand. Ingrid wasn't the sort of wife who took no interest in her husband's business, and she knew all about the problem, although she had yet to learn how it had suddenly escalated. She had some news of her own, she believed, that would make him put it on the back burner.

'Bad day at the office?' she asked, seeing his face.

'No worse than usual, but I'm going to have to do something ... what are you grinning about, woman?' He took the glass and smiled at her. 'Found the secret of the universe? I wish!'

'Not exactly, but I have got something to tell you.'

He grunted, and flopped down to relax in his favourite chair. 'Something good, I hope.'

Ingrid perched on the arm, her own glass of sherry in her hand. 'Very good. And very funny, too, if you're in the mood to be amused. It's about Dot.'

Alex groaned and took a hefty swig.

'Oh no! Not Dot on top of everything else. She's the last person I wish to hear about!'

'No, listen, you're going to love this. Susan and Debbie came up from Cornwall to visit her today.'

'Unwise of them. They should have left her to get over her tantrum on her own.'

'They did better than that. I *think* they gave her an ultimatum, although she didn't exactly put it like that.' No, she wouldn't. But he had begun to look interested. Ingrid reached for the whisky bottle and poured him a refill. 'Anyway, the upshot is that she's thinking of having a dinner party, probably the Saturday before Christmas. "For my family and all my dearest friends" she said, I suppose that includes us?'

'I should think it's *only* us,' said Alex. His tolerance of Dot Nankervis was beginning to run thin. It was, in any case, largely based on his friendship for the late Henry Worthington, her first husband and Susan's father. In spite of the quarter-century gap in their ages, the two men had got on well together. Alex, then an up and coming young accountant, had been recommended to Henry for the handling of his personal tax affairs by a mutual acquaintance from the Yacht Club, Jerry Nankervis, who had also been Henry's solicitor. Henry's business had been worth having: a wealthy investment broker with his work based in London but with his principle residence in Embridge, his patronage and recommendation had sent Alex's star rising fast, and a mutual respect and liking had grown between the two. When he had found himself an expectant father at the age of sixty-five, Henry had drawn up a trust for his unborn child and Alex and Jerry, together with the child's mother, had been appointed as joint trustees. Up until recently, the duties involved had been fairly nominal, but the recent break-up of Susan's marriage to Tom Casson, who to complicate matters worked in Alex's office, had meant that Alex had seen rather more than he really wished to of her difficult mother. He knew Ingrid liked Dot, for reasons that escaped him, but on the whole, he didn't, much. He considered her to be manipulative and destructive and rejected his wife's insistence that she was really rather a sad person, basing his opinion on the fact that her second husband, father of Debbie and incidentally of her half-brother, Oliver, was that same Jerry Nankervis who had been Henry's solicitor and friend. Dot, Alex thought with hindsight, had always meant to have him; he felt sorry for Jerry's beautiful and talented ex-wife.

There was time for most of these thoughts to replay themselves in his head before Ingrid said, 'I know what you think about her ...' very slowly. Alex looked up into her serious face. The laughter had gone from her eyes, and he was sorry. No point in taking his own problems out on Ingrid.

'So tell me,' he said. 'What's the joke about this dinner party of Dot's?'

'Her son-in-law is doing the catering. And, one presumes, the cooking too.'

'Good God! You mean to say he offered, and after all she's said about him?'

'I doubt if he actually knows what she's said about him, and I don't think he so much offered as was volunteered. Wouldn't you agree?'

Alex thought about this. 'Clever of them, if so. Do you think it will work the miracle required?'

'I think that will depend on him, rather than on Dot. Dot's had some salutary lessons lately.'

'She couldn't have known that he'd pop up on her telly and wow everyone.' It went against the grain to put in even a mild word on Dot's behalf, but he said it anyway.

'I think that's rather what I mean. *Be sure your sins will find you out*, or something.'

'Poor old Dot,' said Alex, but it was perfunctory.

'Lucky old Dot, I think you should say, to have such forgiving children. And lucky old us too, if we get an invitation.'

Alex considered this, and found the reflection pleasing. He appreciated good food and the building reputation of Dot Nankervis's unwanted son-in-law was enviable. He sighed and took a sip of his whisky. Life began to look a little better.

'Of course,' Ingrid was saying, 'she may choose to invite the people she wants to make eat her dust, but on the whole, I hope she doesn't do that. It would be such a waste.'

'Far more satisfactory *not* to invite them,' Alex agreed. He went on, as casually as he could manage, 'Did she say how Susan's getting on?' Susan was his god-daughter; he had a soft spot for her and deplored her recent marital problems, which were not unconnected with his own office ones. But Ingrid shook her head.

'No, she was more taken up with her own affairs.'

That sounded like Dot, Alex reflected. He took another sip, and allowed the silence to develop. Ingrid stood up to fetch the bottle and top up his glass.

'Do you want to talk about it, darling? Have you made a decision?'

Alex turned his glass slowly between his hands, looking at the tipping liquid as if he was studying its amber colour, but did not, in fact, see it at all. Alex's troubles revolved around his retirement imminent in the next year or so. He had once planned that Susan's ex-husband, Tom Casson, the senior accountant in the business, would take over in his place, but recent events had begun to change his mind. Without Susan behind him, Tom had revealed himself as a colourless plodder, and moreover one with a shaky sense of loyalty. He had betrayed Susan consistently with a succession of girls, both in and out of the office, until she had thankfully had enough and called time. Tom would never have taken that step himself, Alex realised. He might not love his wife, he might have ignored the welfare of his children, but he wouldn't have left Henry Worthington's money of his own accord, and for that, Alex was finding it hard to forgive him, even if he hadn't believed that lack of loyalty in one respect implied its possibility in others. But the problem remained: Tom *was* senior, and he had never made a serious mistake in his work, even if he had never, on the other hand, showed any particular flair. His private life should be no business of his employer. Alex's impulse to send him packing rather than award him honours was therefore possibly unjustified. He wished he could be sure about that.

He became aware that Ingrid was waiting for his answer.

'Yes ...' He spoke slowly. 'Yes, I think I have. Only, it isn't going to go down well with Tom Casson.'

'Oh?' Ingrid prompted, after a significant pause. Alex took a bigger sip of his whisky.

'You know I had advertised for someone who would fill the gap when I finally retire?' She did know, of course, but he felt it necessary to set out the cards properly.

'Yes,' Ingrid said, cautiously.

'They've been a run-of-the-mill lot, up until today, nothing to choose between them. That might not matter if I'd finally decided on Tom as my successor ... but then, this afternoon ... well, this afternoon I interviewed an applicant who isn't run-of-the-mill at all.'

'That's good, isn't it?'

'Better than you know. He's relocating from London because he's getting married and wants to make changes to his lifestyle. Excellent references, it sounds as if his present employers had plans for him and are sorry to lose him.'

'So why choose here?'

'He's a local lad.' Alex spoke with satisfaction. 'Born and brought up in the area, passionate about sailing which is one reason he wants to come back. His father is chief superintendent here in Embridge, you probably know his wife.'

'Valerie Harries? Yes, I do. Not well, but I do know her.' She paused. 'So, why the long face? It sounds to me like the perfect solution if you think he'll fit in and do the job.'

'Yeah ...' Alex drew the monosyllable out almost into a groan. 'So, what do I do about Tom Casson?'

'Two options?' said Ingrid, on a query. 'Keep him on, or let him go? It seems to me a simple choice.'

'Oh, it's a choice – a straight choice, even. But simple? I don't think so.'

'Because your god-daughter dumped him? He deserved it. In my opinion, she should have done it years ago.'

'And if I give him the boot hard on the heels of that? How's that going to look?'

'I think that would depend on your precise motive.'

'Exactly.'

'Oh dear.' Ingrid held out the bottle. 'Would another one help?'

Alex shook his head with a rueful smile. 'No. I mustn't let Tom Casson drive me to drink.'

'I think,' said Ingrid, slowly, working it out as she spoke, 'that you need to ask yourself what your motive would actually *be*. Because, you see, I don't think that you kept him on all these years just because of Susan. He must also have been competent, or even for her, you wouldn't have done it.'

'He was. "Competent" describes him exactly. Without Susan, he can be seen as exactly that, and not a jot more. She gave him standing, and that gave him a spurious confidence. Now she's gone, he has no standing, no flair and no confidence either. He's an also-ran who does a passable job, no more.'

'Come on Alex! She didn't do his job *for* him!'

'She entertained his clients; she was the social face of his working life, he warmed his hands at the fire of her natural integrity. People judged him by her place at his side. *I* judged him, God help me. Now, poor man, he's standing naked in the chilly winds of reality.'

'And there's me thinking accountants didn't have a poetic bone in their bodies!'

'It isn't funny, Ingrid.'

'No.'

'I just wish I could see the way clear.'

'If he kept his job,' Ingrid speculated, 'and you put ... what's his name? The Harries son and heir?'

'Valentine, poor bastard. Val.'

'All right, you put Val Harries in over Tom's head, what could Tom do?'

'Put up with it, or ask for his cards and walk.'

'There you are then. No problem.'

'His walking would certainly present none. I'm not sure about his putting up with it and staying on. Tom is very bitter over Susan. He would consider it a deliberate slight on my part.'

'And you're quite, quite sure that it wouldn't be?'

'Good God, of course I'm not! What can you be thinking of? No, I genuinely don't think he could handle the position, but he tried to take Susan for a small fortune, pressuring her over custody of the children. If I could do it without ending up in front of a tribunal, I'd get rid of him tomorrow and it would be for entirely personal reasons!'

'Oh dear,' said Ingrid, again.

'If he had any guts at all, he'd go of his own accord. He must realise he's blotted his copybook irretrievably.'

'And his parents are such nice people, too.'

'Doesn't follow, unfortunately.'

'They'll be so disappointed. Sally hasn't said anything, but I know she must be beginning to wonder about all those horrible things he said about Susan, now she's fallen straight into a new relationship.'

'Tom says she's just trying to prove a point and will come unstuck.'

'And do you agree?' Ingrid heard a chill in her own voice, but it wasn't only for Alex. Fortunately, he didn't disappoint her.

'No. I've never met the man, but Susan has too much sense to fall for a line a second time. And she cares very much for her children's welfare and happiness, which is more than their father does for all his fine words. I would hope, and on the whole, trust, that her new partner is a man of an integrity to match her own who loves her for herself and doesn't care a fig for her money. There must be some around.'

'He went around telling everyone she was frigid – Tom did,' said Ingrid, accusingly.

'Well, he would, wouldn't he? It's the oldest excuse in the book for playing away.' Alex sounded tired: to be truthful, he was sick to death of Tom Casson and his affairs. Ingrid stood up. She knew a full stop when she heard one.

'If Dot invites us to her party, you'll very possibly meet him and can judge for yourself. Finish your drink, I'll go and check the casserole. It'll be on the table in ten minutes.'

Debbie dropped her sister off outside the house on the creek side of St Erbyn's main street after a drive that had been mostly silent, but contentedly so. It had been a nerve-racking interview with their mother, but the outcome had been hopeful. Susan, leaning down to peer in at her sister as she went to shut the nearside door, underlined this conclusion, if with moderation.

'I think we can call it a result, anyway.'

Debbie made a face, shadowy in the dim light from the dashboard.

'It's the next move I'm looking forward to – or am I? Are you coming down to the pub later?'

'Might do. If Gemma can babysit and we feel like it. At the moment, I'm just glad to be home.'

'Know the feeling. Might see you later, then.'

She drove away, and Susan went up the short path to her front door. It opened onto a narrow, stone-flagged passage, a large and friendly dog, and a wonderful smell of curry. The sound of chatter and laughter came from the open kitchen door. Susan smiled, happily. Coming home had never been like this in the old days; Annabel and Sebastian would be shut away in their upstairs playroom with the *au pair* keeping an eye on them, and Tom, if he was even at home, would be reading the evening paper in the drawing room with a drink in his hand, very adult and self-centred. She would greet him without getting much response, and go off like a good wife to prepare his dinner with barely a word to her own children, passing on, she now saw, her husband's attitude. It was one kind of a life. Not this one, though.

Preceded by the bouncing dog, she went to the kitchen door and looked in, and her partner looked up from the pan he was stirring on the stove with a smile of welcome.

'Susie!' He put down the spoon and held out his arms. 'Good trip?'

Susan walked into his embrace and was thoroughly hugged. Sebastian, busy laying the table, looked up with a solemn grin.

'Hullo Mummy.'

Annabel, her face serious, was peering at something in the oven.

'Carl, should these come out now? They look done.'

'And how, tell me young Annabel, does an onion bhaji look "done"?' Carl released Susan with reluctance and went to check on the bhajis and Sebastian moved into his vacated place, hugging his mother round the waist, his grin broadening.

'We've been cooking the dinner,' he announced. 'I think it's ready, Mummy.'

It was Annabel's turn for a hug, as Carl took the tray of bhajis from the oven and set it on top of the stove. Her greeting was silent but warm.

'It just about is,' Carl confirmed. 'Do you want five minutes, Susie? You've only just got through the door.'

'Just time for a quick wash and a comb through my hair?' Susan smiled at them all. She knew that she hadn't answered Carl's original question, and that he had noticed that she hadn't, but it would wait.

'I'll pour you a drink for when you come back down,' said Carl, unruffled.

But it wasn't until the curry and its adjuncts had been eaten, the fruit and custard that followed it was only a memory, and the children had raced upstairs to play on Sebastian's computer, that the subject was reopened over the washing-up. Susan, trying to think if she had ever, in her whole marriage, come home to a dinner cooked by Tom and then companionably shared the washing-up, was brought back to the more cheerful present by Carl saying, 'So, was it a successful foray into enemy territory?'

'Not exactly *enemy* ...'

'Not exactly friendly either.' Carl placed a plate carefully into the rack and set about the next one. He didn't look at her. 'I can see her point about Mawgan, but once the situation was explained, surely ...?'

'She loves Debbie,' said Susan. It didn't really explain things. Now, Carl did turn to look at her.

'And you. Be sure of it. Mothers are like that with their children, you should know.'

'Yes.' Susan let out an audible breath and picked up the draining plate. 'But Debbie is her favourite, because Jerry was her favourite husband.'

'Unjust, when your father seems to have been so much the kinder of the two.'

'Are you trying to pick a quarrel?' asked Susan, with interest, but he only laughed.

'No. Just trying to put in some demolition work on your inferiority complex.' He flicked her cheek with a soapy finger and returned to the job in hand. 'I've told you before, you persistently undervalue yourself. Did you tell her it was Oliver's idea?'

'No.' Susan set the plate aside and picked up the next one.

'You should. Oh, maybe not now – after. When the party has been a success and you're all friends again.'

Susan stopped drying the plate and looked at him curiously.

'Why, particularly? I mean, you said that as if there was a reason.'

'There is. She's your mother. Work it out.'

'I can't,' said Susan, after a pause spent trying.

'I've not met her yet, but isn't it possible that you and she are alike in more ways than the bossiness you say you inherited from her?'

Susan thought about it. 'You mean *she* has an inferiority complex, too? Nah!'

'Consider it as a possibility. Chel says that nobody thought you had, either, until you fell off your perch.'

'Oh did she?' Susan was indignant, but only momentarily. The statement was too true to challenge, for one thing. She had, she knew, hidden her private self behind her talent for organisation, and *that* she certainly had inherited from her mother. Deb too, but Deb had the confidence that came with knowing exactly who she was. Susan, up until recently, had never even known that her natural father had three much older children from a previous marriage. The discovery had been both a shock and a revelation. She thought about it now. The thought took her into an unexpected byway. 'Actually, I know very little about my mother. She's almost as much of a mystery as my father was.'

'Surely not. You grew up with her.'

'Well yes, but she's hardly ever talked about her family. I must have rather taken her for granted, I can't think of one thing I really know about her except that she was an only child.'

Carl considered this for a moment, while continuing to pile plates onto the rack. 'Keep working, we'll be here all night. Didn't you know your grandparents?'

'Depends what you mean by "know",' Susan said, considering. 'They were still alive until I was almost in my teens, and we went to see them, duty visits like Sunday lunch, Boxing Day, you know the kind of thing. Usually just me, and Deb after she was born ... and Mother, of course.' She paused.

Carl picked up her discarded tea towel and placed it back into her hands. 'Dry. Not Oliver?'

'No. Not Oliver, not as we got older. They didn't like him, he was too direct for them. He said what he thought.'

'And they didn't say what they thought?'

'No,' said Susan, thinking back. 'I don't believe that they did. But they did say he was rude, and to be fair, he often was. It was very uncomfortable if he was there.' She picked up a plate and began to dry it. When the pause had gone on for too long, Carl broke it.

'So, what were they like, apart from not liking Oliver?'

'They weren't keen on Jerry, either, come to that. They were very religious, and he was divorced, of course, and Oliver was his first wife's child. Carl, I'm sorry, that's really all I can remember. Grandma died when I was about eleven, some illness, heart or something and

Grandpa followed her not long after, for no particular reason I ever knew. Someone said that he couldn't bear living without her, I remember, but people do, don't they? Say that, when ...' She tailed off and picked up another plate. 'I can't remember missing them. Sad.'

'Go on,' prompted Carl, after a pause.

'I can't. There's nowhere to go *to*, that's it.'

'It can't be. She's your mother, for God's sake! You have to know more than that.'

'She went to boarding school,' Susan offered. 'All very jolly-hockey-sticks, she was Captain of Games or something. I don't think she was particularly academic. I get that from my father.'

Carl asked, idly, 'And did you go to boarding school, too?'

'Oh yes. Oliver and I both did. Oliver went to Winterbourne, and then on to uni, and I went to a B-list place called Griffon College and then got married to the first man who offered.' She had named two public schools, one big and eminent, one not. She had stopped drying the plates again.

'Now, stop that!' Carl commanded. 'Lots of people feel that education is less important for girls, even today, and we already know your mother is one of them. And Griffon College is OK, even I've heard of it. What about Deb, did she go there too?'

'No,' said Susan. 'No, she didn't. She went to the college in Embridge – not the Art School, a posh private school for girls. And she was a daygirl, at least up until the fifth form she was.'

'Didn't she want to board?'

'I don't think she was ever asked. Mum just didn't want to part with her.' She put down the tea towel again and turned to him, and Carl gathered her into his arms, tossing the dishcloth into the sink with a splash behind her back.

'Come on, that's enough. Snap out of it!'

'Sorry.' She stayed where she was for a moment or two, and then pushed him away. 'I'm tired, and it's not been an easy day.' She resumed the drying of the plates, and went on, more lightly, 'Did you go to a public school?'

'Me? Heavens, no! We didn't have that kind of money – or ambitions, come to that. I went to the local comprehensive – it was a good one, but even so, and on to a redbrick university – one up on Mawgan, though, if you look at it like that. Personally, I don't.'

'*Several* up on Mawgan,' said Susan, on a sigh. 'And Oliver didn't exactly go to Oxbridge, come to that.'

'What did he study?' asked Carl, curiously, and Susan made a face.

'Social Science, can you imagine it?' She dried the last plate and placed it on the pile. 'He only did it to annoy everyone. He nearly got sent down for drugs, scraped a third class degree, and then ran away to sea.'

'And he's been running ever since, if you want my opinion – which I daresay you don't.' Carl pulled the plug and spread the dishcloth to dry. 'That's that, then. D'you want to go down to the Fish later, mull things over with the tribe?'

'No,' said Susan, considering. 'Not really. Deb did suggest it, but I think I'd rather chill out in front of the telly once the kids are in bed. Chel and Oliver will be minding their young anyway.'

'Deb must be shattered too, if you are.'

'Oh, come on Carl! You know her better than that! She's thriving, even the prospect of moving house in the New Year doesn't seem to bother her – even though they've no furniture worth mentioning. She just says she's looking forward to hitting the January sales, I ask you!'

'Not having any furniture will make it that much easier,' Carl pointed out. 'The stores will simply deliver it. She's a one-off, your sister, I'll say that, so what will she make of being someone's mum, do you think?'

'A right pig's ear, I would suggest. Are you coming?' She paused on her way to the door, suddenly aware of a space behind her. 'Carl?'

'Just something I've been wondering about,' said Carl, slowly, not moving to follow her.

Susan bit her lip. She thought she knew what was coming: she had been waiting for it, since Carl was an intelligent man, but please, not tonight! Today had been bad enough.

'What's that?' she asked.

'I *haven't* met your mother. Not even spoken to her, and yet we've been living together for quite a few months now. Your Dad, yes, often. Your brothers and sisters and cousins, but not your mother.

Does she ... well, put it another way. Is Mawgan her only problem?'

The problems her mother had with Carl ranged from his age – three years younger than Susan – through his living on a boat when she met him, all the way to his not being Tom Casson. Susan, said, on a note of desperation, 'I think she'd prefer it if we were married.'

'Well I'm with her on that one,' remarked Carl, by the way. He saw her face and took a quick step across the room towards her. 'Don't look like that, Susie.' He caught her outstretched hands in his. 'It's not a criticism, just a comment. I know how you feel on the subject, and that's fine too. So, did she ban me from the house as well?'

'Sort of,' muttered Susan. 'Not just like that, not like with Mawgan, she just said, well, if we got married ... but she's no right to – to *bully* us like that.'

'No,' said Carl. 'She hasn't.' And it had made Susan even more stubbornly opposed to the idea, he could feel it. He said, trying to speak lightly, 'Well then, she'll have to learn to make the best of things, just like the rest of us. And don't look at me that way. I love you, I'm not going anywhere.'

'It's not about you,' said Susan, but they had covered this ground many times already. Carl gave her hands a squeeze and dropped them, spinning her round to face the door.

'March. It's time for a drink, if we're not going out.' He made his voice deliberately light, for of course it was about him, at least in the sense that it was about any man who wished to marry her, and even more, the one who had done so. But he wouldn't push her, and he was angry that her mother had. Surely she realised what Tom Casson had put Susan through? Or did she put the blame on Susan, so carelessly sidelined all her life? For a second, Carl felt quite murderous, but where was the point, really?

'Did those two do their homework when they came in from school?' Susan was asking.

'So they said. I confess I didn't check. Have you done yours?'

'I should hope so! I did it yesterday, I've college tomorrow.'

The awkward moment had passed. They went into the living room together and Carl poured two brandies from the bottle on the bookcase. He handed Susan's to her and raised his own.

'To tomorrow,' he said. 'From the looks of you, it can only be better.'

'Amen to that,' said Susan.

Just as Susan had done, once she was away from her sister and in the peace and comfort of her own home, Debbie began to suffer from reaction. It was all right to begin with; the friendly familiarity of the flat above the bars at the Fish was welcoming, and Mawgan had drawn the curtains and left the lights and the fire switched on. She sank into one of the big leather armchairs, propped her feet on the coffee table, and prepared to be lazy. She was tired, she realised; Susan had insisted on doing the bulk of the driving but she had done her share, and even just sitting in the car, when some other party was kicking seven bells out of your intestines, wasn't exactly restful. Travel seemed to excite the young Angwin; just like his father he was shaping up to be a live wire. She gave a deep sigh of contentment and wondered if she was hungry.

Then the goblins began to gather in the corners, and her contented mood evaporated.

It wasn't a very happy feeling, remembering what she and Susan had just done to their mother. Yes, Mum had been stubborn and intractable but surely, the ultimatum they had issued had been unforgivable? They *loved* her, for God's sake – yes, in spite of everything, they *did*. Had that undutiful confrontation been a suitable expression of filial affection?

No, it probably hadn't.

On the other hand, what had been the alternative? To leave her lonely, or to bow to her decree and only visit her on their own, without Mawgan, the father of her own unborn child, or Carl, the star of Susan's suddenly summer sky.

Acceptable? No. But neither was what they had actually done. She hated to think how their mother must have felt, must be feeling now. Her eyes went to the telephone – but no. They had administered the medicine, better not to interfere with its effect or the dose might be wasted. She couldn't do it again, that was a dead cert.

Looking at the phone seemed to have set off a chain reaction; it rang. Debbie dragged herself from the depths of the chair and picked it up. 'Fisherman's Arms.'

'Deb,' said her brother's unexpected voice. 'Tommy said you were back. I'm in the bar, fancy a drink?'

'Oliver! Honestly, I'm shattered, I don't think I could face the crowd, but thanks anyway.'

'I'll bring one up then. I suppose you'd better not have alcohol, orange juice?'

Suddenly, Debbie wanted his company. She said with relief, 'Pineapple, please. With ice.'

'And have you eaten?'

'Not yet. I'm not hungry really, and I can't be bothered to cook.'

'Be honest, you *can't* cook! I'll order you a steak down here, they can send it up. Five minutes.'

Before she could argue, he had gone. She went back to her chair and flopped back into it. She was surprised that Oliver was here, he and Chel weren't such regular visitors since the birth of their daughter, but she was glad that he was. Come to think, Oliver was about the only person she wanted to see right now, and that included her husband.

It was nearer to ten minutes before he finally appeared, bringing with him three cans of beer and two bottles of pineapple juice but no glasses. 'I knew you had some up here,' he explained. 'Where are they? In the kitchen? I'll find them.'

'The bottle opener is in the drawer,' Debbie mentioned, without getting up. He grinned at her, sympathetically.

'Not been a good day?' He diverted into the tiny kitchen, appearing soon with a glass in each hand. He handed the juice to his sister before sitting down in the armchair opposite. Debbie said, 'Did you leave a message where we are – in case Suse comes in?'

'Tommy'll tell her. So *you* tell *me*, how did it go? I felt a heel leaving you both to do it when it was my idea, but it really wouldn't have helped if I'd come too.'

Debbie shuddered at the bare idea, and took a gulp of juice. 'To start with, she just harped the old song, but when we said we weren't prepared to visit her on our own, she ... well actually, it was rather sad. I felt awful, Oliver.'

Oliver said, gently for him, 'You'd have felt worse if you hadn't done it. Believe me.'

20

'Yes. You're right of course, but that doesn't seem to make it better.' She paused. 'I thought at one point, Suse was going to chicken out, and I'd have been glad, Oliver. I really would.'

'But she didn't, I take it. And neither did you.'

'No.'

'So is the party to take place?'

'So it seems. I don't quite see what you mean it to achieve.'

'Reconciliation – of a sort – obviously. Surely that'll be worth something?'

Debbie let out a long, unintentionally weary, sigh. 'I feel it all goes a whole lot deeper, and honestly, it makes me feel tired. Just tired. What can we do? Really?'

Oliver considered before he answered. There were two ideas in his head, but he wasn't sure where either of them was going. He and his stepmother had never got on, in fact he actively disliked her, but he also considered that she was a very unhappy woman, some of which was his fault. That was one thing. The other was more difficult to pin down. He had – no, not exactly *disliked* Susan, but found her very easy to quarrel with, for most of his life. Susan was like her mother in some ways, but not, it now appeared, in others. She had turned out to be bitterly unhappy too, and frustrated which might have been more fundamental. In retrospect, ninety per cent of her confrontational attitude had been defensive. Now, with a different partner, happy children, a new family and a satisfying career as an archaeologist in her sights, she had become another person. Still abrasive, but that was Susan. Strong, loyal, level-headed and ... well, fun to be around. And he and Chel owed her the survival of their marriage and also, he had a suspicion, the survival of their baby daughter, who thanks to her quick wits had been born safely in a hospital, and not messily beside the road on the way home. The big question was, how far could you equate Susan with her mother? Or the other way about? None of them, not even Susan, had ever met her father, which made it hard to evaluate.

A lot of Susan's problems had stemmed from her feeling herself to be an outsider. Insecurity, in fact. He didn't want to follow that path to its logical conclusion.

Fortunately for Oliver, before he found himself too deep in the mire, the door opened to admit his brother-in-law, bearing a tray that he dumped unceremoniously onto the coffee table before stooping to salute his wife.

'Deb, I heard you were home, everything OK? I got five minutes, then I must go back down.'

'The party's on, if that's what you're asking.' Debbie leaned forward and lifted the cover off the plate that sat on the tray. 'Wo! That never came from the pub.'

'I thought you might need cheering up.' Mawgan exchanged a glance with Oliver. 'Hi, glad you're here.' He didn't enlarge on this, but went on to ask, ever practical, 'I don't suppose you've any idea of when she wants it?'

'No, but knowing her, she won't consider your priorities, so be prepared for just before Christmas.' Debbie knew her mother well enough to know that she would only concede what had been forced from her, and while she grieved for it, she also slightly sympathised: it must have been a bitter pill to swallow. She was relieved when Mawgan took her guess calmly. He had, she knew, been forced into agreeing to the plan – *plot*, rather – in the first place, although she fortunately had no idea of exactly how little love was lost between her mother and her husband, or for what reasons. Oliver, who had done the forcing, had no idea either which was perhaps fortunate too, for he would have found his stepmother's behaviour impossible to condone, and come to that, might have had trouble with Mawgan's, too.

'Not a problem,' Mawgan said now, cheerfully enough. 'One advantage to having a top quality chef, with enough experience to trust, is the chance to slope off now and then. Doug will love it.' Doug was Australian, highly talented, and in Debbie's opinion the best thing that had happened to Mawgan for years; he might even have the chance to know his own son when the time came, which hadn't looked like an option before.

'Does that mean we can take more than one night?' she asked, hopefully, but Mawgan only laughed and said "We'll see, shall us?" and stood up, ready to leave. 'See you later bird. Have an early night; I'll probably be late, we've a full pack tonight.' He was gone, leaving behind a sensation that the air was settling in his wake. Oliver grinned.

'He doesn't improve, does he?' he observed. 'Eat your dinner. It looks too good to waste.'

The subject of Dot seemed to have been shelved, rather to Debbie's relief. She picked up her knife and fork and looked with appreciation at the juicy fillet steak sitting on her plate, that she should probably not be eating at this time of night, but intended to enjoy anyway.

'So how's the family?' she asked, digging in. She had only seen Chel and little Zoë yesterday, but it felt as if she and Susan had been away for a year after the day they had spent.

'They're fine,' said Oliver. He opened his second beer and poured it expertly. 'Chel's up in the air – she had a piece of good news this morning that set her off.'

'Oh?' asked Debbie, when he didn't go on. Oliver took a swallow of his beer. 'Her mother rang, it seems that brother Mike is quitting the army and coming home for good.'

'That must be a relief,' said Debbie. Chel's brother Mike had been in some hotspots and given his family not a few bad moments over the years. She looked at her own brother curiously. 'You haven't ever met him, have you?' It seemed unlikely, when you considered how long Oliver and Chel had been married.

'No. It's never worked that way. Tracy and Tom and the monsters, yes, often. Richie and Louise and that small child whose name I can never remember, once or twice. Mike and I have always managed to miss each other.'

'He's Chel's favourite,' stated Debbie.

'I know.'

'What's he going to do when he's home? Help run the shop and take over when Chel's Dad retires?'

'I don't know, but I would doubt it. After the life he's lived the past fourteen years, I imagine a village shop will be very small beer. On the other hand, since I don't know him, perhaps that's his dream for civilian life.'

Debbie smiled, she was feeling better by the minute. 'Looking at the rest of the family, I think I'm with you. For heaven's sake, he's Candy's uncle!'

'A sobering thought. It almost makes you sorry for the enemy, doesn't it?'

'What was he? Royal Artillery, or something, wasn't it?' It was an idle question; since neither of them had ever so much as set eyes on the absent Mike. A pause filler, Debbie, thought, and Oliver said, as idly, 'Engineers. REME.' All right, make that an *awkward* pause, then. Debbie decided that she was too tired to backtrack to her original question, and that it would be a shame to spoil a good steak. Mawgan's brief interruption had been timely, she decided; if they tried to talk tonight, they'd only get bogged down, and it was becoming apparent by now that Susan had decided to call it a day. It seemed that Oliver had come to the same conclusion, for he smiled across at her and raised his glass.

'Here's to your bright eyes, Deb. You're looking better, when I came up you looked grey and shattered.

'*Merci du compliment!*'

He stayed for another half hour, talking about this and that, but never Dot, until Debbie had finished eating and set the tray aside, declining his offer to make coffee on the grounds that it gave her indigestion these days if she drank it in the evening. 'It's the one thing he can't seem to take,' she explained. 'He tosses and turns all night. It's such a weird feeling, having another person inside you.'

'It must be,' said Oliver, unable to imagine it.

'I can't believe how Chel overlooked it.' Her sister-in-law's child had come as a complete surprise – not to say shock.

'She had other ideas in her head,' said Oliver, quietly. 'Deb ... there's something we need to discuss with you, I'm not sure if this is the moment.'

'Depends what it is.'

'The christening.'

'Sounds simple enough to me. You are having one, then?'

'Chel wants it, and it'll please all the parents. Anyway, we want Suse to be Zoë's godmother.'

'So where's the problem?'

'We thought,' said Oliver, not meeting her eyes, 'that it might be nice to leave it a month or so, and do the two of them together.'

Debbie thought about this, on the face of it, practical idea, and immediately saw the big snag that made it questionable. She

24

understood Oliver's reticence. 'I can see the advantages, of course,' she said, feeling her way. 'A lot of people will be asked to both, so killing two birds with one stone is the obvious thing to do ... but Oliver, you do realise, it'll mean asking Mum. We can't not.'

'That,' said Oliver, carefully, 'was the general idea.'

The first thought to enter Debbie's head was that she really didn't want to think about this one tonight, the second was that she might sleep better if she did.

'I see .' She hesitated, and was relieved when Oliver gave her a sudden brilliant smile.

'No you don't. I'll tell you.' But even so, he hesitated. Debbie waited.

'The thing is,' said Oliver, feeling his way towards something that he only half-understood himself. 'The thing is, Chel and I think she ought to be there for Zoë's christening ... but the way she's going these days, if we asked her, she'd very likely throw the invitation in our faces. This way, she's got – well, space to manoeuvre, I suppose it would be.' Then, as Debbie was still silent, he said, impatiently, 'Oh, come on Deb! She brought me up, for whatever reason, and she tried to do her best. It was me that didn't, and look where it's got us all!'

Debbie found her voice. 'You want to offer an olive branch?'

'Not want to, no. I just think – and Chel agrees – it's something we have to do. Me, particularly. It's time to bury the hatchet, deep, deep down where hopefully we can never find it again. If last summer's shenanigans proved nothing else, it proved that.'

'Last summer's ...?' Debbie felt herself to be in such alien territory, she was almost afraid to speak.'

'All that business over Annabel and Sebastian. She'd slammed the door in your face, she'd finally bullied Susan into a full-scale revolt, she was desperate not to lose all of you. That stood out a mile. Chel said she'd ridden her horse into a canyon, and knew it was one way only, no room to turn round. I only know that it all had a distinct flavour of total panic. However unlikely it sounds, she was shit scared of losing everyone, is all I can think of.'

'Manipulating Tom over the custody issue wasn't the best way to deal with it.' It felt odd to be arguing with Oliver against her mother, but it had to be said. Oliver laughed, without mirth.

'Deb, darling, your mother has never worked out the *best* way of doing anything. That's her problem. Nonie says she was often almost certain that she meant well, she just didn't have the knack of bringing it off.' Anona Theodorakis was his own godmother, once a close friend of his mother, privy to all the secrets and uncomfortably clear-sighted. His father thought so, at least. She wasn't afraid to speak out, either, and some of the things that she had said had brought Oliver up short, as in the past they had made Jerry break stride and sweat a little too. She had once said, among other things, that Dorothy Nankervis didn't know how to be loved – not *be lovable*. *Loved*. Oliver was still trying to work this one out. He didn't repeat it now to Debbie.

'It all ended happily, that's one thing,' said Debbie, now. Almost, both she and Oliver thought, as if she was making excuses for her mother.

'Yes,' said Oliver, not without relief to be past that hurdle. 'So, shall we do that?'

Their conversation had covered so much ground in such a small space of time, that for a moment Debbie couldn't think what he was talking about. She stared at him for a blank moment, and then said, in relief, 'Oh, the christening! Yes, of course. It's only common sense when you think about it.'

Oliver had finished his third pint. He put the glass down. 'Then, if you've finished licking that plate clean, I'll put all this in the kitchen and go home to my wife and daughter. And you should follow your husband's advice and take yourself to bed. You've had a long day.'

Debbie grinned at him.

'Pregnancy isn't an illness, you know. But if you insist, I'll probably have a good soak in the bath and take a book to bed. Will that satisfy you?'

'Yes.' He gathered all the glasses and plates onto the tray and picked it up, standing for a moment looking down at her. 'Sleep well, Deb. Sweet dreams.'

'Oh, go home and polish your halo, you!' She stood up so that she could reach to kiss his cheek. 'You want to watch it, brother mine. You're in danger of turning into a normal human being since you became a daddy!'

'That'll be the day.'

When she had shut the door on his departing back, Debbie wandered back into the flat and stood for a moment, uncertain what she wanted to do, in spite of what she had said to Oliver. She felt better, for in spite of its slightly curious final direction, their talk had done her good, she wasn't sure why. She no longer felt as if they were banging their heads on a brick wall over their mother; although she couldn't see how, she began to hope there might be a way through, over, or even under her intransigence. If they could find it, that is. She made a face, although there was nobody there to appreciate it.

And then, an odd thought came into her head.

Since their father had returned to his first wife, he had become a different man. With his parents reunited and his mother in a way reconciled with him, so too had Oliver. There was a clue there, if only she could find it. And Susan, reunited with her natural father's family, stretching her intelligence on a degree course, and living with a man that she had chosen for herself, was unrecognisable.

So, what had their mother been trying to achieve?

The answer to that question might be interesting to know. She thought no further than that.

II

Two days later, her natural father's family turned up on Susan's doorstep, in the form of her niece, Liz.

'I guessed you'd be here,' she said, stepping over the threshold into her aunt's embrace. 'How are you, Auntie Sue?'

'I'm fine.' Susan was almost two years junior to her niece, something about which Liz never failed to tease her. 'What are you doing here? You should have rung, we might have been out.'

'On a wet November Saturday? Worth taking a chance, wasn't it? I made an excuse to Paul, and I don't put any money on his not checking up on me. I've brought my toothbrush, may I stay? Is there any coffee going? I'm parched!'

Swept into the kitchen in the path of her impetuous relative, Susan reached for the kettle. 'There soon can be. What do you mean, you made an excuse?'

Liz plonked herself down on a chair by the table, pushing her fingers through her mop of dark, curly hair in a gesture of despair. 'I just wanted a break from him. He wanted to come down to Devon for the weekend, and I didn't want him there. That's all.'

Susan raised mocking eyebrows. 'Love's young dream on the wane?'

Liz giggled, regrettably, and made a funny face. 'Oh, blah, you sound like a novel!'

'You should know,' said her aunt. Liz was a best-selling novelist.

'A *bad* novel,' said Liz, severely. 'It never was love's young dream Suse, you know that. Just fun, while it lasted.'

'And it isn't fun any more?'

'I just need a break from him,' Liz repeated, suddenly moody. 'Where's the lovely Carl?'

'Upstairs, correcting proofs. And the kids are off with their mates, rehearsing for the pantomime; Annabel's going to be some kind of apprentice genie, Seb is first urchin or something, under protest, he wanted to be back row of the chorus. So if you want to tell me about it, I can listen and we won't be interrupted.'

'I don't think there's anything really to tell.'

'No burning resentment? No regrets? No spent passion?'

'No. None of those. I don't know.'

'Boredom, then?'

'Not even that, really. Just ...'

'You need a break. I get the picture. Well, you're always welcome here.'

'It isn't,' said Liz, accepting a cup of coffee, 'that I don't quite like the man, although I do realise the family don't, much. It's just that I think he rather makes use of me. I've heard him, you know, showing off to people – "Liz and I are off to *our* country cottage this weekend" – our cottage, you notice. It's *my* damn cottage!'

'Well, he is a bit of an arsehole,' said Susan, cheerfully. 'Even Carl says he's a pretentious idiot, and he's Carl's publisher!'

'Not exactly,' said Liz, cynically. 'One of the senior partners snapped him from under Paul's nose. But I take your point.'

'Why not just give him his marching orders, if you feel like that about him?' asked Susan, curiously.

'Because ... oh, because he's someone to go to parties with. He's a good lover. He's better than being alone.'

'That sounded really, really sad, Liz! There's lots of good fish in the sea.'

'Not swimming my way, there aren't. Waldren Stavey is a bit short on storybook heroes.'

'Does it have to be a hero?'

'Of course. My standards are high, you know.' She grinned, suddenly. 'I don't know, Suse. I just seem to have fallen into a bog, somehow.'

'Welcome as you always are, running away doesn't seem to me the best solution.'

'I'm not running away, I'm taking temporary cover. I might feel better, after a weekend off.'

Susan doubted this, but she didn't say so. Instead, she said, 'Why don't we go upstairs and disturb Carl, and drag him down to the Fish for lunch?'

'What about the kids?'

'Not a problem. It's Ben's birthday, Morwenna is taking them all to the Kaff for lunch when the rehearsal is over.' The Kaff was actually the Rosebud Café-Bistro, a spin-off from the more prestigious *An Rosen Gwyn*, alias the Rose down by the water, and these days belonged to Mawgan, but in the eyes of the village it would always be "the Kaff", harking back to its deplorable past as the Kosy Kafé. Ben Jenkin was Seb's best friend, Morwenna well on the way to being one of Susan's. Liz heaved a half-envious sigh.

'It all sounds so ... so like real life.' Absently, she removed the glasses she wore in preference to her contact lenses for driving, and began to polish them on her sleeve. Her eyes, without their protection, looked big and lonely.

Susan said, gently, 'But it *is* real life, Liz. Friends and kids' parties, and lunch at the pub. Pantomimes and going to work and coming home again. Family on your back all the time.' She paused there. Liz looked at her curiously.

'You said that last bit with real feeling. Problems?'

'Yes and no. Not really, or maybe yes ...'

'Make up your mind, why don't you?' Liz looked amused.

'It's just a bright idea that Oliver had. He seems bent on reconciling Deb and me with Mother, and the other way about.'

'Gracious!' Liz returned her glasses to her nose, the better to contemplate her aunt. 'That sounds like a recipe for disaster! But then, I've often wondered if Oliver is entirely in this humdrum mortal world.' She paused. 'Why does he want to? I wouldn't have thought he even cared, one way or the other.'

'It seems that he does. I was a bit surprised too – and the odd thing is, Liz, that I don't think it was entirely about Deb – *or* me, come to that. It was about her as well.'

'That proves it. He *is* bonkers! I knew it.'

Susan wasn't prepared to discuss it too much with Liz: Liz didn't know Dot, even though she was, sort of, Liz's grandmother. All Liz knew was the family lore she had grown up with, none of it flattering, and inherited prejudices are the very worst kind. 'I'll go and get Carl,' she said.

Carl was perfectly happy to be interrupted, correcting proofs is nobody's favourite job. He came downstairs with alacrity and Susan's dog, Clinker. Carl's study had originally been Seb's bedroom, and when Seb wasn't home, the dog often oozed his way in, apparently for comfort rather than company. Several times now Carl, on getting up to find something, had stumbled painfully over a large black labrador lurking quietly and unobserved in the shadows at his feet. Neither of them, as Susan didn't hesitate to point out, seemed to learn from their experience.

'Are we taking Clink with us?' asked Liz, eyeing the animal doubtfully. Liz was more of a cat person herself.

'Might as well.' Susan swept the empty mugs into the sink. 'It won't be busy down there, not in November. I'll just find my coat and put a comb through my hair.'

Left alone together, Liz and Carl eyed each other. 'I didn't know we were expecting you,' said Carl, not accusingly but more in query.

'You weren't. I invited myself for a couple of nights. Do you mind?'

'No, not at all. Paul not with you?'

'Not this time. No.' There was a pause. Then Liz said, against her inclination, 'You asked that almost as if you expected he would be.'

'No, not really. I just thought he said he was going to Devon this weekend when I spoke to him the other day, that's all, but I must have got it wrong.'

'He thought he was,' said Liz. 'He hadn't actually been invited.'

'Does he have to be?' Carl sounded surprised.

'He doesn't seem to think so, at least.'

'That old taken-for-granted thing? Beginning of the end, Liz, trust me. I'm a bloke.'

'I would call that one of the best reasons on earth for *not* trusting you,' said Liz, with a sudden grin. 'To be honest, if he upped and offed with some other woman, I wouldn't cry about it. But he doesn't.'

'Then you do it. Get a life.'

'The thing is,' said Liz, thinking it out, 'I'm convenient. He likes his country weekends – mostly at my expense, come to that.'

'Good God! Get rid of him!'

'But then I'd be a sad thirty-something without a partner, like someone in one of my own books.'

'I would have thought you were the expert on that situation,' said Carl, with deliberate mischief. Liz gave a reluctant laugh.

'You'd think so, wouldn't you? But I don't have to tell you, of all people, that life doesn't, on the whole, imitate art, not even our art.'

'True. Not word for word, certainly.'

'All I want,' said Liz, plaintively, 'is a bit of time to myself the odd weekend, to do what I want to do. It's not much to ask, surely?'

Carl narrowed his eyes at her, to be truthful slightly startled by this artless confidence.

'As bad as that? That's not –' He broke off, with a slight shake of his head. 'No, forget I spoke. He probably just likes to get away from London, I know I would.'

When Susan came back to the kitchen, the three of them, four with Clinker, strolled down to the Fish together, and the subject of the persistent Paul was shelved. Not entirely to their surprise, they found Chel and Debbie there, sitting at a table by the fire with their heads together.

'What, deserted your litter?' Carl said. 'You've never left that poor baby with Oliver!'

Chel looked round, smiling. 'Oh, hullo! Of course not, he's in his studio, working, I wouldn't trust him with a budgie when he's up there! Gosia has her, and anyway I'm off home in a minute. I've just finished in the office, I only stopped for a word with Deb about yesterday.'

'Too much information smacks of a guilty conscience,' said Liz. 'How are you, Chel? How's motherhood? I never fancied it myself, I have to say.'

'Have you time for another before you dash off?' asked Carl, preparing to head for the bar, and Chel said that she probably had since her babysitter was the best on the block. 'And since you asked,' she added, to Liz, 'motherhood is all I hoped. What are you doing here?'

'If anyone else asks me that, I shall go home again,' Liz complained, sitting down.

'She's avoiding Paul,' explained Susan.

'It sounds awful, when you put it like that,' said Liz, ruefully. 'True though. I am.'

'Couldn't you just have asked him if he'd like to stay in London this weekend?' asked Debbie, curiously.

'I did. He just said he needed to get away and he'd see me this morning.'

'Does he know you won't be there?' asked Chel.

'I told him so. I'm not certain he was listening though, he might turn up there anyway. Tough!' She saw Chel's face. 'Look, I told him. Can I do more?'

'It sounds as if he wasn't so much not listening as he didn't believe you.'

'Bit of both, on current form. Forget him, I want to.'

It came into Susan's head that Liz, just as she had accused Chel, was protesting too much. Maybe she had a genuine problem with the absent Paul. She hadn't time to consider this properly before Chel said, 'Deb's been telling me about yesterday. It sounds as if the party is on, then? Oliver seemed to think so, last night.'

'It looks like it. Although, I can't say I'm looking forward to it with anything but trepidation.' Susan picked up the beer mat in front of her and began to play with it abstractedly. 'It could be an utter disaster. Quite possibly will be, in fact. But I suppose we have to try.'

'What party is this?' asked Liz, and listened to their explanation wide-eyed. Debbie had none of Susan's inhibitions, the Worthingtons weren't her family after all, and expounded Oliver's startling idea in detail. Carl, returning with the drinks half way through, brought up a chair and sat down in silence, pint in hand; the plan had smacked to him right from the start of a last ditch enterprise; it might well end up in the kill-or-cure category. He had never met Dot, of course – Dot had seen to that – but he had heard about her, and seen the misery she had wrought in Susan during the summer. He wasn't entirely sure that he even wanted to meet her, come to that, except that it was obvious he would have to, sooner or later.

'Goodness,' said Liz, when she had all the details in place. 'That's ... that's ... well, would *daring* be too strong a word?'

'What else could we do?' asked Susan. 'Think about it Liz: she wasn't going to give way on her own, we had to make her somehow.

And this fell into our laps, when Mawgan went on the telly and all her friends saw what he was really like and laughed at her.'

'Some friends,' observed Liz, with unexpected sympathy for Dot.

'That's another thing, of course.' Susan looked pensive. 'It seems she hasn't that many after all. Not what any of us would call friends, anyway.'

'*As ye sow, so shall ye reap,*' Liz suggested, but Susan only sighed.

'Sometimes, I think that all her good intentions got good-intention fly, or something. I'd swear she means well most of the time.'

'She's your mother,' Chel pointed out. Debbie said nothing, she seemed to have distanced herself from the conversation, allowing her mind and her eyes to wander. She wasn't sure she agreed with Susan anyway, their mother's intentions over Mawgan had been overbearing and without sympathy, not *good* at all; Susan hadn't been there, she didn't know. She didn't want to condemn Dot outright, but she wasn't prepared to concede mitigating circumstances on such slender evidence either. She simply reserved judgement and hoped for the best while preparing for the worst. Then all of a sudden, her wandering eyes became fixed in surprise.

'Liz?' she said, interrupting Susan who had begun to speak – in defence of Dot or not, nobody was ever going to know. Something in Debbie's voice brought the discussion to a halt.

'What?' asked Liz, surprised.

Debbie, still looking beyond their own group, said, 'Did you actually say to Paul where you were going to be?'

'I can't remember. Possibly. Why?' Debbie met her eyes, and she turned hurriedly to look over her shoulder. 'Oh *God*! *Now* do you see what I mean?'

Paul had spotted them. He walked easily across to join them, sure of his welcome; lean, darkly good-looking and well aware of it. 'Liz!' he said, stooping to kiss her affectionately. 'Hullo everyone. Surprise!'

'Shock, more like,' muttered Liz, but almost inaudibly.

'Carl!' Paul gave Carl a familiar slap on the shoulder that made him wince and spill his beer. 'Good to see you! We're all very excited about the book!'

Liz gave him a sardonic look, being familiar with that particular old bromide from her own early days; it was just something that publishers and agents tended to say automatically, and nearly always in that same enthusiastic voice that no sensible person would ever take seriously. It was the publishing equivalent of "hullo, how *are* you?" and meant about as much. She was pleased to see that Carl had all the cynical appearance of a man who knew a conditioned reflex when he saw – or in this case, heard – one.

'Hullo Paul,' said Susan, feeling that one of them ought to say something. Paul threw himself, uninvited, onto the seat beside Liz and put an arm round her shoulders to give her a quick squeeze: Liz looked wooden. He beamed around the company, pleased with himself.

'I guessed I'd find you all here when there was nobody at the house. Would you believe it, this silly girl thought it would be too far for me to drive to Cornwall on top of a week's hard work? Little does she know how far I'd go to be with her! Eh, Liz?'

'Apparently,' said Liz. She looked across at Susan a little wildly. 'But I'm staying with Auntie Sue, you know, not here in the Fish.'

If that had been a cry for help, Susan couldn't throw a lifebelt, her impeccable upbringing forbade it. She mumbled something about Liz's friends always being welcome.

'I knew you wouldn't mind,' said Paul, inaccurately. He leapt to his feet again. 'Who's for a drink? Chel?'

Chel, too, stood up. She said, 'Not me thank you, Paul, I was just going.'

'Me too.' Debbie jumped to her feet beside her. 'Got work to see to, letters to write. See you, Paul.' Their departure was swift and businesslike. Paul raised enquiring eyebrows at those who were left.

'Carl, my friend, another beer? Liz? How about you, Auntie Sue?'

Susan wouldn't let that pass, manners or no. 'Make that Susan,' she said, not as nicely as she might have. 'I'm not your aunt, after all. Actually, we were just about to order lunch.'

'Great, I'll fetch the bar menu, shall I?' He gathered the empty glasses together. 'What was your tipple – *Susan*? G'n'T?'

It was hopeless. Susan said she'd have a glass of house white, thank you Paul, and Paul betook himself to the bar.

'Ought I to go and help him?' asked Carl, irresolute.

'Certainly not, he can manage four glasses perfectly easily – or make two trips, who cares?' Liz sounded cross. 'I'm so sorry, both of you. Would you like me to take him away?'

'Can you?' asked Carl, interested, and Susan shook her head.

'Since he's here, you'd better stay, it might look odd if you didn't. But what on earth did you say to him?'

'I was trying to let him down lightly,' said Liz, guiltily. 'I just said ... well, more or less what he said I said, I suppose. I never thought ...'

'Letting people with the hide of a rhinoceros down lightly never works,' Carl told her. 'You'll have to do better than that.'

'Like what, for instance?'

'A good kick up his pretentious backside might do the trick.'

'Ooh, Carl! And there's me thinking you were Mr Nice-Guy!'

'Never mind Liz, it was a nice try. We can bear it.' Susan sounded resigned. 'Only I have to make it quite plain, if he wants to eat out tonight, you're on your own. Saturday night is family night in our house, the children come first except on really special occasions.'

'Oh goodness, of course that's understood. I suppose,' Liz added wistfully, 'it wouldn't be fair if I refused to go out, too.'

'Serve him right if you did, except we'd all be stuck with him – oh, ssh! Here he comes.'

Lunch wasn't the cheerful occasion it might have been; it became dominated by Paul. Paul had plenty to say on every conceivable subject (although his favourite was Paul Attwood) and was happy to say it at length. He beamed on the company and patronised Carl with an encouraging pep talk for "new writers", totally disregarding Carl's previous successful career as a journalist, drawing Liz by inference into a conspiracy of superiority, and he more or less ignored Susan, who had no connections to his world of books and publishing. By the time they all got up to leave, he had every one of his companions thoroughly irritated, and Liz, in desperation, suggested that the two of them might go out for the afternoon, have dinner somewhere, and leave Susan and Carl to get on with their work and look after their children.

'Great!' said Paul, expansively. 'We'll take your car, mine's running a bit rough, I was planning to take it into the garage in your village, but as you weren't there ...' He shrugged his shoulders. 'I expect it'll get me home, but let's not push it, shall we?'

Liz gave a snort of laughter, she couldn't help it. 'Oh Paul! If you were planning to let Ole Jarge Pryor dig around in your engine, you're a better man than I am! He's the mechanical equivalent of a large and destructive landslide.'

Carl and Susan parted from their unexpected guests, the welcome and the unwelcome, in the pub car park where both of them had left their cars, Liz by arrangement, Paul by assumption, and walked up to the house with Clinker, who had been unusually quiet under the table all through lunch. Clinker didn't think much of Paul; he wasn't alone.

'What she sees in that self-aggrandising plonker, I shall never know,' said Carl, as they reached the gate. It was the first thing he had said all the way. Susan tried to be fair.

'He did get you a contract.'

'He did. Mainly because it made him look clever, be sure.'

'At least he's not your editor.'

'No. Interesting, that.' Carl said no more, but went straight upstairs to his study, and Susan wandered into the front spare bedroom to check that it was ready for guests. Once there, she sat down on the bed and contemplated the wrecked weekend. It would have been great if it had just been Liz, but there was something about Paul, quite apart from his boastful manner, that she simply couldn't like. She thought that it was possibly the way he sponged off Liz; she had very little doubt that there was nothing whatsoever wrong with his car, but if they used Liz's (which was a sports convertible, fast, powerful, eye-catching and fun), it was cheaper – from his point of view it was cheaper. In fact, in a word, that was what Paul was. Cheap.

Something needed to be done, but the only person who could realistically do it was Liz herself, and so far, she wasn't being very successful; for some reason her heart wasn't in it. She needed, thought Susan crossly, someone to step out of one of her own novels, sweep her off her feet and punch Paul on the nose very hard indeed to make him go away. If only life was really like that! She had once punched her own ex-husband on the nose with a similar end in view; she thought about it now with nostalgia. Shame, really, you couldn't make a habit of it.

Annabel and Sebastian, returning tired and over-excited from the pantomime rehearsal and Ben's birthday lunch, greeted the news of their unexpected visitors with sulks; like the dog, and everyone else come to that, they didn't think much of Paul.

'Oh Mummy, must we?' Annabel whined.

'Yes, we must,' said Susan, firmly. 'Anyway, you like Liz.'

'We *love* Liz,' Annabel contradicted. 'Couldn't Poncey Paul stay at the Fish?'

'*Who?*'

Annabel went red and muttered something inaudible.

'Anyway,' said Susan, 'they won't be home until after you're in bed, I daresay, and tomorrow they'll be gone.'

'Liz too?' asked Seb, but Susan said she didn't know, and almost added that by this time, she didn't care, either. 'Go up and do something quiet until teatime,' she ordered. 'And don't disturb Carl, he's meant to be working.'

'It's Saturday,' said Annabel, sticking out her lip.

'It's starting to rain,' said Susan, as if that ended it.

'But –'

'Look,' said Susan. 'We aren't any happier about it than you two are –' she caught Annabel's eye, and her parted lips, and continued hastily '– about Paul *or* the rain. Just go upstairs and be quiet for an hour, give us a break, then we'll think of something. OK?'

Reluctantly, they went. She went into the dining room, where her work station occupied a corner by the window, and switched on her computer. On opening up her email for a quick check before beginning work, she found one from her sister.

Sorry we ran out on you, rats from the sinking ship, but that Paul could bore for England! He's just parked his car in the car park and gone off, the presumptuous moron, Mawgan isn't amused. Watch this space! And cheer up, it can only get better! Love and squeaks, Deb: Chief Rat xxx'

Susan smiled, she couldn't help it. Then she dismissed the message and brought up the website she wished to consult, and an hour passed happily. At the end of it, feeling calmer, she shut down the computer and, as she had promised, went in search of the children.

They had their bedrooms in the converted loft space, and both of them were in Seb's, playing on his game boy. The rain rattled down on the sloping window in the ceiling, there might even be hail in it; Liz and Paul would be having a miserable afternoon. Susan knew that she should have told them to come up to the house and relax in the warm on such a horrid day, and was ashamed to find that she wasn't sorry she hadn't. Paul really did bring out the very worst in her. Annabel jumped to her feet when her mother appeared. 'Hullo Mummy! Are we going out?'

'I shouldn't think so. I thought you might like to come downstairs, the pair of you, and make fudge, and some biscuits for tea. You can tie some of the fudge into little packets to give your friends at Christmas, I've got some coloured transparent paper and some ribbon.'

'Oat biscuits!' These were Seb's great skill, he got to his feet eagerly. It seemed that the hour's quiet had done everyone good, Carl too. They found him already downstairs in the kitchen, making tea and whistling under his breath, and so the four of them spent a sticky, happy afternoon together, more of a family, Susan caught herself thinking uncomfortably, than the original family had ever been. The children were full of anticipation for Christmas, only a few weeks ahead now, chatting happily of what they would do with their cousins in Devon, the ponies they would ride, the fun of having Christmas on their Uncle's farm. Unlike last year, when Susan had felt a desperate need to be with her Nankervis family, and drawn them all together under this roof, this year would be spent with the Worthingtons. Oliver and Chel and their little daughter would be going to St Ives, where Jerry and Helen, finally reconciled, would welcome them for the first time under their shared roof: Debbie and Mawgan would be off to St Austell as usual as soon as the restaurant closed on Christmas Day. Once, this would have made Susan feel insecure and unwanted: how her life had altered!

The evening meal had been cooked and eaten, four rounds of Cluedo had followed it; then baths and bed for the children, disgracefully late as it was a Saturday. Susan and Carl had settled down for a peaceful evening of books, music and a bottle of wine, since there was nothing but soaps and game shows on the television, and the level in the bottle had fallen noticeably before Liz reappeared, alone. Susan, hearing the front door open and close, got up to greet her returning guests and found her niece standing in the hall, dripping, and dashing the wet out of her eyes with her hands. For an instant there, Susan would have sworn she was crying, but on seeing her Liz's face broke into a smile. 'I'm wet,' she said, unnecessarily.

'I see you are. Leave your coat in the cloakroom, it's warm in there, it'll dry.' Susan paused. 'What have you done with Paul?'

'He's parking his car,' said Liz. She turned away abruptly, and Susan remembered Debbie's email. For the first time, she wondered if it had been meant as some kind of early warning.

'Uh-oh.'

Liz had vanished into the small cloakroom but she hadn't closed the door. Her voice, floating back into the hall, sounded muffled, but that might have been the coats. 'We went into the bar for a drink when we got back, and Tommy said he couldn't leave it there.'

'What, just like that?'

'He was quite polite about it. He said the restaurant was busy, and the car park was for customers only. And Paul said, he *was* a customer, he was buying a drink.' Liz emerged at that point, and met Susan's eyes ruefully. 'Well, he had a point, didn't he? But Tommy said, he'd just driven up in *my* car, and his own had been parked there all day.'

'So?' Susan prompted, when the dribble of information seemed to have dried up, and Liz simply stood there, looking miserable. 'Oh, come on!' she said, taking Liz's arm, 'come and sit down and have a glass of wine, and tell us all about it. That isn't all, I know!'

Seated in a comfortable chair with a glass of a rather good red in her hand, Liz continued with her unhappy tale. 'You know Paul. He hates to be caught wrong-footed, and especially in front of other people, and they were all listening. Instead of just saying "sorry mate, I'll shift it when we go," like any normal person would, he put on that awful talking-to-the-peasants voice he has, and said "My good man, I'm family!" And Tommy said, "No you ain't. *She* is" and just nodded at me.'

"Oops," mentioned Carl, and Susan asked, 'So what did Paul say to that?'

'He said, we always left our car there. And Tommy said, "*her* car", and then there was a sort of deadlock. Tommy hadn't got our drinks, and he and Paul were eyeballing each other and the bar had

40

gone horribly quiet. Somebody had to say something, so I said I'd move mine then, I didn't mind, and Tommy just said no need, I had the boss's permission to park it down here when I came, and Paul somehow decided from that, that Tommy was acting on his own authority and demanded to see the manager. Well, Chel was long gone, so that left Mawgan.' There were definitely tears in her eyes now, of fury or of remembered humiliation, or simply misery Susan wouldn't have liked to guess.

'I can see Mawgan'd have really liked that, with the restaurant full to overflowing,' said Susan, when Liz had fallen quiet again.

'He was very reasonable to begin with – when he finally accepted he had to come away from his kitchen,' said Liz. 'Impatient, but reasonable. He said what Tommy said, that it wasn't a public car park, and he didn't like his customers having to park where they could in the village. He said he was sure Paul would understand he couldn't start making exceptions or there'd be no end to it and he even managed to sound friendly when he said it. But Paul–' She broke off.

'Wasn't having any? Well, there's a surprise.' Carl looked cynical.

'He asked where else he was going to park it, did Mawgan think? – asked quite rudely, actually. Because there were no spaces down the street. And Mawgan said that he didn't really care, just shift it, please, or he'd have it towed away – this is the abridged version, you understand. You really don't need to hear it all.'

'So what happened in the end?' asked Susan, curiously.

'I don't know. I left when Paul claimed again he was family and we always parked there, and called Mawgan "some upstart so-called celebrity chef from the boondocks, too big for his clogs", and the people in the bar began muttering. I just ... left, and walked here in the rain.' She made a helpless gesture. 'I'll never dare show my face in there again. How *could* he?'

Carl got silently to his feet and refilled her glass, and Susan said, bracingly, 'Of course you will! It wasn't *your* quarrel.'

'Guilt by association?' said Carl. 'Susan?' He held up the bottle and she picked up her glass and offered it for a refill. 'I wouldn't worry, Liz. Mawgan is nobody's fool. As the saying goes, he knows how many beans make five.'

'I felt I ought to move my car, too,' said Liz. She wiped a hand under her eyes. 'Sorry, I'm being a fool. But it's always been so great down here, and now I shan't ever feel quite the same. Why couldn't the idiot stay in London?'

'I hope you didn't,' said Susan, forcefully. 'Move your car, I mean.'

'I couldn't. Paul had the key.'

'Well good. Mawgan said a long time ago that you could park there whenever you came, he won't go back on it, whatever Paul said, even if the restaurant has rather taken off lately. And I doubt if he blames you for anything Paul does, either.'

'I feel as if I'm taking advantage now.'

'Well, don't. You aren't. Oh bother, who's that?' as the phone began to ring. Susan went to answer it, and came back into the room with it in her hand. She held it out to Liz.

'It's for you. Mawgan.' Liz took it as if it was red hot, so that Susan felt constrained to say 'He doesn't bite, you know.'

Liz said nervously, 'Hullo?'

'Liz! Sorry you had to listen to all that. I just wanted to say, you're welcome here any time, car and all.'

'Well ... thank you.' She hesitated. 'Did he move it – the car?'

'Did'n have much choice, did he? Blokes in the bar was all set to go out and move it for him, so he had to, you could say. Reckon that'll be a while before he comes back.' He spoke with satisfaction.

'I thought you might ban us,' said Liz, uncomfortably.

'No need for banning you, bird. I told him he could come back when he was ready to apologise to Tommy – and everyone else too, time he'd done! If it weren't for you, he'd have found himself banned for life, no messing.'

Liz thought about the scene in the bar. 'That's generous of you. He was way out of order.'

Mawgan said, gently for him, 'See him off Liz, he's no good to you, then none of us don't have to put up with him. Look, I got to go, I've a full restaurant. Just don't be upset about it none.' He was gone, before Liz could find a word to say. She switched off the phone and handed it back to Susan. The tears she had been trying to fight back ever since she returned from the Fish trickled unheeded down her face.

42

'How could he,' she said.

'Mawgan? Or Paul, are we talking about?' asked Carl. He refilled her glass and put it back into her hand. 'Come on Liz, cheer up! It's only a storm in a teacup, for God's sake!'

'Is it?' Liz took the glass and sniffed, inelegantly. She brushed angrily at the tears. 'Sorry. It's not being a good day, is it? And I was so looking forward to being here.'

'It wasn't your fault he followed you – and without being invited,' retorted Susan, with more heat than she had intended. 'Carl, be an angel and go and fetch Liz a tissue, there should be some in the cloakroom.' She waited until he had gone, and then put her arms round her tearful niece. 'Come on Liz, nobody's blaming you. He'll have to go back to London tomorrow, and we can enjoy the rest of the weekend just like we planned.'

'I think I'd better go too. Go out and come in again, don't they say?' Liz managed a laugh. 'Mawgan's banned him, did he tell you? Until he apologises. Hell'll freeze over first.'

'That's good, then. He won't bother us again.'

'I wouldn't put money on it. I know Paul better than you, he'll turn it all round. It'll be Mawgan's fault, or maybe Tommy's, you just wait and see.'

'Why do you put up with the arsehole?' asked Carl, returning, but that scene had already been played, there was nothing more to add.

It was some time before Paul finally appeared, far wetter than Liz had been and seething with rage. When he had hung up his soaking wet jacket and dried himself as best he could on the cloakroom towel, he came into the living room and flung himself into a chair.

'What a bloody awful evening!' he exclaimed, leaving it unclear whether he meant the weather or the recent *fracas* at the Fish. Carl poured him a glass of wine and handed it to him with a smile.

'Should've stayed in London,' he said, apparently guilelessly, and Susan gave him a look. Liz said, because someone had to say something or it would look odd, 'Did you park the car OK?'

Paul snorted. 'Eventually. I had to go right up by the church before I found a slot, and even then some old bat came leaping out at me to say it was "her man's" parking spot, and I had to move. I told her straight, it was a public road, she didn't have rights in it, and she went off.' He sounded satisfied with himself.

'It took you long enough,' observed Susan, thinking that poor Paul wasn't having a very good night one way and another. It turned out it was even worse than that.

'I went up to your sister's place first,' said Paul. 'I thought she wouldn't mind, but soon as I turned the engine off, that sailing instructor bloke – what's his name, Ronnie?'

'Roger,' said Carl, quietly.

'Roger, then,' said Paul, impatiently. 'Whatever his name is, he erupted out of the door and asked my business. As if it was any of his!'

'It was, actually, if you were on our premises,' Carl pointed out.

'I told him I was just parking the car for the night, and he said what that oaf at the pub said, it wasn't a public car park! I told him I was staying with you.' Paul sounded hurt. 'He said, did I have permission! I ask you!'

'Sounds a fair question.' Carl took a lazy swig of his wine. 'And then?'

'I said I was staying with his boss's sister, and he said, did Carl give you permission then? And I said nobody would mind anyway and blow me down, he took out a mobile phone and rang your sister then and there!' He looked at Carl severely. 'You should have a word with that young man, if you're Deb's partner. He takes too fucking much on himself!'

'Roger is an equal partner,' said Carl, and left it there.

Susan asked, 'So what did Deb say?'

'The idiot asked, had she given permission for anyone to park there, then he just turned to me and said, "she says no. So I'm sorry, you'll have to go somewhere else." Then he said to try up by the church, where I'd already been, and he stood there waiting until I'd driven away. Stupid idea, living in a place where you can't park a car, anyway! All those narrow streets, and no car park! What do people do in the summer, for God's sake?'

'Park in a field at the top,' Susan told him. It was true that parking in St Erbyn was tight: only the main street, whose residents, including herself, parked their cars down one side, was wide enough to do so, the rest of the roads being mere lanes and too narrow. People with houses set back from the road were luckiest and could park off-road. Carl left his car permanently at the sailing school, where Paul had tried to park. It was hard luck on Paul, but on the other hand, nobody had asked him to come.

'And that's not the end of it,' said Paul, turning to Liz. 'Your aunt's precious brother-in-law has banned us! What a carry on just over a car!'

'Banned *us*?' asked Liz, before she could stop herself.

'Tommy told him some tale that we had been abusive, which *you* know isn't true, although I didn't hear you standing up for me!' He glared at her.

'You *were* abusive,' said Liz, unable to help herself. 'You spoke to him as if he was some serf from the Middle Ages.'

'Rubbish! I was simply trying to reason with the moron! God in his heaven, he's only the barman! He took too much on himself.'

'What do you mean, "only"?' Liz asked, but Paul ignored her.

'When Angwin came in, he didn't even ask me for my side, he was looking for trouble, and we all know what *he's* like!'

'Do we?' asked Susan, apparently of the ceiling.

'Of course we do! Everyone knows, it's in the public domain! I tell you, I wasn't going to argue with him!'

'But you did,' said Liz, still contentious. She met his fulminating eye and explained further. 'You did argue with him. You said –'

'Never mind that!' Paul interrupted, brushing her unwelcome intervention aside. 'The upshot was he said we needn't go back, because we were banned – but you'd gone by that time, of course.'

'He didn't ban me,' said Liz. 'I'd done nothing.'

Paul said, as one who was making a great concession, 'I suppose Angwin had to back up his staff, but he took it way too far! He made me look a fool in front of everyone! I tell you, I shan't be going near his pub *or* his restaurant again until he apologises!'

'That'll teach him,' murmured Carl, almost to himself, and it was Susan's turn to glare. He grinned back at her, unabashed. Liz got to her feet.

'I'm going to bed, I think – it's nearly eleven, good gracious, look! It's been a ... a long day,' she ended lamely. Susan hurriedly leapt to her own feet.

'I'll come up with you – see you've everything you need,' she said, hastily. Paul held out his empty glass.

'Is there any more, where that came from? I need to get very, very, drunk.'

'So generally speaking,' remarked Carl, when their guests, the welcome and the unwelcome, had finally left around mid morning on the Sunday, 'you wouldn't call that a successful visit?'

'Definitely not.' Susan shuddered. 'I wish Liz hadn't felt she had to go too, though. It makes me feel awful.'

'Don't. She was wise. And she'll be on the phone tonight, you wait and see, or if she isn't, you can ring her. It's all right.'

'I suppose so,' Susan agreed, on a sigh. 'Aren't families the limit, really?'

'I sometimes think it's what they're for,' said Carl.

'And *you* didn't help,' Susan accused him, but he only laughed at her.

'Now don't you try and pick a quarrel with me! Cheer up Susie, the man's a conceited oaf with the manners of an opossum and all the charm of a black widow spider, let's forget him.'

Alas, it proved impossible. Within ten minutes, Paul was back on the doorstep, incandescent with fury and practically incoherent.'

'Just come and look at this!' he spluttered, gesturing angrily to the street. He had parked, or possibly simply abandoned, his car with its nearside wheels on the opposite pavement, obstructing traffic and pedestrians alike so it was fortunate it was Sunday.

'Another smart bit of parking,' said Carl admiringly. Paul hardly noticed.

'Just come and look what those bloody vandals have done!'

Susan and Carl, with Annabel and Sebastian crowding curiously behind them, followed the furious Paul down the path and out into the street. Once there, it was obvious what had angered him: the offside of his gleaming BMW was decorated with a message, etched deeply into the paintwork: EMiT GO HOM. They all stared at it, with various degrees of blankness.

'Oh my goodness,' said Susan, stifling laughter, for if it had been anyone but Paul it wouldn't have been particularly funny. 'What an atrocious bit of spelling.'

'Bloody kids, up on that estate there!' Paul fumed. 'They should be locked up until they learn some respect! Of course, nobody knows a thing about it! In fact, they were bloody offensive!'

'Never mind,' Carl offered, consolingly. 'You had to take it to a garage anyway, you can have it resprayed at the same time.'

Paul stared at him, uncomprehending. 'What? What are you talking about?'

'You said you had engine trouble,' Carl reminded him.

'Oh yes, that.' Paul reddened, and to cover his embarrassment, swung round on the children. 'This is probably the work of friends of yours! If you hear them boasting in school tomorrow, you just tell me, I'll sort them out!'

Annabel backed away a step. 'Our friends wouldn't do something like that.' Both she and Seb, and come to that, Susan and Carl too, could have made a guess at the villain responsible, but the name of Damien Tregear wasn't going to pass any of their lips; this time, for once, they were all on Damien's side. In any case, her statement was technically quite accurate, she comforted herself: Damien was hardly a friend.

'Well, you just tell me! Oh damn everything!' This to a car that had driven down the street and was hooting to pass. 'Why didn't that idiot wait? Now he'll have to back all the way up!'

'I doubt it,' murmured Carl, to Susan, as Paul got into his own car and banged the door. The engine roared angrily into life. The other driver, a local farmer on his way down to the Fish, had folded his arms, grinning as Paul lurched his car off the pavement, narrowly missing Susan's Range Rover, and came nose to nose with him; he obviously had no intentions of shifting, quite possibly he had been in the bar last night. Carl took Susan's arm and turned her round.

'Let's not watch his humiliation, I don't think I could bear it. I think it's time for coffee and some of Seb's biscuits, don't you?'

As the door closed behind them all, they heard the hideous scrunch and howling engine of an angry man slamming his expensive car into reverse.

III

One bright morning in early December, Debbie walked up the hill to cadge a cup of tea off her sister and to relay some interesting news. It wasn't one of Susan's days at college, and as it happened she was well ahead with her studies, with time to chat for once. The children were at school, Carl down at the sailing school doing some maintenance work on his boat, laid up ashore there. The sisters could settle down in the conservatory with no fear of interruption.

'So, what's new?' asked Susan, for it was apparent that Debbie had arrived with a purpose.

'Mum rang last night,' Debbie told her. 'It seems the party's on. Saturday before Christmas, trust her!'

'Good choice!' Susan thought with awe about Mawgan's permanently packed restaurant with its three-month-minimum waiting list, and the approaching festive season. 'What did Mawgan have to say to that?'

'Actually, he took it pretty calmly. For some reason he seems set on doing whatever she wants, however inconvenient – which is an awful lot more than she deserves, Suse.'

Susan, who knew the reason, mentally applauded her brother-in-law, for his courage as much as his devotion to her sister, but made no comment. Instead, she said, 'What form has she decided it should take?'

'She's having fourteen people to dinner,' Debbie told her. 'That includes the four of us, of course, and herself. Nine friends.'

'She can get twenty round the table with all the leaves in,' Susan observed.

'I know. I just wondered ... well, perhaps she can't raise as many as fifteen friends at the moment.' Debbie took a sip at her tea, which allowed her to lower her eyes. Susan said nothing in direct reply, she had been wondering the same thing. She took refuge in idle speculation.

'I wonder who she'll ask? Not Tom's parents, I don't suppose, that would be too awkward under the circumstances. Uncle Alex, probably, and Aunt Ingrid. Seven others.'

'Canon Plessey and his sister,' offered Debbie.

'Of course, they won't have fallen out with her. Who else?'

'Joanna's parents, do you think?' Joanna Clarke, *née* Rendell, had been Susan's great friend in Embridge: it had been Dot's dearest wish to see her married to Oliver but Chel had got in the way: Joanna's parents were very much "county", it would have been a boost to her standing in the town had her ambition succeeded. That incident, too, had caused some ribaldry among her detractors, as both Susan and Debbie remembered, which was probably not unconnected with her feelings towards Chel. Susan considered the older Rendells now.

'Which camp would they be in, do you think? They were a bit ambivalent over Oliver's defection, Jo was pretty upset over it.'

'I'd say they aren't the kind to jeer openly,' said Debbie, judiciously. 'After all, it turned out right in the end. Mark them down as a possible?'

'Three to go. Does she know any single men to make up the table?' Susan wasn't prepared to discuss Joanna's business: it was her considered opinion that, married or not, her friend still carried a torch for Oliver. She didn't plan to say so now.

Debbie considered the question. 'I wouldn't think so. Would you? Single women, then.'

'There's a wide choice there. There's a fair few on her committees, terrifying, most of them.'

'One or two of them are quite human,' said Debbie. She didn't know the ladies in question as well as Susan did. Susan made a face.

'So long as she doesn't pick on that terrifying Mrs Vachell-Chillingworth – you know the wicked witch of the west who lives out at Tildown – what's the name of the place? Oh, of course – *Vachells*, that says everything you need to know about her, doesn't it? Isn't she the mother of a friend of yours?'

'Francis Chillingworth is no friend of mine, thank you! We belong to the same sailing club, is all. He's scary stuff, that man, for all he looks like an archangel! Way out of my league!'

Talking about their old home town, their old life, old friends (or otherwise) with the soft Cornish wind sighing past the windows and the quiet grey view of the winter river spread in front of them, was like visiting another planet. Both of them felt it. Debbie shifted in her chair.

'It'll be strange – going back. They say you never can, don't they?' She looked at her sister, thoughtfully. 'I don't know how you feel about this, Suse, but that Friday night is Christmas Party night at the club. Do you fancy going?'

Susan's eyes opened wide in surprise. She said, 'Are we talking the yacht club – or Ember Valley?' The Ember Valley Sailing Club was mainly concerned with dinghy racing; Debbie had sailed there before her move to London. Susan was a member too, although rather lapsed since most of her sailing of late had been in bigger boats under the aegis of the Embridge Harbour Yacht Club where their father was Vice Commodore – Commodore, this year, indeed, unless he resigned due to his changed circumstances.

'Ember Valley, of course. *Do* you want to go? We can still get tickets I expect – after all, since we're going to be over there anyway ...'

'I would have thought, the question was do *you* want to go,' said Susan. 'You're bound to meet Tim, you must realise.' Debbie made a face at her.

'Got to do it sometime, I suppose.'

'You pirated his sailing school! He hasn't forgiven you, you know.'

'I didn't *pirate* it. The bank sold it over his head, and I bought it. That's not quite the same.'

'But you refused to lend him the money to save it first.'

'It wasn't like that!' Debbie protested. 'Nobody in their senses would have invested in that disaster, thanks to Lesley's incompetence with the catering side it was unsaveable! Come on!'

'It's how he sees it,' said Susan. 'And he wrecked his marriage before the ink was fairly dry on the certificate because he thought he was still in love with you. And he hates Mawgan's guts, you have no idea how much!'

'I think that's his problem, not mine. I'd like to see my friends again.'

Since Susan knew that she felt rather the same, she merely said, 'All right, on your own head be it. You get the tickets, and then pray that you can drag Mawgan out of Cornwall in time to make an appearance.'

'We thought we'd try and get there for a late lunch. He wants to do a bit of preliminary preparation on Friday afternoon. What about you?'

'I don't see why we shouldn't, but I ought to talk it over with Carl first, before I say yes.' She paused. 'You're changing the subject, Deb. So, fourteen people for dinner, did she say what kind of a do she had in mind?'

'A traditional-style Christmas dinner, but she doesn't want turkey, nothing so commonplace. I put her on to Mawgan, catering isn't my department.'

'Wow!' said Susan, awestruck at such daring – but of course, Deb didn't know the worst. 'How did that work out?'

'Considering it was the first time they'd ever spoken, it could have been worse,' said Debbie, blissfully unaware. 'I only heard one end of the conversation, of course. Mawgan was incredibly formal and businesslike, as if he was talking to a complete stranger.'

'He was,' Susan pointed out.

'Oh – yes, of course. It was all about what she wanted, where it could be got – I think we're going on an expedition to the Farmers' Christmas Market on Saturday morning for fresh vegetables and things, that'll be fun: I love that market, as a child it was like Santa's Magic Land! And we're travelling to Embridge in company with eight brace of pheasant from a local shoot, because that way he can be sure they've been hung for the right time and not rotting on their bones – rather disgusting technical stuff. Not my scene.' She hesitated. 'Suse, do you think we're going to get away with this? Really? It's all very well for Oliver, coming up with wonderful ideas. He isn't going to be there to see that they work.'

'We may have to sweat over it a bit.'

'The thing that keeps me awake at night is, in this context, both Mawgan and Carl are unknown quantities.'

Susan privately thought that, in this context as Debbie chose to put it, so was their mother, but she didn't say so. Time would reveal all, the one thing certain was that if they didn't try, even though they both felt that it was Dot, not they, who should be doing the trying, there was too much to lose. There was no future in discussing this, both of them felt too hurt by, not to say resentful of, the treatment they had received. She was relieved when Debbie didn't pursue the subject, to which they could add nothing but conjecture, but changed it entirely, this time deliberately.

'Have you heard from Liz since she left here? Mawgan felt bad about what happened, but it wasn't his fault; he didn't have a choice, not in front of everyone like that. The unspeakable Paul was way out of order!'

'She rang me when she got back, just to say that Paul had gone straight back to London in a really foul mood. I don't blame him really, did you hear what happened to his car?'

'I think the whole village heard. Well, he should have known better than to give a back answer to a local – and a Tregear, at that! It was Richard Tregear's spot he pinched, did you hear? Damien's dad, and his mum that he cheeked. You can guess who's the prime suspect!'

'Was there ever any doubt?'

'Why doesn't she give him the push?' asked Debbie, not the first person to do so.

'Don't think we haven't asked, believe me. No real answer was forthcoming, just a lot of stuff about "someone to go to parties with."'

'I suppose she's got a point there, somewhere. Single women don't get asked to dinner parties, apparently, some married women see them as a threat, or something. Do you feel like that?'

'No,' said Susan. 'On the other hand, it can be pretty miserable being on your own at parties.'

Debbie looked at her curiously. 'You said that almost as if you had personal experience.'

'I was married to Tom Casson, remember. Anyway, I think this weekend was a bit of a one-off, he doesn't usually behave quite so badly as he did this time. The car business was only Paul being Paul, it just escalated.'

'He tried to park it at our place afterwards, did you hear? Roger rang me, but he didn't say who it was –' She broke off, and looked slightly guilty. Susan looked at her thoughtfully.

'And you didn't ask, I don't suppose.'

'Why should he take advantage of us, particularly when he'd made such a row in the bar? We don't even like him much – certainly not now!' Susan didn't answer a rhetorical question to which there was in any case no sensible reply, and Debbie went on. 'But that's all well and good. There's a lot of good fish in the sea, why doesn't she let this piranha go and catch a different species? She's an attractive woman, surely someone would fancy her.'

'I think,' said Susan slowly, thinking it out, 'that there's several different things at work there. One, of course, is the old Catch 22 – she's got Paul, their relationship seems to suit her in a lot of ways, even if it wouldn't do for thee and me, so why should she bother? And just *because* she's got Paul hanging round all the time, why should anyone else? Bother, that is, unless, I suppose, they were swept off their feet – and I think that kind of thing mainly happens in the sort of books she writes, or come to think, *doesn't* write. And another is, as you should very well know Deb, that if you're a woman with money of your own, as Liz rather obviously has to be, you're never absolutely sure of people's motives. She can be sure of Paul's – he's out for what he can get – and as she doesn't care very deeply, that's fine. But anyone else ... perhaps being well known, and the rumours you hear, even if they aren't exactly true, about fantastic advances and so on are ... well, inhibiting. To both sides, Liz and anyone who might fancy her. I don't know. But that's what I think.'

Debbie said nothing to this, she could think of nothing it was possible to say, for Tom Casson, she was morally certain, had married Susan primarily for her money. Mawgan of course, the other side of the coin, hadn't realised that she herself had any until they were well and truly committed, and anyway, these days he could probably buy her at one end of the street and sell her at the other. About Tim Howells, whom they had already discussed, she had never reached any conclusion, and Robin, with whom she had lived for a while in her London days, had certainly had an eye on the main chance. Only one eye, probably, to be fair to both him and herself, but one was enough. On the other hand, Carl, she was fairly sure, was one of those rare and happy people to whom money didn't particularly matter anyway: he was totally self-sufficient, quite content to live aboard his boat if push came to shove, and the reason he was with Susan was quite simply because he loved her. But men like Carl did not grow on every bush, and how could you decide which category a man fell into anyway?

Susan said, when the pause had gone on too long for comfort, 'I suppose we could make it our mission to introduce her to suitable young men, but actually, I don't think I know of any. And Liz is an intelligent woman, some men don't like that.'

'And yet, she goes out with Paul,' said Debbie, raising her eyebrows.

'I suspect it goes with the territory.'

'What – terminal naïveté?'

Susan wanted to say, her grandfather married our mother, I married Tom, think it out, but didn't, she wasn't sure that Debbie would understand. Debbie came from hardier stock; a lot more resilient and more likely to laugh at herself: an ability to see the funny side was always an advantage. Their mother noticeably didn't seem to have a sense of humour at all, but that was a different argument. 'Something like that, I suppose,' she said.

A silence fell, while they thought their different thoughts; Debbie broke it, leaning forward to place her empty mug on the table. 'I ought to go. You wouldn't think it, but I've got work to do. We're working on next year's programme, we thought we'd make a few changes.'

'Oh? In what way? I thought you had it pretty much sewn up.'

'We did and we didn't.' Debbie sat back again, not averse to putting off the evil hour. 'It was OK to start with, but it's different now. Phil is a married man, and Carl has you and the children to think about these days, and there's another thing, too. We had several enquiries last year from people who were complete beginners with yachts – dinghy people, quite a lot of them, planning flotilla holidays and wanting a bit of hands-on experience with bigger stuff before they went to Greece or somewhere and made idiots of themselves. So we thought we might with advantage introduce a shore-based pre-flotilla course. It would work too for people planning to scale up a bit from dinghies – there's plenty of those around. They'd stay at the Fish, Chel's agreeable, come to our evening talks if they wanted, but the main thing is that it would mean that whoever was in charge could go home at night like a normal person – the way we plan to work it, not less than one week in four, perhaps as much as every other week if the idea catches on. What do you think?'

'Sounds a great idea to me, but then, I have a vested interest.' Susan looked interested.

'We thought,' Debbie continued, warming to her theme, 'that if we ran one every fortnight to begin with, Carl and Phil could take it in turns. If the punters want to go on and do Competent Crew or Day Skipper afterwards, they can book the second week separately, but that's up to them. And ...' she paused, smiling at her sister. 'Want an early Christmas present, Suse? I thought, one week of the summer I could do the shore-based course, and maybe you and Carl could take the children off to the Scillies, or Dartmouth, or somewhere – France even, if you felt like it, or the Channel Islands. Gosia can look after his nibs from ten until five just for that five days, she'll love it, and you and Carl and the children should have some quality time in the summer, not just the odd weekend. You can squash quite a lot into eight days, if you try hard'

Susan saw a snag. 'But if we go to France, you won't have a boat.'

'Well,' said Debbie, 'that's another thing, of course. We were thinking of getting something a bit more user-friendly for absolute beginners than the Feelings; they can be a bit of a handful if it blows, although I love them dearly. Because, you see, we always knew that Carl probably wouldn't stay with us more than maybe a couple of years, and we need to think ahead ... I mean, if his book takes off, he won't want a full-time job that takes him to sea half his life, and anyway, when we started this, he didn't have a family, he didn't have *you*. We hope he'll stay as a partner, help with the administration and see to the publicity, maybe do the odd week here and there to give Phil, and whoever else we take on, a bit of a break ... but I don't really see him as a permanent full-time instructor, and Roger, of course, never did.' She paused. 'You're not saying anything.'

'I'm speechless, actually,' Susan confessed. 'Is Carl in on your plots?'

'We've obviously discussed the shore-based courses. The rest is conjecture by me and Roger.' She grinned. 'No Suse, he's not keeping secrets from you, and he hasn't said anything to us either. But we're right, you wait and see. I give him one more year, starting from now.' She heaved herself to her feet. 'Oh, roll on February, I feel like a hippopotamus! I'm off to my office, I can't put it off any longer.'

When she had gone, Susan carried the empty mugs back into the kitchen and put them in the sink, but didn't immediately set about washing them It had never occurred to her that Carl might give up his job at the sailing school, but now it had been pointed out, it was an obvious possibility – probability, even. Carl was a writer, primarily; the job with Debbie had been a godsend at the time, but if his book was successful he wouldn't need it. He had never chosen it deliberately; indeed, as she knew, it had often got in the way of his ambitions. If he gave it up, or even just drastically modified his commitment, it would make her own life, and her children's, completely different. They could be a family, not just in the winter months, but all year long; take the children to magical places, on proper cruises ... Debbie had mentioned flotillas in Greece, well, why not? Annabel and Seb would love it. They were not the only ones.

Happy Christmas, indeed! Even if the reality of the gift was maybe as much as eighteen months ahead, the promise was wrapped in stars and angels.

Dot ran into Sally Casson while on a shopping trip to Borden's, the big department store in the centre of town. The two women had always been friendly, but the marriage of Dot's daughter to Sally's son, that had once brought them together, had on its rather contentious dissolution pushed them apart. These days, they tended to avoid each other, so their meeting head-on in Ladies' Fashions wasn't entirely happy. Sally had been psyching herself up to ring Dot, but that didn't mean she wished to confront her nose to nose; Dot, feeling a little short of friends after the Mawgan *débâcle*, had been missing Sally, but uncharacteristically wary of her reception should she get in touch. The unexpected meeting rendered them both speechless. Dot, predictably, found her voice first.

'Sally! How nice, it's been an age!'

Sally wasn't sure that "nice" was the word she would have chosen herself: Tom's behaviour towards Susan, and some of the things that he had said about her, that she now understood to be untrue or at the very least much exaggerated, made her wary. Dot would be perfectly justified in taking exception, and Sally had no wish to be on the receiving end of her opinions. She had known Dot for many years now, and it said much for the quality of their friendship that it had lasted in spite of all. She said, 'Oh!' and then went on, lamely, 'I was going to ring you,' just as Dot said exactly the same thing. They looked at each other, and the silly coincidence shattered the ice between them.

'Then we may as well save the money, and go and talk over a nice cup of coffee,' said Dot, briskly, and Sally refrained from pointing out that the cost of two coffees at Borden's would probably fund a long distance call to Alaska lasting roughly half an hour.

'I was just –' she began, and then shrugged her shoulders. 'Why not? It can wait.' She could hardly say that she was on the hunt for a suitable outfit for her son's wedding to Dot's daughter's supplanter, an event in which she had, in any case, steadily diminishing faith. Sally had been on a steep learning curve with regard to Tom just lately. It's hard to find your own child indefensible.

The two women, by common but unspoken consent, made their way upstairs to the Garden Restaurant on the top floor. It really was a garden, since it was built on three-quarters of the flat roof, and a pretty roof garden occupied the last quarter; in summer, this was a pleasant place with tables and chairs under bright umbrellas where one could sit and eat outside, but in December the doors were firmly closed and the plants slumbered, waiting for spring. Looking out at the bare twigs and empty tubs, Sally shivered. Life wasn't looking good at the moment, and the winter garden reflected her mood.

'So,' said Dot, when coffee and little cakes had been brought and set in front of them. 'What were you going to ring me about?'

Sally lowered the pastry she had been about to bite back onto her plate. 'It's a bit awkward,' she said. Not a good beginning. She began to fiddle with her teaspoon.

'Out with it,' said Dot, bracingly. 'Whatever it is, it can't be so bad you can't tell me in public.'

Sally nearly laughed. 'It practically is,' she said. They exchanged a smile, and then it was easy. 'It's about Susan, actually. Susan and the children. And this man, Carl Colenso. Have you met him?'

'Not yet.' Dot paused, wondering if she would explain, and then decided not to. 'But they're all coming up from Cornwall just before Christmas to spend a weekend with me, so I shall meet him then. I think Susan is planning to bring the children over to see you on the Saturday, let Tom have them for the day. We're going to be busy, I'm giving a party, you know.'

Sally hadn't been invited. She began breaking her pastry into flakes. 'Then I wonder ... when she brings them over, would she bring him ... Carl ... with her, do you think? I'd like to meet him, so would Irwin. After all, it looks as if he's going to have a big say in bringing up our grandchildren.'

Dot looked at her with a certain amount of sympathy, for of course, the same thing applied to her now that she came to think about it, and perhaps in banning him from the house she had been negligent. It was a new and slightly uncomfortable consideration. She said, 'I was wondering about asking you both to the party. I hesitated only because ...' Not normally sensitive, she paused here to choose her words carefully. Sally didn't meet her eyes.

'I don't think so, thank you Dot. It would be too awkward, don't you think? Like Banquo, sitting at the feast only nobody could see him.'

'Tom, you mean,' said Dot, ever forthright, and Sally nodded. Dot had time to wonder, inappropriately, whether Sally was right about nobody seeing Banquo, because surely *somebody* must have, before Sally went on, 'It feels so strange, so ... different. I should have been in touch with you, but really, I didn't know what to say. The things Tom said about Susan – Lorraine says, they weren't true.'

'Does she know that?' asked Dot, interested. The question was justified, since one of the things Tom had said was that Susan was frigid, and he had "needs".

Sally said, dryly, 'I think she is morally certain. Naturally Susan is hardly likely to confide in her, but her ex-husband said the same about her, she says it's the oldest excuse in the book for playing away.'

Dot said nothing to this. Jerry, as she had known at the time, had played away, but he had never made excuses about it that she had ever heard. She had only known at all because he had been careless about leaving clues around; restaurant receipts and used theatre tickets, she had never confronted him. Since he was a solicitor, and therefore should have known the pitfalls, she had often wondered about it, but she had never made an issue of it: if Jerry wanted out, he had to try harder than that. The physical side of their marriage had been long dead by that time but so long as they kept up appearances, she hadn't had the heart to care. This was not because she was frigid, no. They simply didn't fancy each other any more after Deborah was born. She found herself wondering if Susan and Tom had felt the same after Sebastian, and knowing the arid wasteland that would have ensued, was for the first time sorry for her daughter rather than censorious. And Tom wasn't Jerry, "discretion" was not a word in his vocabulary, half the town had known about his succession of young women, Susan included. Dot realised she couldn't have named even one of Jerry's, or even known if there was more than one, and was grateful to him. Of course, it was different now, with Helen, but maybe with Helen it always had been.

'Tom's met him, you know,' Sally was saying. 'Back in the summer, little Christina went down to stay with Annabel while Tom and Lorraine went off together – I thought that was so generous of Susan, you know. Taking in the child of the woman her husband left her for while they went off to enjoy themselves together. But apparently she and Annabel get on really well.'

'And what did he think?' asked Dot, ignoring this byroad, for there was reasonable doubt, according to both Jerry and Susan herself, as to who had left whom in the case of Tom and Susan, and this she could hardly discuss with Tom's mother.

'He didn't say much. Just said he thought the children would be all right. I got the impression he hadn't liked him, but then, he wouldn't, would he?'

'Hadn't liked him, why?' asked Dot, sharply.

'That, I don't know, of course. But I suspect it was because he was young and good-looking and had set Susan alight. He has, you know. When she brings the children now, she's a different creature. She's glowing, I suppose it's with happiness.' Sally sounded desolate.

'Or sex,' said the more cynical Dot. 'He's several years younger than she is, you know.'

'Yes.' Sally finally bit into her pastry to give herself time. She spoke on impulse, muffled by a mouthful of pastry flakes. 'Tom said he was a grown-up though.'

'Of course I'll tell Susan to bring him to meet you,' said Dot. 'Indeed, I shall be interested to meet him myself.' The subject needed to be closed. She changed it, therefore. 'So when is the wedding to be?'

It happened that this topic was very little better than the other. Sally said, 'Easter – if it ever happens.'

'Do you think that it won't?'

'I don't know. I just begin to think that my son is handsome and charming, but has no constancy in him, and that if Lorraine marries him she'll end up like Susan did, an unhappy, lonely, neglected wife.' She looked at Dot, horrified at what her mouth had said, almost of itself. 'We've been friends a long time, Dot. I know you won't repeat that.'

'Of course I won't,' said Dot, and might have added that gossip was vulgar, and she was never, ever vulgar. Instead, she asked, curiously, 'You mean, he's seeing another woman before he's even married this one?'

'No,' said Sally. 'I wish I did. I mean – I *think* I mean – that's he's sorry now he broke up with Susan. And if Carl Colenso is really a serious contender, my heart will bleed for Tom, but he brought it on himself. And that, I suppose, is really why I've been avoiding you, so now you know.'

'Have some more coffee,' said Dot, pouring. The action gave her space to think, but the only thought that came into her head was, 'He hasn't asked Susan to marry him. There has been no mention of it.'

'Perhaps Susan has had enough of marriage,' said Sally, more bitterly than she had meant. 'Perhaps he has asked her, and she turned him down.' Dot looked at her.

'Or perhaps the young man has no such intentions.'

'Whichever it is, I doubt if it will make any difference. Susan would be a fool to go back to Tom, I say that even if he is my son. What's over is over. You can't breathe life into the dead.'

'The children –'

'The children,' Sally interrupted forcefully, for it was a subject on which she felt deeply grieved, 'are quite different since the young man came into their lives. Surely you've noticed?'

Dot hadn't, not really. She didn't have the kind of mind that looks beyond the obvious, and she saw what she wished to see; to a large extent that was what she had always done.

'What do you mean?'

Sally groped for words. 'They're ... more like other children, I suppose. Confident. Happy. I don't know quite what it is, they seem to ... to believe in themselves. Sebby, particularly.'

'They were always happy,' said Dot, seizing on the most obvious point.

'Were they? I'm beginning to wonder. We *thought* they were. Perhaps they thought so, too. But looking back, I suspect that most of their happiness, and their security too, certainly latterly, came from that girl my son dismissed so easily – so *thoughtlessly*.'

'Susan was always an excellent mother!' Dot was indignant.

Sally was relieved to find someone else at fault besides her own son. 'Susan was always too busy with her charity work to be there for them the way they needed. She went through the motions without understanding – in both departments, if you want my opinion. Now, from somewhere, she's found both understanding and direction. And Annabel and Sebby laugh and chatter and behave like – like present-day children, and not something from a 1950's children's book. And is it coincidence that it's all happened since Carl Colenso came into their lives? I don't think so. I wish I did.'

Dot was silent. Sally, wondering if she had let her mouth run away with her again, addressed herself to her pastry, which had slowly disintegrated into a flaky heap beneath her restless fingers and was really quite uneatable now. She stirred the flakes round, concentrating. After a while, Dot spoke. 'One always does one's best for one's children.' She sounded uncertain.

'I think,' said Sally, who had thought about this a lot lately, 'that sometimes our conception of "best" may be at fault.' She sounded so miserable that even Dot noticed. She looked at her friend more carefully.

'You can hardly be held responsible for what a grown man chooses to do.'

'Can't I?' Sally asked. 'Irwin says I spoiled him. Did, I Dot? Do you think so?'

'I didn't know him as a child,' Dot pointed out. She recognised this for a get-out and said, with unintentional bitterness, 'I think that most men have an eye to the pretty girls, it's born in them, and it's born in the pretty girls to play up to them, there's nothing that can be done about it. After that, it's simply down to strength of character.'

'Which Tom doesn't have' said Sally, studying the flakes on her plate.

'It's difficult bringing up an only child, I imagine,' said Dot.

Sally said, as if the information was being forced out of her, 'Tom's weak, he's always been easily led. He's a bully too, when he finds someone vulnerable, it's the only way he seems to know to assert himself. He was far too hard on Sebby. It's an awful thing for his mother to say, Dot, but Sebby is much, much better away from him.' She put up a surreptitious finger to wipe under her eye. Dot noticed, of course, Dot always did notice things you wished she wouldn't, but mercifully she didn't comment.

'Annabel misses him,' was all she said. It was consolation of a kind – only a kind.

'Annabel was always his pet. It's hard on the siblings, that kind of thing.'

Dot found herself thinking, without meaning to, of her own attitude to first Oliver, Jerry's beautiful son, and then to Deborah, his beautiful daughter. She thought about the daughter who wasn't Jerry's. It would be too much to say that she suffered a sudden enlightenment, but she did find herself feeling slightly uncomfortable. She realised that she should say something encouraging to Sally, who looked about to burst into tears and cause a scene.

'Nobody is perfect, Sally. Look at Susan, suddenly rushing off to get herself a career! Children, even one's own, are so unpredictable!'

As she had hoped, this was firmer ground. Sally stiffened her back almost visibly. 'I'm on Susan's side. She had her children very young, any minute now they'll be growing away from her. She could be left with a very empty life if she doesn't take steps to fill it.'

Relieved at the success of her gambit, Dot said, argumentatively, 'She may have more children with this Carl.'

'I doubt it.' Sally, equally relieved, rose to the bait. 'Susan isn't naturally maternal. If you ask me, she's pleased to see the end in sight, and is getting herself a life. And no, I don't blame her. She's a very clever girl, your Susan, only you never seemed to notice for some reason.'

Didn't I? A sudden feeling of discomfort, stronger than before, swept over Dot. She hastily reached for her bag. 'It's been good to talk like this, Sally, but I have to move on, I've a meeting this afternoon.' She paused. 'You're sure you and Irwin won't come to my party? Deborah and her husband are coming too, you know, they offered to do all the work for me, Mawgan will be doing the cooking.' The name almost choked her: it was the first time she had brought herself to use it, preferring to call him "That Man" or in selected company "The Disaster", but she made herself smile as she said it. Sally gaped at her.

'What – that wonderful new chef off the television?'

'That's the man she married, I believe.' Dot smiled more easily now, enjoying her triumph.

'Oooh!' Almost, Sally was tempted. But no, it would be a bad idea, everyone would feel uncomfortable; Dot wouldn't understand that. Regretfully, she declined. 'No Dot, it's sweet of you, but I think it would be too awkward – for everyone, really. Just tell Susan we'll expect them both for coffee when they bring the children. I'll make sure Tom won't be there, I'll tell him to pick them up at lunchtime, not before.'

They settled the bill between them, and parted at the foot of the stairs, Sally knowing that she had pushed her luck a time or two there but not got her head bitten off, and wondering why not. Perhaps Dot hadn't been listening properly? To be fair, she often didn't.

On the other hand, Sally thought, as she looked hopelessly along the racks of elegant coats and skirts for something to wear at a wedding in which she no longer believed, it was true that, in one way at least, you could always say what you liked to Dot. She was insensitive, domineering, opinionated, officious and misguided, and she spoke her mind at all times and on all subjects without either fear or consideration, but she was also utterly safe as a repository for one's private thoughts and always ready to rise to a crisis even if you never knew quite what she would do, and that, Sally realised, was why she called Dot a friend. She handled both people and delicate situations like a regimental sergeant-major on speed, but her heart, and she definitely had one in there somewhere, was in the right place.

But Dot had lost interest in her shopping expedition and drove herself back to her big, beautiful, empty house that had never really been a home, and later in the day, found it very difficult to concentrate on the speaker at the meeting she attended.

IV

Now, for better or worse, the Friday before Christmas had arrived, and Dot awaited, with very mixed feelings, the arrival of her two daughters, their partners, and her grandchildren. They had said they would arrive in time for lunch; Dot spent the morning fussing round the house, driving her domestic help mad with her unpredictable appearances just where she was least wanted or expected, and unable to settle in one place for more than ten minutes. She would have denied that she was on edge, apprehensive and on at least one level – the level of her son-in-law – actively scared. However, since there was no one to challenge her she was free to explain her restlessness to herself as anticipation if she so wished.

Some time had passed since her conversation with Sally, which had given plenty of opportunity for its implications to sink in and Dot, if she was honest with herself, was more than a little horrified at these. Sally's uncomfortable honesty about her son had started a train of thought on which Dot would rather have been spared the journey. There was no escaping it, she had acted on the premise that what Tom had said was true and that Susan was at fault; now it appeared that Tom had lied, so where did that leave Susan? It began to dawn on Dot that Susan was being uncommonly generous now, given the circumstances, and to wonder why.

And if she had been wrong about Susan, had she also been in the wrong over Deborah? The man had been acquitted on appeal, and Jerry had been very forthright on the subject, on several occasions; Dot knew that she had simply chosen not to listen, for what some would call outdated reasons connected with class, education and means of employment. Of course, he had tried to – no, he *had* applied blackmail to get her to the wedding, but on the other hand, she was glad that she had gone, she had come to see that it would have been unforgivable to stay away – although, she assured herself, she would have reached the same decision without his intervention, of course. And she had given him provocation, she couldn't deny it. Susan ... a wave of heat went over her as she thought about *why* Susan should have said such a thing, but she had said that the man ... Mawgan, she had better get used to it, had been close to a breakdown, he hadn't been acting rationally.

She could barely face Susan if, on top of everything else, she had to believe that she *knew*.

Thoughts like these, and others similar, had been her constant companions just lately. Today would be the moment of truth, and she couldn't imagine what they would, either of them, do or say. Deborah had even more cause than Susan to turn her back on her mother: she hadn't done so either. Dot couldn't escape a fear that they would use the opportunity to have things out with her; she would far, far sooner not confront them. It never even occurred to her that both Susan and Debbie were on their way to Embridge now simply because they loved her in spite of everything, and of course she had no idea either that the original suggestion had come from Oliver, who had also fallen foul of her in spectacular fashion.

Then there were the two young men: Mawgan Angwin, whom she had already met although, please *please* God, only the two of them knew that, and Carl Colenso, whom she now realised she *should* have met, if she truly had her grandchildren's interests at heart. She had taken up a position, that was the trouble, and when one did that, it was often impossible to back down gracefully. Dot knew this, for she had often done so, and by no means always intentionally.

Troubled and perturbed, Dot wandered restlessly into her big, elegant, lonely drawing room, which there was no longer a family to fill. By the window, a Christmas tree, decorated with coloured lights and glittering ornaments, its base piled with gaily wrapped presents for them all, met her eyes. She had made an effort for her grandchildren, but she felt cold as she looked at the result. It could all turn out to be a mockery, a hollow sham. Dot was aware, anyway, that she had never really got the hang of Christmas: it had always been a highly decorated, over-fed, traditional occasion with good intentions behind it, but it had never ... well, never what? Never met her expectations, perhaps? A lot of things had failed to do that, all her life; Christmas – or marriage come to that – was only the tip of the iceberg. There had never been the warmth behind either that she had always longed for, somewhere at the back of her mind where the dark places lurked. Dot seldom visited dark places on principal, believing it did no good to brood on them, but this Christmas they seemed to be coming to visit her. To distract herself, she looked at her watch. Quarter to twelve. They would be here soon, she had been expecting them this last hour. Her feet, apparently of their own accord, took her to the window, but the drive was empty. Soon now, either Deborah's yellow Golf or Susan's maroon Range Rover would appear through those gates, and there would be no going back.

Dot felt as if she stood at the top of an endless helter-skelter with only one way down. She also felt slightly sick, and wondered if the egg she had eaten for breakfast had been quite fresh.

And then a car did come through the gates, and it was one she had never set eyes on before. A sleek silver-grey sports coupé – it was an Alfa Romeo, but Dot didn't know that – swept in from the road and up the drive, and parked with what she could only call a vulgar flourish at the foot of her front steps. The driver was a stranger, but on the back seat she could see Annabel and Sebastian waving to her, and Susan leaning back to see her, smiling a greeting. Dot pulled herself together and went to the front door to greet them. Pay-up time had arrived.

Annabel hurtled out of the car and flung herself up the front steps into her grandmother's arms in a wholehearted way that she had surely never done before.

'Grandma! Did you think we were never going to get here? We did! The road was up and there were lights and lots of traffic –' She kissed her startled grandmother soundly, and moved aside to make room for the quieter approach of Sebastian from the other side of the car. He hugged Dot warmly but swiftly, and in his turn stood aside for his mother. Dot, accepting this third embrace of apparently untarnished warmth, was aware of the young man waiting in the background. She kissed Susan and turned to meet her first challenge. 'And you must be Carl,' she said.

He was a good-looking man: very blue eyes and dark, crisp, very short hair; chunkily built and of only average height, but strong and fit – and the latter in every sense of the word. Dot, against her expectation, and possibly even her will, was impressed. He had a firm handclasp and a friendly grin, and his voice when he returned her greeting was free from the Cornish accent she had dreaded. One regional accent in the family was surely a heavy enough cross for them all to bear! It was a shame, though, about what she believed was known as "designer stubble", of which she didn't approve, considering it slovenly. She was surprised that Susan condoned it: it gave the man a swashbuckling appearance that didn't fit in with her idea of the responsible head of a family, particularly if it was her family. She would have been both disappointed and grieved to learn that it had been Susan's recent suggestion, on waking up late after a heavy night at the Fish and seeing her unshaven partner in a completely new light. The children were delighted with it, they said it made Carl look like a pirate – not a high recommendation in their grandmother's book.

'I'm so sorry we're a bit later than we said,' Susan was saying. 'Annabel's right, the roads were awful. Debbie and Mawgan will be caught in it too, so don't expect them for a while yet – they left later than us, because Mawgan had to check with his staff first and see that everything was OK to leave.'

'Never mind, you're here now,' Dot smiled, not sorry for a short reprieve. One of the young men at a time, she could maybe cope with better. 'Fetch your things inside, out of this drizzle and then Carl can put his nice car in the garage.' She was favourably impressed with the Alfa too: she hadn't expected anything like it.

Annabel and Seb had headed indoors out of the cold and away from any danger of being asked to carry something, but before they had made good their escape, Carl hailed them back.

'Oy, you foremast hands! No jumping ship, please! Come and help unload your share of the cargo.' Had Tom said anything of the kind, it wouldn't have been said so good-naturedly, and there would have been moans and groans and dragging feet, or even pretence not to have heard: to Dot's astonishment, Annabel and Seb stood smartly to attention with a brisk 'Aye aye, sir!' and ran back down the steps, giggling. Susan caught her mother's eye and laughed.

'Magic, isn't it? It's not Carl, you know, it's the influence of Arthur Ransome! We run a tight ship, these days.'

'So I see,' said Dot, faintly.

Laden with luggage, they all surged into the hall, while Carl, with Seb insisting on going too "to show him the way", took the car along to the big triple garage that now had only one lonely car left in it. Dot, bemused, went with the tide, directing Annabel and Seb to their usual rooms, and Susan and Carl to the blue spare bedroom. There were too many spare bedrooms in this house, she found herself thinking as she did so. The blue room, the pink room, the yellow room, there was no end to it. Well, this weekend they would most of them be occupied, and she was startled at the surge of satisfaction the thought gave her.

While they sorted themselves out upstairs, she briefly visited the kitchen to instruct young Mrs Adams (she had inherited the post from her mother-in-law, "old" Mrs Adams, who still came in to help out occasionally and was actually younger than Dot herself), otherwise known as "the girl", to hold back lunch a little while, before going back out into the hall. Upstairs, she could hear movement and laughter and running feet; the whole house felt different, it had come alive. She stood there, listening and trying to analyse the change, and was still standing there when Annabel and Sebastian came hurtling down with Susan following more slowly. Susan linked her arm through her mother's, and walked with her to the drawing room door.

'Carl's just hanging up his suit,' she said. 'Annabel and Seb, you stick around and show him where to come when he comes down here, will you? He doesn't know his way about yet, remember.' They were through into the room, so smoothly that Dot wasn't quite sure how it had come about. 'He only has the one good suit, we treat it with reverence. You don't really need things like that when you live on a boat, do you?'

'I suppose not,' said Dot, who had never considered this, naturally enough. She looked at Susan. 'He seems very pleasant. Good manners, and the children obey him.'

'I suppose they do,' said Susan, sounding surprised. 'He's wise, you know, Mother. He doesn't try to be a father to them, they've got one of those. But I suppose, he's the captain of the ship just the same, and they heed him accordingly. Love him too, although I don't think they quite know it yet.'

Burdened with the knowledge that Sally had given her, Dot didn't dispute this as she might have done a week ago. Instead, she said, 'I believe I owe you an apology, Susan.'

'You do?' Susan stared at her, for yes, her mother probably owed her several apologies, come to think, so which particular one had she in mind?

'I shouldn't have listened to those unkind things that Tom said about you when your marriage was in trouble,' Dot said. She added, because it was so manifestly true that she couldn't avoid it. 'I should have been more supportive, and I'm sorry. There!'

Susan found herself caught at a disadvantage. She said, awkwardly, 'Well, it all turned out for the best, so shall we put it behind us?'

Dot couldn't resist saying, 'Sally thinks that Tom is regretting it now. I don't suppose ...?'

'Never in a million years!' said Susan, firmly, but Dot knew in any case that she had abandoned that hope, if it had ever existed, the instant she set eyes on Carl, for between the two there was no comparison. Tom had been right, Carl was a grown-up. Tom's continuing behaviour manifestly betrayed that he wasn't, for all his seniority. Dot had never expected to feel glad for her errant daughter, she must see what could be done to consolidate the position now. Before she could say anything ill-advised on the subject, fortunately, Carl and the children appeared from the hall, and the children stopped in their tracks when they saw the beautiful tree.

'Grandma!' cried Annabel, awestruck. 'Oh Grandma, it's *beautiful*! Did you do it all for us?' Sebastian grinned without words, Dot found herself thinking that it made him somehow unfamiliar, and felt jolted; surely he had never grinned like that in the past? Was it really so new, or was she just on edge? Annabel ran forward and fell on her knees before the pile of parcels, in the age-old family tradition known as "making your presents felt", and Seb joined her. Dot, shaken, invited Carl to sit down.

'I asked the girl to bring some coffee, since it seems we have to wait for lunch,' she said. 'You must be hungry, I expect you started early didn't you?'

'We stopped for breakfast on the way,' Susan informed her. 'It breaks the journey for the children. But coffee will be great, I'd kill for a cup right now!' Talking for the sake of talking, she knew it. She felt awkward, and thought that Carl did too.

In fact Carl, unusually quiet for someone who generally had a lot to say for himself, was simply gathering impressions. He had heard a great deal about Susan's mother and been given an idea of her that he was beginning to think wasn't entirely accurate. Several things that had already happened had, to his mind, contradicted received intelligence. The way the children had run to her, the way she had greeted them. The straight, summing-up look that she had given to him, the thought and effort she must have put in to create this magical Christmas tree for her grandchildren who would only be with her for two nights. Most of all, the way she had almost grabbed at Susan out there on the steps, as if she had feared to lose her. There wasn't enough data yet to form a theory, but he had become interested. He realised that Dot was speaking to him and hurriedly turned his attention to what she was saying.

'... that you've written a book, and it's going to be published next year. That's very clever of you, you must be pleased.'

Carl admitted that he was more astounded than simply pleased, in the present post-modernist climate, and the talk became literary. Dot was genuinely interested, as it happened, and contributed a well-thought out point of view to a discussion of present-day publishing that made her daughter look at her in astonishment: she had never suspected Dot of having any views on the subject at all. The coffee came, and the discussion continued, and Susan it was now who simply sat back and listened. Annabel, bored with talk that went straight over her head, got up from the floor and peered out of the window. Her excited yelp brought the company to attention.

'Here they come now, Grandma! Here's Uncle Mawgan and Auntie Debbie!'

Abruptly brought back to a somewhat fragile present, Dot rose to her feet and came to join her granddaughter, unconsciously standing slightly back so as not to be seen from outside this time. Yet another strange car was drawing up at the foot of the steps. She blinked in shock.

'It's very ... very *noticeable*, isn't it?' she said, and Annabel giggled.

Seb, coming to stand beside his grandmother, slipped his hand into hers and informed her, 'It's a Porsche 911 Careera 3.2 litre, and it goes like shit off a shovel!'

There was a dead silence. Seb turned scarlet with horror at what had slipped out of his mouth, Annabel looked at Susan round-eyed, and Susan held her breath, but either Dot hadn't heard properly, or she decided, unusually for her, not to rock the boat. She said, 'Don't exaggerate, Sebastian,' automatically, her eyes on the monster. Not only was it dangerously sleek and sophisticated, it was a particularly vibrant shade of scarlet; a beautiful object, but unashamedly both extrovert and, to her way of thinking, flashy, and a phrase she had once heard Deborah use, and chastised her for, jumped fully fledged into her head – *a mobile penis*. Her mind slipped into panic mode, not for the first time in connection with her son-in-law. Surely, the last time she had met him, admittedly in the dark, he had been driving something cream and commonplace and far from new?

He was getting out of the car now, walking round in front of the bonnet to open the door for his wife, helping her haul herself out, both of them laughing. They held each other for a moment, unaware that they were observed, and the way that they did it made Dot feel like a *voyeuse*, she turned away.

'Come along then, children, let's go and give them a hand with their luggage shall we?' She led the way briskly to the door. Best to get it over with, but she found that her heart was beating so hard that she thought she could actually hear it. The aura of fear that Mawgan had created on their first meeting was as palpable now as it had been then and to add to her distress she found herself thinking, if Susan knew, did Deborah also? But Debbie's greeting as they met on the steps dispelled this idea immediately; there was a slight, understandable reserve in her greeting, but genuine warmth nevertheless. Dot kissed her youngest and dearest daughter, suddenly poignantly aware of how much she had missed her this past two years. Her son-in-law had gone to unload luggage from the back seat – and a few bits and pieces, though not a lot, from under the bonnet, which made Dot blink, but it was only one more anomaly in a day suddenly full of them – apparently as reluctant for the meeting as she was herself. Seb ran down the steps to help.

'I'll carry that for you, Uncle Mawgan.' He staggered under the unexpected weight of a cold box and lugged it up the steps again into the hall, where he dropped it with a gasp. 'Wow, that's heavy! What is it?'

'Bodies,' Mawgan told him ghoulishly, coming in behind him. 'Eight of 'em for tomorrow's dinner.' He put down the luggage he was carrying, and he and Dot looked at each other. The moment had arrived. Mawgan held out his hand. 'Mrs Nankervis! I saw you at the wedding. Thanks for coming, I know you didn't like it none, but it meant a lot to Deb.'

'I saw you, too,' said Dot, with a grim smile. She took the outstretched hand. 'Well, you're here now, so let's say no more.' She added, matching courtesy for courtesy, 'It was kind of you to volunteer to do this party for me, I appreciate it very much.' *Volunteer*, had she known it, wasn't quite the right word, Oliver had needed to bring considerable pressure to bear, luckily unaware of any hidden overfalls or even he would possibly never have dared. Susan, with an unidentified conviction that this first encounter needed to be brief, intervened here.

'Get your luggage upstairs, and let's have lunch, we're all starving! Annabel, show Uncle Mawgan the way – which room, Mother?' Susan at her organising best – or worst. Carl hurriedly suppressed a grin of appreciation; he knew his Susan well by this time.

Dot said, 'I put them in the yellow room, Annabel dear,' and felt overwhelmed. Seb heaved up the cold box again.

'Shall I take this to the kitchen, Grandma?'

'I'll do it, it's some heavy for you,' Mawgan jumped in swiftly, perhaps with the aim of escaping to draw breath for a minute. If so, he was out of luck.

'Tell you what,' said Debbie, laughing. 'Don't quarrel about it, the pair of you, please! Carl can carry the luggage, I'll show him the way, and Annabel can take you to the kitchen and you can bury your dead in the fridge.'

'We left a shelf empty for you,' said Dot, bustling forward. 'Just bring the box this way.' She led the way. Annabel shrugged her shoulders and exchanged a grin with her mother, remarking with a disconcertingly adult perception, 'That went off all right, didn't it Mummy? You were scared, weren't you?'

'Rubbish!' Susan denied. She resumed the upper hand, slightly shaken. How much had Annabel observed or overheard just lately? 'Go and wash your hands ready for lunch, please – you too, Sebby. It shouldn't be long now.'

Lunch, predictably, was an awkward meal, although it never reached the point of being actually uncomfortable. The family assembled around the table was a newborn entity, unsure of its feet in an unfamiliar world, at least two of its components treading very carefully indeed. The brunt of the conversation was borne by Debbie and Carl, even the children feeling an atmosphere and being very quiet. Towards the end, Dot said, in a firm tone more like her usual self, 'Deborah, after that long drive I think you should rest this afternoon, if you intend to go out partying this evening.'

'Come on Mum, I'm not feeble!' Debbie began to protest, but Mawgan unexpectedly gave his support to Dot.

'No, she's quite right, bird. You want to enjoy yourself tonight, and we don't want to be worrying over you none. Do what you're told, for once.' He smiled at her, taking the sting from the adjuration. Dot looked at him with approval, something she had never expected to feel.

'Your husband will want to be in the kitchen in any case,' she said, putting an end to the discussion and Mawgan in his place at the same time. 'The girl will help him, she has agreed to stay on.' Had leapt at the chance to score so many points with her friends, in fact. Dot was still having trouble with "Mawgan", she needed to work on it. There was something about both young men that was so alien to her experience that she didn't know quite how to treat them for each of them did come from another world in one very real sense, but with her son-in-law, of course, there was another consideration too. He sat there at her table, smiling pleasantly at her and bearing his part in what conversation there was like a Christian, but he made her nervous. Nervousness made her unnecessarily brisk, and unusually aware of it. She looked towards Susan, as the only one apart from the children with whom she felt relatively at ease at this precise moment, and asked, 'What time is this "do" of yours this evening? Because I have tickets for the pantomime at the Winter Gardens for myself and Sally and the children, why should you people have all the fun? But we shall need to eat early if we are picking up Sally on the way.'

A squeal of delight from Annabel greeted this announcement, and a contented grin from Sebastian. 'What is it this time, Grandma?' Annabel demanded.

'Robinson Crusoe,' said Dot, smiling at them, and Susan added. 'What a lovely idea! Say thank you to Grandma, both of you.'

The thanks being enthusiastically given, Dot returned to her original question. 'So, what time will you be leaving?'

'It's seven-thirty for eight I think – but don't worry about us, there'll be a buffet, there always is. We can last until then, and we'll lock up. I've got my keys with me.'

Dot nodded her approval of this arrangement, and the meal being over, Mawgan and Debbie retired upstairs to the yellow room to unpack and settle in, and Carl was deputed to tidy the Porsche away into the last of the three garages. Dot noticed that Mawgan looked around him with interest as he followed Debbie upstairs. The first – and last – time that he had seen this house it had been almost dark, she recalled, just the light at the foot of the stairs and the shadows

... and when she had put on the light in the drawing room he had never come into the room, but stayed in the doorway and ... she closed her eyes. It was not a good memory. He had succeeded in scaring her witless without coming anywhere near her, and every time she looked at his pleasant, smiling face now, be it on her television or in the flesh, as at present, she felt sick. The necessity to grapple with this was looming like a bull elephant. They had to find some common ground on which to stand, only, she didn't want to do it; put bluntly, she knew him for what he was, or what he could be at least, and she was afraid of him. End of story. But at least he seemed impressed with her home. Good! That might serve to keep him in his place.

Dot had yet to know her irreverent son-in-law.

Up in the yellow room, Debbie had flopped onto the bed and kicked off her shoes, leaving Mawgan to sort out the hastily dumped luggage and unpack what he needed before he went down to do some preliminary work on tomorrow's dinner. 'This house is amazing,' he said, heaving Debbie's suitcase onto a chair ready for her to unpack, and his own modest overnight bag onto the bed. He unzipped this and looked at the contents as if he had never seen them before. 'It's huge! How big – six bedrooms?' He had realised it was big on his previous visit, but exactly how big had been to a certain extent disguised by the night and the lack of lights.

'Seven.' Far from unpacking, Debbie still sat comfortably on the edge of the big bed.

'And she lives in it all on her own? She must be mad!'

'She hasn't always, of course, don't be silly!' Debbie smiled at him. 'We all lived here when we were children, naturally. Oliver left first, then Susan got married, then I went to London, then Dad, last year ...' She paused, listening to what she had been saying. 'I see what you mean. But she won't move, you know. She loves this house, she's been polishing and perfecting it for over twenty years. It's her life.'

'Pretty pointless life,' observed Mawgan. 'Your Mum's got a problem, Deb, if you ask me. She's high and dry and the tide hasn't come in. She needs rescuing.'

Debbie had never considered it like this: for one thing, until today she had never been back since her marriage nearly two years ago. It now seemed to her that Mawgan was right, and her mother must be not only mad to live here alone, but terribly lonely as well. The fact that it was to a large extent a self-inflicted wound was merely sad on top of everything else.

Mawgan had extracted clean jeans and a T-shirt from his bag, leaving the rest of his things in chaos, and was heading off to the en-suite bathroom. 'You need to do something about it, bird, you and Susan,' he told her. The bathroom door closed behind him, leaving Debbie wondering, like what, exactly? She began to unpack, extracting Mawgan's suit from its zipped carrier and hanging it in the wardrobe. Tonight would be cheerfully informal, but tomorrow Dot would be expecting the full regalia. She sighed. Mawgan had a point, but how on earth did one change the convictions of a lifetime in someone as intransigent as their mother?

Mawgan reappeared ready for action, grabbed a striped butcher's apron from the muddle on the bed, and disappeared to spend the afternoon in the kitchen with "the girl", a basket of shopping bought by Dot in accordance with a list forwarded by Debbie, and tomorrow's pudding course, both Dot's choices of which could be conveniently started in advance and finished off before the dinner, leaving tomorrow morning clear to visit the market and source farm-fresh vegetables, local cheeses, and other goodies. Debbie wondered if Dot would appear in her kitchen to supervise, and on the whole, hoped not. She stuffed Mawgan's empty bag inside her case and went downstairs to the drawing room to do as she had been told, and rest. She had just settled herself on the big sofa with *Country Life* when Susan put her head round the door.

'The rain's stopped, we're just going to take the children for a breath of air by the water. They've been cooped up in the car all morning, they need a run. Will you be OK?' She had made Annabel and Seb sound as if they were a pair of dogs, and Debbie laughed.

'Of course I will, silly!'

'Don't get in an argument with Mother while we're gone,' Susan warned her, before withdrawing her head. Out in the hall, Debbie could hear the cheerful sounds of a family getting itself ready for an outing: with a contented sigh, she snuggled into the sofa cushions and resumed her magazine.

Dot found her there later, and said approvingly. 'Good girl. Now, are you quite comfortable?'

'Of course I am. Bit bored.' Debbie yawned. 'How's things in the kitchen?'

'It all seems very organised,' said Dot, as if she had expected something else. 'I just asked the girl to make us a cup of tea, I daresay she'll bring it in a moment.' She seated herself in an armchair where she could see her daughter. 'He's very competent, your husband.'

'He is, rather. Poetry in motion.' Debbie smiled at her mother, tempted to retreat into *Country Life*, but it wasn't an option.

'He seems pleasant enough.' It was said grudgingly, but at least it was said. Debbie didn't build too much on it, rightly as it happened. Dot hesitated, never a good omen. 'Are you happy, Deborah darling?'

'Blissfully,' said Debbie, meeting her eye.

'It's just that he seems so very different from what you have been brought up to expect,' said Dot. She sounded fretful. 'Susan's young man now, he's another thing. He's been to university, he's educated. Which is not to say that I approve of their lifestyle,' she added severely, in case Debbie got the wrong idea. 'But ...' she hesitated, and then went on, 'Mawgan comes from a completely different background. I find it hard to believe that you have much in common.'

'Maybe we don't,' said Debbie, thinking about it. 'Maybe that's why it works? Lots to talk about.'

'At least he seems to be doing quite well for himself,' said Dot grudgingly. If she was honest, it was another thing she was beginning to resent about him; she couldn't completely despise him and it made things very difficult. The television series, *Six Courses*, thankfully ended last week, had changed her life in too many ways. Changed her thinking. Changed her conception of friendship. Changed everything. She blamed Mawgan, but she was rapidly running out of anything more to hold against him, apart from the obvious one, naturally. She spoke with extra firmness to compensate for this unusual vacillation. 'You mustn't let those three keep you out until all hours tonight, Deborah. It seems to me that your sister is getting positively irresponsible!'

For a moment Debbie wondered whether to murmur a diplomatic "No Mum, I won't", but then she thought, if we're here to negotiate new terms, I shouldn't let that pass. If we want Mum to behave like a normal human being, perhaps we should treat her as if she *is* one?

76

So instead of diplomatic evasion, she said, 'Yes, I know. It suits her, don't you think? She's having fun at last.'

Dot was so startled that she didn't know what to say. Eventually, she found her voice. 'Whatever can you mean?'

Debbie set *Country Life* aside carefully to give herself time to think. She had started this, she didn't want to make a mess of it. She said, 'Susan hasn't exactly lived life to its last drop, has she? Married so early, children straight away – there's been no room to do the silly things the rest of us did when we were young, she had to be a grown-up before she really got a chance.'

'What nonsense you do talk, Deborah,' said Dot, and wondered why she suddenly felt uneasy. It was her talk with Sally all over again, and she was glad when "the girl" arrived with the tea on a tray and she could change the subject.

Later in the day, her complacency received yet another jolt. Susan was upstairs organising the children to get ready for the pantomime, and Dot, going into the drawing room to wait for them, found Carl, like Debbie earlier, passing the time with *Country Life*. He too laid the magazine aside as his hostess came into the room.

'They won't be long. I'm keeping out of the way,' he confessed. 'Susan in head-girl mode frightens me to death!' He smiled at her, and Dot, thus encouraged, stepped bravely out on what was to become yet another quicksand.

'You're very fond of Susan, aren't you?' she said, directly.

'I love her,' said Carl. He kept his tone neutral, and waited.

'But not enough to marry her,' said Dot, meeting his eyes. He read the challenge in her face, but he had expected it to come sooner or later, would have thought less of her, in fact, if it hadn't.

'I would marry her tomorrow, if it comes to that,' he said. 'It's Susan who is against the whole idea.'

'What nonsense!' Dot exclaimed, briskly. 'I'll speak to her. You can't go on like this, such a bad example for the children. I suppose she has some silly idea that it's daring and modern!'

'No,' said Carl. 'I mean, no, don't speak to her. She has no ideas, she's just afraid of it.'

'*Afraid* of it?' Dot stared at him.

Carl stopped lounging in the comfortable armchair and sat up straight. He chose his words with care. 'Susan found marriage to be a totally humiliating and largely unrewarding experience. She therefore values the freedom she now has very highly.'

'Nonsense,' repeated Dot, but with less conviction.

Carl said, 'I think, if she's left alone to sort it out for herself, eventually she'll change her mind. Right now, Susan is healing. I believe she'll be best left to do it in her own way.'

'But the children —'

'You must see for yourself that the children are fine. But that's another problem anyway.' He leaned forward, taking Susan's mother into their confidence as he had done with his own on a similar occasion. 'Annabel loves her father. She can accept me as a friend, but she isn't ready for a stepfather. As things are, we can function as a group and nobody needs to feel threatened, and I think that's important.'

'And what about you? Doesn't what you want count for anything?' Dot demanded, thinking that Susan was being incredibly selfish – but then, so she had been all along, over her marriage, over her children, over everything really. But she liked this young man, she found, he had a good feel to him. Unlike his predecessor ...

'More important than what I want,' Carl amended.

'And Sebastian?' said Dot, confrontationally. She was losing the battle and it made her want to push it to the limits – a conditioned reflex that had got her into trouble before this.

'Seb is a quite different problem. He doesn't much like his father, he's scared of him.'

Dot said, 'Rubbish!' for a change, but there was no conviction in the word. Sally had said much the same, but if it was true, how had she herself never noticed it?

'I'm afraid not.' Carl didn't explain further. Dot sat still, her thoughts in confusion, and after a while, Carl went on. 'These are problems that will sort themselves out, but only with time. You can't force any of the three of them, and neither can I. But I appreciate how much you must be worried, and I promise you this much; I'll look out for them all and take care of them, and if she ever learns to trust me enough, I'll marry Susan and be proud to. She's been badly hurt, but she's brave and strong and compassionate and clever, and you must be very proud of her.'

Was she? Dot had never thought about it. Deborah, yes, but Susan? It was a new idea. She deployed the first argument that came into her head. 'She wants to be an archaeologist.'

'Yes, I know. I think she'll be great at the job.'

'The children –'

For the second time, he interrupted her. 'The children will be practically grown up and living their own lives before she's fully qualified. She's timed it well. And face it, Mrs Nankervis, she isn't housewife material. She doesn't know which way up to hold a broom!' He smiled at her, inviting her to share the joke. Dot said, helplessly, and almost without volition, 'You had better call me Dorothy.'

'Thank you – Dorothy. I should be honoured.'

This time, it was the noisy arrival of Annabel and Sebastian, well-wrapped against the cold outside and full of excitement about their unexpected treat that saved Dot from further confusion. She rose to her feet with alacrity, picking up her bag and gloves.

'Come along then, children, we should be on our way to pick up your Grannie!' She swept them back out into the hall, where Susan had just reached the foot of the stairs. The sight of Susan further confused Dot, whose preconceived ideas had now added themselves to the mental mush caused by close contact with Mawgan, thanks to her brief but telling exchange with Carl. Those two young men had a lot to answer for! Something, however, must have crystallised into a definite concept somewhere in the sludge, she found herself smiling at Susan with a warmth normally reserved only for Deborah. Clever, brave, strong, compassionate ... if Susan was all those things, a mother *should* be proud. Her father would have been.

'There you are, Susan. Now you have a lovely evening, and don't worry about these two rapscallions. And take care of your sister, for she won't take care of herself!' Susan, startled by the unwonted warmth in both the smile and the words, said,

'And you have a good time too. We'll try to be quiet and not wake you when we come in, but I don't suppose we'll be that late. Behave yourselves, you two.' She kissed the children and pushed them towards the door in their grandmother's wake. 'Be good for Grandma, enjoy the show.'

The front door closed behind the three of them, and Susan, left standing a little blankly in the middle of the hall, became aware of Carl leaning against the frame of the drawing room door. She turned slowly to face him. 'What's got into her?' she asked, not expecting a reply but simply because the question was in the forefront of her mind.

'Why do you ask?' Carl enquired.

'I don't know ...' Susan hesitated. 'Because ... because she treated me ... I don't know.' She was used to being sidelined, reproved and bossed, and kept in her place, but loyalty forbade her to say that. She shrugged her shoulders helplessly. 'She was just different.' Changing a subject that was unexpectedly difficult, she looked at her watch. 'We've got an hour before we need to get ready to go and watch our reluctant celebrity chef being lionised, how shall we spend it?'

Carl stood up straight, away from the doorframe.

'Do you need suggestions from the floor?' he asked.

'I hoped you'd say that,' said Susan, contentedly, and turned for the stairs.

V

But, in the event, and rather to Mawgan's relief and Susan's surprise, in tonight's company, as it turned out, it wasn't Mawgan who was the lion; it was Carl. Introducing him to a group of her friends, his distinctive name made ears prick in recognition.

'Carl Colenso,' mused Merlin Ravenscourt, thoughtfully. 'That rings a bell. Weren't you on *Orb Technic* a few years back, the time she won the Round the World?' Carl admitted that he had been, and Val Harries, whose threatening position in regard to Tom was as yet unknown to Susan, as to himself, remarked, 'Largely thanks to a rather a brilliant young tactician, I seem to recall. You, wasn't it? I remember the name; come to that, it's hard to forget it.'

Carl admitted to the further charge, but added that the skipper, not to mention the rest of the crew had quite a lot to do with it as well.

'Yeah, Larsen was good,' Val allowed. 'Even if he was a second choice, he was a good choice.'

Carl looked surprised. 'Was he a second choice? I never heard that.'

'According to the grapevine, he was. I assumed it was true.'

Carl shook his head. 'Who told you?'

'James Filedale-Brown, he was the chap who set it all up, but you'll know that, of course. I supposed him to know what he was talking about. He was an associate of mine when I worked up in London, sort of.' Val looked at Susan, with an apologetic shrug. 'I suppose Susan doesn't know either, or you would by this time, too. They asked Oliver Nankervis first – about a week before he met the crunch that put paid to him ever racing again. They never got a reply. I imagine he didn't want to talk about it anyway, it was a bloody tragedy, what happened to him.'

'Well, that explains that, then,' Carl remarked, half to himself, unexpectedly shaken.

'Explains what?' Merlin's wife asked, curiously, but Carl only laughed, and said, 'Nothing.' Impossible to say in this company of strangers that what it explained was Oliver's attitude towards him, even if it had slightly abated over the past summer. Poor old Oliver!

He wondered if Oliver thought that he knew, but whether he did or whether he didn't, he would either have to get over it or do the opposite. There was no future in discussing it with him; they weren't on terms of intimacy. What he did say was deliberately controversial in what had been Oliver's home club, but a genuine opinion nonetheless, and had the desired effect of diverting the course of the discussion. 'Actually, Larsen was probably the best thing that happened to *Orb*. I wouldn't rate Oliver as a racing skipper, unless it was single-handed. He isn't what you'd call a team player, he only plays against himself. Larsen has bigger teeth.' There was a murmur of objection, but put so bluntly, few of those present could find a valid argument against.

'He used to race a Finn,' Merlin remarked, and made a face. 'He was good, that goes without saying, but you're right, his heart wasn't really in it. You must know him very well: that was a swingeingly honest estimation, and probably deadly accurate. But he was a Name back then, of course, after setting a record circumnavigating the globe. It was sponsorship they were after.'

Carl didn't think he knew Oliver well at all, and from her face, neither did Susan, but he supposed it was true that he *understood* him, because of their common, but not shared, experience. He didn't think it was quite the same, and had nothing to say.

'Are you planning to race *Silver Spirit*?' somebody else asked. 'That'll make them sit up in Embridge! Tom Casson was scared to take her off the mooring! Sorry Susan, but it's true.'

'She's up for sale,' said Susan, offhandedly, for truth to tell, the fact that her beautiful classic ketch had been a casualty in her divorce from Tom was a sore point. 'Carl has a boat of his own. We don't need two.' It was a brave show, but Merlin gave her a grave look.

'Even so, I can imagine how you're feeling. She's a lovely boat, have you seen her, Carl?'

'Not so far.'

'No point. She's for sale, and that's that.' Susan sounded more brusque than she had intended. She added quickly, 'But of course, we can look at her if you like. She's in the marina, they've got her on the books at the agency there. But Hierax is more practical for us, with the children and everything. More fun for them.' *Hierax* was Carl's boat, and there was no question of doing a deal over *Silver Spirit*. *Hierax* represented Carl's independence.

'Much interest?' Bob Chase, who, together with Merlin, owned the Taverners' Shipyard at Emberton, asked the question casually, and Susan lifted her shoulders in negation.

'Not so far, she's not exactly going for peanuts and most people look, yearn, and walk away, apparently. Maybe after the Boat Show next month.'

'Only,' said Bob, more purposefully, 'we might know of somebody who'd like her, and more important, can afford her. Should you really want to sell.'

'Oh? Anyone I know?' Susan looked interested.

'I can't really answer that until I've put out a few feelers. But if he buys her, she'll be in good hands. The best.'

'I suppose that'll be some consolation.' Susan sighed, regretfully. 'If she's got to go – and she has – I'd sooner see her go to someone who would love her and make real use of her.'

'No question about that,' Bob assured her. 'Pity in a way, though. I'd've been interested to see your friend here put her through her paces and maybe knock the smug expressions off some of those toffee-nosed stuffed shirts at Embridge Harbour.'

Susan grinned at him, like Carl earlier happy to move the conversation on. 'Do I sense a little inter-club friction here?'

'It's a long story,' said Merlin, rising to his feet. 'Time to get in another round. Carl? What are you on? It'll be a real pleasure to buy you a drink.'

'I'll come and help you carry them,' said Val, already standing. They collected orders and headed for the bar, and the talk veered again, back to Ocean Racing, and *Orb Technic*, and Susan sat back and listened, enjoying being among old friends again – old friends, she now realised, from whom Tom Casson had to a certain extent cut her off, preferring as he did the more rarefied atmosphere of the town yacht club. There were some new faces too, but then, she had been out of the dinghy racing scene for some years now, witnessing her ex-husband showing off on *Silver Spirit*, and yes, that had mainly been on a mooring, being the Committee Boat while others raced. Carl was unexpectedly giving her a VIP passport back into a past life, and it felt good; how had she come to let herself drift away after her marriage? She settled down to enjoy herself.

Debbie, some years younger than her sister and far more of a dinghy sailor anyway, had run with a different crowd. It included Val's younger sister Penny, his racing crew Rob Lambert, Jake Thomas, who had crewed for her old friend Tim Howells and probably still did, and among others, although he had not yet appeared, Tim himself of course. She wondered whether to ask Jake if he was expected, and thought better of it. Best not to draw attention and hopefully he wouldn't be here anyway. Acquitted of burning down his business premises for the insurance money only due to lack of evidence, poor Tim must still be lingering under a small, rather smoky black cloud of doubt and probably kept a low profile these days. Debbie, who had never been absolutely certain in her own mind whether he was guilty or not, could only be grateful, since he and Mawgan were like two tomcats, and her own obvious pregnancy wouldn't help.

The pleasure of her friends when they saw her had been heartwarming. She had been in Cornwall nearly three years now, and had wondered if they might have forgotten her. No chance. 'You should have come back long ago,' Penny told her, firmly 'Just coming to your wedding wasn't good enough! We've missed you lots, you know.'

'And you missed all the fun,' Jake added, with a grin.

'What fun? What have I been missing?' Debbie asked, and was immediately and horribly aware of a sinking feeling as she thought, *Tim*. She would know far more about that than they did, and even then, not everything. But once again, no chance. Penny was smiling wickedly.

'Look about you. See anyone not here?'

'How can you see someone who isn't here?' Debbie objected, but she looked around her all the same. It seemed to her that all the usual suspects were assembled in their accustomed places, and she said so. 'Nope. Looks like a full house to me.'

'Look again.'

Debbie shook her head. 'I don't know, you'll have to tell me.'

'No stray farmers propping up the bar?' Rob prompted her, and Debbie was forced to admit that no, there weren't.

'Francis Chillingworth isn't here. So what? There's still time, and anyway, he quite often isn't.'

'In the summer, when he's harvesting or something. You don't harvest in the depths of winter – except cabbages I suppose, if he grows anything so mundane, but they're hardly urgent.'

Debbie would never have attached any significance to the absence of Francis Chillingworth, he was in any case very much a loner and not exactly a friend of any of them – or anyone else, now she came to think about it. She explained to Mawgan, who was a stranger here, 'Francis is a farmer, his family own half this part of Dorset, he sails a Moonraker – that's a kind of racing boat, they've a fleet here, and Penny's brother was the national champion until this year. He's older than us – quite a bit older, practically middle-aged, and lives with his mother, but so far as we know anyway, he's straight.'

'*Definitely* straight. And loaded,' Penny put in. 'Don't forget that.'

'And reputedly loaded,' said Debbie, more temperately.

'And the committee invited him to resign,' Penny went on, bright-eyed.

'Good gracious! Why ever?'

Penny had opened her mouth to reply, when she was interrupted. 'Hullo Deb,' said a familiar voice, and Debbie jumped, turning her head so suddenly she nearly cricked her neck. Tim Howells, hands in pockets, looked at her coolly and then at Mawgan. 'Evening, Angwin. Didn't expect to see you two here.' He went on smoothly, making mischief, Debbie thought, but couldn't see how. 'You've met Jake, have you?' His eyes were on Mawgan. 'His father is in the same trade as you, runs the Crown & Anchor in Eastbridge back in the town. You'll have a lot to talk about.'

Debbie got to her feet. She said that she felt like a hippopotamus, elephant, or other ungainly beast, but actually she was still a long way from that. Even so, her pregnancy was obvious, and she saw a look of pain cross Tim's face. He said, 'I see you are to be congratulated, both of you.'

Mawgan had risen too, to stand beside Debbie. He had kept a low profile in this gathering, feeling, to be truthful, immeasurably older than his wife's friends and knowing nothing of the people they were talking about, which almost seemed to set a gulf between him and his wife, but none of that meant that he was prepared to let Tim Howells take the piss. He knew exactly where Tim was heading, and there was no way but the direct way to forestall him. He said, easily enough, 'Yes, I remember the Crown & Anchor. We ran into each other there once.' He half-turned towards Debbie. 'It was the day I come up to see your Dad, remember? A couple of years back now, before we was married.'

'I'm suprised you even remember it,' said Tim, dryly. Mawgan laughed.

'I don't, that clearly, Susan told me which pub – probably so as I shouldn't go there again. That weren't a good day.' He paused. 'I b'lieve I owe you thanks.'

Tim gave it up. He had no genuine wish to hurt Debbie, and he had no real idea what all that had been about either, it had just been reaction from the sight of her, pregnant, more beautiful than ever, and completely out of the blue and his reach. He echoed the laugh, but it wasn't a good effort. 'Not surprised you can't remember. You were royally out of your head.'

Debbie had found her voice. 'You never told me.' She sounded accusing, as well she might, Mawgan thought, wincing inwardly.

'Didn't seem no point. You'd seen it all before anyway.'

'Do sit down, you three,' Penny interposed, plaintively. 'You're blocking the light. You can talk just as well down at our level. Aren't you going to say hullo to us, Tim?'

They sat, there seemed nothing else to do without drawing attention to themselves. The seating arrangements unfortunately left Tim confronting Mawgan, but the only one who shot them an apprehensive glance was Debbie, the others were unaware of any history, of course. They immediately began to distract Debbie's attention, filling her in on events since she had left for Cornwall, a subject which tended to exclude Mawgan, who knew none of the people they were discussing, and upset Tim, who had of late deliberately excluded himself where he had not been excluded. Mawgan was content to sit back and listen and learn more about the woman he had married, whose alien life previous to their meeting was to a great extent a closed book to him, but Tim felt wrong-footed and therefore confrontational.

'You look as if you're doing all right for yourself,' he said, and made it sound like an accusation. 'Although I hardly need to ask, what with your face all over the telly.'

Mawgan said, neutrally he hoped, 'Oh, the devil looks after his own. And you?' It was a natural question, but he could have kicked himself immediately afterwards. Tim looked as if the kick had landed painfully on his shin.

'What do you think? You've been here.' He went on, with bitter resentment, 'Only, your friend the devil was with you then, too, wasn't he? You had your own business, you didn't have to go crawling round begging for a job!'

Mawgan was taken aback by the venom, and indeed, the pain, in this speech. He said, momentarily bewildered, 'But you were acquitted, surely?'

'Because of insufficient evidence – that is, nobody could prove I did it. By the same token, I can't prove I *didn't* do it. Believe me, an arsonist isn't everybody's favourite job applicant!'

Mawgan, for various reasons, mostly unflattering, had never believed that Tim had set fire to his business premises, and although he didn't like Tim, he was suddenly desperately sorry for him. He didn't know quite what to say, so he said nothing. Tim looked at him sardonically.

'See what I mean? You don't even want to discuss it, because you think you don't want to hear more excuses and lies. Just like everyone else.'

Mawgan said, carefully, 'Is that what they say?'

'No, of course not. But you can see it in their eyes, and the way they turn away. And the way nobody will employ me, come to that. Would *you* – employ me?' It was a direct challenge, eye to eye. Mawgan spoke even more carefully than before.

'I'm in the restaurant business. You're an engineer, so Deb tells me.'

'Very neat,' said Tim, approvingly. 'Congratulations. It overlooks, of course, that I am also a sailing instructor, and *your wife* –' with deliberate emphasis, '– runs a sailing school.'

Mawgan shook his head. 'Not a good idea, you must see that. For your own sake, leave alone Deb's.'

'Oh well. I suppose I can be grateful you didn't give me an outright "no", anyway,' said Tim, and there was something hopeless in the way he said it that rang a warning bell in the back of Mawgan's mind. For Tim was right, he had been there, and nearly paid the penalty too, had the luck not gone with him. He spoke on impulse, without really thinking it out.

'OK then. You and me haven't never been friends, but tell me this. Suppose I sponsored you through a business management course, and then arranged for you to learn *my* business in a top restaurant, would you *want* to work for me? And I don't mean as a chef.'

Tim simply stared at him, shocked. He didn't even know if Mawgan had asked a serious question; he did know that he himself had spoken to this man – this man that he disliked – with less protective reservation than he had to anyone for quite some time, even if it was simply because he was the only person he knew who had shared his own bitter experience. After a minute or two, he found his voice. 'You don't mean that.'

Mawgan had said the first thing that came into his head, now he found that he *had* meant it. His ill-thought out question had set off an idea, fizzing like a rocket the second after a match had been applied to the touch paper. It would require an able assistant if it was to work: he didn't like Tim but would he need to? He had respected Tim's ability in his own particular field, that was what really mattered. He decided on the instant to pursue the hare he had started and to see how it ran. He said, 'Well, would you?'

Tim swallowed. If this was a joke, it was the cruellest joke he had ever heard, and he didn't think Angwin, whatever his other faults and he had many, would do that.

'I'd work for your friend the devil himself, just so long as it was a halfway decent job I could take some pride in,' he said.

'Even if it meant working out of the country, maybe, for a while – a year, say?'

Tim opened his mouth, but no words came out. He swallowed again, although his mouth had gone dry. After the miserable year just passed, and the long sequence of rejections he had recently received, his thought processes seemed to have shut down. He wasn't sure that Angwin meant what he was saying. Absurdly, he wanted to burst into embarrassing tears, here in front of everyone.

It was at this moment – inopportune, or opportune? – that Susan noticed the unlikely juxtaposition of Mawgan and Tim, and the tension that showed clearly between them. She touched Val, to whom she had been talking, on the arm. 'I think it might be merciful to break that up,' she said, nodding in their direction. 'Those two hate each other's guts, I can't imagine what Deb is thinking of, and anyway, my brother-in-law is about a hundred years older than any of that lot. Shall we rescue him?'

Val was well aware that Debbie and Tim had once been an item, and like most people, had a pretty good idea why Tim's marriage had broken in pieces so soon after its inception. He saw Susan's point straight away. They moved to the rescue: neither Tim nor Mawgan was sure whether this was a good thing or a bad, but it effectively ended their conversation. Debbie, Susan thought, looked startled, as if she hadn't realised what was going on, too busy enjoying herself no doubt. There were times when her little sister needed a good shake, she took far too much for granted!

'Come and join the grown-ups for a bit, Mawgan,' she invited. 'That crowd over there are all Oliver's friends, come and say hullo – this is Val, he's one of them. He's just been telling me, he's going to work for Uncle Alex in the same office as Tom in the New Year. Deb can join us when she's ready. D'you mind, Deb?'

'No, you take him away,' Debbie waved a lazily dismissive hand. 'I'll join you in a sec.' She turned back to her interrupted conversation, and Tim, thus abandoned, got to his feet and went over to the bar for a refill. He found to his shame that his knees were trembling. He still wasn't sure what all that had really been about and he knew he could never ask, in case it turned into yet another humiliating disappointment. If Angwin meant what he said, and hadn't just been talking because he liked the sound of his own voice, it was up to him to take it further.

Later, when the buffet was but a memory and the band had warmed up, Debbie, dancing in her husband's arms, said, 'I thought Tim looked bloody awful. What was he saying to you?'

'I think your friend Tim's come face to face with real life,' said Mawgan. 'Seems he's not the most popular job applicant in the queue right now.' He had no intention of telling her exactly what Tim had said, fully aware that it had only been said because he, Mawgan, was who he was, but that was near enough.

Debbie looked troubled. 'Poor Tim, that's pretty rotten. But he was acquitted. Surely ...?'

'For lack of evidence, Deb. I know that scene, been the lead in it myself.'

'You weren't acquitted, not at the time.'

'Of murder, I was. I could've gone down for twenty years, not just three and there's still those as think I should've. You know that.'

It didn't bear thinking about, let alone discussing. Debbie said, 'So what will he do, do you think?' When Mawgan said nothing, she went on, 'Perhaps I should offer him a job at the Phoenix. We'll need instructors come the summer, and he's good. The best; we know he is.'

'No Deb. I don't think so.'

Debbie looked at him with serious eyes. 'Because of all that business over Lesley? That's history, Mawgan. He hardly spoke to me earlier on.'

'And that's the way you need to keep it, bird. Anyway, think about it. Working for you he'd be working for Roger, too.'

'And Carl,' said Debbie, argumentatively.

'Carl don't matter. He don't know Carl. But Roger worked for *him*. Come to that, so did you. No Deb, you leave it alone. Anyway, it's a proper job he needs, not tempor'y.'

They circled to the music for a turn or two. Debbie said, moodily, 'Ain't life a bitch? Tim and I were such good friends back when.'

'Were,' said Mawgan, firmly.

'We practically grew up together,' said Debbie, wistfully. Mawgan looked down into her beautiful face and said nothing at all. In this alien place, among these strangers he was seeing another Debbie, one he hadn't met before. He would, he thought, like to know her, and the idea that had come to him earlier while speaking to Tim came back and sat squarely in the forefront of his mind. People shouldn't uproot too finally, there was no need for it. Deb had almost the whole of her life, until she met him, set against the background of this town. There was her mother too. Mawgan had Dot down already as a very lonely woman, whatever else she was. It occurred to him that his half-formed plans for making good use of Tim Howells, if they came to anything would clear the air and allow Deb to come home in peace. Shipping Tim off to Italy, which figured in them at some point, would get him right out of the way, and hopefully cure him of the last of his infatuation, best thing for everyone. He took Debbie a little closer into his arms and felt her response. She laid her cheek against his shoulder.

'Love you, Mawgan Angwin. Just you.'

On another part of the dance floor, Susan was dancing with Merlin Ravenscourt.

'Now tell me,' he said, 'how do you come to know Carl Colenso? And so well too!'

'He's Cornish,' Susan pointed out. 'My family has migrated to Cornwall. QED.'

'I'm technically Canadian, but you wouldn't meet me if you went to Canada, so that doesn't prove anything. So where did you meet?'

'At Deb's wedding, actually. He was one of the ushers – and before you ask, he's a partner in her sailing school project.'

'Blimey, is he really? No wonder she's making a bit of a name for herself! So how did *she* meet him?'

'She didn't – not just like that. Her other partner, Roger, knew him already, they met in the bar of a sailing club further up the river.'

'Life is full of surprises.' Merlin looked down at her thoughtfully. He remembered that he had never set much store by Tom Casson. 'He's done you the world of good, anyway – I always thought Debbie was the beauty between you two, but now I'm not so sure.'

Susan was unused to such compliments; she felt herself blush. They danced in silence for a minute or two.

'She's looking very happy,' Merlin observed, after a while. 'I like her celebrity chef, he seems a good bloke – although he has come as a bit of a surprise. We all thought, being such a stunner as she is, she'd ride off into the sunset with a handsome prince, but she seems to have settled for the frog. Probably a wise move, I never did care that much for princes, come to that.'

Susan couldn't help it, she burst out laughing. Merlin, looking at her critically, decided it suited her to laugh, and it did occur to him that it was a sight too seldom seen in the past. She said, 'You shouldn't say things like that, but I know what you mean. He wouldn't win first prize in a beauty competition, but he's no ambitions that way either. He's a star just the same.'

'Very likeable,' Merlin agreed, but Mawgan interested him less than Debbie's connection with Carl. 'Did Debbie know, when she took your Carl as a partner, that she had a tiger by the tail?'

'I think, at the time, she was so desperate for help she didn't even ask – or think about it,' said Susan, after a moment's thought. 'She found out eventually of course, but it was a done deed by then.'

Merlin asked, curiously, 'And does she have Oliver, too, on her payroll?'

'He takes the odd masterclass in advanced navigation in the winter. For the local sailing community, that is – they're generally packed out.'

'I should think so! Well, well. Not just a pretty face, your little sister, is she?'

'She has turned out to be unexpectedly shrewd,' Susan agreed. The sequence of sentimental sixties tunes came to an end at that point, and changed to something more up-tempo, bringing more people onto the floor. Merlin shook his head.

'Unless you feel like giving the meal you've just eaten a good shake-up, I suggest we call it a day for now,' he said. 'It's not that I'm getting old or anything, but I could do with a drink.' Susan was in agreement, and as they left the floor they fell in with Debbie and Mawgan and together made their way back to the bar, where they found not only Carl, but several more of their particular friends, and the evening continued on its merry way.

'What did you mean back then?' Susan asked Carl, under cover of the general talk, for at least one thing he had said had startled her a little. He looked at her quizzically.

'What did I mean back then, when?' he countered.

'When you said that Oliver only played against himself.'

'Oh ... that. Come on Susie, you must know what I meant. He's your brother.'

'I don't know,' said Susan. 'Tell me.'

Carl thought for a moment before he spoke; there was no point in starting an argument, after all. 'I think I meant that he pushes his personal boundaries beyond what is reasonable, but doesn't pay much attention to the competing ambitions of those around him. He's not a leader of men, he's a one-man band. Will that do?'

Susan considered this, and had to admit that as an estimation of her brother's character it had a certain amount of justice in it.

'You mean, you don't think you'd have won, if he'd been skipper on *Orb Technic*?'

'I didn't say that. I just think it wouldn't have been a foregone conclusion.'

'I see,' Susan, as well as Carl, realised that this would go nowhere. She put her glass down on the table and smiled at him. The DJ had returned to sentimental mode. 'I love this corny song – shall we go and smooch to it?'

Some time later, Debbie, finding herself by her sister, speculated on how the pantomime might have gone. 'For I'm not sure if Mum has quite caught up with the new Annabel and Seb,' she said. 'She might have had a bit of a shock, she's always been very much a "little children should be seen and not heard" sort of person.'

'I think,' said Susan, after consideration, 'that Mother is finding this weekend a bit of a mystery tour. She's very muted, somehow.'

Debbie made a face. 'I don't know about that. She seems almost afraid of Mawgan, have you noticed? I can't work out if it's just because he's an alien, or she's in awe of his fame – which seems unlikely – or what it is. But I definitely get that impression.'

'Don't be silly, Deb,' said Susan, in her best big-sister fashion. She hesitated, for Debbie had given her an opening to say something that she had an instinct needed saying, but which Debbie wasn't going to like. 'Deb ... about tomorrow.'

'Yes?' prompted Debbie, after a long pause. 'What about tomorrow? Apart from its being a minefield, that is – but it should be OK if we can keep Mum and Mawgan apart, or at least, not leave them alone together.'

'That's the point,' said Susan, seizing the bull by the horns since it was strolling past. 'I think we *should* leave them together. I think ... you might not like this.'

'Suse, for heaven's sake, come out with it! Get it off your chest, what's bothering you?'

But that, Susan couldn't actually tell her. She compromised by saying, 'I've been thinking. It might be a good thing if you could *not* go with them to the market tomorrow. Say you're tired after the party, or something ... just let them go and fight it out in private. I know you'll be disappointed and probably bored to tears as well. I just think, they need to talk on their own.'

Debbie looked at her for a long moment. Then she said, in an odd voice, 'What do you know that I don't, Suse?'

'Nothing!' said Susan, hastily. 'I just think ...' she broke off, helplessly. 'Anyway, that's what I think.'

'You seem to have been doing a lot of thinking,' Debbie remarked, caustically.

'Yes,' said Susan, with a meekness that made her sister look at her suspiciously.

'You might tell me, if it concerns me,' she said.

'There's nothing to tell. It's just –'

'– what you think. I'd grasped that, thank you!'

For a moment, the seeds of dissent fluttered almost visibly down from the rafters, but Susan looked so innocent that Debbie suddenly decided that she was being paranoid. What could Susan possibly be hiding from her anyway? She said, judiciously, 'Well, maybe you've got a point. Perhaps if they had a good old wingding, it might clear the air.' She ended on a doubtful note.

Susan said bracingly, 'That's just what I was thinking!' and they both burst out laughing.

The dangerous moment was past – for now. Relieved to have got it behind her, and with comparative ease too, Susan changed the subject back to the pantomime. Truth to tell, she was more than a little apprehensive about what she had just set in motion. Almost, she hoped that Deb would back out at the last minute and make one of the marketing party.

Except that, if Deb did that, this weekend would have achieved, in real terms, precisely nothing.

The pantomime was going rather more smoothly than the sailing club party; it had the advantage of being familiar ground peopled with no unknown quantities, whereas Carl and Mawgan had caused definite ripples in the social stream, each in his own way. Dot and Sally made a mutual effort to give Annabel and Seb a wonderful evening, so that everyone had a good time. It was only when Sally had been dropped at her own home and Dot had seen her grandchildren safely into bed that it occurred to her to wonder what had been different about it.

What had so subtly but so unmistakeably changed Annabel and Sebastian? What, indeed, had needed changing, for the change was definitely for the better. Dot, rather against what she considered her wiser judgement, had been impressed with Carl, but she knew that he wasn't the whole answer, he couldn't be. There had to be something else. She wished she knew what it was; she could use some of it herself, she thought with a sigh. It was a pity that it wasn't a particular essence that could be sprayed around at will. She had an unfocussed feeling that it was more a kind of Philosopher's Stone that she had been seeking since the day she was born and in spite of her efforts, had never found. It had come into the house today ...

It had come into the house today in the wake of one, or both, of those young men whom she had done her best to exclude. It had a name, but Dot was a stranger to it, she had never been properly introduced. It was called "happiness" and it had eluded her, if you discounted one short period in her schooldays, ever since she was a very small child.

Without conscious thought, she glanced at the clock on her mantelpiece and saw, with an unfamiliar pang of disappointment, that it was only half past ten. They wouldn't be back for some time yet, if she knew her daughters. They would dance the night away – or Deborah would, at least – and return, like Cinderella, at midnight or even later. She might as well go to bed as sit here lonely.

The word brought her up short. Unlike "happiness", it was one with which she was well acquainted.

It had been slowly dawning on Dot for some time now that she had made a monumental mess of her life. She wasn't sure how, or why, but the reactions of those around her had made it apparent. Helen had hated her, Nonie Fingall had despised her, Henry had died, although that was hardly his fault; Jerry had left her, not once, but twice, and for the same woman; her children had gone to live over two hundred miles away, her friends laughed at her. Not much to show for almost sixty years of living. Just a huge, beautiful, empty house, the handful of friends who remained, and ... nothing. And yet, she had meant no harm. She had only wanted to protect them.

Dot pulled herself together. This wouldn't do! She was a fortunate woman, by any standards, she should look on the positive side. She had a lovely home, her grandchildren were upstairs now, sleeping in their beds; her daughters would be here tomorrow, helping with her party. The sadly few friends who remained were the ones who were worth having, the rest were better gone if that was how they felt! As Susan had once pointed out, the road to Cornwall ran both ways, and although she hadn't married him, and his lifestyle was unusual, her Carl was far from the opportunistic hanger-on that Dot had expected. She had sensed both strength and goodness in him, and knew she should be glad for Susan. Her husband, whom Dot had herself hand-picked, had failed to make her happy, after all.

Dot moved restlessly around the room, picking things up and putting them down again, unable to settle. It wasn't Carl who was the problem, as it happened he seemed to present no problem at all. It was the other one. The one that Deborah, the core of her heart, had married so precipitately. Deborah was unmistakeably happy, but how, Dot asked herself, was she, or come to that, Mawgan, to get out of the pit they had dug to their mutual disadvantage? There was no way! And if there was, they would still have nothing in common beyond Debbie.

For the second time, she thought that she really ought to go to bed. She was getting maudlin, and that she despised. Things were as they were, and it was no use wishing back the past because really, that had been no different. People just never seemed to understand her motives, they automatically appeared to think the worst.

It hadn't yet occurred to her that perhaps her motives were at fault. Things had always seemed so obvious to her: Helen had been a silly little thing, very young, and selfish too, and she herself had only wanted Jerry to be happy even if he had dumped her. Anona Fingall had led a most irregular life with that dreadful Sutton man, she was a totally unsuitable influence for an impressionable little boy. Mawgan had killed a man and gone to prison for it. Divorce was wrong, and so was living with a man without the bonds of matrimony, however pleasant he seemed to be.

Her own life had begun when Jerry entered it. It had somehow managed to end, twice now, when he left. She didn't think back further than that.

Dot resolutely left the drawing room, checked the locks on the back door and, leaving the front door on the latch and the lights on the stairs burning, made her way upstairs to her lonely bedroom.

Even when she was in bed, she couldn't sleep. She lay in the dark, eyes open wide, knowing that she was waiting for them to return, to bring the house to life again. She despised herself, but couldn't help it.

In the depths of the dark, quiet house, silence reigned. The children slept, but Dot did not. She fancied she could hear her heart beating in the lonely room that once she had shared with Jerry.

It was well past midnight when she heard, at last, the purr of a car and the scrunch of its wheels on the gravel of the drive. It drove straight past the front door to the garage, so that the slam of the doors was muted. There was a burst of distant laughter, swiftly hushed. It had been Carl's car, Dot knew, the scarlet monster had remained in the garage, and Deborah would be driving; she hadn't been drinking of course. She realised that she was lying rigid, and tried to relax.

Footsteps crunched on the gravel now, the latch on the front door clicked. Soft voices spoke in the hall, more laughter, very quiet. They were coming upstairs now. Dot heard someone stumble and a squeak of surprise, a giggle, swiftly cut off, and someone else said 'Sssh!', she thought it was Susan. Two doors opened and as quietly closed. For a short while, the plumbing gurgled, then the house fell silent again.

That feeling was back, like a wave of warmth reaching into a cold place. The house no longer felt empty but full of life, full of people as it had been meant to be. Seven souls slept under its roof and for the moment, Dot almost fancied she could feel its contentment.

But early on Sunday they would all be gone, back to their own lives. In a sudden rush of feeling, quite unlike her usual self, disregarding entirely for a brief moment her problems with her son-in-law, Dot wondered how she was going to bear it.

VI

Susan had wondered if Debbie would back out of their agreement when it came to it, but she didn't. It was Mawgan and Dot who caused the problems. In retrospect, perhaps she should have expected that.

Debbie remarked at breakfast time that she thought she might chicken out of the morning's expedition, and spend a quiet morning at home with a book. Mawgan leapt in first, with an alarmed look in his eyes – of course, there might be more than one reason for that, if it hadn't been for what he actually said. 'Oh, don't do that, bird – you know how much you've been looking forward to it.'

'That was then,' said Debbie, reaching a languid hand for the toast rack. 'This morning, I seem to have run out of enthusiasm. I don't think Daniel likes late nights.'

'Daniel?' asked Dot, before she could stop herself. Debbie smiled at her.

'Your grandson. Hopefully, it means he isn't going to be a party animal like his dad.'

Dot was not amused. She looked at Debbie severely. 'I trust that doesn't mean that you overdid it. You were back very late.' She paused, seizing on a heaven-sent lifeline. 'Perhaps I had better stay here with you. Susan will be out, of course, and I'm sure your husband can find his way perfectly well.' She made it sound like a deliberate plan on Susan's part to escape her sisterly duty.

Susan held her breath. Debbie raised her eyes from her buttering, and innocently returned her mother's stare. 'It's sweet of you Mum, but you go. I just want peace to be honest – and Leanne will be here, anyway. I shan't be on my own.'

Dot was successfully sidetracked. 'Leanne?' she sounded disapproving.

'Mrs Adams' daughter-in-law,' Debbie explained. 'We can't call them both Mrs Adams; Mrs A Senior will be here helping this afternoon and tonight. She said I should call her Leanne.'

Dot, of course, had the same problem, which was why she referred to her domestic help as "the girl". It hadn't occurred to her to call her by her given name, and it didn't occur to her now.

'You shouldn't have let her be so familiar, Deborah,' she said firmly.

'Mum, she's my age, and we don't live in the dark ages! I *can't* call her Mrs Adams, it would be ridiculous!' Was there a glint of rebellion there? Dot wasn't sure. She looked down her nose.

'And will she call you Deborah in return?' she asked, sarcastically, but Debbie only laughed.

'Debbie, more likely,' she said.

'I'm not sure that I approve,' Dot said, firmly, realising she was on a hiding to nothing here, and Debbie wisely kept silent. She accepted the marmalade from Annabel and went serenely on with her breakfast. Dot went on, 'Just the same, I'm not sure you should be left on your own with just the staff. I think perhaps I shall stay here. I won't bother you, darling, just be there if you need me.'

'There's no need,' said Debbie. 'I'm fine. Don't fuss, Mum! And Mawgan *will* need you to show him the way to the market. He'll never find it on his own, whatever you may think.'

'Draw me a map, I'll find it,' said Mawgan, immediately.

'Oh, do stop arguing, all of you!' Susan interrupted impatiently, 'Deb will be fine on her own, she's not going to give birth here and now, she just wants a bit of peace! Stop fussing over her, the pair of you, and stick to the original plan! You know you want to anyway, Mother, you know what you're like about having everything perfect when you entertain!' She felt Mawgan looking at her, and resolutely turned her own eyes away. Mawgan hadn't been fussing, and now, she thought uneasily he was more suspicious than anything. She suppressed the instinct to start humming, something she had always done as a child when she felt wrong-footed. That would never do, their mother had a memory like an elephant for things like that. She said, with a subtle shift of subject, 'We'll be back after lunch, I'll help Deb lay up the table if you like, Mother, and you can tell us how you want it done. Carl can carry chairs for you and take things down from high shelves, he's useful like that.'

Carl grinned at her across the table, but when they were about to get into the car later, he paused with his hand on the door. The children were safely in the back, arguing about who was going to choose what they did with Daddy this afternoon – a fruitless argument,

Susan thought, since Daddy would decide anyway – and Carl met Susan's eye across the roof and asked, 'So what was all that about at breakfast? Are you planning to let me into the plot?'

'What plot?' asked Susan, hurriedly opening her own door and preparing to get into the car.

'Don't play the innocent with me, Susie darling. This whole weekend has a strong flavour of an undercover operation. All three of you are up to something, you can't kid me!'

'All three?' asked Susan. She slid into her seat and Carl got in beside her. He looked at her assessingly.

'Oh yes, all three. You, Deb and Oliver. I exempt Mawgan, I don't think he has a clue what's going on, but he *does* know something. Doesn't he?'

'I suppose he does,' muttered Susan.

Carl had fastened his seatbelt and now started the engine. He said, 'You can tell me about it later. That way, I'm less likely to put my foot in it.'

'Was that a threat?' asked Susan, surprised.

'No. But when someone has only half a tale, they can bugger the whole works without even meaning to. Unless you don't trust me.'

'I trust you. It's not my secret.'

'Mmm. Deb doesn't know everything either, does she?'

'No. Come to that, neither does Oliver. So you're in good company. And I won't be telling either of them, either. I'm sorry.' She added, after a moment's thought, 'How did you know that?'

'She's at ease. You're not.'

So that's what you got, if you lived with a man who observed people as a necessary part of his working life. She must remember that.

The car slid away from the front steps, down towards the gate. Carl said, 'I would never force a confidence from you Susie, or make you break your word to anyone. I just wish you would trust me so that I can maybe help you.'

Susan thought about Mawgan and her mother, preparing to set forth in the Porsche in search of supplies, and then tried not to think about it. It suddenly seemed a monstrous arrangement.

'It's already too late for that,' she said. Annabel and Seb had stopped their argument and begun to listen. It was time to change the subject. 'After we've had coffee, and after Sally and Irwin have finished looking you over, we could go down to the marina and look at *Silver Spirit* if you like. There'll probably be time before we meet Joanna and Ian at the club.' This time she was referring to Embridge Harbour Yacht Club, that had come under such censure last night.

Carl recognised this for an olive branch, the lesser of two evils, maybe. He said, 'Yes, I would like. Thank you.'

Annabel leaned forward so that she was speaking practically in his ear. 'Couldn't we come too, Mummy?'

'No, you couldn't. You've seen her before, and you're meant to be spending time with your grandparents and your father.'

'They wouldn't mind.'

This whole day, so far, was making Susan's hair stand on end. She didn't mean to snap, but that's how it came out. 'I said *no*, Annabel!'

Annabel subsided into a hurt silence, and Carl shot Susan a swift sideways look, but made no comment, much to her relief. She said, 'Sorry, everyone. Maybe I got out of the wrong side of the bed this morning.'

Seb said, wisely, 'It was last night's party, I expect. You drank too much, like Uncle Mawgan does.'

'God, I hope not!' Susan regarded her brother-in-law's capacity for alcohol with awe but no admiration. 'But we were very late to bed, I suppose, after our journey.'

'That's what Grandma said to Auntie Debbie,' said Annabel, bouncing back with aplomb. 'Mummy, why is Carl coming with us to Grannie and Grandad? Won't Daddy mind?'

'They want to meet him, why wouldn't they? He's living with us all.'

'But he's not our Daddy,' said Annabel, on a note of contention. Once more, Seb came to the rescue.

'I expect they want to know he's not a bad influence. We'd better not say he's taught us to play gambling games.'

'What, strip Jack naked?' asked Susan, and thankfully, they all laughed. 'Turn right here, Carl – it's about four houses down on the left.'

There was no way that coffee with Sally and Irwin was going to be a relaxed occasion. Since Annabel and Sebastian, perhaps feeling an undercurrent, refused to go outside to play in the sunshine it was even more awkward than it should have been. They talked about Cornwall, about the sailing school, and about Seb's boat *Swallow*. This led to Annabel's pony Penelope Peppermint, who lived at present with their cousins in Devon, and it proved impossible to get the conversation back on track when nobody was sure what the track should be. Irwin wanted to ask all sorts of questions which, as Susan's ex-father-in-law, it wasn't his business to ask, and Sally was unusually subdued. Dot had told her last night that she thought that Carl Colenso would "do", and that she liked his influence on the children. It had made Sally feel dreadful, and meeting him now, she could see exactly why the usually judgemental Dot had said it. She grieved for her unfaithful and self-centred son, aware that there was no way back for him, and smiled with lips that felt stiff as she offered more coffee. The children had taken charge of the occasion, and thank goodness for that. It was a relief all round when Susan and Carl felt that they could decently take their leave and drive down to the marina. Glancing back for a final wave to the children as she got into the car, Susan caught a glimpse of Sally's sad face, watching them. Her wave was therefore perfunctory, and she bit her lip as she got into the car.

'I can't say that I enjoyed that,' she said.

Carl, belting himself into his seat, said, 'No. But they were right. It had to be done.'

'I'm not their daughter. It doesn't concern them.' Susan sounded argumentative. Carl started the engine and pulled away from the kerb before he answered.

'Yes it does. They wanted to know that Annabel and Seb would be OK.'

'And do you think they're convinced?'

'No telling. Let's hope so. Where now?'

'Oh, just turn right at the end here and keep going until you come to the road along the harbour.' Susan fell silent. There was one thing about this so far rather awful day that needed putting right, she had to work out a way to do it without breaking faith. Carl, she knew, would never bring the subject up again, but it would still be there between them. The drive to the marina was therefore very quiet; Carl didn't disturb her thinking, perhaps he was doing some of his own. They parked the car in the marina car park and collected the keys to the yacht from the office, and it wasn't until they were walking along the pontoon that the silence was really broken.

'I can't tell you everything,' said Susan. 'It isn't my secret. And what I *am* going to tell you, you mustn't say to a living soul.'

'You don't have to tell me anything at all,' said Carl, gently. 'I'm sorry if you think I was making an issue of it. If it's private family business, it's no affair of mine.'

'But it is,' said Susan. 'You're family now. You see, what Debbie doesn't know, and must never know, is that this isn't the first time that Mother and Mawgan have met.'

Carl might reasonably have responded with shock or amazement, but he didn't. Susan stole a sideways glance at him. Their pace had slowed. 'You aren't surprised.' It was a statement.

'Well ... yes and no. For two strangers who are supposed to be trying to make the best of things, they do seem very wary of each other. I couldn't help wondering.'

'They met just before the wedding. That's why she came, just to see them married, she didn't stay. Well, you know that anyway. She did it for Debbie, because she loves her.'

Carl found himself wondering what else she had done for Debbie because she loved her, there was something in the way Susan said it that opened up a wide field for conjecture. He knew he mustn't force a confidence she felt she couldn't give, and contented himself with saying, 'And I presume, he brought pressure to bear for the same reason?'

'Something like that,' said Susan, with relief. Carl thought about this.

'Then was it the wisest thing to turn them loose together without a referee?'

'Neither of them knows I know. Mother thinks only Jerry does, Mawgan knows Helen does too, but that's all. So who would you suggest for the position? They've got to settle it, you must see that.'

'So how come *you* know?' Carl asked, curiously.

'I was the one who ended up picking up the pieces in the Crown & Anchor that night.'

It was only half an answer. Although true as far as it went, Susan knew because she had done exactly what Carl had refrained from doing; made it a point of issue, in her case with Jerry. From neediness, not curiosity, but she had done so just the same. Privately, she was ashamed of it now, and fairly punished too, for it was an uncomfortable item of knowledge.

Carl decided to let the subject drop. He thought that Susan might have gone out on a limb over this, and be busily sawing at the branch behind her, but it wasn't for him to say so. He had already deduced that it was a family failing, both Deb and Susan were sometimes guilty of acting without thinking, and he suspected that their mother was the same only worse. He wondered a lot about Dot; she reminded him very much of Susan when he had first met her, all prickly defences and trying to run the world. He wondered even more, but only to himself, what was happening at the farmers' market.

Susan had brought them to a stop beside a big white-painted wooden ketch, sleek and immaculate and so obviously cherished that Carl, just for a moment, couldn't meet her eyes. He said, 'This is her? She's beautiful.'

Susan said, 'Yes,' and cleared her throat. 'Do you want to go aboard?'

'Not if you don't want to.'

'The gangplank is on the deck, but we can climb over the boat beside her.' She turned abruptly away to *Silver Spirit*'s smaller neighbour.

They climbed aboard and stood together on the foredeck, looking aft along the graceful curve of the deck. Carl said, 'I can see that it hurts to part with her. Do you really have to?'

Susan shrugged her shoulders. 'There's no point in keeping her, is there?' She managed a smile. 'A two-car family is OK, but a two-yacht family is ridiculous. Anyway, the upkeep on a wooden boat is horrific, you have no idea ... or perhaps you have, come to think.'

'What made you buy her in the first place? I know she's beautiful, but from what I heard at that party, she was too much for your husband to handle, so ... well, why?'

'I think I was trying to prove a point. Debbie and Oliver were so popular, I always felt overlooked, and this was my way of saying "Look at me". I'm ashamed of it now, and it got me nowhere, but I still love her for her – well, her loveliness, I suppose.'

Carl said, carefully, 'But presumably you could handle her, or you *wouldn't* have bought her.'

'Yes. But Tom ...' she left the sentence unfinished.

Carl said, quietly, after a long pause, 'I can always sell *Hierax* to the sailing school,' and Susan was silent for so long that he turned to study her, and saw that she was close to tears. 'Susie?'

Susan said, half choking, 'Do you truly love me that much?'

Carl took her in his arms, very gently. He said, 'Susie, can I ask you something?'

'If you want,' said Susan, muffled.

'How long is it since you were at that sailing club we went to last night?'

Susan was surprised; she had expected something different. 'Oh ... years. It's more a dinghy club. Tom preferred Embridge Harbour, it's very prestigious and quite hard to get into.'

The more he heard of Tom Casson, the more Carl was beginning to despise him. He let it pass, however, and asked what he had intended to ask to begin with. 'Did you even recognise the warmth with which all those people greeted you? Or are you so busy putting yourself down always that you can't see beyond it?'

'That was because of you.'

'The hell it was! Yes, when they realised I'd been on *Orb*, they were interested, of course they were, but they didn't know that just by looking at me, did they? They welcomed *you*, Susie, and don't tell me it was just because of Oliver and Deb because I shan't believe you.' Susan said nothing, and he went on. 'Listen Susie, because I'm not going to go on and on saying this. You aren't like Debbie and Oliver, you never will be, I don't even know why you want to be. You're a different person, a different *kind* of person. They're vivid and noticeable, but that doesn't mean that you're negligible by comparison, or that people don't recognise what you are, too. Whatever makes you believe they don't?'

Susan shook her head, unable to answer.

'Well then,' said Carl, knowing the answer but unable to push the point further. He wondered if confidence lost in childhood was ever entirely regained. 'Be an archaeologist,' he said. 'Be the best archaeologist in Cornwall, just for your own satisfaction and forget about trying to compete with them. What they want has never been what you need anyway, you're not even playing in the same game. And now, show me what goes on down below on this very beautiful boat.'

So Susan showed him, and when they had finished the tour, they sat down on the bench seat in the saloon, and Susan said, 'So now you know all about her – except for the instruments we have, of course, they're taken ashore for the winter for safety, and put back when she comes out for a scrub in the spring. What do you think?'

'She's a lovely ship, but I think I've said that already.'

'She is,' Susan agreed. She had herself in hand now, and was sorry for her stupid behaviour earlier. It occurred to her that this breakdown in confidence happened every time she came to Embridge and within the orbit of their mother, and she needed to confront it. But not right now. 'She is very beautiful, but she's not as much fun for the children as *Hierax* is, she's too big for them to sail properly. And I wouldn't ask you to sell your boat, Carl, she's not just a yacht, she's your insurance policy. Mine too.'

'In what way?' asked Carl, not sure he understood her correctly.

Susan replied simply, 'While you have her, I shall know that you're staying with us because you want to, and for no other reason. Is that clear enough for you?'

Carl was on the point of asking her if she really needed that assurance, and then he remembered Tom Casson again and knew that the answer was "yes". Knew why, too, and was enraged with Tom all over again, and with her mother who all her life had failed to protect her – not just against Tom, but Oliver too. He knew he would never be close friends with Oliver, and that this was why far more than Oliver's bitterness and grief over the blue-water sailing he would never experience again. He said nothing. Susan got to her feet.

'Now we've decided that, we'd better lock up again and go across to the club. It's only over the road, we can leave the car here, nobody will mind this time of year. I expect Joanna and Ian will be waiting for us by this time.'

The farmer's market was outside the town to the north, situated conveniently beside the road that led, eventually, to the big dual carriageway along the south coast, and not that far in actual distance from the avenue where she lived, but it felt like a hundred miles to

Dot. For one thing, quite apart from the man beside her, handling his outrageous red car with relaxed and confident skill, she very soon became aware that the car itself turned heads. Male heads, mainly. That, coupled with the fact that her companion was totally silent, made the short journey very embarrassing. She found herself wishing that he would say something – anything – which was unfair of her, since she couldn't think of anything to say either. It wasn't until they parked in the big car park beside the market that he switched off the powerful engine, unfastened his seatbelt, and turned to her. 'You and me've been set up,' he said.

'Yes,' Dot agreed. She reached for her handbag. 'So, let us concentrate on the job we have come to do.'

She received the glimmer of a smile that startled her. Nothing like the ferocious, unamused grin she had received on their first meeting; one that showed her a fleeting glimpse of an entirely different person.

'Right,' he said. 'And when we've done that, d'you think we might try an' go out and come in again? For Deb's sake, and the baby's?'

Dot said, darkly, 'It's Susan that's at the back of this.'

'I think so, too. She was there that night, did you know?'

It had sounded almost like a warning. Dot shook her head. It had never occurred to her to wonder what had happened after he left her; she had assumed, without thinking about it, that he had gone straight back to Cornwall, but that was only because she didn't know him at all. She wanted to ask "where?" but didn't, and reached hastily for the door handle. The man she had designated variously as a yahoo, a Neanderthal and a yob removed her big carrier bag from behind the front seats and thereafter carried it for her as a matter of course; and once again, she was thrown out of her stride. She led the way towards the sprawling red-brick building that housed the market.

The Embridge farmers' market was a permanent structure, open seven days a week. It consisted of a large open area where local produce from meat, fish and cheeses, through vegetables of all kinds to honeys, jams and chutneys was displayed for sale and, at one end, a row of internal shops selling various crafts. On the upper floor there was a restaurant that did morning coffee, light lunches and teas, with everything home-made, cakes and scones and home-baked bread, samples of which were also for sale below if people had liked them. Outside was an area where plants were sold. It was always busy. Mawgan regarded it with approval.

Going round the stalls together, deciding on what Dot should give her guests as a starter, as vegetables with the pheasant, whether or not there should be a soup to begin the meal; picking a selection of local cheeses to end with, discussing the merits of brussels sprouts against cabbage fried in butter with crispy curls of home-cured bacon and slices of crunchy red apple – something that was, so far, outside Dot's experience, but on which she was prepared to be flexible as she liked the idea of it – talking about these things, they found some common ground at last.

'Sprouts,' Dot observed, at one point, 'are traditional at Christmas. People expect them.'

'Surprise them,' said Mawgan, cheerfully, and she gave him a look that he didn't quite understand.

'That's what you're here for. Cabbage, then.'

Mawgan chose three pointy cabbages with drops of water clinging to their fat, green sides; Dot added parsnips and he said, 'Good idea. Roast or mashed with butter?'

'Oh, with butter, certainly. And freshly ground black pepper corns.' She sounded like Delia Smith, she realised, but Mawgan grinned appreciatively. 'And some of those tiny carrots – for colour, you know.'

'Right. That's enough, if you're serving an *hors d'oeuvre* with a salad garnish.' He spoke knowledgeably with the stallholder on the subject of potatoes, made his selection and added them to the bag. They moved on to lettuces and wild rocket, and then fell out briefly over a display of locally smoked fish. Dot fancied smoked salmon, Mawgan preferred hand-dived scallops still in their shells from a neighbouring stall; he won. They finished at the cheese counter, with the dawning of a mutual respect in this area, at least. There was still, however, a long bridge to cross, and so far they weren't even on the road that led there. It had all been done with such charm that Dot hadn't realised how many times she had been overruled, and on impulse, as they loaded their purchases into the space under the bonnet of the car, she decided to take the plunge.

'Now that's all done, shall we go and find ourselves a cup of coffee?' she asked. 'I think we've earned it, don't you?'

Mawgan hesitated; his conscience was quite as uneasy as hers, and he had less nerve in this situation than she, simply because Debbie was involved and he had taken himself way out of his depth. But he saw, quite as well as Susan, that something had to be done.

'Fine. If you'd like.'

He paid for the coffee without even querying it, and Dot, who had expected to pay for them both, had to remind herself about the television series and the lovely old pub she had seen by the water in Cornwall, and forcibly repudiate her original picture of a seedy publican who ran a café on the side and hadn't two pence in his pocket to rub together. The comforting residue of this image had been dying, hard but nonetheless, over the last twenty-four hours and was leaving her feeling rather defenceless. Once she had actually seen the Fish and the adjacent Rose back in the summer it had begun to waver anyway, but she had clung to it because in some way she hadn't properly considered it had seemed to justify her; now she was losing it altogether. But he had still tried to blackmail her, she told herself stoutly, and wished that she hadn't suggested coffee. It was too intimate, sitting at the little table by the window. She turned her eyes outward to the rolling downland of Dorset, at least that was immutable.

Mawgan said, equally concentrating, but on stirring sugar into his coffee, 'I don't want to talk about it neither, but we've got to. I was half off my head, what's your excuse?' He sounded merely interested. Dot swallowed. It had already been borne in upon her that this weekend was not, as she had imagined, a kind of capitulation but a way of giving her a chance to make peace. She had no idea what would happen if she failed to do so, but she did know that she dreaded whatever it would be. She therefore answered as honestly as she could bring herself to do.

'I wanted Deborah to be happy. And I was afraid I might lose her entirely if she married you.'

Mawgan looked at her properly then, and she met his eyes, she hoped, without flinching. She was surprised to see kindness in their golden depths, but she had once seen another emotion there and stiffened her defences. 'Why? You're her mother, she'd never of backed off if you hadn't of forced her.' The words *to choose between us* hung unspoken in the air.

Inwardly wincing at the repeated grammatical error, Dot said, 'I thought that you were after her money. I still think that – then.'

'Yes, you made that pretty obvious, with your private detective an' all.'

'Jerry says I was wrong,' said Dot, stiffly.

'But you don't believe him.' It was a statement, not a question. Dot was spared the necessity for answering by the approach of one of her friends – her ex-friends – smiling warmly and extending her hand. She had been one of the ringleaders in Dot's humiliation, and was the last person Dot wanted to see now. Her body language was expressive, and Mawgan took due note.

'Dorothy! It seems an age since I've seen you! How *are* you, my dear?' She air-kissed Dot effusively on both cheeks. 'Mwah, mwah! And this must be your oh-so-talented son-in-law!' She turned to Mawgan, a charming smile on display. 'I've seen your programme on the television, so interesting and amusing, and so clever of you, all that mouth-watering food!'

Mawgan had risen to his feet politely, he shook her hand with murmured thanks, but he noted that Dot did not introduce them. The woman said, 'May I join you? It's such an *age* since I spoke to dear Dorothy, I don't know where the time goes!'

Dot gave her a cynical look. 'That would have been lovely, Jenny, but another time maybe? We were discussing family matters, you have to excuse us this time.'

'Oh!' Jenny looked taken aback. She had thought that Dot would be glad to welcome her, to see an end to what had amounted to social ostracism, and would then invite her to her dinner party that everyone was talking about, but it seemed that she wasn't glad at all. 'Oh,' she repeated. 'Another time then. So lovely to meet you, Mr Angwin – or may I call you Mawgan? Such an unusual name! And Dorothy and I are such old friends!'

Mawgan had resumed his seat opposite to Dot, and since neither of them said anything, she became flustered and took herself off with what looked suspiciously like a flounce. Once again, Dot found herself meeting her son-in-law's eyes. 'Friend of yours, is she?' he asked, sympathetically.

'I thought so,' said Dot, acidly. 'It seemed that I was wrong. It was you she wanted to talk to, of course, so that she could go away and boast to the rest of her clique.'

'I know. Miserable old cow,' said Mawgan. He gave her what she could only classify as a cheeky grin. 'Friends like her, you can do without. Hope she's not on the menu tonight, or come to that, we could poison her, maybe.'

'She certainly is not!' snapped Dot, but the interruption, unfortunate on the surface, had melted some of the ice between them, made him, in a sense, her ally. She went on, 'Those you will meet in my house tonight are the people who have proved themselves my true friends. There are sadly few of them.'

'There always are,' said Mawgan, unexpectedly. 'You don't need to tell me, I been there. The ones you got left are the ones as you hang onto.'

Dot sipped at her coffee to give herself time to think. Some things were going to be irreconcilable. There was no future, for instance, in discussing whether or no he had initially wanted to marry Debbie for her money; he was hardly likely to admit to it, but in Dot's experience, recently confirmed by Susan's, that was one of life's constants. Although neither Henry nor Jerry had married her for what she had, after Henry had died and left her so wealthy she had become suddenly popular with certain men. Knowing that she was no beauty, was encumbered with a small child, and had nothing else to recommend her but the money, she had retreated into herself and focussed, unfortunately, on making sure that Jerry was happy with Helen, never quite grasping that the endeavour was both tactless and interfering. She believed it was Helen's resentment and jealousy that had ditched that plan from the outset, but at least with Jerry she had always known where she stood.

Maybe that was why she had accepted Jerry's proposal. He hadn't loved her, she had been aware of that, although she had thought she loved him, but his motives were at least straightforward. Oliver needed a mother, Susan a father; both of them would be better for siblings. She had believed that love would grow, thinking that, before the arrival of Helen on the scene, they had been on the brink of it. She had been wrong on both counts.

None of which had anything to do with the man now sitting opposite to her.

Not one of Dot's detractors, and she had many, had ever impugned her courage, not even her difficult stepson. She had known almost from the start of this weekend that there was only one thing to be done if she was not to emerge, in one important sense, destitute. With Carl, partly, she admitted, after Sally's confidences, it had turned out to be easy. With Mawgan, not so, but it still had to be done. She replaced her cup in the exact centre of its flowery saucer.

'I think perhaps I owe you an apology. I acted for the best, for Deborah's interests. Even so, it is something I should not have done.'

'Then that makes two of us,' said Mawgan. Without looking at her, he spooned more sugar into his already sweetened cup, thus rendering the contents undrinkable, and stirred it round. 'I was way out of order too, but that don't make it right. Shall we just forget it ever happened?'

Dot would have liked to, but she wasn't sure that she could. She said, as neutrally as possible, 'Do you still have that letter I wrote you?'

Mawgan shrugged his shoulders and didn't reply. He didn't wholly trust Deb's mum yet, he realised. She had all along worked in her own interests rather than Deb's; probably, she still was. The big question was, of course, *why*? Was she simply an over-possessive control freak, or was there something behind it? No good asking Susan or Deb, they obviously didn't know the answer. Even less, Oliver or Chel. Perhaps he should talk to Carl, a stranger here like himself. They weren't close friends, there had been no opportunity, but they were in this together.

Dot didn't push her question. She said, without quite meaning to, 'Your marriage to Deborah had wide-reaching repercussions. Everyone knew I was against it, everyone knew why. I still believe I was justified in my objections.'

'Yes, I think you probably were.'

'She seems very happy, however,' said Dot, grudgingly.

'Yes. I think she is.'

All this agreement was disorientating. Dot seized on an issue with which, if he agreed again, he would be in the position of the engineer hoist with his own petard. She wasn't sure what a petard actually was, but it sounded both uncomfortable and final. She said, confrontationally, 'I should say to you, I don't at all approve of my grandson being brought up in a pub,' and waited for his reply.

'He won't be,' he said. 'Maybe Deb hasn't had no chance to

tell you. We're buying a house up on the cliff, completion in early February. We should be well in by the time he's born.' He saw the hurt in her face and was angry, with Debbie as much as anybody. He added, 'Maybe she meant it for a surprise. I'm sorry, I seem to have jumped the gun.'

'I see,' said Dot.

Mawgan saw that she was near to tears. He didn't like Deb's mother particularly, and "tact" was not his middle name, but he realised that in all compassion, having talked himself into that one, he now had to think on his feet. But she was speaking again. 'Deborah is almost twenty-seven years old, a married woman with her own business. I am not one of her trustees. She does not have to discuss anything she does with me if she doesn't wish to.'

'Who said anything about not wishing to? Of course she does; she wants you to feel comfortable when you come visiting.'

'You neither of you need to worry about that. I may always stay with Susan.'

'Of course you can, but Deb wants you with us when the sprog gets here.'

Dot was really fighting with the tears now: she couldn't look at him. She was amazed at the pain she felt over Debbie's secretiveness, even though she knew she had deserved it. 'I'm sure your own mother will give her all the help she needs,' she said, stiffly.

'She would, but that's not the point, is it? It's you that's Deb's mum.'

'Susan will be there. She seems to deputise very efficiently.'

'Susan has her own life. And Deb will want *you*.' They seemed to be quarrelling. Mawgan pulled himself together. Up until this moment, the last thing he had wanted was Debbie's mother under his roof, he would have endured it for Debbie's sake. Seeing Dot sitting there trying to disguise the fact that she was bitterly – and justifiably – hurt was too much for him. They had neither of them drunk their coffee, which was cold and disgusting, and in his case, desperately over-sweet. He stood up. 'I'll get some fresh coffee. Back in a moment.'

The relief of his departure nearly brought on the storm that she had been fighting back. Dot fumbled in her bag for a handkerchief and blew her nose. Then she folded her hands in her lap and stared out of the window. There had been something in that last exchange that was unfamiliar; instead of having to apply pressure to achieve what she wanted, the pressure had seemed to be coming the other way. The view outside was unexpectedly hazy; she blinked hard.

The chink of china a precious few minutes later, as Mawgan placed the fresh cups on the table, brought her head round at last. He had been longer than she expected; deliberately? She didn't know, but was grateful anyway. Mawgan sat, and with a complete change of subject asked, 'Why d'you always call her *Deborah*, 's if she done something wrong?'

'It's the name she received at her christening,' replied Dot, rising to the bait with relief.

'I know it is, but *Debbie* is more friendly. You should try it.'

It had never occurred to Dot to think of her children as *friends*; you do not pass on what you have never received. The idea was revolutionary. On the point of saying something crushing, she found herself hesitating. But her deplorable son-in-law hadn't finished speaking.

'It's time for a change all round,' he was saying. 'You want to jump on the band wagon, make a few changes with the rest of us.'

This was carrying his impudence too far, Dot considered. She said icily, and with considerable sarcasm, 'In what way, would you suggest out of your wide experience?' and was disconcerted when he answered her quite seriously. Mawgan, as Tim Howells could have told her, didn't recognise sarcasm when it came up and bit him, he assumed people meant to be taken literally. It had got Tim into trouble in the past, it was about to do the same for Dot.

'Get rid of that great house, would be a start. It's a nice enough house, but you rattle round in it like a pea in a can on your own,' he said.

'Its size is essential if you all come to stay together, even you must see that,' said Dot, immediately on the defensive, while at the same time wondering if such a thing would ever happen again. She was proud of her home, she had worked hard on it, and it was situated in a most exclusive part of town. She sensed that he was unimpressed and, her moment of weakness behind her, was ready and willing to cut him back down to size.

But – 'Giss on!' said Mawgan, irreverently. 'You still got rooms empty now. And anyway, some of us can always stay somewheres else – Annabel and Seb can go to their dad, come to that. You aren't happy there on your own, anyone can see it's getting you down.'

Was it? Knocked off course again, Dot foundered for a moment, but came back fighting. 'You know nothing about it,' she told him, firmly.

'Oh yes, I do. You know what made you grab after Deb – and the children too, come to that? Loneliness. Don't tell me different, you're talking to an expert here.' Suddenly, it was important to convince her, for everybody's sake but most of all, her own. He closed his eyes and then opened them again on her flushed, indignant face. 'You know what you should do?'

'I'm sure you are about to tell me,' said Dot, as he paused to take a breath before he metaphorically jumped off the roof.

He had gone too far, he realised, to back off now. He said, 'Divorce Jerry, get your freedom back. Sell that house and buy another one, smaller and friendly, with no bad memories. Then take yourself off on a world cruise or something, meet new people, lie in the sun, work out what makes you happy. Then get on and do it.'

Dot was too taken aback to find a ready answer. She reverted abruptly to her normal self.

'And that is quite enough impertinence from you, young man!' she said. She had drunk her fresh coffee without noticing, she now rose to her feet and picked up her bag. 'It's time we were leaving, you have work to do, remember.' That should put him back in his place.

'Yes, ma'am!' He leapt to his feet beside her, taking her arm like a gentleman, guiding her towards the door, throwing her out of her stride again, but when he had settled her and stowed the shopping, he slid into the driving seat and gave her another unmistakeably cheeky grin. It had a certain charm to it this time, which only made it more infuriating. 'And that,' he said, 'I'm not going to say sorry for. It needed saying, if you ask me, a long time back.' And he started the engine and drove out of the car park without another word.

When they arrived back at the house, it was to find that oh, so tired Debbie had gone out with a friend – unspecified – and left a message to say that she would be back for lunch. The implications of this had

Dot and Mawgan simultaneously: they had both identified Susan as the one behind this weekend, and since both of them, at some time, had already wondered about the extent of her knowledge, in a way they could live with that, even if uneasily. They hadn't compared notes, naturally, and perhaps naïvely, both of them had accepted Debbie's excuse this morning as genuine. Now they were faced with the knowledge that it hadn't been, and the implications of such a discovery. They couldn't confront her, they might be wrong, and since they both loved her, it brought home to each of them exactly how stupid they had been. Dot sniffed.

'Well, there's a thing,' she said, wishing to hurt. 'I just hope it isn't Tim Howells she's with at this minute!' and Mawgan said nothing at all.

VII

Mawgan carried the bag of shopping along to the kitchen, and Dot, deeply worried, wandered restlessly into the drawing room, where Debbie was meant to be resting on the sofa. That she had initially done so was obvious by the squashed cushions, an empty glass on the coffee table sticky with juice, and an abandoned magazine tossed folded open onto the top of the previously neat, now haphazard, stack at its south-western corner. She picked it up and folded it tidily closed; an old *Country Life*, she subconsciously noted, she could have sworn she had banished that one to the recycling bin long since. Dot did not treasure and store out-of-date periodicals.

When she had folded it properly, she didn't immediately carry it away to add it to the pile of waste paper in the utility room. She stood holding it, and became lost in some bitter thoughts.

She didn't like Deborah's husband, and neither was she under any illusions that he particularly liked her. They came from different worlds, and although she conceded that he seemed decently brought up rather than the animal she had expected after their first meeting, was demonstrably a hard worker, and probably genuinely loved her daughter, he was still very much from the wrong side of the tracks. Some of the things he had said to her this morning had been outrageous! But if Deborah knew what they had both done, and had deliberately thrown them together to give them the chance to resolve their differences, it put a whole new perspective on the situation.

It would be impossible to ask Deborah. If they knew that she knew what they had done in the run-up to her wedding and had deliberately said nothing, it might have been possible, but neither of them, presumably, did know that. If she *didn't* know, to ask would simply be to tell her anyway, and that, Dot couldn't face. She didn't think that Mawgan could either, although she had read the uncomfortable speculation in his face just as he had in hers. It went through her head now that perhaps they both had got what they deserved.

Without thinking, she tossed the magazine she held back onto the heap, but she had unconsciously held it with her thumb in the page that Debbie had folded back, and it flopped open again. With an irritated '*tsk!*' Dot went to close it tidily and carry it away.

And paused.

From one cause or another, houses had figured largely in this morning's uncomfortable coffee break: the one that Deborah and her husband were buying, that Deborah hadn't seen fit to tell her about; her own, and the hypothetical house that her son-in-law thought she should find in its place. Now, here was yet another. Dot picked up the magazine again to take a closer look; maybe it was Deborah's dream house and that was why she had been looking at it; her chances of achieving it had to be small.

It was a low, white house with a grey slate roof and pointed central porch, a long garage block to the left and a high wall with a door in it to the right. Above its wide, single-storey front aspect the roof rose in a long, shallow slope, with Velux windows in it. Another picture showed the back of the house, and here, the land fell away and it stood two storeys high, with a verandah along its width and a partly-recessed balcony above, curving stairways leading down at each end to a wide patio, shaded by the balcony and by a loggia tangled with passion flower vines that rioted up the supporting white pillars. The room beyond would be cool in summer, the room above with its wide windows and french doors, warm and bright with sunshine. A further picture, of the garden, showed a swimming pool on a lower level, and a spectacular view of what appeared to be the mouth of a river and the sea beyond with a distant coastline hazy in the background and tiny sails dotted around. There were also two interior shots, one of the large, light sitting room that opened onto the balcony, the other of a dream kitchen with the same spectacular sea view. Half on auto-pilot, Dot read about an entrance hallway with spiral staircase to the first floor, two large reception rooms and a total of five bedrooms distributed on two floors, one of them with dressing room and en suite bathroom, a separate bathroom on each level, modern kitchen with spacious dining area. All the doorways in the pictures were arched, with light oak doors, very Mediterranean: it was a house for summer days, designed to garner sunlight. Price on Application. Well, that was no surprise, it looked extremely expensive. It was in a place called St Anthony in Meneage, of which Dot had never heard. It was a very, very desirable residence indeed.

'Oh,' said Debbie's voice, behind her. 'You've found it! I brought it down to show you when you got home.'

118

Dot swung round, the magazine in her hands, and met her daughter's smiling eyes.

'I'm sorry, did I startle you?' Debbie came forward and took *Country Life* from her hands, smoothing the page which had got a little crumpled. 'Did you have a good morning?' The query was perfectly innocent, but Dot had a guilty conscience and found herself unable to reply. Debbie didn't notice, nor did she pause for an answer; she turned the page round so that her mother could see it too. 'What do you think? It's even better when you see it, you just wait!'

Dot stared at the house, and felt as if its pictured windows were staring back at her. She said, and knew that she sounded breathless, 'This – *this* is the house that your husband told me about?'

'Did he?' Debbie sounded disappointed. 'Oh well, I didn't actually ask him not to but I did want to surprise you. Yes it is, do you like it?'

Dot was still having trouble breathing. 'It must have cost a million!' she said, her mind reeling.

'Just about – enough anyway.' Since Dot had made no attempt to take the magazine, Debbie turned it back to face herself. 'Mawgan's wanted it for years, and you can see why, can't you?'

Dot said, in a bewildered voice, 'Deborah, you can't possibly afford it! Does your father know?'

'Of course he does. And I'm not affording it, Mawgan's affording most of it. He's the one who'll be making the mortgage repayments, I don't make enough yet.'

Dot's mouth opened and closed helplessly, she was past speech. Debbie took her arm and led her to the sofa, they sat down together and Debbie spread the magazine across their laps. To give her mother time to recover from what seemed for some reason to be a considerable shock, she began to point out the attractions of the place. After a few minutes, Dot collected herself together and found her voice again. She felt the need to find something to criticise, to bring Deborah down to earth, and the first objection that came into her head was, 'Shouldn't you have looked for somewhere in St Erbyn? You both work there, after all, your child will need to be looked after, and even if you employ a nanny you should be close – unless, of course, you plan to give up work, which would be best of all.'

119

Debbie paused to choose her words. She didn't want to mess this up, so decided that the best idea was to take it a step at a time. 'It's only a few hundred yards up the hill from the lane that leads to Chel and Oliver's, actually,' she said. 'A few feet further west, and it would have been our side of the parish boundary. And think about it Mum, my business is just that, mine. If I want a baby gurgling in a pram under the trees on the foreshore, or playing in the corner of my office, that's my affair. Carl and Roger won't care one way or the other, they'll be out on the water most of the time.'

'You're not planning to leave the poor child with that Maria girl, I hope!'

'I daresay, sometimes. I shall cut back on my teaching, of course, but I shall want to keep my hand in, and I can't think of anyone better, offhand.' That was a challenge, she realised, but to her amazement, Dot didn't rise. The name of Maria started her thinking: Tom had lied about Susan, had he also lied about Maria? Debbie looked at her with compassion: the house seemed to have knocked her mother endways.

Leanne Adams, "the girl", appeared tentatively in the doorway to say that lunch was on the table and Dot, folding away the seductive illustration with what was suspiciously close to a slam, rose to her feet. She didn't want to believe that Cornish oaf could possibly afford a house like that! It was against probability, expectation, and the laws of nature! 'That husband of yours,' she said, resuming the upper hand forthwith, 'is a very outspoken, cocky young man! Watch that he doesn't overreach himself, if you're wise!'

Debbie got meekly to her feet beside her. Whatever had Mawgan done? She quailed inwardly, wishing for the support of Susan, and followed her mother to the dining room.

Lunch, however, went off reasonably well. Whatever had happened at the market this morning, and something certainly had, it hadn't totally shut down the lines of communication, Debbie even imagined she felt a kind of respect between the protagonists that had certainly not been there earlier. She wondered what Mawgan could possibly have said and then immediately wondered if she really wanted to know.

'Did you have a good morning, bird?' Mawgan asked, casually, over the fruit and cheese that concluded the meal. Debbie cut herself a small chunk of cheddar and nibbled it appreciatively.

'Yes thank you.'

'You were supposed to be having a rest,' said Dot, with disapproval. 'And you shouldn't be eating that cheese, Deborah, not with Baby on the way.'

'I was bored,' Debbie explained, ignoring most of the burden of this speech. 'There was nobody to talk to, and Penny rang up and said, did I want to go for a drink at the club if Mawgan was busy, so I did. I only had pineapple juice,' she added, quickly.

Dot frowned. She barely knew Debbie's sailing friends, and among those she did know, Penny she would have described as "a silly girl" had anyone asked her. She knew that Penny had a brother who was something of a sailing hero, although not in Oliver's class of course, and who worked in London, but she had no idea of what work he did, no idea of the threat he represented to Tom Casson. She said, austerely, 'Penelope Harries is totally irresponsible. I thought she had a job, anyway.'

'Yes,' Debbie agreed meekly. She caught Mawgan's eye across the table; he looked amused. 'She finishes at lunchtime on a Saturday. And she's good fun, and also she picked me up and brought me back too, and so I can't be said to have overdone it. Anyway, I'm fine, I keep telling you both.'

'Hmm,' said Dot, but Mawgan laughed.

'All right, we'll let you alone. I know you are, anyway.'

'As if a man knows anything about it!' said Dot, and listened to herself and was horrified. She had sounded as if she was speaking to Tom in the distant heyday of his popularity. That would never do!

Susan and Carl came home soon after lunch, to find Mawgan in the kitchen, Dot upstairs in the linen cupboard counting out napkins, and Debbie sitting at Dot's desk in the drawing room window, writing place cards. She put down her pen with relief when Susan walked in.

'Oh good! I've been hoping you'd arrive.'

'Why? Has there been murder done in my absence?'

'No. Mum's fussing about putting the leaves in the table, she says it's too heavy for me to do and for some reason she won't ask Mawgan, it's almost as if she's afraid of him.'

'As bad as that?' Susan wasn't travelling that road, and anyway, Debbie looked far too placid to be taken seriously.

'Well, no. But there's a bit of an atmosphere.'

There was the sound of voices, and footsteps on the polished parquet of the hall floor. Susan peered cautiously round the drawing room door. 'She's caught Carl. She's marching him off to help her with the table, we're safe for the moment. So what happened this morning, do you think?'

'I don't know, but she said Mawgan was cocky and impertinent. Or outspoken, or something. Sounds about right, don't you think?'

'That's hopeful, then,' said Susan.

'*Hopeful*?' Debbie raised her eyebrows.

'Come on, Deb. It's almost friendly, considering what she's said about him in the past.'

Debbie conceded this was true, but still looked doubtful. 'She sounded offended,' she said.

'She frequently does,' Susan pointed out. 'Don't worry about it, Deb: remember, this weekend is kill-or-cure, and nobody promised that the cure would be pleasant. And we've all survived so far.'

Debbie heaved a sigh so heavy that it blew the slips of card she had placed on top of the desk into disarray. She said, 'I suppose we shall go on surviving until breakfast time tomorrow, then.' She picked up the scattered cards and began to form them into a neat stack. 'I've finished these, should we go and help?'

'Who's coming?' asked Susan, and Debbie silently handed her the list from which she had been working. Susan ran her eye down it.

'Uncle Alex and Aunt Ingrid, good, they'll help keep us all afloat. Canon Plessey and his sister, we expected them. A bishop! My goodness, she's flying high.'

'He's staying with the Canon,' Debbie put in.

'Sounds suitable. Convenient, too, he makes up the numbers! Who are Ernest and Benita Vachell? I don't know them, do you?'

'They sound like relations of that ghastly Mrs Vachell-Chillingworth – and Francis, I suppose, too. Did you hear about Francis?'

'Yes. Some, anyway, but I don't know exactly what it was he did to be excommunicated.' Susan's mind was still on the list. 'Joanna's parents. Ooh, and the General and Mrs Law! I thought Mother and Mrs L were at daggers drawn!'

'Dear enemies?' suggested Debbie. 'They love to hate each other – and they hate each other so much that it really couldn't get any worse, so I suppose it's understandable, in a way.' She looked at her sister, and they both laughed.

Susan said, thinking it out as she spoke, 'There was always something almost enjoyable in their spats, of course, and I can imagine Mrs L standing up for her enemies if she felt they were in the right.'

'Mum wasn't,' said Debbie. Her laughter had died. Susan looked at her seriously, but someone had to say it.

'In a way she was, Deb. You've got to look at it from both sides. *You* believed that Mawgan was innocent, but face it, not many other people did. Even his own family were having trouble with it. You have to be fair to Mother, or we're going nowhere, she was only trying to protect you – all this flack she's taking now is with hindsight.'

'Did you believe it?' asked Debbie, on a challenging note, but Susan only shook her head.

'We've gone too far down the line for me even to remember,' she said. 'Come on – bring those cards, let's go and lay the table.' She took another look at the list. 'There's sixteen names here, not fourteen.'

'She added the Vachells at the last moment. She hasn't said why.'

'Hmm. Has she told Mawgan?'

'Luckily, we brought four brace of pheasants with us. Hard luck on Mrs Adams and Leanne, but they'll have to make do with the soup and fish.'

It seemed that every simple action of this weekend was to be disturbed by undercurrents. It was impossible, too, to tell which way these were flowing. Dot set her daughters to laying out cutlery and Carl to polishing glasses, while she herself arranged flowers; a tall vase of orange hothouse lilies, trailing variegated ivy and slender branches of pine for the sideboard, two low arrangements of holly, ivy and mistletoe for the long table. Because her kitchen quarters had been taken over by a professional chef of whom, in his working persona at least, Dot was slightly in awe – although she would have died rather than admit it – she arranged her flowers on the end of the sideboard, their cut stalks resting on carefully spread newspaper. While they worked, it was natural for them to talk.

'I see you have a bishop among your guests,' Susan said, busy setting out forks. 'Nice work, Mother – that'll fix the tabbies!'

'Yes, it will, won't it?' said Dot. She paused, rearranging a spray of lilies and standing back to look at it. She spoke casually. 'Yes, he was at university with dear Canon Plessey, he has just returned from abroad for a conference. He will be helping to conduct the Family Christmas Service in the church tomorrow morning.'

'That's nice.'

Dot went on purposefully, addressing herself mainly to Carl, it seemed. 'It's a delightful service, all the old carols, and the Sunday school children make a procession up the aisle and lay gifts at the foot of the tree for children less fortunate than themselves – children in the bishop's own diocese, this year.'

Carl only resisted with an effort the impulse to echo Susan. Instead, he called up all his creativity and said, 'That's a good gesture. Friendly.'

'The church here has a very strong connection with Africa,' Dot told him, firmly. There was a short silence.

'Where do you want the spaces left for your table decorations, Mum?' Debbie asked. 'I'm just putting the mats out for the serving dishes.'

'Divide the table into equal thirds,' Dot directed, and Debbie squinted at the expanse of spotless cloth, wondering if a few inches either way would matter. Knowing her mother, probably yes. Dot asked, 'Do you attend church regularly, Carl?'

Thus put on the spot, Carl answered with unwise honesty. 'I used to go with my mother at Christmas, if I was home.'

'But this year, I understand, you'll all be in Devon,' said Dot, pronouncing the name of that beautiful county as if it was the armpit of the western world. Realising that he had stuck his neck out in a way different from the one he had expected, Carl simply replied, 'Yes.'

'I hope you will be taking those children to a service on Christmas Day, Susan,' said Dot.

'I don't know what we will be doing, exactly,' said Susan. 'Isobel said something about the midnight service.' Wrong again! Dot sniffed.

'Far, far too late for those children,' she said disapprovingly.

124

Debbie, looking up from her mathematical equation with the dinner mats, unexpectedly found herself eye to eye with her husband. He was leaning against the doorframe, listening as if he was enjoying the entertainment. Nobody else had noticed him come in; Dot had Susan and Carl against the ropes, and Dot herself had her back to the door. Debbie made a face at him, and he grinned back at her.

Dot was speaking again. 'Such a shame that they can't come to the service here tomorrow,' she said. 'Do you really have to rush off so soon?'

'Mawgan has to get back to his restaurant,' said Debbie. Dot dismissed Mawgan, probably the nearest thing to a believer among her family here owing to his background and lack of exposure to higher education, as if he was an unconverted heathen from the bishop's African diocese. 'But you, Susan, and Carl. Do you have to rush back?' There was an unfamiliar note in her voice that made Susan and Debbie exchange glances, and Carl look up from his polishing. Mawgan unstuck himself from the door frame and stood upright.

'Let's all go,' he said.

Dot visibly nearly jumped out of her skin, and Susan and Carl turned abruptly. He moved out into the room, casual and, Debbie thought, bent on stirring the pot, although which of them he was planning to annoy was an open question. Susan, who had decided that the sooner they were out of here tomorrow, the less chance there was for a major meltdown, looked at him despairingly. But Mawgan had recognised that note of unexpectant pleading for what it was, and it had touched a chord. He said, 'We don't have to get back, Deb, Doug can manage Sunday lunchtime easy this time of year, and we're closed come evening. And your mum'd like it.'

Susan looked wildly in Carl's direction for support, but he disappointed her. Unlike the rest of them, Carl had no preconceived notions about Dot, he knew, in fact, very little about her beyond the obvious, he hadn't been one of the family for long enough to have absorbed family lore, nor had he ever crossed swords with her. He simply saw a lonely woman who loved her children and grandchildren rather too possessively, and would have none of them around her this Christmas, and he saw no reason why she shouldn't have a wish that was so easy to grant.

'Fine by me,' he said.

Dot, who had been hoping without hope for just those few more precious hours with them all, was more astounded than anything, but she recovered quickly. 'And then you can all have lunch before you have to leave,' she said, with satisfaction.

'After what we're eating tonight, will we *need* lunch?' asked Susan, giving up, and Dot said, 'Of course you will, Susan, don't be absurd! Two grown men, and those children will be hungry, if you aren't. I'll take a joint out of the freezer this minute!' She bustled towards the door and Mawgan stepped aside to let her pass. When her mother had gone, Debbie scowled at him.

'So, what got into you?' she asked him. 'What are you doing out of your kitchen anyway?'

'I just came up to say that Leanne was taking tea into the drawing room,' he replied, meekly.

'A pity you didn't just say that, then. Now look what you've done!'

'Ah, come on Deb. It won't hurt us none!'

'It's playing right into her hands,' Susan objected. 'She's like that, always. She manipulates us all like ... like puppets.'

Carl put his arm round her shoulders. 'There's a saying, Susie,' he said. 'It goes, onlookers see most of the game. She's a very lonely woman. Humour her a little.'

'If she is, it's her own fault!'

'Actually,' said Carl, apologetically, 'I'm not so certain that it ever is.' Then, as Susan and Debbie stared at him, he went on. 'Everything starts somewhere. I just think that we don't – that's you two as well as Mawgan and me – we don't know where it *did* start.'

'She's our mother!' said Debbie indignantly. Carl grinned at her.

'True, she is. And you know what she reminds me of?' Debbie shook her head, mutely. 'Susie here, when I first met her. Think about it before you knock my head off, I would.'

Susan stepped away from him and laid down the spoons she was holding very carefully on the sideboard. 'Let's go and find that tea,' she said. As she passed him, she gave Mawgan a grim smile. 'I have to tell you, you will be knocked off your pedestal as favourite uncle when Annabel and Seb hear what you did.'

126

'Rubbish, it won't hurt them, neither,' said Mawgan cheerfully. 'Come to that, a bit of organised religion will do the lot of you a power of good.' He turned to go back to his kitchen.

'The lot of us?' asked Susan, indignantly, of his retreating back.

'He's a Methodist,' said Debbie, gloomily. 'They have a direct line to God.' She cheered up immediately. 'Anyway, actually, he's right Suse, when you think about it. It *will* be nice to go to the family service all together. Nice for Mum, good for the children, and it won't do us any harm either, will it?'

'And it'll make a great extra Christmas present for your mum,' said Carl, clinching it.

Having won a point that she had fully expected to lose, Dot was in a benign mood over the teacups. It was only when they all went back to work that the going became sticky again.

The table was finished, except for the holly that Dot was still arranging. Susan picked up the little stack of place cards. 'How do you want this arranged?' she enquired. 'The bishop, I suppose, at the head of the table, and you at the foot?'

'Certainly not!' said Dot, as if Susan had said something very silly. 'Since your father isn't present on this occasion, the head of the table must be taken by our son-in-law in his place.'

'Urg?' said Susan, unintentionally, and Debbie stared. Dot went on, making things clear.

'As the senior male member of the family present, it's his privilege and duty,' she said, firmly. 'Of course, if you were married Susan, it would fall to Carl, but since you are not ... The bishop on my right, if you please, and dear Joanna's mother on my left.'

'But,' objected Susan, 'Mawgan won't join us until we get to the main course.'

'Which makes it an even more convenient place for him,' Dot pointed out. 'It will leave no awkward empty chairs among the company. And put Ernest Vachell near to David Rendell, please, they are both landowners, and will have something to talk about, and his wife next to Carl. The Vachells are new friends, and we must look after them for they will know none of the others, of course. Your Uncle Alex on the other side of Benita, please.'

Susan scurried round the table, following instructions as best she could; half expecting her mother to insist that Mawgan had Mrs

Law beside him to terrify him, but perhaps Dot felt she owed him something, for she didn't even suggest it. When it was done, Dot looked at the table arrangement with a frown. 'It's the best one can do, of course, with the numbers, but I always feel it is better to have men and women alternately around the table. But among friends, it is permissible.'

'You should have asked a couple more, Mum,' said Debbie, without thinking, and Susan kicked her on the ankle.

'I could have, of course,' Dot agreed. 'I asked Ernest and Benita on impulse, only a few days ago, without thinking about placements I'm afraid. They are such kind people.'

Since in the past, kindess hadn't figured highly on Dot's list of desirable qualities in a friend, both Debbie and Susan felt suddenly sorry for her.

'Nobody'll care anyway,' said Susan. 'Dinner for friends goes by informal rules. You need to do it more often, Mother, it's far more fun than all that socially correct stuff.'

Dot looked unconvinced, but it was too late to argue. No way was she going to admit that these people named around the table were, at present, the only friends she felt she had, although she was aware that they must all realise and that it was very possibly why they were here in the first place. She covered her unease with a new attack of bossiness.

'You should put your feet up between now and dinner time, Deborah,' she instructed, firmly. 'You've worked very hard this afternoon, you want to enjoy the party.'

'Mum, I've only polished a bit of cutlery and helped to lay a table!'

'Nevertheless, you were out all morning,' said Dot. She turned her attention to Susan. 'I hope you put in some good clothes for those children, Susan, I want to see Annabel in a pretty frock, please, and Sebby in proper trousers, not those jeans. I know they're not sitting at the table with us, but they will be coming into the drawing room to greet everyone.'

'I put their best clothes in, Mother, but it will depend on Tom whether they have time to change or not.'

'I shall ring Sally, and tell her to make sure that he brings them back in time,' said Dot, and on the word, marched out to the telephone in the hall. Susan and Debbie exchanged a look and a shrug of the shoulders. Susan said, 'Come on, Deb – better do as you're told for once,' leading the way to the drawing room as she spoke, and the others followed meekly.

'A great organiser, your mum,' Carl remarked. He was beginning to envy Mawgan, safely in the kitchen with the Adams ladies and nothing more threatening than a dead pheasant to deal with. Any minute now, he feared, he was going to find himself under attack along with the girls.

'She's always been like this,' Susan tried to explain. Carl looked at her sympathetically.

'There's no need to sound as if you were apologising for her. I think she's amazing.'

Debbie sat down obediently on the sofa. 'Don't you mean astounding?' she asked ruefully.

'Anyway,' Susan clinched it, '*you* don't need to worry. You're her white-headed boy at the moment, although I can't think why.'

Debbie picked up *Country Life*, still lying abandoned where Dot had dropped it earlier. She said, 'Have you seen this, Susan? It's got our house in it. I brought it to show Mum.'

'I thought your house was already sold – to you,' said Susan, but she took the magazine.

'It's a back number,' Debbie explained.

'And was she impressed?' asked Carl. Debbie looked thoughtful. 'Actually, she seemed more indignant than anything, but that's Mum.'

Dot came into the room then, in her element and beginning to revel in it. Susan hurriedly dropped the magazine again, indignation was an emotion she could do without just now.

'Everything seems to be going well in the kitchen,' she said, although nobody had expected anything less. 'Deborah, I hope that husband of yours intends to make himself decent too, before he joins us.'

'Yes Mum, of course he does. He'll slip upstairs and have a shower and change into his suit while we're getting through the soup and fish a bit. Don't fuss. It's all under control.'

Dot gave a sigh of pleasure that surprised even herself. 'I'm really looking forward to this evening,' she confessed. 'And it's lovely to have you all here with me. I just hope nothing goes wrong!'

'It won't,' said Debbie, with conviction. 'You have an expert at the helm, just sit back and enjoy it.'

Tom did bring Annabel and Sebastian back in plenty of time, but he didn't stay for more than a moment, having no wish to see Carl occupying what used to be his own place in the family and pausing only to deposit a box full of wrapped Christmas presents under the tree, which the children insisted on showing to him. As soon as he had gone, Susan chased the children upstairs to get dressed up. There was a certain amount of grumbling, particularly from Annabel, but a little to Susan's surprise, they took the news that they were to go to the family service tomorrow morning and then stay to have Sunday lunch with Grandma in their stride. The pretty frock decreed by Dot caused far more commotion.

'I've got nice trousers that aren't jeans,' Annabel pleaded, but Susan was firm.

'It's Grandma's party, so you'll do as she wants. And you can take it off again the instant we go in to dinner.'

'But get upstairs first, I would,' suggested Carl, who was an amused audience at the dispute. Annabel scowled at him.

'We *always* do what Grandma wants!' she said.

'And quite right, too.'

'It's all right for you,' she told him, unanswerably, 'nobody expects you to wear a silly frock!' Seb seemed to find this inordinately funny, throwing himself onto Annabel's bed and waving his legs in the air, shrieking with laughter. Both Seb's mirth and Annabel's dark scowl brought Susan up short: it reminded her of the bad old days before Carl. She said, 'That's enough, Seb! Now, sit down properly, both of you, and tell me what's wrong, please.'

Seb sat up immediately, responding to the tone of her voice, and Annabel sat on the bed beside him. They said nothing.

'Shall I go?' asked Carl, of Susan. She shook her head.

'No. You took us all on, you can stay and help sort this out! Now then, Annabel?'

'Nothing,' said Annabel, sullenly.

'Seb? Didn't you have a good time with Daddy?'

Seb looked down at his feet, and mumbled, 'Daddy wasn't there.'

'He brought you home,' said Susan. Seb began to kick his feet, watching them intently. It was left to Annabel to answer, which eventually she did.

'Lorraine picked us up. She took us back to her place, and then Daddy came back for lunch and they had a row and he stormed out again. Then she took us to the Leisure Centre and we went rollerblading. Chris too.' Christina was Lorraine's daughter, and rather unexpectedly, had become Annabel's friend.

'*Lorraine* picked you up?' asked Carl, when Susan said nothing. Susan had asked for his input, after all, and it seemed an obvious question. Tom was the children's father, for heaven's sake and he hardly saw them these days.

'He said he was busy in his office,' muttered Annabel. She looked up and met his eyes. 'That's what the row was about, but I think he didn't want to meet *you*.'

Susan was swept with a wave of such fury that for a moment she was speechless. How *dare* Tom, when he must surely know how Annabel adored him? Maybe it hadn't been intentional, but it would nevertheless leave behind it a feeling that Carl was responsible for the family break-up. All the more unjust since on a Saturday, at least in the afternoon, it was highly unlikely that he had been at work: far more probable that, and not for the first time, time with his children had been sacrificed for time spent with his latest girlfriend; she knew that ploy with the row over nothing all too well. It was too bad of Tom! Worse still, to leave poor Lorraine holding the fort. Susan didn't like Lorraine, for several reasons some of which were obvious, but she was bitterly sorry for her. Been there, done that Lorraine. Face up to it, get out now while you can! None of these things was it possible to say.

Somebody, however, needed to say something, for Annabel looked about to burst into tears. Carl said it. 'That's reasonable,' he said casually. 'In fact, I think he was wise to keep out of the way. '

Annabel stared. 'You do?'

'Certainly. Your grandparents wanted to run their eye over me, Annabel – make sure I wasn't going to beat you, or be a bad influence or something, I expect. They'd have asked your Dad to give them a clear field, I would have. Wouldn't you?'

Annabel's stare intensified, but she was obviously thinking about it. She looked at Susan.

'Was that right, Mummy?'

'Near enough. Grannie and Grandad care very much what happens to you, you know. And as for later on, if Daddy had to work, then it was very nice of Lorraine to take you all out.'

Annabel, left without a shot in her locker, looked uncertain. Susan took advantage of this. 'So go and get a quick shower and put on your frock for Grandma, and let's have no more nonsense. You too, Seb.'

'What – put on a frock?' asked Seb, grinning. What his father did, so long as it was at a circumspect distance from himself, troubled him far less than it did his sister.

'If you insist. Use our bathroom, Annabel, and be quick about it. We have to change too remember.'

Annabel ran off, giggling, to find her towel, and Susan swept Seb into the bathroom that the children shared. The crisis was safely past, and hopefully Annabel would now let her grievance go, but Tom was going to hear about it, no question. Oh yes!

When the children were clean and had started to change into their good clothes, Susan left them and rejoined Carl in their bedroom. She linked her hands behind his neck and pulled his head down to kiss him.

'Thank you for that. I really thought we were in deep trouble there.'

Carl returned the kiss with interest. 'That husband of yours is a bit of a one-off, isn't he?' he observed.

'Ex-husband,' said Susan. 'Do you mind if I use the shower first? Then I can get downstairs and give Mother a hand.'

'Good gracious, I thought she'd organised everything to the *nth* degree already!'

'You don't know Mother,' said Susan, darkly, and disappeared into the bathroom. A few minutes later, the shower started to run. Carl took his suit out of the wardrobe; it was getting a lot of use he reflected, tomorrow too, no doubt. He was wondering if Dot – or come to that, Susan – had realised yet that he didn't actually possess a tie, and had no intention of doing so either, and if Dot would mind, when a light knock came on the door, and Annabel slipped round the edge. She looked at Carl, and he looked back at her. For a moment, he thought she was going to demand where Susan was, but she didn't. She stood poised for a second, and then without warning rushed across the room, flung her arms round him and hugged him tight, burying her face against his chest. She said nothing, however, releasing him as suddenly as she had grabbed him, and standing back smiling. She held out her skirts and shook them at him.

'Do I look nice?'

Carl looked at her critically. He said, 'You don't look like Annabel. But you look very pretty.'

'Ugh!' said Annabel.

'Never mind,' said Carl. 'You aren't alone. I have to wear a suit.'

'Awful, isn't it?' Annabel sounded sympathetic. And then she said, 'Where's Mummy?' and the world slipped back to normal. Carl, wondering what all that had been about, wished that he had Tom here so that he could tell him what he thought of him. He said, 'In the bathroom,' and Annabel nodded, and ran back to the door.

'I'll go and see if Seb's all right, then,' she said, and was gone.

Twenty minutes later, Susan ran downstairs to find her mother, as she had expected, fussing around in the drawing room, shaking up cushions that didn't need shaking.

'There you are, I was beginning to wonder where you and Deborah had gone to! All these people coming, and neither of you in sight!'

'I'm here now,' said Susan, soothingly. 'Carl will be down any minute, and you know Deb, she's always last. So what would you like me to do?'

'There's the sherry glasses to put out. I left the tray on the sideboard ready.' Dot gave the last cushion a shake and put it back in place. 'Is Carl planning to have a proper shave before he comes down?' It was a challenge.

'I shouldn't think so,' said Susan, peacefully, refusing to rise to it. 'It's designer stubble, Mother, and very trendy. High maintenance too, to keep it looking good.'

'I would call it slovenly,' said Dot, firmly.

'It's fashionable,' said Susan. Dot was following her to the dining room to fetch the glasses, shame really. She said, 'The same goes for his shirt, before you start on that as well. Carl isn't into the collar and tie thing, but that's OK. It's not disrespectful, it's –'

'Trendy!' Dot interrupted. 'Don't tell me again, Susan, please. And I suppose that Mawgan will be wearing that sharp foreign suit he got married in.' She sounded in despair, and Susan turned away to hide a grin that would definitely not have gone down well. 'I dread to consider what my friends will be thinking!'

'What hip young bucks your daughters have chosen, let's hope,' said Susan. Mawgan's despised suit was, she knew, Armani. She had the glasses on the tray, all sixteen of them. They rattled together as she picked it up, and Dot said, 'Be careful, Susan!'

'Sherry?' asked Susan, seeing only the empty decanters beside the vase of lilies.

'I shall ask Carl to decant it when he comes down,' said Dot. Man's work, of course, designer stubble, trendy shirt and all, presumably. Susan, suddenly finding that she was enjoying herself and, rather against expectations, looking forward to the evening, led the way back into the drawing room.

'I suppose,' Dot was saying, apparently to console herself, 'they are both very cosmopolitan young men who have been about the world, but I don't hold with it, Susan. One must have standards!'

Susan, thinking of the way in which Carl, particularly, had been about the world, which had definitely not included gents' fancy suiting, decided, yet again, to let this pass. She wondered if her mother actually knew about the ocean racing, and tried to remember if she had ever mentioned it. When her mother did hear, what she would make of it? She had disapproved of Oliver's footloose, wandering life afloat, as it appeared she also disapproved of Mawgan's smart Italian tailoring, but Carl, as she had already noticed, seemed to get away with things that they did not. Pick of the bunch of the rotten apples, no doubt. Fortunate Carl!

Annabel and Seb came running in before Dot could find anything else to criticise, and while she was assuring them how nice they both looked, Debbie and Carl came in behind them. Dot, eyeing them both quite as critically as she had inspected the children, conceded that Carl looked very handsome, but a good suit with an open-necked shirt was something she could not condone, he looked like some jumped-up young pop star on the television! "Trendy" wasn't a word in Dot's vocabulary, although it seemed to have found its way into Susan's. And that scruffy ... well, it wasn't even a beard! Even Oliver had never sunk that low!

Susan had taken him away to decant the sherry, and Debbie went over to her mother, linking her arm through Dot's, smiling. 'Everything looks great, Mum. Looking forward to it?'

'Thank you, Debo –' She stumbled on the name. 'Debbie. You've all worked very hard. I appreciate it.'

Debbie stared at her, but before she found her voice, the doorbell rang and the first guests were upon them. Dot said, 'Off you run and answer that, Annabel, if you please. Show them in here and then take their coats into your Grandpa's old study, lay them down on the table – carefully, mind!' Annabel ran off, and Dot turned to Debbie. 'Yes, since you ask, I think I am looking forward to it, Deborah.'

Oh well, you couldn't win everything, every time.

VIII

The bishop was tall, handsome and charming, and looked as if he had been carved by a master from seasoned ebony.

'Do you think Mum knew?' Debbie whispered to Susan, under cover of the general buzz of conversation.

'Oh, I'm sure she did,' replied her cynical sister. 'This is just a test for Carl and Mawgan, how will they react?'

'Carl seems to have passed it, anyway,' Debbie observed, seeing him for the moment in easy conversation with both bishop and canon, but Susan didn't answer. A long-forgotten memory had stirred in the very back of her mind, a very old memory that dated back to her childhood. She reached for it. Debbie was still speaking. '... and you can say what you like about Mum, Suse, but she's never been racist. Far from it!'

Susan said, slowly, 'No, but Grandfather was. I remember ...' but what she almost remembered escaped her again. She said, 'Come on Deb, let's circulate. Toss you for Mrs L!' Dot came up to them, smiling and in her element.

'Susan dear, come and look after the Vachells for me, introduce them to a few people while I catch Annabel. She must go down to the kitchen and bring her Uncle Mawgan here to meet everyone, they're all asking for him.'

'Jeans and all?' Debbie asked, but Dot only murmured, 'They'll understand that he's working, dear,' before she was off. Susan, obediently following, gave her sister a grin over her shoulder. This party, she realised, already had the hum of a successful one: a group of friends, all expecting a good meal and mellowing under the influence of their mother's excellent, if dated, sherry, but more than that. She sensed behind the immediately obvious a goodwill that for some reason surprised her. These people really *were* their mother's friends. They cared about her and were happy to help her climb her way out of the pit she had dug for herself. And if that were so, Susan was all at once extremely glad that Oliver had come up with the idea for this party, and that she and Deb had agreed to it, and thus given them all the opportunity. The only obvious absentees, she realised sadly, were Sally and Irwin, and only time, and Tom pulling himself together and behaving like a reasonable human being, would heal that.

The Vachells were a pleasant couple, rather younger than most of their mother's friends. As Dot should have expected, they knew David Rendell and his wife already, but the rest of the guests were strangers to them. Susan, chatting to them, learned that they ran a family-owned farm called Shortlanesend, near Shearwater, a large village a few miles to the west, which among its other claims to fame boasted the Ravenscourt family seat, Ravenscourt Place, and a pub called the Ravenscourt Arms, with both of which, for one reason and another, Susan was familiar.

'So how did you come to meet Mother?' she asked, naturally enough. Benita Vachell, to her surprise, failed to meet her eyes, but Ernest said, 'Some disagreement at a committee meeting, I understand. Bennie rushed in where angels fear to tread – she often does that. Never learns.'

'Oh?' Susan obscurely felt that it was necessary to know more: she wasn't sure why since it was arguably none of her business, but the feeling persisted. Pause. Ernest looked at his wife.

'Tell her, then.'

Benita said reluctantly, 'It was my first committee meeting for that campaign that helps people in Africa,' she said. 'I'm not really a committee person, but I let myself be over-persuaded by Jenny Carruthers. I believe you know her, she's got a great line in sob stories.'

'Yes,' said Susan. She hesitated. 'She's one of Mother's mates, they seem to be in everything together.'

'Ex-mates,' said Benita, flatly. There was a pause.

'So, what happened?' Susan prompted.

'Are you sure you really want to know?'

'To be honest, I never much liked Jenny. She always struck me as a two-faced cow.'

'Oh, I know!' Benita looked relieved. 'To be perfectly frank, and we might as well be, I'm pretty sure that she only took me up because she wanted the inside story on all that trouble over at Vachells so she could knock Mary off her perch too, and move one more step up the pecking order! I never asked for her patronage, but she sort of weaseled her way in, and it's a good cause and

everything – nobody could fail to be moved by those poor people.'
She sounded defensive, and Susan nodded sympathetically. She had
been suckered on to that committee herself by the persuasive Mrs
Carruthers – who, she was pretty certain, was on it rather for her
own aggrandisement than out of genuine compassion. Probably,
Benita was occupying her own vacated seat. Benita's next words
made it a racing certainty. 'She said it was always nice to have
somebody young on the committee.'

'Ha! So she can hand them all the dirty jobs! Been there, done
that.'

'Yes, I know.' Benita gave her a sympathetic look. '"Wonderful
Susan, always ready to cope, such a shame she lost her head and ran
off with that dreadful young man!". Poor Dot squirmed in her chair
and said that you had "provocation".'

'Did she really?' Susan was surprised, and rather touched. She
hadn't expected such loyalty from her mother.

'Yes, she did. It cut no ice, though. And then, when your sister's
husband appeared on the telly and wowed the nation with his cheeky
grin and his wonderful cooking – well! It was open season, and I
really couldn't sit and listen, and see poor Dot almost in tears and
all the other cows lining up behind the leader, so I'm afraid I blew
my top. Then we both walked out, and I took your mother to the
nearest pub for a stiff drink and she pulled herself together. She has
immense courage, you know.'

'Thank you,' said Susan, trying to imagine her mother all to pieces
in some pub, and failing.

'Don't mention it. We decided then and there to send in our
joint resignation, shook hands, and became ... well, sort of friends.
It's actually quite hard to be a real friend of your mother's. She puts
up a wall, fends you off, you know? In case you get too close, but
I haven't worked out why. Maybe because she's afraid of being let
down again.' Susan was silent. Benita patted her arm. 'Don't worry
about it. She's a natural survivor, full of shit, if you'll pardon the
phrase. And Ernest's cousin Francis has knocked her off the top of
the scandal chart anyway, so the talk is dying down now.'

'I heard.' They exchanged a sympathetic look. 'Families,' said
Susan. 'Who'd have 'em?'

Ernest had moved away during this exchange to talk to General Law, and Susan took her new friend by the arm, guiding her across the room to where Debbie was entertaining the Bishop. 'Come and meet my little sister. Do you know Bishop Okaro?'

'No.'

'Then let's meet him together.'

The bishop was delighted to make their acquaintance, and Debbie slipped away to relieve Carl, who was moving easily through the crowd with the decanter, keeping people topped up, but before she reached him, spotted her mother sitting for the moment on her own and went to perch on the arm of her chair instead. She asked, 'All right, Mum?'

Dot looked up and smiled at her, but her smile was absent-minded. Truth to tell, Dot was a little bewildered; twenty minutes into its inception, her party seemed to be going off the rails. In the past, her entertaining had been of a far more formal nature, with the people whom she had once considered to be her friends chatting politely over a drink, and then filing obediently into the dining room to sit around the table in their appointed places and talk together with well-bred restraint: boring, she had sometimes thought, and been ashamed of herself, these people were the cream of Embridge Society! Or thought they were, she was belatedly beginning to realise: it wasn't quite the same thing. Jerry would go round with the wine, and maybe towards the close of the meal one or two of the men would get a bit loud and silly, and the women a bit bitchy, particularly Jenny Carruthers come to think, and then the men would be left to their liqueurs while the ladies retired to the drawing room. Something was already telling her that tonight was going to be different.

She couldn't put her finger on why: it could have been the presence of Debbie and Susan – and Carl of course. It could have been that Jerry had never really liked her choice of friends – and how right he had turned out to be! – and his courteous formality had set the tone, but she didn't think it was either of those things. It was *something* to do with the young people, of course; Susan's Carl had pleasant manners, thank goodness, stepping easily into the position of deputy host in Mawgan's absence, attending to the glasses and making people laugh as he went among them. But far more, she had begun to see, it was the guests themselves. Canon Plessey, with Annabel on his knee, listening with apparent interest to the tales of her pony, Peppermint. David Rendell having a joke with Ernest Vachell, the canon's sister listening, smiling nervously. Susan and Benita with their heads together over something, none of it anything she could put her finger on, but indefinably different from the usual. It must surely be her imagination.

Seb was sitting on the window seat all alone, just watching, and she frowned: Sebastian had always been an onlooker, but he should try to do his bit. She was just about to tell Debbie to go and make him join in and be polite to the guests when Mawgan came through the door to say hullo to everyone on his way upstairs for a shower. Thank goodness, Dot thought, he had got rid of that apron, there was something totally out of place in an apron on a man, except perhaps at a barbecue – so servile! But the jeans and T-shirt stood out like a banner among all the suits and elegant frocks. She smothered a sigh, and rose to her feet to introduce him, unaware that the sigh had verged on being indulgent.

'And here comes the hero of the hour,' she said, smiling. Talk had faltered away to nothing, began again; they all wanted to meet him and shake his hand. Thankfully he, too, seemed to have been brought up to know his manners, a bit too easy-going for Dot's taste, but he would pass. When he had spoken to everyone he withdrew to "make himself decent" – his own words. She shook her head over him, caught Joanna's mother's eye, and smiled a rueful smile.

'What a charmer,' Elise Rendell said, returning the smile. Dot found herself unable to respond to this comment, too much rather turgid water had flowed under the bridge that might lead to open approval of her son-in-law, but fortunately, before her failure became obvious, Leanne appeared at her elbow to announce that dinner was ready to serve; on cue, Susan rounded up the children to say goodnight to everyone, and sent them off to get ready for bed.

'You can read until I come up,' she told them, as they ran off, and then the company crossed the hall to the dining room and took their places round the table, and the hurdle was past.

The relaxed, informal mood seemed to travel with them. Dot found she had to be firm about them paying attention to her place cards, ably seconded by Susan, who after all the trouble that she and Debbie had gone to wasn't going to see it wasted. Good-naturedly, the company allowed themselves to be organised, and Carl went round with the wine as Leanne came in, bearing the big soup tureen and wafting a heavenly smell along with her. Cream of mushroom: Dot's choice, her favourite, but lifted to a level far beyond the tinned or packeted. Leanne placed the tureen in front of the hostess, put a basket of equally fragrant hot rolls fresh from the oven on the table. and withdrew once she had carried the plates. For a brief interval. the soup kept the company deliciously busy, apart from appreciative comments, until Mrs Law, seizing her chance, looked beadily across the table at Carl, and asked. 'And what do you do, Carl?' with the force of a bullet fired from a rifle. There was not, to be fair, or so Susan thought, any malice behind the delivery; it was simply Mrs Law's normal abrupt way. With such a wide choice of answers available. she was interested to hear which Carl would choose.

'I'm a journalist,' he replied tranquilly, picking the most controversial and possibly, for himself the most important.

'A *journalist*, how interesting.' Mrs Law made it sound like the lowest of the low, deliberately provocative. She liked what she had so far seen of Dot's daughter's young man, but that didn't mean she wasn't prepared to put him to the sword if necessary. But Carl. unruffled, allowed another spoonful of soup to intervene between himself and his response, which was to the tone of her voice rather than her exact words.

'Not *that* kind of journalist,' he said, perfectly aware that he was on trial here among Dot's wellwishers. 'A sporting journalist. I write about watersports and things associated – like Deb's sailing school venture, for instance. And yacht racing.'

'For a newspaper? Or a magazine?' Ernest asked, becoming interested. 'I do a bit of sailing myself when I have the time, perhaps I've read some of your stuff.'

'Both. I'm a freelance, but I do a now-and-then column in one newspaper.' He looked apologetically at Mrs Law. 'I'm afraid it's a tabloid. Have I sunk beneath reproach?'

'Certainly not, I admire your courage in admitting it.' She needled him again, happy to find a foeman worthy of her steel Everyone was listening with interest now. 'And do you plan to write a novel one day? That's what most of you scribblers dream about, isn't it?'

'I already have.' He was about to say that it would be in the bookshops in the coming summer, when little Miss Plessey chimed in with, 'Oh, how exciting! What is it about?'

'Ocean racing.'

'And do you know anything about ocean racing?' enquired the General, genially. 'Or have you just picked it up from books and the internet, like a lot of you writing johnnies seem to do these days?'

'Four times across the Atlantic, and twice on the Round-the-World have helped, certainly,' Carl admitted, he hoped without sounding boastful. The general raised his eyebrows.

'So you were a grinder, were you?' he enquired.

'No. Not exactly, although I did my share of the heavy work too, obviously.'

'What were you? Not another cook! One in the family is enough, surely!' cried Elise, laughing, and Susan answered for Carl, 'He was the tactician.'

'And did you win?' asked Mrs Law, unperturbed.

'Yes,' said Carl, and added, with strict honesty, 'The second time we did.'

Susan heard a snort, quickly smothered from Ingrid Hetherington. Mrs Law conceded victory, with one last, on this occasion unintentional, barbed comment. 'You must get on very well with Oliver. So much shared experience.'

Wrong.

'You must find a publisher for this book of yours so that we can all read it,' said the canon, smiling. 'Although, I hear it isn't so easy these days,' and it was Debbie, rather than Carl or Susan, who said, 'He already has.'

There was a short silence, mainly, Susan surmised, from surprise.

'Well well,' said Mrs Law. 'So this is the "unsuitable young man" that abysmal idiot Jennifer Carruthers was telling us all about so gleefully, is it Dorothy? Dear me. Poor Jennifer.'

Canon Plessey, perhaps feeling that the conversation should move on before anyone had time to wonder where Jenny Carruthers could have got such an idea, made a comment on the excellence of the soup and the talk became gastronomic. Carl, catching Debbie's eye

142

across the table, grinned at her, and then caught Mrs Law watching him. He included her in the grin, there seemed nothing else to do, and she smiled back. Not such a battleaxe as she tried to make out, but a wicked old stirrer just the same, he concluded, and turned his attention to Miss Plessey on his left, who seemed scared of her own shadow but possibly wasn't. Dot turned her own attention to the bishop, but had an uneasy feeling that he had read between the lines and was maybe judging her. But nobody had bothered to tell her all that, she defended herself in her head.

You never asked, some hitherto dormant part of her brain reminded her. You simply assumed the worst. You always have where Susan is concerned, because she isn't Jerry's child.

Unfair, when you consider how Jerry has treated you.

She wondered if just sitting beside a bishop could bring answers to questions you never realised you needed to ask, told herself that anyway, she hadn't been looking for answers, of course not, and tried to think of a sensible question to ask him about Africa. The middle of a dinner party was no place to start having seminal revelations about your past conduct. The bishop however, in uncomfortable confirmation of her suspicion, jumped the gun.

'What interesting and pleasant young men your sons-in-law are,' he said, smiling. 'You must be so happy for your daughters.'

Dot found herself saying, helplessly, 'Carl isn't my son-in-law.'

The bishop took this confidence calmly. 'But he and your daughter Susan are partners, isn't that so?'

'Does it shock you?' asked Dot, uneasily.

'Should it?' he gave her another smile, kindly this time. Dot considered his question, trying to be objective.

'Yes. I think it should.'

'It shocks you?'

'Not shocks, no. Saddens me.'

'And why would that be?'

This was such an odd conversation to be having with a bishop, of all people, at a dinner party that the truth popped out of Dot's mouth before she could stop it. 'Because Susan's husband made her so desperately unhappy that I very much fear she won't ever trust anyone, not even Carl, enough to marry again. And I wonder if it was my fault.'

'How can it possibly be your fault?' he asked, still kindly.

'Because I talked her into it.' Dot sighed regretfully. 'And then, when it all went wrong, I didn't support her. I thought that marriage should be taken seriously, for better or worse.'

'I don't think,' said the bishop, reflectively, 'that Our Lord ever intended that it should make people "desperately unhappy". I think "for better or worse" means through the good times and the bad, not through love and hate. If there is no love, then there can be no true marriage. And if there is love –' he shot a glance across the table to Susan, laughing across at something that Carl had said, her face eloquent, '– if there is love, a genuine love, that transcends everything else, then that is a kind of marriage, and the Lord will bless it accordingly.'

'You believe that?' asked Dot.

'I think that He does not require a ceremony to bless the true union of two hearts that, as they say, beat as one.'

'Surely that's a revolutionary view for an Anglican bishop to take?' asked Dot, recovering her poise with an effort.

He looked thoughtful. 'And I believe too that He can see deep into a marriage, however sanctified by the Church, that is not true, and grieves for it.'

Jerry popped immediately into Dot's mind, which this weekend seemed to be going on a journey all on its own, and she was relieved when Susan rose to her feet to collect the soup plates. The slight disturbance broke the company into different discussion groups, and when next she spoke, it was to Elise on her left.

The scallops followed, simply cooked and garnished with wild rocket salad drizzled with a lemony dressing, and the murmurs of appreciation effectively dismissed the lingering discomfort that her conversation with the Bishop had left behind it, and directed her attention towards the man who really was her son-in-law. She recognised – had recognised for some time if she was honest – that the thought and care he was directing to her little dinner party was a peace offering, and that if she could accept it gracefully and make some reciprocation, then the past would remain the past, never mentioned again.

I seem, she found herself thinking, to be rather good at misunderstandings. How many more?

She became aware that Elise was speaking to her, had been speaking for some time. '… absolutely wonderful food, how lucky you are, Dot! And this is a terrific party, too, and what lovely women Debbie and Susan have become. It seems ages since I saw them both –' she broke off, as another pitfall in this evening so full of them yawned beneath their feet. The reason she hadn't seen them was at least in part because of the way Oliver had behaved towards her own daughter Joanna, creating a coolness in her friendship with Oliver's stepmother, although on reflection it had hardly been Dot's fault. She met Dot's eyes and Dot, gathering wisdom from some unfamiliar source, found herself, for once in her life, grasping the proffered nettle.

'You know, I used to think it was a pity we couldn't have more control over what our children do, but I'm beginning to believe that once they're grown up, it's up to them and we should leave them to it – unless we're asked, of course. And Joanna is very happy with Ian, so Susan tells me – and I am never quite sure that Cheryl is, with Oliver, you know. He's such a volatile man. Gets it from his mother, I imagine; artistic temperament I believe it's called.' She smiled, and perhaps harking back to her brief but uncomfortable conversation with the bishop, added, 'God moves in a mysterious way, you know. It's very true.'

Elise shared with Susan a belief that Joanna had never quite succeeded in putting Oliver behind her, but it was true that she was probably much better off with kind, steady, level-headed Ian Clarke. Oliver Nankervis had always been a bit of a loose cannon. She sighed.

'Yes, perhaps you're right. It's silly to expect your children to cement your own friendships, after all. Joanna was hard hit at the time, but we've all survived. Friendship too, or why are we here?' And she smiled.

'Children,' said Dot. 'What can you do with them?' and returned the smile.

There was no answer to that, and Elise didn't try to find one. She addressed herself to the last of her scallops instead. Just like the soup, they really were out of this world.

For a moment, Dot was left to herself. The bishop was laughing at some dry, academic joke with the canon, Elise was busy with her scallops and her thoughts, in apparently equal measure; there was time to check that the party was still going well. As it was; remarkably well, considering that the guest list had to a certain extent been forced on her by circumstances and few of those present knew each other well, if at all. Even Marie Law was behaving herself, Dot was pleased to see, but you never knew exactly what she would say, she had a way of speaking her mind perhaps too forcibly. Unaware that it was a fault that she herself shared, Dot allowed herself a little complacency; it was always satisfying when a party was being a success, and she couldn't recall one around this table that had gone as well; she wasn't used to being on the receiving end of so much goodwill. She couldn't imagine that it would or could improve, but then Leanne appeared to clear away the fish plates and she and her mother served the pheasant.

Canon Plessey looked at the plates of fragrant meat – a small fan of breast slices juxtaposed with an artistically placed leg, a twist of crispy bacon and a ball of herby forcemeat stuffing, all drizzled with a redcurrant gravy – the dishes of *Pommes Dauphinoise*, buttery cabbage, glistening orange carrots and heaped golden parsnip that accompanied them, and rubbed his hands together. It was traditional food, not fancy "cheffy" stuff, just as Dot had promised it would be, and he appreciated that.

'Aaah,' he said, with anticipatory pleasure. 'Dorothy, this isn't simply a dinner party – this is a banquet!'

Mawgan made his entrance as the vegetables were going the rounds, looking rather smarter than on his last appearance; he, at least, had a tie to his name Dot was pleased to see, and it was decently sober too. He took his place at the head of the table, and with his arrival the party moved up a notch. There were things that Dot hadn't fully realised – or wanted to realise, maybe – about her despised son-in-law, such as that he was socially adept, very much a party animal; and ran a highly successful pub, however unwillingly. All of that should have told her something but hadn't. Also, having worked abroad for so many years he was cosmopolitan in his outlook and able to talk easily on a surprising variety of subjects. He soon had his end of the table eating out of his hand, and Dot realised that there had, after all, been a lack in her unexpectedly splendid party: in spite of the support of her daughters and of Carl, there had been no host to balance herself. Now, suddenly, there was, and although not quite the society ornament her friends might be used to, an expert one. *A finished performer*, she told herself wryly, and then unexpectedly caught his eye along the length of the table. He gave

146

her a saucy grin and a swift thumbs-up sign, and against her will, she found herself smiling in return. For no reason, she remembered suddenly that he was the one who had backed her up over going to church tomorrow.

'I should think,' Elise remarked quietly, in her ear, 'that that one is a rare handful.'

'I think that I have yet a great deal to learn about him,' Dot countered.

'You don't sound wholly disapproving.' Elise looked at her curiously.

'Socially, he's a disaster,' said Dot, knowing that it was a feeble answer. Elise laughed.

'Rubbish, Dot, socially he's a diamond. Some Cornish mother back there in the west country has done a pretty impressive job!'

'He comes from a council estate,' Dot murmured.

'All the more credit to her, then.'

Dot said nothing. She had never met Cally Angwin, had never expected to although this weekend the possibility had maybe come closer, and couldn't believe they would have much in common if they ever did meet. She had seen her at Debbie's wedding, that was all. She had, Dot now recalled, come as a surprise, just as her son was now doing. Although there was no doubt that if he really was a diamond, it was a rough one.

'Cheer up,' said Elise, kindly. 'Worse things happen. Remember, I thought I was going to get your Oliver for a son-in-law.'

Dot had never considered Oliver to be hers. She looked at Elise with a double surprise. 'Didn't you want him?'

'Good God, no! Oliver is a recipe for disaster! And unfortunately, I don't believe Jo has ever really got over him.'

'But she's happy?'

'Oh yes, she's happy. A wistful hankering for the one that got away is, if anything, an essential ingredient of her marriage to Ian, it gives him a touch of the knight in shining armour. Jo is an incurable romantic.' She looked at Dot consideringly. 'If it's of any interest, or help even, she thinks Carl Colenso is the best thing that ever happened to Susan.'

Dot looked wry. 'I think I may agree with her.'

'That's good, then.'

'Divorce is never good,' said Dot, on a sigh. Elise speared the last piece of pheasant on her plate with her fork, and paused with it on the way to her mouth.

'Sometimes it's the only cure. Perhaps you should try it for yourself.'

She was the second person who had said that today, or possibly the third, even. Dot was silent.

The pheasant having gone to its last resting place, Susan looked at her watch and got up with a brief apology to go and see to her children. Her departure shifted the balance of the conversation at that end of the table, when she came back, Ernest Vachell, David Rendell and Mawgan were deep into a discussion on organic farming and Ingrid, trapped among the three of them, was trying to look interested. Susan slipped back into her place and caught Carl's attention.

'They want you to go up and say goodnight,' she told him.

'Right,' he pushed back his chair, excused himself to his neighbours, and left the room. Mrs Law turned to Susan.

'I like that young man,' she told her. 'Take care of him Susan. Don't let him slip through your fingers.' It was so much an order that Susan had no answer. Mrs Law turned away to speak to the Canon, on her right, and Susan looked across the table at her godfather.

'You're being very quiet tonight, Uncle Alex. Cares of the world?' She smiled, and was surprised when he returned the pleasantry with a wry face.

'Cares of the office, more like. Sorry, was I being rude?'

'Not rude, no. Just a little distrait. I'm sorry you're having problems.'

Since his main problem was Susan's ex-husband and what to do about him, Alex had no real reply to this. Instead, he said, 'You're looking well, Susan. Much better than the last time we met, Cornwall must suit you.'

'Was I looking such a hag?'

'Would I be so unkind? No, not a hag, but you did look rather fraught – understandably. Things better now?'

'Things are unbelievably better, thank you. It's only Annabel I worry about a little. She's always been such a Daddy's girl.'

'He didn't deserve it.'

'No. But try telling that to Annabel – if you can be so cruel.'

Bloody Tom Casson! Alex found himself thinking. If I could think of a way to lose him without ending up in front of a tribunal, by God, I'd do it! He said, 'But she seems to have accepted Carl, or hasn't she?'

'She's accepted him as a friend. We leave it at that for now.'

'Wise. And Sebastian?'

'Oh, Tom never made any effort to endear himself to Sebastian. He could see no good in him at all and treated him as a silly baby! Taking him at the valuation of that God-awful school he insisted they go to – he and my mother.' She spoke with bitterness, the damage that Summerlease had done to Seb would lie on her conscience for ever.

'Was it so awful? I always understood it to have a very good reputation.' He sounded interested. Susan sighed.

'Oh, it isn't so bad, I suppose, Annabel liked it all right. But Seb is like Oliver, he's not a team player and they didn't like that – not the other children, or the staff. His form teacher even said he was a special needs child. Turns out, at his new school – which is just a village school, by the way, not a bit posh but good just the same, and a lot more sympathetic – they say he's unusually bright. Not wanting to join in hearty ball games doesn't mean you're an idiot.'

'No, it doesn't. Seb doesn't like sport? He might find it helped his image if he would try to.'

'It turns out he's a natural sailor. Roger – that's Deb's chief dinghy instructor – says he's quite likely going to turn out really talented, if he sticks with it.'

'And he's no blood relation to Oliver,' said Alex, musingly. 'Well well, isn't life peculiar sometimes?'

Carl arrived back at the same time as the pudding made its entrance. Dot and Mawgan had diverged in their views on this, and ended on a compromise: a smart and fashionable tiramisu was Dot's choice, a cold lemon soufflé served with brandy snap curls had been Mawgan's; since he had worked in Milan, and even gained a Michelin star there, the tiramisu was a jewel of its kind but it had never been his favourite. The assembled company had no complaints on either count.

The arrival of the pudding course had moved the pieces on the conversational board yet again. The General, looking appreciatively at the portion of tiramisu on his plate, took advantage of a pause in the conversation to ask a question that had been in his mind since the scallops. He spoke down the table to Mawgan.

'Ever thought of opening a restaurant here, Mawgan?' he asked, with hopeful interest. 'I could live with the thought of food like this on my doorstep very happily, and I'm sure I'm not alone.'

Everyone looked at Mawgan. He twirled the stem of his wineglass and said, 'Matter of fact, it had come into my head to do something like that.'

Debbie's jaw dropped. 'You never said!'

'Haven't had time, bird.' He raised his head and grinned at her. 'Only thought of it last night. Been no time to think it out properly myself yet.'

'What kind of establishment did you have in mind?' asked David Rendell. 'Something on the lines of your place in Cornwall?'

'Honestly, I don't know. It's just an idea.' Mawgan looked thoughtful. 'It was when we was at that party last night. All those people, involved in the water. And then there's the marina here ...' His mind was working almost of its own volition. 'Somewhere more like the Fish, maybe, with a bar, but a really good restaurant not just bar meals, handily placed for sailing people, somewhere on the waterside. I said, I haven't really thought.'

'Right here in Embridge?' Ingrid asked.

'Not necessarily. That place we went last night was an option, too. I'm sure there'll be others in the area. What do you think, bird?' He looked across at Debbie.

'Even if you put in really good staff, you'd need to come over and check it out every now and again,' she said, considering. 'It would give me a chance to come with you maybe, see Mum and my friends.'

'That's what I thought, too.'

Dot sat still. A most unusual feeling of warmth was stealing over her, for a moment she thought in horror that she was actually going to burst into tears. To cover the moment, she said briskly, 'Well, that sounds a splendid idea. We must all keep our eyes open for a suitable property for you.'

For a second time, Mawgan met her eyes down the length of the table. He said, 'Thanks. I'd appreciate that.'

The discussion became general. Dot, spooning up her tiramisu, accepted with remarkably good grace, for her, that there was no chance of the ladies withdrawing and leaving the men to their port after the cheese, realised too that she had no wish for them to do so anyway. The bishop, smiling at her, said, 'This is a splendid party, Mrs Nankervis. You must be very proud of your young people. They have such ambition and such talent to go with it.'

'Oh, do call me Dorothy,' she heard herself saying.

'I should be flattered. And I am Nicholas.'

Debbie, noting the exchange, wished she was close enough to Susan to mutter into her ear, 'Mum's getting off with the bishop!' but she wasn't. This weekend could have been a nightmare, but it was turning out to be great fun instead. Mum was behaving well, more like someone else really. and Mawgan was being amazing. Even without knowledge of his reason for having a guilty conscience, she had to concede that he had surprised her. He would never be anything but himself, never be posh like she supposed the rest of them must seem, but he was socially adroit and was using his gift for being immensely likeable to its full extent and she was grateful to him. He might well be doing it on purpose, but he had the company eating out of his hand – partly, by this time, because they had hopes of eating off the plates in his new restaurant, of course. And what a startling idea that was! She thought about it in silence for a moment or two, until Benita Vachell reclaimed her attention.

'What a star your husband is!' she said, laughing. 'Wherever did you pick him up?'

'From the floor,' said Debbie. It was the literal truth, but Benita looked startled.

'I beg your pardon?'

The tale of how she had become snowbound in her car outside a deserted cottage – after the thaw, it had turned out to be not so deserted after all, in fact – and found Mawgan unconscious on the floor, was a good one, and lasted well into the cheese, attracting interest from Canon Plessey as well as Benita. At the finish, when the Air Ambulance had arrived to the rescue, the canon remarked, 'You make it into a funny story, but it seems to me that he was a very lucky man.'

Mawgan had caught the drift of the conversation from his end of the table. 'You telling tales out of school again, bird?' They exchanged a smile.

'You must admit that as "How I met my husband" stories go, it's a winner,' Benita told him. 'Just meeting Ernest at a family party sounds dreadfully dull in comparison.'

'Yeah, well, maybe you've got more sense than Deb to be driving around in a blizzard,' said Mawgan, but he grinned as he said it.

'Ungrateful swine,' said Debbie, appreciatively. Both of them knew that he could very well have died if she hadn't driven around in a blizzard, but there was no need to say so here. The rather alarming tale of how she had met Mawgan had sparked off a round of similar stories, and Susan had her fingers crossed that nobody would ask her how she met Carl, or the other way around. To say that he had picked her up at her sister's wedding while she was still married to Tom might be the truth, but was unlikely to go down a storm in a company that included her mother, a bishop, the Plesseys and the Laws. She didn't dare look across the table to Carl in case she caught his eye, and stared down at her plate instead. But perhaps Dot had her suspicions, for before the game, as it had become, reached either Carl or Susan, she had swept everyone away into the drawing room for their coffee, giving in to the mood of the moment and allowing Leanne and her mother to clear away. The move changed the balance of the company yet again as they all mixed more freely, while Mawgan and Carl did the honours with the brandy and port and Susan poured the coffee.

Alex Hetherington, watching the interaction between the two men appreciatively, murmured to Debbie, 'Those two make a great double act. I should think they must both be right outside your mother's comfort zone, how's she doing?'

'Remarkably well, actually,' said Debbie, reflectively. 'She likes Carl, that's for sure.'

'So do I. I think your sister will be all right now.'

'Did you think she wasn't?' asked Debbie, curiously.

'Debbie, your brother-in-law – ex-brother-in-law I should say, works in my office. I knew what he was up to before any of you.'

'It's a terrible indictment of us,' said Debbie, slowly, 'that not one of us – not Mum not Dad, not me, not Oliver, not even Chel and she's pretty perceptive, realised how unhappy she was.'

'You were too close, you all thought you knew her. Don't beat yourself up over it, Susan is a good dissembler. And remember, I knew her father very well. She's a lot like him in some ways.' He didn't elaborate.

'I suppose, because I'm younger than her, I've never thought of her as not being Dad's daughter.' Debbie looked thoughtful. 'He was a good bloke, this Henry, was he?'

'The best.' Alex looked at her seriously. 'And don't let anyone try to tell you he wasn't very fond indeed of your mother. I think the period of her marriage to him was probably one of the happiest in her life – so far.'

'Now you're mortifying me again,' Debbie accused him. She thought suddenly that several of the people here tonight could be here not necessarily because of her mother, but because of old loyalties to Susan's father, and it shook her. If it was true, it opened such a wide field for speculation that it made her feel dizzy, and unexpectedly she was desperately sorry for Dot, without being quite sure why. Alex touched her arm sympathetically.

'Your mother is a bit like a swan,' he told her. 'Controlled, bossy, and even threatening on the surface, and paddling like hell under water in order to beat the tide and stay afloat. Be kind to her.' He smiled at her and moved away to speak to Elise Rendell and Debbie, suddenly adrift, looked round for Susan and instead saw Dot, laughing with Benita with an expression on her face that her daughter realised she had never seen before. She sought for a word that would describe it, and came up with "happy", which seemed in the context to be sad. A conundrum.

Mrs Law appeared at her elbow. 'If the wind changes, Deborah, you'll be stuck for ever with that scowl on your face,' she told Debbie. 'You look tired, you should sit down.' She took Debbie's elbow and moved her towards the sofa. 'Your mother is doing well, don't you think? Hopefully, she'll learn from tonight just who her real friends are.' She gave Debbie a sharp look. 'I hope you and your sister are among them. Your husband, too. You must let bygones be bygones.'

'I think we all realise that,' Debbie told her. She hesitated. 'This party was Oliver's idea, you know.'

'Was it really? Hmm.' She didn't sound impressed. 'I don't see him here. Now, sit!'

They had reached the sofa. Debbie sat down obediently, and Mrs Law sat down beside her, not entirely a felicitous arrangement from Debbie's point of view. Carl came over with the brandy bottle, and a glass of pineapple juice which he handed to Debbie.

'Brandy, Mrs Law? Or what's your fancy? There seem to be most things on the tray there.' He grinned. 'I've left Mawgan with the vintage port, he's better qualified to deal with it!'

'Very wise,' nodded Mrs Law. 'And you may send him over here, young man, if you will.' Carl moved away to carry out her instructions, and she turned back to Debbie, now pinned into the corner of the sofa without means of escape. 'What you have to bear in mind, Deborah, is that the fault is not all on your mother's side. I like your husband, I imagine most people will, but what were you thinking of? My sympathies lie with Dorothy: however charming, I wouldn't wish him for a son-in-law.'

Debbie was indignant. 'Why ever not? You just said you liked him!'

'Don't fire up at me, young lady. It's done now, and no use giving out awful warnings after the event. What I am saying is that, however delightful he can be, he isn't from your world, nor you from his. So, be happy, but be circumspect, and consider your mother's point of view. Be kind to her.'

Debbie felt herself redden, because she knew that she could have handled her mother better had she not let herself get so fired up in the first instance; she had known it for some time. Oliver's devious plan had come as a relief, if she was honest; that it seemed to be working was a minor miracle. You gave thanks for miracles. And Mrs Law was the second person tonight to tell her to be kind to her mother, which made her wonder if, in the eyes of other people, she maybe hadn't been. Mrs Law patted her knee as if in approval and made to get to her feet.

'Good girl,' she said, although Debbie had committed herself to nothing, and thankfully moved away, leaving her place to be taken by Miss Plessey, who was fluffy, but meant well, and was a vast improvement on her predecessor, who undoubtedly didn't. Meddling old witch!

The unexpectedly merry evening began to draw to a close. The eclesiastical group were the first to take their leave, claiming the need to work the next day.

'And I trust we shall see you in church tomorrow after this dissipation, Dorothy,' said the canon, clasping Dot's hand in his.

'Of course. We shall all be there.'

If the canon was startled, he hid it. 'Well, well, I had better ask the sidesman to save you enough seats!' He smiled, moved on to kiss Susan and Debbie, whom he had known for many years now, and to shake hands with Mawgan and Carl. The party began to break up, gather their belongings and take their leave. Finally, the family had the house to themselves. A dinner party in this house, Susan thought in amazement, looking at the clock on the mantelpiece, had surely never before ended after midnight because nobody wanted to go home.

Debbie yawned. 'Well, I'm for bed.' She gave her mother a swift hug. 'Lovely party, Mum. Aren't you glad we came?'

'The general said the dinner was one of the best he had ever eaten,' Dot said. Mawgan was quietly gathering up the glasses onto a tray, he paused.

'Do it again next year, shall we?'

Old traditions had gone by the board. Maybe it would be good to instigate some new ones. Dot said, 'That would be very pleasant, thank you Mawgan,' wondering if it would ever happen. She had gleaned enough, listening to her friends, to know that she had been granted a very big favour given the circumstances of their first meeting, but she couldn't help thinking too that such an annual event would go a long way to restoring her social position.

It wasn't until she was in her big, lonely bed later on that it occurred to her that yes, it would be hailed as a social triumph, but the best part of the evening had been seeing her family and friends around her table, and all of them so obviously enjoying themselves, too. She fell asleep on that unfamiliar thought.

IX

'That all seemed to go off very well last night, considering,' remarked Carl, the following morning. 'What do you think? Were you pleased?'

Susan stirred in the cosy depths of their shared bed, and opened half a reluctant eye. The shadowed corners of the blue bedroom were mysterious in the cold early light, and her subconscious was telling her that it was far, far too early for a post mortem. She had very mixed feelings about last night anyway. The party had certainly been a tremendous success, it was the reasons for it that she was having trouble with. So she said, 'Mmph,' and shut her eyes again..

Carl was obviously very wide awake. Keeping watches at sea, Susan often suspected, had forever shattered his ability to lie-in when the opportunity offered. Then she remembered, and gave a groan, burying her head under her pillows. No lie-in, no time to waste on making love to welcome the day; they all had to get up, get breakfast, clear it away, peel vegetables, get the joint in the oven, make the beds and be on the parade line dressed in their best by ten o'clock ready for the Christmas family service. What on this *earth* had Mawgan been thinking of? He came from a large family himself, he must know the score!

'What does *mmph* mean in this context?' Carl was asking. Susan pulled her head out from under the pillows and tried to think of an answer. In the pause thus created, Carl sat up, releasing a draught of freezing air into the bed beneath the duvet, and wedged his own pillows behind his back so that he could see her better.

'I hate you in the mornings,' said Susan, but without either rancour or truth. She sat up too, since there was no help for it, drawing the duvet up round her neck for warmth. 'Last night? Well, you saw for yourself, it was a great evening. I just ...'

'Just what?' he prompted, when she didn't continue.

Susan said, 'Why don't you go downstairs and make us a cup of tea? You know where everything is by now, and it'll give me time to wake up.'

'Suppose I run into your mother? She looks like an early riser to me.'

'Make her one as well.'

Carl gave her a thoughtful look, but obediently got up and reached for his bathrobe – not the smartest item in his wardrobe, since it had led a hard life on his boat and become faded and tired along the way, much the way Susan felt this morning, in fact. Although still marginally decent, it would make a poor impression on her mother if they met, but she said nothing, and when Carl had gone, drew back the curtains, jumped hastily back into bed, and tried to get her thoughts into order. It said much for her reluctance to face up to last night's subliminal messages that the first thing she thought was that the dog might as well buy Carl a new bathrobe for Christmas. She pulled herself together with an effort.

Last night. That was a hard one.

First and foremost, you had to consider the guest list. Among those present, the Vachells and the bishop were total strangers, Uncle Alex and Ingrid old friends. In between you had Joanna's parents, whose relationship with Dot had been seriously compromised by Oliver, the Plesseys, who had in the past been invited only to quiet family suppers or charity lunches, and the Laws, who to Susan's knowledge had never crossed the threshold of her mother's house before. And themselves, who had never attended one of their mother's more formal dinner parties in their lives. Oliver left home at the earliest opportunity, Deb had her own life and lived it to the full, she and Tom had been the wrong generation. Those who were absent were equally significant, including Jenny Carruthers and her husband, and other members of her particular set. Social high-flyers, mountaineering up the scale to a man – or woman. Not people she herself had particularly liked, although she had worked with them in the past. Benita Vachell, on the other hand, who had been present, was a completely different proposition, and how she had ever become involved was a mystery.

And Sally and Irwin. They hadn't been there.

Had she expected it? Realistically, no, she hadn't. But if Sally and Irwin had refused the invitation that Susan was certain they must have received, it was down to what Tom had done, not anything that Dot had done, and probably rather more to the presence at the party of Carl.

The overall impression left by the evening was one of supportive warmth and goodwill, true friendship, in fact. She seriously wondered what her mother had made of it all, and also, what she had made of Mawgan. Mawgan had been amazing: perhaps not exactly what Dot was used to at the head of her dinner table, but very entertaining, keeping things moving along with a practised hand, making them all laugh and join in. Well, he worked in catering didn't he? He ran a pub, and a very successful restaurant – no, make that two restaurants, don't forget the Kaff – and he had worked his way around Europe while he learned his trade, he was bound to be – well, *professional* was the word that came to mind first. She wondered what Dot had expected, and knew she would never find out. She didn't, however, insult her mother's intelligence by supposing that she had expected a complete yob. If she had, she didn't believe Dot would ever have placed him at the head of her table, not even to make a point.

What had passed between them at the Farmer's Market? She would never know that, either.

Carl returned with two steaming mugs of tea (they were the ones Dot kept for the gardener, Dot herself was a cup-and-saucer person) and climbed back under the duvet, handing Susan hers as he did so. He said, 'Impressions in order now?'

'Yes.' Susan took a sip and let out a sigh of pleasure. 'That's good! Was Mother around?'

'No. So what do you think? Were you pleased with the way it turned out?'

Susan allowed a few moments to pass while she sipped her tea and framed her answer, and Carl waited patiently. At length, she said, 'I honestly don't know what to think. It was so far away from past experience it could have been someone else's party.'

'Your mother enjoyed it, that was obvious. But I think I know what you mean, she did look every now and again as if she'd accidentally beamed down on the wrong planet.'

'I wish I knew ...' Susan allowed the sentence to tail off, but Carl didn't let her get away with that.

'You wish you knew, what?'

'You'll kill me when I tell you. I wish I knew what it is I wish I knew – or remembered, I suppose. I wish I'd paid more attention when I was a child.'

158

'You know what,' said Carl, after thinking about it, 'This may sound mad to you, but if what you want to know is a bit more about your mother, why don't you ask your father's family?'

'What, Aunt Emily and Auntie Anne? I don't suppose they know any more than I do.' Susan sounded surprised that he should even suggest them.

'I didn't mean Jerry's family. I said your father's. I meant the Worthingtons.'

'What would they know?'

'Quite a lot, I should think. After all, she was married to their father, as well as yours. For several years, as I understand it. He must have talked with them about her, I just thought it might be interesting to know what he said. For instance, they probably know exactly why he married her in the first place.'

'I never thought of that,' said Susan, considering.

'It could be informative. You never know.'

'Jerry's never said anything. He was married to her too.'

'Did you ever ask him?' He saw the answer in her face. 'No, you didn't. And maybe it wouldn't have helped, Jerry has been carrying a torch for Helen Macken longer than I think any of you realise. But Henry ... I get the feeling that he really cared about her. Or you could ask Alex Hetherington, he's been a friend to all of them, and he's your godfather as well as a trustee. There are people out there who know things, Susie. Do a bit more detective work, but do it yourself this time.'

Susan said, thoughtfully, 'It wouldn't change her, of course, but it might make *us* more understanding if we knew a bit more about her.'

'Ask Carol,' said Carl.

'*Carol*?' Susan stared at him. Her sister-in-law, wife of her half-brother Anthony, was a barrister with a very low opinion of Dot. 'Carol hates her guts!'

'Carol doesn't like her, certainly,' Carl agreed. '"Hate" is putting it a bit high. She will, though, probably give you the truth without trying to protect you from it, and I think she'd be straight with you. I think that Owen, or Isobel, possibly wouldn't say anything that they thought would hurt you.'

'No ...' Susan thought about it. 'All right then, I'll ask Carol. And if she blasts me out of the water, I shall rely on you to collect the bits. And now,' she regretfully set her empty mug aside, 'we had better get up. It's going to be a busy morning.'

'I thought we were all going to church,' said Carl, an only child. Susan got out of bed.

'You poor, innocent lamb! There's a large family to organise first and to feed afterwards. No time even to show you how much I love you.' She sounded regretful. Carl grinned at her.

'I thought you said a while back that you hated me.'

She picked up a pillow and threw it at him. 'Oh, I do! Now get your act together, please, and it's me for first turn in the shower!'

In the yellow bedroom, there had been no such political start to the day: Debbie had far less hang-ups over their mother than Susan, her quarrel was more straightforward, and Mawgan, of course, had far more hang-ups than Carl, so without discussing it they had adopted a mutual policy of "let's wait and see what happens next". And too, Debbie, following in Oliver's footsteps, had spent a great deal of time away from home since she grew up and that altered her take on things: she also had less of a conscience than her sister over domestic chores. All of this allowed them a far more lustful start to the day and they arrived down to breakfast last, when everyone else was way past the cereal stage and on to the scrambled eggs and toast, looking fresh and rested and as if yesterday had never happened.

Dot was in organising mode this morning, and the children excited by the proximity of Christmas, the enlarged family group that was so unfamiliar in this familiar setting, the prospect of going home after lunch, the imminent visit to Devon, and the general unusualness of everything. The combination had made breakfast an electric occasion. Dot, her mind on everything that needed doing before they left for church, had been fussed by the absence of her younger daughter and her husband.

'What are those two doing?' she asked the company at large, plaintively, and Carl looked hastily down at his plate. Susan, hardier, struggled to answer without choking on her cereal.

'I expect Mawgan was tired after yesterday,' she offered. Dot looked disbelieving.

160

'He certainly didn't *look* tired!' she said. 'Anyway, Susan, it's his job. He must be used to far more work than that in his kitchen at his restaurant.' Unable to argue with this, Susan wisely said nothing, and Dot continued. 'If they don't come down soon, Susan, you'll have to go and knock on their door. We need to get this all cleared away, so that Carl can take the leaves out of the table for me.' Her mind had already moved beyond breakfast: she really must see about turning Jerry's old study back into the breakfast room for which it had originally been intended then things like this wouldn't happen. It was obvious by this time that he wasn't coming back, after all: the thought depressed her. Annabel reached for another piece of toast.

'I'll go and call them, Grandma, if you like,' she offered helpfully.

'No you won't,' said Susan, quickly, but fortunately at that moment the latecomers made their appearance, apparently unaware that they were late at all. Dot set them right.

'Good, here you are – we were all wondering what was keeping you so long.' She gave Debbie, who had turned a becoming pink, a hard look. 'There's a lot to do before we leave for the church, and we mustn't be late or we won't get seated together, so eat up quickly and we can clear the table.'

Debbie, not daring to look at Mawgan, Susan or Carl, took her seat hastily, wondering if her mother could really have forgotten what it was like to be young and in love. Perhaps she had never really known, which would be sad. Mawgan, luckily, had more self-control, or possibly more bare-faced cheek.

'Sorry if we're late,' he said easily. 'Deb was asleep, I didn't want to disturb her none.'

Debbie's lips shaped the word "liar!" but Dot looked at him with approval – something she had never expected to feel.

'Just don't dawdle over your breakfast now,' she ordered, and Susan ventured, pushing her luck in this unfamiliar atmosphere, 'They could put it all on a tray and take it in the drawing room. Then we can get on with the work.'

Dot thought about this, on the face of it reactionary, suggestion, and so far was the atmosphere of last night still hanging in the air that she said, 'That's a good idea, Susan. Annabel, run and fetch a tray from the kitchen – and put the kettle on while you're there, to make fresh tea, please.'

Debbie and Susan exchanged a surprised glance over the tablecloth. Seb slid off his chair as Annabel ran off to do her grandmother's bidding. 'Grandma, please may I get down?'

'Of course you may. You can start clearing the table.' Dot looked round at the rest of the team. Time to deploy the troops. Debbie was already pouring cereal into two bowls and assembling milk, sugar and toast in a group ready for the tray. 'And be careful not to make crumbs on the carpet,' Dot told her.

The morning was under way.

Dot soon had the jobs allocated: the children to clear the table, Susan on the washing-up, Carl to help her with the table first and then into the kitchen to dry what wouldn't go into the machine, Debbie, when she had finished crunching toast, to sit at the kitchen table with a pile of sprouts. It was only Mawgan that she appeared to hesitate about finding a job, but he soon settled that for himself, retreating into the utility room with a colander of carrots and some parsnips, the potato peeler, and Seb. Gales of laughter soon issued from the room. Dot herself prepared the joint, a noble sirloin of beef.

'And when you have finished with those sprouts, Debbie, you can peel the apples for the pie. Can your husband make a good Yorkshire pudding?'

As it happened, Debbie had no idea, although it was a fair guess that he could, and she was so taken aback by hearing her name shortened for the second time this weekend that it was left for Susan to reply.

'I should think so,' she said. 'Since he has a carvery in his restaurant every Sunday lunchtime, I'd call it a foregone conclusion.'

'Somebody else might make it,' said Annabel, contentiously. Annabel had been set to her least favourite job: putting things away as they were dried. Her face was set in a mutinous scowl. Debbie raised her voice.

'Can you make Yorkshire pudding, Mawgan?' A muffled shout answered her, and Seb's head popped round the scullery door. 'He says, yes.'

It was all so – well, so like a family, that Dot began to experience

162

the peculiar feeling of having got into the wrong life that she had experienced the evening before. She shut the oven door on the beef with a snap.

With so many people on the job, the work was finished in double-quick time, and the family lined up ready for church parade on the stroke of ten o'clock. The service was at ten-thirty, and likely to be crowded: Dot allowed no quarter. Mawgan and Carl were despatched to fetch cars to the door, Seb was squeezed into the back of the Porsche, and Dot took her place in the passenger seat of Carl's Alfa. The procession was ready to roll.

The church was already filling up when they arrived, but as he had promised, Canon Plessey had asked the sidesman to keep Dot's usual pew and the one behind free for her party, with the hymn sheets for the special day laid on the seats. Their walk up the aisle had something of a royal procession about it: Dot, knowing that within the church were quite a few of her detractors, including Jenny Carruthers and some of her clique, walked with her head held high and her accustomed resolute step, and the family, taking their cue from her, formed up behind. She left an atmosphere in her wake that wasn't entirely in keeping with the season but neither Susan nor Debbie could help admiring her. Social humiliation had been hard for their mother, but she obviously had plenty of fight left in her.

Dot had intended to sit in her usual aisle seat, but having allowed Debbie to pass ahead of her into the pew, she found that Mawgan, whose upbringing had been careful in spite of his rough-and-ready beginnings even if he hadn't always lived up to the fact, was standing aside for her; she ended up sitting between the two of them, while the grandchildren, Susan and Carl occupied the pew behind. It felt good. The walk up the aisle had been in the nature of a defiant gesture, now she found herself able to look around her from a position that felt unexpectedly secure. The Carruthers woman was right in her line of vision, Dot bowed to her with a smile. She knew Jenny for what she was now and found herself wondering, for the first time, about the points of view of others whom Jenny had frozen out of their circle, and with her own connivance. Maybe she should look some of them up and listen to the other side. Dot had no intentions of sitting meekly back and allowing Jenny Carruthers to be Queen of Embridge Society. Oh no!

There was a scuffling in the pew behind, and a loud whisper from Annabel. 'Mummy, do we have to take presents up to the tree?'

'Bit late for that. You haven't brought anything with you.'

'But I want to.'

'Sssh.'

Dot had come prepared for this, she opened her handbag and fumbled inside, removing two gaily decorated envelopes. She turned, and gave one to Annabel, and the other to Seb. 'There you are Annabel. And you, Sebastian. Put them in a safe place.'

'I don't want to,' said Seb, pushing out his lip.

'Nonsense! You always have in the past.' She caught Susan's eye, and was surprised at the softened expression on her daughter's face. Beyond her, Carl looked enigmatic. Susan said, with genuine gratitude, 'Thanks Mother. I never thought of it.'

'What is it?' asked Annabel, feeling her envelope which seemed to her to be empty, and Dot said, firmly, 'A donation,' and turned back to face the pulpit. She would, she thought, have to find a way round this "Mother" thing of Susan's, it felt somehow cold and it had deservedly grown out of actions that she had come to regret bitterly. Since Susan wouldn't say "Mummy" in the old way, that left Debbie's rather plebeian "Mum", oh dear. Now she came to think of it, Deborah had always had a leaning towards the common. Perhaps that explained the man now sitting on her left.

The very possible millionaire sitting on her left. Dot wished she hadn't had that thought in church, of all places.

There were a lot of fences to mend. Perhaps this moment was a good one in which to take a resolve to fetch out the moral toolbox. Dot genuinely believed in the God in whose house she sat, she wondered now if she was possibly a disappointment to Him, and offered a quick prayer for guidance. It had to be a quick one, for the organ voluntary had tailed off and metamorphosed into the first notes of *Once in Royal David's City* sung in a clear, childish treble. The congregation arose as one to its feet and the processional began.

Dot was about to get a surprise; she hadn't thought of her son-in-law as a church-goer, more of a heathen, but as soon as he opened his mouth to join in the second verse, the strong, true tenor in her left ear nearly made her forget the words. The long choir tradition in Mawgan's Wesleyan Methodist family had ensured that a voice true as a bell to start with had been not so much trained, as guided in the right direction: like the Welsh, the Cornish take their singing seriously. Dot had a good ear for music, and appreciated what she was hearing; she also appreciated that the family black sheep knew all the words without consulting the hymn sheet. Perhaps he wasn't so disastrous after all, and since they all seemed to be landed with him, maybe it was time to find ways to make the best of it? It would be hard, but she didn't want to lose Deborah – no, she must try to get used to *Debbie* – and she undoubtedly would if she couldn't make the effort. She thought of her unborn grandson: for his sake – for Daniel's sake – she would try. Running off at a tangent, her thoughts recognised and approved the solid, biblical sound of the name. She had feared for something less traditional: Darren or Wayne, or even something totally inappropriate like Charlene, if the child was a girl.

We all have our crosses to bear, Dot thought philosophically. Mine happens to be called Mawgan Angwin. If I'm stuck with him, as it seems I am, maybe I should look on the credit side.

Another, possibly less admirable but certainly understandable idea floated in past the Christmas message of the hymn: television personalities were the new aristocracy. So, the old two-fingered salute to Jenny Carruthers! Dot frequently thought things that she would never dream of saying; most of which she had learned from Jerry: this was one of the times. It gave her a secret satisfaction to know how she would shock and astound her circle – and indeed, her family – if she actually came out with one. Perhaps, she thought to her own surprise, she should give way to the impulse occasionally. It might make her seem more human.

She hadn't intended to think that last bit. She hadn't even known it was there to think.

Canon Plessey, last night's dinner guest at his side, was passing slowly down the aisle, his eyes fixed on the way ahead. Dot managed to feel not one whit of shame for her uncharitable thought a minute ago. Mrs Carruthers had proved herself to be a fair-weather friend. Such people didn't deserve apologies; rather, they should be offering them.

The fact that she had called up the storm for herself, she didn't consider, as she had also conveniently filed, at least for the present, the recollection of the storm petrel she had called up with it, now sitting at her side looking as if butter wouldn't melt in his mouth, listening to the collect for the day. He didn't, she noticed, with a slight return of disapproval, appear to know his way around the prayer book: it had taken him a minute or two to find the right place.

Sometimes, the only way to live with yourself is to ignore things. Quite often, it was the only way to live with other people, too, if they were close to you.

The service continued on its way: a smiling Annabel and a mutinous Seb joined with the Sunday School children, many of whom had been their friends in the past, on their journey up the aisle to lay their offerings under the big, decorated tree with the Christmas crib nestling under its laden branches. Canon Plessey thanked all the givers, and told them that the gifts this year would be going to needy children in the African diocese of Bishop Okaro, here with them today, who would convey them home when he returned there next month. The bishop would now be giving the Christmas address for them, and he hoped that all the children, and indeed, the adults, would listen very closely.

Some hopes, Susan thought, glancing along the pew. Seb was already off in a world of his own, Annabel making faces at another child who had screwed herself round to see her from a pew diagonally across from them on the other side of the aisle. She frowned at Annabel, decided to ignore Seb, and settled herself to listen to what the bishop had to say.

The Bishop spoke about reconciliation.

It couldn't possibly be deliberate, Dot thought in shock. No, of course it wasn't; he was talking about war and its innocent victims, and the need to make peace, to become reconciled, so that people could help instead of hurt each other. But remembering some of the things that he had said – or someone had said, she didn't exactly recall who – last night, she felt as if the message had been directed straight to her, and a very strange thought joined all the other strange thoughts already in her head.

Was it at all possible, when it was so diametrically opposed to the teachings of the Church, that letting someone go – that is, divorcing them and leaving them free to move on – was a form of making peace? She already knew, in fact for many years she had known, that she should never have married Jerry, so if, according to the Bishop, that wasn't true marriage ...? But it seemed very specious reasoning, an easy let-out to salve an uneasy conscience.

Jerry had been married to Helen first. If you didn't believe in divorce – and she really, really didn't – then he still was. What would that make her? In the particular circumstances? Apart from a hypocrite, that is.

Too many people, too many events, had made her think too many uncomfortable things this weekend. The man beside her, her son-in-law, heaven help her! – he had been the first of them.

Divorce Jerry ... work out what makes you happy, and do it ... Impossible advice.

Impossible!

But she found herself wondering – just wondering – if it was, in spite of its absurdity, *good* advice.

From *him*? From that Neanderthal yobbo from the wrong side of the tracks?

He must know a bit himself about making mistakes and rebuilding from the wreckage afterwards. Always listen to the man who knows.

The sermon continued, and Dot went on thinking some most unaccustomed thoughts.

The Christmas Family Service always ended with coffee and mince pies for those who wished to partake. The congregation on Christmas Day itself was always quickly dispersed: there were turkeys to baste, puddings to put on to boil, custard to make, so a pleasant tradition had grown up around the Sunday before. This one was no exception.

Dot found herself caught on the horns of yet another dilemma. Although quite a large part of her didn't wholly approve of her plebeian son-in-law, he was a celebrity, after all. The desire to show him off fought with her equally strong wish to sweep him under the carpet: the former won. In spite of an attempt at escape on the part of Susan, who murmured about checking on the joint and getting the potatoes in, the family found itself in the adjoining church hall. It turned out to be a bad idea.

Mawgan, of course, had already encountered Jenny Carruthers, and hadn't been impressed; he had her down straight away as a snake in the grass, and since then, he had learned a bit more about her and hadn't seen cause to change his mind. His loyalties were not so much to Dot as to Debbie, her daughter, but even so, given the choice, he would have avoided this woman. He wasn't to be given the choice: she pounced on him as if he was her dearest friend.

'Mawgan! How lovely to see you again, and this time we mustn't let Dorothy keep you all to herself, so mean of her wasn't it? Come and let me introduce you to everyone!' *Show you off to my friends and steal Dorothy's thunder*, read the subtext. Her scarlet-nailed fingers rested possessively on his arm.

Debbie, watching this with her mouth open like an idiot, for of course she had no idea the two of them had met, thought that Mawgan's body language was amazingly expressive. He almost visibly recoiled from the encounter, every muscle tensed on to the offensive. She found herself wondering apprehensively what he was going to say, and flinching in sympathy with the importunate Mrs Carruthers. She had witnessed Mawgan dealing with troublemakers in the bar of the Fish and of course there was the famous encounter with poor Tim, too, which she hadn't actually witnessed, but which had passed into St Erbyn folklore. He didn't suffer fools, gladly or any other way. She held her breath.

'Kind of you, but we needn't trouble you none,' he said, almost politely. 'Deb's mum is waiting for us.'

'Oh, but she can spare you for a little moment, surely!' cooed Jenny, putting her head on one side. Her hand was still on his sleeve, the fingers tensed. Mawgan looked down at it. She removed it hastily and began to fiddle with the clasp of her bag. 'We all so much enjoy your wonderful programme.'

'Thanks,' said Mawgan. He turned slightly away from her, taking Debbie's arm as he did so. He smiled, what Debbie mentally termed his "professional" smile. 'We'll see you around, I expect.' They moved away smoothly, and he muttered, for Debbie's ear only, 'but not if I see you first.'

'Oh, ssh!' exclaimed Debbie. 'She'll hear you, and she's real poison!'

'She don't worry me none.'

'She should. Look what she's done to Mum.'

'Your mum is the equal of that one, don't make no mistake. She's marshalling her army, didn't you notice last night? And good for her, if that's the enemy.'

Debbie, regrettably, allowed a grin to spread across her face. 'You won't have much of a fan club, if that's how you treat them all.'

'Never wanted no fan club anyhow. Let's go and look after your mum, if that cow is on the warpath.' He steered her towards Dot. Their path led them quite close to the Carruthers clique; Jenny's voice floated across to them quite clearly. Deliberately so, Debbie thought.

'... yes, I ran into him yesterday at the Farmer's Market, such a delightful man – but of course, Dorothy tried to keep him all to herself. Now she's realised what a star he is, she's changed her tune a bit! Poor Dot, she really did drop herself in it, you have to smile, don't you? I wonder if he knows about the dreadful things she said about him ...?' The heads drew closer together. Debbie saw laughing looks directed at her mother, and seethed quietly.

Mawgan made a tutting noise. He said, quite loudly, 'Don't think that's quite the attitude for church, is it Deb? We don't say things like that at home, I wouldn't never tolerate it in my pub!'

Susan materialised between them. 'What have you two been up to? Mrs Carruthers looked as if she was going to choke on her false teeth when you spoke to her.'

'Good!' said Mawgan. 'And she spoke to me. Be clear on that.'

'Have a cup of coffee,' said Susan, soothingly. 'You can't have an attack of spleen in church. Let Mother show you off to all the tabbies.'

'Thanks a bunch!' said Mawgan, but he came with her obediently. To be sacrificed in this way was what he supposed he was here for, and probably less than he deserved, although being lionised wasn't really his scene.

But Dot showed no disposition to show him off to anyone. She introduced him to a few people, mainly those who filled positions in the church hierarchy and others who came up to speak to her and to exchange greetings with Debbie and Susan, but made no move to embarrass him, thus scoring a subtle but definitive point over her enemy. Mawgan wondered if it was on purpose, but eventually decided not. Dot, he concluded, was in spite of all what his mother would call "a lady". There was a surprise: you lived and learned. Nevertheless, it was a relief when she called time on the occasion and hustled them all off to see to the lunch.

The time was going too quickly now; Dot almost believed that the clocks were speeding up, ticking faster, rushing ahead to the moment when she would be alone again, facing Christmas with nobody, in an empty house. Her heart felt so tight behind her ribs that she seriously wondered if she was about to have an angina attack – not that she had ever had such a thing, but the only other explanation, that she would miss them all so painfully, was ridiculous of course. Why, they hadn't even left yet! Briskly, she set the children to laying the table, Susan to seeing to the vegetables and the pudding batter that Mawgan had made earlier, Carl to opening a bottle of wine. Once again, she hesitated to find a job for Mawgan. Seb noticed this, and pointed it out, indignantly.

'He's doing something anyway,' said Annabel, rattling forks. 'He's out in the hall, reading the yellow pages.' Susan, who had just slipped into the dining room to check on progress, looked sceptical, but Carl, busy at the sideboard, said, 'Checking out the competition, I expect.'

'You didn't really believe all that, did you?' Susan asked. 'He always says he isn't interested in empire building.'

'Maybe national fame has given him ideas,' suggested Carl. Susan would have gone into the hall to check this out, but by now both Mawgan and Debbie must have gone upstairs to pack their things, and if he really had been studying the telephone directory, it was back on its shelf. Immediately lunch was over they would need to be on their way. When Dot went out into the hall later on to call upstairs that lunch was ready, Mawgan was already coming down with their bags. She wondered how she was going to bear it when they drove off.

As they did, of course. Lunch was over too soon, and while Susan and Carl stacked the washing-up machine, Debbie came and put her arms around her mother and hugged her.

'It's been a lovely weekend, Mum, I'm so glad we made the effort. Are you?'

Dot returned the hug, her heart too full for words. She met her son-in-law's eyes over Debbie's shoulder, they were golden, like a lion's, but on this occasion with none of the lion's threat. He wanted to be off, she knew, but he wasn't hurrying Debbie. She found her voice.

'It's been lovely to have you all here, you know it has. Thank you so much for doing all that work for me, it was a great success.' That was directly to Mawgan's address. 'Now you go safely, and give me a ring when you get back to let me know you've arrived.' That was an instinctive harking back to when the children first learned to drive and set off on their own adventures. All but Oliver, who never rang, and was never asked to either.

'We'll be all right, don't fuss Mum!' Debbie sounded as indignant as the teenager she had once been, but Mawgan said peaceably, 'Of course we'll ring your mum, bird, she'll want to know you're OK.' He shook Dot's hand formally, but the gesture was friendly compared to his arrival. 'Have a good Christmas, Mrs Nankervis. I expect Deb'll ring on the day.'

Now was the time to say, as she had said to Carl, *call me Dorothy*. The words stuck in Dot's throat. 'That would be very nice,' she said.

They were gone. The outrageous red car had swept off down the drive, waved cheerfully on its way by Annabel and Sebastian and watched sadly by their grandmother. But Annabel and Sebastian would see them again very soon. Dot turned away.

Susan came out of the kitchen to chase the children upstairs. 'And make sure you've got all your things while Carl brings the car round – look under the beds and in all the cupboards, what you leave behind, stays behind.' The children ran off and Susan turned to her mother. 'I hate having to rush off, but the weather forecast was more rain and we want to be home before it gets really dark.' She paused, unsure whether to ask her question in case the answer was "No". 'Do you have something nice planned for Christmas Day?'

'I shall go to church, as usual, and then spend a quiet day here,' said Dot. It sounded bleak. Susan hesitated. 'Would you do something? On Christmas morning, would you take flowers to Jeremy? I used to do it, but I suppose nobody did last year.'

Dot caught her breath. Jeremy was Oliver and Cheryl's little boy, born prematurely and only surviving for a few hours while his father lay fighting for his own life and his mother wept inconsolably expecting to lose them both. But she lost only Jeremy, and quite suddenly, Dot ached for her. She didn't think much of Cheryl, a shopkeeper's daughter, but to lose a child was unthinkable! It was almost too much, on this day already so full of parting. She said, 'Of course,' and didn't recognise her own voice. She said, more strongly, 'I should have thought of it myself. Please tell Cheryl, I'll make it a regular visit, particularly on his birthday and at Christmas, now I'm the only one left here with him. He won't be forgotten, I promise.'

Carl, now, was coming downstairs with a load of cases. He said, 'Susie, Annabel's lost her bunny slippers, and she's having a hissy fit saying Seb's hidden them, could you ...?'

'I was just going to get the boxes from under the tree – Mother, I don't suppose ...?'

Dot turned briskly towards the stairs, relieved to have something definite to do rather than stand around waiting – for the blow to fall, it rather felt. 'Of course I can,' she said.

Once peace was restored between the children, Annabel's slippers weren't far to seek, under her own bed, thrown right to the back against the wall. Dot tutted at her for her carelessness, made her take a last look round for anything that had been overlooked, and followed both children down the stairs. Time to say goodbye.

Hugs and kisses all round – Carl kissed her too – children loaded into the car, more waving as the Alfa roared down the drive in the wake of the Porsche, then they were gone. All of them. Dot walked back into the house and went into the drawing room; it felt very quiet. The lights on the Christmas tree twinkled in the corner, she could hardly bear to look at them, they seemed to accentuate the emptiness of the big house. The girl – Leanne, she must get used to that – wouldn't be here until tomorrow. It was hard to remember, in this dead silence, how full of warmth this room had been last night. Dot sat down in an armchair, but then, unable to settle, stood up again to move where she wouldn't have to look at the glittering tree. Perhaps if she turned the lights off it would be better, maybe she could ignore it then. She walked round the big sofa to get to the switch, and then stopped. Those children! They'd lose their own heads if they weren't screwed on, they had forgotten the box of Christmas presents! Susan must have taken one and forgotten to come back for the other, how silly of her! Now they would have to be posted – and then she pulled her thoughts up abruptly. This wasn't the same box. This one was covered in Christmas paper and tied round the middle with a large bow, the one that Tom had left had been plain cardboard, the one her own presents had been piled into for transport, the same. So all

172

that business with the slippers had simply been a carefully arranged ploy to get her out of the way.

Hmm ... but the thought of them all ganging up together to surprise her when they were gone was unexpectedly heartwarming. To her own irritation, she felt tears sting behind her eyes.

The box was stacked full of gaily wrapped parcels, some tied with tinsel, some fastened with Christmassy sticky tape, some in pretty bags. At least one of them was certainly a bottle; there had been no bottles among her own offerings. After a minute, Dot knelt beside it and picked up the one from the top; a small rectangle about half an inch thick, it felt like a flat box of some kind. It was decorated with a silk Christmas rose, and had a brightly coloured label dangling from it. The label read *To Grandma, with love from Zoë.* For a moment, Dot couldn't think who Zoë could be. Then she remembered.

Zoë was Oliver's daughter – and Cheryl's. Born at the end of the summer, a small miracle for a couple who, after Oliver's terrible accident four years ago, had believed they would never have children. Dot remembered that she hadn't even sent a card, had believed, and said out loud too, that Cheryl must have played away, and was bitterly ashamed of herself now. How could she have been so small-minded? Even if Cheryl had done so, was it her place to blame her? She, who had two children of her own and, now she came to think about it, by different fathers. She put the little parcel gently back on the pile and explored further.

There were presents from Susan, from Debbie, from Susan and Carl, from Debbie and Mawgan, from the children. There was one from Cheryl and Oliver, and a flat, rectangular parcel about eighteen inches by two feet – Dot still thought imperial in the time-honoured way – from Oliver alone, that felt as if it was framed under the paper. One of his beautiful – and costly – paintings? Unlikely. A nice print, or a painting by a lesser artist he considered promising. The bottle-shaped one was from Mawgan alone. There was even a parcel from the dog.

She was still kneeling there, looking at the colourful boxful, which had become a little blurred in front of her eyes, when the phone rang and she got up to answer it. It was Ingrid.

'Dot! How are you doing, have they all gone?'

'Just ten minutes ago.'

'I bet the house feels empty!' Ingrid hesitated, but then decided to go straight on. 'I just rang to thank you for last night, it was wonderful. What gorgeous food! And great company, too.'

'I enjoyed it myself,' admitted Dot. 'Of course, the children did most of the hard work.'

'Lucky you! Look, Dot, Alex and I were thinking. You're on your own this Christmas, aren't you? Would you like to come and have Christmas lunch with us? We were going to cheat a bit and go out to the pub, let someone else do the cooking for a change, since none of the kids will be here this year, and I expect we can easily book another seat, after all, we've booked the table already, one more chair isn't going to bring the organisation crashing down. What do you think? And then come back with us and we can all watch the Queen's Speech and eat chocolates.'

Ten minutes ago, Dot would have leaped thankfully at the chance not to be alone on Christmas Day of all days. Now, she suddenly realised that she felt quite differently. 'It's sweet of you Ingrid, but I've already arranged what I shall be doing. And the children will ring me during the day, I'd like to be here to take the calls. So may I, very gratefully, refuse?'

'So long as you won't be moping on your own,' said Ingrid.

'Certainly not!'

Before the afternoon was over, she had refused another invitation, this time from the Laws. It was pleasant to be invited, but Dot was feeling much better since the discovery of that unexpected box under the Christmas tree – the tree which still twinkled merrily, but now in what she considered was really quite an encouraging way – and she was even quite looking forward to spending the day on her own. She had a great deal of thinking to do.

X

Another day, another journey, this time in another car. Susan's Range Rover was loaded to the gunwales with boxes of presents, luggage, children, dog, and Susan and Carl, the only ones in comparative comfort in the front – and perhaps that only really applied to Carl, Susan thought, for her own feet were resting on a holdall belonging to Seb, and Carl's laptop was sitting, appropriately enough, on her lap. On the back seat, Annabel and Seb had nearly disappeared under a pile of winter coats and were pushed into the corners by boxes; in the boot, Clinker was uncomfortably wedged in with the main luggage, a mute testimony to the complicated logistics of a large family visiting another, even larger family, at Christmas. The children had refused to leave even one parcel behind for their return, and Carl had even suggested taking both cars. It was a nightmare, only resolved by Liz, when Susan had despairingly recounted the problem over the phone the previous evening, offering to come back with them if all else failed, and maybe even spend New Year.

'That's if Paul will let me,' she had added. 'But anyway, I can slip down for a night, probably, just to transport the surplus.'

'Will Paul be with us for Christmas?' Susan had asked, trying not to sound tepid, and Liz had said no, he wouldn't be. 'He had a terribly not-to-be-missed invitation to stay with some aspiring celebrity writer who he wants to impress,' she said, cynically. 'I was invited too, but I said I was already tied up with family.'

'And how did he take it?'

'He said he wouldn't go, then, he'd come and join us.'

Pause.

'How did you circumvent that?' asked Susan, with interest, and Liz laughed.

'I told him he'd hate it – that Cecy and her boyfriend would be in my bed and we'd have to squash up in the spare room unless he wanted to sleep on the sofa.'

'And will they? Be in your bed?'

'No. Charlie's going to his parents' place. Cecy was invited too, but she wants to meet you all; she'll be sleeping in the spare room, but Paul doesn't need to know that. Anyway, he never really meant to come, it was just flannel! His other invitation was far more interesting.'

Cecilia Worthington was Susan's half-brother Anthony's daughter, and therefore, like Liz, her niece. So far, they hadn't met; apart from Liz herself and her sister Alice, the younger generation were scattered half across the world by this time: Australia, Canada, France, plus one in Yorkshire. Tony, Owen's younger son, and Anthony and Carol's son Richard were based in London, along with Cecy. They had all sent Christmas cards and enthusiastic greetings, together with photographs of themselves and their families where appropriate, and requests for photographs in return. Jill, Owen's youngest daughter, sent regular emails from Brittany; she was almost like a friend these days although they had never met. It was, thought Susan, trying to find a better position under the laptop, very strange. Heartwarming, but strange all the same.

As a lot of things had been this Christmas. She and Deb had still not got to the bottom of their mother's Christmas party, and it hadn't been for want of trying. Talking it over with Oliver and Chel, as Deb had already done, had produced nothing useful; Deb had said she almost thought that they hadn't believed her. Chel, to be sure, had murmured something rather profound about people, like animals, responding to the way they were treated, but Oliver had turned the discussion very adroitly. Oliver, Susan suspected, was feeling guilty. Reflection was making her wonder if he was being too hard on himself. She was trying not to think it, but she had a feeling that probably Jerry – and Helen too – had contributed as much to the situation as he had. He had only been a child when it all began, children, even the impossible child Oliver had been, didn't have that much clout.

If that was where it *did* begin. She was beginning to wonder about that, too, and looked forward to a chance to talk to Carol. Something was desperately wrong with the Nankervis family when one compared it, for instance, with the Worthingtons or with Chel's family. There is never just one cause for things like that, Susan was quite certain.

An excited squeal came from the back seat, drowning out the sound of the radio which Carl had left on for weather and traffic reports. 'Ooh, Mummy, look, it's snowing!'

'Sleet,' said Susan. She glanced sideways to Carl. 'Is it going to get thicker, do you think?'

'Snow's not forecast. Let's hope.'

'For what?' asked Annabel, but under her breath, then louder. 'We like snow.'

'Maybe there'll be some for you on Dartmoor,' Carl suggested. 'We don't need it on the A30, however.'

'Auntie Debbie didn't mind,' said Annabel, rebelliously. The tale of how Debbie met Mawgan had passed into family lore. Susan laughed.

'I think you'll find she did, if you ask her,' she said. 'How she tells it, she was terrified from start to finish, and I'm not surprised. I would have been, too.'

'She met Uncle Mawgan,' said Seb.

'So she did. But as it turned out, she would have done that anyway, and I think both of them might have preferred it.'

'Our family is very interesting, isn't it?' Annabel speculated, and Carl gave a snort of laughter.

'If that's the word. Other people's families find it easier to be merely boring.'

'Is yours boring?' asked Seb, with interest.

'Very. You'll find out the dreadful truth on New Year's Day.'

The children fell silent, watching the sleet come down and hoping for it to get thicker and be snow, and Susan considered Carl's last statement. She hadn't met any of Carl's family, apart from his mother. Grannie Julie, as the children called her – a shorter version of Seb's tentative "sort of our grandma" and Annabel's slightly more contentious "you aren't old enough to be a proper grandma, and Carl isn't our daddy" – had gone to her brother and his family for Christmas this year, but she would be with them in St Erbyn for the New Year. The day after, the Colensos were holding a big family get-together in their home town of Redruth, it would be ... she hesitated in her thoughts, and then borrowed a word from Annabel ... an *interesting* occasion.

The sleet was turning to rain as they crossed Dunheved Bridge and left Cornwall behind them. Carl took the left-hand fork to Lifton, remarking, with thankfulness, 'At least it doesn't look as if we're going to be snowbound outside an apparently deserted cottage, like Deb. Good thing too, I don't think I could stand finding another of your Uncle Mawgans.'

'You like Uncle Mawgan,' Seb accused him.

'Certainly do. But I believe that one is enough.'

'Grandma doesn't, much,' remarked Annabel, to the window and the falling rain. Susan let that pass, it was true anyway even if she did wish Annabel wasn't quite so observant these days. What wouldn't be true any more was to say that she didn't like him at all. And that was interesting – that word again, how useful it was. Her attitude, by the end of their visit, had begun to resemble that of Carl to Oliver, and come to that, Oliver to Carl: best described as an armed truce. She thought about what they had learned at the sailing club party, and her heart ached for Oliver. What a disastrous coincidence that was, no wonder Oliver had backed off! He would certainly have realised, the instant he heard the name of the boat Carl had sailed on; she couldn't imagine him not having taken an interest in her performance, however bitterly it must have been. She wondered if he would have liked Carl any better had they sailed together on *Orb Technic*, if Carl had even been on board had Oliver picked the crew, and found no answer. They were too unalike, and at the same time, too alike to be easy with each other. Probably, that wouldn't have been different. Mutual respect was probably the best to be hoped for, and she thought they might have achieved that much.

The car was leaving the secondary road and heading into the lanes. There was water everywhere, running in the verges and sluicing down the slopes and still it rained down. Even the children had fallen quiet now. Carl was concentrating on driving, and Susan was glad that considerations of space had precluded their travelling in the Alfa; at least her car had the power to get them out of trouble with its four-wheel drive.

Apart from a row of cars parked outside the shop and a huddled figure hastening to the postbox, Waldren Stavey, when they reached it, was deserted. Only Seb ventured to mention, as they drove past Liz's cottage, that they could stop in and see her. 'We like Liz,' he said. Nobody answered him.

It was a few miles further to Stavey Tor Farm: they passed silently. The lane leading to the farmyard was muddy and running with water;

as they drove into the farmyard the back door of the farmhouse opened and a shaft of yellow light darkened the gloom of a midday more like late evening. Owen, Susan's half-brother, came dashing out, the hood of his rainproof jacket pulled over his head and his heavy boots on. He was calling as he came, 'Back right up to the door and then make a dash for it, we'll do the luggage when this eases off! Dreadful, isn't it? We thought you might have trouble in the lanes.'

Everyone tumbled out and made a dash for the door. Carl, releasing Clinker, grabbed at his collar before he could hurtle off into the mud. The farmhouse kitchen was suddenly full of people, laughing and greeting each other. Owen's wife, Sarah, hugged them all warmly, and Owen smiled with an arm round each child. Clinker made for the Aga and flopped in front of it, startling a tabby cat that was already there.

'It's so good to be here,' said Susan, returning Sarah's hug. 'It's been a frightful journey, and it's just like coming home at the end.'

'What a nice thing to say! Oh, it's so lovely to have you for Christmas! I never believed it would happen, with all your other commitments! Coffee?'

'Oh, please.'

'Can we go and see the ponies?' asked Annabel, and Sarah and Susan spoke in unison, 'When it stops raining.'

'Then can we go upstairs to the playroom and watch telly?'

'That sounds dry enough,' said Owen. 'You don't want a drink, either of you?'

'We could take it with us,' said Annabel, hopefully.

'What a splendid idea! I'll bring it up to you,' said Carl immediately.

The children ran off, headed for the big attic at the top of the house, stocked with games, music, television and toys to ensure peace for beleaguered grown-ups on days like today. As they ran, Annabel called, over her shoulder, 'Will Katie and Lulu be coming round?'

'And William,' put in Seb.

'Later,' said Sarah, and the kitchen door swung shut behind them. There was the sound of feet clumping swiftly up the wooden stairs, and silence settled on the kitchen like a comforting blanket. After a short pause, Owen remarked, 'Phew! How can two children fill a large house the moment they come into it?'

'You just wait, you ain't seen nothing yet,' Sarah told him. She poured coffee into four mugs and addressed herself to Susan and Carl as she handed them round. 'It's been a right carry-on, finding beds for everyone! Carol and Anthony are staying with Isobel and George, but they've only the one spare room because George uses the other for an office, and then Cecy decided to come too and there's no way Alice can fit an adult-sized bed in that slip of a room of theirs, so Cecy will stay with Liz – and actually, that's great, because it means we don't get Paul –' She broke off. 'I shouldn't have said that, should I?'

'Feel free,' said Carl. 'In fact we said something quite similar, not so long ago.'

'Oh dear – what happened?' asked Owen, looking amused.

'Mawgan banned him from the Fish,' Susan told him. Nobody looked particularly distressed – or surprised, for that matter.

'Wish we could do the same, and ban him from the house,' said Sarah. 'What did he do?'

'Made a big scene in the bar,' said Carl, without going into details.

'Sounds just like him – pretentious prat! I just don't know what Liz sees in him.'

'I think she's beginning to wonder about that, too,' observed Susan, and Sarah gave her a quick look.

'What makes you think so?' She sounded hopeful. Susan shook her head.

'Not sure. On the one hand, she's still making the same old excuses – someone to go to parties with, better than spending the weekend on her own –' She broke off as Sarah interrupted, 'She wouldn't! Liz should know better than that.'

'Maybe.' Susan wasn't going to be judgemental on this one, she had done a bit of going about on her own, and hadn't enjoyed it. And she had been married. It had been, she fully realised, largely down to lack of confidence and not standing up for herself, but Liz had no cause to be like that, surely? Did her own mother? she suddenly wondered. She gave no sign of it, but such people often didn't. Quite often, they became bullies to compensate ... oops! And where had that gem come from?

180

'What's the matter?' Sarah asked, looking at her curiously, and Susan said, nothing really. 'A goose walked over my grave. You know how it is.' She frowned, remembering a conversation she had had with Debbie, and deciding on impulse to try it out on Sarah and Owen. 'We have wondered if Liz being ... well, well-known and presumably fairly well off, is at the bottom of it. She doesn't trust men to love her for herself alone.' And I don't blame her, she thought, but didn't say. Tom Casson was a perfect example of the species hanger-on.

'You think that's why? It seems a curious way of dealing with the problem – Paul Attwood is blatantly out for what he can get!'

'So she knows exactly where she stands,' Carl observed. There was a short silence.

'Well,' said Owen, judiciously, 'we can put up with him if we have to – he isn't that bad, and we've been doing it for long enough to get used to him – but it does seem rather a final solution. While he's hanging around, nobody else is going to get a look in, are they?'

'It's a problem that Liz has to resolve for herself,' said Sarah, firmly. 'Whatever we say ... well, while he's her friend, we can't slam the door in his face. Not unless he gives us cause, and he doesn't. He's always very pleasant, really. I just can't like him, somehow.'

'Join the club,' said Carl. Footsteps rattled on the stairs and Susan put her finger to her lips. A moment later, Annabel burst in through the kitchen door.

'It's stopped raining, can we go and see the ponies now – *please*?'

The rain hadn't really stopped, just abated a little, but Owen good-naturedly fetched his coat and wellies and Carl extracted the children's from the back of the car. The three of them and Clinker went off happily towards the barn where the three ponies lived in winter and since he was already out in the rain, Carl unloaded the car into the back porch and reparked it beside Owen's. Sarah, meanwhile, asked Susan to help her with the lunch. 'We need to get it over, because Alice and the kids will descend on us before you know it – they can hardly wait to get together in their unholy alliance with yours again!'

'God help us,' remarked Carl, passing through with load of luggage on his way upstairs.

'How are you at carving?' Sarah asked Susan. 'There's a ham here that needs attention.' She dumped it in front of Susan with a carving knife and fork and turned to washing lettuce in the sink. 'Ugh, I hate slugs! Although, I suppose they're quite beautiful if you study them –' She hesitated. 'How did your mother's party go? I know you were a bit doubtful about the idea.'

Susan thought before answering, but eventually said, 'Actually, it went off rather well. This knife needs sharpening.'

'There's a steel in the drawer. Can you use it?'

'Yes.' Finding the steel and attending to the knife gave her breathing space in which to think. She hadn't intended to broach the subject of the party with Sarah, but why not? Sarah, like Carol, wasn't a blood relation but an in-law, Susan had found her sensible in the past. She said, 'Sarah, can I ask you something?'

'Of course you can. Why shouldn't you?' There was a pause, as Carl passed back through the kitchen, throwing over his shoulder a question about where to put the boxes of presents. 'Just dump them on that end of the table for now, Owen will help with them later on,' Sarah told him. The back door closed behind him, and she turned back to Susan. 'So? What is it?'

The brief interval had given Susan time to frame her question, but even so, she spoke it hesitantly. 'When Owen's father married my mother, did he give ... well, any explanation?'

Sarah looked at her without speaking for a moment. Then, 'What a curious way of putting it,' she said.

'Maybe. But when you look at it, it was a curious thing to do. After all, she was – what, forty years younger than him?'

'Near enough. But it's been done before. *Shall I be an old man's darling*, and all that.'

'But from what I can work out, she was already *a young man's slave*. Even if he had dumped her for a trendier model.'

Sarah shook her head. 'Don't think we didn't wonder about it. He never really said outright, he wouldn't say anything against her, but obviously we discussed it among ourselves.'

'And did you come to any conclusions?'

'That he was sorry for her,' Sarah said slowly. 'Oh yes, he had enjoyed being married, that came into it too, he was that kind of man. But there were women nearer his own age who wouldn't have turned him down. He was a sweetie, and rich with it. Carol says it was the money that attracted her, but then, Carol would.'

'So? What did you think?'

'I thought that lots of women get dumped, and nobody feels they have to marry them out of pity. Or not often. And Owen's father wasn't that daft.'

'But he did marry her.'

Sarah said, musingly, 'I think he did pity her. But I'm not sure it was for that.'

'What, then?'

'Search me. If you really feel it's important to know, try asking Isobel. It's no use asking me, I was the daughter-in-law.'

'Carl said, ask Carol.' It came out like a challenge, which Susan hadn't intended. Sarah tipped the lettuce from the spinner into a bowl and turned round, resting her back against the worktop, so that she could look at her.

'That would be a good suggestion, except for one thing. Carol would tell you the truth without trying to dress it up, no problem, but she and Ant weren't married then, she wasn't around that often. She's a non-starter, she knows sod all. And she can't stand your mother.'

'It's mutual,' Susan mentioned. It was time someone put in a word for Dot. 'So, why Isobel?'

'Because fathers are very close to their daughters.' She saw Susan's face and winced. 'Sorry, I didn't mean to rub it in. If Dad confided in anyone, it would be Isobel. But don't get your hopes up, he was very loyal. He wouldn't have offered any criticism.'

'It's not criticism I'm searching for,' said Susan. 'It's reasons. Reasons why he should have done it, because I'm beginning to be sure it wasn't just because Jerry dumped her for Helen and she was feeling sore, it isn't enough, given the sort of man you all say he was.'

'Ask Isobel,' Sarah advised again. 'Now, how's that ham doing?'

'I've carved enough for six of us, but it's not going anywhere until those boxes are off the table.'

'I'll give Owen a whistle,' said Sarah, and went to the back door. Her shrill whistle brought not only Owen, Carl and the children, but a muddy Clinker and two damp border collies and the kitchen was suddenly full of people and dogs.

'Should've left them,' Susan remarked. Sarah shrugged her shoulders, she was used to scenes like this. She made her dispositions accordingly. 'Carl, can you take the dogs into the scullery and give them a rub down, you'll find a towel hanging on the door, and Owen, can you and the children please move those boxes into the sitting room and give us room to lay the table.'

Carl had some trouble with the dogs, who wanted to follow Owen and the children, but peace was finally restored and the scullery door firmly closed on them. The subject of Dot was swept away in the disturbance, and as they laid the long kitchen table for lunch, Susan and Sarah talked only about uncontentious things such as the family and the coming Christmas celebrations.

Lunch was a cheerful meal, but disorganised; a great contrast to lunch with Dot. The cat had retreated to the back of the Aga, and the heap of damp, only slightly less muddy, dogs piled up on the rug in front. Susan looked at Carl critically. 'Better have a shower after you've eaten. You look as if you've been wrestling a hippopotamus.'

Carl had washed his hands, but since there was no mirror in the scullery, he was unaware of the muddy smear across his cheek. Sarah took the cloth from the sink and wiped it off. 'There – that's better. Sit down and eat your lunch before the others get here! You must be starving after that awful drive!'

The others arrived while the adults were sitting over their coffee, in the shape of Liz's sister Alice and her three children; William and the twins, Kathryn and Louise. Sarah dealt with the invasion with practiced competence. 'Annabel and Seb are up in the attic, off you go and join them. Coffee, Alice?'

'Oh, please! I've been cooking all morning, I feel like a rag!' She turned to Susan. 'Have you been warned, you're all eating with us tonight? Only a buffet, paper plates so we can throw away the washing-up. You can come back with me and lend a hand if you want, Susan. Liz said she'd be over later and I'll bring you back when I collect the children.'

'It hardly seems fair to leave Sarah with all five.'

'They'll be OK, William will keep them in order.'

'You go, Susan,' said Sarah. 'Alice can probably do with the help, Liz isn't much use, she's too impractical, and you can all have a good girlie gossip. Owen will find something for Carl to do. All the lambing ewes are inside in this wet, there's plenty of work.'

'Oh, great,' said Carl, making a face. Sarah smiled at him.

'Or you could put your feet up with a good book.'

Carl laughed. 'I'll give the sheep a go, if Owen wants to risk it. So long as it doesn't entail actually delivering any lambs.'

'The girls aren't due for a week or two yet,' said Owen placidly. 'Have some more coffee – you need to keep your strength up.'

'It's quite an undertaking, dishing out the work fairly with all the family coming,' Sarah said, but she didn't look as if she minded. 'I don't think we've ever been quite so many – Ant usually gets tied up in his constituency, and of course, you haven't been able to come before. It seems so strange to think we've only known you a couple of years –' she broke off, and looked thoughtful.

'Such a waste, all that time we didn't know you,' remarked Alice. She smiled at Susan. 'It's you coming here that's brought everyone out of the woodwork, of course, even Richard was muttering about coming from London on Christmas Day apparently, although where he thinks he's going to sleep that night if he doesn't go back again, I hate to think.'

'Liz and Cecy will have to share a bed if he stays,' said Sarah, briskly. 'That'll make it eighteen of us on Christmas Day.' She looked at the big farmhouse table measuringly. 'Good thing the children are only quite young. We can stack them up on the ends.'

'Paul would have hated it,' said Alice, reflectively. 'Probably have tried to drag Liz away to some posh restaurant somewhere, run by one of his "contacts".'

'On Christmas Day? He'd be lucky to get a booking!'

'Somehow, people like him always are.'

'But he's not here, so we needn't worry about him,' said Owen. He stood up and put his mug in the sink. 'Well, you may all have time to sit around gossiping, but I must get on. Coming to give me a hand, Carl? You don't have to.' The two men went out into the rain together, and Alice got reluctantly to her feet.

'Shall we help you with the washing-up, Aunt Sarah?'

'Don't bother, it'll all go in the machine.' Sarah began collecting the mugs. 'You get off, after all, I haven't got to do anything tonight. I can spend the afternoon restfully.'

'With those five in the attic, I wouldn't bet on it,' Alice said. 'If you're sure, we'll be on our way. Got your coat, Auntie Sue? Then let's go, before that lot upstairs realise we're escaping!'

Alice's husband Gil ran a substantial plant nursery just outside Waldren Stavey, their house was conveniently right next door and Alice helped out when the children were at school. The house was new, built as part of the nursery complex, and the garden, in the summer months, was naturally a picture, although Alice claimed that she did all the hard work. 'Gil just supplies the plants and issues his orders,' she was wont to say. On a wet winter's day it wasn't looking its best, and she and Susan rushed indoors at speed. Liz was already there, as witnessed by her car parked on the drive. She didn't seem to be doing much, and greeted them with pleasure.

'Coffee? I've just switched the kettle on.'

'Hope you filled it first, then,' remarked Alice, hustling into her kitchen, which looked as if a bomb had hit it. 'I think I'd drunk it dry! I see you've been doing some cooking. Why do you never clear up?'

'I made the sausage and egg pie while I was waiting for you to get back. It's in the oven. I made two.' She repeated her previous offer. 'Coffee?'

Alice hesitated. 'We've only just had one, really. Susan?'

'I like the idea of a cup without the threat of children hanging over me,' said Susan firmly. She flung her coat over the back of a chair and pushed up the sleeves of her sweatshirt. 'You get on with that, I'll clear up Liz's mess.'

'Liz is a good cook,' said Alice fairly, reaching for mugs. 'Her sausage and egg pie is to die for. But she'd never survive in a professional kitchen. Your brother-in-law would strangle her as soon as look at her – or rather, at the mess she leaves behind. Just look at it!'

'It's not that bad.' Susan was gathering up rolling pin, bowls, spoons and knives with practised ease and piling them into the sink. 'It's scattered rather than deep – where do you put eggshells – how did you get them in so many places, Liz?'

'And speaking of the devil,' said Liz, giving a perfunctory poke at the pile in the sink with the dishcloth, 'how did your party go?'

186

Sarah had asked the same question, and Susan was aware that she hadn't really answered it. To Alice and Liz, who were her contemporaries, she felt she could be more direct. They could add nothing to the sum of her knowledge, but they might make useful comments. So she replied with total honesty. 'It was the oddest party I've ever been to in my parents' house. I don't know why – possibly the people who were there. I don't think more than half of them had ever been there before.'

'But they're your mother's friends,' Alice objected.

'Not her usual ones. Except for my godfather, and Oliver's ex-girlfriend's parents. And four of them were us, which hasn't happened before either. One of them, I would have said was Mother's sworn enemy. Two were total strangers. Weird, or what?'

'Different, anyway, but was it successful?' asked Liz.

'Strangely, it was. There was even a bishop.'

'Sounds like she's decided it's time for a change, then,' said Liz. The kettle had boiled, and into the silence that followed this comment there fell only the rattling of mugs. Then Susan gave herself a shake, as if to rid herself of something.

'That was uncommonly insightful, Elizabeth Ballantyne,' she said. Liz put the mugs on the kitchen table and added the sugar bowl. She pulled out a chair.

'Sit down – you too, Alice. The three of us can finish the job in a trice between us, let's take time out.' When they were seated, she looked at Susan. 'Of course, it doesn't mean that *she* will change, but bearing in mind that people tend to take their tone from those around them, she quite possibly will. So, given the company, would that be for the better?'

'The bishop should be a beneficial influence,' offered Alice. She sugared her coffee and stirred it thoughtfully. 'Of course, we've never met your mother.'

'Perhaps we should,' said Liz, idly. 'Oh, I know there was all that trouble over Grandad's will, but that's years ago. And Aunt Carol was at the back of that, from all we hear. Why should we all be ruled by Aunt Carol?'

'You're suggesting that healing old wounds would solve the problem?' Alice sounded sceptical.

'Help, anyway. Even as Susan tells it, this Dot sounds unlovable. People like that are often unloved.'

'And ask for it, generally,' said Alice, briskly.

'That's not quite what I meant.'

Alice and Susan thought about that for a moment, and not for the first time, Susan felt a flicker of knowledge at the back of her mind, but she had been too young, it was too long ago. She lost it again, but that time it had felt closer, almost within reach. She considered what Liz had just said with objectivity. 'Who wouldn't have loved her then? Apart from Jerry, and it couldn't have been him. Everyone gets jilted at least once, unless they're very lucky, and survives.'

'It's generally the parents,' said Liz, without looking at her.

It was like a physical jolt. Susan's memory quite suddenly began unreeling pictures. When you are a child, you take things for granted, but she wasn't a child now, she was an adult, searching for answers. And there they were. She drew a breath. 'Bugger! I think you're right.'

Alice looked at her severely. 'You've been spending too much time with that sister of yours,' she told her. 'It's not like you to swear. Right about what?'

Susan's mind was whirling. She had been very young, of course, but she recalled that it had seemed as if her mother could never do anything to please in her childhood home. At the time it had been just the way things were, but now, constant criticism and stinging put-downs echoed in her head, and she remembered how she had never really wanted to go there. Some of it would have been down to Dot's handling of Oliver, who had always played up in that house, but surely, not all of it. Their grandparents had treated their daughter as if she was a rather unsatisfactory servant, it seemed to Susan now, and herself and Deb as a duty rather than a joy. From an adult point of view, it suddenly all looked awful. But it had been a long time ago, perhaps she was bending the past to fit her own ideas? She didn't want to believe her mother to be the woman she appeared to be, after all. She took a gulp of coffee, and choked. Liz watched her seriously.

'Of course,' she said, 'when you start looking for answers, it's easy to imagine things that aren't really there to build up your case.' It was so much what Susan was thinking herself that she nearly choked again, from surprise this time. Alice patted her back. 'Choke up chicken. Isn't there anyone around you can ask?'

'Sarah said, your mother.'

'Well, you'll see her tonight. Do that. Although actually I meant someone who knew your mother as a child.'

Susan shook her head. 'I think they're all dead. Gone away, anyhow, even if I knew who they were.'

Alice swept the mugs together, and Liz gave a sigh. 'That looks like coffee break is over.' She got to her feet. 'I'll wash up, shall I? What's to do next?'

'Two roast chickens to dismember,' said Alice. 'Salad to wash. Mince pies to make. Potato salad to prepare. Tomatoes to slice. Table to lay.'

'So, what were you doing all morning?' Liz demanded. She turned on the tap and whisked up the suds in the sink with her hand. Susan watched her critically.

'You need fresh water, that's disgusting, Liz. Pull the plug out and start again. How many people are coming tonight, Alice?'

'You. Us. Uncle Owen and Aunt Sarah. Mum and Dad. I make that fourteen, how about you?'

Susan counted up on her fingers and found Alice to be right. 'Is it always like this?'

'Not usually, no.' Liz watched the last of the water gurgling down the sink and put the plug back in. 'You're not usually here for one thing, nor Uncle Art and Aunt Carol, nor Cecy and Richard if it comes to that. And there's usually Paul.' She didn't add that apart from his irresistible alternative invitation and the lack of accommodation, it had been the advertised presence of Susan and Carl that was really keeping Paul away this year, but just the same, she thought that it was true. His humiliation in St Erbyn had gone deep.

Alice gave her a sisterly look. 'Well, we won't miss him, that's one thing.'

'He's a friend of mine,' said Liz, on a dangerous note. Susan jumped in to avoid a family squabble, not entirely happily.

'Why *don't* you have New Year with us, Liz? Have you thought about it? You could stay when you come down at the end of the week, make the most of it. After all, it may not happen like this again for a year or two; for one thing, I think next year we may find ourselves going to Embridge for Christmas.'

Coming from what could be classified as a "normal" family, neither Alice nor Liz saw anything unexpected in this. Liz said, 'No thank you, Auntie Sue, it's tempting but I don't think it's a good idea.'

'Why ever not?' asked Alice.

'I should have thought that was obvious. New Year in St Erbyn centres around the Fish. Paul's been banned.'

'Surely your brother-in-law wouldn't enforce that, not at New Year?' Alice turned to Susan.

'Don't bet on it,' said Susan, and Liz said, at the same time, 'Paul wouldn't go in there, he'd die first. Everyone was staring at him and listening.'

'Then go without him,' said Alice, to which Liz made no reply. Alice gave a big-sisterly sniff. 'Why do you stay with him?'

'The sex is good,' said Liz, half to herself. 'What else is on offer?' Alice exchanged a look with Susan and raised her eyes to heaven. The oven timer chose that moment to ring, and Liz busied herself taking her pies out of the oven, and the moment passed. Susan found herself wondering if, with Paul banned from the Fish, he and Liz would ever visit St Erbyn again, and was irritated with him. She could do without his company, no question, but if it meant that Liz wouldn't come either it would be sad. It didn't seem to be the right moment to have this out with her: there was too much to do, but after the holiday was over and New Year too, Susan decided that she would address the question. It wasn't even as if Paul was worth it, their relationship was transparently one of convenience – Paul's convenience, that is – it was going nowhere. Liz herself freely admitted it. "The sex is good" was no good reason if she didn't even like Paul that much, and both her aunt and her sister were beginning to seriously question that.

The three of them worked hard all afternoon, avoiding any more controversial subjects, and at five o'clock Alice, looking at the dining room table spread with food, heaved a sigh of satisfaction. 'That's it, then. I can collect the kids and drop you off, Susan, and then we can all have a rest – ha, some hopes for me!'

'It all looks fantastic,' said Susan.

'But will we ever eat it all?' asked Liz. There was some justification for this, for there were not only the fruits of their own concerted labours that afternoon, but bread rolls and trifle made by Alice in the morning, and it looked enough to feed an army. Alice, however, merely said, 'What, with five children, one farmer, one gardener, and one tractor dealer? Don't be silly, Liz!'

There was some justification for this comment, too; turning the family loose on the spread later certainly didn't leave much over for the pig, as Owen philosophically remarked.

'I thought you weren't supposed to feed pigs on leftovers these days,' Susan said.

'We don't have a pig,' Sarah pointed out.

'Good thing! Poor piggy,' contributed Annabel, dancing up in time to hear this exchange, and then unexpectedly flung her arms round her mother and said, 'Mummy, this is a lovely Christmas – going to Grandma, and the pantomime and everything, and now this, there's never been such a good Christmas in the history of the whole world!'

Susan and Sarah exchanged a look. Susan ruffled her daughter's hair, laughing at her because she could think of nothing else to do. 'Come on Annabella, last Christmas was pretty good.'

'Yes, it was.' Annabel released her and made to dance away again to join the twins, 'but there wasn't William and Katie and Lulu.'

True, thought Susan, watching her run to join the other children and fall into a heap with them beneath the laden Christmas tree in the corner. She found Sarah still looking at her, and said, defensively, 'I didn't deprive my children, did I?'

Sarah didn't answer directly. She said, 'I suppose that depends on what you think they should have.'

'Oh, very profound!'

Gil and Carl rounded up the children and took them off to play a game on a cleared end of the table before they became out of hand, and Alice looked, with a sigh, at the decimated remains crammed onto the other end. 'I suppose we'd better clear this lot up,' she said.

'If you leave it, most of it will disappear on its own,' suggested Owen, helping himself to a lonely slice of Liz's pie. 'George is good for another round, aren't you George?'

'Dad should be watching his weight,' said Alice, severely, and her father grinned at her.

'Oh, I do. Every morning on the bathroom scales. And talking of rounds, another beer, Owen?' They went off to the laden sideboard to see about it, and Sarah shrugged her shoulders.

'And it'll get worse,' she mentioned. 'A quiet day tomorrow to gather our strength and wait for everyone else to arrive, and then the next couple of days will be chaos! Annabel's right, we always have a good time at Christmas, but this one is going to be either incredibly special or a total disaster!'

'Do you notice,' said Liz, coming up with a double handful of dirty glasses, 'how cunningly the men have deployed themselves? Uncle Owen and Dad, so called "in charge of the drinks" while they quietly knock it back, and Gil and Carl playing with the children and behaving like kids themselves, and all of us women carrying the debris out to the kitchen? Where's Mum?'

'On current form, probably loading the washing-up machine,' said Alice, running a swift eye over the assembly. 'Come on girls – let's go and lend a hand! There's some rather good coffee beans in the fridge.'

'We'll soon have them out!' Liz led the retreat.

Isobel was indeed in the kitchen, but not loading the washing-up machine since apart from the glasses and the odd plate there was as yet little to load. A loosely tied bag full of discarded paper plates and napkins and a clear expanse of worktop bore witness to her industry, but Isobel herself was sitting quietly at the table listening to the kettle coming to the boil.

'I was just going to come and see who wanted coffee,' she said. 'Glasses straight into the machine please, Liz. Are the men still on the beer?'

'What do you think?' asked Sarah, joining her at the table. 'We thought we'd take five, we think we've earned it.'

Alice was already getting coffee beans out of the fridge and lining up mugs on the worktop. Susan, seeing nothing useful to be done, sat beside her sisters – and there was a peculiar thought, even if one was a half-sister and the other a sister-in-law. She was so used to there being just herself and Deb, and of late years, Chel, that it felt extremely odd, especially so when you realised both Alice and Liz were older than she was. Isobel, apparently picking her thought out of the ambient air, said, 'This must all seem very casual to you, Susan. I imagine your mother runs a tighter ship than we do, she had that look.'

It may or may not have been a deliberate bait, but Susan decided on impulse to treat it as such. Never mind the presence of the other three; Sarah she had confided in earlier anyway, and Liz had already made one insightful remark today. She said, 'It's true, but I think maybe it's just that she doesn't know how to let go and have fun. The party the other night was a bit of an eye-opener.'

'Sarah said you wanted to talk about it. Is this a good moment?'

'Could be.' Susan paused, as the roar of the coffee grinder interrupted them. When it had stopped, she went on. 'It was a great party. That isn't the problem.' She looked down at her hands, resting on the table. 'I asked Sarah this, she probably told you. Have you any idea why your – our – father married my mother in the first place? It seems such an odd thing for him to have done – her too, come to that, she can't have been even as old as Deb at the time.'

'Twenty-five,' said Isobel.

'And he was?'

'Sixty-three.'

'See what I mean?'

'Well, of course he did have his reasons,' said Isobel. 'I don't know how much you know about those days, Susan. Dad was a client of … of your adoptive father's father. That's how he knew her.'

'Jerry,' said Susan, not for the first time, 'Call him Jerry.'

'I'm starting this from the wrong end,' said Isobel, ruefully. 'Your mother worked in the office, did you know *that*?'

Susan hadn't. She was surprised. 'I never knew she studied law!' She sounded indignant, for when she had wanted to study law herself, years ago now, her mother had slapped her down on the grounds that "women get married" and then seen that she did.

'She didn't,' said Isobel. She made tea, and typed the letters. Dad said she seemed totally out of place.'

'Then why was she doing it?' demanded Susan, and Sarah said, 'She was waiting for Mr Right.'

'Oh, him,' Susan was dismissive. 'Yes, she is a bit hung up on that mythical creature.'

'It's the way she was brought up.' Sarah hesitated. 'Look, Susan, you could be about to hear things you won't want to listen to.'

'I've heard a lot of them lately. You might just as well come out with it, and get it off your conscience, for one thing I suspect we all need to know. Things can't stay as they are. We need to get to the bottom of it all.'

'Perhaps you do. Tell me, how well do you remember your grandparents?'

Bullseye! Not sure whether she was glad or not to have this independent confirmation of her guess, Susan considered her reply with care. 'Not that well,' she said, finally. 'I don't think they were very ...' She sought for a word. 'Very *cosy*.'

'Funny you should choose that word,' said Sarah. 'That's exactly what Dad said – at least, he said they were cold, actually, but it comes to the same thing.'

'They were religious,' put in Isobel. 'Not the nice, friendly, normal sort of religion, just a comfort in the background and a few hymns on Sundays. Joyless stuff, very serious, evangelical. No love in it, Dad said, unless it came from God – and even He seems to have been very censorious.'

'Dreary, then?'

'It gets worse. They hadn't really wanted Dorothy, children would interfere with the Lord's Work, and they were quite old for having a child, but it was "the purpose of marriage" I think was the phrase, so when it happened they bit the bullet and got on with it. They raised her as a duty, to serve their God; not fun for her, and sent her to boarding school at soon as they could.'

'I knew that bit,' said Susan, relieved to see a familiar landmark. 'She was captain of games, all very jolly hockey-sticks.'

'Yes, that figures.' Isobel took a sip of her coffee, and replaced the mug on the table with care. 'Do you also know that she was an absolutely brilliant tennis player? I mean, really, really, good, national competition standard?'

Susan gaped at her, feeling stupid. She had had no idea. Thinking of her mother, she saw no connection. Isobel watched her thinking about it for a moment, and then said, 'I see that surprised you. The school recommended that she take it seriously, they said she had a real chance of a brilliant future. Do you know what her parents said?' Susan shook her head, speechless. 'They said that to spend your time in playing games was both wasting your life on childish pursuits and against the teachings of the Bible, and in any case, a woman's pre-ordained destiny was marriage to a good man and the procreation of children – and recall what I just said about their attitude to *their* child. They sent her to a secretarial college instead so that she could be "useful in the community" while she waited for this Mr Right person. When she qualified, Jerry's father gave her a job out of sheer compassion. Dad said, he thought it broke her heart, giving up all her wonderful hopes and ambitions. Her exceptional talent for tennis was the only good thing in her life.'

It certainly explained a lot about their mother, Susan thought. Poor Mother! No wonder she was so difficult to understand, or to put it more bluntly, so difficult, full stop. What a mixture of different things had gone to the shaping of her character! Puritanical religion and parental rejection on the one hand, and a brilliant future in sport snatched away on the other. Of course, she might never have fulfilled her potential, but it was downright wicked that she had never been permitted to try. Susan felt furiously indignant on her mother's behalf. She said, 'Go on. That's not the finish.'

'Dad knew her right back then, of course. He saw her when he visited Jerry's father's office and he knew her parents slightly – as slightly as he could conveniently arrange, actually. He had no time for them and their preaching, and he thought the way they treated Dorothy was appalling.'

'I'm surprised she put up with it,' said Susan. Sarah raised her eyebrows.

'I can't see why. From all accounts, you did similar.'

Susan felt her colour rise, she couldn't control it. It was true, of course. Her mother appeared to have left most of her parents' religious beliefs in the past, she was standard C of E these days, but Mr Right had remained with her and she had married him to Susan. Except that he had turned out to be Mr Entirely Wrong. There was something else she had done, too. Susan mentioned it now.

'I wanted to study Law at university. She said ... well, almost exactly what her own parents said to her. *It's a waste of your time and your father's money. Women marry, children come along, that's what happens.*'

'Old injuries die hard,' said Sarah, and Susan said, 'Yes.' There was a pause.

'So, go on,' said Susan. 'It can't finish there. What happened next?'

'Your adoptive father happened. He had been away, gaining experience with a big London firm, and he came back to join the family business. Of course, he met Dorothy, took her out a bit and naturally, after the way she had been guarded from real life all the time, and considering how unhappy she was at home, she fell in love with him. Her parents encouraged it, they wanted her off their hands and safely married, producing more little soldiers for the Lord – but he met another girl when he had been home for long enough to find his feet, and that was that. She was very beautiful.'

'She still is,' said Susan. Isobel, who of course must have seen Helen at Henry's funeral, gave her a long look, and continued her tale.

' Dad went in to see Jerry's father about something, and found her crying her heart out in the outer office. He was a kind man. He took her out for a coffee and listened to her, he said he thought he was the first person who ever had. She spilled it all out, blighted ambitions, blighted love, blighted life, the lot. Nobody had ever bothered with her before.' Isobel spread her hands, with a slight shrug of her shoulders. 'You can see what happened then. He saw that she needed help, needed rescuing. He said she wasn't fit to fly, his exact words, nobody cared about her. The young man in the case didn't even know what he had done, he was treating her as if she was nothing more than a casual friend –'

'– as he thought she was.' Susan spoke up in Jerry's defence, but she did think he had been unforgivably thoughtless. He wasn't a fool, he must have known. Isobel echoed the thought.

'He's a fool then. Mind you, most men are if it suits them. So Dad picked up the pieces and eventually married her simply to get her away from her dreadful parents and give her a life; he said, if somebody didn't help her, she'd just go under, and anyway, he was the kind of man who had enjoyed the companionship of being married, he'd been lonely since Mum died, so it was as much for him as for her. He offered to help her go back to her tennis, pick up where she left off, but it was probably too late by that time, and this Jerry had introduced her to sailing anyway ... and she stuck with it, as it turned out, as a means of keeping in touch with him, although she didn't actually enjoy it much. She threw all Dad's kindness and generosity back in his face, and went on being infatuated with another girl's boyfriend, and then husband, and eventually, the stress of it all killed him. Just before you were born. Such a shame, he would have loved you.'

'You can't know that's what killed him,' said Susan.

'They said it was executive stress,' Sarah put in, fairly. Isobel let out a long sigh.

'All right, perhaps it was. But she can't have helped, she made him so sad. And he was still dead. And he was such a darling, he didn't deserve it.'

Liz said, quietly, 'Perhaps it's time to rethink, Mum. She must have been devastated too, and you can't help infatuation, it's like a disease.'

'And you should know,' put in Alice.

'I am not infatuated with Paul Attwood. And nobody can say, on the evidence just presented, that she was streetwise. Can they? All that religion, and women's-fate-is-to-marry stuff. And they should have let her play tennis, if she was that good. She was as much a victim as Grandad, but unlike him, she didn't ask for it. And before you say anything, I know you all loved him to bits, but facts are facts. Maybe we should all look at them. From the little that Susan has said, she's not had a happy life, and it isn't entirely down to her if you ask me.'

'Were we asking you?' asked her mother, raising her eyebrows.

'No,' said Sarah. 'Liz has a point. Dad wanted to help her, he wanted us to help her, and did we ever? Or did we just let Caro., who was a latecomer and didn't really know anything, wind us all up? We never totally agreed with her reading of it all anyway, you know we didn't, so why not try it Liz's way?'

'I imagine it's way too late for that,' said Isobel, but she said it almost regretfully.

'It does rather explain the way she is,' observed Susan, thinking about it. 'She's always on the defensive – trying to hang on to us all, afraid we'll slip away. Like my father did. And Jerry. And leave her with nothing.'

'She got Jerry in the end,' Sarah pointed out, unwisely.

'No she didn't.' Susan had long ago come to terms with this. 'He married her for the sake of me and Oliver, and when that didn't work, he stayed with her for Deb. And all the time, he really wanted Helen. Well, now he's got her. And what has my mother got? Sod all!' She got to her feet. 'Shall we go and see what's happening in the other room? Perhaps we can clear away now and sober them up with the coffee. It smells about ready.'

Isobel reached out and laid a hand on her arm. 'Susan.' Susan paused. 'Dad did love her. That was genuine.'

'I'm glad about that,' said Susan, collecting up mugs as if she was on autopilot, 'because it does seem to me as if he's the only person who ever did, apart from me and Deb.' She was annoyed to hear her voice shaking. Nobody else said anything. She rattled the mugs into a line, and then was furious to find that tears were running down her face. She scrubbed at them with her palm. After a moment, she felt an arm round her shoulders.

'Come on, Auntie Sue,' said Alice. 'You can't cry in front of the children, and at Christmas too. It'll all sort itself out. Things do.'

'I don't see how,' said Susan. The thing that had upset her most, she realised, was the tennis. All these years, and none of them had even known, never shown enough interest to know. It seemed a terrible indictment of not just their, but everybody's, treatment of Dot. Nobody had cared. Neither had she ever mentioned it, which probably measured the depth of her disillusionment. They had just, she told herself, dismissed her as a no-hoper that even her husband didn't care about. She had no idea how to set about putting it all right, or even if it was possible. Dot herself was the biggest obstacle, and how did you get around that?

'I think,' said Sarah, 'that it's time to join the men. Forget coffee, I'm sure there was some wine left in those bottles, let's go and drink it. Never mind the clearing up, Susan, it can wait. And cheer up, there's nothing new here, it's just that you didn't know it.'

'I should have done,' said Susan, sniffing, but obediently heading for the door with the others.

'Yes, you should, but it's not your fault that you didn't.'

But it was, Susan thought, and the knowledge cast a cloud over the pleasant family evening that followed.

XI

On Christmas Eve, in the office that he and Chel shared at the Fish, Mawgan took a small piece of paper from his pocket and dialled the number that he had extracted from yellow pages in the hall of Dot's house in Embridge.

'Crown & Anchor.'

'Good morning,' said Mawgan. 'I'm sorry to trouble you, I'm trying to get hold of Jake. Can you tell me how to find him?'

'Jake? He's around somewhere, hang on.' There was a short pause, and then a different voice said, 'Hullo?'

'Jake! It's Mawgan Angwin here, Deb's husband – we met the other night, remember?'

'I remember,' said Jake. He remembered very well indeed, whatever Deb's husband had said to Tim had sent him off on a real downer. He therefore sounded cool.

'I'm trying to get hold of Tim Howells,' said Mawgan, aware of the coolness. 'I asked him a question, and he was going to give an answer when he'd thought, but we was interrupted and I never got his number, and there's quite a few Howellses down your way.'

'You could have asked Deb, surely,' said Jake, hostile.

'Yes I could, but it was private business, not sure Tim'd want her involved.'

There seemed little point in not telling him, Jake decided. He would only ask Deb anyway, and if Tim *didn't* want her to know whatever it was ... his mind was filled with a great big question mark, but remembering Deb's husband, who, although pleasant enough, looked as if he might be a right bastard if he set his mind to it, he decided not to ask questions. He gave Mawgan the number of Tim's mobile phone and went back to restocking the shelves behind the public bar, filled with curiosity. It was time Tim had a break, Jake considered, but was Deb's husband the man to give it to him? From what Tim said, they disliked each other intensely, and certainly the body language at the sailing club party had been eloquent, particularly on Tim's side. He hoped he had done the right thing, except that it was hard to see what else he could have done.

200

Tim had never expected to hear from Mawgan again, so that finding him on his mobile came as a shock.

'Just wondered if you'd thought any more about working for me,' said Mawgan, and Tim nearly dropped the phone. He asked, stupidly, 'What'd you want me to do?' because it was the first thing that came into his head.

'I'm thinking of opening a place in Embridge, maybe next year,' said Mawgan, and Tim's jaw, already slack, dropped. 'I'd need someone to manage it, be in overall charge, someone I could trust, because I can't be around all the time. Interested?'

Tim found his voice with an effort. 'I know nothing about your business.'

'I know as you don't,' said Mawgan, and might have added, none better, but refrained. 'That's why I said I'd sponsor you through a short course in catering management and accounting, then send you to work in a good restaurant to learn the business from the bottom up. I can fix that, but it'd be abroad somewhere probably, that's where my best contacts are. What d'you reckon? You'd have a year, near enough, to learn before it was needed.'

'You're not just winding me up here?' asked Tim, his voice loaded with suspicion but no hope. Mawgan felt for him, been there, done that, got the T-shirt. He said, 'No. I wouldn't do that, not to no one.'

Tim had thought the original casual query hardly worth thinking about, Angwin couldn't have really meant it. The realisation that he had, and of exactly what he had in mind, choked him for a moment so that he couldn't speak. Mawgan waited. When he had waited long enough, he prompted, 'Well?'

Tim took a deep breath. 'It's right out of my field, but I'd like to give it a go. Doesn't look like anyone wants me in engineering right now.' He added, on a challenging note, 'They don't trust me. Might set fire to the shop, you know.'

'You didn't,' said Mawgan, with such finality that, had he been there, Tim could have hugged him. Strange, that the one person who wholly believed in him he would have called a sworn enemy. He was speechless. Mawgan, understanding, filled the gap in the conversation.

'Right then. I'll get Chel to send you a letter you can show the college, about fees and that, and another about money –'

'Money?' echoed Tim, blankly.

'Can't live on air,' Mawgan pointed out. 'Give me your address – or I can get it off of Deb.'

'She doesn't know it,' said Tim. 'I've got a flat.' He gave the address. It was a good flat, lent by a friend as a refuge from the unspoken reproaches of his parents, not so much for him, although he wouldn't have put money on their complete faith in him, as for the many people who hadn't given him a job. And if Mawgan actually paid him while he studied, he could keep it for the moment. Quite suddenly, Christmas had come, with the best present he could have wished for, and the most unexpected. He said, 'I'll wait to hear from you then.'

'Right after the holiday. Merry Christmas.'

'And to you.'

For a long time after Mawgan had rung off, Tim just sat there, looking at the phone in his hand as he didn't recognise it. Right out of the blue, he had a future. He wasn't entirely sure what it was going to be but it was there, within his grasp. He felt breathless, stunned.

Bloody Angwin! Who'd have thought it?

After a while he got to his feet. Time to share the good news and inject new life into what had been looking, up until a moment ago, like a rather miserable Christmas. As he left his flat and ran downstairs to the street door, it occurred to him, knowing Angwin's history, it might be an idea to sign up for classes in conversational Italian, and a great burst of optimism nearly knocked him off his feet. For the first time in months he was smiling as he walked to his car.

In the office at the Fish, Mawgan, too, was pleased with his morning's work. Over the intervening days, he had come to believe that his impulse in offering work to Tim had been a sound one. Tim was intelligent, he got on with people, he knew what made the sailing crowd tick, he could manage what he understood superlatively well; you couldn't ask more of anyone for what he had in mind. What he would make of catering remained to be seen, but Mawgan felt hopeful. He put down the phone and looked at Chel, tidying up ends on her computer before heading off to St Ives for Christmas. It should have been Shirley, their office assistant, he spoke to now, really; Chel managed the Fish, she wasn't his secretary, but he didn't want his business all round the village.

'Can you do me a favour, Chel? Just a quick couple of letters?'

Chel had heard, with half an ear, enough of the preceding conversation to get the general idea. 'OK. Who to, what about?'

'One to whom it may concern,' Mawgan was brisk. 'Guarantee the fees for courses in accounting and catering management for Tim Howells. The other to Tim, I've his address here, offering him eight hundred pounds a month on top of the fees while he studies and asking for his bank details so I can set up a standing order.'

'Fine.' Chel looked at him. 'Is this a good idea, Mawgan?'

Mawgan didn't ask, why not? 'He won't be working around here. I want him in Embridge.'

'Yes, Deb said you had some mad idea ... why Tim?'

'Oh, lots of reasons. He knows the town. I want to target the sailing community, he knows them too, and can talk to them. I'd trust him not to louse it up.'

'He didn't do that well with his first essay into catering.'

'His wife handled that – mishandled that. His sailing school was OK. From all accounts, he was a good engineer too. Someone's got to help him. You didn't see him Chel, you weren't there. Nobody gives him a hand, he's going to capsize that boat of his right out in the middle of that sea out there, when nobody's around to see. Trust me, I been there.'

Chel said nothing for a long moment, then, 'I see,' she said. 'Well, I'd better get these letters written then. You personally, or just *pp*?'

'Me personally. I aren't cocky, Chel, but I want them to take notice of him. My name'll do that these days, so get on with it and then you can push off.'

'You always manage to surprise me,' Chel remarked. 'From the Fish or the Rose?'

'The Rose.'

'Where'll you be when I've finished, the Rose kitchen?'

'You'll find me behind the cooking pots as usual. Bring a decent pen.'

Tim's future was under way. Chel, typing the letters briskly into her computer as requested and printing out on the Rose letterhead, thought that it had a good feel about it. It was an unexpected turn of events, and she wondered what Debbie made of it – or even if she knew about it, for she had said nothing – but it had the makings of an interesting game plan. Well, she would have expected that from Mawgan, he was nobody's fool. Obviously, the springboard for it had been fellow-feeling, but he was essentially unsentimental and if there had been nothing else in the package, he wouldn't have fallen for that old line. She would watch Tim's progress with interest, but for now she must get these letters out of the way and get off home. There was a most unusual Christmas to celebrate in St Ives.

Oliver's mother, Helen, had bought herself a double-fronted terrace cottage in a sunlit square in St Ives, with a small garden at the rear and a couple of outbuildings against the far garden wall that she had converted into a studio. She had done so partly to realise a lifelong dream and partly to resume a friendship that she had thought lost for ever with portrait and still-life painter Anona Fingall. They had been at college together; events had conspired to end the friendship some years later. Dot hadn't been uninvolved, but then, neither had Jerry, and Jerry now lived with her for part of the time, as she occasionally spent time in his penthouse flat overlooking the harbour in Embridge. They were nothing so final as a couple, not yet, but they were certainly lovers. Thinking about this, and about the tentative reconciliation that had taken place with her long-estranged son, a casualty of the same set of circumstances, Helen had a smile on her face as she set about stuffing the first turkey she had stuffed for her family for nearly thirty years.

Her family. Not only Jerry and Oliver, but Chel and baby Zoë too. The smile had spread into an out and out grin. They would be here soon, all four of them; Jerry from Embridge and the children from St Erbyn. She and Nonie, who, together with her husband Dimitrios Theodorakis would be here with them tomorrow, had decorated the house with celebratory extravagance and not a little artistic flair. If it all lived up to expectation, it was going to be the best Christmas for many years. But the undertaking was not without risk, as Helen was all too well aware.

A knock fell on her front door, which immediately opened and footsteps sounded in the hallway. A moment later, Nonie came into the kitchen, her arms full of parcels,

'Hi, how're you doing? I had to come into town for a couple of things, I thought I might as well drop these off for tomorrow.' She lowered the armful onto the worktop. 'I couldn't bear to wrap the teddy bear, but she's too young to understand Christmas parcels anyway, bless her.'

Helen spared a glance from her stuffing to appreciate the bear; she wouldn't have been able to smother him in paper either, she decided. He was a splendid bear, almost as big as Zoë herself, and with an appealing expression on his furry face. 'Sentimental idiot,' she said cheerfully. 'There, that's done – let me get this in the fridge, and I'll put the kettle on. Time for a break anyway.'

Nonie pulled out a chair and sat down with her elbows on the table. 'Looking forward to it?'

Helen paused on her way to the fridge, considering. 'Yes and no. It's all new territory, and I just get a feeling that some of it is still mildly hostile.'

'He agreed to come,' Nonie pointed out.

'Yes ... yes, he did. But perhaps, maybe Chel over-persuaded him a little. Oliver is going to find it quite hard to let bygones be bygones, I think.'

If you want to know what *I* think,' said Nonie, 'which I don't suppose you do, since it would create a dangerous precedent, both you and Oliver have some outstanding business to resolve. And it all centres around the same person.'

'Bloody Dot.'

'Dot, yes.'

Helen pushed the turkey into the fridge and closed the door, it gave her an excuse for turning her back on her friend. 'Susan is on a mission to rehabilitate her, Oliver says.'

'Good for Susan. I hope she succeeds.'

'You do?' Helen flicked the switch on the kettle and slipped into the chair opposite. 'Why on earth?'

'You know why. I never painted her as black as you did. A pain in the arse, yes. But I never saw her as the deliberate destroyer that you had her down as. Ill-advised, interfering and misguided, yes; actively malicious, I was never quite convinced. I always found Dot a bit like one of those infuriating puzzles that has half the pieces missing. Nobody could be as awful as she seemed.'

'Why not?' asked Helen. She picked up a stray ball of pastry left over from the quiche she had made for supper and began to work it into a rough shape.

'Because they couldn't. That kettle's boiling, you can't have had enough water in it.'

'I'll see to it in a moment.' Under her restless fingers, a tiny weasel was beginning to take shape. Nonie said nothing, and after a moment, Helen went on. 'I suppose I did blame her for everything that went wrong, and some of it was certainly her doing.'

'Not all of it, however. You were jealous –' She broke off as Helen raised her head and gave her a dark look. 'Yes you were, and I can see why, but listen to me. No, I didn't like her – much, anyway – so don't get me wrong. But Jerry quite obviously worshipped at your feet, so why did you let her bother you so?'

'He didn't worship me enough to shut her out of his life.'

'No, and do you ever find yourself wondering why that would be?'

'It seemed obvious. Why are we talking about Dot, anyway? She's a dreary subject at the best of times.'

'Because she hasn't mattered for years, and now she does. Jerry hasn't divorced her.'

'No,' said Helen, again. 'For some reason, in spite of the way she's behaved over Debbie – and Susan too – he "doesn't want to hurt her". Well, he never seemed to mind hurting me!' The pain in her voice was tangible. Nonie winced, but persisted doggedly.

'And he never did want to, did he? Listen, Helen, don't scowl at me like that. I think this is important. I think you and Oliver both need to get Dot straight in your heads, and you can't do that with half a story.'

Helen set her weasel carefully on his little feet. He was exquisite. She said, 'I wonder if there's money in baking pastry animals? You could ice the stripes on the tigers and –'

'Stop changing the subject. And don't be ridiculous! Of course you could, but would you want to?'

Helen sighed. She screwed her pastry back into a ball and put it carefully aside, then got to her feet to refill the kettle. She said, 'You always did want to set us all straight, didn't you?' in a tired voice that made Nonie sit up straight.

'Did I? How awful!'

'What was even more awful is that you were quite often right,' Helen told her. She turned round from the kettle and leaned her back on the worktop. 'All right, I'll think about it, because I think you might be right yet again, and I want things sorted out between me and my son. But not now, not at Christmas. And don't look so smug!'

'Oliver feels guilty about her,' said Nonie, hurriedly adjusting her expression, and Helen said, unexpectedly, 'And so he jolly well should! Now, can we drop the subject?'

But this Christmas it was turning out to be a subject impossible to drop. Whatever wind of change was blowing across the west country, it blew here too. That evening, when supper was over and Zoë safely in her cot, it was Jerry who brought it up over the quiet glass of sloe gin that ushered in the night before Christmas. 'So, how did the party in Embridge go, do you know?' he asked. 'Any blood shed, or did Debs and Susan get away with it?'

'Actually,' said Oliver, thoughtfully, 'it seems to have gone off rather well. Deb said she'd never seen a party like it in that house before.'

'And what did Susan say?'

'I don't know. They were straight off to Devon the day after they got back, I haven't spoken with her.'

Helen and Jerry exchanged a look. Helen said, with elaborate casualness, 'No showdown between Dot and Mawgan, then?'

'Should there have been?' Oliver looked surprised.

'Oh, well, you never know with those two.'

'Really? Deb seemed to think they got on OK.' Oliver didn't want to talk about Dot's party, but Jerry didn't seem to be able to let it go.

'Many people there? The usual crowd, Jenny Carruthers and her coven?'

'Debbie said not,' Chel put in. She sipped at her orange juice thoughtfully, she was still breast feeding and this Christmas had to be a teetotal one. 'She said it was an almost totally new selection of people, and they were all great.'

'Good. I never liked Jenny, couldn't see why Dot was so thick with her.' Jerry sounded pleased. He added, casually, 'Alex and Ingrid there, were they?'

'Of course. And a clutch of clergymen.' Oliver's voice cooled. 'And the Rendells.'

'Some, anyway, of the usual suspects then. Well, I would have expected all of those to rally round.' Jerry sounded sad. 'Poor Dot.'

'You always did pity the silly witch,' said Helen, but without rancour. She remembered what Nonie had said that afternoon. 'I never understood why.'

'Yes, you made that very obvious,' said Jerry, shortly. Helen said, 'Perhaps if you had explained it to me, I might have found it easier.'

'Exactly what did you want explained?' asked Jerry. 'She was an old friend, that should be enough.' Like a number of other people, he had a conscience about Dot, complicated in his case by the fact that he also had one about Helen.

'You hadn't known her *that* long, Jerry,' said Helen. 'OK, explain me this one. I find it fairly fundamental.' She paused. 'Henry's funeral – remember it?'

Jerry did. He fidgeted with his glass. 'Is this the moment, Helen? Really? Chel and Oliver don't want to hear us squabbling over an old bone like that.'

'Christmas is a good time for *burying* old bones,' Chel suggested. 'Oliver and I can go somewhere else.'

'No. Please don't.' Helen didn't look at Oliver, but she went on, 'Henry's funeral, Jerry. Let me remind you: what Dot said to Nonie was absolutely unforgivable. We left – Nonie and I – and you stayed. Take it from there.'

Jerry said, quietly, 'Nonie was never a fan of Dot's, Helen. I didn't know why she came, either.'

'She came, because she knew how Dot must be feeling, out of sympathy.'

'I can't think why. She was always against Dot.'

'Yes, because she was my friend – and what you say is not absolutely true, either. But that's not the point. You stayed on all through the wake –'

'– I told you at the time, I was her solicitor.'

'It isn't a solicitor's job to stay on at a party, of whatever kind, after everyone else has gone in order to take a woman in labour, not related to him in any way, to hospital and stay with her half the night. Jerry. She had perfectly good parents. Where were they? Why did it have to be you?' She broke off, and made an expressive face. 'God, it sounds so petty at this distance, but it hurt at the time Jerry, and a lot.'

Jerry had never considered this particular event in their married life in quite this light before, but being accustomed to evaluating evidence of one kind or another, he had to concede that Helen had a point – only to himself, naturally, but the realisation tempered his response.

'It wasn't quite like that,' he said. 'Look Helen, it was a long time ago. Does it really still matter?'

'No, go on,' said Oliver. 'I'd like to hear the explanation, too. This is all news to me.'

'And it does matter,' said Helen. 'Draw the sting, Jerry. Let's hear the truth. What was all that really about, if it wasn't Dot playing off her tricks as usual?'

Jerry took a moment to put the facts in order in his mind. It wasn't that every event of that day wasn't graven on his memory, it was how to present it so that what was obviously both a too-long festering resentment in Helen, and a new and inimical curiosity in Oliver, should both be disarmed. If he could achieve this miracle, maybe his curious relationship with the woman he had never ceased to love would establish itself on firmer ground and Oliver would ease up on his lifelong dislike of his stepmother. If Susan, who had the makings of a redoubtable woman, was indeed on a mission, it behoved the family to pull together, instead of in about ten different directions. He said, 'If you really want to know the truth, I was pretty well pissed off with her as well. I wanted to get home, I knew you'd be seething and an early return was my only way of making peace. And as a matter of fact, I said exactly what you've just said, why didn't you say you thought you were in labour while your mother was here to be with you? Do you know what she said?' The question was so obviously rhetorical that none of his hearers bothered to answer, and after a short pause to collect his thoughts, he went on. 'She said, she'd sooner not tell them, so that she wouldn't have to listen to them telling her they were sure she was just imagining things, but to call her doctor if she was worried, they had to be off to some terribly important church social where some evangelist or other was going to speak. And remember here, please, that she had just buried her husband only a matter of hours before, and if she really was in labour, and believe me, it was pretty obvious by then that she was, the child, the only one Henry would ever give her, would be five weeks premature. And when you've taken all that on board, tell me what you would have done.'

'Her parents wouldn't have done that!' cried Helen, horrified, as much as anything by the way, as she saw it, Dot had twisted Jerry round her little finger yet again, but Jerry said, 'Oh yes, they would. Think about it.'

Helen did think. She couldn't imagine her own father or her stepmother having left her alone to go to a church social on the evening of her husband's funeral, were she pregnant or not. That didn't mean that Dot's parents hadn't done it, and if they had, and if it was par for the course as Jerry seemed to be saying, what did that say about Dot?

'Oh shit,' said Oliver, who had also been working this out. Chel said nothing, and it was left to Jerry to add the final straw.

'She was really touched when you came along later to be with her. And whatever you were feeling towards her, you were really kind.'

'With her in such a state, I hadn't much choice,' Helen muttered, remembering. 'But her parents *did* come, in the end.' It sounded like a challenge.

'Yes,' said Jerry. 'I found the number of the pastor, or the leader, or whatever they called him, in the phone book and rang him while you sat with Dot. I lied. I said I couldn't get a reply from the Shiphams: I hadn't even wasted time ringing them. He went to fetch them in his car, and he drove them to the hospital, I doubt they'd have come for anyone less. And I lied to Dot too, and never mentioned him. And then you bitched at me all the way home.'

Into the silence that followed this final accusation, Chel said quietly, 'Was her whole life like that, until she met you?'

'It seems so,' Jerry replied.

'That would explain some things,' Helen said, trying to be fair. 'But it still doesn't excuse her behaviour to Nonie, to me, to Debbie or to Susan. Does it?'

'No, it doesn't,' said Jerry. 'But bear in mind this; you can't give what you have never received in the first place. And in the course of her life, remember, she had lost me, Henry, your friendship –'

'– which she never had in the first place,' put in Helen, with a momentary return of spirit.

'Maybe not, but she imagined she had, and that's only to name but a few. And now, she saw herself also losing her daughters and her grandchildren, and as a spin-off from that, she has also lost her friends. She has no idea how to compromise; nobody ever compromised with her all the time she was growing up. It seems Susan is now rather belatedly trying to teach her, well good luck to her. I'm on her side.'

Oliver had been feeling increasingly guilty about the way he had treated his stepmother from childhood up for some time now, although wild horses wouldn't have got him to admit it. He didn't like her, couldn't see that he ever would, but she had, he admitted to himself now, tried hard to make up for the loss of his mother, and with no chance of succeeding. He had blamed her for the break-up; he now saw that there had been more behind it than he had ever been permitted to know – or Helen either, which had maybe been Jerry's mistake. Would that younger Helen have been more sympathetic had she been fully informed of all the circumstances? Nobody would ever know; Oliver, recognising how much of his mother there was in himself, thought probably not. But the things that he, particularly, had done in response to his mother's perceived attitude had not only made life a burden for Dot, but had made Susan's childhood into a battlefield. Remembering now what Susan had recently done for him, he cringed inwardly and not for the first time. It was because of her actions that he had come up with the idea of the Christmas party. He now saw that it wasn't enough if the situation was ever to be resolved.

It was time to do something more fundamental about it all. If nothing would change Dot, as he rightly or wrongly believed, then they must learn to live with her, if only for the sake of Debbie and Susan and the children. Chel had already made him make the first, reluctant move by insisting that they, too, contributed towards Dot's box of presents, and as if they really meant it; he had agreed because he could see the wasteland that Dot had created for herself. And when it came down to it, it was perfectly true; if you didn't know him, at the time of Deb's engagement Mawgan had looked like the very last person anyone would want their favourite daughter to marry, so score one to Dot. Oliver now had a daughter of his own, small, yes, but he could visualise the years ahead. For the first time in his life he had a little sympathy for his tiresome stepmother. They needn't see a lot of her, after all. He said nothing of any of this, but continued to brood into his wineglass.

Chel could sense that the family teetered on the edge of a catastrophic quarrel that would effectively ruin Christmas for all of them. There are only so many skeletons that can be liberated at one time, this was the moment to slam the cupboard door.

'It's not as quite desperate as it looks,' she said. 'From what Deb said, there were one or two surprises at the party as well as the people Oliver mentioned.'

Jerry, perhaps feeling the same as Chel did, responded thankfully to the change of subject. 'Sally and Irwin, I suppose, I'd forgotten about them.'

'No,' said Chel. 'She didn't mention them.'

'I suppose that would be down to Susan and Carl,' said Jerry sadly, thinking about it. 'Shame. They were good friends of hers, Sally particularly.'

Helen nearly spoiled it. She said, tartly, 'I imagine it was more down to Tom actually, Jerry,' and for a moment, dissension shivered in the air once more. Oliver stepped in smoothly, ably seconding his wife. 'Some people called Law, she mentioned. And an African bishop.' It was a better ploy than he realised. Jerry's jaw dropped in astonishment. Never mind the bishop.

'*General* Law? Dot and his wife are sworn enemies!'

'Apparently not. According to Deb, she's rallied to the flag with enthusiasm, and a rather scathing criticism of Deb's headstrong behaviour. But she liked Mawgan, although she said words to the effect that Deb should learn to think before she acted. Fair enough, when you think about it.'

'Well well,' said Jerry, still astounded. 'Good for Marie! With her on her side, Dot's got a powerful friend!'

'And a younger couple, Deb said even Susan didn't know them before,' Chel put in. 'He's a farmer, from over Shearwater way. Ernest Vachell, and his wife.'

Jerry nodded. 'He farms at Shortlanesend. I've met him a couple of times, surprised Dot knows them though.'

'I think it's a fairly new friendship. It seems to have arisen out of a fracas at a committee meeting. The name Carruthers came up,' Oliver said.

'Bloody woman!' said Jerry.

Throughout this brief exchange, Helen's thoughts had still been revolving around Dot. It didn't sound as if Dot could have experienced a particularly happy childhood, to put it at its highest, but Helen had been on the receiving end of her attentions, and wasn't going to let go of her resentment that easily. More argumentatively than she had intended, she said now, 'She may have had the childhood from hell, but she's still a bully. And a control freak.'

'People who are bullied and controlled often are,' Chel suggested. She was getting mildly annoyed with Helen's determination to dig the last ounce out of the ... well, what would you call it, she wondered? Discussion? Almost. Argument? Not quite. It had overtones of confrontation without being a confrontation, it was as if Helen was purging something. What? And where was it going to lead? More, why did it have to lead anywhere on Christmas Eve, of all days? It occurred to her that Jerry didn't know Dot as well as he thought he did, but she didn't say so. It also occurred to her, and not as an original thought, that to bring Jerry, Helen and Oliver together as a family group for the first time for around thirty years at such an emotive time of year might have been a mistake. She was still trying to see how to defuse the situation, when Helen, whose thoughts had maybe been running on similar lines, did it for her.

'And did Mawgan manage to stay sober throughout the proceedings?' she enquired, with reason for Mawgan had a bit of a reputation.

'According to Deb, he did pretty well,' said Oliver. 'Of course, Susan may have a different version. But they all went to church the next morning, so perhaps she felt that was expiation if he did fall by the wayside.'

Nobody made the mistake of thinking "she" referred to either of his sisters.

Jerry picked up the bottle of sloe gin and quietly topped up the glasses. He picked up his own and rested the base in the palm of his other hand. 'A toast,' he said. 'To happier times and a better understanding.'

'Of Dot,' said Helen, obediently raising her glass.

'I think a better understanding of Dot is fundamental to the exercise,' said Jerry solemnly. Their glasses clinked together.

Oliver lifted his own glass. He said, with a wicked grin, 'To peace in this place.'

'Amen to that,' remarked Chel, sipping orange juice, and as if on cue, a most *un*peaceful wail came from the baby alarm on the bookcase. They all laughed. Chel got to her feet.

'Bring her down here,' said Helen. 'We don't mind.'

The discussion was dead, and without actual bloodshed. Well, Chel thought as she made her way upstairs, probably you could call that a result.

St Ives wasn't the only place to have a rocky start to Christmas. The same thing happened in Waldren Stavey and its environs, and any one of the Worthington family could have put money on it's being Anthony and Carol's daughter Cecily who would be the cause.

She arrived at Liz's cottage very late on Christmas Eve, having left London after she finished work and miscalculated the amount of traffic she would find sharing the roads with her, but being Cecy, she arrived with her energy undiminished. Eight years younger than her cousin, she had frequently found herself being used as a model in Liz's particular form of literature which often featured feisty young girls living it up in London, but apart from this, they were too far apart in both age and outlook to be close. Liz was at heart a country girl, Cecy of the town. Nevertheless, they were friends of a kind, and pleased to see each other.

'You can have the spare room tonight,' Liz told her, 'but if Richard wants to stay, you'll have to spend tomorrow night in with me!'

Cecy, heaving her bag up the narrow stairs behind her, said, 'So long as the bed's had time to cool down after Paul, that's OK.'

'Paul isn't here,' said Liz, and right at that moment, Cecy said no more than, 'I know.'

It was too late by this time to start cooking a meal, and Cecy in any case claimed not to be hungry, so they sat in the kitchen with the cat and drank a Christmas glass of wine as a nightcap, eating some shortbread that Liz had made earlier. Cecy wanted to know about Susan, whom so far she had yet to meet. 'Is she nice, this junior league aunt of ours?' she asked. 'I mean, like, one of us? She's younger than you, isn't she?'

'Actually, she's more like yet another cousin. She's nice, you'll like her, and she has this lovely bloke as a partner –' She caught a gleam in Cecy's eye, and said, 'And you leave him alone! There's children involved here, and anyway, you haven't a prayer. So just don't go rocking the boat!'

'Would I?' asked Cecy, outraged, and then laughed. 'Yes, you're right, I would. But I won't. Let's have a happy Christmas!' Which turned out to be ironic, when they both looked back on the evening, for if ever a boat was rocked, it was rocked in the farmhouse kitchen on Christmas morning – although it was admittedly a different boat.

Susan and Alice, who appeared to share the same gift for organisation (so possibly Dot had been unfairly blamed for some of it?) had decreed that Sarah, Isobel and Carol should spend Christmas morning taking the children to church, in spite of Annabel complaining loudly that they had already sat through one Christmas service with Grandma.

'Never mind,' said Susan, firmly. 'There's a saying, the better the day, the better the deed. And it will keep you all from under our feet while we get the lunch.'

'I could help,' offered Annabel, but Susan refused to be beguiled. The church party left at ten, and Anthony and George went with them. Carl, who subscribed to Annabel's view, opted for helping Owen outside, for the work of the farm continued irrespective of Christmas, Gil retired to the sitting room with yesterday's paper, and the four younger women adjourned to the kitchen, where lunch for eighteen – Richard had phoned to say he was on his way – would keep them fairly busy until the rest of the company returned.

'No holier, of course,' said Alice, 'but they might be calmer. And perhaps they could go out and ride round the meadow for a bit after we've done the presents, it's a lovely day.'

'You'll never get them in and cleaned up in time for lunch,' objected Susan. Alice grinned at her.

'You think lunch will be a moment before three o'clock? Think again!'

'Really,' said Cecy, busy peeling sprouts at the sink, and a lot more efficiently than Debbie ever had, as Susan noticed, 'it's hard to know where to put you, Susan. You're younger than most of us – not me, of course – but technically, I suppose you belong with the older generation. Perhaps we should have sent you to church, too.'

'You could have tried,' said Susan. 'Anyway, Sarah and I went to the midnight service while you were snoring in your bed.'

'Did you indeed? You mad thing, you!' Cecy tipped her sprout peelings into the compost bucket. 'What's next? Carrots, I suppose, why do I always get the dirty jobs?'

'Rubbish, you're never here,' said Liz, elbowing her out of the way to fill a saucepan with water for the pudding.

'That's because I have a life,' Cecy told her. 'And anyway, every time I come here for a weekend, I trip over that arsehole Paul Attwood, and it's enough to trip over him in the week. What do you see in him, Liz?'

'Do you trip often?' asked Alice, before Liz could reply.

'Often enough. I see him around with that stupid Ash sometimes. You'd think, in a place as big as London, I could avoid him, wouldn't you?'

'Ash?' asked Alice. Liz had gone very still. Cecy said, 'She's a model, not a very good one. Her real name's Ashley, but she likes Ash better.' It seemed to dawn on her that they were all looking at her, particularly Liz. 'You did know about her, didn't you Liz? He said you did. He calls you his "weekend woman", and Ash his "everyday elf". But I have said already he's an arsehole.' She paused. 'I've put my foot in it, haven't I?'

Liz, to her credit, managed to smile. She said, 'I didn't imagine he lived a celibate life during the week, no.'

'You shouldn't sleep with people who sleep around,' Alice told her, shocked. 'You don't know what you may catch these days!'

'Oh, thanks! I'm not an idiot, you know!'

Cecy narrowed her eyes at her. 'What else don't you know, Liz?'

Liz felt ice crack beneath her feet. No, she wasn't in love with Paul, and she had been finding him a bit tiresome lately, but he was a part of her life – her comfortable life, arranged as she wished it to be arranged; she didn't want the bother of a major commitment after all. But she felt now that Cecy knew things that she did not, and that perhaps they were things she ought to know.

She didn't like being referred to as a weekend woman.

Susan, the onlooker here, couldn't acquit Cecy of deliberately stirring things up, but she did think too that Cecy had brought to the surface rather more than she had meant. She had been enjoying herself being scathing about Paul, much as her mother could be in one cause or another, but had gone too far. She looked contrite, but it was too late. The damage was done.

'Such as what?' asked Liz.

'Oh, nothing,' said Cecy, airily, reaching for the carrots. Liz moved them out of her reach.

'Come on, you can't get away with that. What?'

'Give over you two,' ordered Alice, firmly. 'It's Christmas day, don't let the prat Paul ruin it, please!'

'You none of you like him, do you?' asked Liz, challenging. Every one of her three hearers left it to the others to answer, and she said defiantly, into the resulting silence, 'Well, he's my friend, so you can put up with him. I don't ask you to see a lot of him, do I? Well then! Mind your own business, Cecily Worthington, and leave me to mind mine!'

Cecy, stung, retaliated with, 'Some friend! Oh, wake up Liz! Smell the coffee!'

'And don't talk in silly clichés!' retorted Liz, the writer, and then caught Cecy's eye and they both collapsed with laughter.

'We sound like the twins and Annabel,' said Cecy, giggling. Liz gave the pile of carrots a push in her direction. There was no telling what either of them might have said next, but fortunately, there was the roar of a sports car out in the yard at that moment. Cecy cocked her head, listening. 'That'll be Richard. In time for the presents and lunch, but too late for the work, that figures. Come on Auntie Sue, come and meet your little nephew.'

Susan and Richard had been born in the same year, Richard being the older of the two by a month or so, and he wasn't Susan's idea of a nephew. Tall, dark, and blindingly handsome, and; older than Carl by three years, which felt bizarre. He greeted his new aunt with enthusiasm, flinging his arms round her in a huge hug and planting a smacking kiss on her cheek. 'Aunt Susan! Where have you been all my life?'

'In blissful ignorance of your existence,' said Susan, laughing as she disentangled herself. 'Put me down, or Carl will beat you up!'

Carl and Owen had emerged from the barn at the sound of the car, and introductions were made. Owen looked at his watch. 'The others will be back from church any minute and we're about done in there. Time to splice the mainbrace, do you think?'

'What a splendid idea!' Richard thumped Carl, who was nearest, on the shoulder to turn him in the direction of the back door. 'Come on, Uncle Carl, let's go and drink a toast to the family!'

'Who?' asked Susan, on a spurt of laughter, and Richard grinned.

'Oh, come on!' he said, still grinning. 'The relationships in this family couldn't get more complicated if they tried, let's try and keep it to its simplest, shall we?'

'Don't tempt fate,' Liz ordered, as they all followed to the door. 'I can almost hear it rubbing its hands.'

'Does fate have hands?' Cecy wondered, 'and wasn't it three sisters, so shouldn't it be "them?" They sat spinning, or something, didn't they?'

'If they spun, then they must –'

'Enough!' ordered Owen, 'this is a Christian festival! Alice, catch those dogs! They're filthy!'

The arrival of Richard, followed by the return of the church party soon after, was the signal for the festivities to really get under way. Any hope that the children might have calmed down during the service turned out to be vain, Richard was the kind of cousin who stirred things up – much like his sister, but perhaps kinder. Cecy had sharp edges, much as Carol had.

218

'That'll do!' called Sarah. 'Sit down and be quiet, all you children – that means you too, Richard! – or there'll be no presents! Owen, find Carol a drink. Oh dear, what a crowd of people!' but she was laughing as she said it. The family disposed itself around the armchairs and sofas, and the children sat expectantly in a row on the floor. Owen thrust the wine bottle into the hands of his brother Anthony, and took up his traditional duties at the Christmas tree. The rustle of paper and squeals of delight took over from the previous chaos, and Alice ordered the children to please write everything down. 'Or you'll never remember who gave what to write your thankyou letters.'

'Everyone's here,' Katie objected. 'We shan't have to. We can say them.'

'Everyone isn't here,' Alice told her. 'Write, please!'

Susan, snug in the corner of a sofa beside Carol, found herself thinking, *could* there be any more of them? There seemed at least four families-worth here already, and knew that there could be, indeed, that there was. She felt rather overwhelmed.

'What are you thinking?' asked Carol, quietly, in her ear. 'You look very pensive all of a sudden.'

'I was thinking what a lovely family this is,' Susan confessed, 'and I don't even know you all yet.'

'Isn't – I won't say *your own* because you're one of ours too – but your *other* family like this at Christmas?'

Susan shook her head. 'No. They're different: Annabel and Seb are the only children, until this year anyway, and we're all ...' She sought for a word to describe what she was trying to say, failed to find one, and had to settle for 'less of a family.' She made a face at her own honesty. 'Just the way it is. I *wish* I'd known you all years ago,' she ended, unexpectedly, and Carol said, 'So do we,' and smiled at her.

The small disagreement in the kitchen seemed to have been glossed over and forgotten, much to everybody's relief, and the rest of the day went well, if noisily, with a sumptuous lunch, at three o'clock as predicted, followed by a riotous card game organised by Carl and Richard into which everyone but the older generation was dragged willy-nilly, a calming-down period with a good family video, a light supper, and then Alice and Gil took their over-excited and over-tired offspring back home to bed, and Susan turned briskly to Annabel and Seb.

'You too. Say goodnight, and off you go. Tomorrow is another day.'

Isobel yawned behind her hand. 'I think we'll go home too, if you don't mind, Sarah. Anthony and George are asleep already, look. It's been a wonderful day, and we'll see you all at ours tomorrow afternoon. Not too early, if you have any mercy.'

'Could you use any cold turkey tomorrow?' asked Sarah.

'Goodness, is there any left? I would have thought the poor thing was reduced to mere bones!'

'We cooked two of them. I'll bring some along, shall I?'

'What a lovely Christmas!' said Annabel, on a blissful sigh.

'Bed!' said Susan.

Dot's Christmas Day hadn't been exactly blissful, but she had enjoyed it, more or less. Debbie and Susan had both rung her by lunchtime, she had spoken to the children, and she had been to the church service in the morning and wished her friends, those that remained to her, a happy Christmas, and ignored the rest, which had given her a certain satisfaction too. She had placed a bunch of Christmas roses, appropriate since Chel had used one to decorate the present from his sister, on Jeremy's lonely little grave, offered a short prayer and wished him well on Christ's birthday. She lunched alone on a stuffed chicken breast left ready for her by Leanne Adams, and the last of the *tiramisu* from her party, rounded off with some rather good brie eaten with home made oatcakes, also from her party, the whole accompanied by two glasses of perfectly chilled white wine and a CD of her favourite carols, and felt quite Christmassy in a quiet way. She stacked the washing up carefully in the machine, looked round to make sure that the kitchen was immaculate, and went into the drawing room to listen to the Queen's Speech on television. After that, and not a moment before, she allowed herself the pleasure of exploring the bright box of gifts beneath her Christmas tree, augmented now by one or two parcels from her own circle, spinning out the Christmas feeling for as long as she could.

She had never been alone on Christmas Day before, she had always thought it would be a sad thing to be, but it hadn't really been like that at all. Partly, this was because she had been offered other alternatives so that being alone was her deliberate choice, partly because she had so much to think about and partly because of the box full of goodwill that she now began to unpack. Nobody could feel unloved or alone when their children had left such a comforting pledge of their affection. She picked up the parcel that lay on the top.

To Grandma, with love from Zoë.

Carefully Dot detached the silken hellebore and unstuck the tape that held the parcel together. It contained a box, which contained a photo frame, which contained a photograph.

Dot sat with it in her hands for quite a long time. It was a picture of a very young baby, dark hair, dark eyes, delicate flyaway eyebrows that came from another grandmother via her father, her father's passionate mouth in miniature ... Dot was conscious of such a jumble of mixed emotions that she couldn't even begin to sort them out, for in spite of what she had thought, and said which was perhaps worse, this was undoubtedly Oliver's child. She was both ashamed and delighted that her uncharitable conclusion had been so inaccurate and honest enough to recognise that it was another lesson to add to those she had recently learned.

After a while, she set the little picture aside, laid the flower carefully upon it, and picked up the next parcel, but even as the gifts piled up on the sofa beside her, her mind was still working – working things out, indeed. She left until last the rectangular parcel from her stepson, almost afraid now to open it for fear of what it might contain, and when she finally reached it, it was only slowly that she unwrapped it. It might be a family photo, of course, of the three of them together, although it was big to be that, but it turned out to be nothing of the kind.

She recognised the subject immediately, it was a scene with which she had been familiar all her life, but painted in a medium she didn't recognise: surely too robust and vibrant to be water colour, certainly not oil and anyway, it was glazed; her artistic knowledge, rudimentary at best, stopped short of gouache, her stepson's preferred medium these days. The sandy finger of Taverner's Point reached across to the harbour mouth, with the cluster of buildings that was the Ember Valley Sailing Club, and the remains of the old Roman signal station on the furthest tip; safe within the curve of the sandbar, the rows of yachts swung on their moorings. The water shimmered in a light that was unquestionably dawn, and a single trawler, brown sail slack in the still air, chugged almost audibly across the unruffled water that reflected a pinkish early-morning sky, heading for the open sea, her crew, blackly silhouetted, working on deck or manning the wheel, the V of her wake sparkling behind her. It was tranquil and beautiful and essentially, she realised with a shock, painted just for her. Why else would Oliver paint Embridge, a place she believed he rather disliked?

It was some time before she moved, and then it was to pick up the little photograph and carry it to the mantelpiece. Moving a school photo of Seb, taken some two years ago now, to one side to make room, she put Zoë beside him, and placed the hellebore carefully in front. She stacked most of the presents onto the coffee table, collected the paper wrappings into the box and carried it out into the kitchen, where she made herself a pot of tea. Then she returned to the drawing room with the tray, and sat down again. Propping the picture where she could see it, she sipped her tea and thought, long and unhappily, about the past and all the things that could have been done differently. Fruitless to do so, she knew. What's done, is done, and it hadn't only been done by herself, either. It wasn't until she came out of her unhappy reverie some time later, pulled herself together, and got up to turn on the lights and the television that, for the second time now, a rather presumptuous piece of gratuitous advice drifted unsought into her head.

Lie in the sun, work out what makes you happy. Then get on and do it.

Fine words.

At the New Year, Chel and Oliver broke with a newly established tradition and took themselves and their baby daughter to Suffolk, to Chel's family, where Oliver and long-absent brother Mike made each other's acquaintance at last, and where Mike told the family about the interesting plans he had for his future as a civilian.

Back in St Erbyn, Susan, Carl, Carl's mother Julie, Debbie and Mawgan foregathered as planned at the Fish with their friends and half the village too, but this year, not just Oliver and Chel, but Jerry and Helen too, were absent, attending an annual New Year shindig in Nonie Fingall's studio in St Ives. Nevertheless, the Old Year was sent on its way with traditional celebration, and the New Year welcomed in similar fashion. And what a year it looked like being, Debbie said to Susan, with a wry grin. Moving house, baby Daniel to bring into the world, Roger and Gosia getting married! Not to mention Mawgan's plan to expand his empire into Dorset, and did Susan know he had offered Tim a job?

'Good heavens!' exclaimed Susan, astonished. 'What as, for goodness' sake?'

'Some kind of manager. For his new place in Embridge.' Debbie sounded doubtful.

'Well, good for Mawgan. Time something went right for poor Tim! Have another pineapple juice.'

'When this is over,' said Debbie, pushing her glass across the table, 'I shall never drink fruit juice – or milk -ever again!'

Liz, on the other hand, had a less amusing time. She went up to London to spend the New Year in her flat, with Paul. Not in his expensive waterside apartment, and this not for the first time, although she had in the past spent the odd night there. He shared this apartment, in an expensive riverside warehouse conversion, with a friend, whom Liz had never met since he apparently worked out of London during the week. At weekends, Paul had said right from the start, ushering in what had turned out to be an enduring tradition, it was better to be at Liz's place where they could be alone. It had never seemed odd at the time; now, with Cecy's dark hints still lurking in the background, it seemed less reasonable.

Who was Paul's mysterious friend? Could it be *Ash*, whoever she was? Liz dismissed this suspicion as paranoia, but the question remained: who? Also, why the big mystery? And now she came to think about it, Paul had other explaining to do, too, such as the existence of his "everyday elf", stupid phrase! She had staked no claim on Paul, to be fair, and she had never assumed that he led a monkish existence once she had given up permanent residence in town, but she had thought that he was honest with her – reasonably honest. She knew he occasionally took out other women, usually writers or women who were like himself in publishing, in the line of business, but he had never mentioned anybody called Ash, and Liz knew that she would have remembered if he had. The name alone was too silly to forget.

She couldn't be any good. Liz had never heard of a model called Ash, she probably modelled for some cheap catalogue or other. The thought gave her a momentary satisfaction.

Perhaps she was writing her autobiography, everyone even remotely celebrated seemed to be doing that these days, or maybe a romantic novel? There was only one way to find out.

'Cecy was down for Christmas,' she said casually, after they had greeted each other, and Paul had put his bag in her bedroom. 'She said to say "Hi". She says sees you around.' Had she not been watching carefully, she might have missed the slight, calculating narrowing of Paul's eyes. He said, 'Yes, she does, but we move in different circles. Bit of a live wire, your young cousin, too hot for me!'

Liz was sitting at her dressing table, fixing her make-up before they went out to celebrate the New Year at a nightclub. She watched him in the mirror as she said, 'She sees you about with some model. Can't remember the name, something made-up, more like a nickname.'

Paul didn't miss a beat. 'Ash. Ashley. Yes, she probably has. She's new to London, daughter of a friend of my mother's, she asked me to look after her, keep an eye on her, sort of thing. She's trying to break into modelling, which her mother considers a den of iniquity, I'm deputed to protect her from the wicked world.'

It sounded so specious, so probable even, that Liz might have taken it at face value, if it hadn't been for the thing, or things that Cecy *hadn't* told her. 'You never mentioned her,' she said.

'Should I have?' Paul raised his eyebrows. 'Jealous, are we, Elizabeth? You needn't be.' He put his arm across her shoulders, and his face close to hers, grinning at their combined reflections in the mirror. 'You're my weekend woman, Liz, how could I do without you?'

'So, what's your everyday elf to you?' asked Liz acidly, and Paul gave a snort of laughter.

'Cecy did try to sell me down the river, didn't she? Well, she never liked me – she makes that very clear. Don't listen to her, Liz, she just opens her mouth and the words come out, I wouldn't believe a word she says if I was you.'

There was no point in pursuing the discussion, Liz realised. Paul had disarmed all her arguments, and although she was indignant about his opinion of her cousin, Cecy's of him was as bad and possibly no more accurate. Why, though, did she have this sudden sensation of being a helpless fly, stuck in a spider's web? If she wanted Paul to go, she had only to tell him "go". Didn't she?

Paul glanced at his watch. 'If you've finished painting your face, we ought to be off. There won't be a table if we're late, not on New Year's Eve.'

Liz sighed as she put the top carefully back on her lipstick. There was no feeling of celebration about this New Year, and she wished she was in St Erbyn, living it up in the more bucolic atmosphere of the Fish with people –

She swallowed. Where had that thought come from?

With people she really liked.

XII

One day when the year was still young, Liz sat with her elbows resting on the kitchen table, nose to nose with her companion who was sitting on it, against all rules. She had no heart to push him off. 'I'm sick of it,' she told him, with deep feeling. 'Sick, sick, sick of it! Do you blame me?'

Her friend, who was tabby and white and furry, and engaged in washing his paws, made no reply, and thus encouraged, she continued. 'It's all very well for him. He comes down here whenever he wants, all the convenience of a cottage in the country without the expense of paying for it, and really Tib, he makes shameless use of me, and that's all. My family don't like him much, and I'd far sooner have been in St Erbyn on New Year's Eve. So what's in it for me, I ask you? What?'

Tib placed his paws, now cleaned to his satisfaction, carefully adjacent on the table top and looked at her with what Liz chose to take as sympathy, his yellow eyes luminous. 'I knew you'd understand,' she said, and removed one hand from its supporting position under her chin in order to stroke him. He purred and jumped down from the table, crossing the kitchen to stand expectantly beside his bowl. Liz got to her feet and opened the cupboard where the cat biscuits lived, waxing philosophical as she did so. 'Cats have the right idea, no problem in the world that can't be solved by the application of more biscuits – and actually, that seems to be the general view, most of the time. Not sure it's right though, come to think, or not for people.' She poured the biscuits rattling into the bowl, and Tib crouched down to attend to them. Looking down at his broad, stripy back, Liz was swamped with affection. Wise Tib. He gave his love in return for food and shelter and was perfectly honest about it. She was expected to give hers for nothing and pretend it was for something – the dubious satisfaction of the great Paul Attwood's company when he could tear himself away from the pleasures of London. She had begun to realise that she was onto a loser when she found herself wondering, in the face of her combined family's criticisms and Cecy's unlucky revelation over Christmas, just what those pleasures were, and discovering that she didn't particularly care.

This reflection brought her thoughts full circle. 'I'm sick of it,' she said. 'I'm sick of *him*!'

So involved had she been in the passion of her own resentment, that she had failed to hear either the front door opening or the footsteps in the tiled hall and crossing her tiny study, so that the voice from the kitchen doorway made her jump.

'If you're talking about Paul, three rousing cheers,' said Alice. She placed her bag of shopping on the kitchen table in Tib's place and looked at Liz with sympathy. 'Sorry if I startled you. I had to take the car to the garage for its MOT and I've got time to kill. I went to the shop, then I thought I'd drop by and cadge some coffee, it's too cold out there to just stand around. January, brrr! Any going?'

Liz switched on the kettle without replying and took two mugs from the draining board, and Alice pulled out a chair and sat down. She looked at her younger sister's back with an understanding and, on the whole, sympathetic eye.

'What now?' she asked. Liz sighed, without turning round.

'I've just come to the conclusion that I'm thirty-three years old, and nothing but a convenient habit. I feel as if I'm living in one of my own novels, except that if I was, this would be the moment when my life changed dramatically and after various interesting tribulations, all my pigeons came home to roost as birds of paradise.'

'No love?' asked Alice, raising her eyebrows.

'Not with Paul. He only loves one person: Paul Attwood. He's not even a friend, in any real sense, just a user, and it seems I'm the only one who's not realised it before.'

'Then congratulations,' said Alice. 'We've all thought that for a long time now.'

'So why didn't any of you say?' demanded Liz, turning round at last. She spoke with curiosity rather than resentment. 'I mean, I knew you didn't like him especially, but ...'

Alice said, with equal interest. 'Would you have listened?' and Liz replied, 'No.'

'There you are, then.'

Liz came back to the table, a steaming mug in each hand, and sat down again. Tib gave them a look, decided that his moment in the limelight was past, and headed off into the garden through his cat flap. Alice spooned sugar into her mug and stirred it thoughtfully. She said, following on from where she had left off, 'You seemed to know what you were doing, to be set on it, in fact. You're a grown-up. Why should we say anything – more than we did, that is?'

'None of you usually hold back. Look at the way you all set about Auntie Sue.'

'Auntie Sue was married to an arsehole, she needed rescuing. You're a free woman.'

Liz said, with a touch of regret. 'From where I'm sitting, being a free woman equates with being a lonely one.'

'Goodness!' Alice looked at her, round-eyed. 'Is the independent Elizabeth Ballantyne ready to settle down and raise children?'

'Not children, no,' said Liz, taking the easiest part of this question first. 'I think my biological clock was never issued with a battery, to be honest. Anyway, there's plenty of children in the family already. Nor settling down, really. I want ... what do I want? A good companion, I suppose. A *real* friend. Someone to love who loves me back and shares my life, not just good sex, and not taking advantage or under my feet all the time ... oh God, I'm sounding like a novel again!'

'An occupational hazard,' Alice diagnosed. She paused. 'So, what brought this on? All this wishing for the moon?'

'I'm not sure. Spring on the distant horizon, perhaps? Sap rising, and all that jazz? Boredom?'

Alice said, cautiously, 'You and Paul have been an item for years.'

'Yes. Too many years.'

Since Liz was a best-selling novelist, and her long-term, not-quite-live-in partner in publishing, Alice asked the obvious question, but cautiously. 'Dumping him wouldn't dig a pitfall under your career?'

'No. He's not my publisher anyway.' It seemed boastful to say that her position was too secure for such as Paul Attwood to damage it, but she said it all the same. 'Nobody would listen to him in any case. He'd hurt himself more than me if he tried anything.'

'So, dump him.'

Liz looked wistful. She said what she had said to Carl before Christmas. 'That would leave me a sad thirty-something without a partner.'

'There's lots of good fish in the sea.'

'Yeah, sure. All looking for dizzy young blondes.'

228

'Now, even I think you're talking like a novel! Anyway, you're gorgeous when you bother to wear your contact lenses. And famous. And earning good money. That's why Paul hangs around.'

'There's more to life than being a trophy, however. And I'm still thirty-plus, and I found a grey hair yesterday.'

'You poor old thing!'

Liz made a feeble push back. Older sisters need keeping in their place every now and then. 'If you left your poor car with Ole Jarge, you've got more than time to kill. You've got the car as well. Probably yourself too; last time he touched mine, I ended up calling out the RAC.'

Alice looked at her calmly. 'It's no good demolishing poor Ole Jarge to make yourself feel better. He's a nice old boy. And anyway, he's convenient.'

'Sure,' said Liz. 'But it's time he retired. He thinks so too, did you know the garage was up for sale?'

'Yes,' said Alice, taking the wind out of her sails.

'It's meant to be a secret!'

'Most open secret in the world. Anyway, why?' She added hastily, before Liz could misunderstand her, 'Why a secret, I mean.'

'He thought he might lose business. But it seems he told everyone anyway. Ha!'

Alice shifted to make herself more comfortable and took a sip of her coffee. 'He's losing business anyway, too. He doesn't seem to mind.'

'Only because he *is* retiring. But he won't have anything to sell, if he doesn't sell it soon.'

'He's got someone having a look round today,' said Alice.

'Hopefully, just in time!' Liz wished no actual harm to George Pryor, but the RAC man had been very explicit about the state of her Mercedes convertible's electrical system. She was slightly put out that Alice, who lived outside the village, should know more about what went on than she did herself and her reply had a waspish ring to it.

'Hopefully, much more competent and they'll buy it,' said Alice, unmoved.

'And thinking that, you still gave him your car for its MOT?'

'You're still going out with Patronising Paul,' Alice pointed out.

Liz came to a decision. 'No, I'm not. He's had his chips.'

'Don't believe you!'

They eyeballed each other for a moment, and then Liz, unconsciously bracing her shoulders, said, 'No, I've had enough. He's wasting my life.'

Alice clapped. 'But I'll believe it when I see it, all the same. Habits are hard to break – particularly bad ones.'

'Oh, he's not *bad*,' Liz protested. She added, more honestly, 'Just boring,' and looked pensive.

Alice said, precisely, 'He's conceited, condescending, calculating, creepy and cold. That's just my opinion, of course.'

'You *really* don't like him, then?'

'You could say that.'

Liz thought for a moment.

'Not *creepy*,' she objected. 'He's quite cute, really.'

'He's slimy,' said Alice. There was a silence.

Alice happened to know, from rigorously interrogating Cecy behind Liz's back at Christmas, that Paul Attwood, since Liz had moved her main residence to Waldren Stavey, had filled the evenings of his weekdays very pleasantly, and not in the line of business either whatever he chose to tell Liz, and she wasn't even sure that Cecy had told her everything then, she had become evasive as only Cecy could. She didn't say so, where was the point? To have mentioned it then would have made Liz angry, she had become very defensive under the family onslaught: to mention it now would be shutting the stable door after the horse had gone, but it was this inside knowledge that had shifted her previously take-him-or-leave-him view of her sister's partner – if that was his position. She was fairly certain that Liz's attitude to Paul had been one of familiarity rather than passion for a while now; the two of them had fallen into too comfortable a rut for Paul, at least, to have wished to climb out. After all, his weekends under the shadow of Stavey Tor had been not only pleasant, but largely free. Had he found something better to do in London, he would no doubt have done it. It was up to Liz whether she put up with it or not.

And now, it seemed, she wasn't going to put up with it. Three rousing cheers!

Obscurely feeling that the occasion required a celebration, although she wasn't, of course, going to put it quite like that, Alice glanced at her watch. 'The car'll be a while yet, the speed Ole Jarge works. Fancy having lunch with me at the Three Bears?'

'It's a bit early for lunch, surely?'

'Then we can have a drink until it isn't.'

Liz looked at her askance. 'And you driving, too! Moreover, driving a car that Ole Jarge has been at. You're a brave woman, Alice Ballantyne Hogg!'

'The word "drink",' said Alice, pedantically, 'applies to liquid, not necessarily to alcohol. A best-selling writer like you should know that.'

'In the context of pubs,' said Liz, gathering the empty mugs together, 'it means alcohol.'

'Well good, then. We can drink to your emancipation before I move on to orange juice! And while we're at it, you can check out the talent. After all, you're a free woman now.'

Liz gave a snort of laughter. 'Thank you! Retired colonels, grockles, and ruddy-cheeked farm workers with maybe the odd rep on a good day and with the wind behind us! Not my style, thank you.'

'A good lusty farm worker might do you good.'

'My name is not Lady Chatterley. Anyway, great blokes though most of them are, they feel about me like I feel about them. We don't go together.'

'Ooh, you snob, you!'

'Not at all, it's common sense. What do any of them want with a woman with a university degree in English? They want a proper partner who can take an intelligent interest in sheep.' She put the mugs down again, and looked at her sister in sudden apprehension. 'Oh God, Alice, what am I going to do? I'll hate being a sad singleton. At least Paul was somebody to go to parties with.'

'If that's all you can find to say by way of a valediction, then it's high time he was gone,' said Alice, briskly. She picked up the mugs herself and put them into the sink. 'Come on, misery. You need a good stiff drink!'

The Three Bells inn, aka the Three Bears, was only a few steps along the village street, they walked there slowly enjoying the chilly winter sunshine. 'New year, new beginning,' said Alice.

'Don't be so twee,' said her sister.

Alice said nothing to this. She was thinking about that final comment on Paul, *somebody to go to parties with*. It occurred to her that the sooner the vacant space at her side was filled, the less likely Liz was to backslide into her old habits. Liz and Paul were party animals; it was about the only thing they had in common. Insufficient, in Alice's opinion, even had Paul not been a creep.

It was still quite early for lunch, but even so the small bar was well patronised. Alice, securing a table beside the smouldering fire by dint of slipping into it ahead of a man approaching with a glass in each hand, settled herself comfortably and looked around with interest. She gave the approaching man a sunny smile and he shook his head at her and walked away. Liz said, 'And now, I suppose, you're going to ask me to go and buy the drinks and fetch you a menu.'

'If you don't,' Alice pointed out, 'we'll lose this table and end up trapped in the restaurant and you won't be able to view the talent properly.'

'I don't intend to view the talent, as you so elegantly put it, thank you.'

Alice took no notice. She looked meditatively at her late opponent, now propping up the bar with his back ostentatiously towards her, talking with another man. 'How about him, for a start?' she speculated, nodding in their direction. Liz followed her eyes and gave a snort of derision.

'Bright red hair and a ginger moustache? Thank you for nothing!'

'Not him, silly. The one with his back to you. Rather smooth, I thought. You could chat him up when you fetch the menu. Apologise for your sister's pushiness, or something.'

Liz slipped onto the bench facing her, sitting down firmly. 'You may apologise for your own bad manners. You can chat him up too, for all I care, but don't do it on my behalf.' She hadn't expected Alice to take her seriously, but to her horror her sister immediately rose to her feet.

'All right. You sit there, I'll be back.'

232

There was no way of stopping her, Liz realised. She sat back in her seat and watched with resigned interest as her sister wormed her way through the small crowd to the bar.

With cunning and persistence, Alice wriggled her way in alongside her selected victim's back and ordered two glasses of the house white. While they were being poured for her, she deliberately stepped aside to allow someone else to approach the bar and jostled him, harder than was strictly necessary. He turned round and she gave him a dazzling smile.

Not bad, Liz admitted from her seat in the audience, and she wasn't just thinking of Alice's technique. Crinkly fair hair, smartly cut, unlike the fiery, close cropped bristle of his hirsute companion. Nice face, brown from a sun that had never shone on an English landscape, firm chin. Good body, lean and hard, and a nice neat bum, she had already noticed.

Watch it, you lonely saddo! You're getting as bad as Alice!

Alice was talking, spreading her hands. 'I'm so sorry, did I spill your beer? I've really got it in for you today, haven't I?' She smiled; Alice had a friendly smile. The man smiled back.

'No problem, ma'am. All's fair in love, war and a busy pub.'

Ma'am? Alice just managed not to stare. The barman came with the two glasses of wine.

'And the bar menu Jamie, please. Thanks.' She paused with it in her hand. Behind her selected prey, Ginger Moustache was grinning at her in an appreciative way that made the hairs on her neck stand on end. 'There are two spare chairs,' she said. 'It's only fair if I invite you to sit on them. My sister won't mind.'

'That's very kind of you.' The Prey's eye roved across to Liz, sitting on the bench behind the table and he turned to his companion. 'What do you reckon, Sergeant? Shall we risk a sortie into enemy territory?'

Sergeant? This time, Alice didn't so much stare as goggle. Was she chatting up the fuzz on her sister's behalf? She recollected herself hurriedly, and gathered up the drinks, slopping one onto the counter as she tried to hold it with the bar menu. The man addressed as "sergeant" smoothly appropriated the glass from her. 'I'll carry this for you, shall I?' he said.

The matter seemed to be settled: Alice led her trophies back to the table. She took the seat beside her sister, and the two men sat opposite. The fair one manoeuvred himself adroitly into the seat facing Liz, and Alice was left to look at Sergeant Ginger Moustache. There was a short pause. Liz was first to speak; somebody had to be. 'Hullo,' she said.

Alice, suddenly uncomfortable with the result of her scheming, thrust the bar menu at her. 'Better choose something. There's quite a lot of people here for the time of year, we might wait ages. They don't have the staff on.'

While Liz ran her eye down the already familiar menu, The Prey said, politely, 'I take it you're locals, the two of you, since you know the barman by name?'

'Yes. At least, my sister is. I live just west of here – my husband runs a nursery – plants, not toddlers.' Too much information. She fell silent. The silence became noticeable. 'You?' she asked, to break it.

'The sergeant here and I, we're homeless men at present. Just discharged from the army.'

There were things in that short speech that were questionable, Alice thought. The word "we", for instance, that made them into a pair. They didn't look ... well, gay, if you wanted to put it bluntly, but of course you never knew. She said, 'Oh,' and the silence fell again. Liz broke it, handing back the menu and looking The Prey squarely in the eye. Alice had brought them over here, it was no use her pussy-footing round them. 'So what brought you to darkest Devon at this time of year?'

'Just spying out the land, you might say.' He smiled, and unexpectedly extended his hand across the table. 'I should introduce myself. Captain Anstruther, late of the Royal Electrical & Mechanical Engineers. The sergeant here was my right-hand man. There's no better man with machinery in England, that's a fact.'

Something went "click" in Liz's head. She took his hand and shook it warmly. 'I know who you must be! You're the people who have come to view Ole Jarge's place.'

'If Ole Jarge is the character who owns the garage up the street, you're spot on, ma'am.'

'Liz,' said Liz.

'Liz.' He released her hand and picked up his half-finished pint.

He did not, she noticed, make her a present in return of his own christian name.

Alice, meanwhile, left to make the best of Ginger Moustache, was making heavy weather. There was something about his face that told her he knew exactly what she was up to, and was deeply amused. Already thrown off balance by the – let's face it – unexpected success of her mission, she floundered miserably, seizing on her sister's casual question and its reply as a lifeline. 'So will you make an offer?' she asked, which was really not her business.

'Should we, do you think? Is it a good garage?'

There were three answers to that; Alice knew she could make none of them. *Yes*, which was manifestly untrue. *I don't know*, which would be an outright and possibly obvious lie. *No*, which had the virtue of truth, but would be unfair to Ole Jarge, who desperately wanted shut of it. She hedged. 'I take my car there. In fact, it's there now.'

'Is there much competition?' he asked, casually.

Another facer, he had a gift for them. Almost anyone who knew one end of a spanner from another would be competition for Ole Jarge. In fact, quite a few of the locals took their cars to the local tractor dealer, who happened to be their own father.

'There's a lot of people with cars around,' she said, and in desperation carried the war into the enemy's camp. 'So are you going into partnership, you and Captain Anstruther? Is that the idea?'

'In a way. He'll run the business, whatever we settle on, that's not my scene. I'll be in charge of the workshop. A couple of the lads will come along with us, at least to start with.'

'What, all ex-army?'

'They don't come much better than the REME.'

It sounded like potential good news for her car, but the village might not like it. Local businesses, in their perfectly valid view, should provide work for local people. Alice said, curiously, 'It seems an odd choice for a man like the Captain. I'd have put him down for a big city man, or at least a sizeable town.'

'Well, you never can really tell with people on short acquaintance, can you?' He smiled at her. He was a country boy himself, she could hear it in his accent. Nothing overt, just a faint suggestion of east coast ... not Essex; somewhere more rural. Norfolk? Suffolk? Somewhere on that side of the country, anyway. Ignoring what could be construed as a snub, she said, 'You're a long way from home, Sergeant ... Sergeant ...?'

'Wainwright,' he said helpfully.

Liz jogged her sister's elbow to get her attention. 'What are you eating? I'll go up and order.'

'Crab cakes, did you need to ask? I'll go if you want.'

Liz was already on her feet. 'You got the wine. Do you want another, or are you sticking to your threat about orange juice?'

Captain Anstruther rose to his feet as well. 'Let me get this round – no, really, you were kind enough to invite us to sit with you. Sergeant, a refill?'

He and Liz walked across to the bar together, and Alice and Sergeant Wainwright watched them go. He said, idly, 'Tell me about this garden centre. Do you work in it too?'

'It's not a garden centre, it's a nursery. We supply garden centres. And yes. Part-time, anyway.' She was relieved at the change of subject, she hadn't liked the feeling she was prying she had begun to have – quite deservedly, of course: she had been prying. 'We have three children, they take up the other part.'

The sergeant laughed at that. 'Yes, I can imagine. I'm no expert, I've not been home much since I joined up, but my brother and sisters all have kids, and they seem to have their hands full. One of my nieces, particularly, is a real handful.'

'The female is deadlier than the male?'

'Much. Candy was making waves in her cradle.'

'You'll be able to see much more of them now, I suppose.'

'Thanks for that happy thought!'

They both laughed. He picked up his glass and took a pensive swallow. 'So your sister lives here in the village?'

'Yes. Just up the road.'

'And is she part of the market garden thing, too?'

Nice to feel she wasn't the only quizzy one, thought Alice. She said, 'Nursery. And no. Liz is a novelist, she writes best-sellers.'

'Really?' He looked interested. 'Would I have read any?'

'I very much doubt it. She writes what they call "chick-lit".'

'Never heard of it.'

'There's a surprise!'

Captain Anstruther and Liz came back, laden with glasses. The sergeant looked at Liz with more interest than he had hitherto shown. 'Your sister tells me you're an author,' he said. Liz sat down and pushed Alice's juice in her direction. The captain, too, looked interested.

'Really? And what do you write?' he asked.

Liz resisted the temptation to reply "books". There are three questions your average writer doesn't want to hear: "And are you writing anything now?", "So what is your new book about?" and "What do you write?". 'Novels,' she said, which was only marginally better.

Captain Anstruther smiled kindly. 'Ladies' novels, I suppose? Romances, or – what do they call them – bodice rippers?'

'Those tend to be historical,' said Liz, seething inwardly.

'And are you writing anything now?' he asked. Alice flinched. Not a well chosen question, Captain Anstruther! But Liz only returned the smile, very sweetly.

'It's my job,' she explained, which was mild for her. 'Do you go to work at yours every morning, after all? Or did you, when you had one?'

'Ouch, nasty!' said the sergeant, and grinned, but his superior officer showed courage, even foolhardiness, in the field.

'So, what is your new book about?' he enquired genially.

He had blown it, thought Alice sadly. Blown it right out of the water with a perfect set of three, before it had fairly got under way. Shame.

'Now, would I be likely to tell you?' Liz asked, still smiling. 'You'll have to go out and buy it when it comes out – that is, if you really want to know.'

'Fair enough.' He obviously had no idea that he had offended, and Alice mentally wrote him off. Try again with someone else, if the opportunity arose, she decided. There were lots of good fish in the sea, if you bothered to put out a line and a good, big hook. And baited it with an attractive woman, of course.

The conversation went downhill from that point, until it reached the nadir of discussing the good weather for the time of year and the number of strangers around for the beginning of February, and when the waitress came with knives and forks and table mats for the women, Captain Anstruther emptied his glass and looked ostentatiously at his watch. 'Time to keep our appointment, Sergeant, and leave these ladies to eat their meal in peace.'

The sergeant's glass was already empty. He smiled at the sisters across the table. 'Must go then, duty calls. Maybe we'll have the pleasure of meeting you both again some time.' Both men stood up and took their leave. Alice and Liz watched them go.

'Nice try, Alice,' said Liz, grinning.

'You shouldn't be too picky – at least, not on a first acquaintance.'

'If I'm not being picky, then I might as well stick with Paul,' Liz countered.

'No you mightn't. Don't even consider it!'

'Give him credit, he never called us "ladies".'

'He knew we weren't.' She hesitated. 'The sergeant wasn't so bad, when you talked to him.'

Liz shook her head. 'Alice, as you very well know, there are two things I could never, ever, stand in a man – a military background and a ginger moustache, the two biggest turn-offs in the catalogue! So forget it. And you can add to that list, anyone who talks about "ladies' novels", by the way.'

'Shame.'

'No it's not. I'm not that desperate, I haven't even finished with Paul yet, so keep your oar out of the water, please.'

'Fine.' Their meal arrived then, probably a good thing, and Alice decided to back off. While they were eating, she changed the subject to a gymkhana at the weekend in which her twins would be riding; they parted on a friendly note, and Alice walked back up to the garage to collect her car.

They were there, she saw as soon as she arrived, standing in the workshop with George Pryor, engrossed in talk; if either of them saw her, they didn't acknowledge it. She went into the office where the girl who attempted to keep order in the chaos greeted her with a fistful of paper. 'Mrs Hogg! Your car's ready, the certificate's here with the bill. Not much wrong this time.'

'Hi Angie, thanks.' She checked the bill, trying not to think "nothing wrong when I brought it in, anyway", then hunted for her credit card in her purse. While thus occupied, she said, 'Those two men in the workshop – we just met them in the pub. Having a look at this place, they said; are they interested, do you think?'

'If they are, they'll be the first,' Angie told her, gloomily. 'So far, people have taken one look and run for it. I think myself that it'll close, and then bang goes my job.' She looked at Alice speculatively. 'I suppose you don't need anyone in the office at the nursery, do you?'

'You'll have to ask Gil. I generally do it, but he might.' And he might not want to employ someone who had worked for chaotic Ole Jarge, but that was his business. 'Here you are –' she put the card down on the desk. The transaction completed, she picked up her key and the paperwork and turned to leave. Her car was parked in front of the office, she took the opportunity, as she opened the door, to steal another look into the workshop, but the three men had vanished into the depths.

Oh well. He had been a prize pillock anyway. Too much time spent bossing blokes around and charming "ladies" at gatherings in the officers' mess no doubt. Liz would never go for that.

Shame, she thought, not for the first time.

Alice got into her car and drove away. She never expected to see the two men again.

Liz, meanwhile, had returned home with the admirable intention of getting down to work, only to find that her mind wouldn't settle on the doings of her latest heroine but instead had fixed itself on Paul. He was taking over her entire day, bother him. Her tabby confidant was fast asleep on the sofa in her sitting room; she sat and stared at her computer screen

Paul was a problem that she needed to resolve. Good sex was no reason to waste your entire life, and even if she had wanted to marry Paul, or anyone come to that which she certainly didn't, she knew very well that he had no intentions of marrying her. Their present arrangement suited him perfectly. Paul was understandably content to spend his weekends in her house, arriving on Friday night with his bag and a couple of bottles of cheap wine, departing on Sunday with his clean washing for the week, done in her machine because, he said, it was so much easier to do it at weekends. If they went out in London, it was always Dutch treat, something that dated back to their early days together, and when they went on holiday, the same applied: Liz paid for Liz, Paul paid for Paul. He claimed he didn't want to encroach on her independence.

But here in Devon, Paul preferred to eat in rather than go out to the pub, or a restaurant. He said he liked the feeling of being at home in her cottage, and needed the break from anything resembling his manic London life in order to relax. Well, fine, as far as it went, but what Paul was actually doing was freeloading every weekend. He never offered her anything towards the food he ate, or the electricity and gas that cooked it for him or did his washing. It wasn't just what she had said to Tib that morning: it was far, far more than a free weekend in the country. It was free board and lodging for nearly a third of his time. She might not have grudged that had anything ever gone the other way, from him to her. It didn't. There was always a reason why she couldn't spend a weekend with him in London unless it was in her flat, when usual terms applied. Unreasonable, she now thought, when her flat was decidedly small, and his was huge and far more comfortable. His classic excuse was "I know you like to have your own things round you, Liz,' said with an understanding smile. Or alternatively, "It keeps the place aired." Am I being petty here? she asked herself, and answered herself, no. But you have been stupid, and you have been manipulated, and believe me, that's a lot sadder than being a singleton.

He was supposed to be coming to Devon this Friday. Perhaps she would ring him this evening and tell him she wouldn't be here. If she did that a time or two, although it hadn't been exactly successful the first time she had tried it, maybe he would get the message without her actually having to fall out with him. She could gradually ease herself out of the relationship and they would just drift apart. That would be the best way to do it, with no unpleasantness to leave a bad taste behind on the closing of an arrangement that had, to be fair, suited them both in the past.

Come to that, she could ring him right now. He would argue less, maybe, if he was in his office. Perhaps he wouldn't argue at all, and that would be just fine.

Paul, when she finally got him on the line, wasn't happy. He listened to her explanation and then said, with calm certainty, 'That's not on, Liz. You'll have to reschedule, I've already made my arrangements.'

'Then you'll have to *un*make them. I'm sorry Paul, I told you, something came up. I've got to be away.'

'Away, where?' His voice was loaded with indignation. She said the first place that came into her head. 'Cornwall.'

Paul laughed. 'That can't be so important, come on Liz! Or come to that, I could come with you, it was quite fun last time until that crashing oaf started up in the pub, and we needn't go there, after all. I'd like a word with that chap, Carl Colenso, that your aunt is living with. I was going to ring him, but this would be better.'

Paul's publishing house was, of course, handling Carl's book, due out in the summer. Liz realised that she couldn't challenge Paul as a liar, even if he was one, and so had painted herself into a corner. She hurriedly changed course. 'I didn't say I was going to St Erbyn. Cornwall is a big place.'

'Where? Why?'

'Paul, is that really your business?'

'Since it's oversetting all my arrangements, I think it is.'

'I do have a life of my own, you know.'

'I never said you didn't. So, where are you going? You at least owe me an explanation.'

'I don't owe you anything, Paul, if it comes to that. Look, it's quite simple, I'm sorry but I've got to be somewhere else this weekend.' She felt him hesitate.

'All right then, I could come down to the cottage and look after the cat for you. You could leave some food, and I could have a meal ready for when you get back. At least I could do my washing.'

'You can do that anyway. There's a perfectly good machine in your apartment, it wouldn't hurt you to use that for once.'

'I'll come down,' said Paul, firmly. 'I've got my key, it won't matter if you aren't there. It will save you making arrangements with your neighbour.'

'*Paul*! There's no point, I shan't be back until Monday morning.'

When she finally put the phone down on the argument, she still wasn't sure that she had made her point. Paul seemed determined to come to Waldren Stavey, and she really didn't want him in her house when she wasn't there.

At this point in her resentful thoughts, she was brought up short. Why was that? She *liked* Paul, didn't she? Even if she didn't actually love him. Was it just his insensitive insistence on invading her space in her absence, or what was it? They had, after all, drifted along together without incident for some time now, getting on for three years it must be.

Drifted, of course, was the operative word. She had suddenly decided to stop drifting, and he didn't like it. Well, he could lump it, then!

But perhaps, tomorrow, she would get Gil to put new locks on her doors.

And where had that gem come from?

Liz sat and thought about that, and discovered its origin in what her sister had said of Paul: *conceited, calculating, condescending, creepy and cold*. Something like that, she might not have remembered the indictment one hundred per cent correctly. She thought some more.

She placed no reliance on Paul not coming anyway, although why he couldn't just stay in his smart riverside apartment for one weekend was a mystery. That meant that she would have to be somewhere else, which was a nuisance, as she hadn't planned on going anywhere.

Well, that was easy. She had said she was going to Cornwall, she would go: he would never know exactly where, and anyway she didn't think she had actually said she *wasn't* going to St Erbyn, simply implied it. Auntie Sue would have her for the weekend, the neighbours would feed Tib. Satisfied with her arrangements, Liz made a note to remind herself about the locks.

It would all work out fine.

XIII

Benita Vachell, strolling round the Square in Embridge on a fine winter's morning, looking at the shops and wondering if she fancied a cup of coffee in Borden's, caught sight of Dot staring into the window of an estate agent, and decided on impulse to scoop her up and take her along. Coffee on your own was never that much fun, and she liked Dot. She also had a great admiration for her after seeing her annihilate the awful Jenny Carruthers, and then sweep out of the committee meeting with her head held high, even if she broke down later. Bennie thought she had never seen a more feisty fighter, and being on Dot's side on this occasion, for Mrs Carruthers had been way out of order, she had immediately proffered her own resignation and followed her. She had a feeling that she hadn't been the only one to feel this way, but none of the others had had the guts to speak up. She wasn't much of a one for sitting on committees anyway, there were more interesting things to do with your life.

'Dorothy!' she said, stopping beside her quarry. 'Fancy running into you! Isn't it a lovely day! You'd never think it was February, would you?'

'The forecast isn't good,' said Dot, in a distracted tone of voice, and then turned to look at her. 'Benita dear! How nice to see you, are you in town shopping, or are you on business?'

'Both. I came in on business, and now I'm shopping.' She peered into the window with Dot. 'Thinking of moving, or just passing the time?' She smiled at the absurd suggestion that Dot should move from her beautiful home. 'I was just off for a coffee, fancy joining me?'

'Oh ... yes, why not.' Dot gave one last glance into the estate agent's window and visibly redirected her attention to her young friend. She was lonely these days, she missed having Susan within call more than she would have believed, and the idea of company was welcome. 'Yes, that would be pleasant.'

'Borden's? Theirs is the best, don't you think, and we could have a sticky bun as well.'

'No, no bun,' Dot said regretfully, as they fell into step along the pavement. 'I really must get rid of some weight. It creeps on in the winter months, you know how it is.'

Bennie nodded sympathetically, but privately she thought that Dot had lost enough weight since she had known her to be going on with. Lose too much too quickly at her age, she thought critically, and you could end up looking a hag. Dot had the makings of a handsome woman if she would only lighten up a bit; good bones and so far, she hadn't let herself sag. Bennie wondered how old she actually was, she must be at least twenty years older than herself, if her daughters were anything to go by. Susan must be in her thirties, to have children that age, although she didn't look it. A lusty young lover might be the explanation there, of course. Perhaps Dot should find herself one.

By the time her thoughts had reached this point their steps had reached the portals of Borden's, where they ran into Sally Casson, just coming out. Dot greeted her warmly. 'Sally! We were just going in for some coffee, do join us! Have you met Benita Vachell?'

Sally hadn't, and during the introductions found herself swept to the lift and up to the restaurant. They ordered their coffee, and when they were happily settled at a table, Bennie said, 'You never answered me, Dorothy. *Are* you thinking of moving?' She still didn't believe it, but it was something to talk about. She turned to Sally. 'I found her staring at Hallidays' window display as if she'd seen the holy grail.' They both looked at Dot with alert interest. Thus put on the spot, Dot had no option but to confess.

'I thought I might just have a look around. My present house is very big for one person, and Debor – ie – moving into her new home this week set me thinking.'

'Deborie, eh?' said Benita, grinning at her. 'That's a new one! Do you have any ideas, or were you just looking for inspiration?'

'I must have a big garden, of course. And room for the children, when they come.'

Sally looked sceptical. 'Sounds as if you might as well stay where you are to me,' she said.

'Four bedrooms would be ample,' said Dot. 'I hardly need seven, Sally, it's unlikely they will all descend on me at once very often. And Debbie's husband is looking to set up a restaurant business locally, and presumably that will have accommodation.'

'Is he indeed!' Sally looked impressed. 'That news will make Irwin's day! All right then, a big garden and four bedrooms. Any other priorities?'

'A pleasant area, of course.'

Bennie said, idly, 'Why don't you look in Shearwater? There are some lovely houses there. I could plug you into the grapevine, and get you priority viewing if anything good came up.'

'Shearwater?' Dot spoke as if Shearwater was at the ends of the earth. 'I'm not sure I would wish to be that rural, Benita.'

'Why not? Think about it, you could make a whole new set of enemies, reorganise the W.I., who need it, believe me, terrorise the Garden Club, boss the Drama Group around ... I think you'd find it right up your street – or lane, I suppose, out there in the boondocks.'

Sally was interested to see that Bennie's irreverent approach left Dot smiling, and made a mental note to tell Irwin this too when she got home, and Dot said, 'I wouldn't want Jennifer Carruthers to think that she had driven me out.'

'Don't worry, there's no chance,' said Bennie. 'She's horrified at the success of her attack, particularly since your son-in-law has been forgiven. She was mad as a wet hen about that, and I'm told by my spies that he handled her beautifully, squashed her flat as a jaywalking frog!'

Dot couldn't help looking pleased. While she was savouring this interesting news, Ingrid approached their table with a cup in her hand. 'May I join you?' She set the cup down and pulled out the fourth chair. 'How lovely to run into you. Hullo Sally, hi Bennie.'

'You two know each other?' asked Sally, surprised and feeling strangely left out.

'We go to the same art class,' explained Ingrid. 'Painting in Oils for Beginners, Thursday afternoons at the college, but I don't think either of us is a serious threat to your stepson, Dot.' She hesitated, but then said it anyway. 'We were both at Dot's party, which is when we really got together. Up to then, we just stared at each other across the room and never knew each other's names, how you do, you know?'

'Stared in mutual confusion,' put in Bennie. 'Heads spinning on a colour wheel.'

'Dot was just telling us she's thinking of moving,' said Sally, when Ingrid was seated. 'What do you think of that? We were just discussing the pros and cons of moving out of town.'

'Oh, what a lovely idea! I'd love to do that, but Alex won't budge, he wants to be near to his precious office. Maybe when he retires ... where were you thinking of, Dot?'

'I suggested Shearwater,' said Bennie, immediately. 'Not too far out of town, and plenty going on. Emberton is nice too, but that's all yachting, not quite Dorothy's scene really. But it's a thought.'

Dot said, coming to a decision, 'Perhaps I might go into Hallidays' and just put out a few feelers when we've finished our coffee.'

'I'll come with you,' said Bennie, immediately. 'I can point you in the direction of the best parts of the village. February is a dead month for selling houses, but you never know, you might strike it lucky.'

Sally and Ingrid looked as if with the slightest encouragement they would have come too, but they didn't volunteer: four women intent on a search might have been two too many. Bennie lived in – or near anyway – Shearwater; she was the best one to accompany their friend, but, 'Mind you tell us how you get on,' said Sally, when she and Ingrid got up to go. 'I think it's a great idea, anyway, Dot, go for it!. You can always drive into town when you need.' They said goodbye and walked away to the lift, and Dot picked up her gloves. 'Well, if we're going to do it, let's be on our way,' she said.

As they passed through the book department on their way out, Bennie had another idea. 'Come on Dorothy, I tell you what you need: a really good book to cheer you up. Let's find one.'

Dot's taste ran to biography and the more respectable novelists, but Bennie headed straight for the best-seller section. 'I don't think these are quite me,' Dot murmured, swept along with her, but Bennie, like Susan before her, was on a mission.

'No Dorothy, I've seen the kind of thing you read,' she said, firmly. 'You need to branch out – new days, new ways. Let's see what we have here, now ...' She ran a practised eye along the shelves of new books. 'Oh, she's good – how about this one? I enjoy her books, anyway.' She took a fat paperback from the shelf. 'You don't want to go for a hardback unless you know you really like an author, if you don't like this one you can put it on the WI stall and never feel a thing.' She dumped the book into Dot's hands. Dot, accepting it since it was either that or dropping it on the floor, murmured that she didn't belong to the WI.

'We can soon fix that,' said Bennie. 'They're the backbone of the nation – just where you belong! Have a look, see what you think.'

Dot looked at the book in her hands. *What's in a Name?* by Elizabeth Ballantyne. She felt a sudden hot flush coming on, but no. It couldn't be. She opened the front cover, and there, looking up at her, was a picture of a dark haired, dark eyed young woman who could – no, of course she couldn't! – quite possibly be related to her own daughter Susan. Her heart began to thump uncomfortably, how ridiculous! She read the biographical note beneath it.

Elizabeth Ballantyne was born and grew up in Devon, and after gaining a BLit with Honours from University College, went on to work in London as a literary agent. Her first novel, published six years ago, was an instant success, enabling her to give up real work and devote her time to enjoying her favourite hobbies of writing, partying, and watching the grass grow. She has now moved permanently back to Devon to be near her family, where she lives à deux with her cat and tries not to overtire herself with gardening.

Dot turned the book over and read the short synopsis on the back.

Aminta has always been confident, outgoing, and certain of her place in the world, but when a terrible tragedy strikes out of the blue, she makes the disturbing discovery that her whole conception of herself so far has been built upon sand. The parents whom she has loved and respected all her life are not, in fact her own: her heredity is very different from the secure middle class background against which she has grown up.

Shocked by the unexpected revelation coming hard on the heels of personal disaster, Aminta sets out on a quest to find her roots, but what she finds is a great deal more than she had ever expected ...

'Aminta,' said Dot. 'What a ridiculous name.'

'It's a made-up name,' Bennie explained. 'Her parents – her adoptive parents – are called Amy and Nathan, they named her after both of them, they're that kind. A bit twee, you know? I think so, anyway. Her real name is something quite different.'

There was a dedication, too, among the front pages. *For Susan, who came on a Quest.*

'What d'you reckon?' said Bennie, unaware of undercurrents. Dot tucked the book into her arm and took out her purse. 'I'll buy it,' she said.

'Is anything wrong,' Bennie asked, for something in the way that Dot had spoken had finally alerted her powers of observation. She added, acutely, 'You don't know her, do you? Elizabeth Ballantyne?'

Dot said, slowly, 'I believe I may have been at her christening.'

'So you do know her! What fun!'

'I haven't set eyes on her since she was two years old if this is she, so no, I don't. But I suppose, in a way, you could say she is my granddaughter.'

'How amazing!' cried Bennie, intrigued. Dot went to the pay desk without answering, and Bennie, taking the hint, allowed the subject to drop, but she didn't forget about it. There was a mystery here, and it intrigued her. Not for the first time since she had made her acquaintance, and still more since she had met her children, she wondered about Dot.

Debbie rang her mother that evening, bubbling with excitement and full of news.

'We're in, Mum! The furniture looks lost and half the rooms are empty, but we're home!'

'Well, that's good news,' said Dot. 'I hope you didn't tire yourself out, Deborah. You've two weeks to go yet, you know, we don't want any accidents.'

'Two weeks is nothing!' said Debbie, carelessly. 'Anyway, I did hardly anything, I didn't have to. Mawgan was here, and Gosia, and Mrs Tregear, who's housekeeper at the Fish, came and cleaned up after the men and left everything shining. I just made the tea, and now I'm sitting here in my gorgeous new armchair by a lovely log fire with my feet up on an antique footstool, and Mawgan is getting supper.'

'Where was your sister while all this was going on?' asked Dot, with disapproval. 'I thought she was going to help you.'

'She was at college, of course. We didn't need her, we've hardly any furniture anyway and most of it was delivered by shops, a bit at a time, so there was plenty of time to unpack our boxes of personal stuff, and Gosia did most of that while Mawgan sorted out the kitchen; I swanned around ordering them about! We left most of Mawgan's furniture in the flat for Gosia and Roger, they're going to live there, and be in charge at night. Goodness knows when we'll find time to buy anything else, next winter I shouldn't wonder!'

It occurred to Dot that if she moved into a smaller house, she would have a lot of surplus furniture needing a home, but she said nothing. It was early days, and maybe Deborah wouldn't want it anyway. Young people seemed to like new things these days, apart, perhaps, from the antique footstool of course, and it would be interesting to see what Deborah had done with her new house. She had never seen the flat above the bars at the Fish, had no clues to go on, and for the first time the thought sent a thrill of shock through her; she should have seen it, it had been her daughter's first married home and she had lived there two years. She said, shaken by this realisation, 'It sounds as if you have everything worked out, then. Now you keep your feet up, and get to bed early. You need your rest, remember, for you won't get any when Baby arrives.'

'So everyone keeps telling me,' said Debbie. She laughed, a happy sound. 'Have you got a pen handy? I'll give you our home telephone number.'

Dot put the phone down ten minutes later, and looked around the big hall where Debbie's voice still seemed to echo. Yes, it was time to be gone from here. Mawgan had been right; the ghosts in this house were not necessarily happy ones, she would be glad to leave them behind her. She thought about a house in the country, green fields, village life. Benita Vachell could be a disrespectful young madam of course, but she was very entertaining and was turning out to be a good friend, and the Vachells owned land and property in and around Shearwater. To have Benita on her side would ensure her respect and welcome. She went into the drawing room and settled in a big armchair with the book that her new friend had made her buy, and as she sat down, she found herself thinking that this huge, luxuriously comfortable suite was one of the things that would have to go; a smaller house would never accommodate it.

Elizabeth Ballantyne's book held her attention happily until quite late into the night. The adventures of rather stuffy, uptight Aminta as she travelled from her middle-class roots to Europe in search of her Bohemian heritage were entertainingly told, and intelligently thought out: Dot would have said that it wouldn't be her kind of book at all, but she would have been wrong. Of course, Henry had been an intelligent man.

She wondered, as she read about Aminta's shock when she discovered she was adopted as she sorted out family papers after her parents' simultaneous death in an air crash, how much of all this was based on Susan, and found the idea sobering. Of course, Susan had known about the adoption, but she hadn't known about her brothers and sister, and for the first time it fully dawned on Dot how high-handed that had been of her. It was almost midnight before she finally put the book down and took herself to bed.

Just before seven o'clock in the morning, she was abruptly woken by the telephone on her bedside table shrilling in her ear. Groping for it sleepily, she put it to her ear. 'Hullo?'

'Did I wake you?' said her son-in law's voice. 'Sorry about that, I thought you'd want to know.' His voice sounded odd, as if he was drunk. Dot, who was nobody's fool, thought that he probably was, she may have been right.

'Know what?' she asked, but she already knew in her heart.

'You've one more grandchild. A couple of hours ago, all the excitement of moving in brought it on last night. Both of them are fine, but I'm not sure I am. What a carry on! Enough to put you off sex for life!'

'You surely weren't there at the birth!' said Dot, amazed.

'Course I was, what d'you think I am? My son, isn't he?'

'Quite the new man,' said Dot, verging on approval. She really wouldn't have thought it of him.

'At the moment,' said Mawgan, on a groan, 'I feel like a very, very old man. And they said it was an easy birth, easy as shelling peas, the midwife said. I tell you, you don't get all that shouting and yelling and stuff shelling peas in my kitchen!' He pulled himself together. 'They said they could come home tomorrow, my Mum said she'd come over to be with Deb if you couldn't get here at such short notice but Deb'd want you, I know, if you can.'

'I'll be there,' said Dot, briskly. Then her voice softened. 'Who does he look like?'

'Me, sorry about that. Living spit. Deb said you'd think to look at him she'd had nothing to do with it at all.'

'I expect I can live with that,' said Dot, thinking about a squarish, dark, miniature thug with tenderness. Dot loved babies, something

250

that had come as a surprise, for her first close encounters with one – Oliver, to be her perennial *bête noir* for ever as it turned out – had been unfortunate, to say the least. She thought wryly that Helen would be astonished if she knew how much Dot had learned from her observed example and put to use with her daughters – particularly Debbie – and with her grandchildren. 'You go and get yourself some sleep,' she said now. 'You sound exhausted.'

'Got to go and do some work,' said Mawgan, and Dot heard herself saying, 'Don't be silly! You need sleep! Phone whoever is your second in command, tell them you'll be along later. That's not advice, that's an order, you'll poison somebody or cut your fingers off if you try to cook in your sleep! We can't have you falling apart, Deborah will need you!'

She heard the faint ghost of a laugh on the line. 'P'raps you're right. See you tomorrow then, sorry if I woke you.'

Dot replaced the phone and sat up. Sleep had gone, there were things to arrange, if she was going to be away from tomorrow! Time to get up and start arranging them! She flung back the duvet and headed for her bathroom, and as she prepared herself for the day ahead, she thought that she was deeply impressed with Mawgan, although it would never do to tell him so. Jerry had never done that, and Henry certainly wouldn't have even had he been there to do so, quite out of the question for men of his generation. She allowed herself a brief, regretful twinge; she had been fond of Henry and recently she had found herself, to her surprise, wishing that he was still there, which, she had also noticed, was something she didn't wish about Jerry. Of course, in her day the term "birth partner" had yet to be invented, but she privately considered it a very good idea. Not only did it give support to the women, but it showed the men exactly where their lustful ways could lead! Salutary for them – it had certainly sounded as if it had been salutary for her son-in-law!

How would Carl react in the same circumstances? she found herself wondering as she went downstairs to get her breakfast. Carl was her favourite, no doubt of it, but she did fear that he would never be put to the test. Susan seemed to have decided against more children, heart set on this archaeology business, selfish girl! Then she had a thought that was so novel, it made her falter in her tracks. *It's not my business, however.* She dismissed it, but it would return.

Dot spent a busy day, arranging with Leanne that she would come in every other day to check the house while its owner was absent, ringing round her friends to announce the birth of her new grandson, and packing carefully for the west country last-stand-of-winter weather; muggy and damp, she understood. She went carefully through her fridge and gave all the perishables to Leanne. There would, she realised, be no point in going to her daughter's house bearing supplies; she was married to a chef after all, and by this time, whatever her other remaining reservations, Dot had no doubt that he would feed her properly. She took her car to the garage to fill it up with petrol for her journey, cancelled a hair appointment and one with her chiropodist, and by the time evening came was more than ready to settle down again with her really rather entertaining book and a background of irreproachable music on Classic FM.

By this time, Aminta had reached Italy and met up with her artist father in a waterside village that Elizabeth Ballantyne had described with such loving care that Dot could almost see it. She had met a dashing young Italian fisherman, and Dot found herself shaking her head: that would never do. But now there came, hotfoot in pursuit, the heroine's rather stodgy *fiancé*, determined to bring her quest to a close and take her home. Easy to guess what would happen next, Dot thought, somehow disappointed in this easy solution; Aminta, now trying out her original baptismal name of Gianetta for size, would send him on his way and settle for life in Tuscany with her young Italian, and learn to paint and be artistic and carefree and live the Bohemian life. Probably Dot decided from what little she knew of popular fiction, the young fisherman would turn out to be the son of a rich man, or possibly someone very well-known on the stage or in the arts, fleeing from fame to recover from a breakdown, and they would all live happily ever after.

But no. When she came to the end of the book and turned the final page, there was the dull, plodding Edward living it up with a Hungarian singer called Magda, and Aminta, having kissed her fisherman goodbye with no hard feelings on either side, waiting at the airport for a flight. Nurture had won over nature: she hadn't felt at ease with Gianetta, or like a real daughter to her charismatic but self-centred Italian father, and was returning home to be Aminta, and to her teaching post in the small west country town where she had been born and had grown up. The final scene had her sitting in her seat on the aeroplane thinking about her adoptive parents, and saying to them in her head, *It was good to find out where my roots are, and I think I learned a lot about living and loving, but you were my real parents, and I'm glad I have your names.*

Dot closed the book. It had been intelligent, funny, thought-provoking, and ultimately, as Gianetta/Aminta left her natural father behind to return to the happy memories that constituted home for her, moving. She wondered if Susan felt like that about Jerry, and thought with a slight feeling of guilt that she probably didn't. She had made Jerry betray Susan in the same way that she herself had done, keeping her heritage from her; she didn't think Susan was finding that easy to live with. Unlike the parents of Aminta, they hadn't managed to give her anything better in return; Susan, she knew, had always felt second best and she might as well admit, had grown up in a breaking home not surrounded by love like Elizabeth Ballantyne's heroine.

She tucked the book carefully into a space in her bookcase and again went thoughtfully to bed.

Armed with directions that Susan had given her over the phone, Dot found her way up to the headland without difficulty, although she did nearly miss the turn off. She hadn't been expecting such an insignificant approach to the fine house in the picture she had seen, and was astonished when at the last minute she spotted the signboard, *Waterways House*, with its arrow that pointed down an unpromising little lane. There was a car parked on the tarmac outside the house when she reached it, but it was neither Debbie's nor Mawgan's, and it was Chel who opened the door to her.

Some of their history had been epic; on one occasion Oliver had rejected her kindly meant advice and help with the threat of actual violence, and Cheryl had virtually thrown her out of the house, Dot recalled, and was surprised and wasn't pleased to find that the recollection made her uncomfortable rather than righteously indignant. Well, she had travelled a long road since, she thought grimly, and at least Cheryl was smiling now. She came forward and kissed Dot on the cheek, not exactly warmly, but at least it felt mildly friendly.

'You've got here safely! Did you have a good journey? Let me get your bag for you.' She lifted Dot's suitcase out of the boot of her car and led the way through the front door into a cool, slate floored hallway with a spiral staircase curling upwards on the left and a ceiling that soared away to a raftered roof – a roof that from the looks of it, went the entire depth of the house, for the staircase ended on what seemed to be a balcony. Chel led the way through an open door into a sitting room with a log fire blazing in a wide hearth and opened a door on the left, leading the way into a small lobby with more doors on every side. 'That's the bathroom,' she told Dot, nodding to the one straight ahead. 'The two bedrooms share it, but there's nobody in the other one – actually, there's no bed. This is yours, Deb put you down here because it's warm.' She pushed open the right-hand door and stood aside to let Dot pass ahead of her.

The room was big and full of light from a window that faced towards the sea. Built in cupboards with a dressing table, and a bed but very little else. One small table beside the bed to take a lamp, tiles underfoot with a cream flokati rug to step onto in the mornings. A wonderful view down a terraced garden to what appeared to be a low wall bounding a cliff edge and then the sparkling water of Falmouth Bay stretching to a hazy coastline with a lighthouse, tiny at this distance, visible on a headland. No radiator to be seen, but the room was certainly comfortably warm; Dot surmised the existence of underfloor heating, very sophisticated.

'This is very pleasant,' she said.

'Gorgeous, isn't it?' agreed Chel. She hesitated, she never felt at ease with Dot, never even knew quite what to call her. 'Mawgan said to apologise for his not being here, he had to go down to the Rose, and then he's straight off to collect Debbie and Daniel, he asked me to be here to welcome you and give you some lunch.' She didn't add that the choice had been between herself and Gosia, and they had decided that she was the lesser of two evils. 'I'll leave you to unpack then, shall I? Come through when you're ready. I'll be in the kitchen.' She left the room.

Dot unpacked and hung her clothes carefully, had a wash in the beautifully fitted bathroom supplied with fat new towels, and went back into the sitting room. A door beside the fireplace was open onto a room beyond, and she could hear someone moving around and talking, so she followed the sound. At first, she thought that Cheryl was listening to the radio, but as she walked through into a spacious kitchen/dining room, she realised that there was someone else present. A very small baby in a reclining baby chair sat on the worktop where she could see what was going on, and it was to her that Cheryl spoke. She broke off as Dot came in.

'This is Zoë,' said Chel. She lifted the baby out of the chair and held her out to Dot. 'Give her a cuddle, while I finish the lunch, she's grumbling I'm not paying attention to her.' Dot held out her arms and Cheryl placed the child in them. 'There Zoë darling, this is your Grandma – your third grandma, aren't you a lucky girl?'

The child was warm and light, wriggling in her arms. Dot said, 'I'm not really her Grandma, Cheryl, but that was kind.'

'Of course you are.' Chel and Oliver had had a talk about this, and Oliver had come, reluctantly, round to Chel's point of view – and Susan's and Debbie's – that a new approach might produce a new reaction, and a happier one. 'You brought her father up from a small child, what else are you?' She noted that Zoë snuggled into Dot quite happily, and that Dot held her gently and, it had to be faced, lovingly. She said nothing, however, and after a pause, Dot said, 'She's very small, for six months, Cheryl.'

'I know,' said Chel. She looked rueful. 'You should have seen her when she was born, she was like a little doll, she could nearly lie in the palm of Oliver's hand. It seems you were right all along, I'm not the best breeding female on the planet, hormones all out of step or something, and she's lucky to be here, but she's doubled her birth weight and she's here to stay.' She laughed then. 'Only Daniel is already nearly as heavy as she is, and he's only a day old!' She added, without looking at Dot, 'I think it made Oliver feel a little ... well, less responsible I suppose, when we were told that, and by the way, thank you so much for looking after Jeremy at Christmas. Susan told me. It was dear of you.'

'It was a pleasure to do it for you both,' Dot murmured, her attention on the living child in her arms. 'She's a beautiful little girl, Cheryl. You must be so ...' She couldn't think of a word, and said, 'pleased,' knowing it to be inadequate.

'The living image of her daddy, however,' said Chel. She turned away from the stove, a steaming saucepan in her hand. 'I can see I'll have my hands full before long! Mawgan says Daniel is the same – the image of him, that is. Apparently it's a ruse of nature so that the fathers don't desert the young, dead cunning, old Mother N, wouldn't you say?' It seemed odd to be having a sensible conversation with Dot, she couldn't remember ever having one before. She said, 'Oxtail soup, Mawgan thought you might be chilly after that long drive, is that all right?'

There was a pause while Chel poured the soup into two bowls, which gave both of them time to think that if Chel had listened to Dot at the time, maybe Jeremy would be here, a lively four-year-old racing around the place, but it wasn't something that either of them felt able to say. Chel carried the bowls over to the dining table, where places were laid for two.

'How about madam, here?' asked Dot, and Chel said, 'I'll feed her later, she's fine now – she's a bit young for oxtail soup, particularly this oxtail soup.'

'It smells home made,' said Dot appreciatively, taking her place at the table.

'Mawgan made it.' Chel held out her arms for the baby. 'No tins and packets in this house! Give her to me, I'll put her back in her chair, where she can watch us,' but Zoë objected to this plan with noisy indignation, and Dot said, 'Let me hold her, Cheryl. It's such a long time since I had a baby to cuddle.'

'She'll spill your soup,' Chel warned, but Dot smiled and said no, she wouldn't, and Chel thought how different she looked smiling and tried to remember if she had ever seen such a kindly look on her face before. People are at least partly how you treat them, she thought, and remembering Jerry's abiding love for Helen, and Oliver's continuing resentment at the loss of his mother, she felt all of a sudden very sorry for Dot; lovely Helen had been an ongoing disaster for her. She thought that her recent behaviour and the resultant salutary shock had mellowed Dot in a way, but it hadn't made her whole. She wasn't sure what would – or could. Beneath the chastened exterior there would still be the woman that life had made her: confrontational, bossy, totally lacking in understanding of other people.

But perhaps, Chel thought unexpectedly, it was lack of understanding *in* other people, such as Jerry and Oliver and Helen, for instance, that had hardened her attitude over the years. Nonie, she knew, had always had reservations, although Helen and Oliver had shouted her down. But Jerry ... he had married her for some reason, so also Henry Worthington, for whom only hearsay evidence remained.

256

Nobody, Chel reasoned, threw themselves into the pit of hell for no reason, so there was another Dot. Too late to change her radically now, but if they could *understand* her, as Susan maintained, would she be easier to live with? Certainly it would be impossible to shut her out of the family circle, Susan and Debbie would never allow it – for which they, too, must have their reasons. She looked at Dot, talking to the baby between drinking her soup, and felt herself softening. Perhaps they should all throw a six and start the game again?

The fruit and cheese that followed the soup being eaten, Chel washed up, refusing help -only two bowls and the side plates, no problem – made up the fire, and then looked at her watch.

'Will you forgive me if I leave you now? Deb and Mawgan'll be here soon, and I ought to be doing some work after taking the morning off. I've a business to manage down the hill.'

'What about the baby?' Dot asked, reluctant to relinquish her, but Chel said that Gosia would look after her for a couple of hours after she had guzzled her lunch.

'She usually does that every morning. It's a brilliant arrangement, she's wonderful with children, then when I'm not working she goes down to the sailing school and helps there.' It sounded very casual to Dot, but the baby looked contented enough. No doubt Deborah would do something similar with little Daniel when the spring came. Dot couldn't approve, but she appreciated the practicality of the arrangement, even if it did involve the Maria girl. She contented herself with saying, 'Life was very different when I was bringing up a family,' and they parted, if not on friendly terms, at least closer to that happy state than ever before, and Dot was left alone.

She stood listening to the sound of Cheryl's car receding up the lane, taking that darling little baby with her, and then the silence of the house closed around her. There was no traffic noise so far from the road, no distant human voices, nothing. Just silence.

Dot sat by the fire for a while, listening to the crackle of the logs and thinking how quiet it was. Then after a while, the quiet began to get on her nerves; in Embridge there was always some sound, aeroplanes overhead, passing cars, lawnmowers, dogs barking. Here on the headland, in the middle of February, there was nothing, not even birdsong. After a while she got to her feet and began wandering around the room.

It was a pleasant room, even a beautiful one. Good furniture, Dot noticed approvingly, not too much of it. Nice pictures, not too many of them. Just the right amount of books in a polished bookcase, Deborah had good taste. A guitar was propped against this last item of furniture; knowing that Debbie had never played such a thing, she presumed it belonged to her grandson's father. Hmm ... She ended up by the window, looking out into the early afternoon sunshine.

The winter sunlight dappled through the slatted pergola outside onto a tiled patio, beyond was the distant view of sea. Some climber, dry and dead at this time of year, twined around the stone supports at the corners and across the slats above, dark green covers disguised and protected what must be patio chairs and tables. It would be lovely out there in the summer. She imagined herself sitting there, the baby in his pram beside her, summer warmth on her face and the cool sea breeze fanning across the sunlit garden while Mawgan and Debbie went with easy minds about their respective businesses. There would be birds singing, and small boats darting across the now almost deserted expanse of the bay. Only a couple of big ships lay at anchor today.

Dot turned away to find something else to inspect. She had already seen the kitchen and the dining area, very nice. She wouldn't pry behind closed doors, Deborah would want to show her round herself, but she thought she just might go upstairs to the room above this one, which was, after all, totally open to inspection. The view from there should be wonderful.

Tutting a little over the spiral staircase, for she considered such things dangerous, particularly for small children, Dot made her way upstairs to the big room above. As she had thought, the open rafters went the whole way over from the entrance hall beneath the ridge of the roof, but she was pleased to see that the divider above the stairwell was too high for a child to climb over, and there was also a built-in bookcase running its whole length, pretty well filled with books and magazines. Above a fireplace that was this time little more than a square hole in the wall hung a beautiful oil painting of a row of moored boats and some deep looking, very clear water; peering at it, Dot noted without surprise the signature, *Nankervis*, and a tiny date that she couldn't read without her glasses. Apart from an impractical cream carpet, which Daniel would no doubt soon put in its place, the only other furnishings were the oatmeal linen curtains hanging beside the french windows that formed the whole of the outside wall. There were three doors; one either side of the fireplace, one on the centre of the opposite wall. The doorways were arched, the doors of pale golden oak, matching those downstairs. It was a huge space, very beautiful and very empty. It occurred to Dot that her big suite would look good up here, *if* she really did move, she hadn't yet made up her mind finally. The suite needed a big room, this enormous room needed a suite. But perhaps Debbie and Mawgan wouldn't want second-hand furniture. Perhaps they had different ideas of their own.

Unaware that this last thought on its own was a huge step forward, allowing as it did space for the opinions of other people, Dot returned downstairs to inspect the bookcase there and enjoy the warmth and comfort of the fire. Debbie had a line of four paperbacks by Elizabeth Ballantyne, none of them the one that Dot had already read. She selected one and settled back in her armchair. This book had been signed by the author, *to Debbie with my love, Liz xxx*, and her full signature. Dot studied it for a long time, her thoughts full of Liz's grandfather.

It must have been half an hour later that the sound of voices at the front door brought her out of her reverie. Setting the book aside, she rose to her feet and was there to greet her most beloved child as she came into the sitting room with a child of her own cradled in her arms.

'Mum!' Debbie walked in, and straight into her mother's embrace, the child she held snuggled between them. 'Look what I've got!' She gently eased the baby into Dot's arms and stood back smiling. Dot looked down and fell in love. After Zoë's light, wriggling weight and delicate feminine features, this one was every inch a boy; heavy and warm in her arms, a perfect little replica of his Cornish father; dark, chunky, and if Dot wasn't much mistaken, trouble on the way. *All* the way too, she thought, and was slightly shocked to realise that she had also thought, he could do worse than take after his father. This would never do!

'Well! There's no blaming this one on the milkman!' she said, and Debbie laughed.

'Never fancied the milkman anyway,' she said.

'He was too posh for 'er liking,' said Mawgan, coming through the door with Debbie's bag, and leaving, thought Dot with resignation, his aspirates on the doorstep. She only stopped herself laughing with an effort, and looked down at the child in her arms. 'Sit down Deborah and I'll give this big lad to you while I make us a nice cup of tea. Your husb – Mawgan, can take your bag upstairs. Do you have a cradle down here?'

'There's a pram in the front room.' Debbie sat down obediently and held out her arms for her child. 'Mawgan'll fetch it in a minute. What do you think of him, Mum?'

'Mawgan or Daniel?' asked Dot, moving towards the kitchen, and Debbie looked at her in surprise. 'And I never thought to hear that expression on the lips of a child of mine! *Front room* indeed!' The accompanying shudder was implicit in the tone.

'Front room, as opposed to the back one where you're sleeping,' Debbie explained, grinning. 'Do you like your room, Mum? We thought it would be nicely distanced from all the squawking at night.'

'It's a lovely room, Deborah,' said Dot, and went hastily into the kitchen. Once safely there, she stood for a moment with her hands resting on the black marble worktop, staring at the kettle without seeing it. She had put the unfamiliar warmth of Christmas largely down to Susan and Carl and the children, but here in this unfamiliar, beautiful, empty house, it was here again. Not just Debbie, which might be expected. Cheryl too, and little Zoë, and now Mawgan as well, surely a symptom of a whole new approach. And if that was so ... if that was so, it behoved her to make an effort too. She had nearly laughed out loud just now, next time she would let herself do so. You never knew, it might feel good to climb down off her dignity, dear Benita had said that she was always riding her high horse. She had said it laughing, but she had then added that Dot should dismount occasionally, look around and see the flowers. Dot wasn't certain that she would be very good at seeing the flowers, but she could make the effort to try, surely, when everyone else seemed to be trying.

They wouldn't try, any of them, if they didn't feel there was something to be gained from it. The thought was oddly comforting. She switched on the kettle and looked around for cups and saucers, finding only mugs. She lifted three down and ranged them beside the kettle, shaking her head, just as Mawgan came through into the kitchen and caught her at it. She looked at him with a challenge in her eyes. 'I'm sure you don't serve tea in mugs in your restaurant,' she told him. Mawgan tried to look chastened, and failed.

'They are the very *best* bone china,' he wheedled. Dot looked at the mugs, feeling that unfamiliar laughter in the background again. So they were.

'Hmm,' she said. He was different on his own territory, she decided; people often were. The question was, was she a match for him? She certainly hadn't been over the wedding, a recollection which made a hot wave of shame run across her face, and she looked away from him swiftly. Mawgan didn't appear to have noticed, he was quietly assembling a bottle of milk, golden sugar, and a tin of biscuits – home-made biscuits, Dot noted approvingly as he removed the lid, and pulled herself up short. It would never do to *approve* of him! He was a chef, that was all, doing what chefs do.

Mawgan swiftly gathered the mugs of milked tea, the sugar basin and the biscuits onto a tray and stood back to allow his mother-in-law to pass ahead of him into the big living room, Dot was glad to see that he left the milk bottle where it was. Debbie, in the meantime, had fetched the pram from the eponymous front room and tucked her new baby snugly in a blanket before resuming her comfortable armchair. Dot felt an urge to assert herself in this new atmosphere, and looked disapproving. 'You should have waited for one of us to do that for you,' she scolded. 'I'm surprised that Susan isn't here to lend a hand.'

'Susan's at college, and she's a family of her own to worry about,' Debbie pointed out. She accepted a mug of tea with a smile. 'Thanks Mum. Look, I can't stand around like a barn door, I'm a woman who's used to an active life. I can't turn into a couch potato – a *mashed* couch potato. Have a heart!'

'You should rest up while you have the chance, while I'm here to look after you. Your life will be active enough soon, believe me! In my day, you wouldn't have even been allowed home for a week yet.'

'Then I'm glad this is *my* day,' Debbie retorted, with spirit. 'Come on Mum, don't try and wrap me in cotton wool! It's a perfectly natural process, having a baby!'

'That's not what you were saying two days ago,' Mawgan remarked. 'A biscuit, Mrs Nankervis? You've had a long drive, you must need stoking.' Dot looked at him suspiciously.

'Are you setting up as a diplomat, young man?'

'No way.' Mawgan grinned at her, he was certainly very charming when he tried! 'Not me, I value my hide too much. Me, I'm going to start on the dinner,' and on that word, he rose to his feet and retreated into the kitchen.

Dot settled back into her chair. The biscuit was melt-in-the-mouth delicious. A snuffling noise came from the pram – not what Dot would have called a pram, more a fancy pushchair – and Debbie leaned over to inspect her son. Dot watched her, and unexpectedly felt her heart swell with a love that took her by surprise. She realised that she had viewed this inescapable visit with something approaching trepidation, and now that she was here, it seemed that she had been worrying over nothing. And she hadn't expected that her son-in-law would be taking such a hands-on attitude towards his new family; although it was no doubt of necessity temporary, it showed a proper attitude and boded well not only for the future but for the catering over the next few days. Life was not so bad.

Maybe Benita had a point.

See the flowers ...

XIV

Liz arrived in St Erbyn on Friday evening, as yet unaware that Daniel had made his slightly premature appearance in the world and that she was about to run the gauntlet of Dot. Susan hadn't rung to inform her; although Liz was the one of the Worthingtons who knew Debbie best, even that wasn't well, she had felt the news would wait until she saw her; of the others, only Alice and Gil and the children had even met her. Nor was she certain that there wasn't a more subtle reason for her omission: if Liz didn't know that Dot was likely to be there, there was no reason for her to postpone her visit. She put it to herself no more plainly than that. There was also, of course, the irrational apprehension that she had harboured of Liz never visiting again after Paul's behaviour in the Fish to weigh in the scales of her judgement.

'So long as he doesn't just turn up again,' said Carl, voicing a secret fear that Susan shared.

'I shouldn't think he would,' said Susan, but doubtfully, for Paul's personal arrogance was phenomenal.

'You don't sound certain,' Carl observed. 'Don't worry – I agree with you. And if he does, we needn't offer him a bed this time.'

'Then Liz will go, too. Like she did last time.'

Carl made no comment on this. He thought that Liz would have to sort herself out over Paul, nobody was going to do it for her. Then, when she did arrive, it appeared that she had done so – up to a point, anyway. 'I thought I could gradually discourage him until he gets the message,' she told them, over a glass of wine round the kitchen table, after the children had gone upstairs. 'There's no need to fall out, we still have to meet each other after all, and we've been together a while. Some of it's been fun – a lot of it has, really. But I haven't told him where I am, I let him think it wasn't here ... and if he does turn up, after that, I shall ... I shall ...' She broke into nervous giggles and took a sip of wine.

'That'll fix him,' said Carl admiringly. Liz put down her glass.

'The trouble is, he doesn't seem to listen to anything I say,' she said.

'He doesn't, does he?'

'Even after I said I wouldn't be home, he said he'd come down anyway and look after the cottage for me, feed Tib and everything.'

'And what did you say?' asked Susan, with interest, for this sounded to her almost like stalking. Liz shook her head, trying to shake off a memory.

'I said he needn't bother.' She gave them both a guarded look, and added, 'Then I got Gil to change the locks for me.'

There was a silence.

'Wasn't that a bit ... extreme?' asked Susan, to break it. Liz shrugged her shoulders. 'So what if he does go down, and can't get in?' Susan pursued

'He'll have to go home again. Maybe he'll believe me then.'

Carl and Susan exchanged a look. 'He'll certainly believe *something*,' said Carl. 'Did you tell your neighbours what you'd done?'

'Of course, they feed my cat for me. I didn't say *why*, naturally. Why do you ask?'

'No reason.' He looked at Susan. 'What do you think?'

It was now Susan's turn to shrug. Liz said, changing a subject that had begun to make her vaguely uncomfortable, 'So tell me about this baby of Deb and Mawgan's. Annabel and Seb seem to think he's wonderful, they've been telling me all about him. Seb's a bit offhand, mind, but you can see he's impressed.'

'Not that there's a lot to tell, really.' Susan reached for the bottle and refilled Liz's glass. 'He's just a baby. Yells a lot, sleeps a lot, makes a lot of washing. There's something the matter with me, I can't get excited over babies even if they're quite sweet, like this one.'

'Me neither,' admitted Liz. 'It must be some sort of gene thing. Alice wasn't rapturous either, and she had twins! Although come to think, that might've had something to do with it.'

'Mother thinks he's perfect, thank goodness, in fact it all seems to be going very well up there,' said Susan, without thinking, and Liz looked up. The children hadn't mentioned their grandmother, and come to that, neither had Susan and Carl up until now.

'Your mother? Has she been down already?'

'She's here now,' said Susan, as airily as she could manage.

'Oh,' said Liz, taken aback. Carl grinned at her.

'This *is* going to be an interesting weekend, one way and another, isn't it?' he observed.

'Come on Liz,' said Susan, with some justification. 'It was you who said at Christmas that perhaps you should all go out and come in again.'

'Whoo!' said Liz. 'I didn't expect you to take me literally.'

'How else did you mean me to take it?' asked Susan, with interest, and Liz said lamely, 'Some warning would have been good.'

'It can't be that bad,' offered Susan, after a pause. 'She's sitting up there reading her way through your novels.'

'Is she?' said Liz, faintly. Her heart was bumping, she realised. She hadn't meant to put herself into the centre of a family feud, she'd have been better off at home with Paul. After another pause, she added, 'But why should your mother read my books?'

'A good question.'

'She must know who I am.'

'Presumably, or – forgive me – she wouldn't be doing it. But she hasn't said.' Liz said nothing, and after waiting for the response that obviously wasn't going to come, Susan went on, 'We'll go up after breakfast tomorrow to introduce you to Daniel. And take it from there.'

Carl diplomatically poured more wine, and Susan got up to put the kettle on. 'Let's have some coffee – Liz?'

'You really think I need something more to keep me awake tonight?' Liz asked, looking at her askance. 'Oh, all right then. And now, can we talk about something more soothing? How's Mawgan doing in the dad stakes?'

'Fine. He can't exactly take time off, but it's not *too* busy at the Rose in February and he manages to spend a fair amount at home – cooks the dinner for them before he heads down the road, generally makes himself useful. Mother is mildly approving, particularly as he was there at the birth.'

'Good heavens, was he? Whatever did he make of that? I shouldn't have thought it was his kind of thing, I'd have said he was the classic unreconstructed alpha male!'

'You'll have to ask him. He came home a gibbering wreck, that we do know,' said Carl, with all the complacence of a man who was never likely to be put through the experience.

'Don't blame him,' said Liz, shuddering.

'It can't have come as *that* much of a shock to a man who's accustomed to skinning rabbits and gutting pheasants,' Susan contributed, more callously. She resumed her seat at the table while she waited for the kettle, but her comment had turned out to be a bit of a conversation-stopper, and nobody seemed able to come up with a response. In the minds of her two more imaginative literary companions, who in any case had no hands-on experience, she had called up some fairly graphic horrors, and they found nothing to say.

After a moment, choosing the lesser of two evils, Liz said, out of the blue, 'Does she know I'm here?'

'Probably. Deb will have mentioned it,' said Susan. Carl, who wasn't certain that Susan was approaching this situation from the right direction, made no comment, and Liz heaved a sigh.

'You're right, Carl. Tomorrow is going to be interesting.'

Annabel came with them the next morning. Susan wasn't sure if this was a good thing or a bad, but there was nothing she could do about it. There was no school, being a Saturday, and Seb had sloped off somewhere with his friend Ben from the village, Carl claimed somebody needed to put in some work in the office down at the sailing school – taking the coward's way out, Susan considered – and Annabel had wanted to see the baby again, and her grandmother, and it was really quite impossible to say no, so it was three of them got into Susan's car after breakfast.

Dot knew that they were coming. For all she considered herself a sensible grown-up, and one moreover who had originally been in the right, the thought of meeting one of the contentious Worthingtons after all these years had given her a bad night. The few days that she had spent in her son-in-law's house had set her to wondering if you could be both right and wrong at the same time – right, that is, in her initial attitude to the man whom Mawgan had seemed to be, but wrong in her approach to the problem. She had wondered, in the still, three o'clock watch of the winter night, if she had done the same with the Worthingtons. She had been in the right over the will, of that she had no doubt: what Henry had chosen to do with his money was entirely down to him, not to her, and not really the province of his children either. And yes, Carol Worthington had made trouble; yes, she had been in the wrong to do so, but in the period immediately following the row she had caused, both Owen and Isobel had tried to keep in touch and it was she, hurt and miserable and feeling, not for the first time in her life, betrayed, who had put up the barriers. At this distance, she wasn't sure exactly why: she had liked Henry's children before he died, and Isobel, she remembered, had always been sweet to her. Liz was Isobel's daughter, how was she likely to behave?

But it was at this point that Dot began to lose her way. For Mawgan, when it came down to it, had behaved to her with what she was beginning to realise was characteristic generosity. He had agreed to make the initial step towards resolving their problems, and he had done it, she now saw, because he loved Debbie in a way that made Dot, who had never been loved, she believed, in any way at all, want to sit down and cry, except that she would never let herself do anything so feeble. Liz, however, was a different matter. Liz was here on her own business, not Dot's, she wasn't directly involved in the family feud having been only a toddler at the time, she was a wild card. Dot had no idea how much, or how little, Liz might know about first causes, nor how such information would have been presented to her. The only things she knew about Liz at all were first, that it was she who had given Susan her passport back into the Worthington family, and second, that her books were written with insight and compassion.

Mawgan, whose presence might have put a brake on the situation, was down at the Rose, like Carl attending to his business; there was only Debbie, reeling under the reality shock of broken nights and her child's total dependency, albeit with rueful laughter; Susan, torn both ways in this quandary, and the oblivious Annabel to cushion the impact. Annabel, fortunately, came up trumps. She rushed into the room and ran to hug her grandmother. 'Grandma! Look, it's me, are you surprised?'

Dot, staggering under the collision, had barely time to glance at Liz, who caught Susan's eye, shrugged her shoulders with an almost imperceptible lift, and went with the flow. There was really nothing else to do. As Annabel stepped aside and ran to peer into the pushchair, Liz stepped into her place. 'Am I allowed to say the same?' she asked with a smile, and leaned forward to kiss Dot lightly on the cheek. 'Hullo Gran, remember me? And I bet you're surprised to see me, too!'

Annabel stared. It hadn't occurred to her to work out the relationship between her grandmother and her mother's niece, possibly she wasn't consciously aware that there was one. Susan thought you could almost see the cogs revolving behind her eyes. Dot's hand went to her cheek where Liz's kiss had landed. 'Of course I remember you,' she said, briskly to cover her confusion, and ventured on one of the first jokes of her life. 'How you've grown, Elizabeth!'

'I should hope so! How old was I? Two?'

'About that. How very nice to see you again now.'

'But,' said Annabel, puzzling it out, 'Grandma isn't *your* grandma, Liz.'

'Oh yes she is – well, near enough.' Liz grinned at her. 'Think about it, if your mother is my aunt ...?'

'But that's just a joke ...' said Annabel, uncertainly now.

Explaining the relationship glossed over any awkwardness, consigned it to history. It was then that Debbie made her entrance from the kitchen, her arms full of neatly folded baby clothes, looking so unfamiliar in this mumsy guise that Susan burst out laughing, partly from sheer relief.

'Good grief, look at you! Quite the yummy mummy!'

'Don't you start.' Debbie put her pile down on the coffee table. 'Hullo Liz, on your own this time?'

'Hopefully. Congratulations on your son. May I see him?'

'Of course you can.' Debbie rootled purposefully in the pushchair and hauled him out. 'Here he is. Isn't he gorgeous?'

'Deborah, you clear that table and I'll make some coffee for us all,' said Dot, and escaped to the kitchen. It was a lovely room, she considered, spacious and light and beautifully fitted, with a wide and soothing view from its windows over the garden and the bay beyond. A scarlet Aga against the inside wall kept it warm and added character, and in the centre, a more sophisticated dual fuel cooking stove took up part of an island unit. At the other end, a scrubbed refectory table and eight antique ladder-back chairs occupied what would, with the addition of a bit more furniture, make a pleasant dining area. Concentrating on its charms was soothing, and prevented her from thinking of other things, for truth to tell, Liz's greeting had taken her aback. She busied herself with the kettle and the despised mugs and tried to put space between herself and the incident, but before the kettle had boiled the door was pushed open and Liz came through, the very last person whom Dot was ready to see. They looked at each other. Both of them knew that Liz was right, there was only one way to handle this, but both of them hesitated. It was Liz, finally, who spoke first, an uncontroversial opening designed to defuse potential dynamite.

'I came to see if there was anything to do. They're all baby-worshipping in there.'

'He is a dear little baby,' said Dot. The kettle boiled, and she poured water into the *cafetière*, very carefully.

'Yes.' Liz hesitated. 'I think that Mum would like it if you got in touch. Now we've met Susan ... well, a lot of dirty linen has had an airing. I think it would be a good thing to do.'

'I don't think so, Elizabeth,' said Dot, concentrating on what she was doing.

'Why not? It's all a long time ago, and Susan gave Carol a right rollicking anyway. You could try,' Liz coaxed. 'If you sent a letter, you'd never know how it was received, it's hardly going to tell you, is it? And if you never got a reply, what have you lost? Although you would.'

It was what the reply might deservedly be that bothered Dot's conscience. She said, 'Your mother can't possibly want to hear from me after all these years.'

'She loves Susan,' said Liz, gently. 'We all do.'

'That's very good to know – but no, Elizabeth. There's too much history.'

'Water under the bridge,' said Liz.

'Cannot be called back,' replied Dot. She picked up the tray. 'If you would just open the door for me –'

'Just think about it,' Liz persuaded, going obediently to the door. Dot didn't reply, but walked past her with the tray to rejoin her family in the living room. Liz sighed, and followed. Well, nobody could say she hadn't tried. She just found herself wondering if perhaps she should or could have tried harder, although it would have been hard with someone who simply walked away. She wondered how much walking away Dot had done in the past, and if it was a habit, and if so, why.

Over the coffee, they all kept to safely non-contentious subjects; the baby, how Debbie was coping (remarkably well, said Dot approvingly), how Annabel was getting on at school, where she was now in her last year before going on to senior school in Truro. When the conversation began to flag, in part because Annabel, who had been keeping things afloat very nicely, seemed to have run out of steam, Liz said, 'This is a lovely house, Deb. I never realised it was so big, just seeing it in pictures.'

'Not that big,' Debbie contradicted. 'It's more spacious than lots of rooms. Only five bedrooms, and we'll be using one of the downstairs ones as an office, so we can spend more time here.'

'Only five bedrooms, ha!' said Liz. 'I've got two.'

Debbie grinned at her. 'I'll show you round, if you'd like. Make you really jealous.'

'Thank you, I would like.'

Daniel was sound asleep, so they all went on the tour, and Liz was impressed. 'What a fantastic place, and so simple! And just look at that view, it's to die for!'

They were standing in the big, empty upstairs room – one of three big, empty upstairs rooms, for the bedrooms to the left, a repeat of those below, were bare of anything beyond carpets and curtains – and the view was looking its best, bathed in sunshine, the sea sparkling and swathes of brave daffodils blowing in the garden. Debbie heaved a great sigh of satisfaction. 'It is, isn't it? Do you know, to start with I wasn't sure about it, it was Mawgan that had set his heart on it, but now we're really here, I love it. I can't imagine how I ever thought I wouldn't.'

'Hard to please, some people,' Liz observed. 'But how are you ever going to furnish it? It's huge!'

'Slowly,' Debbie replied, and they all laughed, and as they did so, the idea that was up until that moment still only tentative in Dot's mind suddenly crystallised and became a definite resolve. She said,

270

'If it would be of any help to you, Deborah, I shall be clearing out some of my larger pieces of furniture, maybe you could accommodate them?' She looked around her at the big empty room. 'My big suite, for instance, would be just right in here.'

Debbie and Susan both gaped at her, this was news to them. 'Why would you clear out stuff?' asked Susan, and Debbie said, 'You mean that lovely big squashy one in the drawing room? Mum it would look perfect in here! You don't mean it?'

Dot said, pleased with the sensation she had made, 'I have been seriously considering moving to a smaller house now that you are all gone away. I really don't need seven bedrooms just for me and the occasional visit from you people.'

It was Liz's turn to gape now. '*Seven* bedrooms! It must be a mansion!'

'It is a very large and handsome house,' agreed Dot complacently. 'Too big for me now, however.'

'But where would you go?' Susan asked, sounding indignant. She hadn't intended to.

'Have you looked at anywhere?' Debbie asked, more practically.

'I have looked at some details, but not so far of anything I wished to take further,' Dot replied, smiling.

'Seven bedrooms would be a hard act to follow, I imagine,' said Liz, almost to herself, and Annabel giggled.

'It's not a good time of year for buying and selling houses,' said Susan, thinking. 'It'll be better next month, I daresay. Would you stay in the same part of town you're in now?'

'Actually, I thought I might move further out, into the country,' said Dot, enjoying her moment in the limelight. 'Shearwater or Emberton, maybe.'

'It might be a good move,' said Susan, considering. 'Your house must be worth a fair bit, property in Emberton would be cheaper. You could get something really mouth-watering on the waterside and walk away with the change.'

'Something like that, I intend to do,' Dot admitted.

'How long have you been planning this without telling us, Mum?' Debbie wanted to know. The strictly correct answer, of course, was about seven minutes, but Dot said, 'It has been in my mind since Christmas. It felt very big and lonely at home when you had all gone,' which was near enough.

'Well!' said Debbie. 'I think it's a wonderful idea, and we'd love the suite Mum, if you really don't need it. And if there are any spare beds going, we can use them too.' She put her arm round her mother and gave her a hug. 'A new beginning, how exciting. Aren't you impatient to get started?'

To Dot's surprise, she found that now the decision was taken and out in the open, she was impatient. 'Yes, I confess I am. And now, Deborah, I think you should go downstairs and put your feet up, you've been very busy this morning.' Having thus restored the *status quo*, she led the way down. Susan picked up the tray of used coffee mugs and headed for the kitchen.

'I'll just do these, and then I think we should go. Daniel will be waking up soon and demanding attention, if he's anything like the rest of the family, and Seb will be back too. Come down and see us later on, Mother, if you'd like, have a cup of tea. Let Deb deal with her child on her own for a bit, see what it's like!'

'I'm sure she will manage perfectly,' said Dot. 'Thank you Susan, I should like that.'

On the short drive back to the village, Liz and Susan would have remained silent from choice, giving themselves time to mull over the morning's somewhat surprising revelation, but Annabel had no such inhibitions. 'Mummy, did you know Grandma was planning to move?' she asked, leaning forward as far as the seatbelt would allow. 'You never told us!' She sounded reproachful, and Susan laughed. It sounded like an effort.

'Then join the club, for *she* never told me and Auntie Debbie, either,' she said. Liz glanced at her, and then away again. She thought that Susan, and possibly Debbie too, had been hurt by that carelessly imparted piece of news and its implied lack of confidence and she didn't blame them, but she had already deduced, from what she knew of Dot before she even met her, that she had a gift for putting her foot in it. She may even have had her own personal reasons for not stating her intentions too soon, but on balance, Liz thought that her sympathies were with Susan and Deb. She had liked Dot, rather against her expectations, but she saw her for what she was, which perhaps Dot's daughters did not; somebody permanently on the defensive, liable to attack out of the sun. Not for the first time that morning, nor the first person to do so, Liz found herself wondering why.

'But we love Grandma's house,' said Annabel, contentiously. 'Why does she want to leave it? We've always gone there.'

'I expect she feels it's time for a change,' said Liz, when Susan remained silent. 'It's one thing when you're all there, Annabel. If it's got seven bedrooms, like she said, she must rattle around on her own like a dried pea in a drum!'

Susan found her voice. 'If she moves out into the country, it'll be even nicer staying with her. Boats, if she goes to Emberton. Ponies maybe in Shearwater. Think about it.'

Annabel thought for at least half a minute. 'Well, perhaps ... but she could have asked us.'

'Why? It's her house.'

'What about Grandpa?'

'Well, *what* about Grandpa? He's doesn't live there any more.'

'He might go back,' said Annabel, in a very small voice, leaving Susan wondering if she hoped that her own father would return to his ex-wife. But Jerry wasn't an ex, so perhaps in his case Annabel felt she had some justification; he was still married to his second wife, even if he was now virtually living with his first. But there was no future down that path. 'No he won't, Annabel,' she said firmly, and the rest of the journey, all five minutes of it, passed in silence.

Seb wasn't yet back, and without his company to distract her, Annabel hung around downstairs, making it impossible for Susan to discuss Dot's bombshell with Liz, and setting everybody's nerves on edge. She trailed into the kitchen behind them when Susan went to start the lunch and leaned on the worktop, getting in the way. 'What are we going to do this afternoon?' she whined.

'I don't know. I haven't thought,' said Susan. Liz gave her a look; it seemed to her that Susan's parenting skills were failing her here, when the child was obviously upset. 'What would you like to do?' she asked. Annabel muttered, 'Go riding,' and Susan made an impatient tutting sound. Liz, slightly bewildered by all this angst over somebody selling a house several hundred miles away that they didn't even live in, stepped in again.

'It's not a very nice day for riding. It's cold, and it looks as if it's going to rain.'

'There's nothing to do when it's raining,' said Annabel, crossly, and Liz grinned at her.

'No pleasing you this morning, is there? Haven't you got any friends to hang out with?'

'That's a good idea,' said Susan, briskly, opening the fridge to peer inside it for possibilities. 'Why don't you go and see Rosie? Or ask her to come over here.'

Annabel said nothing, and began to kick the cupboard door. 'Stop that,' said Susan, automatically. Liz got up from where she was sitting by the table and went over to Annabel.

'Come on. Come and sit down here with me, out of Mummy's way, and tell us what's the matter. There's surely not all this fuss just about Grandma selling her own house.' Annabel came away from the worktop with all the enthusiasm of sticking plaster from a sore spot, and trailed across the tiles with Liz, but then she just stood drooping in a new position, and Liz had to drag her down onto a chair. 'Come on, out with it! What's the problem?'

For answer, Annabel burst into tears.

Susan slammed the fridge door shut. For a moment, Liz thought she was going to stalk out, but instead, she came and sat down on the other side of Annabel and pulled her into her arms. 'This isn't just about the house,' she said to Liz, above Annabel's sobs. 'This has been coming on all morning. I thought it was odd when she didn't want to go off with Rosie.'

Annabel gave a howl. 'Everything's going wrong! Auntie Debbie and Uncle Mawgan aren't at the Fish any more, and Grandma's moving, and Rosie doesn't want to be friends with me any more! And Daddy hasn't written or phoned since Christmas and everything's *horrible*!'

Susan was silent, rocking Annabel in her arms as if she was a baby again.

'If Tom Casson was my ex-husband,' said Liz, conversationally, 'I'd kill him, and chance the consequences. It'd very likely be brought in as justifiable homicide anyway.'

Susan shook her head, but said nothing. It seemed to her that Grandma moving house and Debbie and Mawgan leaving the Fish had both simply been a catalyst that had released the grief over two bigger problems, and she wasn't certain what to say about either of them. While she was still floundering, the front door slammed and footsteps sounded in the passage, and a moment later Carl came through the kitchen door. He paused at the scene that met his eyes. 'Oops! Shall I go?'

To everybody's astonishment, including Carl's, Annabel's response was to tear herself out of her mother's arms and fling herself into his. He picked her up and sat down on her vacated chair with her on his knee. His eyes met Susan's over the top of her head. 'I take it this is about Rosie?' he said.

'And Tom. How did you know about Rosie?'

'How does anyone know anything in this place? Shirley told me when I dropped into the pub to have a pint with Mawgan.' Shirley Pengelly, Mawgan's receptionist, was also Rosie's big sister.

'Grandma's going to move,' sobbed Annabel.

'Is she?' Carl sounded interested. 'That's a good idea, she doesn't need that big house. Surely that's not what this fuss is about?'

'Everything's changing,' cried Annabel, with such pathos that for a moment she silenced all three of her hearers. Liz found her voice first, following an instinct that this scene needed to be kept on track.

'So what's with Rosie? Have they fallen out?'

Carl cradled Annabel's head against his shoulder, stroking her hair as if she was a frightened animal. He looked bleak. 'It's about Annabel going to school in Truro this autumn. Apparently she was a bit too cocky about it, and they're all picking on her.'

'Oh dear,' said Liz.

'Oh God,' said Susan. 'That's all we need!'

'You might like to consider a more helpful approach,' Liz suggested. 'Poor Annabel, she's the outsider here, the incomer. Kids gang up on each other, she doesn't need that.'

'It sounds as if she invited it,' said Susan, in a tired voice.

'I'm sure she didn't mean to.'

'I thought they'd be pleased for me,' said Annabel, in a very small voice. 'I thought they were my friends.'

'I daresay they were. I daresay they *are*,' said Susan. 'It'll all blow over, Annabel. Just try and be a bit less upfront about it in future.'

Carl said, 'Could one of you two pass me a bit of kitchen roll? I'm getting drowned here!' and Annabel gave a very small giggle. Susan got to her feet and pulled a piece from the roll on the wall, and handed it over without speaking. Annabel blew her nose loudly and mopped at her eyes, and then sat up, but without releasing her grasp of Carl.

'That's better,' Susan said. 'Come on Annabel, cheer up. A couple of days from now, someone else'll put their foot in it, and you'll find yourself back in favour.'

'What on earth did you say, to upset them all so?' asked Liz, curiously. Annabel sniffed.

'We were all talking about where we were going to go after the summer. They're all of them going to the comp in Helston. And all I said was that I was going to school in Truro.'

'Did you just happen to mention that it was a public school?' asked Carl, and Annabel went red. 'Enough said.' He lifted her off his knee and stood up, holding out his hand to her. 'Come on you, you'll just have to live it down. Come upstairs with me and play spider on my computer while I check some stuff, and let these two see to the lunch.'

When they had gone, Susan looked at Liz in despair. 'I never know what to do for the best these days. I thought it was good for Annabel and Seb to go to the village school, and up until now they've been fine.'

'Seb still is fine,' Liz pointed out.

'But Annabel isn't. Seb fell on his feet, he straight away made friends with Ben Jenkin, and he found something he could do superlatively well, and from all accounts he hated his old school anyway. Annabel is just a fish out of water, and she's finding things very hard at the moment – at home as well as at school. I don't know what's the best thing to do, I'd hate to have to think that Mother was right all along. It really shook me just now when she left me and ran to Carl '

'Annabel is looking to fill a gap. Whether she knows it or not. Your Tom is a real bastard.'

'He's not my Tom. I wouldn't have him as a gift!'

Liz said, 'Aren't there any other children more Annabel's kind in the area? Surely there must be, there's big houses on the other side of the creek.'

'If there are, we haven't met them. Our lives revolve round the Fish and the sailing school. People come and go all the time.'

'You should think about it.'

'Annabel's enjoyed the village life. She was in the pantomime, and she made friends at school easily to start with –'

'– and lost them just as easily, it now appears. Seb's fine, he's intelligent and he's going to be a brilliant sailor and his peers respect that, but he's not necessarily academically clever so he doesn't shine people down. Annabel's like you. She went to that school from a good prep school, and it's a miracle she settled in as well as she did.'

'Oh God!' Susan put her head in her hands. 'I do screw up, don't I? I don't even have to try!'

'Girls are always more difficult, so Alice says,' Liz tried to console her. She reached out and touched Susan on the shoulder. 'Come on Auntie Sue. You did the best you could at the time, and it was a pretty good best on the whole. Shall we get the lunch and leave time to do its job?'

Mawgan left the Fish by the rear door at lunchtime to reclaim his motor bike, that he used for everyday transport, and return to his new family for the afternoon, and found a thin, dark, wiry boy of around twelve sloping shiftily around the car park with the air of someone looking for trouble to get into.

'Afternoon, Damien,' he said. 'What you doing around here?'

'Waiting for my dad.' Damien Tregear kicked casually at a nearby tyre, and tried to sound airy. 'Mum said to meet him and see he come straight home.'

'Set a thief to catch a thief, I see. Well, your dad will come out the door of the bar, so maybe you better go round and wait there.' Damien had a certain respect for Mawgan, one of the few people it has to be said that he did respect, if for all the wrong reasons, and he was about to do as he was told when Mawgan was visited by a sudden inspiration. Listening to Shirley in the bar earlier he had been very sorry for Annabel, who had enough problems without her friends turning on her, even if she had been silly. He knew from personal experience how social ostracism felt. He said, 'But just before you go, what's all this about Annabel Casson at school?'

'Oh, her!' Damien snorted. 'Your niece or something, i'n't she? Silly little cow, shooting her mouth off, boasting about her posh school. She'd of done better to of kept it shut. Not that it bothers me none,' he added, hastily, meeting Mawgan's eye. 'Girls never know when to shut up!' He spoke with scorn, playing, had he but known it, right into Mawgan's hands.

'Really,' said Mawgan. 'Well Annabel does, and you should be glad.'

Damien, who had been about to slope off round to the front as instructed to wait for his dad, paused at that. He looked back at Mawgan over his shoulder. 'What you saying?'

Mawgan moved casually towards his bike.

'Remember that car you scratched all over outside your place, in November backlong?' he asked.

'What car?' asked Damien, stonily. 'I don't remember no car.'

'Oh, I think you do. Nice car it was, expensive, parked legal by the roadside, where your dad likes to think he owns the road.'

'Oh – that one,' said Damien, uneasily now.

'Bloke was staying at Annabel's mum's place. He was pretty angry, shouting and stamping all over. Annabel knew you done it and he knew she knew, but even when he yelled at her she didn't give you away none. If she had, you'd of been in big trouble. He's not a nice bloke, he'd've had the police in before you could whistle. You might like to think on that.'

Damien did think about it, for all of half a minute. 'And Annabel didn't say nothing? Nothing *at all*?'

'Not to no one. No.' He didn't add that everyone else present at the time had come to the same conclusion, and Damien's reasoning powers didn't prompt him to ask how Mawgan came to know, then. He said, 'Blimey!' and relapsed into thought.

Mawgan straddled his bike and began to fasten his helmet before kicking the engine into life. He raised his voice above the noise. 'You might like to give that a bit of thought while you're waiting for your dad,' he said, and roared off out of the car park. Damien stood there looking at the dust he had left swirling in the air, and then, obedient to a deep instinct for safety, made his way round to the front of the Fish to wait for his dad as instructed.

XV

'Your mother seemed very full of her new plans when she came over for tea yesterday, after keeping them so dark from you,' said Liz.

'What I wonder is, why did she?' Susan replied. 'She can't have thought we'd mind, surely!'

'Maybe she hadn't quite decided,' offered Liz, more shrewdly than she realised. 'Maybe it was seeing Deb's lovely new place that made her mind up for her.'

'It wouldn't just have been that. Someone must have put the idea into her head to start with.'

'Why? Doesn't she have ideas of her own?'

Susan thought about this, it wasn't something it had occurred to her to wonder about before. After a while, she said, 'No ...' very slowly. Liz raised her eyebrows.

'I find that hard to believe, she seems a reasonably intelligent woman to me. I liked her.'

It was Sunday morning, they were sitting over the remains of breakfast, putting off the moment when they would have to get to their feet and wash up. Carl had taken the children off to give the dog a run along the foreshore and up into the woods, making the most of the sunshine that had replaced yesterday's clouds. He had some work to do on his boat after that, he said, and Seb and Annabel could help him when Clinker had had his turn. Susan had been relieved: Annabel, she was certain, was working on a good reason not to go to school tomorrow and she didn't think she could face it. She had great sympathy with Annabel over the predicament in which she had landed herself, but she couldn't see any way out of it other than facing up to it and living it down – two things which she knew Annabel would find very difficult. A sneaking sense of guilt because her mother seemed to have foreseen it and she had not wasn't helping, and it was this as much as anything that made her pause now, so that it was Liz, in the end, who spoke first.

'Perhaps she didn't tell you because she thought you might rain on her parade. Perhaps she's used to that kind of thing.' Susan winced, recognising that this might well be true. Liz hadn't finished. 'What she needs is the kind of friend who encourages you into doing things you never did before. Broaden her horizons, boost her confidence, give her courage.'

'She's never been short of those qualities,' said Susan, defensively.

'Really? From what little you've told me, I wouldn't agree. Confrontational, yes. Confident? No, I don't think so. And people watching is part of my job, remember.'

'But she is changing now,' said Susan, slowly, thinking. 'That party ... thinking of selling the house ... reading light fiction ...'

'Then perhaps she's found the friend like that,' said Liz.

Susan shook her head. 'Except for one, all the friends at the party were people she already knew.'

'All right,' said Liz. 'So who was the one? Maybe you ought to think about it.'

The only thing Susan knew about Benita Vachell was that she had taken her mother's side in a run-in with Jenny Carruthers, but that was a good start. But Benita couldn't be much older than herself, at the very least fifteen or twenty years younger than Dot. From what she knew of her mother – although she was beginning to wonder if that was all that much – Susan couldn't see it. She was about to say so, when the phone extension rang from its place on the end of the worktop. She got up, relieved to be spared answering Liz, and lifted it to her ear. 'Hullo?'

'Susan,' said a familiar male voice. 'I need to speak to Liz. It's urgent, is she there?'

Susan looked across at Liz, sitting peacefully at the table. 'Oh, hullo Paul,' she said. Liz sat up, shaking her head violently and waving her hands about in a vehement negative. Susan equivocated. 'What made you think she would be here?'

'She said she was going to Cornwall,' said Paul. He sounded momentarily taken aback.

'Big place, Cornwall.'

'That's a nuisance. I need to get an urgent message to her. Are you sure she's not there?'

'How can you be *not sure* about a thing like that?' asked Susan, reasonably she hoped. 'Have you tried her mobile?'

'She's got it turned off. Most inconsiderate, and rather stupid too.' Paul sounded cross. Susan looked across at Liz, now sitting with her head in her hands.

'You could give me the message if you wanted. She did say she might drop in on her way home, but of course, I can't guarantee it.'

'She is there, isn't she?' said Paul, deeply suspicious. 'Come on Susan, stop playing games, and just put her on! I need to get back to London, I haven't time to muck about with kindergarten playtime!'

'I thought you were in London anyway this weekend,' said Susan. Liz raised her head, suddenly watchful.

'Well I'm not, and it's a bloody good thing too! Just tell her then, when I got to the cottage late Friday night, the lock was jammed and I had to break in. I've had the lock changed for her and left the bill on the worktop, and it cost me a bit, I may tell you, at a weekend. The new key is with her neighbour. I'll just hold on while you tell her all that.'

Susan almost fell for it, but saved herself in time. Her hesitation was infinitesimal, she wasn't sure if Paul had noticed it or not. She said, 'I'll tell her if she comes by. You'd better leave a note on the door for her, just in case.'

Paul slammed the phone down. Susan put her own phone very gently back on its rest. Liz said, 'He went there, didn't he? To my home?'

'Yes, he did.' Susan went back to her seat and picked up her now cold mug of coffee. 'He couldn't get in, so he broke the lock.'

'Bugger!' exclaimed Liz. 'How dare he? He must have realised ...' she tailed off. Susan took a sip of cold coffee and shuddered.

'I daresay he did, but you'll never prove it.' She got to her feet again and reached for Liz's mug. 'I'm going to make some more coffee. Want one?'

'Please. Black. And strong. So what am I supposed to do when I get back? Is he planning to leave the house wide open to burglars, or is he going to wait for me?'

'He said he had to get back to London.' Susan switched on the kettle and began to rinse the mugs. She didn't look at Liz. 'He's changed the lock, he said, and left you the bill, I don't know if he paid it, and he's left the new key with your neighbour.'

'The swine!' Liz sounded furious. 'So now he's got the key again! And I'll have to change the lock again. What are people going to think?'

'Don't change it,' said Susan. She turned to lean against the worktop while she waited for the kettle. 'Put another lock on as well. A different one, one that he can't break so easily. You can get them, I know, ask your friendly neighbourhood DIY shop. You can tell Paul, he broke the other one so easily you thought it was best. Or you can just be totally honest and say that you resented his being there when you'd told him you wouldn't be.'

'How did he have the *gall* to do it?' Liz raged. 'It's not his home, it's mine! And I hope he was nice to Tib.'

'Why wouldn't he be?' asked Susan.

'He doesn't like cats much. And Tib is afraid of him, a bit.' Liz was suddenly uneasy. 'He can be very spiteful, Paul.'

'Why did you stay with him so long?' asked Susan, but it was a rhetorical question, she already knew the answer. 'OK, OK, someone to go about with, the sex was good, don't tell me.'

'I'm bothered if I know.'

Susan poured boiling water into the *cafetière* and carried it with the mugs to the table. She sat down again, looking at Liz seriously. 'You'll have to get rid of him once and for all.'

'Like, how? I've just tried. You can see for yourself how well it worked.'

'Perhaps you didn't try hard enough.'

It was Liz's turn to hesitate now. When she did speak, it was in one sense a *non sequitur*. 'I ought to go back and check things out. But how do I know it isn't all a trick to make me do just that, and he'll be lying in wait for me? Then he'll know I lied to him and ...'

'And what?' Susan asked.

'And I don't know. I feel quite suddenly that I don't know him at all. What sort of a man would break into someone's house like that? Surely a normal person would have gone to a hotel for the night and dealt with it properly in the morning, told the neighbours or my family, or just left a note and gone home.'

Any or all of those things, Susan thought, or come to that a normal person probably wouldn't have been there in the first place. Which raised a question that she could see had already occurred to Liz. They looked at each other uncomfortably. Susan said, 'Would you like Carl to come back with you? I'm sure he would.'

'I think that might be over-reacting,' said Liz, after a pause. 'Paul wouldn't *hurt* me, and I can always stop off and pick up Gil to come with me if it comes to that.' She realised that this equivocation revealed her own unease. 'Pour that coffee. I think I need it.'

Susan poured. 'It could, of course, have been a genuine misunderstanding over the lock.'

'But you don't think so,' said Liz.

'No. Even the arrogant bastard that Paul always is wouldn't break in, in that case. He'd do what you said, find a bed for the night and leave a message with someone, if he really believed it was jammed. So ...'

'He didn't believe it.'

'Probably not, in my view.'

'Mine too.'

They drank their coffee in silence. Then Liz said, 'If it wasn't for Tib, I'd put off going home until tomorrow morning. Then I know I'd not run into him.'

'Ring your neighbour,' Susan suggested. 'Get him or her to check, say you've been delayed or something. Then if Tib is OK, you can stay with an easy mind.'

'Paul changed the lock. She can't get in.'

'She's got the key, he said. She can.'

Liz hesitated. 'May I use your phone? I just think, if I switch mine on and he chooses that moment to ring me again ... well, he'll be pretty stupid not to know where I must be.'

'He knows anyway. But use it, no problem.'

'There's no need to prove it,' said Liz, getting to her feet. She picked up the phone and entered the number, and after a moment said, 'Tina, it's Liz ... what? ... Paul? ... oh, I see ... yes, it was lucky, wasn't it? Is he still there? ... No, no, definitely not. And don't tell him I rang, I'll get in touch ... no no, it's just, I could stay another night here, but I just wanted to check that Tib was OK before I said yes ... yes ... is he? Well, that's good ... do you mind one more night of cat-feeding? ... you're a star, Tina! Keep an eye on him until Paul leaves, will you? ... No, no, of course not, it's just that he hasn't much time for animals ... that'd be great. Thanks Tina. See you tomorrow. Oh, and remember – don't tell Paul you've spoken to me. Just see him off the premises and check he's locked up properly ... I'll explain when I get back, I promise.' She put down the phone. 'Tina doesn't like Paul much either, she says he patronises.'

'He does,' said Susan. 'He was lucky Carl didn't flatten his face, last time he was here.'

Liz resumed her seat and picked up her mug. 'She told me about the lock, she sounded pretty doubtful about Paul's motives but I couldn't really go into it on the phone. She said ...' she hesitated. 'Anyway, she said she'd catch Tib, he's mooching around her garden, and shut him into her conservatory until Paul leaves. And now, I'm left wondering why.'

'Ring her again, and ask,' offered Susan.

'No. I won't do that. I know he's safe, and she'll look after him, even if Paul hangs around until dawn tomorrow – which is quite possible.'

'You know,' said Susan, slowly, 'you sound almost as if you think he's stalking you.'

'I think that's overstating it a little.' Liz swept the mugs together, regardless of the fact that Susan hadn't quite finished, and carried them over to the sink. 'It's just that this weekend, it's felt a bit like it. I just need a serious talk with Paul, let him know it's really over between us and he might as well concentrate on this Ash, whoever she is. Sponge off her for a change!' She laughed, trying to sound light-hearted. Susan didn't laugh with her. She remained seated at the table, studiously watching her own finger tracing whorls and circles on its wooden surface.

'I've been thinking. Something Cecy said at Christmas, that he called you his "weekend woman". That sounds to me like taking the piss, Liz. You say he's in Devon every weekend, or up in your flat with you in London. Why not his flat? Why never during the week?'

'Because I'm at home in the week, of course, and he works in town,' said Liz, answering the easiest question first.

'And?'

'And what?'

'Why your flat? Why never his?'

'He says it keeps mine aired,' said Liz, realising that this sounded lame even to herself, and that she had never properly considered it before.

'Have you ever been to his? It does exist, doesn't it?'

'Of course I've been to it. 'This was firmer ground. She turned round. 'It's gorgeous, down by the river in one of those warehouse conversions. I've had meals there, slept there even –' she broke off. Susan looked at her for the first time in this exchange.

'At a weekend?'

'No,' said Liz. It had never struck her as strange before.

'I think you should talk to Cecy,' said Susan.

'Why ever?'

'Because I think she knows something that you don't,' said Susan, more forthrightly than she had intended. Their eyes locked across the space between them.

'Ho hum,' said Liz.

'And,' went on Susan, having gone this far, 'I think it's something you *should* know.'

'Then why hasn't she told me already?' demanded Liz, defensively.

'Most probably, because she thinks you know.'

'Why don't you come and dry up?' asked Liz. They finished the washing up in silence, each of them taken up with her own thoughts, but before the atmosphere had time to become strained, they were interrupted by the unexpected arrival of Debbie, Dot and Daniel.

'We're off to show Mum a bit of the countryside,' Debbie explained. 'We thought we'd drop in and cadge a cup of coffee on the way. Daniel's first real outing, he likes riding in the car! Look at him, isn't he darling in his little woolly suit?'

Both Liz and Susan were pretty much awash with coffee already, but the diversion was timely and Liz reached for the kettle while Susan ushered the newcomers into the comfort of the living room; she couldn't see their mother slumming it at the kitchen table. Back in the kitchen she viewed Liz's preparations critically. 'Cups and saucers, not mugs. They're in that cupboard.'

'Can't we have mugs? I much prefer a good mug.'

'Only if you want to have your ear chewed off about the scruffy habits of today's young people,' Susan told her. 'Anyway, cups are smaller, and I don't know about you, but I can't hold much more coffee.'

'Your mother is a terrific lady, isn't she?' commented Liz, which could have been taken two ways. Susan rubbed her nose thoughtfully.

'The trouble with Mother is that she hasn't really mixed with people like us. You don't often find them sitting on charity committees.'

'You found you, apparently.'

'Yes.' Susan looked back on that arid period of her life and shuddered. 'It's no life for a young girl. I don't know what got into me.'

'Then that makes two of us,' Liz remarked, under her voice. Susan looked at her.

'If you want to know what I really think, I think that the only one of us about to drink this coffee out of posh cups who hasn't screwed up big time, somehow, somewhere, is Daniel, and no doubt his turn will come. Now can we call a truce?'

'Daniel,' observed Liz, picking up the tray of cups, 'isn't going to drink it.'

Susan prepared to follow her with the *cafetière*. 'Deb probably shouldn't either. Perhaps I should have made tea?'

Debbie said that she would drink her coffee very, very weak, thank you Suse, with one eye on their mother as she said it. To Susan's surprise, Dot didn't challenge this, and after a few commonplace preliminaries, Liz took the conversational initiative. 'So, tell us about this new house, Mrs Nankervis,' she said. 'What are you looking for, apart from less bedrooms?'

The new house had become more real since its possibility became common property, Dot was happy to talk it over with what she saw, unusually, to be friendly, genuinely interested company, although she wasn't sure Liz should be calling her *Mrs Nankervis*. But then,

Grandma didn't seem right either. Dot wisely decided to leave the question to look after itself for now.

'A big garden is essential, of course,' she answered Liz, 'and I would like a house with some character. Pleasant views.' Staying with Debbie and Mawgan and their stunning sea views had given her some interesting new perspectives.

'Older, or newbuild?' Susan wanted to know. 'Town or country?'

Dot confessed to something that she had never mentioned before, deeming it of no interest to other people. 'I have always liked the idea of an older house, somewhere with some history behind it, but properly modernised of course. Plumbing, and drains, and central heating.'

Susan and Debbie both stared at her. That didn't sound like the mother they knew, except about the drains, naturally. 'But we always lived in smart modern houses,' objected Debbie, always the more outspoken of the two.

'Yes dear. Your father preferred it.'

Did he? Debbie found herself wondering. She had seen the fisherman's cottage that her father now more-or-less shared with Helen, although Helen had chosen that of course. But there was also the old cottage that he and Helen had lived in when they first married, of which she had seen photographs in that volume of the family album devoted to Oliver's childhood. Jerry, she now thought, had distanced himself from the past, but perhaps not out of personal preference, which was a bit unfair on his second wife if she liked old property too.

'So,' Liz was saying, 'If you want views, that's country not town. It's easier to start afresh in a village, much easier to make friends than in a town too.'

Dot remembered that Benita had said something similar. She wondered if it was true, and if so, what it would be like to live that way, in a small community. Of course, if she moved out to Shearwater, Benita would introduce her to people, make sure she was welcomed and known. She felt an unexpected warm feeling around her heart: when her children came to visit, as she by this time was sure that they would, she would have a proper life to show them – to share with them.

Which rather begged the question, hadn't her previous life been a proper one?

But that was something that she wasn't yet prepared to face up to, for if it hadn't been, she had inflicted the same emptiness on Susan. Looking at Susan now, happy, relaxed and fulfilled, prettier than she had ever been, Dot felt a shutter come down in her mind. 'Well, we shall see,' she said. 'I shan't move unless the perfect property comes on the market, of course.'

'But you're definitely looking?' said Debbie. 'How exciting! Perhaps Daniel and I can take some time out and come and help you.'

'That would be lovely,' said Dot, meaning it. She smiled, and ventured on another little joke, the second in two days. 'I'm sure that Daniel's opinion will be particularly valuable.'

'Dear of him,' said Debbie, smiling at her son, snugly tucked up in an armchair and oblivious to the conversation around him. 'Isn't he good?'

'Better than either of mine ever were,' mentioned Susan, looking at her snoozing nephew with a touch of envy. 'Both of them were yowlers. All the time.'

'Deborah – Debbie – is much more relaxed over her baby than you were,' Dot told her. 'You were never at home with young babies, admit it. Deborah has taken to motherhood like a duck to water.' One day she would get this "Debbie" thing consistently right. It is hard, changing the habit of a lifetime. One other thing that she failed to see she had not got right, and not for the first time by any means, was comparing Susan unfavourably with her sister. Liz picked up on it at once, and also noticed Susan's face.

'It's a family thing,' she said swiftly. 'Alice nearly left home after the twins were born, and Mum always says that she didn't sleep at night for four years on the trot when we were small and could quite easily have thrown us out of the window if Dad hadn't stopped her – that's both of us, on separate occasions or together.' Thus placing Susan firmly in the camp of the Worthingtons, and bringing Dot up short. Liz was pleased to see a startled look cross her face, and was wise enough to leave the subject lying where it was. Instead, she said, 'Well, when you do move, if you need help just call on me if Auntie Sue and Deb are busy. I work for myself, I fix my own hours – and anyway, I can bring my laptop with me if I have to. I can do some granddaughterly duty, it must be heavily in arrears by this time.'

'I notice you say "when" and not "if",' said Dot, dryly.

'Oh yes. It's the sort of idea that, once it takes root, it takes over like ground elder. You'll move. You'll find the perfect house and that'll make your mind up.'

Dot wondered if she would and what it might feel like, and to cover the moment looked at her watch. 'You should drink that coffee if you're going to, Debo – Debbie. We're going to run out of time of you're not careful.'

'Come on Mum, we're hardly here.' Debbie was in no hurry, she was enjoying the novelty of being out of her own house for a couple of hours. She took an obedient, but small, sip from her cup. 'Anyway, the scenery will still be there.'

'That's one thing. Having a bawling hungry baby in the car with you is quite another. And don't give me that line about feeding him anywhere, it's not decent.' Dot sounded more like herself. 'Come along now.' She reached for her bag, and Debbie sighed.

'Oh, all right then. I'm coming.' She replaced the cup on its saucer and went to pick up Daniel, cradling him on her shoulder. 'Good to see you anyway, Liz. When are you coming down again?'

'Who knows? I'm a working girl, unfortunately, if I'm to meet my next deadline.' Liz had risen to her feet, she unexpectedly leaned to kiss Dot on the cheek. 'Lovely to meet you at last. And don't forget what I said.'

'It's very sweet of you to offer,' said Dot, not committing herself. She returned the surprise kiss briefly and swept Debbie towards the door. 'Thank you for the coffee, Susan. I shall be seeing you again before I leave, I expect.'

'I should think so,' Susan muttered, and Dot, remembering herself, came back to kiss her too. Liz and Debbie exchanged a glance, neither spoke. When the visitors had gone, Susan rattled the cups and saucers back onto the tray with unnecessary noise, and Liz watched her compassionately.

'Your family is a right mess,' she ventured, at last. 'What on earth was the solicitor thinking of?'

'Jerry?' Susan straightened up with the tray in her hands and the crockery rattled together ominously. Liz took it from her, gently.

'Going by what you've told me, he always loved his first wife. Why mess up your mother's life – and yours, come to that?'

'Mother –'

'Don't put everything on your mother,' Liz interrupted her. 'No, she's not perfect – but if you analyse the situation from start to finish, I think you might find that he's as much to blame. Maybe *more* to blame. Whatever your mother may have done, if he loved his wife, why did he let her? Think about it. His wife too, if *she* loved *him*, she's culpable as well.'

'She suffered –'

'Probably. But if you want my opinion, the main sufferers are you, your mother and probably your brother, and there's no excuse for that.' She turned abruptly and headed for the kitchen. She had said too much, and it had all happened so long ago, there had probably been no point in saying anything at all. She wondered if Susan would follow her, and was relieved when, after a few minutes, she did, even though she looked, and sounded, controversial.

'She deliberately broke up the marriage –' she began.

'Did she? How do you know that, you were only about three at the time!' Liz realised that they were quarrelling, and was conscious of shock. She never quarrelled with Susan, she liked her. Susan, too, realised that she had been betrayed into repeating something heard long ago when she was too young to understand, and never confronted. She paused, and took the information out to consider it more carefully. Finally, she spoke.

'Grannie used to say so – Jerry's mother. Not *to* me, of course not, but when I was in earshot. And my father's sisters, Auntie Anne and Aunt Emily.'

'Hearsay,' said Liz, but more temperately this time. 'Now I'll tell you some more. *My* family lore has it differently, you remember; my grandfather married her because she was dumped, and heartbroken, and couldn't deal with it, and because she had never been taught how to cope with real life and he was sorry for her. Yes, he must have loved her as well – but he wouldn't have married a woman so much younger if there hadn't been a good reason.'

'And his children let her down in the end, even so,' said Susan, bitterly, and Liz said, '*Too*,' and a silence fell.

'Anyway, he didn't dump her.' Susan broke the silence, and to her own horror, sounded sullen when she did so. Liz raised a quizzical eyebrow.

'Who says?'

'He says. They were only friends.' Defensively.

Liz laughed. 'Oh come on, Susan. You know better than that! It's the second rule in the Man's Book of Self Justification.' She paused. 'The first is "she was frigid and I have needs".'

'Oh shit,' said Susan.

'Indeed.'

It was like a gigantic game of patience, Susan caught herself thinking. First you had neat columns of this card and that card, in no particular order; you shifted one here, one there, picked up another and found a place for it, shuffled the pack and repeated the process – and suddenly you had an orderly pattern, quite different from what you had started with. She didn't know what to say. Fortunately, Liz said it for her. 'It's a pity the two halves of your family didn't get together years ago. And that's everyone's fault, but probably not yours or mine.'

Susan was saved from replying by the crash of the opening front door, and childish voices chattering in the passage; Annabel and Sebastian, and it sounded as if Ben was there too. But not Rosie, and Susan's heart ached for her daughter, silly though she had undoubtedly been. A moment later Clinker came pushing through the kitchen door, tail wagging furiously and river mud adorning his paws and, by association, the floor. Carl's voice shouting 'Grab that dog, Seb!' came too late.

'Oh God!' cried Susan, seizing the dog by his collar. 'Liz – that towel, the black one – oh God, Clink, don't do that!' as Clinker tried to jump up on her. Any lingering bad feeling flew out of the window straight away as Liz, laughing, brought the towel and tried to trap the excited dog in its folds. Carl and the children came in through the door, Seb looking a bit shamefaced.

'Sorry Mummy, he got away from me. He got in the mud.'

'No, really?' asked Liz, towelling briskly. 'You could have fooled me!'

'I'll clean the passage,' Seb added, quickly, and Carl said, 'I'll do it, you'll only make it worse – you take Clink into the garden and keep out of the way.' He headed purposefully for the cupboard which held mops, brooms and buckets. Susan, who had been kneeling by the dog, rose to her feet brushing mud from her shirt. It was wet, and she saw that she had made things worse. She made a face.

'Now look at me! I shall have to go and change. Did you all have a good morning?'

The sudden silence made her look up abruptly from her stained shirt, but before she got a word out, Annabel let out a wail of despair and ran from the room, slamming the door behind her. Her feet could be heard hammering up the stairs, to the accompaniment of sobbing, and Seb grabbed Ben and headed for the back door. 'Come on Ben, let's go and play in the garden.'

Liz released Clinker, only very little cleaner, from the towel so he could follow, and as the three of them vanished out of the back door, Susan called, 'And don't let him go back down to the creek – chase him around until he dries, *properly*, then brush him!' Then she turned and looked at Carl, leaning against the broom cupboard door with a resigned look on his face. 'So, what happened? What's upset Annabel? Has she been like that all morning?'

'No,' said Carl. 'We had a good morning. It was when we were coming back up the street – I wish we'd gone round by the foreshore now, but I thought it would stop Clink getting even muddier ... anyway, we ran into the Pengellys, on their way back from church, with Rosie and a couple of her friends in tow. Annabel called out to them and they cut her dead. Just pretended they hadn't heard her, even when she was right beside them. She was gutted.'

'Oh dear, poor Annabel,' said Liz, immediately sympathetic. Susan bit her lip.

'She did boast a bit, of course, but it does seem rather hard. I wonder if it would help if I had a word with Shirley?'

'I wouldn't,' said Carl. He straightened up and opened the cupboard, reaching for the broom. 'I think it might make things a whole lot worse. She'll just have to ride out the storm. It'll pass.'

'You think she was in the wrong, don't you?' Susan sounded confrontational.

'She was in the wrong,' said Carl. 'Or at the very least, boasting was a silly thing to do.'

Susan opened her mouth to argue, and closed it again. Carl carried the bucket to the sink and began to fill it with hot water. He said, 'She needs to regain their respect, Susie, and she won't do that if Mummy runs to Rosie's big sister. Think about it.' He withdrew out into the passage with the mop and bucket and Liz looked at Susan.

'What on earth is the matter with you this morning, Auntie Sue? Are you premenstrual or something? You were about to bite poor Carl's head off just then, don't tell me!'

Susan made a helpless gesture with her hands. 'It just doesn't seem to be turning out to be a good day, somehow.'

'Then we'll improve it. Let's all go out after lunch and do something interesting.'

'Such as what? It's February.'

'For goodness sake!' Liz was openly laughing. 'Cheer up, do! Go and find yourself a clean shirt and then go and comfort Annabel. I'll wash the cups. Go on.'

'How can I comfort Annabel? She's made a fool of herself and lost her friends. How can she come back from that in any kind of hurry? And that's what she needs to do.'

'Sounds just like her grandmother,' commented Liz, and Susan left the room at speed, almost tripping over Carl as she made her exit. He leaned the mop against the wall and caught her as she tried to hurry past, pulling her into his arms.

'Hey, not so fast! I'm sorry Susie, I probably shouldn't have said that. Can we kiss and make up?'

'No, you were right.' Susan returned his kiss with interest. 'I wasn't thinking, that's not the way to sort things out for her.'

'You *can't* sort things out for her. She needs to do it for herself.'

'That's what Liz just said, sort of. But I wish I could.'

'I can see that. But if anyone helps her, it can't be you. Not this time. You'll only make it worse for her.'

'Poor Annabel,' said Susan.

'One of life's big lessons. Someone will come to her rescue eventually. Or she'll move schools and start again.'

'She'll still have to live in the village.'

294

'Then hope for the first.'

But who? Susan wondered, as she made her way upstairs. Annabel was an outsider here, an incomer from upcountry. The village children would close ranks against her, much as their parents had against Mawgan in similar circumstances. And then she thought, there was a certain amount of truth in what Liz said, it is more or less what Mother has done, but she found a friend to help her – she had friends who stood by her. Who's ever going to stand by Annabel?

Mawgan, to tell the truth, had been slightly surprised by the result of his casual advice to Dot at the market. Surprised, and rather taken aback. Recalling what else he had said on that occasion, he found himself wondering, slightly apprehensively, what might happen next. He had never meant, or expected, to be taken quite so literally, had indeed almost forgotten that he had said anything at all until she had announced her tentative plans to move house. There was something else that he had said, not to Dot, that he had also more or less forgotten. That, too, was about to come home to roost.

On Monday morning Annabel, as Susan had feared, started early. She came trailing down to breakfast, clutching her stomach and trying to look ill. 'Mummy, I feel sick. Do I have to go to school?'

Susan looked her up and down. She did look a bit subdued, and quite possibly did feel sick too, but only from nerves. And Carl was right, she would have to face up to it. 'There's nothing wrong with you that a bit of breakfast won't cure,' she said briskly, feeling unbelievably hardhearted. She wanted to hug Annabel, she looked so sorry for herself, but knew that it would be a bad move. Instead, she pointed to the table where Seb was already well away with his cereal. 'Sit down, and I'll bring you a drink.'

'I don't want any breakfast.' said Annabel, but she did sit down. Susan poured tea and placed the mug in front of her daughter, pushing the toast rack in her direction.

'Just have a piece of toast. You must eat something.'

Annabel pushed the toast rack away, pettishly. 'I said, I'm not hungry.'

Susan put a piece of toast on a plate, buttered it, added jam, cut it into four and put it down under Annabel's nose. 'Eat, please.'

'I'll have it if Annabel doesn't want it,' said Seb, eyeing the plate greedily. Annabel raised a hand to push it across to him, but found it resisting her efforts as it met her mother's hand on the other side. She looked up, her eyes pleading. Susan gave the plate a little push back into position and told Seb, 'If you want toast, you can spread your own. Now finish your crispies.'

She went over to the worktop to pour Seb a mug of tea, keeping tabs on Annabel out of the corners of her eyes. She saw her push the toast around her plate, pick up a piece, put it down again. She made no comment, but she could see Annabel watching her for a reaction. Annabel made a heaving sound. 'I don't want it,' she muttered.

Susan was desperately sorry for her, but she knew there was no point in making concessions. It had to be faced. She said, 'Yes, you do,' bracingly, and tears came into Annabel's eyes.

'I *don't*, Mummy. You don't *know*!'

'For someone who's feeling sick, you look remarkably pink and healthy. Now, eat something.'

'You can go pink when you feel sick, it's a bad sign,' said Annabel contentiously. Seb sniggered into his cereal, and Susan snapped, 'Don't do that Seb, eat properly!' rent with sympathy and determined not to give in. Annabel sat there. There was the annoying tap, tap, tap of her heels hitting the chair, and Susan said automatically, 'Don't do that.' She picked up the cereal packet and poured some into Annabel's bowl, pushing the milk jug towards her. 'Try this then, if you don't want toast. Now eat, and you'll feel better.'

Annabel poured milk and then pushed the contents of her bowl round with her spoon until it resembled a soggy mess. She pouted, and let a tear escape to run down her cheek. Susan looked the other way. Liz drifted through the door, yawning, felt the atmosphere and woke up abruptly. She saw Annabel's face.

'Oops, would you like me to go away and come down later on?'

'Depends if you like drama with your breakfast,' said Susan, smiling a greeting with what looked uncommonly like relief. 'Sit down, I'll make some coffee.'

'Where's Carl?' asked Liz, taking a seat beside Annabel. She looked at Susan's back, rigid with the effort of her self control, and gave Annabel a nudge and whispered in her ear. Annabel took a reluctant mouthful and choked on it, deliberately. Seb it was who answered her question.

'He's taken Clinker for a run on the foreshore,' he said, and reached hungrily for a slice of toast. Seb had no problems with school, whatever Annabel had called down on her head had not affected him. If it did, Susan thought she would be very angry with Annabel; Seb was so happy, so different, at this school from what he had been at his preparatory school in Embridge. She wanted him to keep his new confidence, believing it to be little more than skin deep at present. She made the coffee and carried it to the table.

'Here – have this to be going on with. I'll make us some fresh toast when the children have gone to school, we can have our breakfast in peace.' She pushed a mug towards Liz.

'I'm not going to school,' Annabel muttered mutinously. 'I'm ill, you can't make me.'

'Want a bet?' asked Susan cheerfully. She smiled at her daughter. Another tear ran down in the wake of the first. 'Come on, cheer up, it'll all blow over. You mustn't run away, or you'll hate yourself afterwards.'

'I'll be sick all over everyone,' Annabel threatened. Susan sighed.

'If you aren't going to eat that cereal, stop messing it about and go upstairs and get your things together, or you're going to be late. Ben will be here any minute. You too, Seb, you've had enough toast – no –' as Seb opened his mouth to argue the point. 'Go! Do as you're told for once.'

'The joys of Monday morning,' Liz murmured, as the children left the room, Seb running, Annabel dragging her feet and sniffing. 'I feel so sorry for her. Couldn't you just for once ...?'

'No,' said Susan. She poured her own coffee and took a sip. 'Don't think I don't feel for her, I do, but if I let her get away with it they'll all know and despise her even more. Much better to face it out.'

'Little girls can be so bitchy. Particularly ex-friends.' Liz considered. 'They're envious of course. They don't want to go to school in Truro, but they resent that she is.'

'I know. It's unreasonable, but she has to learn not to boast about things just because ...' she broke off, shrugged her shoulders, took another sip.

'Just because you have money, and their parents don't.' said Liz, quietly.

'Some of them do. And I can't help it, can I?' She paused, staring down into the swirling brown depths of her coffee. 'Perhaps Mother was right all along, when she said it was a mistake to come here.'

'She wasn't. You just have to learn how to live here,' said Liz. A silence fell, broken by the rattle of the knocker on the door.

'That'll be Ben and Morwenna. They usually just walk in these days.' Susan got to her feet. 'Maybe I didn't unlock the door.' Liz watched her leave the room, nearly as sorry for Susan as she was for Annabel. She heard her footsteps clacking down the slate floor of the hallway, heard Seb's feet running down the stairs, heard the door being opened, but no sound of unlocking. Then silence. Then Susan's voice, surprised. 'Oh – hullo. What can I ...?' and a loud, confident, Cornish voice saying, 'I come for Bel. Is she ready?' Intrigued, because that certainly wasn't Rosie Pengelly's voice, Liz went to the kitchen door and looked out into the hallway.

Susan stood by the open door, her body language expressing surprise bordering on shock. On the doorstep in front of her stood a stout, florid, dark-haired girl of about Annabel's age but with ten times her confidence. "Brash" was the word that sprang to Liz's mind. Not one of Annabel's regular circle, she looked as if she could easily be the school bully if one was honest. Fascinated, she waited to see what would happen next.

Seb arrived in the hall. He looked taken aback, even recoiled a step. 'Oh, hullo Kayleigh, what're you doing here?' More forthright than his mother, he called the girl's attention to himself.

'Hi Seb, how yer doing? Damien sent me, said I was to look after Bel.'

A second's pause that seemed to last for ever, then Susan, realising her presence, turned to Liz. 'This is Kayleigh Tregear, Damien's cousin – you remember Damien, he ...' her voice trailed into silence. Liz said, 'I never actually met him. Hullo Kayleigh.'

Kayleigh, unafflicted by inhibitions, said cheerfully, 'She made a right fool of herself, but Damien says it's not her fault none. She'll be all right, Mrs Casson, I'll look after 'er. I'll thump anyone what sneers at 'er, they won't dare do it twice.'

'Oh... er... well, thank you, but perhaps ...' Susan had never felt more out of her depth.

'I'll go and fetch Annabel,' said Seb, and bolted up the stairs. Liz, unable to think of anything useful she could add to the situation down here, and seeing Morwenna and Ben approaching along the street to the rescue, followed him. Upstairs, she might be more successful than Seb with Annabel, although she wouldn't have put money on it. Susan and Kayleigh confronted each other in silence, Kayleigh's *sang froid* far in excess of Susan's.

Liz found Seb standing rather helplessly at the foot of Annabel's bed, where she lay with shoulders hunched and face buried in the pillow. 'I'm not coming,' she was saying, muffled. Liz said, 'Your friend is waiting downstairs for you,' and then wished she hadn't, as Annabel sat up abruptly, her face transformed.

'Rosie?'

'No,' said Liz, sorry, 'not Rosie. Kayleigh?'

Annabel's jaw dropped. 'Kayleigh *Tregear*?'

'That's the name.' Liz turned to Seb. 'Off you go, Seb, Ben's on his way. Annabel will be down in a moment, tell Kayleigh.' As Seb, relieved, shot out of the door, she turned back to Annabel, sitting aghast on the bed. 'Come on, there's no need to look like that. She won't hurt you, she's come to look after you, she says.'

'What?' said Annabel, huskily, and cleared her throat to repeat more clearly, 'What?'

Liz sat down on the end of her bed. 'You never told about Paul's car, did you? Damien must know you'd've guessed, he's put her up to it.'

'None of us told. We ...' She stopped. Paul was Liz's boyfriend, after all.

'This isn't about the rest of you. It's about *you*. If I were you, I would continue to say nothing and cash in on the benefits because it seems to me you desperately need some help here. Now come on, your friend is waiting for you. You'll make her late, that wouldn't be a good start.'

'She's not my friend,' said Annabel, but she swung her legs off the bed and reached reluctantly for her school bag, giving way to a stronger will than her own – not so much Liz's, or her mother's, as Kayleigh's.

'Oh, I think she is,' said Liz. 'Come on now, get moving – put a comb through your hair quickly, you look as if you've just got out of bed.'

Annabel still hesitated. Kayleigh, as Liz had surmised, had a reputation as a bit of a bully; she had so far left Annabel alone for all that she was an incomer, partly from a respect for Mawgan that Annabel didn't recognise, partly because of Annabel's friendship with Rosie Pengelly and Seb's with Kayleigh's cousin Ben. Such lines of defence were fragile at best, as Rosie had just conclusively proved, and the idea of Kayleigh as friend and champion so novel that Annabel didn't quite believe in it. It could all be an elaborate and cruel hoax to make her look even more stupid than she looked already. But oh! she couldn't help thinking, how wonderful if it was true! Nobody, but *nobody* argued with Kayleigh Tregear!

Liz slapped her comb into her hand, and mesmerised by conflicting emotions, Annabel obediently hauled it through her curls before finding herself, she wasn't certain how, at the top of the stairs and then on her way down them.

One more flight ...

In the passage below, her mother waited with Kayleigh. It was impossible to retreat, as Liz was behind her. Ben and Seb had already gone ahead, fine friends they were! She went as slowly as she dared down the second flight of stairs.

'Hullo Annabel,' said Kayleigh, with a beaming smile. 'Come on then – we're going to be late if we don't hurry.' She made an urging gesture with her arm and Annabel, as helpless as a mouse in front of a snake, walked down the hall and out of the door.

Liz and Susan repaired to the kitchen. 'Was that good, or bad, do you think?' Liz asked.

'It was unexpected,' Susan replied, which was no real answer. She reached for the loaf and the bread knife. 'Toast?'

'Just a quick slice.' Liz added, regretfully, 'I must be on my way. Go and look at what Paul's done to my door and see my cat.'

'It's been a strange weekend.'

'A learning experience.'

'It's weird,' said Susan, slapping bread into the toaster. 'A lot of things have happened, but there's nothing really to discuss. It's wait and see time over Mother's house, over you and Paul, over Annabel and her alarming new friend ...'

'It gets like that sometimes. It's called Life.'

'Inconclusive, you mean?'

'Totally. We never really know what will happen next.'

'I'll tell you one thing that will happen next,' said Susan, picking up the butter dish to put it on the table. 'Mother will get wind of Kayleigh Tregear and do her nut! Ben is bad enough, but Kayleigh!'

'Then, if you want my advice, make sure she doesn't. Annabel needs someone like Kayleigh right now.'

'Don't we all,' said Susan, gloomily.

'You could try explaining to your mother,' said Liz, after a pause.

'No. You don't explain to my mother.'

'Have you ever tried?'

Susan thought of the million and one things she had tried to explain to Dot over the years, and quailed at the sheer number of them. 'Some things, Mother would never understand.' The toast was done, Susan put it in the rack and sat down opposite Liz, placing it on the table. 'It's very sobering to realise she was probably right about the village school. Seb is fine, but Annabel ...'

'Annabel was fine too, until this happened,' Liz told her, firmly. 'Good for her to mix with real people. And as for your mother being right, it's only her point of view. Valid maybe, in one way anyway, but it doesn't have to be yours.'

'I should like to be a fly on the wall at school right now,' said Susan, reflectively.

'Me too. You must ring me this evening and tell me what happens.'

'I will.' Susan sighed, unintentionally gustily. 'Why do things never go smoothly?'

'Because they don't. Now for goodness' sake, eat your toast and cheer up!'

'Oh, I shall miss you when you're gone!'

'Me too,' said Liz, again. 'Me too. But you've got Carl, Auntie Sue, lucky you.' She put on a mock-sad expression. 'Me, I've got nobody. Just a cat.'

Susan didn't reply to this, and Liz didn't pursue it. They were still contemplating in silence the many queries their brief exchange had raised when Carl and Clinker came in through the door, fresh and chilly after their morning walk, and the chance passed.

XVI

The first thing that Liz had to do, when she arrived home some two hours later, was, of course, to visit her neighbour and collect her new key. 'He's a strange one, that,' said Tina, as she handed it over. 'You'd've thought, wouldn't you, that when he couldn't turn the key, he'd've come for help to Sid, not just bust his way in.' She gave Liz a shrewd look. 'Keeping him out, weren't you? I know as you'd changed the lock, was that why?'

Liz hesitated. She liked Tina, but they weren't more than good neighbours; there was an age gap of thirty years or so between them, apart from a huge cultural gulf. On the other hand, if Paul was going to do things like this, maybe she should have Tina on her side.

The thought brought her up abruptly. If Paul was going to do things like this, what Susan had said about stalking would come uncomfortably close to the truth. But he wouldn't. Would he?

She realised that Tina was still waiting for a reply and made a swift decision. If she had nobody here to watch out for her interests, she would never be able to leave home in peace. She said, 'Come in and have a cup of coffee when I've had a chance to unpack and check the post. How's Tib? Out on the rampage, slaughtering things?' She caught a flicker of something in Tina's expression. 'He is OK, isn't he?'

'As to that, I'm no expert, but if he was my cat, I'd be taking him to the vet this morning. Sid was all for taking him Saturday night, but I said no, it's not as if it's that serious, best not to interfere. But in my view, he's had a knock. Of course, it could have been a car, or a kid on a bike.' She obviously didn't think so. She said, 'I've kept him in while that man was still around. Maybe you'd like to come in and take a look. He's out in the conservatory.' She turned on the word and led the way through the cottage to the back, where she and her Sid had built a fine conservatory to sit in on sunny days. Liz followed, her mind whirling. Paul didn't like cats, but he wouldn't hurt Tib, surely?

Tib was curled comfortably into a deeply cushioned chair, looking smug. An almost empty food bowl was on the tiled floor alongside, and a bowl of fresh water. Liz was relieved. 'At least he isn't off his food.'

'No, it takes a lot to put that one off his food,' said Tina, with grim amusement, 'but if you touch him wrong, or try to pick him up, he cries. I'd say he'd been kicked, myself.'

Liz squatted down beside the chair and stroked the soft, stripy fur gently. 'Hullo Tibby, what've you been doing? Getting into trouble?' A rich, throbbing purr rewarded her, but when she tried to move him, he cried and lifted a warning paw, claws flexed. She sat back on her heels, biting her lip. 'See what you mean. He's not happy, is he?'

'You leave him here, while you get yourself sorted out,' said Tina. 'Then you come over with the cat basket and we'll get him in, and you can take him down the vet. He'll be all right with me.' She narrowed her eyes. 'We'll have that coffee another time.'

Liz let herself into her own cottage with her new key and stood in the tiny hall, wondering if it was only in her own imagination that she felt an alien presence. She was half-tempted to ring Susan and tell her about this new development, but then changed her mind. Perhaps Tina was wrong about Paul kicking Tib, and the vet would tell her so. She dropped her weekend bag onto the tiles and walked through into her study.

Someone had been at her desk, she saw at once. Perhaps Paul had used her computer; she tried to remember if he knew her password, but he had been in and out so much that she wasn't certain. Automatically, she reached out to put her pens back where they belonged and straighten the pile of the printout for her new book. He had read it, probably. She wondered why she should mind, for the reason she wrote books in the first place was for people to read them. Not sneakily, though, before she had finished and while they were still unedited. No first draft was ever perfect – no last draft either, in her experience, but that was another story. It was an invasion of privacy to do what Paul had done, he wasn't connected with her publisher, he had no right.

He took a lot of things as his right that actually weren't.

There were signs of him in the kitchen, too. An untidy stack of dishes waiting to be washed by the sink – Paul never washed up, it was women's work – a subtle misplacing of her pots and pans, a folded newspaper left on the table. Silly to feel as if she'd been burgled, but that's the way it was. Moreover, she found herself with a distinct feeling that the slight disorder was deliberate. He had meant her to remain aware he had been here.

'Bugger,' said Liz aloud, and with the word, a sudden wave of fury swept over her. How dare he! How dare he break into her home uninvited, kick her cat, and leave his mess all over the kitchen! Just who did he think he was? She had told him, hadn't she, she didn't want him here? Really angry now, she picked up the newspaper, scrumpled it up and pitched it into the bin. He had made free with the contents of her freezer, she immediately saw from the abandoned packaging already there, and she stalked across to the fridge and flung the door open. No milk, not even enough for a cup of coffee! No bread either, which she normally kept in a freezer bag on the shelf, although he had kindly left the bag. Not a mushroom or a tomato in sight, good thing she'd had breakfast in Cornwall! He'd done himself well, there were no eggs in the crock beside the stove either.

She found that she was shaking, and was even more furious to discover she wasn't entirely sure what with. She sat down at the kitchen table and tried to gather her ideas together.

On present form, she'd be needing to change the sheets on her bed too, he probably wouldn't even have made it. The thought was depressing. She put her head in her hands, fighting a storm of mixed emotions of which the chief appeared to be indignation, but there was a nasty little twist there somewhere that gave her reservations. Now I know, she thought, how people feel when their homes are broken into. *Bugger* Paul!

The ring of the phone made her pull herself together. She went into her study and picked it up. 'Liz,' said Alice. 'You're back! Did you have a good weekend?'

'Interesting,' said Liz. 'I met Auntie Sue's mum. She's ...'

'She's what?' asked Alice, with interest, when Liz failed to finish her sentence.

Liz thought, and eventually, said, 'Not what I expected.'

'In what way?'

'I'm still trying to work it out. It felt as if I wasn't looking at her through the same window as everybody else, does that sound silly?'

'Well, you weren't, were you? The rest of them, Susan and all of them, they're carrying baggage that you don't have.'

'I suppose so.'

'Come over and have a cup of coffee and tell me all about it,' Alice enticed.

'I can't. I have to take Tib to the vet.'

'Come over afterwards. Come and have lunch with me. I can't come over there, I have to mind the shop, Gil's gone off somewhere on business. Someone wanting lots of lovely expensive plants for a new garden.'

'Maybe. I'll ring you.' She hesitated, then said, 'Did you realise Paul was here over the weekend?'

'No, was he? I don't get out much at the weekends, we're busy, even at this time of year.' Alice paused in her turn. 'But you were away.'

'Yes.'

'Come to lunch,' ordered Alice. 'Look, must go, the other phone's ringing. See you later, and have I got news for you!' She was gone before Liz could either argue the point or question her further. She sighed, disconnected, and then dialled the vet's number. Perhaps lunch with Alice would clear the air a bit, it certainly needed it. She hoped the news was good news.

The vet said that Tib was certainly bruised in what might euphemistically be called his armpit, but that nothing appeared to be broken.

'Took a knock, did he?' he asked, fixing Liz with an accusing eye.

'I don't know, I was away for the weekend. My neighbour was looking after him.' She hesitated. 'Could it have been from a kick, do you think?'

His suspicious look narrowed. 'You think someone kicked him? Your neighbour?'

'Good heavens, no! Just someone. You know what people can be like.'

Sadly, the vet did; he saw a lot of it in his line of business. He said, 'Well, try to keep him in for a couple of days, just to give it a chance to mend. And if you find out who, report them!'

'Oh, I will,' Liz promised, but she knew he knew she already knew, and wouldn't.

Feeling that she had disappointed somebody she rather liked, she took Tib home and settled him in the best armchair, put an earthbox in the kitchen by the barricaded cat flap, and went out to the village shop to replenish her denuded larder. Here, she learned Alice's interesting news before Alice had a chance to tell her.

'So what d'you make of the latest, then?' Mrs Pinkerton asked her, when she approached the counter to pay for her basketful.

'Not heard it,' Liz admitted. 'I've been away, only just got back – hence these iron rations. So, what's been happening?'

'George Pryor had a firm offer on his place at last, that's what's happened,' said Mrs Pinkerton, rattling the till. Liz was surprised, probably in company with the rest of Waldren Stavey's inhabitants, who had largely given up hope and taken their business elsewhere.

'Good heavens! Who was daft enough to make an offer on that disaster?'

Mrs Pinkerton gave her a cynical look. ''t'idn' a good offer, mind.'

'So who, then,' Liz urged.

'Some army bloke, came and give it a look last week gone. Moving into the area with his family, looking for a business now he's out of the military.' Mrs Pinkerton sniffed. 'Hope he's got capital, just. That place never made a penny in all the time it's been there. We all thought as it'd go for a building plot in the end, and that'd be that.'

'Could have been something to do with George,' Liz ventured. 'He's a dear chap, do anything for anyone – but he knows sod all about cars.'

'Had a bit of a do yourself, your sister was telling me.'

Trust Alice. Liz grinned. 'The RAC man was quite poetic,' she said, gathering her shopping into a bag. 'Is Ole J – is George planning to accept the offer?'

'Him!' Mrs Pinkerton snorted. 'Says it's a joke, he's holding out for better. Well, he's done that before, and here he is a year on and the place still on his hands. Some of us never learn. That'll be seven pounds and fifty-three pee thank you, Elizabeth.'

Liz left the shop and carried her shopping home with a grin on her face. That was one in the eye for Alice then, Captain Anstruther had a family – of course, it could be his old mum and dad and his dear old Gran, but Liz didn't believe it. Wife and kids that sounded like. Hard luck, sis! She wondered where he was moving to, exactly, and if it was here in the village or out in the hinterland. He had had that glossy look that probably meant he had a bob or two, she admitted to herself now. Sergeant Ginger Moustache, on the other hand, was definitely one of the lads. She wondered where he was planning to live. For some unidentifiable reason, she couldn't connect him with a wife and kids; if so he'd have every unattached girl in the village eyeing him up if he settled here. She thought he could probably handle it.

Liz put her shopping away, checked Tib, who yawned in her face and went back to sleep, told Tina she'd catch up with her later, and then drove her car to the nursery, where she found Alice tossing salad. She sat down on a chair by the kitchen table to watch, and Alice said, 'Have a good weekend then?'

'Except for Annabel falling out with her best friend and Paul breaking into my house and kicking my cat, great thank you.'

Alice raised her eyebrows. 'Not a classic, then, I take it.'

'No.'

'Are you going to tell me?' asked Alice, after a pause.

'Oh ... Annabel's going on to a public school in Truro in the autumn, and she was boasting about it a bit unadvisedly. They all sneered at her and called her a snob, and her friend Rosie cut her dead in the street. She didn't want to go to school this morning.'

'Don't blame her! Poor Annabel, it's no big deal for her, of course. Just how things always were but aren't any more, but will be again come autumn.' Alice, who had received a private education herself, as had Liz, saw nothing out of the way in Annabel's behaviour and was sorry for her. 'In the school she was at before, Truro would be very small beer, probably.'

'True, but even Annabel didn't really understand that.'

'So what did Auntie Sue do?'

'Auntie Sue isn't Grade A mummy material, as you know. She took the view that Annabel had to live it down, and the sooner she got to grips with it the better.'

'She's right of course,' said Alice, thoughtfully. 'Even so, it's a bit hard. So what happened?'

'What happened is that some female thug from Annabel's year, who apparently rules the class like Attila the Hun did the marauding hordes, turned up on the doorstep and swept her off under her wing, I suspect because of all that business with Paul's car back when; the villain Damien Tregear is her cousin, he's the one who wrote all over it. Annabel never told on him, even to us – although we all guessed, of course.'

'So, out of evil, good may come?'

'Let's hope so. Annabel looked terrified when she left with this Kayleigh.'

Alice finished tossing her salad and placed the bowl on the table. She added bread, knives and forks, plates and a platter of smoked fish, and then sat down opposite Liz. 'Now tell me about Paul   I hadn't heard about it.'

'Well, you wouldn't. It wasn't exactly the crime of the year. He *says* he thought the lock was broken, but actually, I'd asked Gil to change it for me – as you know.'

'Mmm,' said Alice. 'Have some salad.' They ate in silence for a few minutes, then Alice said, 'You made it clear to Paul you were going to be away, I take it?'

'Of course I did. What do you take me for?'

'Then why ....?'

'God knows. I wish *I* did.' Liz paused. 'I didn't tell him where I was going, in fact I deliberately misled him because I didn't want him following me again, but he rang yesterday morning anyway. Susan implied I wasn't there, but he didn't believe her.'

'So, did you speak to him?'

'No. I wasn't there, remember?'

'You're going to have to do something about him,' said Alice, after a pause. Liz gave her a look.

'Suggestions from the floor, please.'

'Easy. Just tell him.'

'I have.'

'In so many words?'

'Well ...'

'You're going to have to spell it out to him, in words of one syllable. Like F U C K O F F,' said Alice, which was easy for her to say when she wouldn't be the one doing it. Liz said, 'I have tried. Truly I have. He just doesn't listen.'

'You're too kind to him. Just tell him to go bother Ash, whoever she is.'

'He said she was nobody. Just some kid he'd been asked to keep an eye on by her parents.'

'And you believed him?'

Liz thought about this. She said, 'On the whole, yes. It didn't actually disagree with what Cecy said, and you know she doesn't like him. She'd put the worst slant on it she could, short of telling an outright lie, just to spite him.'

'Would she indeed?' Alice paused. 'I think it's time you had a serious talk with Cecy. Why don't you go up to London, and suss the whole thing out?'

'I hate London.'

'You're going to have to do it sometime, or have him round your neck for ever. Your choice.'

'Tib –'

'I'll look after Tib. Or Aunt Sarah will.'

Robbed of her excuses, Liz looked mutinous. 'What gives you the right to push me around?'

'My older sister status. And the fact that somebody has to, or Paul will still be around, wasting your life, in your old age. Do you want that?'

'No, of course not!'

'Right, then,' said Alice, on a note of triumph. 'Now tell me about Susan's mother. It sounded almost as if you actually liked her.'

'I did,' admitted Liz.

'Why, particularly? What grabbed you about her?'

'Oh, lots of things. And Grandad was fond of her, everyone says, and he was nobody's fool from what I know. I wish I remembered him.' She sounded wistful. Alice frowned.

'You're changing the subject. Go on. Lots of things, you said, that's only one.'

'Well ...' Liz frowned, thinking. 'She's very defensive. Leaps into the fight before anyone's offered battle, as if she's used to fighting her corner ... and she always expects the worst, I noticed, even in small things.'

'Which is two ways of saying the same thing,' Alice pointed out. 'Come on, there must be more to it than that. She's the family ogre, for goodness' sake!'

'She loves them,' said Liz, slowly. 'She loves them all, even Oliver, but I don't think they realise how much. She's not too good at showing it, as if she doesn't quite know how.'

'Like Susan, when we first knew her,' said Alice, nodding.

'Yes, but worse than that. She doesn't even seem to *expect* anything back. As if she's never had it.'

'We know she did, from Grandad,' Alice objected.

'Perhaps she didn't recognise it then, either,' said Liz. The discussion seemed to have run out of steam, there was no future in discussing somebody neither of them knew except by reputation, for Liz couldn't claim more than a swift glimpse. Alice shrugged her shoulders.

'Not our problem,' she said, with which Liz didn't necessarily agree, but she didn't argue the point. Instead, she said, 'So, fill me in on Ole Jarge. Mrs P in the shop said the REME were on the job.'

'Early days yet,' said Alice, not at all disappointed at having her thunder stolen, she had rather expected it since Liz had been home for the best part of the morning. 'Jarge has rejected the offer, they might not want to play his game.'

'Depends how much they want it,' suggested Liz.

'Can't be very much. Mrs Jarge says the offer was an insult '

'So is the state of Jarge's business.'

'You can't expect him to agree with that. Fun if they did buy it though – apart from the benefit to our transport, it'd give you a second chance with the gorgeous Captain Anstruther.'

'He's married,' said Liz, with some satisfaction.

'What? How do you know?'

'Heard it in the shop. *Moving into the area with his family,* only one sensible conclusion to draw from that.'

'Oh,' said Alice. 'Oh well, he was pretty much a non-starter anyway. How about Sergeant Whatever-his-name-was?'

'Wainwright,' said Liz. 'And no. Never in a million years! Now stop hogging the salad and pass it over here, and tell me all about Gil's rich new client.'

A few days after this Dot, too, made her way home, and like Liz, with a lot to think about. It had been a strange week, she had seen aspects of her children that she had never seen before for one thing. She had seen Susan, at peace and much loved in her own simple cottage, surrounded by computers and books and happy children, not all of them her own, with the man who surely ought to be her husband working away upstairs; a cluttered, contented life in which Annabel and Sebastian so obviously thrived – although she wasn't too certain about Annabel's friend Kayleigh. A real rough diamond, that one, but probably when Annabel went on to her new school that would all come to an end, and a good thing too in Dot's opinion. She knew trouble when she saw it, and Kayleigh Tregear was it. Ben, she had become used to; he was a nice little boy on closer acquaintance, well brought up, and she liked his mother too. Morwenna Jenkin was a good friend to Susan, as her son was to Sebastian. Dot appreciated that, knowing in her heart that she herself had in some respects failed them both.

Then there was Debbie. Debbie was a completely different person from the Deborah Dot had thought she knew so well. A casual but competent mother, who loved her baby without letting him rule her life, and loved her amazing husband without letting him rule her life either. Dot had come to terms with Mawgan, and believed he had done the same with her; there would always be a mutual reservation between them but they also now had a mutual respect. Debbie's life, and those who shared it, had achieved a workable balance, Dot envied her.

She had gone with Debbie down to her sailing school and been shown around, and been impressed. She was proud of Debbie, Susan too. So different, they were: Debbie the business woman, Susan the academic, each in her turn following in the footsteps of her respective father. It occurred to Dot with increasing frequency that Henry the default husband had been pure gold, Jerry the first choice some far

312

more dangerous metal, and not for her. Not, she thought wryly, the only or indeed the first mistake in her life. Would Henry be alive now if she had recognised it earlier? Probably not – he would be over ninety – but he might have lived both longer and happily, and she would have known the delightful Elizabeth Ballantyne and her relations all her life – all Susan's life. Would that have been a fair exchange for Debbie, who would then never have been born? Dot didn't know. There are some questions to which there is no answer.

She had, she realised, undervalued Susan in exactly the same way as she had undervalued Henry. The realisation was humbling.

But the biggest shock of the week, if she was honest, had been Oliver. She had never really understood Oliver, for all she had brought him up, and no wonder! He wasn't only Helen's son, wild, untameable Oliver, he was Jerry's too, and the resemblance between them, as Oliver grew older, was disturbing. She had never fathomed Jerry either, if she was being truthful. It was, she thought, a good time to be truthful, at least with herself. No need to spread it around.

She thought about Oliver now. She had always considered that Helen and Jerry between them had made such a mess of their son that he had no hope of ever amounting to anything, whatever his potential. A rebellious child, in trouble with the police as a teenager, a drifter as an adult, moving from one exotic job to another – delivery skipper, diver, flotilla skipper, nothing normal or carrying a sensible pension. He could have studied law, he had the brains for it, gone into his father's firm as a partner, been a responsible citizen. Instead, he had studied some Mickey Mouse subject at university, nearly been sent down for using drugs, finally achieved a rather mediocre degree, and then run away to sea. No. Correction. Run away, full stop. He had crowned this series of disasters by ditching Joanna Rendell, a girl from his own world, and running away – again – with a receptionist from the Queens Hotel on the waterfront, marrying her out of hand and in the teeth of opposition from both his own family and hers. They had lived in a bedsit – it was no more – above a shop by the harbour, where Oliver worked on a professional diving team and achieved accidental fame by first, finding an important historic wreck, and second by getting himself mugged and nearly murdered, resulting in his present disablement and the ending of what career he could ever be said to have had. He and Cheryl had ended up living in a caravan, for heaven's sake! And once again, he had run away, this time to Cornwall.

But now ...

Cheryl had invited Dot to tea so she could see little Zoë again and get to know her, more out of politeness and a wish to establish some kind of acceptable relationship than any real wish to entertain her, as Dot was well aware. But all three of her children, if you counted Oliver as one of them, were making an effort, it behoved her therefore to make an effort back, and so she had accepted the invitation in the spirit in which it was given. She wasn't sure what she had expected, some cottage perhaps, maybe terraced like Susan's, but smaller and more humble. She couldn't imagine a struggling artist being able to afford much more, and she knew that Cheryl had to go out to work, running Mawgan's pub for him. She had had no high expectations. It had come as a shock, therefore, to find that Oliver and Cheryl lived in a modest but beautiful stone-built period house beside a tranquil creek, with Oliver's studio above the adjoining garage, approached by a set of curving steps beside the wall. The studio had a balcony that overlooked the water and the opposite wooded shore, and afforded glimpses of the river mouth beyond. Oliver had taken her up there, a courtesy she hadn't expected, and shown her his work. He hadn't said much, true, but he had done it, although possibly at Cheryl's instigation. Cheryl hadn't come up with them. Dot wondered then, and wondered again now, if she had hoped that they might effect a reconciliation if she wasn't there. And maybe they had, in a way.

She had not been invited to Oliver's first exhibition, nor any subsequent ones either, and so she knew his work mainly by report. She had been shown the catalogue of that first public show, but the photographs therein hadn't done Oliver's work justice: in real terms, it was breathtaking. Dot had stood in the door of the studio speechless, and Oliver had leaned casually against a workbench along the wall and watched her. Finally, she had found her voice. 'I never thought it would be like this,' she had said, for "struggling", she now saw, had been the wrong adjective. Oliver had made no reply, and she had walked around the studio, studying the walls that glowed with colour and shimmered with light, and the unfinished work on two separate easels, one in oils, the other, smaller, in what he informed her was gouache, and had been rendered completely speechless. So this, then, was what Oliver was all about. Helen Macken's son, and all her talent transmuted into this tide of beauty and colour, this storm of love and empathy with sea, ships and shore, the things that had formed the background of his life since he was old enough to decide for himself. She had been humbled, she admitted it. She had also realised, which she had not expected, how Helen's defection had diverted the course of his life and made him what he was – what he had been. He had needed Helen, he had always felt she had let him down and deserted him, and for the first time ever Dot completely understood this and her heart went out to him. She couldn't see how Helen, whatever she did now, could ever make that up to him. Perhaps he didn't even want her to try. Oliver had always been a loner; only the Wainwright girl, Cheryl, had ever breached his defences.

Strange, that. Perhaps it was her practicality that anchored him. Dot would have been very surprised had she known how very unpractical Cheryl could be. But then, she had never really bothered to get to know Cheryl.

The turning off the motorway for Embridge was coming up, Dot brought her full attention back to her driving. It had been an interesting week, illuminating even, but now she was nearly home. She braked for the turn, and as she did so, the last thought of her journey that wasn't to be concerned with town traffic and wandering pedestrians flashed through her mind quite without her own volition.

They were all of them such talented young people, each one a star in their own firmament; Oliver, Mawgan, Debbie, Susan, Carl ... and she had thrown away her own chance to shine among the stars because she hadn't had the courage to stand up for herself and fight for something she had wanted so much that it actually hurt. The familiar bitterness of it choked like bile in her throat.

The house seemed very big and empty when Dot returned to it; it had never struck her before how unnecessarily big it was. She had talked glibly about downsizing, and latterly had even begun to mean what she said, but for the first time she realised without reservation how much happier she would be without all these empty rooms lowering over her. She walked through the echoing hall and in contrast with the week she had just spent in Cornwall, ached with its loneliness. The family that had once occupied the space had gone west – literally gone west, and there was no option for her to follow; she had find a new, different life of her own or waste the rest of her time as she now saw she had wasted the time up to now. They would come back for visits, of course they would, but she had to accept that her children, all three of them, had finally and irrevocably left home and made their own lives elsewhere. It happened to everybody. Only, the lucky ones had a husband beside them to share the changed circumstances and make something new of them. For her own sake, she must stop merely going through the motions and do some serious house-hunting, it was time, more than time, to change ... *for* a change, she hastily corrected the thought. Suddenly overcome by a painful wave of empty-nest syndrome, she carried her suitcase to the foot of the stairs and noticed, for the first time, the red light flashing on her answering machine. Even a recorded voice, at that moment, was better than nobody. She pressed the button to listen.

'Dorothy!' Bennie's voice greeted her, 'Dorothy, are you home? Give me a ring, talk to me. Better still, come over to lunch. I've something to tell you – to show you. Be in touch!' A click ended the message, and the resulting silence closed in once more.

Dot picked up her suitcase again and carried it upstairs. She wasn't used to people leaving messages like that, friendly and personal, issuing casual invitations to lunch. She was more used to committee business, people who wanted to make use of her. It felt strange to be wanted – for herself alone, she thought cynically – and then realised that it also felt rather pleasant. She unpacked thoughtfully, stowed her suitcase back in the spare bedroom, and returned to the telephone downstairs. She looked at it for a minute as if it might bite her, and then picked it up and dialled Bennie's number.

It turned out that Bennie had left her message two days earlier. 'But it doesn't matter,' she said. 'You're here now. Did you have a nice time? Is the baby beautiful? Who is he like?'

'He takes after his father,' said Dot. 'Cheryl tells me that this is a trick of Mother Nature to discourage fathers from rejecting their children, but she has some very strange, mid-Suffolk notions sometimes. And yes thank you, Benita, I had a very pleasant week. Very ...' she hesitated, over the next word but then said it anyway, 'informative.'

Bennie, for all that she had known Dot for only a very short while, had seen her with her defences down which most people hadn't, or if they had, had failed to recognise it. She filed the comment for consideration later, and said, 'Is it too late to ask you over for lunch?

I suppose it is, really, if you're only just back. Tomorrow? There's something I want to show you.'

'You said so in your message. What can it be, I wonder?'

'Wait and see,' said Bennie. 'I promise you, it's good. A date, then?'

Reflecting that she had no other demands on her time since Jenny Carruthers had frozen her off so many committees, Dot agreed, and they fixed a time; twelve o'clock at the farmhouse. Bennie gave her directions and then very meanly hung up before Dot could question her further. She stood in the hall with the phone in her hand and wondered. It was most probably a house, she thought. It would be interesting to see how closely Benita had listened to her; most people didn't bother. She would find out tomorrow.

On this, on the whole pleasant, thought, Dot made her way to the kitchen to see what Leanne had provided for her lunch. After she had eaten, she would attend to the accumulated post, mostly junk mail for recycling from the look of it, and then put her feet up and enjoy the peace and quiet of her own home. A house with a small baby in it, however good the baby, wasn't a restful place, and neither was her son-in-law a restful man. Not that he had been home that much, he had two restaurants to attend to and a pub to run, for all that Cheryl managed the last for him, and how she did that with a child to look after beggared imagination! Dot had seen none of them, except from the outside, but she thought that her children had been breaking her in gently and had therefore not pushed the point. Pubs hadn't figured largely in her life to date, and she had made it very clear at the time of Debbie's wedding what she thought about such places, although she would have liked to see the restaurant – the Rose, they called it, although that wasn't its real name – *An Rosen Gwyn*, very Cornish – and the mural that Oliver had painted. Next time ... there would be a next time.

She needed to work on her relationship to every one of them, and over the past week they had shown their willingness to meet her halfway. She wondered what changes this would make in her life, but one thing was certain: they might make peace, all the signs were there, but they would never return on the old terms and nothing was ever going to be the same again.

*

Shortlanesend lay in the rural area between the village of Emberton, at the western end of the harbour, and the village of Shearwater a few miles inland. As Dot already knew, it was part of a huge area of land held by the Vachell family, who had been around even longer than the rather more aristocratic Ravenscourts, owning almost everything in the immediate area that the Ravenscourts didn't. Their holdings lay to the south and west of Shearwater, the Ravenscourt land lying north and east, with Shearwater itself in the Ravenscourt belt. If the Ravenscourts were aristocracy, the Vachells were good English yeomanry who could trace their origins back to the Domesday Book, and the Vachell land, rather than being one large estate, was comprised of separate farms owned and worked by individual members of the family, now administered over all by a limited company with a board formed of family members. Bennie's husband, Ernest Vachell, had been born at Shortlanesend, as had his father and grandfather before him. Very feudal, Dot reflected, as she drove down a winding lane towards what she hoped was the right place. Why couldn't Deborah and Susan have met somebody like that? Too late now.

The farmhouse at Shortlanesend was old, the kind of house, in fact, that Dot fancied for herself. Built of warm golden stone with a grey slate roof, it snuggled into the edge of the downs like a cat into a cushion, its small mullioned windows blinking out thoughtfully, watching for who came. Over the centuries, various marauders had tried to dislodge the cat; so far, none had succeeded. It grew fat and sleek and prospered.

Dot parked her car outside the house and got out. Bennie had told her to go round to the farmyard, where she would find the back door.

'Nobody ever uses the front door,' she had said, blithely. 'Except for Jehovah's Witnesses and people selling things, that is. The sound of the knocker is like a warning signal, take cover!' Dot, who had never used a back door in her life that she recalled, approached the five-barred gate to the farmyard and pushed it open. The yard was big and cobbled, a bank of outbuildings flanking it on two sides, some of which were stables; three horses looked out at her with interest, and the door to the last stable stood open. Then there was the clop of hooves behind her, and she turned to see Bennie approaching through another gateway, leading the fourth horse.

318

'Hi, you found us then! Just let me see to this girl, and I'll be with you!' She paused beside Dot, smiling. 'Do you like horses?'

Dot reached up to stroke the soft nose nuzzling at her sleeve. She said, wistfully, 'I haven't ridden in years. I had a friend at school who had a pony, she used to let me ride it, I never had a proper lesson. My granddaughter has a pony now, but I've never seen it.' And had thought that she never would, since the pony lived on Henry's eldest son's farm in Devon, but after having met Liz, she was no longer so sure. For a second she had a sensation of all her securities crumbling around her, but then she pulled herself together. She had no time for people who crumbled. 'This is a very beautiful horse, but surely, too big for you.'

'She's Ernest's,' said Bennie, 'although I have ridden her. But you're right, it is a bit like sitting astride the ridge of a rather high roof. Say hullo to the others while I see to this one. Second on the left is mine.'

Dot obediently cruised the stable doors, stroking velvety noses poked hopefully over the top and gathering impressions. She paid special attention to the second on the left, and Bennie came to join her with a handful of carrots. 'Here – give her one of these. She'll be your friend for ever.' She held one out, and Dot extended her hand, palm up, with the carrot sitting on it. The horse lipped it off and crunched contentedly. Bennie nodded approval. 'I can see you've seen a horse before.' She handed carrots to the last two, and then turned to lead the way to the house. 'Lunch – Ernest is in town on business, so there's just us. I thought we'd have it in the kitchen, it's far cosier, and warmer too. It's chilly today, isn't it?'

The sun was shining, albeit from a cloudy sky, but it was true, the wind was cold. Dot followed her to the back door, thinking that she wasn't used to being asked to eat in kitchens, the nearest she had ever come was Deborah's kitchen/dining room, but this was a day of new experiences – so far, a year of them indeed. She went with the tide.

The kitchen was a period piece, and Dot thought that the period concerned must be almost the same as the outside of the house, with the single addition of a rather more modern Aga to replace what could quite possibly even have been a turnspit originally. The Aga stood looking lost in a great arched fireplace with ample room for a boiler beside it, and the pipes and wheels that fed and controlled it looked severely out of place. There was a distinct lack of worktops, a lot of old oak cupboards lolling against the walls as if they had seen all of life and were tired of it, a big chest of drawers beneath the biggest window with a bowl of fruit on it, and a huge, scrubbed table that could seat a small army, probably of farmhands. An enormous dresser took up most of one wall, and accommodated an assortment of antique china plates and dishes which on their own, Dot estimated, could have raised enough at auction to refit the entire kitchen in a more modern and convenient style. Bennie saw her looking, and grinned.

'Like something from *Upstairs, Downstairs*, isn't it?' she said. 'Not up-to-the-minute, of course, but it's friendly.' Which was true, Dot conceded. There were curtains at the windows, pictures on the walls, and the window sills were crammed with pot plants and growing herbs; the two wing chairs either side of the Aga were piled with bright cushions, the obligatory farm cat curled among them. No dogs, Dot was pleased to see. She searched for and found something nice to say. 'Attractively traditional, I would describe it.'

'Be honest,' said Bennie cheerfully. 'You think it's caught in a probably unhygienic time warp – and you're right, of course. But it works for us, and anyway, we haven't time to think about changing it, we're too busy. Do sit down. Lunch is all ready in the larder. Just let me wash my hands –' she vanished through a door that probably, Dot guessed, led into an old-fashioned scullery. She pulled out a chair and sat down, wondering how many people these days boasted a larder. And there were dogs, she now realised, their baskets, but thankfully not themselves, were tucked in beside the stove. There was plenty of room for them. She was wondering what she would do with this kitchen if it were hers when Bennie came back, bearing a dish with a cold chicken on it and with a salad bowl tucked into her other arm.

'Only something light, we have dinner in the evening when the work is finished for the day – could you get some cutlery out, Dot? Left hand drawer of the dresser – that's it.'

The cutlery was mismatched, old, and rather beautiful. Bennie rattled a couple of priceless plates onto the table and began to carve the chicken. 'Breast or leg? This is Chloe, by the way, she was a poor layer.'

Dot admitted a preference for breast, thinking that she had never been formally introduced to her lunch before and then said, trying not to sound critical, 'Should you be using those plates, Benita dear? They're valuable, you know.'

'Are they?' Bennie looked surprised, pausing to look at them. 'Goodness, there's a whole stack of them in the drawing room! Vegetable dishes, great big carving dishes, soup bowls, the lot.'

The chicken, Dot was relieved to note, sat on a metal dish. She said, 'They're Davenport, and worth a great deal of money if you have a full service.'

'Goodness!' Bennie heaped chicken and stuffing on one of them and pushed it towards Dot with the salad bowl. She sat down herself, and then got immediately to her feet. 'I forgot the bread. Sorry!' The cat woke up while she fetched it from a crock on the stone floor, and smelling the chicken, jumped on the table to investigate. Dot pushed it off firmly and it gave her a look before stalking off in the direction of the scullery.

Another new world. Dot wondered how many more of them there were.

There was home-baked peasant bread, farm butter, cider which Bennie claimed they made themselves. The stuffing was delicious. They talked about Daniel, and Dot's Cornish visit, and Dot enjoyed her lunch and the cheese, also made on the premises, with the crisp apple which followed it. 'They grow in the orchard,' Bennie told her. 'We store them in the barn – some of them don't keep, but these ones do. We're not sure what they are.'

Dot couldn't help her, she knew nothing about apples, although rather more about old china. She said, 'So are you going to tell me why I'm here? You said you had something to show me.'

'I do.' Bennie spoke round a mouthful of apple, then swallowed, and continued more clearly. 'It's a house. It isn't on the market yet, but it will be soon, and I think it might be just what you need. There's a cottage goes with it, if you wanted it, where you could keep a married couple, or they'll sell it separately.' She made the putative married couple sound like Chloe the chicken. Then she went on, 'It has just about everything you need – four bedrooms, three reception, conservatory, big kitchen, lovely garden too, but not too big because they've turned the bottom of it into a hard tennis court – your family would enjoy that when they come. I don't suppose you play much tennis yourself!' She smiled as she said it, and then saw Dot's face.

'What have I said?' she asked, but Dot had mastered her expression almost immediately.

'I played a lot at one time,' she said, off-handedly. Bennie narrowed her eyes at her. She had touched a nerve, she divined, but how? She said, with less certainty, 'You could play again. You'd soon get back into it.'

'I don't think so. It's too late for that.' Dot already hated the house, without even seeing it. She smiled to disguise it. Bennie didn't know her well enough to realise, but she would not be alone; nobody else around Dot would have realised either. Dot was used to dissembling.

They went to see the house in Bennie's car when the lunch was cleared away. It was down a winding lane that led off the main village street, and was known as Haymans Lane. The house, too, was called Haymans. At the beginning of the lane there was a certain amount of new building, which Dot thought with relief would give her an excuse to turn the house down out of hand, but it swiftly came to an end, and fields lay to either side. Haymans, said Bennie, as they drove, was the old farmhouse for what had once been Haymans' Farm, but the Hayman family were long gone, and the farmland was now part of the Ravenscourt estate.

'I see they've built on some of it,' said Dot, hoping for a reprieve, but Bennie said, 'Yes, they did, but only close to the village. All this land is let.'

Dot frowned at the fields. She didn't know a great deal about farming, but even to a layman the fields looked overgrown and neglected. 'Really,' she said. Her tone spoke volumes, and Bennie laughed. She drew up outside the gates of a square stone house, the same golden stone and grey slate as her own home. 'Don't look too closely: up until recently, the man who leased them was a so-called organic farmer, which in his case, meant "leave it to nature" – he went bust, naturally enough, and his farm has recently been sold, and the leases went with it, plus a bit more. These fields are leased by one of Ernest's cousins as of now, he'll get round to them soon. There's just too much to put right all at once!' She opened the door on her side and got out, Dot did the same. Bennie pointed across to a nearby hill, prominent among the other rolling hills of the downland. 'The farm is the other side of that. There's an Ancient British encampment or something up there, Susan will love it.' She pushed open the five-barred gate that guarded a gravelled drive. 'Come on.' Dot stepped back, alarmed.

'But people live here! Won't they mind?'

'They're away,' said Bennie, walking through. She saw Dot's expression. 'Don't worry, we aren't trespassing, they said we could look around. I think they'd be quite pleased, actually, if someone loved it and they sold privately, without agent's fees. Wouldn't you?'

Dot said nothing. She wondered, a little wildly, if it was actually possible to hate the idea of something while falling in love with the reality, for the house was delightful. Much later in date than Shortlanesend, but still a period house; Georgian, she thought, it had the proportions. Where Shortlanesend snuggled into the downland, Haymans stood proudly against the background of the fields, surrounded by flowering shrubs and manicured green lawns. There was a double garage, Dot noted, that was good. And a path that meandered round through a shrubbery heading for the rear garden and, presumably, the tennis court. The cottage Bennie had mentioned nestled on a small patch of land beyond the garages, and could, Dot noted, easily be sold as a separate parcel. Not many actual trees; the aspect was open, and if the fields were put in order, would be rural and beautiful, with the rolling downs on the near horizon. Having the Ravenscourts, or even one of Ernest Vachell's cousins, as a neighbour would be one in the eye for Jenny Carruthers.

She realised all at once that she didn't care about Jenny Carruthers' opinion, she could think what she liked. It was a great release. If she bought this house, it would be to please herself. She took a deep breath of clean country air and listened to the silence. Bennie waited. After a while, when Dot said nothing, she ventured, 'I haven't the key, but we can peer in the windows, they won't mind. Then we can go round the back and look at the conservatory, and the court, and all that. There's apple trees too, though not as many as ours. I don't know what they are, either.'

Under normal circumstances, Dot would never have dreamed of peering into the windows of a stranger's home, but Bennie's certainty, and her irrepressible enthusiasm, swept her forward. The rooms were a good size, as far as she could see, and when they got around the house, the conservatory made Susan's look like a back porch, it was huge. The garden, too, contained all the features that Dot particularly liked; a pond and marsh area, the apple trees, an old-fashioned rockery with an amazing variety of saxifrage, a patio with a wheeled iron barbecue, where she imagined Mawgan, or Carl wielding the tongs while the family sat around and chatted with her friends or, in the case of Susan, Debbie and Oliver, their friends maybe. She almost heard the thud of balls from the tennis court, mercifully hidden behind shrubs, and wondered if she could bear it, if all this lovely house and garden would be worth it.

'So, what do you think?' asked Bennie, smiling.

'I think it's very beautiful,' said Dot, thoughtfully. 'I shall keep looking, of course, but when it comes on the market, if I have found nothing, then maybe ... when are they thinking of selling?'

'In the Spring. They'll get a better price. But if there's no agent to pay, that won't be so critical. Think about it, there's no immediate hurry.'

'I will,' said Dot. They turned and walked down the path that led back to the drive. Bennie didn't press it, and Dot didn't discuss it. From the gate, she took a last look at the house. Like Bennie, it appeared to be smiling, welcoming. She turned away undecided, unusual for her, and pulled the big farm-style gate closed behind them. She had a premonition that its ghost would always be there with her. Like the ghost of her lost ambitions.

She could always break up the tennis court and turn it into a wildflower meadow.

XVII

Liz took the full five days to decide to act on her sister's suggestion, but on Friday afternoon she rang Paul and told him she would be in London over the weekend and wanted to talk to him. She could almost hear his eyebrows rising down the phone. 'Really? About what?'

'About us,' said Liz, seeing no reason to equivocate. 'I'll be at the flat on Saturday.'

There was a long silence. At the end of it, Paul said, 'I'll see you for lunch then,' and abruptly replaced his phone.

On Friday evening, Liz had a date with her cousin. They met in a wine bar, Cecy's natural habitat along with nightclubs, pizza emporia and Indian takeaways. Cecy was already there waiting when Liz arrived, two glasses and an opened bottle of Pinot Grigio, sitting in a cooler, on the table before her and an expression of expectation on her face. 'I've been waiting for you,' she said. Liz apologised.

'The traffic was bad. It took my taxi simply ages to get from the station to the flat.'

'Since Christmas, that is,' said Cecy. There was a silence. During it, she picked up the bottle and filled the glasses, picking up her own and raising it in a toast. 'To Truth,' she said. Liz didn't move to pick up her own glass. She looked at Cecy steadily.

'If you know something I don't, why didn't you tell me then?'

'In front of the family? Would you have thanked me? Anyway, at the time, I thought you knew it too.'

'What makes you think, now, that I didn't?'

Cecy twirled her wineglass on the table top and didn't look at her. Liz said, directly, 'Is this about Ash?'

'No. Ash is nothing. Just a way of keeping up his image, an attractive blonde on his arm, and she's found something better to do anyway. That was a family thing, it turns out. She's a star, is Ash. Not much of a model, but a star just the same. You'd like her.'

Liz refused to be side-tracked. 'So what, then?'

Cecy didn't answer her directly. She said, 'I never expected you would be so naïve, but perhaps you just didn't want to see it.'

'Naïve in what way?' Liz tried hard to sound curious rather than indignant, and didn't quite succeed. Cecy took a sip of her wine and nodded towards Liz's glass.

'Try it. It's good. Unless, that is, you don't want to drink with me?'

'I'm not sure I do.' But she drank anyway. 'Now stop beating about the bush, and tell me all the dirt. I feel sure it is dirt, the way you're carrying on.'

'Am I carrying on?' Cecy looked surprised. 'All right then. How much do you know about his precious apartment?'

'His *apartment*? I've been there. If you're going to tell me it's a myth, then you're wrong.'

'Only in a way,' said Cecy. 'It exists all right. Only, it isn't his.'

'What?' Liz was so startled her voice went flat with shock. 'Of course it is. He owns it jointly it with a friend.'

'No, he doesn't. He moonlights as a caretaker during the week, for one of his firm's best-selling authors. He just lets everyone assume it's his, and as that suits the owner very nicely since it protects his privacy, he gets away with it.'

Liz was so totally bewildered that she stared like an idiot. She took another hefty swig of wine. If what Cecy said was true, it explained a great many things that had previously been no more than mildly intriguing. She said, blankly, 'But why not tell me? Why would he do that?'

'Because he's a conceited oaf. He likes people to think he's rich and successful.'

'But I was bound to find out,' Liz objected.

'Were you? It's taken you over two years. You wouldn't be finding out now if I wasn't telling you.'

'Of course, I've not been living in London ...' Her mind creaked back into gear. 'So he's been making use of me, you're saying. Why just me?'

'*Because* you were out of London, I expect. And besotted enough to underwrite his weekends living on your earnings instead of his own double ration.'

Liz went scarlet to the roots of her hair. 'How dare you!' She swallowed, although her wineglass sat on the table before her, untouched now. 'How many other people know this?'

'Some. Most of them think you love him so much you don't care.'

Liz found an objection to this humiliating scenario. 'But why only during the week? Most people want to be out of London at the weekend. It's the wrong way round. I don't believe you.'

Cecy gave her a cynical look. 'Keep drinking. You're going to need it. The author in question has a bit on the side in the country somewhere. Think about it carefully before you answer.'

But Liz was ahead of her. 'And her husband is in town during the week, so, this author ...?'

'Got it in one. They share the honours, but only one of them knows it.'

'And Paul *knows* this?'

'You're not the keeper of his morals, Liz. Of course he does.' She paused. 'The man's a best-seller, I told you. It's in Paul's interest to accommodate him. And while he's got you to field him every weekend, why should he worry?'

'He's got other friends,' said Liz, defensively.

'He'd worked through them before you came along. And from what I can find out, most people think he's a pillock anyway.'

'Then that explains –' Liz paused there.

'Explains what?' asked Cecy, narrowing her eyes, and Liz, after only a brief hesitation, told her.

'I told him I was going to go away for the weekend, and I went to visit Auntie Sue and Carl. He went to Waldren Stavey and broke into my house.'

Cecy looked sceptical. 'Why? I mean, why did he break in? He's got the key, hasn't he?'

'Yes,' said Liz. For the first time, she realised that the obvious explanation she now had of why Paul had invaded her space last weekend was incomplete. He also had the key to her flat, he could have gone there, and with less trouble. She might never have known. It could only be that he had been trying to make a point – but what point? She said, slowly, 'I'd changed the lock,' and Cecy made an expressive face.

'Oh Liz, you are an idiot,' she said.

They looked at each other, Cecy with pity in her eyes, Liz with confrontation in hers. Liz spoke first.

'So tell me,' she said. Cecy answered with care, picking her words.

'Look, I only found this out since Christmas, so don't jump down my throat. I never thought much of Paul, you know that already, but I do believe that when you were first together it was because he was genuinely attracted to you. He liked your growing reputation, of course he did, but you're a nice-looking bird, Elizabeth Ballantyne, you've got style, and any man would be happy to be seen with you. And you had interests in common.'

'Look, Cecy, stop letting me down lightly. You're patronising me.'

Cecy sighed. 'All right then, after what you said at Christmas, I made a few enquiries about poisonous Paul. I knew about the flat already, but that's not all, it turns out. The word is that Paul Attwood is in trouble, he needs to get his finger out and bring in some serious money, a really important client, or he's out of a job. His performance, as they say, has been inadequate – in that department, at least.'

Liz stared at her. 'What? But he brought them Carl.'

'Carl, at the moment, is pie in the sky, he may not fulfil expectations. And Paul didn't bring him in directly, Carl's agent did, and he sent the book to Paul's boss apparently, not to the rank and file. On the face of it, Paul had little or nothing to do with it.'

'How do you know all this?' Liz was indignant. Cecy placed a finger against her nose and winked.

'I have my sources.' She saw Liz's expression, and went on hurriedly. 'I chatted up the girl in his office. She hates his guts, she was quite happy to gossip until the cows came home.' She looked complacent. 'I think I missed my vocation. I should have been a Miss Marple.'

'I still don't see what all this has got to do with me,' said Liz contentiously.

'Oh come on, Liz, you're not that stupid! You're a best-seller. Paul's your best-beloved.'

'But I have a publisher already. Beck would never hand me over to Paul anyway.' Rebecca Studley was Liz's agent and friend. But even as she spoke, a little cold chill ran down Liz's spine. 'He'd have to be a nutter,' she said, but slowly.

'He *is* a nutter,' said Cecy. 'Look what you just told me, for a start. Who but a nutter would have broken into your house, knowing you weren't there?'

It was much what Tina had said Liz said, 'And kicked my cat. And gone through all my things.' They looked at each other.

'Uh-oh,' said Cecy. 'You're in big trouble, cousin Elizabeth. Big, big trouble.'

'He was just being nosy,' said Liz, wondering why she was excusing him. Cecy laughed.

'Really? Then why kick poor Tib? He's never done that before, has he?'

'No. But I've always been there up to now.'

'Look Liz, maybe I've been reading too many thrillers here, but that sounds to me as if he was maybe looking for something.'

'Tib would hardly try to stop him.'

'Maybe he didn't find it. Maybe he took it out on the cat. Maybe Tib miaowed out of turn or got under his feet at the wrong moment.'

Liz said, slowly, 'Auntie Sue said it sounded as if he was stalking me.'

'And is he?'

Liz said nothing. She picked up the bottle out of the cooler and refilled both glasses. She replaced the bottle very carefully and didn't look at Cecy.

'If love won't bring you into the fold, maybe blackmail will.' Cecy was derisive.

Liz took a sip of her wine. She still said nothing.

'Get rid of him,' said Cecy, as many had said before her.

But it wasn't to be that easy.

Liz slept badly that night, not only because an evening spent with Cecy tended to be overly stimulating. There were a lot of things on her mind.

She and Paul had had some good times, she conceded, and she

would stick to that whatever they all said, but if what Cecy had deduced was correct, he had always had a hidden agenda. Or if not that, he had devised one when his circumstances changed. It really didn't matter which, for if either was the truth, he had used her and manipulated her, and on the whole, made a fool of her in front of everyone, and no amount of good times really excused it. And he had, unforgivably, broken into her home and gone through her private papers in her filing cabinet, and quite possibly the files on her computer. She found herself trying to remember if the details of her contract were in either place, when it was due for renewal and the setting out of its terms. She was slack about locking her filing cabinet, but in any case, Tib could probably break into that if he tried and had the motivation. About her computer, she wasn't so sure. Paul might know her password, or he might be clever enough to hack in without it, or to guess. He knew her pretty well – as she had thought she knew him.

She hadn't. Even if Cecy was wrong in her conclusions, she hadn't. The man she had thought she knew wouldn't have broken into her house when he knew she was absent.

Had he also entered this flat? Not to spend a weekend, but to pry into her affairs? Liz sat up abruptly. She had noticed no signs of it, but then she hadn't been looking, she had been in a hurry to meet Cecy, and in this case at least he wouldn't have had to break in, he still had the key. She could ask for it back, but he could have taken a copy. After last weekend, he probably had. All of a sudden, she felt terribly insecure. She would, she thought, always feel insecure here now, whatever she did, because she already knew that changing the lock would be pointless – was quite likely already pointless. If he hadn't been in already, if he could break in once he could do it again, and who would ever pin it on him? She wasn't here that often, and he was a familiar figure coming in and out of the building.

She didn't think he would actually hurt her, but "stalking" was an ugly word.

Oh rubbish! Of course he wasn't stalking her!

Susan and Cecy both thought that he was. *Imagined* he was? She could dismiss Cecy's colourful fabrication as mischief-making, but she couldn't dismiss Susan's more soberly reached conclusion that way.

Liz felt for the switch of the bedside lamp, and turned it on. She wasn't going to sleep anyway, so she might as well check round the place.

For what?

Ten minutes later, Liz was wishing she had stayed in bed and taken an aspirin to make herself sleep in spite of everything. The signs of Paul's presence were slight, but unmistakeable; so slight that it was impossible to decide whether he had left them on purpose to let her know he had been there, or been unaware of having done so. Small things, subtly out of place – books on the wrong shelf, which she might have thought to have been misplaced by her cleaner, or by herself in a careless moment, had there not been other things. A newspaper she never read on top of the pile for recycling, carrying a date on which she had been in Devon. A mug on the wrong shelf. Water left standing in the electric kettle. A minor rearrangement of the, fortunately unimportant, papers she kept in her desk.

Imagination? Carelessness on her own part? She wasn't the most organised bunny in the warren. Carelessness on the part of either her cleaner/caretaker or Paul? Or a subtle intent to apply pressure, to tell her that he had been here?

No way of telling. No point in asking her immediate neighbours either, they wouldn't admit to seeing anything untoward even if they had done so; they wouldn't want to be involved. Come to that, nor would they think seeing Paul coming and going untoward.

Liz went back to bed and lay in the dark, staring at the dim ceiling in the light that filtered through the curtains from the streetlights outside, listening to the muted purr of the night traffic.

In the morning, tired and unrefreshed, she rose from her toussed bed, made herself a cup of strong black coffee and followed it with a phone call. She wasn't certain what made her use her mobile rather than the phone in the flat, but diagnosed it provisionally as paranoia. Whatever his faults, Paul could hardly bug her phone. Could he?

Disconcerting to find that however far-fetched the theory, she wasn't sure.

Cecy answered eventually, with a yawn in her voice. 'Good God, Liz, don't you know what time it is?'

'I couldn't sleep,' said Liz.

'Huh! Well I could. I was.'

Liz's apology was perfunctory. 'Sorry. I think Paul's been here, too.'

'Oh, not him again!' Cecy sounded tired. 'Liz, I've told you what to do, Auntie Sue has told you what to do, we've all told you what to do. Get rid of him.'

'I just think,' said Liz, 'that it might not be that simple, if he doesn't want to go.'

There was a pause, while Cecy finished waking up. Then she said, 'I know we talked about this last night, but it's nonsense really. Stalkers happen in tabloid newspapers, to other people. Not to us.'

'Is it exactly stalking, if he has the key and we're supposed to be friends?'

'Not sure. I've never been stalked. I know you don't want to believe it.'

'He's taking me out to lunch.'

'Then confront him with it. You can phone at a more reasonable hour, and let me know what he says. I'm going back to sleep.'

'You won't be in. I know you, it's Saturday.'

'Write down my mobile number.' She gave it briefly, and Liz scribbled it down. 'It's permanently at my side, like a favourite lover – or even a determined stalker. Now go away.'

Thus dismissed, Liz walked down to the shop on the corner of the street and bought the essentials for breakfast, returning to her flat to find her phone ringing. It was Cecy.

'Where are you lunching? Would you like me to be around with back-up?'

'What, some of your scatty friends? No thank you!' Breakfast had restored Liz's courage. She could imagine Cecy and her friends waltzing in on a private discussion between herself and Paul, and shuddered at the thought.

'I was thinking more of Richard. And we wouldn't be obvious; if he spotted us, we'd just nod in passing.'

'It sounds too Miss Marple to be true. And still no thank you.'

'You're sure about that?'

'Yes.'

'Right. Well don't say I didn't offer.'

Reflecting that if Paul *had*, however improbably, placed a bug, he would soon know pretty well the lot, since Cecy, no able conspirator, had used the land line and not her cousin's mobile number, Liz replaced the phone and ate her breakfast, thinking hard. She couldn't live like this, in constant fear of being invaded in her private space, she'd always be worrying about one of her homes when she was in the other, but there was one simple answer. She hardly used this flat, except when she came up to see her agent or her publisher. She could always beg a bed from Cecy, or Richard, or any number of other friends, any of which alternatives would probably be more fun than being here with or without Paul, or she could stay in a hotel. She wondered what the flat was worth; it wasn't big, of course, but it did have two bedrooms, one of them *en suite* even if the other was more of a box room, a small sitting room and a modern galley kitchen, and it was in a desirable area and handy for restaurants and shops. It would sell easily. She didn't think she would miss it, and the money from it would help her buy a bigger place in Devon if she ever felt the need, which at present, she didn't. Paul wasn't going to drive her out of her beloved cottage. No point anyway, anyone in the village would tell him where she was if he asked, unless she left the area completely. She could hardly involve them all.

Liz realised where her thoughts were taking her, and pulled herself together. Oh no! But if Paul was really stalking her she could consolidate her defences by getting rid of this place, and even if he wasn't, it was a good idea. When you came to look at it, it was a pointless expense, and she wondered why she hadn't thought of it long since. She finished her breakfast more cheerfully and before she had a chance to change her mind, walked back down to the shops and entered the first estate agents' office she came to. They were very pleased to see her. There was only one thing better than a seller in their ideology and that was a buyer, and in this area they had plenty of the latter and not enough of the former. She returned home to find the phone ringing yet again, but this time it wasn't Cecy, it was Paul. He sounded cross.

'I've been ringing you for the past hour! Where have you been?'

Liz decided it would be better to tell him that face to face. She said, 'Shopping,' and Paul snorted in disgust.

'I would have thought you had enough junk already!' he said. 'Look, I've only got a moment. I'll meet you at that place round the corner from here – you know the one. We've been there before. It's called Jimmy's Place. Half past one.'

Trust Paul. Two steps from his office, half an hour from her flat. Liz wondered if it was grounds for taking a stand, but it was hardly worth it when he was history anyway. She agreed and yet again, put the phone down. She half expected it to start ringing again, it was that kind of morning, but it didn't. She stood beside it and looked around her. Perhaps she should fill in the time deciding what she wanted to keep out of the contents of the flat, and what she would sell. Uncle Owen would store stuff for her at the farm if she asked him, she was sure. She found paper and pen and began to make lists, room by room, and became so absorbed that she almost forgot the time, and ended leaving for lunch in a rush.

"Taking me out to lunch" turned out to be an optimistic euphemism. It generally was, with Paul. 'We'll have separate bills, then I can pay quickly if I have to rush off back to work,' he told her, as he ushered her through the door of the restaurant after a perfunctory peck on the cheek. 'I know you, you'll take hours to kill a *crème brulée* while I sit and watch you, and we're busy in the office, I can't be late,'

'I would have thought,' said Liz, already incensed with him, 'that after breaking my lock, the least you could do was buy me lunch!'

This unfortunately set the tone for the meal. It put Paul on the defensive – if he hadn't been there already – and their meeting became confrontational almost immediately. Even as they sat down, Paul was saying, 'You owe me for a new lock, by the way. Yours was knackered.'

Liz immediately said, 'No it wasn't. Gil had only just put a new one on for me.'

Paul glared at her. 'You might have told me?'

'Why should I? You weren't supposed to be there.'

'I told you I'd go down to keep an eye on the place!'

'And I told you not to bother. My family do that.'

'You could have warned me. Or sent me the new key.'

Liz took a deep breath, but before she could say something

regrettable, the waiter arrived to take their order. Since they ate there fairly often, neither needed to consult the menu; they ordered without taking their eyes from each other, and as soon as he had gone away, Paul pre-empted anything Liz might have been going to say, by jumping in with, 'Perhaps you'd better give it to me now, before you forget again, so I can get in next time you want to go off somewhere secret on your own, and keep an eye on things for you.'

'I assume you already have it. So perhaps *you'd* better give it to *me*.'

Paul's eyelids flickered, but he only said, 'Why should I have it? I left the spare with your tiresome neighbour.'

'How is Tina tiresome?' Liz knew as soon as she spoke that she should have kept her eye on the ball and not gone tearing off after red herrings. It gave Paul the opportunity to say, 'Bloody interfering old witch! She came ranting round Sunday morning, looking for your stupid cat!'

'Which reminds me,' Liz segued into the accusation, smooth as silk. 'Why did you kick him? Poor Tib, what could he possibly have done to you?'

'Who said I kicked him?' countered Paul. He should, of course, have denied it absolutely. Liz took note; someone could have said it, and wondered who. Not Tina, obviously. But someone else. Not a lot of point in asking round the village, it could be anybody, most likely bet was the postman or the milkman. Perhaps one of them would tell her eventually, perhaps not.

'Somebody did,' said Liz, deliberately ambiguous. Paul let it pass, perhaps knowing he was on dodgy ground. He picked up the water jug and poured water into their glasses, only afterwards asking if she wanted anything stronger.

'No thank you.' Never drink with the enemy, she thought, and then, is he the enemy then? There was a silence, while they each realigned their weaponry. Paul spoke first.

'So, how were Susan and Carl and the kids?'

Liz, as her aunt before her, nearly fell into the trap, saw it just in time, and answered, 'Fine, when last I spoke. Why do you ask?' She added, which was essentially true, if disingenuous, 'She told me you rang her. She seemed a bit surprised.'

Paul said easily, 'I thought you might be with her. She said you weren't,' which was equally disingenuous. Stalemate, Liz thought, and allowed a pause to lengthen. She had read somewhere, probably in a detective novel, that if you did this, the other person might be stampeded into breaking it unwisely, and as it turned out, whoever had written that was right.

'Liz, what's the matter with you?' asked Paul eventually, but crossly rather than sympathetically. 'Has that obnoxious cow been saying things to you?' He narrowed his eyes as he spoke, sizing up her reply before she gave it. In the silent, difficult interval, their lunch had arrived. Liz picked up her fork before she spoke, poking at her caesar salad to give herself time to think. Finally, she said, 'First, if by that you're referring to Susan, what makes you think you're that important that she should even bother to mention you? Second, if she did, she's every reason to be cynical where you're concerned, after the way you behaved last time you visited. She knows we're at the end of our personal line, and so should you.'

Paul went so still that Liz actually began to be alarmed, half-afraid that she had hurt him in slightly more than his pride, but then she looked up from her salad and saw the fury in his eyes.

'Whatever are you on about?' he demanded, in a voice like steel. It struck a spark from Liz, certainly. He had no right to speak to her like that, as if she was some stupid, inarticulate inferior excusing herself for a misdemeanour. She said, 'Come on, you must have got the message by now. Our time together is over. We're going nowhere. Time to say goodbye, and that. I have tried to tell you, you can't say I haven't.'

Paul had gone white. He said, 'How can you say that? You know I love you – you know how I value the time I spend with you – you know you mean everything to me –' He broke off.

For a second there, Liz was almost suckered in, then she recognised the calculation behind it and hardened her heart. She reminded herself what Cecy had told her and snapped, 'Rubbish, Paul, stop sounding like a novel – not even a good novel either. You know and I know, I'm just convenient for you, and I've been treating you the same way, if we're both honest. That's not good enough – for either of us.'

'I could marry you, if that's what you're angling for,' said Paul. Liz had not expected this; as proposals went, it felt more like an insult. She looked blank for a minute, and then summoned her common sense.

'No you couldn't, Paul. Your life is in London, you wouldn't change it. Mine isn't, and neither would I.'

'We've managed all right so far. Lots of married men spend the week in London and the weekend in the country.' Yes, at least one that you know of, Liz thought cynically, but Paul went on, 'And you could always join me in the flat, if you got lonely. You could always come up and do some shopping. Come on –' he spoke persuasively, '– you know we're good together.'

Oh no, we're not, Liz thought, and then wondered, which flat would that be? There was no point in prolonging this, its bare-faced opportunism in view of what she now knew, was sickening her, apart from the unflattering implication that she was so keen to be married that this facile offer would bring her to heel immediately. She said briskly, 'Actually, I'm putting the flat on the market, it's a needless expense when I'm never there. And that reminds me, may I have the spare key for the agent, please?' She held out her hand. For a second, Paul's hand hovered as if he was going to put it into his pocket, but then he picked up his knife and fork.

'I haven't got it on me,' he said. 'Anyway – are you sure you really want to sell it? We've had good times there, we will again.' Defiantly.

'No we won't. The good times are over, Paul, between you and me. It's time to move on.'

'So there's somebody else.' He even managed a wobble in his voice. Liz cringed inwardly.

'No.' Momentarily wondering if she really was hurting him, and finding herself still unconvinced, Liz went on. 'No, Paul, and there never will be – for either of us – while we just make do with each other.' She realised that she could have phrased that more felicitously, and made it worse by adding, 'We're just marking time that way.'

'So that's how you see it.' There was genuine anger underlying the bald statement, but there was only one answer. If she *had* hurt anything, it was only his pride.

'Yes. The good times were good though.' It was useless, she might as well have spared her breath over that last sentence. He hadn't been interested in good times for a while now, only in himself. She had known it, if she was honest, long before Cecy had told her why.

She had just not bothered to do anything about it, in spite of urging from all sides, and now she was ashamed of herself. How spineless was that? She had let the situation go on and on out of sheer apathy, and now she was making a very poor job of getting herself out of the mire. Yet again, she waited for Paul to speak, but this time because she had run out of anything to say. He laid down his knife and fork on top of his almost untouched steak pie.

'Were they? You may have thought so!' Pause. 'I can see there's no use talking to you. You have no further use for me, for whatever reason, so I may pack my bags and go! I would have married you Liz, always remember that!' He stood up abruptly. 'I'll put your keys in the post tonight.' And turned on his heel and marched straight out of the restaurant, to the accompaniment of turning heads and stares, some directed to Liz. So much for separate bills.

Liz felt terrible, but was unable to analyse exactly why. There had been such a mixture of schmaltz, spite, and sheer flannel in that exchange, brief as it had been, that she hardly knew what to think. Even its brevity was disturbing. He had seen it coming, she was sure, and he must have known that breaking the lock would be the final straw. He *had* known, he had banked on the offer of marriage scooping the pool, a last gamble before ...what? If Cecy was right, and Liz had no reason to think that she wasn't, he was fighting in the last ditch, and his backup, herself, was on the run. She couldn't imagine what he would do, knew that even if he sent back her keys, she would never feel safe in either of her homes without a backup of her own. She had no idea what to do next, so she ate her salad. She would have to pay for it anyway.

There had been something rehearsed about the whole encounter, she thought, as she ate, hardly aware of what she was eating. The confrontational mention of the key, the proposal of marriage flung at her out of the blue, the sudden change of attitude before he walked out, as if he had known there was going to be a showdown, and resolved to try everything he could. And stalking out like that was his trump card. Everyone was watching, some might know who she was, she was a celebrity of sorts even if she set little store by it. Had anyone had a camera? Had he arranged that they would? Was it all a tortuous plan to put her publicly in the wrong, pay her out for dumping him? No, even Paul wasn't that devious.

Nevertheless, she was still uncomfortable.

'Will the gentleman be coming back to finish his meal?' asked the waiter, in her ear.

'No,' said Liz. It was hardly worth it, but she added, 'He remembered an appointment he had to dash.'

'Will madam be requiring the dessert menu?'

'No, thank you. I'll have the bill, please.' She sighed inwardly. 'Both bills.'

He nodded sympathetically and left without comment. Liz settled the double bill and left the restaurant trying to look unembarrassed, and failing. Bother Paul, nobody liked to be made to look a fool – but of course, he had known that.

Outside on the pavement, she paused, thinking what to do next. Paul had presumably returned to his office to try to hold onto his job. Cecy could be anywhere by now, and might or might not answer her mobile. She could, of course, contact any of her other friends until she found somebody with a spare afternoon on their hands, but it seemed a sad thing to do, particularly after her parting with Paul. She was still hesitating when her mobile rang, and it was Richard.

'Cecy said you were lunching with Paul and planning some kind of showdown. How's it going? Is he there?'

Liz said tartly, 'If you're wanting to speak to him, try his office. He walked out.'

'Thought he might,' said Richard, with what sounded suspiciously like satisfaction. 'What're you doing now?'

'Standing on the pavement outside the restaurant, feeling like a lemon.'

'Don't do that. Go back to your flat, and I'll meet you there in an hour. I'm tied up at the moment.'

'Richard, are you and Cecy by any chance trying to look after me?'

'Of course we are. That Paul is a nasty bit of work. Never could see what you saw in him.'

'It's amazing how everyone is nodding wisely and saying how nasty he is the moment I decide to dump him. Why didn't any of you speak up earlier?'

'Would you have listened?' asked Richard, with interest.

'Well ... no. Probably not.'

'Anyway,' said Richard, having the last word, 'from what I understood at Christmas, most of them did. See you in an hour.' He rang off. Liz headed for the underground, pleased to have some goal in mind, and took the opportunity, while she sat in the train, to do some serious thinking. It was true that her aunts, her mother, and her sister had all expressed a poor opinion of Paul, but so far as she could recall, it was only Cecy and Richard who had said anything more. Richard particularly. His dismissive phrase "a nasty bit of work" hung uncomfortably around in her subconscious. Had he always thought that, or had he, like Cecy just found out the full truth recently? Just being in danger of losing his job didn't make a person nasty of course, it could happen to anyone, but aiding and abetting an influential best-seller in adultery was cheap, and probably *was* nasty, and all else apart, she didn't want to be associated a moment longer with someone who took such a cynical view of other people's relationships; perhaps the man Paul was helping to betray loved his wife and would be hurt by the deception, and it was shoddy to be a part of it for money and advantage. It wasn't her business, she knew none of the people involved, but the recently acquired knowledge had left a bad taste behind. And Paul had involved her, however innocently; he had flagrantly deceived her for his own advantage, never mind anyone else. Him and his posh flat! Liz hated feeling like a sucker.

Carl thought him a conceited loudmouth. Liz had value for Carl's opinions. She should have taken more notice.

She had thought dumping Paul would be simple. It was turning out to be far from it.

Her flat, when she arrived back there, didn't feel as welcoming and homelike as usual. Edgy and depressed, Liz mooched around and looked at the lists she had made that morning, and the thoughts that now began to crowd into her head were surely ridiculous. She found herself wondering if Richard knew anyone who had a van, if he would help her to move the things she valued into safety, or if he would laugh at her and accuse her of overreacting. She tried to laugh at herself, and failed. When Richard arrived, he found her packing cushions into a bin bag, with a half-full box of books on the floor beside her.

'What on earth are you doing?' he enquired, reasonably enough. 'A moonlight flit?'

There was no point in dissembling. Liz said, 'I put this place on the market this morning. I'm packing up the stuff I want to keep to take home.'

Richard, ever pragmatic, enquired how she meant to do that, since her car was so impractical, and Liz pulled a face. 'I hoped you might know someone with a van.'

'Hire one. I'll drive it for you. When were you planning to do it?'

He hadn't even questioned it. Liz felt the hairs on her neck prickle. 'As soon as possible, really. No point in leaving it.'

Richard was already reaching for the yellow pages, turning the leaves swiftly to find the page he wanted. 'Tomorrow too soon? I can clear it with Linda. Or she can come too.' Linda was his almost live-in girlfriend; Liz knew and liked her.

'Isn't that bit of an unnecessary rush?' she asked. Richard looked at her.

'Let's get the job done, before you change your mind. How much of this stuff are you taking?'

'Oh ... all my books, linen and stuff, these cushions –' she poked the fat bag, '– most of the furniture can go to the saleroom, it isn't special. The desk I want to take, and the pictures. That chair over there. There's some good saucepans here, better than I've got at home.'

'Not a desperately large van, then.' Richard reached for the phone. Liz went on checking things off on her fingers.

'China, the coffee table, that came from the farm, the wine rack in the kitchen, the small walnut chest in my bedroom, all my clothes and ornaments and stuff.'

'Not a desperately small one either, then,' said Richard, pressing keys. Liz had an unexpected surge of panic. Her projected move was at the same time both unreasonably quick, and seeming to lag behind the fair. This morning when she got up she had had no intention of selling the flat, now she couldn't do it quickly enough. It had been invaded, spoiled for her, she couldn't defend it if she was in Devon. What might Paul do? She had no idea. Something to spite her was all that came into her head.

Richard was talking now, she turned away and went into the kitchen, pulling out drawers and opening cupboards and ranging things on the worktop. After a few minutes, Richard appeared in the door. 'I've got a Ford Transit lined up for first thing tomorrow. I'll get some mates to lend a hand loading. Then you can clear up and leave everything tidy for selling, and follow the van down. Where were you thinking of putting it all? There isn't room in your cottage.' He hesitated. 'I'm not stampeding you into this, am I?'

Liz knew she would never want to sleep in the flat again after tonight. She said, 'No.'

'I think you're doing the right thing.' He looked at her gravely. 'Cecy thinks so too. Shall I nip down to the corner shop and see if they've got any boxes?'

The phone rang just after he had gone. It was Paul. 'I've been thinking,' he said, without preamble. 'I was in a rotten mood at lunchtime, I owe you an apology. Problems at work, they're not your fault. I'm sorry Liz, can we go out and come in again? I'll book a table somewhere you like for tonight, and make it up to you. My treat.'

'Paul –' Liz hesitated. How to put this tactfully? 'Paul, I meant what I said. I think we need space. I think if we don't see each other for a bit, you'll see what I mean and we can part friends. It really is time to move on.'

There was a long silence. Then a click, as he put the phone down. Liz was left staring at her own phone in her hand.

That night, the last she would spend in this flat, wasn't a comfortable one. The sitting room, piled up with boxes and bags ready for tomorrow, the empty drawers and cupboards, the denuded state of her bedroom furnishings, all weighed on her mind in the darkness. It was like running away, fleeing before the enemy, taking her belongings with her. Her decision to sell had been sudden but logical; this packing up and heading out bag and baggage was surely unreasonable.

Except that it wasn't. Liz wasn't sure why this was, except that Paul had been here in her absence, and that in Devon he had hurt her beloved Tib. Except that he was proving harder to dislodge than she had expected. Except that Richard's actions, practical and swift, had disconcerted her. There was no actual reason for this last; she had been packing up when he arrived and he had helped her, he had never once said, "get out of here before worse happens to you", or anything silly like that. He had gone along with her wishes, and her problem seemed to be that she wished she knew why she had wished ...

Something creaked in the living room outside her door. She found herself immediately rigid and stiff under her duvet, listening, conscious of the emptiness of the deserted rooms outside her door. If she called out, who would hear her? She held her breath.

There came a faint brushing sound, then silence. It could be one of the stuffed plastic bags sliding to the floor. It could be anything.

Words hammered in her head. *Stalker. Nasty. Blackmail.* Ridiculous! Paul was OK, they were friends weren't they? Had been friends?

Going through her private correspondence wasn't friendly. Invading her space uninvited wasn't friendly either. Kicking her cat was spiteful and cruel. He knew she loved Tib.

Perhaps she was therefore wise to get the things she valued out of here.

One thing was quite clear; if she wasn't fantasising she was, as Cecy had said, in big, big trouble, and unfortunately, outside of her profession, fantasising wasn't one of her besetting sins.

Which left the alternative.

The noises seemed to have stopped. Liz sat up and listened, straining after any sound, however small. She thought, but maybe only imagined, that she heard the click of a latch. It could have been a sound from the street below.

She lay down again and waited for the dawn to come, and with it, Richard and his mates and the van that would carry her possessions to safety.

Or would it?

XVIII

Two or three weeks passed. Dot looked at some houses in the more select parts of Embridge and was noticeably underwhelmed, and Liz spent her weekends at home with her cat. Nothing very much happened except that Dot became somewhat depressed, putting it down to the time of year, and Liz lay awake at nights on Fridays and Saturdays, trying not to jump at every little sound and wondering what Paul was doing, and more immediately, where exactly he was, until the day finally dawned when Dot made an interesting discovery and Liz received both an email and an unpleasant shock.

The email came first. Liz read it with some surprise, and then read it again more slowly and went into her study to pick up the phone. In the west of Cornwall, she heard the ringtone and then, just as she had decided everyone must be out, Susan answered. 'Hullo?'

'Auntie Sue!' said Liz. 'How are you? How are things?'

'We're all fine. What can we do for you?'

Liz didn't immediately come to the point. She said, 'How's Annabel getting on with her scary new friend?' and Susan laughed.

'It's a whole new ball game, but it seems to be working out surprisingly well,' she said. 'Annabel now goes to school with a smile on her face and Kayleigh stands between her and the world with her fists clenched and a scowl on hers. In extreme instances, Damien will appear from nowhere and stand quietly beside them, and the opposition melts away. There's less and less of it every day; Annabel is rapidly finding herself a source of pride to her peers rather than an object of derision. Kayleigh and Damien may be rough, but they aren't stupid, you know. Whatever brought them onto Annabel's side did it thoroughly – although I do think she still misses Rosie rather. Rosie was more her kind.'

'And haven't they made up, if everyone else seems to be coming round?'

'No. Not really. I think Rosie's defection hurt Annabel more than she's letting on.'

'Annabel does hurt rather easily,' said Liz. Susan was surprised.

'Annabel? No, you've got that wrong. Annabel was always the

brash, mouthy one, that's what's got her into trouble this time if you think about it.'

'Was she? Or was she just putting up a better front than even you – or your mother?' Susan went quiet for a moment, and Liz went on, because it was something she had felt needed saying for some time now. 'I know you always thought Seb was the sensitive plant, and yes, your husband did put him down a lot and yes, he did hate his school in Embridge. But Seb is, on the whole, resilient. With Annabel, I suspect it all goes deeper and hurts harder.

Susan said, after a pause, 'You could be right.' She sounded surprised.

'I am right. People watching is my business, remember. And if you're still unconvinced, ask Gosia, she had it worked out long ago. About both of you, if you want my opinion.'

'Annabel has been very distressed about Tom's behaviour ...'

'Hmm,' said Liz. 'And that didn't tell you anything?'

Susan, feeling herself seriously wrong-footed, and guilty about it, changed the subject firmly. 'Have you heard from Deb? She said she was going to email you last week.'

'Yes,' said Liz. She added, hesitantly, 'That's why I'm ringing actually, she rather took the wind out of my sails. She says she and Mawgan want me to be godmother to Daniel.'

'So? What's the matter with that?'

'Nothing, it's a great compliment. I just don't see ... well, why me? She doesn't know me that well, after all.'

'She wondered if you might feel like that – she came over to talk about it as a matter of fact. I told her to go for it, her reasons sounded good to me.'

'So, what were they?' Liz was justifiably curious, for her friendship with Debbie was so far of the most cursory kind; they had met each other, they were connected by Susan. Finish.

'One: no, she doesn't know you that well, but from what she does know, she would like to know you a whole lot better. Two: she'd like you linked in a family way not just with me, but with all of us – and that's for my sake more than yours, and I was touched if you want to know. Three: she and Mawgan feel that Danny's godmother should be somebody who is going to be a familiar part of his life, not a distant stranger he only sees about once a year. And four: we were both impressed with how lovely you were to Mum, and we want to say thank you in a way that will last longer than a bunch of flowers.'

It was Liz's turn to be silent. After a moment or two, Susan said, 'Are you still there?'

'Yes,' said Liz, in a strange voice. 'Do you really mean all that – both of you?'

'Liz, inviting someone to be godmother to your firstborn son isn't something you do without meaning it. Think about it, and then thank Deb and Mawgan nicely, and agree.'

'I can hardly refuse, after that. I feel ... I can't say how I feel. Warm. Flattered. I don't know what to say.'

'Say yes. When are you coming down again?'

'For the christening, from the sound of it.'

'Three weeks time, then. You'll stay with us.' It was a statement, not a question. Liz smiled, although Susan couldn't see her.

'Where else?' She nearly told Susan, then, of her reservations about leaving her home empty over a weekend, but it would sound stupid, she decided, and anyway, there was time to sort something out. Perhaps Richard or Cecy would come down for that weekend, visit with the family or something. She put down the phone after saying goodbye with a mixture of conflicting emotions. Pleasure at the small honour done to her, uneasiness about being away, disgust at herself for her reservations for surely Paul wouldn't come here now, she had made herself quite clear last time she saw him. Stripping her flat in London of everything she valued, she had by this time almost convinced herself, had been overreacting, and Cecy's fault. Cecy should have been the romantic novelist, not herself.

Well, one thing was certain. She couldn't be imprisoned in her home for ever, eventually she – and it – would have to take a chance. She sat down at her desk and switched on her computer to compose a graceful acceptance for Debbie and Mawgan, but she hadn't got much beyond "Dear Debbie and Mawgan" when her mobile rang. It was the agent who was handling the sale of her flat. He sounded troubled.

'Miss Ballantyne, I'm sorry to have to tell you this, but we took a client to see your flat this morning, and ... well, to put it bluntly, you've had vandals in. You'll need to tell your insurance company, and perhaps you should come and have a look too.'

Liz's heart gave one great thump and began to race. Her mind raced too; it was three weeks since she had finished with Paul and she had heard nothing from him since; there was no reason why she should leap to the conclusion that this was his doing now. She said, 'Tell me. What's the damage?'

'Well, as I told you, vandalism more than anything, paint, and what looks like tar, splashed over the walls and furnishings, light fittings wrenched out, things like that. No way of telling if anything is missing. What would you like us to do?'

Liz thought rapidly. She didn't want to go to London, already she felt so far distanced from her flat and its contents that her concern was mainly for her investment rather than a home. There was nothing there that she valued particularly; although it had all been good stuff and it was a shame it should be destroyed, she had planned to let it go with the flat if the buyer wanted it. She was, she discovered, more angry than upset. 'Did you tell the police?' she asked.

'Yes – for what that's worth. They said they'd take a look.'

'Look – I'm down in Devon at the minute. I'll ring my cousin and get him to go round and check it out for me – can you give him the key, if he comes in?'

'If you give us his name. We can't just give it to anyone.'

'Richard Worthington.'

'Perhaps we should go round there with him.'

'That's thoughtful, but I think it's probably service beyond the call of duty. I'll tell him to bring identification with him.' She hesitated. 'Silly to ask this – did the client like the flat?'

'It wasn't looking it's best.'

Silly question. Good answer. Liz thanked him and rang Richard. He would be working, but this was an emergency.

Richard, although indignant on her behalf, took the news with relative calm. 'Of course I'll go and check it out, and ring you back,' he said. 'Good thing you acted on your gut instinct, eh?'

'I thought I was being a fool.'

'And perhaps you were. There's nothing to say it's Paul behind this. The flat's been empty, it's a temptation.'

'It's been empty before without getting burgled.'

'It's in the estate agents' window. Maybe somebody ...? Did Paul give you back the key, by the way?'

'He put it in an envelope and shoved it in the post. No note. No stamp, either. Nothing to say whether he had it copied or not.'

'He'd hardly tell you if he had.'

'That's not quite what I meant.'

'OK Liz.' Richard became brisk, he had work to do after all. 'I'll check it out in my lunch break, ring you back. Meanwhile, try not to worry too much. It's all insured after all.'

'I think it may have lost me a sale, just the same.'

'Tough. There'll be other suckers along.'

He rang off, and Liz was left looking at her rudimentary letter of acceptance. She was annoyed, not upset, about her flat, she had already moved on from there, but if something happened to this house while she was away for the weekend, she would be heartbroken. She loved this place as she hadn't loved her *pied à terre* in London. That had been a convenience, no more. This was home. And there was Tib, too: something happening to Tib was unthinkable.

It wasn't Paul who had vandalised the flat. It couldn't be Paul! Could it?

Liz couldn't be certain either way. Hurt pride, desperation, what might they do to a man who wasn't the most stable person in the world to start with? Perhaps she would never know, but the risks involved in not knowing were unacceptable.

She had three weeks to sort it out, in her own mind or in practical terms, or both. Sighing with frustration, she returned her attention to her letter.

Dot had said at her dinner party that they must all keep a look out for a suitable business opportunity for her son-in-law, but perhaps she hadn't really meant it; it was one of those things that people promise without thinking too hard what it entails. Had she been looking seriously, she would never have looked where she found one, although the moment she set eyes on it she knew that it and Mawgan were made for each other. This was not necessarily a compliment to either.

She was still looking for a suitable house for herself. The ones she had seen in the area with which she was familiar – the "posh" part of town – had seemed to her so lacklustre that she decided to try another tack; there were pleasant houses up on The Cliff, Joanna Rendell and her husband lived in one of them for instance, and the views over the water she knew to be spectacular. She had been taken with the view from Debbie's new home, perhaps something similar would help her to warm to the large three-bedroomed bungalow with room to expand into the roof, the details of which Halliday's had sent her through the post. She made an order to view for Tuesday morning, and it was the impulse that made her decide not to go alone this time that led her into involvement with matters that were arguably no concern of hers. Her chosen companion was Ingrid, she and Alex lived down by the marina. It was therefore more sensible, once she had picked up her friend, to continue on past the harbour to the western edge of town.

It wasn't the route she would have taken normally. It led past the commercial dock to the more rundown part of the town, home to bed & breakfast establishments at the cheaper end of the market, rows of terraced houses, the sleazy alley where Oliver had come to grief, and small corner shops struggling for survival. Cheryl and Oliver, she well remembered, had lived in an attic bedsit three floors above one of these shops, overlooking the dock, when they first married. It had been cheap, and convenient for Oliver's job, which at that point was working on a dive boat. She was thinking of that time with nostalgia as she drove past the marina, for that had been back when Oliver was whole and strong, and free to go where he would. She did realise that the loss of freedom was hard for Oliver, but she had never said so, deeming it pointless to mourn over what was irrecoverably gone. She was wondering if that had been an oversight, when something diverted her thoughts.

'I see the Dock Inn is closed,' she remarked, in passing. .

'Oh yes – didn't you hear about it?' Ingrid asked, surprised, for Dot usually knew everything. 'Or no – I suppose you had other things on your mind.' It sounded better than saying that Dot was rather out of the loop these days. Dot appreciated this but made no comment, and Ingrid went on. 'The landlord did a moonlight flit about a month before Christmas, took the week's takings and the barmaid and vanished into oblivion. His poor wife couldn't cope, the mortgagee foreclosed, and the place is up for a forced sale. So far, it hasn't sold, it's in a real state apparently, and who wants to run a pub these days? The council have been muttering about buying it themselves, they want to knock it down and build some "affordable housing" in its place – it's not quite the place for posh flats like Jerry's, for instance.'

Dot was horrified. 'But surely, it's a listed building?'

'So what? They only have to declare it unsafe – they'd be very nearly right, too. And it's on a valuable double plot, there's quite a big car park at the side – for what it's ever been worth,' Ingrid added cynically. 'Most of the clientele used to come on foot. Roughs and scruffs from the boats and a few hardy locals. It's a long time since its heyday.'

'It's one of the oldest buildings in the town!' cried Dot, with indignation. She was great on heritage, Ingrid recalled belatedly, and perhaps she had been irreverently tactless. It had always been rather easy to be tactless around Dot, nothing changed. She didn't speak, and Dot, too, negotiated the narrow, uphill streets without saying anything further, but her thoughts were busy nevertheless. If the Dock Inn needed money spending on it, then she knew a man whom she believed might have some. She found herself wondering if it was what he had in mind. It wasn't exactly in a prime position, but it was only about a quarter of a mile from the marina, a reasonable distance to walk if there was a good reason, and it was certainly a waterside property, which he had said he wanted. It would be a crime should it be knocked down and replaced with some cheap, modern monstrosity! She negotiated the turn onto the wider road that ran from the town centre with her mind on autopilot and Ingrid had to remind her to turn off to The Cliff.

It wasn't so much a cliff as a small rounded hill, an outpost of the downs from which a large chunk had slid into the sea back in the mists of prehistory, leaving a narrow platform down by the water along which the road to Emberton now ran, and this substantial rise in the ground above it with a sheer drop to the road below. Although well shored up by succeeding councils, in extreme conditions small landslips tended to make the Emberton road hazardous and traffic was re-routed over the hill onto the Shearwater road, but this happened rarely. The cliff itself was deemed to be completely safe, and several pleasant streets of expensive houses occupied its summit. The most desirable ones were closest to the sea, and Dot was on her way to view one of these. It was a luxurious modern bungalow, and although it had only three bedrooms at present, there was room to develop in the roof, and it had other advantages too. It was only a street away from Joanna and Ian, so if the family all came together, Susan and Carl could stay with them, maybe the children too if necessary. It had a good garden, it had splendid views over the harbour to the distant sea. It was a drive away from the town centre and its shops, but Dot didn't mind that. She had had high hopes of it when she set out that morning, but somewhere along the way, she discovered, they had evaporated. A scruffy little abandoned public house seemed to have taken over, or that was what she told herself, unwilling to admit that the Dock Inn might be a displacement ploy.

She and Ingrid were shown over the really rather beautiful house and made all the right noises as the owner pointed out its advantages; the almost-new fitted kitchen with marble worktops, the big drawing room with its fabulous views, the large bedrooms with ensuite bathrooms. They walked around the still wintry garden and admired the sheltered patio, the lawns, the flowering camellias. Ingrid was enthusiastic – too enthusiastic, she began to suspect, to cover for Dot's tepid reaction, which surprised her for this was surely the ideal house for someone in her position. The proud owner pressed coffee and biscuits on them, but her efforts began to have a touch of desperation about them. She knew that it was a lost cause, and showed them to the door in the end with a shrug of resignation. 'You know where to find us, when you've had time to think about it,' she said, with an automatic smile, but Ingrid could tell that she knew she would see them no more. She walked beside Dot to the car, and as they took their seats again, she said, 'Well, I thought it was lovely.'

'So did I,' said Dot. She started the car and set it in motion. 'I don't feel it is what I need, however. Only three bedrooms, and so far out of town.' Excuses. She knew Ingrid recognised them.

'There's room to put two rooms in the roof if you wanted,' Ingrid reminded her, but knew she was wasting her breath. Dot had made up her mind, that was obvious. She said, curiously, 'Are you certain you really want to move, Dot? I'd give my eye-teeth for that house!'

'Perhaps Alex will buy it for you,' suggested Dot, which Ingrid found an interesting idea. She considered it for a moment; he ust might, if approached in the right way, but did she really want to go to all the trouble of moving on what was, at best, a whim? Probably not. Pity, it was a lovely house, but someone would love it.

Dot was speaking again. 'Do you fancy a little more property viewing after we've had our lunch?' she was asking. 'If we can make an appointment, of course.'

Ingrid had nothing much to do that afternoon, she said, 'I'm game. Anywhere in particular, or are we going to trawl the estate agents?'

'Who do you think would be handling commercial properties?' Dot asked her. Ingrid gave her a narrow-eyed look.

'What are you up to, Dot?'

'Do you remember at my dinner party,' said Dot. 'My son-in-law was talking about opening a place here in Embridge.'

'So he was.' Ingrid hesitated. 'What are you thinking? A quick recce of what's available, or ...' She let the sentence tail off, unable to believe what her brain was telling her, and Dot said tranquilly, 'I thought we might have a look at the Dock Inn. Who do you think would be handling it, now tell me? There was no board up.'

'Lacey Forbes handle most of the business properties,' said Ingrid, abandoning herself to the adventure. Nothing would come of it, of course, it was quite the wrong kind of place for a Michelin-starred chef to be interested in, but it would be fun to take a look at it.

'Then we shall park the car and go to see them,' said Dot.

Lacey Forbes were the biggest estate agents in town, and so far Dot had not visited them in her search for a new home. Why this was, she hadn't analysed; possibly because they handled more properties than anyone else she felt she might be overwhelmed with choices, or maybe, she tried not to speculate, she didn't *want* too many choices, and if there was an answer to that conundrum, she wasn't going to look for it. A man on the desk greeted them with reserve and called the manager from his office: he recognised Mrs Nankervis, whose face was familiar around the town, and Alex Hetherington's firm handled their accounts; he felt the mixture too rich for his taste – even more so, when he realised why they were there. There was only one prospective buyer, so far, for the Dock Inn: the council. He feared that Mrs Nankervis, a known campaigner for Preserving England's Heritage, was about to throw a spanner in the works. Buck-passing time. Definitely.

The manager, filled in on the problem in a hasty undertone, handled the situation with suavity. Mrs Nankervis gave no reason for her interest in the property, he in his turn asked for none. He would be available to take them there himself at two o'clock, he said. They left to go to Borden's for their lunch. The two estate agents looked at each other. 'Trouble, do you think?' the junior of them suggested.

'That, we shall see. The council's plans are in their infancy, they have yet to get permission to demolish the building. Mrs Nankervis could demolish their ambitions instead.'

'That place could hang around for ever if she does!'

The manager smiled enigmatically. 'Maybe. On the one hand, commercial activity in the dock itself is limited, right now, to a few trawlers and lobster fishermen and Bill Rowland's diving enterprise. Very few small cargo boats use it and their crews prefer livelier places to drink in these days. On the other hand, more and more yachts use the empty berths when the marina is full – and remember, who is Mrs Nankervis's son-in-law.'

The assistant, metaphorically speaking for he was on his feet, sat up straight. 'You think ...?'

'Let's not,' said the manager, 'theorise ahead of our data. But I will admit I should be sorry to see a pleasant old building wiped from the map if there was a viable alternative.'

'Business is business,' opined the assistant.

'We can be selective, however, as to just what business we engage in.'

'She could be just out to make trouble, you think so yourself. She's a bit of a reputation after all.'

'Who lives will learn,' said the manager, and retired back into his office as an ordinary punter pushed through the glass door.

Dot and Ingrid, meanwhile, had settled themselves at a comfortable window table, ordered their lunch, and unusually for them, fallen into a reflective silence as they waited for it to arrive. Dot's plots in relation to the Dock Inn were no concern of Ingrid's, but Dot's attitude to her avowed intention of finding a new home was beginning to concern her quite a lot. The problem was what to say, if it was wise to say anything at all? Surely she couldn't be hoping that Jerry would return! If so, she would be disappointed;

that relationship had been dead, according to Alex's reckoning, before it had even been born. Jerry had escaped, Dot had to face it. And if she was facing it, which would have been Ingrid's view up until this morning, then what was her problem? That bungalow had been absolutely gorgeous! And she knew from Sally that it wasn't the first gem that Dot had rejected out of hand.

'How many houses is it you've looked at now, Dot?' she asked. Dot looked thoughtful.

'Five, so far. Three of them around the area where I live now, and the one this morning of course, up on The Cliff.'

'And none of them has grabbed you?' asked Ingrid.

'No ... not really. I want something different, I think – they have all been rather the mixture as before.' She didn't repeat what she had said to the family, that she would like an older property; it came too close to home – to Haymans, rather. Their lunch arrived, and in the business of placing it on the table and asking for sauces, she hoped the subject would go away. But Ingrid was following a clue – only a tiny one, but she had spotted it nevertheless.

'And the fifth?' she asked. Dot reached for the condiments, and set about seasoning her salad.

'The fifth?' she asked, airily.

'You said five houses,' Ingrid reminded her. 'What was wrong with the fifth?'

'It wasn't on the market,' said Dot. She saw Ingrid looking at her enquiringly, and went on, against her better judgement, 'It belongs to some friends of Benita's. They plan to move to the south of France, I believe.'

'So it will be for sale.' Ingrid narrowed her eyes. Dot was being suspiciously evasive for one who was usually so forthright. She said, 'Did you like it?'

'I have only seen the outside,' said Dot. She began to eat her fish. 'The salmon here is always so delicious, don't you think?'

Ingrid was no great fan of salmon unless it had been caught in a Scottish river that morning, as Dot well knew, and she knew when she was being re-routed onto a safer subject. There was something about this house then, she wondered where it was. One way to find out.

354

'Where was this house?' she enquired, and Dot, thus put on the spot, said, 'Shearwater. Would you pass the salt across, please?' apparently forgetting that she had already salted her meal.

'And what was it like – on the outside?' Ingrid gave the salt pot a very small push, recognising it for the diversion that it was.

Dot put down her knife and fork. Why had she ever mentioned that first house? Ingrid, she could see, wasn't going to let it go. She said, 'Very nice.' So nice, in fact, that it and what it could stand for were keeping her awake at nights. She had loved that house, all but for the sting in its tail. She began to sprinkle the salt onto her salad again, but for some ridiculous reason her eyes had misted over. Chickens coming home to roost, she told herself, never a good idea.

Except that it was, her commonsense informed her. Chickens came home to lay eggs. Eggs were one of two things, food or the future.

'Dot?' said Ingrid. Dot jumped, and hastily put down the salt pot. There was a neat white cone of it in the middle of her lettuce. Ingrid put down her own knife and fork.

'Come on, tell me. What is it about this house?' and Dot, to whom a swingeing honesty came as second nature, replied precisely, 'It has a tennis court in the garden. Such a ... a waste of space.' She could break it up and turn it into a vegetable patch, but its ghost would always be there, she knew that. She had a horrible feeling that, after all these years and after all she had been through, she was about to burst into tears and howl like a dog. As if the lost dreams of one's adolescence mattered a toss! 'Well,' she said, pulling herself together, 'there will be other houses, I daresay, and I'll find one I like better without the ... the disadvantages.'

Ingrid sat with her thoughts in a whirl. Dot had overlooked something: Ingrid was married to Alex, and Alex had been Henry's friend. If Henry had ever said anything, made any confidences about his rash second marriage, then it could easily have been to Alex – and it had been. On Henry's death, and after his own marriage to Ingrid, Alex might as easily have shared the *un*easy confidence, knowing it would go no further – and he had. Ingrid, alone of all Dot's friends, knew where the bodies were buried. She felt them stirring in their coffins now.

What to say? She could let it pass, of course, and it would never be mentioned again, she knew that. Why, then, this feeling that she shouldn't do it? That she held a moment in her hands now that would never come again, and if she let it slip ... well, something would break?

Nothing ventured, nothing gained. She said, as if casually, 'You played tennis at one time, didn't you Dot? Maybe the tennis court would be fun.'

Dot had herself in hand again, the howl had retreated to the distant forest. She laughed – dear God, she actually laughed! 'Oh, that was a long time ago. I haven't touched a racquet for thirty years or more!'

Ingrid knew she was digging herself deeper and deeper into the shit, but she couldn't stop herself. She said, 'You could take it up again, I'm sure you could, you're fit enough. All that gardening ...' She couldn't look at Dot's face, for fear of what she might see. She picked up her fork again and held it poised. 'You could give tennis parties and invite your friends, and the children would love it, I bet.'

'My children, and my grandchildren too, are like Jerry, they sail,' said Dot dismissively. Ingrid realised she had carelessly lost the initiative. She grabbed it back, expressing a thought that she had often shared with Alex, to no good purpose. 'You've spent all your life, Dot, doing things to please other people – first your parents, making you take a "proper" job when your own ambitions were quite different, then Jerry, so mad on sailing there was no room for anything else, then bringing up children and doing good works because that was all you knew – do something for *you* Dot! You loved tennis! Now here you are, with a tennis court handed you on a plate!'

'I think I have left it too late,' said Dot. Ingrid noticed that she hadn't denied any of the points made to her. She wondered what to say next.

A few mouthfuls passed in silence, Dot thought her salmon would choke her.

'Of course,' Ingrid said, judiciously, 'it's far too late for Wimbledon, you need to be no more than thirty-ish for that, but I bet if you joined the tennis club, you could still thrash 'em!'

'You need to practice, Ingrid, to stay in top form. I told you, I last played serious tennis when I was in my teens, and that, I must point out, is more like forty years than thirty.'

'So what?' demanded Ingrid, well away now. 'I bet none of the other players at the club are much better. And if you join, and have a few refresher sessions with the pro, I can see you running off with the Veterans' Cup year after year after year!'

'And what,' Dot asked icily, 'gives you that idea?'

'Oh Dot,' said Ingrid. 'Henry and Alex were friends – in spite of the difference in their ages, they trusted each other. They talked over the dispositions Henry intended to make with his money, and the reasons for it, Alex was his accountant, for heaven's sake! And Henry would be so pleased for you.'

Dot said, slowly, 'I am beginning to believe that my time with Henry was potentially the happiest in my life, and that I threw it away.' She felt lighter for the admission, maybe it had needed saying for too long.

'Then do it for him. There'll be laughter in heaven, believe me.' Ingrid paused, and then went on more temperately, 'Things are changing Dot, everything about you is set to change. Go with it, it's all positive. Your children love you, they've proved that at Christmas. And they'd love to see you building yourself a new life and having fun. What have you got to lose?'

Dot made a feeble attempt to fight back. 'At the tennis club, I know, they mainly play mixed doubles. I have no partner,' but Ingrid only laughed at her. 'Once they've seen you play, you would have. They'll be queuing up!'

'I'm flattered by your faith in me, when you have nothing whatever to go on.'

'Give it a go,' urged Ingrid, but she thought she had pushed hard enough for now. When next she spoke it was to change the subject entirely. 'Have you seen anything of Sally lately? I don't seem to have run into her for an age. How is the wedding coming on?'

'Sally is a very unhappy woman at present,' Dot told her, feeling herself on firmer ground and thankful for it. 'And as for the wedding, I doubt if that will ever happen.'

'Tom backing off?' asked Ingrid.

'Lorraine, I rather think. But Sally would always defend Tom to the world, whatever she may confide in private.' Dot looked thoughtful. 'I can hardly criticise her for that, however. There was a time when I did the same, and I have lived to be sorry for it.'

'As she will?' asked Ingrid.

'I wouldn't be surprised. Tom Casson can be a pleasant enough fellow, but shallow and cares for nothing but himself. Sally blames herself. Personally, I think it is inborn.'

Ingrid found herself remembering the things that Alex had said to her about Tom, but she didn't repeat them. However much she trusted Dot's discretion, she wouldn't betray a confidence. She did say, however, 'Tom relied too much on Susan to give him status,' and left it at that. Dot, unwilling to travel that road, looked at her watch.

'We should eat our lunch. We will be late for our appointment.'

Mr Forbes himself was waiting for them when they returned to the office, summoned by his underlings, with the keys to his car dangling from his hand. There seemed no question of them making the short journey under their own steam, he called them "ladies" genially – a patonising term to which they shared Liz's aversion – and ushered them to where his Jaguar was parked. Both Dot and Ingrid winced at the term, but obediently took their places. Dot was irresistibly reminded of Mawgan's outrageous red monster, his "posemobile" Seb had called it wickedly, and was horrified to find herself smiling.

The Dock Inn sat at the roadside a few doors along from Chel and Oliver's old home; there was parking for cars in the front, and a bigger space to the side; the beer lorry, Mr Forbes told them, delivered from a road to the rear. Dot wasn't the least bit concerned with the beer lorry, he was interested to see – but then, he didn't imagine Mrs Nankervis was looking at the place for herself. There were only two options here, in his opinion, and for either of them he was glad he had been called from his lunch. He unlocked the door and ushered them inside.

'I'm afraid it has been allowed to run down rather,' he said, unnecessarily for the dereliction was obvious. 'The previous owners failed to make it pay, and rather lost heart, and the regulars gradually took their business elsewhere. The property is put up for sale by the Bank that provided the mortgage, a sad tale but all too common in this industry. A great shame, as it is part of the town's history.'

'Hmm,' said Dot, unimpressed since she knew very well he would sell it to the council to be knocked down and take his commission with barely a qualm if nothing else offered. She stood inside the door and looked around her critically. Dot, although nobody, least of all herself, had really noticed in the past, was good at interiors; she had the knack of seeing what they could be through the distraction of what they were at present. Inside the Dock Inn, this was a useful gift.

Directly in front of the door was the bar, dark and empty at this moment and looking a bit worm-eaten, but one could see what a welcome it could present stocked and lit; it stretched wide enough to accommodate a number of tall stools and still leave room for people to buy drinks. There were two or three tables in this part of the room with old settles for seating, and in the far corner the door to what Dot preferred to think of as the lavatories, but which were labelled as the toilets. To the right the space widened out and there was room, Dot noted, for quite a few more tables and chairs. A big old fireplace dominated the far end, with a rusted electric fire skulking inadequately in its shadows. A set of iron fire dogs had fallen from their stand and lay dustily on the flagstones of the wide hearth. Two wooden steps led up to a door in the back wall.

'So where does that lead?' asked Ingrid, looking at it. 'Out to the back?'

Mr Forbes moved across to open it with a flourish. 'Certainly not, the place is bigger than you think. This used to be the major draw, alas fallen into disrepair like everything else. Come.' He stood aside and held the door for them with a flourish; Dot and Ingrid mounted the steps and found themselves in the pool room. It was a good size, large enough to accommodate two full-size pool tables with plenty of space around them, and more chairs and small tables pushed against the walls for spectators or those waiting their turn. Together with this end of the lower room it would make a fair-sized restaurant. The view, of course, was a downside, straight onto the street behind, where presumably the beer lorry delivered, but one could always put up net curtains. Dot wasn't an advocate of net curtains as a rule, but they had their uses. She turned briskly to Mr Forbes. 'Now, may we see the kitchen, please?'

The kitchen was a disaster. Like everything else about the place it had seen better days, and in addition, it was noticeably dirty. Dot's fastidious eye detected what she was sure were rat droppings on the battered steel worktop and the big gas stove was crusted with grease.

She caught Ingrid's eye. Ingrid shuddered. 'Not good, is it?' she said.

'It is in a disgusting state,' Dot agreed. 'All of this –' she made a wide gesture round the room's equipment, '– needs ripping out and taking to the tip. And those fridges should never have been left closed like that, they will be full of mould!' She opened the door of one to demonstrate her point and closed it again, hurriedly. There had been food left in there, too, when it was turned off. If it had had any air, she reckoned, it would by now be a living organism.

Mr Forbes hadn't realised that the place was in such a state, it was his first visit here. He began to wonder if knocking it down and starting again might not be the best option after all, and decided it was time to call a retreat before Mrs Nankervis gave voice to the adverse comment he could sense hovering on her lips. He said, 'Have you seen enough, or do you want to see the owner's accommodation?'

'Of course we wish to see it,' Dot told him, and he led the way through the kitchen into a tiny rear hallway surrounded with doors, from which the stairs ascended gloomily to the top floor.

'That door leads to the cellar.' He pointed to a door under the stairs. 'The other, apart from the outside door, leads back into the bar past the toilets. Come.' He led the way up the creaking stair. Ingrid remarked, in the rear of the procession, 'It's like the House of Horrors, isn't it?' and he pretended he hadn't heard.

The owner's accommodation wasn't as bad as they had, all three of them, feared. It consisted of two reasonably-sized bedrooms, a living room, bathroom and kitchen, and like everywhere else (except for the fridge) it was stripped bare of all but basic furnishings, and even these, Dot thought eyeing them critically, were probably only left because they were not worth taking. No wonder the man had run off with the barmaid! His home life was obviously as much a disaster as his business! Ingrid, after a long pause, voiced what they were all thinking. 'Their hearts weren't really in it, were they?'

'I think we have seen enough,' said Dot, turning on her heel and leading the way to the stairs, a move which left Mr Forbes bringing up the rear – not his accustomed place. 'If you would be so good as to return us to the town centre, Mr Forbes, we will go away and have a period for reflection. There is a great deal to think about here, and in the meantime, I suggest that you take steps to have that fridge removed. It constitutes a serious health hazard.'

Mr Forbes murmured that it was really not part of his brief, but Dot wasn't listening. She was sure she had actually *seen* a rat in the corner up here, and she only wanted to be gone.

Back in the car and headed for the town centre, Dot spoke her mind 'It is crying shame,' she said, as if, Mr Forbes thought, it was his fault, 'that such a historic old building should have fallen into the hands of people with standards that would have shamed a hyena in his lair! I truly wonder if it is even saveable! There was woodworm in the beams, and the state of the walls was revolting! Centuries of tobacco smoke, and making the place look so dark too!'

Pubs were not Dot's best subject. Ingrid murmured in the background, 'Quite often they paint the walls that colour deliberately you know, to give the impression of age. It's an illusion really.'

'I wouldn't put any money on it, if I were you Ingrid,' said Dot, darkly. 'It is nothing less than a sin, the way that building has been allowed to deteriorate! And it smelt, too.'

She was on the heritage trail then, Mr Forbes thought resignedly. There would be a big fuss over this, but it was unfair of Mrs Nankervis to imply that it was in any way his responsibility. Like many before him, he realised it would be useless to protest, and the journey back to the office was concluded in a fraught silence.

Dot and Ingrid parted from him at his office door; the only good thing, and he wasn't sure about that, was that they took the full details with them. Mrs Nankervis had promised that they would be in touch: no doubt they would. Or somebody would. But he was only required to sell the place; its condition was not his concern!

'Borden's,' said Dot, taking her friend's arm. 'We never had time for our coffee earlier. You can spare the time now?'

Ingrid wouldn't have quit the scene at this point for a fortune. She said, 'Of course,' and they made their way to the big department store. Once seated at a table with a pot of tea and a plate of cakes before them, Dot said, 'So what did you think?'

'It can be summed up in one word – ugh!' said Ingrid, firmly. 'Knocking it down is probably the best option.'

'Do you think so? I thought it had potential.' Dot poured tea, reflectively. 'It has been let go, of course, almost to the point of no return, but its position is excellent, and apart from the woodworm its fabric appears to be sound. The dock is given over more and more to pleasure craft as the fishing declines, and the harbour, of course, is not accessible to container ships and the small cargo boats become fewer and fewer every year. I see a different future for the area.'

'You think your son-in-law would be interested?'

'I have no idea. He does, however, already own one historic inn,' – she had no idea that Mawgan had never wanted the Fish in the first place – 'and he certainly has the vision, and possibly the capital too. Whether he wishes to undertake such a monumental task when he is already so busy is another question.'

'If you want something doing, ask a busy person,' said Ingrid, predictably.

'Exactly.' Dot spread out the details, a double-fold brochure with somewhat optimistic pictures, probably from a long time ago, of a bar full of people and others playing pool, far glossier than its subject merited. 'In its day, it has flourished, you can see that here. I imagine it has declined with the dock. I think it is worth sending him this brochure, don't you Ingrid?'

Ingrid had felt sorry for the old inn, dying on its feet before their eyes. She was used to seeing it there. 'So, will you be doing that?' she asked.

'Oh yes,' said Dot. 'I really think it would be a mistake not to.' She folded the brochure. 'I shall not deceive him, of course. I will give him an accurate report of the state it is in.' She sighed for an oversight. 'I do wish I had thought to take a camera with me.'

'You could go back,' said Ingrid.

'No,' said Dot, who had not been impressed with Mr Forbes. 'I wouldn't give the man such satisfaction.'

And that, thought Ingrid, biting into a bun, sounded exactly like Dot. There had been moments today when she had wondered, but now things were back to normal. She felt quite sorry for Mr Forbes; if Mawgan Angwin showed interest he would be driven hard, poor man. He would certainly earn his commission.

Richard rang Liz after he had finished work that evening.

'So, what's the damage?' she asked. Richard sounded hesitant as he replied. 'It's all rather odd, really. There was no actual break-in, for one thing. The police think the vandals climbed in through an open window.'

'What? There wasn't one, you know there wasn't!'

'Apparently there was.'

'But ...' Liz sounded bewildered. 'Richard, you were there. We loaded the van, we cleared up, we checked all the windows and made sure they were locked. The only thing open was the vents at the top for air, and a beetle couldn't gain access through them! Didn't you tell them?'

'They say your cleaner must have left one open.'

'My cleaner, such as she is, hasn't been. She's the janitor's wife, and she only goes in if I ask her. I didn't.'

'But the janitor has a key?'

'Well, of course he has. It's a requirement of the leasehold – in case of fire, or burst pipes or something. He wouldn't just walk in and open the windows.'

'Nevertheless, they think someone might have gone in to tidy round after you moving that stuff out. The janitor says not, but then, they say, he would if his wife had been negligent. It's a bit of a bugger, because it'll put you in bother with the insurance.' He paused. 'The window had definitely been left open, and someone, or several someones maybe, had definitely come through it, or made it look as if they had. It was still open when the estate agent went round.'

Liz said slowly, 'Then somebody other than us or the janitor's wife must have opened it. Didn't you say that to the police?'

'They would only have asked me who else had a key. And Liz, so far as anyone knows, only the janitor and the estate agent do. As far as you know, too. Paul returned his set, you say.'

Liz's heart began to beat faster, she could feel it banging against her ribs. 'It has to have been him, Richard. It has to be!'

'I agree with you that it's a definite possibility, but there's no point in saying so. Probably nobody would believe you, and you could end up in trouble.'

'So what did they actually do – these unknown vandals?' She almost didn't want to know, but of course she had to.

'Well, that was odd, too.' Richard paused, as if for thought, and Liz said, 'Odd, how?'

'They had made the hell of a mess. The furniture you left was daubed with some black stuff, inside the drawers and everywhere, and the mattresses were slashed, and all the upholstery. There was graffiti all over the walls and the curtains were in ribbons, and they'd pulled the guts out of anything electrical – your TV is a goner, for instance, and that radio you had in the kitchen, and the microwave will wave no more. Your estate agent said they'd ripped out all the electrics, but they hadn't actually gone that far. They had noticeably done nothing at all that might have called attention to the fact that they were there. They smashed nothing that would make a noise, for instance. They didn't interfere with the power. They hadn't broken either the door or the window to gain entrance. They came, they did what they did, and they went and not a soul either saw or heard them. The police asked who you'd upset. I didn't tell them, but they'll be asking someone in Devon to call and see you, and they'll ask you the same question.'

'Should I answer it, do you think?'

'Up to you. If you say you'd just broken up with your partner, that isn't false accusation. You have. On the other hand...'

'On the other hand, what?' asked Liz, after a pause.

'On the other hand, it'll stir up trouble without leading anywhere. Even if they found Paul's fingerprints –'

'-which they almost certainly would –'

'– will you let me finish? Even if they found his fingerprints, it wouldn't prove anything. He's been in that flat countless times. You couldn't deny it.'

'So what are you saying?' asked Liz.

'I think I'm saying, just answer the questions they ask. If they ask about Paul, then tell them. If they don't, use your discretion.'

'It *was* Paul, Richard. It has to have been.'

'Oh, I agree with you. Or if not him in person, he arranged it and let himself in to open the window, but I doubt if anyone will ever pin it on him. I doubt if they'll even try that hard. Nothing was stolen, so far as I can see, and nobody was hurt. It'll be low on the list of priorities.'

'It's not very nice.'

'No. Look Liz, if there's anything I can do, or Cecy, just let us know. Would you like me to arrange to have the place cleaned up and cleared out? It won't sell as it is. I take it you don't want to see it for yourself?'

'No, I don't. I'll just remember it as it was, thank you. And yes, if you would, I'd be grateful. I expect the janitor will know someone.'

'You need a specialist cleaner. I'll see to it. And Liz –'

'Yes?'

'Just take care. I'll be in touch.'

When he had rung off, Liz sat for a long while, cuddling her purring cat for comfort, and wishing Richard had spoken to her for longer. If Paul had done, or caused to be done, all that to her flat – and she thought that Richard had left some things out, and could imagine what they would be – then he was seriously weird, and he was out there somewhere, knowing exactly where to find her. She thought about the particular treasures that she had salvaged from her vandalised flat, and about her home here, and she found herself thinking, he knew there was nobody in the flat and that probably nobody would ever trace it back to him. But he knew that *I* would know, and he knows that I'll never feel really safe in this house again, and she felt very cold.

Dot, too was spending a restless evening. After parting from Ingrid, she had come home and written a long report on the Dock Inn, enclosing it in a big envelope together with the agents' details and addressing it to her son-in-law, but after she had done that, thoughts came crowding in as they did on these lonely evenings. There was nothing on the television, nobody rang. She and the thoughts were on their own.

Had she really lived her life according to the directions and wishes of other people -her parents, Jerry, of everyone but Henry who had had her interests at heart? She had been unfair to Henry, and she felt bad about it now; so easy to be wise after the event. Had she really been so blinded by her infatuation for Jerry that she had let her talents and ambitions slip away, and thereby lost her chances as much by her own fault as by that of her dominating mother and father? Well, it was too late to get them back now, she was too old, too stiff, too long away from the game, but was Ingrid right, that there was still something to be saved? She had loved tennis, it had been her life at one time, she had thought it would be for always. She had dreamed of success, of holding the winner's cup high in every country in the world where the game was played, and the dream had been within her grasp, everyone said so. Without it, had she turned into nothing? Or worse than nothing, into a disappointed bully who wished to coerce those around her as she herself had been coerced?

Could you ever return from that? She thought, probably not. It would be too deeply woven into your character after ... how many years? She didn't like to think. You couldn't go back and live those years again.

There were years ahead that were as yet unlived. What could she do with them? ... *lie in the sun, work out what makes you happy. Then get on and do it.*

She knew what had made her happy in the past, and she didn't need to lie in the sun to work it out. She was just too proud and too scared to return to it. And at that thought, Dot sat up straight in her chair and pulled herself together, firmly. If it would have pleased Henry, who had gone out of his way to please her and received poor reward for it, then she would do it! And if she failed, after all these years, it would be her fault and not anyone else's.

Dot rose to her feet and walked out into the hallway where her telephone sat on its rest. She picked it up, and without giving herself time to think, dialled a number. When it was picked up at the other end, she said, 'Benita! How are you dear? I haven't seen you for an age! Now, you remember that house you showed me – Haymans, was it called? Have your friends decided yet when they plan to sell, do you know? Because I should like to see over it, if it can be arranged.'

XIX

'You lived in Embridge at one time,' said Mawgan. 'What d'you reckon to the Dock Inn?'

Chel looked up from her work on the pub computer, slightly surprised. Her boss had spilled the contents of an A4 envelope, that had come in the post marked "Personal", onto his desk, and was frowning at the papers it had held.

'It's a dive,' she said, and added, after a pause, 'Why d'you ask?'

'Because it's for sale, and Deb's mum has sent me the details. Plus a long written report in which she says much the same as you. But she seems to think it has possibilities, so would you agree with that?'

Even more surprised by now, Chel abandoned what she had been doing and gave the problem her full attention. 'I've never actually been inside it. I know it only by reputation. Ugly.'

'I don't think its reputation really matters. It seems, from what's written here, that it's dead on its feet. Deb's mum seems to think it might be just what I'm looking for, but then she's not got that much of an opinion of me, so who knows?'

Chel thought about Dot, and tried to be fair. 'Actually, I think, from what Deb and Susan say, she thinks more of you than you give her credit for these days. And I *think*, although I haven't any personal experience to draw on, that if she says something is fit for the job, it probably is.'

'Yeah,' said Mawgan, looking at the closely written sheet of paper in his hands. '*She* weren't what *I* was expecting, that's for sure. So you reckon, worth taking a look?'

'Maybe you could get someone to make a preliminary inspection in the first place?' Chel suggested.

'Howells, you mean?'

'You're training him up to take charge of the place. He's the obvious choice.'

Mawgan gave her a long look, and returned his attention to the paper in his hands. On impulse, he handed it to Chel. 'Take a look what she says. See what you think.' He looked down at the brochure still lying on his desk. 'It's a nice old building, it'd be a shame to see it go, and I like the sound of the location.'

Chel paused, the paper in her hands. 'Oliver and I lived along there when we were first married. It's the commercial end, you do realise?'

'So Deb's mum says. Read.'

Chel read. When she had finished, she laid the paper down with a grin on her face. 'I never suspected the Dreaded Dot of having a sense of humour. I like her comments about the rats.'

'She didn't seem to like 'em, did she? So?'

'It sounds a bit of an undertaking, if you believe what she says. But there are other places.'

'I've had details of a few. This is the first I've felt might be a possible. What she says about the marina, and the yachts in the commercial dock, that makes sense. And if the area is a bit workaday, so what? A bit of character never hurt none.'

'You can't lose anything by taking a look,' said Chel, slowly. She wondered whether to go on and ask a question that had exercised her mind for some time now, and decided it could do no harm. 'What I don't understand is why you feel you want to open a place in Embridge in the first place. You always say you don't want to build an empire, but now look at you! It can't be just about Tim. You're not that sentimental.'

'It's not, I aren't that sentimental. Tim Howells just happened to be there when I got the idea. No, it's about Deb.'

'Deb! Deb's made her life here.'

'That's not completely true.' Mawgan picked up a pen on his desk and twiddled it, not looking at her. 'While we was there, before Christmas, we went to this party at that sailing club she and Susan both belong to.'

'I know. That's where you met Tim, you told me, remember?'

He gave her a swift glance and looked away again. 'Deb gave up a lot to marry me. And OK, she gained something too, but one thing was obvious, moment we stepped in that place. She left a whole load of good friends behind her, a whole different life if you like. My friends, they're part of our lives, they belong here. Hers ... they belong there, a lot of them. Good friends aren't so thick on the ground you can just leave 'em and move on: believe me, I know, I tried it, and it don't work. Deb's got a whole life back there I know nothing about. You should've seen her, Chel – all lit up, listening to news of people she'd not seen for an age, she hung on every word – like she was starved or something. Some bloke called Francis something-or-other, got himself into bother; I've no idea who he is, but Deb has, she was all ears.'

'Chillingworth. I've met him,' Chel mentioned.

'There you go, you see. I'm Deb's husband, I've not even heard of him.'

'I wouldn't say he was exactly a friend of hers.'

'Maybe not, but he's part of her past. I don't want her to lose all that, Chel. It aren't fair.'

'She could always go back and stay with her mother if she wanted to see them all,' Chel pointed out.

'So she could. But I wanted to – I wanted *us* to – have a stake in the place. It's Deb's home town.'

'In that case,' said Chel, slowly, 'if you want to spend time there ... I'm sorry if I'm speaking out of turn, Mawgan, but was putting Tim Howells in charge of this stake of yours the best idea you ever had?'

He looked up fully then, and gave her a mischievous grin. 'Ch, I've got plans for Howells, I aren't stupid you know. He don't know it yet, but come the summer he's off to Milan to work with Luigi for six months. Hopefully he'll pick up some luscious Italian bird and bring her home to look good front of house. Best thing that could happen to him, he needs to get Deb out of his head, and that wife of his was just a drag on him. No ambition and bugger all ability.'

Chel stirred. A prickle ran up her neck, but she couldn't have said if it was from what Mawgan had just so outrageously said or from the report on which her hand still rested. Doors opening, sunshine ... but whether for Tim, or for Mawgan himself, or for Dot, she couldn't tell. She removed her hand and folded it into its fellow.

'Mawgan Angwin, you're a devious bastard! And even if your plot is nine parts in ten self-interest, I hope it comes off. Are you going to send Tim to see this place?'

'Don't see why not. He's got eyes, and a head on his shoulders, and if I'm going to give him the charge of the place, he better get a look at it sooner as later.'

Chel looked at him. 'You sound as if you've made up your mind.'

'I like the sound of it. We can deal with them rats. And Deb's mum is bound to know a good builder, Howells can take him with him.'

Chel laughed outright. 'You could appoint her clerk of works, she needs an outlet for her energy now she's been frozen or laughed off all her committees.' She paused, as an unexpected thought followed hard on the heels of what hadn't been a serious suggestion. 'Actually, you could do worse. Deb's mum is a bit of a liability sometimes, but she has good taste, and she's a great enthusiast for conservation, what she doesn't know, she'll know who to ask. You'd want to keep it as authentic as you can I imagine – it's one of the oldest buildings in the town, and even if you got permission for change of use, you'd have to anyway.'

Mawgan looked at her sympathetically as he took note that Chel, like himself, was at a loss as to how to refer to Deb's mum. At the same time he saw some sense in her idea. He gathered Dot's communication together and thrust it back into its envelope. 'I'll give Howells a ring tonight. That's the first step. After that, we'll have to see.'

'You could ring Deb's mum as well. She'd appreciate that.'

The discussion was over, she saw. Mawgan, restless as ever, was heading for the door. She thought he said something about doing that anyway, and the builder, but he was gone before the sentence ended. The door thumped shut behind him. With a shake of her head, as much to clear it as in despair of him, Chel returned her attention to her computer.

In fact, in the event it was Dot who made a call to Cornwall, rather than the other way about. It was purely fortuitous that she caught Mawgan at home, although it was in fact Debbie to whom she wanted to speak. With a reliable chef in his kitchen down the hill, Mawgan tried to be at home at his son's bedtime – Debbie had wondered aloud if he might be a bit of an absentee father, but that didn't seem to be happening so far, although the summer was bound to be different. It was Mawgan who picked up the phone. Dot hadn't expected that.

'I'm glad you rang,' he told her, which took her further aback. 'I was going to ring you later to thank you for that pub you sent me.' He made it sound as if she had sent the whole building in a parcel, no proper regard for grammar or syntax! Dot regained her balance, a feeling of superiority always helped.

'I thought it might be of interest,' she said.

'It is. I'm sending someone round to check it out for me, and what I wanted to ask you was, can you recommend a reliable builder to send with him?'

'You need a rat catcher first and foremost,' Dot told him, with distaste. 'And Ingrid thinks she saw a cockroach under the kitchen sink. I can recommend somebody for those, too, if you wish.'

'That could be handy, but let's make sure they're our rats and roaches first, before we get rid of 'em.' There was a suspicion of a laugh in his voice. Dot sniffed, he heard her distinctly.

'It is all very well to laugh, but Health & Safety would be deeply concerned.'

'Don't worry,' Mawgan told her, cheerfully. 'I've never had no vermin in my kitchen yet. Did you want to speak to Deb?'

'If she hasn't got her hands full. I know what babies are like.'

'She's not doing nothing I can't do for her. Hang on a bit –' He was gone. In the ensuing silence, Dot reached for her phone book and turned the page to the builder she had in mind, and waited with her finger on his name. After a minute, Debbie's voice came on the line.

'Mum! How lovely! What can I do for you, or did you just want a chat?'

First things first. Dot said, 'Have you a pencil handy?'

'Can have. Just a minute ... OK.'

Dot read out the name of the builder and his number, and said, 'Please pass that on to your husband, he was asking about a builder. Now then, first of all I must thank you – all of you naturally – for your invitation to little Daniel's christening and to Zoë's, such a good idea to have them both christened together.' She wouldn't have been able to say that before her visit to Cornwall, and even now found it hard to think about. Zoë implied the presence of Helen, probably Nenie Fingall too: that would be hard, but so were a lot of things just now, and she just had to get on with them. She continued, 'I shall be very happy to be there, of course, and I thank you too for your invitation to stay with you. And that's why I'm ringing you now.'

'Oh?' Debbie sounded surprised. 'You're planning to stay with Suse? I think she's full up, she's having Chel's sister and her family, and Liz, she's going to be Daniel's godmother –'

'Deborah, do please listen, and stop jumping to conclusions! Of course I shall be happy to stay with you, but what I was wondering was, do you need to put up anyone else as well, and if so, are you in need of any beds? I know we discussed this when I was with you last month, but we never took it further.'

Debbie was so surprised that it took her a moment to answer. Then she said, 'Actually, beds would be handy – but –'

Dot said, more in answer to the surprise than anything else, 'I am having a survey done on a house in Shearwater, and if it is satisfactory I shall be making an offer. There is somebody interested in this house, so it is time to start preparing for a move. I can send beds, and anything else you can use from the bedrooms, down to you in plenty of time for the christening. You were interested in my big suite too, I remember.'

'But what would you sit on?' Debbie felt overwhelmed and came out with the first thing that popped into her head. Dot laughed.

'It wouldn't fit in the new house. I shall buy another suite, of course, and sit on that in the interim period. It may look a little lost in the drawing room here, but it won't be for long.'

'You've really made up your mind to this move, then?'

'Oh yes. Benita has found me a charming old place, on the edge of the village with wonderful country views.' She hesitated, but decided not to mention the tennis court. So far as Dot was aware, her daughters knew nothing about her destroyed ambitions, and anyway, she was still not totally at peace with the concept. 'There is a cottage that goes with it; at present it is let for holidays, but I have other plans for it.' She didn't detail what these were, they weren't as yet entirely clear even to herself. She returned to the prime reason for her call. 'I know that your bedrooms have built-in cupboards, but would you like the dressing tables, and the bedside stands? And how about the long glass coffee table from the drawing room? It is of a size to match the suite.'

She rang off eventually, after a long, cosy, domestic chat with her daughter, such as neither of them could ever recall having before, and

Debbie turned to Mawgan, cuddling his sleeping son in an armchair, and still managing to look amazingly undomesticated.

'I expect you gathered what that was about? Oh – she asked me to give you this.' She handed over the scrap of paper on which she had written the number, and Mawgan took it without comment. 'She's going to send the stuff down next week. So we'll be able to put up Chel's parents and her brother Michael, they won't have to slum it at the Fish and someone else can have those rooms. Unless you want to put up your DJ friend and his girlfriend?'

'No no, Con can slum it. I'm not keen on his girlfriend, we can do without her.' Celebrity DJ Con Delaney had been Mawgan's best man, Debbie remembered him – he was fairly unforgettable – but not his girlfriend. Mawgan, seeing her wrinkled brow, said, 'Not that one. This is a new one. He changes them like he changes his socks.'

Debbie sat down opposite to him. She said, 'Mum's found a house. She's really going to move.'

'Did you think she wouldn't?'

'I don't know the answer to that. I find it hard to get my head round the idea.'

'Is she pleased with the house she's found?'

'Benita Vachell found it, apparently – you remember, we met her at the party. Mum says she's looking forward to living in a village; smaller, and friendlier, and Benita has promised to introduce her to "everyone who matters" – and that sounded just like the old mum!'

'Leopards,' said Mawgan, 'don't change their spots none. You can't go expecting it.'

Debbie ignored this, and said, 'She knows one or two already – Val and Penny's parents, Val and Penny were at the sailing club. I think she's met them.'

'This is Penny you went out with and upset your mum? I remember.'

They smiled at each other.

'She's all right really,' said Debbie, not meaning Penny.

'She's certainly coming out of her chrysalis in an unexpected form,' said Mawgan, with dry humour.

'Her new friends are much nicer than her old friends.'

'Then let's hope her new life will be nicer than her old one, too. Here –' before Debbie had a chance to challenge this – 'isn't it time this little feller was in his cot?' And he held out the sleeping baby with such tenderness that Debbie was all over again overwhelmed with grief at the idea that anyone could ever have found him guilty of manslaughter and sent him to prison. You could get such wrong ideas about people she thought, as she made her way upstairs, the child in her arms. And then another thought, unprompted, followed the first.

However well you thought you knew them.

Liz was looking forward to the christening, while at the same time uncertain as to how she could possibly go away. On the face of it, it was absurd to feel she couldn't leave her home in safety, but after what had happened at the flat, over which she was locked in a bitter struggle with her insurance company, it was harder and harder to dismiss a gut instinct that kept her awake at night. If the same sort of thing happened at the cottage, no insurance company would ever believe in her again. According to Richard, the police were sticking to it that the window must have been left open either by herself or by the janitor's wife, and no denials made any impression on this view. The curious nature of the damage simply made them shrug their shoulders; their attitude was that nobody could legislate for what kids did when they were out of their heads on drugs or drink. Liz could never prove that Paul had slipped in behind one of the other tenants, opened her door with the key, and left the window open for the vandals to gain access and haul their materials in over the sill So far as she was aware he didn't know the combination for the main door, but she couldn't swear to that either; he had watched her key it in enough times. Somebody in the block might have noticed him, but the police had only asked them about strangers. Paul, after nearly three years of coming and going, wasn't a stranger.

It was all very disturbing, and not helped by a thought that had come into her head when she couldn't sleep one night. Paul had had access to her computer; had he set a time-bomb among her files? Was there some delayed action virus lurking in there to annihilate all her new book? She would never be able to rewrite it quite the same, you never could. She backed-up every night, of course she did – but could you back-up a virus too? She had no idea. She had no idea, either, how she could check for one in the first place. She had begun to make a hard copy every time she finished work for the day, feeling stupidly paranoid while she did so.

She no longer felt secure in her own home and seriously wondered if she should send her beloved cat to live on the farm for his own safety. She was furious with Paul for creating the situation, furious with herself for maybe being so gullible as to believe it, unable to come to any conclusions that satisfied her or that she felt were safe. The problem seemed to be taking over her life; was that what he intended? Psychological warfare, that would be like Paul.

What had happened to her flat wasn't psychological. She had needed to throw everything out, even the carpets. So maybe Richard hadn't described what they had done in too much detail, but her imagination and knowledge of the street had filled in the spaces. She never wanted to see the place again.

She was thinking along these lines as she walked up to the shop one morning. She would have to resolve her immediate problem soon; there were only ten days left before the christening. She would have to go, she knew that. More, she wanted to, but if only it were that simple! She trailed round the shelves carrying her basket with her mind only half on the job, and ended up at the till predictably no further on with the problem. There was a man in front of her; he didn't seem to be buying much, but he was talking at length to Mrs Pinkerton as if she was his dearest friend. Liz fidgeted; Mrs Pinkerton only ever needed half an excuse to waste everyone's time. While she waited in growing impatience, she studied the man's back. Ginger hair, she noted, typical! Very short hair too, almost as short as ... and then she realised that she knew him. Everyone knew by this time that Ole Jarge had finally shifted the garage to more competent hands, the village had almost declared a festival. This was Sergeant Ginger Moustache, seen from the rear. His hair had grown a bit in the interval, she noted critically, but it wasn't an improvement. The extra length, if you could dignify it by the title, only showed up its flaming red to better – or worse – advantage.

She had reached this point in her thoughts, when he turned round.

'I'm sorry, I'm blocking up the t – oh, hullo again!' He smiled at her with what looked like genuine pleasure. Mrs Pinkerton said, 'You two know each other, do you?' and Liz and the sergeant spoke together.

'Not really. We just met in the pub one lunchtime.'

'Yes. We had a drink together one day, first time we came here.'

Mrs Pinkerton reached for Liz's basket and began checking her items through the till. She spoke over her shoulder to the sergeant. 'I'll ask around for you, but I don't hold out much hope, not this time of year. People like their space while they can.'

'Thanks anyway. I'll keep asking round too, you never know.' He vanished through the shop door and Mrs Pinkerton, always full of news about other people's business, said, 'He wants a bed & breakfast while he looks around for a place of his own to rent, but I told him, everywhere's shut. Seems a pleasant young man, going to work up at the garage for that Captain Anstruther what's buying it. His wife come in the other day for stamps. Seems a nice woman.'

Liz made some suitable reply, paid for her shopping and packed it into her own bag, and left the shop, where she found the sergeant waiting for her outside. She had almost expected it. "Effrontery" was probably his middle name.

'Hi,' he greeted her. 'I was wondering if you fancied joining me in another drink, I don't know many people round here yet.'

'Should that flatter me?' asked Liz, changing her bag to her other hand. 'Sorry, I need to get home with this lot.'

'No you don't.' He took the bag from her. 'Where's your car? We can put it in that, it'll be quite safe.'

'Outside my front door,' Liz told him. He took this in his stride, why had she thought he wouldn't?

'It can go under a table then. Come along.' He took her arm, and Liz found herself marching towards the Three Bells as if she was under arrest. If she was honest, she went quite willingly. After all, she had nothing else to do this morning, and she was a bit short of male company these days.

He paid for the drinks at the bar and carried them to the table where Liz and her shopping were comfortably settled. Taking the seat opposite to her, he said, 'No doubt you've heard, everyone else seems to've. I'm going to become a regular feature of your life in future.'

Liz looked at him over the rim of her glass. 'You flatter yourself. Perhaps I'll take my car to my father.'

He grinned at that. 'Yes, your father is the tractor man isn't he? I think he's going to be quite pleased not to have a stream of cars through his workshop from what he was saying.'

'Well yes, that's true. But I am his daughter.' She smiled back at him, knowing that George was only waiting for the day when he could concentrate on his own business rather than Ole Jarge's.

'We're much better. At cars, that is.'

'That,' said Liz, 'remains to be seen.'

Good relations thus established between them, they sipped their drinks in comfortable silence for a minute or two. Then he said, 'I don't suppose *you* know anyone with a room to let, just for now? Just bed and a bit of breakfast will do. I'm happy to be out all day –'

'– and half the night?'

'Very probably. Just as soon as I find myself a nice bit of totty.'

'Don't look at me,' said Liz.

'Oh no,' he said gently. 'You're not totty.'

Liz found this slightly insulting. 'Why not?' she asked. To her surprise, he looked embarrassed; she had him down as unembarrassable.

'Oh ... you're the kind a bloke needs to take seriously.'

I wish, Liz thought, and then another thought popped into her head unasked. He was looking for a room, he said; well, she couldn't offer him a permanency, of course, but if he had nowhere else to be ...?

Don't be ridiculous! she admonished herself. You don't know him from Adam.

Yes I do. I'm sure Adam never had bright red hair and that rather elegant, even if horribly ginger, moustache to frame his lips. I'm so glad it isn't a bristly toothbrush job.

Why should I be glad? It's nothing to do with me!

'What are you thinking?' he asked, watching her. 'I can see your mind working. Don't say I've offended you, please! I didn't mean to, it was supposed to be a compliment.'

Liz shook her head. 'I'm too old to be totty, is what you're saying. I don't suppose ...'

'What?' he asked, when she didn't go on.

'Actually,' said Liz, 'I've got a bit of a problem.'

'So tell me about it. Problems are my speciality.'

'I can believe that. Causing them, no doubt.'

'Tut,' he said. 'There's no need to be like that!' When he smiled at her, not the wicked grin that seemed to be his speciality, he was so oddly familiar that it seemed as if she had known him for ever. It wasn't a romantic illusion, she realised. It was real. He *did* seem familiar. Well, she had met him before, of course.

It wasn't that.

Shrugging off the feeling, Liz addressed herself to her more immediate problem. 'It's cheek on my part, really,' she said, 'I have to be away over a weekend, and there are reasons I don't want to leave my house empty. I just wondered ...' She faltered to a stop. It was too much to ask of a stranger.

He was quick, that was one thing. 'You need a house-sitter?'

'Yes ... no. I'm sorry, I shouldn't have asked. We're strangers.'

'We can work on that,' he offered, and then immediately became serious. 'So? Why can't you just go away, like other people?'

Liz wondered whether to tell him, and then decided, why not? She needn't mention names, after all, and it wouldn't mean anything to him if she did. 'There's this bloke I used to go around with. He can't seem to accept that "goodbye" means just that. He came and broke into my house when I'd told him I had to be away and so he couldn't come here. He lives in London,' she found herself explaining further. 'He used to come for weekends. It was a habit. It suited him.' She tried to explain about the warehouse flat; it became rather complicated.

'Bit of a freeloader then. On everyone, from the sounds of it.'

'As it turned out. Yes.'

'Not "as it turned out", Liz. All along.'

'Liz?' asked Liz.

'You said your name was Liz the last time we met.' The grin again. 'I'm Mike.'

She let it pass. And then, because he was friendly and she needed to talk to someone, she found herself telling him about her own flat, and watched his face become serious.

378

'What do your family think? Won't they help you out?'

'I haven't told them. Not everything. Not about my flat, anyway, only that I'm selling it.'

'Shouldn't you?'

'No. They'd fuss, and they couldn't do anything. Mum would insist I went home, or something, I can't face that.'

'Home that bad, was it?'

'I've been gone too long.'

He looked thoughtful, and sipped his beer for a while without speaking. Then, 'When you say you've got a problem, you're not joking are you? When d'you need to be away?'

'Weekend after next. I have to go to be a godmother to my Auntie Sue's sister's son.'

'That'd be your cousin, then. Or do you just like to complicate things?'

'I don't need to, believe me. No, he's not my cousin, Auntie Sue's sister is not my aunt. Don't even go there, we've had enough complications already.'

'And we're about get some more, sadly.' He looked at her apologetically. 'It must be something in the air – I have to go to a christening that weekend too, to be a godfather to my little sister's sprog. I'm sorry, I would have been glad to help you out.'

'Bugger,' said Liz. 'Oh well, it was just an idea.'

'Look,' said Mike – she must try to think of him as Mike, "sergeant" was ridiculous. 'If you're really worried, as I think you are ... well, there are a couple of the boys coming down to work with us. I can ask one of them, if you like. I know you don't know them, but you can trust either one of them and they're reasonably housetrained. They certainly won't stand any old buck from housebreakers.'

'Do they like cats?' asked Liz.

'It's never come up, be honest. I take it you have a cat?'

'Tib,' said Liz. He nodded, understandingly.

'I can see how you'd be a novelist, with that imagination. I take it, he's a tabby?'

'What else?' Liz had finished her drink. She put down her empty glass. Hesitated. But why not, if his friends were going to house-sit for her? Calling the army in was perhaps a bit extreme, but since they were going to be working on her doorstep, she felt she could assume she could trust them, for it's well said that it's a dirty bird that fouls its own nest. She could probably trust all of them on that basis. 'I should go home, really. My peas will be melting – do you fancy lunch? Only bread and cheese, but you could check out the territory, so to speak.'

Mike looked at her for a long moment. Then he picked up his glass and drained the last of his beer. 'What a grand idea, thank you. Perhaps we should stake the place out and let your stalker know you'll be away? That'd fix him! Only thing is, I'd like to be here when we did it.'

Stalker. That word again. Liz got to her feet, in for a penny, in for a pound. 'Come on then,'

He carried her shopping for her, and walked between her and the oncoming traffic. Unused to such treatment, Liz felt oddly cherished; Paul would never have done such things. In fact Paul, she was coming to recognise more with each passing day, deserved every insult her family had flung at him, and even then they didn't know the half of it.

Mike looked at the array of locks on her front door with interest.

'Bit like the Bank of England,' he suggested, as one who might have mentioned words such as "overkill". Liz shrugged her shoulders.

'He has the key to the bottom one. The top one is extra.'

'The top one is more likely to keep him out anyway. Unless, that is, he takes an axe to it.'

'That's why I chose it.' She opened the door and led the way inside. 'The kitchen is through here. Bring the bag.' He followed her through her study and down the step into the kitchen. Tib, curled on a chair, raised his head watchfully; Tib wasn't too fond of men these days.

'Nice place,' said Mike, looking around him with approval. He watched without moving as the cat leapt from his chair and headed through the cat flap. 'He doesn't like strangers?'

'Paul kicked him,' said Liz. She took the bag and emptied it onto the table, picking up the rapidly thawing peas to put into her freezer. 'Sit down, do. I'll put this lot away and then get us some lunch.'

Over the bread and cheese and fruit that made up a simple lunch, Paul was not discussed.

380

'When do you take over at the garage?' Liz asked, and earned another wicked grin.

'Why? Your car need servicing? I take it, it's the posh convertible Merc out in the street?'

'Certainly not. It goes to where I bought it, in Okehampton, for its annual makeover. You'll only get the crises in between. You haven't answered me.'

'Week after next, then. It'll take a bit of sorting out, but we should be up and running soon after that. Soon as I get back from Suffolk, we'll be on the job full time.'

'Suffolk?'

'I promised I'd drive Mum and Dad to the christening. I'll be going up a few days before, it isn't as if I'll be spending much time at home from now on. Haven't up to now, come to that.'

'We'll be going in different directions then,' said Liz. 'But you'll fix it with one of your mates before you go?'

'I'll bring him round to see you, soon as I can. That's a promise.'

He would keep it, she believed. 'So what will his name be?'

'Probably Corporal Jones, sorry about that but it has to happen to someone.'

'So long as he doesn't run around shouting "don't panic, don't panic" all the time.'

'Oh, Mark wouldn't do that. Don't think he knows the meaning of the word.'

A comfortable silence fell. Liz broke it. 'Mrs Pinkerton said you were looking for a place to rent.'

'Yeah, that's so.'

'You mustn't mind her telling me. She tells everybody everything.'

'That's village shops for you. I should know, my parents keep one.'

'In Suffolk,' Liz nodded.

'Right. Yes, I'd like a place of my own now, after all those years of army life.'

'You were a professional soldier?'

'Almost half my life. Since I was seventeen.'

'A long time.' Liz allowed the pause to lengthen, and then asked,

'You don't want to buy, then? Renting is money down the drain.' She reddened. 'Sorry, that was rude, it's none of my business.'

'No, it's a reasonable comment. I'd like to buy, when I settle somewhere. Perhaps not yet.'

'You don't plan to stay here?'

He shrugged. 'Maybe. Don't know yet. I told the Captain I'd stay to see things up and running, but I don't see myself working for him for ever. I'd like to have my own business, be my own boss.'

'I expect you get enough of being ordered around in the army – although no doubt you did some of it, too.'

'You could say that.' He hesitated. 'When you find yourself stuck in a war zone, you make dreams for when you get out – you have to, give yourself something to fight for. You wouldn't survive if you had nothing to look forward to. I had a mate, he knew a bit about investments. He used to play the markets for us both when he had the time, made a little bit of savings grow into a nice little nest egg. There's not much to spend money on when you're on active service, it seemed a good thing to do with it.' He shrugged. 'You build yourself a future, and don't stop to think that maybe you won't be having one.'

Something in his voice and in his choice of words made Liz say, slowly, wondering if she should, 'You *had* a mate, you said ...?'

'That's right.' He dismissed it. 'Here comes your cat again. D'you think he'll speak to me this time?'

'Just feed him, he'll be your friend for life.'

Mike pushed his plate away and made to stand up. 'I should leave now anyway, got things to see to, and I daresay you have too. Thanks for lunch, I enjoyed it – and the company. I'll fix things with Mark, and bring him round to see you some evening. You can fill him on the details, or as many as you think is wise.'

She walked with him to the door, waved as he walked away, and then went back to her kitchen and her cat. It had been a pleasant interlude, and it bade fair to solve her immediate problem too; she could go to the christening with a clear mind, but whatever it had promised in the way of friendship, she thought she had blown it in the last five minutes. Perhaps, in spite of his promise, he wouldn't return.

'What d'you reckon, Tib? Will he deliver, do you think?'

Tib gave her a golden-eyed stare. Liz began gathering the debris of lunch together, and caught herself sighing, she wasn't sure why. She tidied up and then went into her study; she wasn't feeling in the least creative, but she could check her emails anyway.

There were five of them. One of them was from her agent, asking how her latest book was coming on. Two were "funnies" forwarded by friends to take up space on her hard drive, she looked at them, smiled, and deleted. One was a special offer from Amazon.

The last one was different.

It appeared to come from a familiar name out of her address book. She opened it in all innocence and was confronted by a picture of such unbelievable vileness that her stomach turned and she was nearly sick all over her keyboard and had to make a rush for the bathroom. Leaning over the lavatory bowl depositing her lunch in its china embrace, the one thought in her head was that Paul had had full access to her address book, and that meant that she would never feel safe opening an email from a friend again. He didn't have to invade her home in person. He was already the enemy within.

XX

Dot, too, was having difficulties over the christening, but hers were mostly of a more practical nature. By this time, she had put down a deposit on Haymans, there was a deposit on her present house, and most of her drawing-room furniture and quite a lot of the furniture from the bedrooms was on its way to Cornwall. The resultant vacuum in her life as well as in her home gave her too much space for thinking, and Bennie, meeting her for coffee one morning, found herself the recipient of her confidence.

Bennie kept in touch with Dot fairly regularly, being not entirely certain that she wouldn't get cold feet and withdraw her offer for Haymans. On the face of it, Dot had already gone too far, but Bennie was aware that she had issues with the place, although she had no idea what they were when she so obviously loved it. A quick injection of encouragement every now and again could do no harm, and anyway, she liked Dot; she admired her two-fingered reaction to the laughter and scorn of her ex-friends, if they could ever have been dignified by the name in the first place, while being at the same time aware, as was Alex Hetherington, that Dot was a little like a swan; floating serenely on the surface, but paddling like hell under water to stay afloat.

'Are you looking forward to your grandchildren's christening?' she asked. 'I hope you've got something stunning to wear, your ex is going to be there isn't he? Make the blighter sweat!'

Dot didn't point out that Jerry wasn't her ex yet. She said, 'I fear that nothing I could do would make Jerry's heart miss so much as a beat. Helen Macken is a very beautiful woman.'

'He dumped her and married you,' Bennie pointed out.

'She dumped him, rather. And it wasn't really over me, I was just the catalyst, and to be honest, if it wasn't for Deborah I would regret it, it made none of us happy. And it was some time later that he married me, too. A catalogue of mistakes, made when we were young.' She shook her head. 'I wish I could think that if we had our time again, we wouldn't do it all again.'

'Doesn't stop you dressing to kill though,' said Bennie. 'Fly the flag. Don't let them think you care.'

'I don't care,' said Dot, who had recently discovered this to be true.

'Not about Jerry and Helen anyway. A little about how I behaved to Henry, a great deal about the children. Children are always the main sufferers, it seems to me. Annabel and Sebastian too, over Tom Casson and his appalling behaviour.' She stirred her coffee thoughtfully. 'I have a little problem with what to wear, however, since you bring the subject up. None of my clothes seem to fit me any more, I shall have to buy a new outfit.'

'Great! I'll help you, I love a bit of legitimate clothes-shopping! What's the problem, eating too many chocolates in front of the telly?'

'No, rather the opposite. I seem to have gone down nearly two sizes.'

'Pining away? Slimming?'

Dot smiled. 'Neither. I put it down to no longer going to lunches and dinners in aid of charities, and to having little to occupy my time but gardening. And also of course, to not having to cook sustaining meals for a hungry man. It seems there is an upside to everything.'

'Great!' exclaimed Bennie for the second time. 'Lucky old you! Now, just don't throw the advantage away.' Out on a limb, Benita, that's the way! Now, where's that saw?

'What can you mean?' asked Dot, fearing that she knew.

'Dot darling, I love you to bits and admire you tremendously, but you dress like your own mother. It's got to stop, and now sounds like a good time.'

'I always aim to look suitable,' said Dot, defensively. 'I have long turned fifty, after all.'

'Fifty's nothing! I bet Helen Macken has turned fifty too, and I bet she doesn't wear neat suitable suits that make her look as if she's been upholstered and sensible shoes.'

No, Helen didn't. But she had the excuse of being artistic, as well as stunningly beautiful. Dot couldn't see herself in flowing ethnic skirts and tight T-shirts. She tried not to feel hurt.

'Suitable is out,' said Bennie, firmly.

'You may come with me to Borden's, if you wish,' said Dot, giving in. 'I shall enjoy the company and your advice.'

Which you have no intention of taking, Bennie thought; well, we'll see about that. 'No, not Borden's,' she said. 'Sophia.'

Sophia was a designer dress shop in the town centre, over whose threshold Dot had never stepped. She looked askance. 'I really don't think ...' she began.

'Just try it,' urged Bennie. 'If you hate everything, we can come back to Borden's. But you won't. You'll love it'

Dot loved it. It did, however, prove to be a rocky road.

'What on earth are you wearing?' demanded Bennie, when they were in a dressing room with several hangers laden with expensive goodies and Dot had removed her coat, skirt and shirt, ready to start trying on. 'Call that a bra? It looks like one of those maternity jobs – and it doesn't fit either. It flattens you out.'

'It would have its work cut out,' said Dot, who found her generous breasts slightly embarrassing when compared to the uninspiring rest of her and tried everything to disguise them.

'It's all built up in front like a Victorian grandma's! And –' Bennie reached her hand into the cup on one side and grabbed a fistful of Dot's breast – 'I don't mean to be personal, but the poor thing is all bulging over the top where you've squashed it with this monstrosity. What size are you?'

'36D,' said Dot, stiffly, and more than a little taken aback.

'I'll bet you're not! Stop there –' She was gone. Dot stood and looked at herself in the mirror; square, stocky, flattened at the top. Sad. To her amazement she found she wanted to cry.

Bennie came back, flourishing a lacy white object like no bra Dot had ever considered buying in her life. 'Try this,' she commanded. 'Get the monstrosity off!'

The new bra plunged in the middle, was padded with gel and underwired, and gave Dot a cleavage that a soap star would have been proud of.

'I knew it, you're double-D,' said Bennie. 'It fits you perfectly, look.'

'It's indecent,' said Dot, faintly.

'It's dead sexy. Now try this on.' She proffered the first dress.

'I really would feel better in a nice suit ... that one.' She pointed to one of her own choices, about the most moderate outfit on Sophia's rack.

'Forget the suit. Just try this.' Bennie lifted the dress over Dot's head and tweaked it into place. She stood back. 'Wow!'

Dot looked at herself in the mirror. The dress was black, in a soft wool, clingy as a jumper; it had a scoop neck that revealed the alarming cleavage given her by the new bra, three-quarter sleeves, and hugged her figure to the hips, from where it flared gently almost to her ankles. She was shocked at the way it made her look, at least from the neck down.

'It's far too long,' she said contentiously, and made to remove the offending garment. Bennie put out a restraining hand.

'No it's not. It's a lovely length for you – all those short, straight skirts you always choose cut your body into thirds and make you dumpy. You should take a lesson from your daughter Susan, she's got your build and she never looks dumpy – you don't look dumpy now, admit it.'

No, she didn't. Dot stared at her reflection, and her own plain, square face frowned back at her. She said, with bitterness, for Helen's beauty had always been a thorn in her side, 'I still have a jaw like a shovel, a forehead like the north face of the Eiger, baby blue pop-eyes like a china doll, and boring hair that's going grey!'

Bennie heard the hurt in her voice without fully understanding the reason. She laid a hand on Dot's arm. 'Don't put yourself down so, it's a habit of yours and you must lose it. All of that is only true because you let it be. Look –' She ran her fingers through Dot's hair, fluffing it out and pushing it into a new shape. 'You put all the curly bit at jaw level, that just emphasises your worst feature. Have it cut so that it's like this, with the fullness above your ears – see now, you look quite different. No, don't say anything –' as Dot opened her mouth. 'Just look. You've got a high forehead, yes, but you don't have to advertise it – have your hair cut in a fringe, like this – look.' Her hands moved again, pulling a swathe of hair across Dot's forehead.

'My mother always said that fringes were common,' said Dot, fighting back.

'Maybe they were, in her day. Times change. Just look, and don't argue so much!' Bennie let go of the swathe and ran her fingers through Dot's hair again. 'You've got lovely thick hair, with a nice wave if you let it do its own thing, it's a shame to have it set it into submission like some sort of war helmet, and so old-fashioned – have it layered and then scrunch-dried, let it find its own way, it'd soften your whole face, and you know Dot, nobody needs to have grey hair if they don't want it. Have highlights put in. Live a little!' She saw Dot's expression in the mirror, and added, more gently, 'It's a time of change for you, Dot. Change everything, why not? A new home, a new life, a whole new you.' And then, without quite knowing the reason, she put her arms around her difficult friend and hugged her. 'Come on Dot. Fight the bastards in the trenches, fight 'em on the beaches. Make Jerry Nankervis wonder what's hit him!'

Dot felt the warmth of the hug and something, some shard of ancient ice, began to melt inside her, treacherously. Tears stung her eyes, she rubbed at them with her hand. Bennie said, 'And while I'm busy insulting you up hill and down dale, Dorothy darling, will you let me give you a special treat?'

'What kind of treat?' Dot asked, immediately suspicious.

'Nothing lethal, I promise. An appointment with a beautician, to teach you how to make the best of yourself. You'd be amazed what cunning make-up can do to alter the way you look. Darker eyebrows, some careful work on your eyes, you'd be a handsome woman if you tried it. Really. And don't cry – please. I didn't mean to offend you.'

'You haven't,' said Dot, between sobs.

'Goodness! I should have! I'd have offended me!'

'No. You meant it all kindly, and you're right anyway. After all, what do I have to lose? I've thrown it all away already.'

'Rubbish. You've got it all to come. Now, we've still all these things to try on, so get that dress off. I take it, that's going home with you?'

'It'll need a coat over it,' said Dot, recovering her backbone. 'It's only March.'

'Not any coat you already own,' said Bennie, firmly 'Not a coat at all, it'll show below any normal coat, very un-smart. A good jacket. And killer heels – *no* Dot, I know you haven't anything like that. You will have.'

They left Sophia laden with bags – none of which contained any selection of Dot's own – and sped on their way by smiling attendants. Out in the street again, Bennie paused. 'Where now, do you think?'

Dot was beginning to get the hang of this. She said, 'If I am going to live in the country, I need some country clothes. Where do you suggest?'

Bennie considered, surprised, if she was honest, that her words had hit home so thoroughly.

She said, 'Borden's is probably as good as anywhere. You want trousers, sweaters, sweatshirts, T-shirts – I bet you've got none of those. And don't offer me twinsets and fully-fashioned jumpers and your gardening trousers, please! I'm getting to know you too well! And there's a good shoe department there, too.'

'Killer heels,' Dot murmured.

'Right. And when we've dealt with all that, we'll make you an appointment with my hairdresser.'

'My own –'

'No, Dot. Your own is obviously stuck in the dark ages. Forget her!' Bennie took her arm. 'Are you enjoying this? I am! I think I missed my vocation as a personal shopper.'

Dot found that she was, and not only because nobody had ever taken so much interest in her before although that was certainly part of it. Some of that was her fault, of course. She had put up a barrier between herself and too much intimacy, fearing to be let down – again. By doing so, she had left a trail of destruction in her wake that she now visualised with a wry grimace that Bennie missed. Too late to do anything about it, but perhaps she could manage not to continue. Certainly she felt at this minute how a water-starved plant must feel when someone came past with the watering can.

It wasn't until she reached home later in the day, that reality rose up and hit her. Dropping exhausted onto her new sofa, the bags of treasure at her feet, she kicked off her sensible shoes and leaned back, closing her eyes wearily. What had she done? What on this earth had she done? She had allowed Benita Vachell to make her over right down to her knickers, that was what she had done! Trying to make a silk purse out of a sow's ear, that was Benita. Dot felt as if someone had pushed her through a sieve, leaving her pulped, disorganised and unrecognisable. She just wasn't the sort of person that Benita had tried to make her into.

She could cancel the hair appointment, Benita would understand. The beautician too, at the same salon. She was who she was, she couldn't change that. And all these clothes, she could probably take most of them back and exchange them for something more suitable.

Not at Sophia. Sophia didn't stock things that were suitable.

That black dress really was rather beautiful. Not for her, of course ... she wasn't that kind of person.

An odd thought drifted into her head then. She wasn't the kind of person that she had been forced into being as she grew up, either.

Benita had said she shouldn't wear a hat to the christening. It had sounded like sacrilege to Dot. People didn't, these days. Benita had said, except at weddings, and nobody else would. Life was more casual than it had been in the fifties.

Disrespectful, Dot considered, feeling suddenly old. And anway, she had been a girl in the sixties, not the fifties.

She felt as if she had never been a girl, ever.

The person that she had tried to be had never been a great success, she had to admit that. In fact some people had seemed to prefer her after her ambitions had hit the skids, so did that say something she should be thinking about? Such as, had her ambitions been unworthy? Charities were good, of course, but she hadn't been in it for the charities had she? She had been in it for herself, and she deserved to trip.

Charity begins at home, they say. You couldn't come closer to home than yourself.

After a while, Dot's energy began to come back, and with it, a cautious optimism. She sat up and poked into one of the bags. She found that even just doing that, and thinking about Benita as she helped to choose the contents, gave her a warm feeling. She would feel very strange going about in these things, but perhaps she owed it to her friend to try? Benita had meant well, after all.

"Meaning well" was a trick of her own. It hadn't got her very far. Two husbands, both gone now, alienated children, an empty house, no friends. No, that wasn't true, she did have friends, it was just that they weren't in the places she had thought they were.

She took out the pale blue jacket that the bag held and looked at it. They had chosen it to go with the black dress – *it will show off your blue eyes*, Benita had said. Dot laid it across her knees and stroked it gently, as if it was a cat. It had been fiendishly expensive.

So, who would she be wearing it for? Not baby Daniel, he wouldn't care. Certainly not Jerry, and her children rather took her for granted: fortunately for her dwindling self-respect, Dot believed that children generally did with their mothers. Herself, then? Or to show Helen Macken something that she wouldn't be interested in knowing anyway?

The newly emptied rooms in the house, although they were out of sight upstairs, pressed on her, the embodiment of a loneliness that she felt right through to her soul.

She wished very much that she had somebody here, right now, to talk to.

Sally phoned the following morning. It was to be a salutary reminder that friendship cut both ways.

Dot was upstairs in her bedroom. A good night's sleep had restored her to a certain extent, and she had resolved that it was time to have a clear out. If none of her old clothes fitted her, as they didn't then now was as good a time as any to sort them out, pack them up, and transfer them either to the charity shop or the bin. Armed with a roll of black bags, she set about the task with renewed energy.

She hadn't unpacked the bags of new clothes last night; there were too many of them: it had taken both herself and Bennie to transport the bags to her car, she recalled. So only the beautiful black dress and its accompanying jacket had found their way onto a hanger, and hung now on the door of what had been Jerry's wardrobe. She looked at them with growing appreciation; really, Benita had excellent taste, it had been wise after all to let herself be guided by her. She opened her own wardrobe, and began to take things out and lay them on the bed. They really did look rather dull and frumpy when compared to the new outfit.

She had filled two bags with discards and was well away on the third when the phone rang on her bedside table. She picked it up, and Sally's voice, thick with tears, said, 'Dot, can you come over for coffee and let me talk to you?'

Dot looked at the pile of clothes waiting to be sorted on her bed, and she hadn't even started on her chest of drawers yet. She really didn't want to stop, but recalling that Sally had stood by her when others noticeably hadn't, she said, 'Sally dear, whatever is the matter?'

'Everything!' said Sally, comprehensively. It sounded time-consuming, and Dot smothered a sigh.

'Why don't you come over here and tell me all about it?' she suggested. 'I'm in the middle of a big clear out, perhaps you can give me a hand and we'll talk while we do it.'

It occurred to Sally that it might be easier to unburden herself if she and Dot weren't actually face to face, although she did wonder if after the storm with Irwin she was in a fit state to drive. 'Half an hour then?' she suggested. That would give her time to bathe her face and recover her composure. If she ever could, that is. Dot agreeing, she rang off and Dot was left wondering what that had all been about. Tom most probably, she thought, condemning yet another dull brown suit that had cost more than its worth to the black bag. She did seem to have a remarkable amount of brown, grey and beige in her wardrobe, what did that say about her? A load of expensive rubbish, she told herself firmly, and then caught sight of her new dress and jacket and smothered a smile. She could have bought two of her dull brown suits for what the blue jacket alone had cost her. She was still smiling when she opened the front door to Sally, but Sally noticeably wasn't. She almost fell across the step and Dot found herself, for the second time in twenty-four hours, with her arms round a friend.

It was obvious at once that there was going to be no more clearing out until Sally had opened her heart. 'Coffee,' said Dot, firmly. It wasn't the girl – Leanne's – day to be here so Dot made the coffee herself, and because Sally had followed her to the kitchen they had it there. It felt distinctly odd, which come to think of it, was exactly how the drawing room looked with the new, smaller suite, so maybe this was fortuitous. And possibly it was the unaccustomed informality that made it easy for Sally to say, straight out, 'Tom's lost his job. Alex sacked him yesterday morning.'

'Oh dear,' said Dot. There seemed little else to say, and it was only after a moment that she gathered her wits and asked, 'Why?'

'One of the assistants reported him for sexual harassment. She's married.'

'Silly of Tom.'

'He said he didn't realise. She was new, apparently.'

'He must have realised that she wasn't interested, however,' said Dot. 'Married or not, women are not automatically fair game.'

'That's what Irwin says.' Sally swallowed a sob. 'He's still saying it's my fault, spoiling him as a child. Dot, it's awfully hard *not* to spoil an only child, however hard you try, and he's one of Tom's parents, too. He's not blameless either.'

This conversation was beginning to sound familiar. Dot asked, 'Did you tell him that?'

'Yes.' Sally hid her face in her hands. Dot gave her time to pull herself together a little, and then said, 'It has always seemed to me that such propensities are as much a matter of nature as of nurture. That would make Irwin equally responsible in my book, maybe more so. Men will be men, after all.' As she well knew.

'I told him that, too. He was furious. He was so furious that it began to make me wonder ... and then we had a terrible row, and he walked out and I don't know where he's gone.'

'When did this row take place?' asked Dot.

'Over breakfast.'

Dot looked at her watch. It was ten to eleven; Irwin hadn't been gone so very long then. I'm sure he'll be back,' she said, a little helplessly. Jerry had not come back. Or Henry, either, although for a different reason. 'And what was Tom doing, in all this?'

'He went out last night and he didn't come back either. He was upset as well, Lorraine dumped him when he told her what had happened, the wedding's off, and only a week to go too.' Dot wanted to say *oh dear* again, but felt it to be inappropriate, and while she sought for something more constructive to say, Sally went on. 'Oh, it's not a surprise – to me, anyway, although it seems to have been to Tom. She's been restless for weeks, and I don't blame her. He's full of excuses, got to work late, got to entertain a client, always standing her up. She'd be a fool not to guess what he's been doing, after all she was one of his other women herself when he was married to Susan.' She was openly weeping now.

'Drink your coffee while it's hot,' said Dot, 'it will make you feel better.' When Sally had sniffed, blown her nose, and taken a sip from her cup, she went on, 'Did Tom himself have any defence to offer?'

Sally gave a kind of wail. 'He says he wishes he'd never left Susan.

He says he wants her back, and the children. He says he was a fool and he's sorry and he's made a mess of his life.'

'How very true,' said Dot. 'I'm glad that he appreciates it. But he won't get Susan back, you know.'

'He arrived on the doorstep with all his things, all anyhow because she threw them into the street after him, and he's coming back to live at home permanently, he says, and Irwin says if he does, he's going, he can't stand being under the same roof – as his own son, Dot! How can he!'

Quite easily, Dot thought, and on the whole she was on Irwin's side; although no doubt some of the row would blow over eventually it wasn't either the time, or her place, to say so. Instead she said, 'No Sally, that won't do. You must be firm.'

'He's lost his job, Dot. Without notice too! How can we turn him away?'

'He may have lost his job, but he is not incapable of finding another. Moreover, by my reckoning he must have received almost half a million from his share of the sale of the family home – to which, in my view, he was hardly entitled under the circumstances. He can easily afford to buy a flat of his own, and the income from the balance should keep him very comfortably even without regular employment. He knows about accounting, let him use his knowledge to support himself.'

'You sound so hard, Dot,' said Sally, miserably.

'Perhaps you should learn to be harder yourself,' Dot commented. Sally sniffed.

'It's easy for you to say. Oliver was all sorts of trouble, I know, but he never caused any woman trouble, you have to allow him that. He never made you ashamed, not that way.'

Dot had never been entirely certain about this. She decided that Sally needed distracting, to give her time to calm down, then maybe they could talk sensibly, and so she said something she had never intended to say to anyone. 'Oh, I think he did, you know. It's only with hindsight that I see it.'

'Cheryl, you mean? But he married her and they're very happy, aren't they?'

'No, not Cheryl. I was thinking more of Joanna. Looking back, you know Sally, that had all the appearance of a transitional fling. Joanna's heart was in it, certainly, but Oliver, when I think about it, had more the manner of someone exorcising a ghost, and when he had done it, and when he had taken himself off on a long voyage alone to put distance between himself and a woman he had used, for there is no other word for it, *then* he was ready for Cheryl.

As she had hoped, she had caught Sally's attention. 'You mean you think there was someone before Joanna? Someone serious? But surely, you would have known about it?'

'With Oliver? No! He delivered a boat to the Mediterranean for somebody, you know, a year, eighteen months, before he set sail round the world. He didn't bother to come back, he fell in with a party of professionals doing an underwater survey of wrecks, or something like that, and from there he took over a flotilla somewhere in the Cyclades – in the middle of the season too! And somewhere in among all that, I think that he learned to care about someone – care very much: it would have been for the first time in his life.' She tried to keep sarcasm out of her voice, and failed. 'He returned home somebody different from the man who set out. It's strange how I see these things now. I have the time for thinking, I suppose.'

'It can't have been that serious, or surely he would have married her?' Sally objected. Dot gave her a quiet look.

'Perhaps she was married already,' she said.

'Well, at least he didn't embarrass you in front of your friends,' said Sally, slightly put out at having her thunder stolen in this way. 'How I shall ever look Ingrid in the face, I don't know, it's too bad of Tom it really is!' She was on the edge of more tears. Dot thought of the coolness that had arisen between herself and Elise Rendell as a consequence of Oliver's fling with Joanna, and made no comment on this, and then, recollecting that nothing is more annoying than confiding your troubles to a friend only to receive theirs in return instead of advice and sympathy, pulled herself together.

'Now come along,' she said. 'You've finished your coffee? Then come upstairs with me, I'm turning out my clothes, you know, ready for the move. If you don't feel like helping me, then you can sit on the chair and talk to me.'

'I ought to go home, maybe. Irwin could be back, wondering where I am.'

In Dot's view, from what she had heard so far, Irwin would be better being left to stew in his own juice for a bit. Let him wonder, he might start thinking then. Men! It wouldn't do to say so, though. She said, 'Give him a ring if you're worried about him. Let him know where you are, then he won't be worrying.about you.'

'You think he will be?' asked Sally, surprised.

'Oh, it's amazing what a guilty conscience can do. You give him a ring, and I'll be upstairs. You know where to find the telephone.'

Safely upstairs on her own, it was amazingly peaceful after the tense atmosphere in the kitchen. Dot filled another black bag, and was hanging her new clothes in her now-almost-empty wardrobe when Sally came into the bedroom. 'He's not back yet. I left a message on the answer phone.' She sounded calmer. Dot nodded her head in approval.

'And when he does come back, the two of you must sit down and decide how you're going to tell Tom that a man who has once left home and is perfectly capable of supporting himself, doesn't return uninvited unless for a very good reason, such as serious illness or overwhelming personal disaster. Tom is suffering from self-inflicted wounds. They don't count.' She paused, reflectively. 'That, and a congenital inability to live on his own resources. It is time he learned.'

'It does feel a bit like kicking him when he's down,' offered Sally. She peered into one of the black bags, without interest.

'If you allow him back, it will very likely be Irwin who leaves,' Dot warned her. 'Which do you want?' To her private relief, Sally didn't hesitate.

'Irwin.'

'Well then. You know what you must do.' She pulled open a drawer and tipped its contents wholesale onto the bed. 'Goodness me, what rubbish one accumulates!'

Sally looked at the row of fat bags ranged beside the bed. 'This looks like a pretty wholesale clear out to me. You'll have nothing left to wear, if you go on like this!'

'Oh, I will.' Dot pulled open the wardrobe door to display the modest row of her new purchases. 'Dear Benita came shopping with me yesterday.'

'I do love a good shop,' Sally observed wistfully. 'So therapeutic.' She sounded as if she was recalling a happier age. Dot felt her patience slipping. She sympathised with Sally, of course she did, but she and Irwin, much as their son had done, had made their own troubles. Neither of them, so far as she could see, had ever been firm enough with Tom, and it was her own Susan who had borne the worst of the fallout! It was unfair too of Irwin to put all the blame on Sally. She would have liked to shake them both, get some sense into them! And as for what she would like to do to Tom, who was a fast becoming a walking disaster area, it didn't bear thinking about! So selfish! She picked up an armful of the knickers that Bennie so wholeheartedly despised and shoved them into one of the empty Borden's bag without even bothering to look through them.

Watching her in amazement, Sally perked up a little, and began to display proper interest. She pulled the one shopping bag that still contained anything towards her and peeped inside. 'Ooh!' She plunged in a hand and pulled out one of Sophia's flagrantly in-your-face bras. She took a second look at Dot, whom she had not really studied earlier, being too wrapped up in her own affairs. She looked back at the bra in her hand. 'Dot!'

'Pretty, aren't they?' said Dot. Sally rose from the chair where she had been sitting, thrusting the bra back into its bag as she did so. There really seemed nothing to say.

'You're throwing out *everything*? Oh, do let me help you, I feel like doing something really *disruptive*!' She picked up a further armful of dismissed knickers and bras and gleefully pushed them after Dot's armful. The two of them working together had purged the entire chest of drawers by the time the doorbell rang, and remarkably little had gone back in. A few personal items, maybe treasured souvenirs, Sally surmised. Even some of those hadn't survived the holocaust. They were working so hard that neither of them heard a car crunch onto the gravel outside, so that the long drawn-out ring at the front door, when it came, startled them both. Dot recovered herself first. There was only one explanation for this, the postman would never dare!

'That'll be Irwin,' she said briskly. 'Come along Sally. We must let him in before he breaks the bell!'

Irwin, like his wife, almost fell through the door, grabbing at Sally and smothering her in a fierce, on the face of it unloving, hug.

'How dare you vanish like that, and not say where you'd gone!' he cried, unreasonably. 'I've been worried sick!' Sally, fighting herself free, retorted, 'You had! Why shouldn't I?'

'I was afraid you'd left me, and I didn't blame you!'

'I thought the same, and I *did*!' Sally retorted with spirit. 'Blame you that is.' Irwin silenced this revolt with a rough kiss, and Dot, watching, felt a twinge of envy. Jerry had never cared enough to be violent, and Henry hadn't had it in his nature, bless him. It wasn't that she wanted to be manhandled, she hurriedly told herself, but it did show that Irwin cared. She was happy for her friend, but this scene didn't require an audience, and she retired tactfully into her denuded drawing room and sat on the edge of an armchair, unsure whether to laugh out loud or burst into tears. Her doubts of yesterday flooded back, she had never felt so lonely.

After an appreciable interval, Sally came into the room. She came over to Dot and bent to give her a swift hug and kiss. 'Dot you're a star, I'm sorry I disrupted your morning, and thank you for being a good friend and listening to me. I'm going home now, we're going to have a proper talk. It's going to be all right, I'm sure. I told Irwin what you said.'

About what? Dot wondered, and with some justification. As she recalled, she had said quite a lot, on several different subjects, and there hadn't been time for Sally to repeat it all, surely! She shouldn't have said some of it, either, she never had known when to pull her punches.

'You always know where I am, if you need me dear,' she said, which was too sadly true to be bearable. Sally didn't notice anything; with a last valedictory kiss, she was off to rejoin her husband. Dot heard the double crunch of their car tyres on the drive as they drove off, and then she was alone again. Irwin hadn't even said goodbye. Hadn't said hullo either, she realised, and a bubble of laughter rose in her throat, but it swiftly died.

After a while, she got to her feet. There was work waiting to be done upstairs. Somehow, it had lost its appeal, but having started she would finish. If she didn't she reflected with a wry smile, she wouldn't have room to go to bed tonight! Not even alone.

Bad news travels fast. It reached Debbie first, via Penny Harries, who, since their reunion at Christmas, had kept in touch sporadically and emailed from work to share it with her while nobody was looking, which was Penny all over. Debbie would have put her sleeping baby into the car and driven down to visit her sister to pass on the interesting news and to cadge a cup of coffee, but before she could put this plan into execution, a small furniture van arrived in her drive. This kept her busy for the next hour or so, as none of the several large items inside it would go up the spiral staircase and had to be carried through the side gate, hauled up to the balcony, and brought in through the french windows on the top floor All of this took time, and when it was all safely in and the van departed she rang Susan instead. It was too late for coffee now anyway, and she had needed to make some for the men in any case.

'Hey, guess what, I've got furniture upstairs!'

'Well, that's good. Mum delivered, has she?'

'Not exactly in person, but yes. Suse, she's sent the lot – bedding. towels, everything! Lamps, dressing tables, bedside tables, the big suite, the coffee table ... I feel quite overwhelmed!'

'Well, she hardly needs pillows and duvets for seven bedrooms. does she, if she hasn't got them?'

'But she's sent the bed linen too. For twin beds and a king-size double, we shan't know ourselves!'

'Your guests will be grateful, come the weekend.'

'Mum being Mum, it's all pure cotton, and it'll need ironing.'

'Never look a gift horse in the mouth. Just leave it to Mrs Tregear. Or send it to the laundry.'

'You bet I will! Suse ...'

'What?' asked Susan, when she didn't immediately continue.

'Have you heard anything from Tom?'

'No, and that's fine by me. Why do you ask?'

'Only I had an email from Penny this morning. He's lost his job.'

'Really? It couldn't have happened to a nicer person. What did he do?'

'Sexual harassment of a married woman, apparently.'

'There's a surprise. I'm glad she had the guts to pin his ears to the wall!'

'You sound very hard. Don't you care? Even just a little bit?'

'No. Should I?'

'And Alex is planning to take Val into partnership. Poor Tom must be liquidised!'

'"Poor Tom" nothing! He brought it on himself.' Debbie hadn't fully realised, until she heard the bitterness in her sister's voice, exactly how much Tom Casson must have hurt and humiliated her; other people's pain is so easy to underestimate. She could think of nothing to say, and after a moment, Susan went on, 'The only reason I care a flying fuck about what happens to Tom, or what he does, is because of my children!'

Susan wasn't given to strong language, even after over a year in the more relaxed ambience of Cornwall she was still far too uptight. Debbie decided, wisely, that the telephone probably wasn't the best medium for continuing this conversation; and she ended on a lighter note. 'And do you know what else Mum has sent us?'

Susan, knowing she had given herself away, was glad to follow the lead. 'No. Surprise me.'

'A whole bone china teaset, complete with cups and saucers! The lovely one with the birds that she had in the corner cabinet. We never used it, remember?'

'You'll be expected to use it now.'

'I take it as a heavy-handed hint that my standards are slipping,' said Debbie, a laugh in her voice.

'Not slipping. Slipped.'

They said goodbye on this light-hearted postscript, and Debbie went off to sort out her new beds ready for visitors while she had the chance, before Daniel woke up. Being domestic wasn't really her scene, she reflected as she shook out duvets and fought them into their covers. It wasn't that she minded work, but this sort of thing was mind-numbing! Roll on Easter, when she would give up breast feeding and Gosia could take some of the strain! And then she started wondering about the weekend, how it would work out. Chel's parents plus one of his brothers were staying with her and Mawgan, which seemed inappropriate, but Chel's brother Richie, his pregnant wife and two-year-old daughter were staying by the creek. She liked Chel's parents, but she didn't know them that well, and neither had they exactly struck up a friendship with her own mother, who would also be here. She didn't know brother Mike at all. She wondered what he would be like. He might find himself something of a buffer state!

Susan meanwhile returned to her archaeological studies, but she found it hard to concentrate when the house was so quiet. Annabel and Seb were out, down at the reawakening sailing school with Roger, and no doubt with Kayleigh and Ben too, possibly even Damien. Carl was down there as well, sorting out the office work while Debbie was busy sorting out her baby and her home. Soon, the sailing season would begin again, and he would be away for most of the week, just as they were all used to him being around. She remembered what Debbie had said before Christmas, and wondered if it would ever happen; it hadn't been mentioned again and Carl had given no indication that he wasn't content to go on the way they were for ever. She found herself smiling at the idea that she was getting so used to a houseful of people and noise that she couldn't work properly without it.

Her thoughts wandered on down byways of their own choosing. Mum didn't change much, she thought affectionately. Cups and saucers indeed! They would only get used when she came calling, but then, that was possibly the idea behind the gift. Mum was trying hard these days, but she really couldn't get to grips with Mawgan – and then, she found herself wondering how she would feel if when Annabel grew up she wanted to marry Damien Tregear, and was brought up short. Oops! That threw a different light on the problem! She thought about it seriously, trying, as they all were in their different ways, to find a way through to Dot. A growing suspicion, that had begun in Devon at Christmas, that they none of them actually knew her had opened up a wide field for speculation. She was being very generous to Debbie, trying to heal the breach between them.

But not to me, Susan suddenly found herself thinking. She has given me nothing, but Deb was always her favourite. She will buy Deb back, if she can, but I don't have a value worth paying. So nothing much at all changes, when you come down to it.

At this ill-chosen moment, the phone rang again, and of all the people she didn't want it to be right then, it was Sally. 'Susan darling, how are you? The children well and happy?'

'We're all fine,' Susan told her, noting there was no enquiry for Carl; well, what could you expect, realistically? She said, 'I heard about Tom losing his job. I'm sorry.'

Sally knew that this would be a lie, but she took it in the spirit in which it was meant, and in any case it wasn't the reason she was ringing. She and Irwin had talked about this long and seriously, and had come to the conclusion that it wasn't fair not to give Susan a chance to think before Tom came pleading to her for reinstatement. Both of them wished he wouldn't do it, both of them knew that he hadn't a chance of getting Susan back, but if she was warned, Sally reasoned, she might be kinder to him. Irwin agreed in principle, but wasn't sure that his son deserved kindness. He was bitterly shamed by Tom's behaviour. Alex Hetherington was – had been? – a close personal friend. He hadn't been in touch. Lost for words, no doubt, Irwin said, with his lips tight. But Tom was their son, and the storm had to be weathered.

'It was a bit of a facer, of course, but he's being very constructive about it.' Sally borrowed words from Dot. 'He had enough after the settlement to get by, and he can always do private work, he thinks he might prefer that to working for somebody else now.' Read between the lines, he won't get a good reference. Sally knew that Susan wasn't deceived, but at least she wasn't saying anything. Sally went on, inwardly quailing,' The thing is, that Lorraine wasn't at all amused –'

Susan did speak then. She interrupted. 'I can see that she wouldn't be. I wasn't either, if you recall.'

There was a short pause. Sally knew that Tom deserved that, but it didn't make it less painful. She said, 'She's called off the wedding.'

'Well, good for Lorraine. I'm surprised she got this far with it.'

'Susan ... you're not making this easy.'

'I'm sorry,' said Susan, wondering why she should pretend to be, or why she should make things easy come to that.

Now or never. Sally took a breath, plunged in. 'Actually Susan, he's relieved. He's been thinking these past months. He misses you, he misses the children –'

'– not enough to ring them, or write to them, or come to see them however,' said Susan, before she could stop herself. 'Annabel's been breaking her heart over him.'

Sally was silent. Susan closed her eyes. It was too bad of Tom, but it wasn't fair to take it out on Sally. Sally had always been kind, when Tom wasn't telling lies and stirring things up. She said, 'Sally, if what you're trying to say is that Tom wants a reconciliation this late in the day, then the answer has to be "No". We – the children and I – have a new life, a happy life, a better life than he ever gave us. We don't need him, we don't want to go back into ... that. I'm really sorry, but that's how it is.'

'Won't you just listen to what he has to say?' Sally pleaded. Susan shook her head, although Sally couldn't see it.

'No, I don't want to hear it. Tell him not to bother, there's no point in putting us both through it. Spare him some of that humiliation he handed out to me. It doesn't feel good, he wouldn't like it.'

'Poor Tom,' said Tom's mother.

Poor Tom, my Aunt Fanny, Susan thought. She said, 'I'm sorry Sally. The children, and Carl and I, will always be glad to welcome you and Irwin here, you know that. But I don't want to see Tom, or to speak to him, except when I can't avoid it.'

Sally's heart clenched at the mention of Carl. She didn't know what she could say, so she said nothing. The silence between them lengthened, and Sally imagined she could feel the gulf between them widening too. Alex, Ingrid, now Susan ... Tom was costing them dear. But at least Dot had stood by her. Dot, of course, knew how it felt to be suddenly bereft of your friends.

'Well,' said Susan, for one of them had to say something, 'If that's all, I ought to be studying. Tell Tom, to spare his breath and his feelings, and that I'm sorry.'

Sorry again. She seemed to have said nothing else. Sally thought that she would never dare confess to her son that she had pre-empted his attempt at reconciliation. She wished she had never started this, knowing each of them was at a loss as to how to bring it to an end. Finally Susan said, in desperation, 'There's someone at the door. I have to go, Sally. Give my love to Irwin,' and that was that.

As it happened, there was someone at the door, but it was the back door not the front, and it was Annabel and Sebastian, closely followed by Ben. Annabel held something clasped to her chest under her coat.

'Look Mummy, see what Kayleigh gave me.' She opened her hands a crack and a small, triangular, furry face peered out at Susan from big green eyes. A whiskery little black face, with a pink mouth that opened and let out a very small squeak.

'A kitten!' said Susan; it seemed to be the only suitable comment that her already overloaded brain could provide.

'Please say I can keep it,' said Annabel, her eyes pleading. Seb gave a small snort.

'Clink will eat it!' he said, and Annabel looked horrified. Susan held out her hands.

'Give it to me. Let me see.'

'It's a boy,' said Annabel. 'Kayleigh promised it was a boy.' She passed over a ball of black fluff, very carefully. 'Isn't he *sweet*!'

Susan accepted the kitten gently, and apparently taking this for a welcome, it began to purr. It was definitely a boy, she noticed, Kayleigh was quite right. On the other hand, so was Seb right; it was very small compared to Clinker, and did they really want a cat?

'I don't know ...' she said. The kitten purred. Tears came into Annabel's eyes.

'Kayleigh's Dad said he was going to drown them if they didn't find homes. Mummy, you *can't* say no!'

'Annabel ...' Susan stood helplessly, the kitten snuggled trustfully against her breast.

'His name's Lucky,' said Ben, speaking for the first time. Seb snorted again.

'Until he meets Clink!'

'Where is Clinker?' asked Susan, suddenly registering his absence.

'We left him in the garden,' said Annabel.

'Licking his lips,' said Seb, with relish.

'Come to that,' said Susan, ignoring him, 'where is Kayleigh?'

'She had to go home.'

'I see.' How convenient for Kayleigh! 'Fetch him in,' said Susan. 'Let's see what happens when they meet, shall we?'

Clinker bounded through the door with his usual enthusiasm, and bustled across the floor to greet his mistress. He paused, when he realised what she was holding, and his ears flattened.

'See,' said Seb. 'Shall I fetch his bowl?'

'Shut up, Seb,' said Susan. She knelt down and held out the kitten – Lucky – towards Clinker, keeping a firm hold. 'See, Clinker. A little friend for you, how about it?'

Clinker sniffed at the kitten. His tail moved hesitantly and he pushed his nose forward. A tiny black paw full of needles flashed out and missed it by a hair's breadth. Susan laughed. 'You can see who's going to be boss.'

Annabel's face became radiant. 'Oh Mummy! Does that mean we can keep him?'

'Oh Annabel, it's hardly the moment! We've a houseful of people at the weekend, he'll be terrified! Someone will step on him.'

Seb had been impressed by the kitten's show of spirit. He said, 'Oh, let him take his chance Mum. He's Lucky, after all.' Seb had abandoned the more childish "Mummy" where Annabel still hung onto it. Something to be learned there? Susan gave in, the kitten was sweet, she would hate to think of it drowning, and why not anyway? It might give Annabel something to console her for her father's behaviour.

'All right,' she said, partly against her better judgement. 'But if he's your cat, Annabel, you look after him. And you can start now by going up to the shop and buying cat litter, kitten food, and a washing up bowl. They won't have a litter tray, so make sure the bowl is shallow or he won't get in!'

Annabel looked as if all her Christmases had come at once. She clasped her hands. 'Oh *Mummy*! He can sleep in my bedroom.'

'No he can't,' said Susan, firmly. 'He can sleep in the cloakroom while he's little. When he's bigger he can go in the kitchen, and we'll put in a cat flap.'

'But he'll be lonely. He'll cry!'

'Give him one of your soft toys. He'll think it's his mother.' Then, when Annabel made to protest again, she said, 'He'll grow up, Annabel, and faster than you'll believe. Cats are nocturnal hunters, he'll want to be out on his own affairs at night.'

'After the girls,' murmured Seb, who seemed determined to stir the pot. Susan gave him a look.

'Not if I have anything to say to it,' she said firmly. She put the kitten down on the floor, where it looked very small beside Clinker. Seb was right, he'd make about one mouthful if Clinker was so inclined, but it seemed he wasn't. He sniffed at the kitten, and this time the two of them touched noses; the kitten had made his point and was prepared to negotiate. Susan wished she had a camera handy.

'Liz will love him,' said Annabel, watching.

'So she will,' said Susan. 'Now off you go, all of you, take my purse, it's on the worktop there. Leave Clink, Seb, let them make friends.'

'Can we have chocolate?' Seb demanded, heading for the door into the hall. 'To celebrate Lucky coming to us?'

Seb would always change his mind if chocolate was involved, Susan thought resignedly, but she said, 'There's already some in the cupboard. Now go, before the shop closes for lunch!'

When they had all pounded down the hallway and out of the front door, she hunkered down on her heels and watched the two black animals making cautious overtures to each other. Why not a cat, anyway? She liked Tib, and at least Lucky wouldn't need walks twice a day. And then she thought, I wonder how Liz is getting on with her Paul problem, she hasn't been in touch since all that hoo-ha over her flat.

No doubt, at the weekend, she would be finding out.

XXI

Tim rang Mawgan on the Thursday before the christening. The builder's report had come direct to him, Mawgan having so far not appeared in the negotiations: Mr Forbes at present believed that he had a third contestant for the Dock Inn, and was rubbing his hands in glee, he had no ambition to find himself referee in a confrontation between the council and the formidable Mrs Nankervis. Tim had forwarded the report as soon as he received it, but he rang anyway to precede it with his verbal impressions. He thought Mawgan would appreciate this and maybe trust him a little more; trust between them was still, in Tim's view, a slightly rocky affair. He had no idea what Mawgan's view was, but then he never had, so nothing had changed there.

Mawgan was interested to hear what he had to say.

'The fabric of the building is sound enough,' Tim told him. 'If the council want to knock it down, they'll have to bend the truth, but maybe they don't realise that so we ought to give them the benefit of the doubt for now. It looks terrible on the surface, but the report indicates nothing that can't be repaired or replaced. It needs money spent on it though.'

'Fine, I expected that.' Mawgan thought for a moment. 'Did he give an estimate?'

'A very rough indication only, it's with the report. I didn't know how far you were prepared to go so we didn't go into it too deeply. The estimate is just for what's essential to put it back into reasonable order, get rid of the woodworm, give it a lick of paint, things like that. In my opinion, the kitchen can't be rescued. The whole thing needs ripping out and starting from the ground up, your mother-in-law agrees with me.'

'You've talked about it with her?' Too sharply. Damn!

Tim made a face at the phone that Mawgan, of course, didn't see. 'She talked to me, rather, she rang me on purpose to do it. She seems to be taking a personal interest.'

'She knew it was you I was sending, then.' Mawgan wasn't certain he was happy with this.

'She knows I'm technically working for you, my mother told her. She guessed.'

'So long as she doesn't spread it about as I'm interested.'

'She wouldn't. That's one thing you can be sure about with her, she doesn't spread other people's business around.'

Mawgan hesitated, but if he was taking Tim on as his right-hand man in Embridge, there was no point really in holding back. He said, 'Chel said I could do worse'n ask her to keep an eye on everything when the builders get started. What d'you reckon? You know her better than me.'

'I could do that,' said Tim, slightly offended. His heart sank, he had known this was too good to last. Bloody Angwin!

'No you couldn't. You won't be around after you finish with the college in June. I got other ideas for you.'

'You have?' Tim asked, cautiously.

'Yeah, I have. How's your Italian?'

Tim's heart gave a great thump, and his blood sang anthems. He said, 'It's coming on pretty well, considering. I've been going to evening classes.'

'I'm impressed,' said Mawgan, meaning it.

'You said at the start you might send me abroad. I can limp along in French, but Italy felt more likely. I hedged my bets.'

'A few months with Luigi in Milan will sort you out ready to open at Christmas. Make you pretty fluent in Italian, too!'

'You're going for it?'

'Subject to the builder's report, yes, I think so. Don't you? I'll take a look for myself first, though; next week sometime after this christening is over. I'll let you know when, or you can arrange it for me.'

'Can do.'

'Right then. I'll wait for the report.'

Tim switched off his phone. For the first time, he felt he was a valued part of an enterprise, not just a lame duck who needed a handout, and it felt good. Managing the Dock Inn, although it wouldn't have been his first career choice, would give him back the respect of his friends, not to mention of himself. The sailing crowd would come initially to support Mawgan and Debbie, but they would keep coming, he resolved, for a damn good restaurant run by Tim Howells! And who in their right mind wouldn't be gleeful at the thought of a whole summer in Italy?

That thought generated another, even better. Mario's Trattoria in the town centre, which was a rather fine restaurant rather than a true trattoria, had enjoyed top spot among the town's restaurants for many years, too many years! Well, watch out Mario, the scruffy old Dock Inn is coming to get you! He realised that he hadn't been so unreservedly joyous since the disaster that was Cornwall.

Mawgan, on the other hand, put his phone back on its rest slightly less euphoric. Tim Howells was still showing signs of trauma; too defensive by half. He should sympathise; been there, done that, but Tim would have to snap out of it soon or they were going nowhere together. This time, he had totally derailed a serious question. Mawgan still didn't know if Chel's estimate of Deb's Mum's abilities was fair, but then, when he thought about it, Tim might not have been able to tell him anyway, he didn't know how well Tim knew Dot or otherwise. On the credit side Tim had put two and two together, made four, and set about learning Italian. One up to Tim.

Well, they would see. So far, so good. All the other truisms. He would talk to Deb's Mum when he went to Embridge, and draw his own conclusions.

Susan too had received a phone call that morning. When she had said goodbye to her caller she stood for a few minutes, deep in thought. Rather sombre thoughts, from the expression on her face. After a moment or two, she turned away and went upstairs. From the top floor, she could hear the cheerful voices of a crowd of children, Annabel and Kayleigh, Seb and Ben, playing something riotous and probably violent on Seb's computer. She really must see about getting Annabel a computer of her own, she would need it for school soon, she couldn't share with Seb once she went to Truro, but that wasn't her immediate concern. She tapped on the door of what had once been Seb's bedroom, lightly, before pushing it open and putting her head round.

'Is this a bad moment, or can you spare ten minutes?'

Carl looked up from his computer with a slightly vague expression in his eyes that meant he had been miles away in his latest book. Susan said, 'Sorry. Shall I come back later?'

He visibly returned from some distant place, and then he smiled at her. 'No, come on in. I wanted to talk to you anyway.' He picked up a sheaf of loose sheets of paper from beside his printer, made to put it in his filing basket, and then returned it to its previous place. 'Damn. He's there again.' The basket, as Susan had already seen, was full of sleeping kitten; he had found the refuge early, and headed for it whenever the children became too noisy. His name had changed in the interval since his arrival; he was now not Lucky, but Loki – the mischief maker, had said Carl, and far more apt.

'You could move him,' Susan suggested. She dropped into the comfortable armchair between the window and an overflowing bookcase. 'Put him on top of the filing cabinet, he'd like it up there.'

'He likes to be near someone.' He reached out and stroked the kitten, gently, with one finger. 'Right Susie, what's the problem?'

'Why do you think there's a problem?' said Susan, contentiously.

'Your face. I heard the phone go, who was it?'

'Bob.'

'Bob?' He looked bewildered, still with half his mind elsewhere.

'You know, Bob Chase – the shipyard. Emberton.'

Carl remembered. He gave her a serious look, completely back with her now. 'This is about *Silver Spirit*.'

'He's got a buyer. If I still want to sell.'

Carl was quiet for a minute. 'And do you?'

'"Want" isn't quite the word. But yes, I shall sell her. We can't have her here, and at least it's to someone I know, and can trust to look after her.' She didn't look as if the idea gave her any joy. Carl said, 'We could keep her in the river. It's deep enough there.

'No. There are all sorts of things we *could* do, but I've made up my mind. Let's not. We're much better off with *Hierax*. It's just sentiment ... because I loved her, and we never got the best out of her. Just quarrels and shouting, and then Tom making excuses not to go out at all. Disappointments. Bad memories. Best put behind us.'

'Tom Casson seems to have been a prize arsehole on all counts,' Carl commented.

'Yes, he was.' Susan wondered whether to tell him now that Tom wanted a reconciliation, and decided against it. Tom wasn't going to get his wish after all.

410

'So, who's going to buy her?' asked Carl, after a pause. 'You say you know them, anyone we met at Christmas?'

'The one you didn't meet. Francis.'

'I remember. The black sheep.'

'He has cows,' said Susan, 'not sheep. He used to sail a Moonraker, quite successfully too, but he's giving it up apparently.'

'Hadn't he made the place too hot to hold him, or something?'

'Something like that, I never heard the full story. But he'll take good care of *Silver Spirit*, I know. He's that kind of person. He wants her hauled out for a full survey, and then we can make a deal.'

'A happy ending of sorts, then,' said Carl, not looking at her. He picked up a pen and began to twirl it between his fingers. 'Have you got a moment for a serious talk, Susie? Is this the right moment, what are the kids doing?'

'Murdering something upstairs, from the sounds of it.' Susan's heart sank. There had been something in the way he spoke that she feared boded no good. The thought that he had had enough of family life and wanted to return to his bachelor existence on *Hierax* was the first into her head. Because she wouldn't marry him, and he didn't want half a loaf. And she couldn't. Perhaps one day, in the far distant future, she would get up the courage but not now. Maybe not ever. Maybe she wasn't going to be given the chance.

Carl didn't notice anything. He was trying to get a sheet of paper out from under the sleeping kitten without disturbing him, and not succeeding. Immediately alert, Loki was making dives at his fingers, claws displayed, tail gleefully aloft. Carl withdrew his hand and sucked it, grimacing. 'The fiend! He's drawn blood.'

'He doesn't mean it. He's only playing.' Susan lifted up the wriggling kitten and, when Carl had rescued his paper – it looked like a letter – put him carefully back in the basket. There was little hope that he would stay there. Carl looked at his trophy, as if it, too, had attacked him. He said, 'This came yesterday. I didn't tell you because I wanted to think about it, but now I've made up my mind what I'm going to do, I need to run it past you. You might not think it a good idea. It ... takes rather a lot for granted.' He held out the letter. 'Read it, but I recommend you stay sitting down.'

Susan took it; it was from his agent. She read it, then read it again in disbelief before exclaiming, '*How* much? It must be a typing error!'

'That's what I thought. So I rang up and asked. It isn't.'

'Your publishers are offering this ... this indecent sum of money, for an option on your next three books?'

'Yep. That's about the size of it.'

'Goodness,' said Susan, inadequately. All kinds of thoughts tumbled in her head; Tom and his freeloading ways, living at her expense and expecting him still to underwrite his life when he had left her for another woman, Carl living on a boat like a gypsy, Carl moving in with her and the children at their invitation, Carl maybe moving out because he didn't need them any more. She sat still, afraid that if she moved something might break. It might be her heart.

But Carl was talking now. Loki had climbed out of the filing basket and tried to walk across the computer keyboard; Carl had picked him up and held him splayed out like a kipper against his sweatshirt, absently stroking him as he talked. The purrs were quite out of proportion to the size of the kitten.

'There's no way I can take on that kind of commitment if I only have four or five months of the year to do it. Some writers claim they can turn out a book every three months, but I'm not one of them. And for that money, I wouldn't need to be. I wouldn't need the sailing school job, I could stay ashore and pay my share here with you, and we could all live happily ever after. Only ...' He hesitated, and Susan said, bewildered now, 'Only, what?'

'Only, it would be letting Deb and Roger down. My investment in the sailing school, what gives me my seat on the board, is *Hierax* and my time and qualifications. If I back out, then that leaves them facing an expensive dent in their funding – a new boat, a qualified instructor, the business is doing good, but it can't stand that kind of shock yet. It's still in its early days.'

'They could still have the use of *Hierax*.' Susan suggested, but Carl shook his head.

'No they couldn't. *Hierax* is mine. If I'm packing my kitbag and leaving, she's coming with me. I don't want us to be limited in our use of her, we'll want to sail as a family at the weekends, and it's time Annabel and Seb had a proper cruise; France, the Scillies, or we could charter in the Med or the Caribbean or the Gulf Islands. We can afford it, in time, if I'm bringing in that sort of money, and anyway

I can claim some of it back on my income tax as research expenses.'

'So what are you suggesting?' asked Susan. Although she knew that Debbie had already envisaged this and made her contingency plans, it wasn't her place to tell him, and she was interested, in any case, in his viewpoint. Carl's hands were full of kitten, so he couldn't point, but he nodded towards the letter.

'I want to invest most of that back in the sailing school, if you agree. Become a shareholder. I can still do the publicity for them, and maybe the pre-flotilla trips occasionally. But basically, I would be a sleeping partner and there would be the money available to replace me. The only thing is, if I did that I wouldn't have a regular income, at least for a while until the royalties began to come in. I'd be back on what I can earn as a freelance journalist.' He grinned at her. 'It's down to how much you love me, sweetheart.'

'Have you talked this over with Deb – and Roger?' asked Susan, playing for time.

'Not yet. I had to talk to you first.'

It was all so very different from what she had imagined when they started out together, or from what her marriage to Tom had led her to expect, that Susan was for the moment unable to frame a sensible reply. Finally, she said, 'So you invest in the sailing school long-term, and I make a short-term investment in you?'

'Something like that, I suppose. Yes. Only I would hope we would both get a return on our investment. And I'm not exactly broke, but there wouldn't be much coming in for a bit, I'd be mainly paying my way out of my savings. It's a gamble. Are you up for it?'

Susan looked down at the letter still in her hands. 'If this is the sort of money that they expect your books to generate, I don't think it's that much of a gamble. Do you?'

'Pie in the sky.' Carl shook his head. 'You can't rely on that until it happens. Personally, I find it hard to believe in. And remember, first I have to cover the advance.'

'Can I think about it?' Susan asked, although she already knew what she would decide.

'I would expect you to. Talk it over with your Dad if you want. But don't never think I'll be like that Tom and expect to sponge off you for life.'

Susan smiled then. 'That's the first time I've ever heard you sound remotely Cornish,' she said.

'Stress of the moment.' He unhooked the kitten and placed him back in the filing basket, where he turned round a few times and then settled back to sleep.

'He seems to have seen Clink off, anyway,' said Susan, for something to say.

'Don't you believe it. Some mornings it's like the zoo in here.' He looked at the kitten. 'Perhaps I should give him a cushion, what do you think?'

'You wouldn't have anywhere to put your stuff.'

'I haven't anyway, if you notice.' He looked at her then, a straight, assessing look that she found hard to meet. 'You're not happy Susie. What is it? *Silver Spirit*, me, or something else entirely?'

Thus put on the spot, Susan said miserably, 'Lorraine has called off the wedding. Tom wants a reconciliation.'

'Does he, indeed.' Pause. 'And do you?'

Susan shook her head, mutely.

'Not even for the children? Annabel still pines for him, you know.'

'I know.'

'Have you told her – told them?'

'Not yet. No. It's between Tom and me, anyway.' The silence this time drew out until she felt constrained to say, 'All Tom wants is his comfortable, sheltered life back. He doesn't want me.'

'Presumably he thinks he does. And the children do come into it, you can't just not tell them.'

'Carl, will you stop playing devil's advocate? Don't think I haven't thought about it, please!'

'How long have you known?'

'A day or two, about the wedding. Penny told Deb, and then Sally rang me just now and told me about the reconciliation.'

'You didn't say anything to me.'

'Neither did you – about that.' She nodded to the letter still lying on his desk. 'Just like you, I wanted to think about it. Not that I expected he'd want me back – and there's no way I'm going back to that –'

414

'Perhaps you'll feel you have, if I pull out of the sailing school,' said Carl.

Susan stood up. 'I think we'd better stop this, right there,' she said. Carl said nothing, and she left the room, closing the door carefully behind her. Carl looked at the kitten.

'At least she didn't slam it,' he told it. He was tempted to get up and follow her, but decided to let her have some time to herself. He wondered, if he murdered Tom Casson would he get away with justifiable homicide? He seemed determined to load Susan with a responsibility that was rightfully his, to prevent her from moving on finally, and it was not, Carl thought grimly, that he cared about her, or even about his children. He hadn't spoken to them since Christmas! No, all Tom Casson cared about was Tom Casson. He would skulk around in the hinterland of Susan's life – of their lives – for ever, asking for sympathy, making Susan and the children feel guilty. If he heard about the sale of Susan's yacht, Carl had no doubt that Tom would be there, holding his hand out. Personally, he would like to take an axe to that hand so that he could never do so again!

Liz had heard nothing from Sergeant Mike, and was beginning to worry about her weekend arrangements. Not just the weekend, either, she was beginning to feel sick every time she received an email from a friend. A couple of times she had even rung the friend concerned to check that they had actually sent one. The one that her friend Lindsey disclaimed, she had deleted without opening, but she couldn't keep doing that, it negated the whole point of emails if you had to make a phone call every time. They were becoming like a slime over her whole life, nasty, clever Paul! She had heard nothing from him. Richard had reported that her flat was well on the way to being saleable again and she couldn't wait to get rid of it. Even if he no longer had direct access, she wouldn't feel comfortable that Paul wouldn't give a repeat performance until the place was safely in the hands of somebody else.

About the sergeant, she was also uncomfortable, but she was disappointed too; she didn't care for people who broke promises and she had wanted to think better of him – although he was no affair of hers, so why was she bothered? And if she had trespassed, he had almost invited her to do so. But even so, she told herself sadly, you should never put your big ugly foot into a stranger's private space, so perhaps she should learn from it.

She wouldn't have had him down as so sensitive. Or maybe it was she herself who was being sensitive, and he had just felt it was time to go, and if that was the case, why was she letting herself get so bothered over it? He had no responsibility for her, if he wanted to forget a casual offer made to somebody he hardly knew, he was free to do so! She never had liked men with ginger hair anyway, but when her thoughts reached this point, Liz began to laugh at herself. The colour of his hair had nothing to do with it of course, she was simply disgruntled because he had left her with a problem that she had hoped had been solved. She was still giggling when her doorbell rang.

The man on the step was a stranger. He was short, dark and square, and when he introduced himself saying, 'Miss Ballantyne? I'm Mark Jones,' she wasn't surprised, if he had been anything other than Welsh, it would have been a genetic miracle. He went on, 'The sergeant asked me to call round. He said you needed someone to look after your house at the weekend.'

'Oh!' said Liz, the wind shaken abruptly out of her sails. So he hadn't broken his promise, why should that make her feel warm all over? 'Come in.' She held the door wide. 'We can talk about it over a cup of coffee, I was just going to make one.' She hadn't been, why did you always say that to an unexpected visitor – in this case, a *very* unexpected visitor?

Mark Jones followed her through to the kitchen, pausing briefly on his way to run a critical eye over her computer and its various adjuncts. 'Nice bit of kit you've got there,' he mentioned.

'Do you know about computers?' Liz asked. 'Do sit down. I'll just switch the kettle on.'

He pulled out a chair and sat at the table. Tib, she noticed, although he raised his head from where he had been snoring in her laundry basket, didn't make a dive for the cat flap; a good augury for the weekend. She clattered about with mugs and the kettle, and Mark Jones said, 'I know a bit. Why, got a problem?'

'Just something I wanted to ask someone,' said Liz, wondering how far she could go. She decided to dissemble a bit. 'I'm a writer. I wanted to know, if someone had stolen your contact list and was setting up different addresses under some of the names, and then using them to send you ... well, say, anonymous letters, is there anything you could do about it?'

'Easy. Just change your own email address.'

'But nobody would know. You wouldn't get any emails.'

'You would if you told them. Just write one email and send it to them all. Magic!'

'How would you do that? I have no idea, although I know people do it.'

'It's not hard. I can show you if you like.' He gave her a serious look. 'Sarge said you were having problems with a stalker. Would this be to do with that?'

Liz didn't answer straight away. She poured hot water into the *cafetière* and carried it across with two mugs. She pulled out a chair and sat down, resting her elbows on the table.

'I see it is,' he said.

'That, I don't actually know,' said Liz, yielding to an impulse she wondered if she might live to regret. 'He was here when I wasn't, and he had access to my computer.' A bit like the open window at the flat, she found herself thinking. On the face of it, obvious, but no proof.

'That sounds pretty open and shut to me.' He hesitated. 'I thought he was worried about you – Sarge. He was going to bring me over to meet you, but his mother had a fall over in Suffolk, and he had to go to the rescue. But he made me promise to come, I hope you don't mind.'

Liz knew she had seldom been so glad to see someone she didn't know, and blessed Sergeant Mike for his thoughtfulness; she was sorry she had doubted him. She said, 'I hope his mother is all right.'

'I think she broke her ankle, or something. Nothing serious. Just badly timed, with the sprog's christening and everything, she needed someone to do the washing up and that for a couple of days while she rested it.' He added, 'He asked me to tell you. He'll see you when he gets back.'

Liz said, 'I just need somebody to be here. Sleep here, feed the cat, keep an eye on everything. Would you? Obviously I would provide for your keep and pay for your services.'

'Glad to, Miss Ballantyne. And you don't have to pay me. Just leave me a fat juicy steak.'

'Liz. And I do. I might need to ask you again.'

'Mark.' He held out his hand. 'OK, I'll submit an account in triplicate. Shake on it.' They shook hands across the table, and Liz began to pour the coffee. He watched her for a minute. Then he said, 'If you like, I could set you up a new email address with a new provider, and transfer your addresses while I'm here. And if you want, I could do a check for foreign bodies while I'm at it; if he knows enough he could have put something nasty in while he was here.'

Liz had no idea how much Paul knew about computers, but she did know she had wondered about this herself. She looked at him in awe. 'You can do things like that?'

'Given the time, yes. You'd have to trust me with any passwords. You can change them afterwards.'

'There's only one that matters. I was going to change it anyway, because ...'

'He knows it?'

'Yes.'

'You should have done it first thing. If he has that, he can access your computer from his own if he has the technology and the skills.'

'Can he? I never knew that!' Liz stared at him, aghast. Mark looked at her enigmatically. No doubt he thought her an ignorant silly woman. But Paul himself, she thought, had set up her present system, and there were probably a lot of things that he hadn't told her.

'We'll do it now, before I go, shall we?' he asked. 'You can change it again later.'

'Oh, please!' said Liz.

'No point in changing your email if we don't,' said Mark, sounding unduly cheerful. He sipped at his coffee and put the mug down. It was scalding. 'How did you fall in with this creep, anyway?'

'He's a publisher,' said Liz. 'Not mine – it's not that bad. But we met at literary gatherings and it just sort of happened.' She looked back to that time, her face thoughtful. 'I think he saw me coming. Hooray, here comes a sucker! I can't believe myself now!'

'Don't be too hard on yourself. We all get suckered sometimes.'

'This thoroughly?'

'Women are more vulnerable,' he suggested, and ducked, grinning. Liz kept her hands on her mug. At least he hadn't said *single* women. 'You could be right,' she admitted.

418

They finished their coffee and he took her, rather than the other way about, into the study. He sat down at the computer and switched it on. 'I'll choose the new password,' he said. 'If you do it, he may work it out if he knows you that well. And when you choose the final one, take a random word out of the dictionary.' His hands flashed over the keyboard. A row of asterisks, six of them, appeared in the box for the new password.

'Let me guess,' said Liz. '"Sucker" – am I right?'

'See what I mean about knowing people?' He looked just like a monkey when he grinned, she decided. A rather clever monkey.

'It'll do for now,' she said.

'You may as well go and do something,' he suggested. 'This will take a while. I'll call you when I'm done.'

Liz went to wash the coffee mugs. When she had done that, she washed Tib's bowl and sat down at the table again; denied access to her workplace, she felt very much at a loose end. She wondered how long it took to do whatever it was that Mark Jones was doing, and then got up again and went to ask him.

'Could be a while,' he said, in a vague way, as if he had hardly heard her. Then he sat back and looked at her fully. 'You've got another email address, on your website, I see. Anything coming in on that?'

Liz shook her head. 'No. I pay my webmaster a vast amount of money to weed out all the spam and the nutters before he forwards it.'

'Would he have told you if you'd received one of those nasties?'

'Not necessarily.'

Mark looked at her, and then down at his hands as if to check his fingernails. 'There's one on your email now. It just came in, and I opened it to check it out, I hope you don't think I was taking liberties. I wouldn't have read it, if it had been personal. What would you like me to do?'

'Just delete it,' said Liz, with a shudder.

Mark gave her a long, quiet look; he said, 'Do you think that's the best idea?'

'Why, what do you think I should do – print it out and frame it?'

'Show it to the police. You should. It's nasty.' He paused. 'Have they all been like that?'

'I haven't seen this one, but probably.'

'I'll print it out and put it in an envelope, if you have one. You can decide what you want to do, you needn't look at it. If you do take it to them ...' he looked at her doubtfully, 'they may want to come and check out this computer too.'

'Why ever? I've deleted them all.'

'You'd be surprised what they can find, even so. When you delete, it goes off the screen, not necessarily off the hard disc. How often do you empty the rubbish box?'

'Not often.' The thought that those horrible things were still lurking in the depths of her computer gave Liz the shivers. She said, 'Would that get rid of them?'

'Might do. I wouldn't bet on it. And there's another thing I thought of, although you may call it paranoia.'

'Tell me. I can take it.'

'Oh, it's nothing awful. Just a precaution. You say he's a publisher?'

'Well, yes. What's that got to say to anything?'

'And you're a writer, and he's had the run of your files – how long ago now?'

'Weeks.'

'Then I'd suggest that you waste no more time in putting any work that isn't already published onto a disc, seal it in an envelope, and lodge it with someone you can trust – your bank, or your solicitor, would be favourite. Get them to sign the envelope and date it, and put it in a safe place.'

'You mean, he might pinch my work?'

'He might have already copied it to disc while he had the chance, or mailed it to himself. It wouldn't create a precedent.'

'The book I'm working on, I haven't finished. He wouldn't be able to get the whole thing until I had.'

'Doesn't matter. If he put a different ending on a recognisable beginning, he'd still hang himself.'

'Surely, the computer itself dates it?'

'And if he managed to wipe it all out with a time-bomb?'

'I see what you mean, but you are devious!' She paused. 'I always make a hard copy.'

'Good, but that won't help you because it isn't dated. Even if you write the date on now, it won't help in an action over copyright, you could have done it at any time. Of course, you could lodge a hard copy with your bank, that would work all right too, but a disc takes up less space. And time, I imagine.'

Liz said nothing. She stood staring at her computer, her thoughts in turmoil. Yes, she did think that Mark was being paranoid, but the hard fact remained that Paul *was* a publisher, and one desperately in need of a book from what Cecy said. It was all a bit paranoid, but it could do no harm. She thought, I could make a disc and give it to Susan's stepdad to look after at the weekend, he's a solicitor and he owes our family. Mark watched her sympathetically.

'It's only a precaution. I don't suppose you'll ever need it.'

'OK, I'll do it. You're right, it can't hurt. Would you like some lunch?'

'Later, that would be grand.' He swung the chair back to the computer screen. 'I'll just finish up here, if I may – say an hour?'

At least preparing lunch gave her something to do. A swift review of her fridge produced cheese and salad, not much else, so to pass the time she made cheese scones to eat with ... well, with cheese, she thought with a wry smile, and there was always plenty of fruit around. The alternative was catfood stew, and she thought he'd prefer the cheese. She laid the table and took a look into the study; his nose was still stuck to her screen, so she opened a tin of soup and poured it into a pan. She was just throwing the can into the recycling bin when he appeared in the doorway. 'Done. Something smells good!'

'Sit down. I'll heat the soup.'

'Before you do that, come and write an email to your friends, and I'll show you how to send it.'

'Couldn't we do that after? The scones are hot.'

'Are they indeed!' He came right in. 'Half an hour won't hurt, in that case.'

Over lunch, Liz asked him, 'When Paul sends another of those ... things, what will happen? It won't arrive. Will it just bounce back to him, like it does when you make a mistake in an address?'

'Exactly that.'

'So he's going to know I've changed my email.'

'I imagine he's not going to be surprised – except that you didn't do it before.' He gave her a funny look. 'What are you thinking?'

'I'm wondering what he'll do instead.'

'If you find yourself in trouble, just call in the army. We're entirely at your service.'

Mike had said something similar, the thought was comforting.

'When I come at the weekend, I'll do a proper search for you, make quite certain there's no hidden extras,' Mark offered. 'I don't think he's got the IT skills, I've found nothing out of place so far, and you seem to be well protected. But it won't hurt to clean everything up for you and leave it sparkling. How's that?'

'Very kind of you,' Liz murmured.

'Your new handle is "wordsmith", I've transferred you onto yahoo. He'll have a job tracking you down again.'

'Thank you.'

'And you know your password.'

'Sucker,' Liz nodded. I suppose I should be grateful I don't figure as "sucker@yahoo.'

When they had eaten, Mark helped with the washing up unasked, and then he showed her how to transfer her address book before he closed down her old provider, and how to email from her new address to all those in it to notify them of the change. All those except Paul.

'You want to keep him on there?' asked Mark, surprised.

'I might want to tell him where to get off!'

'Then don't do it from this computer. You'd be back where you started.'

'Oh sugar, so I would! Take him off then, let's have no accidents.'

Mark highlighted Paul and pressed delete. If only, Liz thought, watching, it was that easy to make him vanish in reality!

'What time would you like me here on Saturday?'

'Oh, around lunchtime, I suppose. It's not far, only just under two hours, I'll be leaving in the early afternoon I expect.'

'Then I'll treat you to lunch at the pub before you go.'

They smiled at each other, both of them aware that there was no chemistry, only mutual liking. 'That'd be lovely,' said Liz.

He left, and she went back into the house. It was absurd, she knew, to think that it felt cleaner. She looked at the envelope containing the printout that lay on her desk. Perhaps she would show it to the police, perhaps she wouldn't. She would wait and see what, if anything, happened next, she decided, and sat down at her computer to play with her new email. There was already one message on it. It was from Richard.

Thank God for that, he had written, *what took you so long? Love R xx*

XXII

Dot drove down to Cornwall on Friday afternoon in a very ambivalent state of mind. There were several reasons for this, the most obvious being that she wasn't entirely sure that Benita's efforts to brighten her image were ... well, appropriate, she supposed. It wasn't that she didn't like the effect, she just felt that it wasn't quite *her*. She certainly liked the way her new haircut softened the rather severe shape of her face; the feathery fringe disguised her high forehead perfectly, and the layered cut, curving into her neck and waving above her ears, drew attention away from her firm jaw line, but she did wonder what her children would make of it all, and not just because of the smart haircut. Dot's hair had darkened over the years from its original blonde to a rather dull mid-brown, subtly designed by nature to show off any grey to the best advantage. Bennie's hairdresser had restored its colour and disguised the grey with sunstreaked highlights; together with the new styling it took years off her age. Too many years? It was all very well for Benita to claim that you couldn't lose too many years, but she didn't want to look ... well, desperate, in front of Helen, and Anona Fingall. Or no, Anona had married at last, hadn't she? Some foreigner, Dot couldn't recall his name, if she had ever heard it.

If it had ended there, that would have been plenty to be going on with. It hadn't. The beautician had dyed her pale eyelashes, shaped and dyed the eyebrows that were too fair to be more than an indistinct shadow, shown her how to make up her eyes so that they looked darker, less ... *bulging* was the word her mother had used, the ultimate put-down for an insecure teenager. The face that looked out at her from her mirror these last few days was not her own. She did like it, but it belonged to a stranger. There was nothing she could do about the dyed brows and lashes, of course, but she could discard the eye shadow and eyeliner that she had been so carefully shown how to use. She hadn't discarded it.

She did have to admit that Benita had been right about her adopting a more casual way of dressing. Dot had always had an athletic build for which smart tailoring had done little, or even nothing. Her new wardrobe of trousers and shirts and the really rather pretty sweaters and the sweatshirts that Benita had helped to choose was far more her style. Dot didn't believe she had ever owned a sweatshirt before. The black dress she had bought for the christening, too, was a style that flattered by its very simplicity. She even had a pair of jeans, that Benita had said she wasn't to keep just for gardening but to wear, like other people. Dot didn't think she ever would, but there they were anyway, before her eyes every time she opened the wardrobe door.

She had not, she thought as she drove, inhabited this new persona for long enough to sustain her through the ordeal ahead. She was to stay with Debbie and Mawgan as before, but this time, she wouldn't be the only guest. Cheryl's parents would be staying there too.

Dot considered that Cheryl's parents would have been better staying with Cheryl, but that wasn't how it had been arranged. One of Cheryl's brothers, together with his wife and young family, was staying in the house by the creek, and Marilyn and Bob would be at Waterways House. Dot found that some of the memories she had of their previous meetings made her cringe in retrospect. How could she have been so tasteless? She had never seen it like that at the time, and failed to recognise that the change in her viewpoint reflected the changed attitude of people to herself. She didn't have to fight her corner with Benita, or Sally, or Ingrid, or even, as it turned out, with Marie Law. She didn't seem to have to fight it with her children any more either. Where once she had felt a need to be confrontational and assertive, now people seemed to be more accommodating. She still was confrontational, she knew that. What was new was that she simply tried not to confront these days. Which brought her back to Marilyn and Bob.

It wasn't Bob so much, he had tended to stay in the background looking miserable, and she had only met him once or twice in the disastrous run-up to Oliver's wedding to Cheryl, and then at the wedding itself. That had been on the television that evening, Dot recalled, on the local news, and then realised that she was adopting a ploy to avoid considering her relationship to Marilyn.

It had to be faced; she and Marilyn didn't get on. On the occasion of the wedding, she had had the upper hand herself, of course, demonstrating in a really rather crass way, as it now struck her, the superiority of the Nankervises over the Wainwrights, and succeeding in making everyone uncomfortable and Oliver downright rude. She had been satisfied with her behaviour at the time, why wasn't she still? Now it seemed unforgivable! None of them had wanted the marriage, they should have joined forces, not engaged in battle! What had she been trying to prove?

And yet, the marriage had worked out well in the end, against all probability. Dot remembered her next encounter with Marilyn, Bob hadn't been there that time. Marilyn had arrived like an avenging angel after Oliver's breakdown following his accident, and a mercifully unsuccessful suicide attempt. She had blamed Dot roundly for lack of support and too much interference, and humble origins or no, had succeeded in wiping the floor with her. And then Cheryl had simply taken Oliver and run away from all the shouting and argument, and left it for months before she let them know where they were. Not just herself and Jerry; Marilyn and Bob too. The shared anxiety hadn't brought them together, Marilyn had again blamed her.

By and large, therefore, it was hardly the best idea to throw her together with Marilyn under the same roof. Even if not Debbie, who hadn't been present on most of the relevant occasions, Cheryl should have realised this.

Perhaps she had realised it.

Dot thought about that as the A30 rolled beneath her wheels. She had felt for some time now as if she had been looking at life through a glass smeared with old hurts and resentments – not necessarily all her own – and misconceptions, failures of understanding arising out of the same failures in other people in the past, and that recently some great hand had picked up a duster and started to clean them all away. She fully realised that Christmas had been a put-up job, and she could think of only one reason for it. This, on the face of it ill-considered, throwing together of herself with Marilyn could be another gambit of the same kind. If it was not, she thought further, she could make it so.

Essentially, she knew, people didn't really change. She wouldn't change, she would always be what she was, lugging the same old baggage along with her, a prey to the old insecurities. What she could do was to try to learn from her past, and be a little more forgiving in her future, a little less insistent on own importance. That ought to be possible, surely, particularly as she had recently found that in a lot of circles she had no importance. And she should do what her son-in-law had implied in that seminal confrontation at the farmer's market; she should make a life of her own, and not try all the time to manage other peoples'.

Work out what makes you happy. Then get on and do it. It was becoming like a mantra.

It was an odd conclusion to reach, when she had felt herself having to shout to be noticed all her life, but perhaps she should resolve to be more humble ... and then it was time to turn off the major road and take to the lesser roads that would bring her, eventually, to St Erbyn and the river, and she had to concentrate properly on the route she must take.

Although, with Easter approaching, she was busy at the sailing school and would have liked to have taken advantage of having a house full of potential babysitters as a change from having the baby sleeping, much like the kitten in Carl's study, in a corner while she worked in her office, Debbie had made the effort to be there when her mother arrived. For this, Susan was mainly responsible: Susan had warned her, after the arrangement had been agreed of course, Debbie thought in exasperation, that the mixture of Marilyn and their mother wasn't necessarily a happy one. The new, improved Dot might, or might not, rise to the occasion. Neither of them knew Marilyn well enough to guess how she might react; Bob would be on her side, naturally, and although Chel's brother Mike, the final guest in the house, could possibly turn out to be a calming influence, being a man, you couldn't rely on it.

Thank you, sister! You could have told me earlier.

It was therefore with a certain amount of apprehension that she heard the ring at the doorbell and went to open the door. For a wild moment she thought she didn't recognise the woman standing on the step with a suitcase at her feet.

'Mum! What have you done? You look *fantastic!*' She enfolded her mother in an impulsive hug that took herself by surprise quite as much as Dot; they had never done impulsive hugs in their family since the children were little. Dot returned it in an unpractised way that spoke volumes about something, if Debbie had had the time to work out just what. 'Come in,' she said, and held the door wide. 'I'll bring your case – go on through, you know the way.' She picked up the case and dumped it at the foot of the stairs before following her mother through into the sitting room fairly speedily. There might be need for a referee.

Marilyn and Bob were both there. Marilyn sat by the fire with a bandaged foot resting on the antique stool, and crutches propped on the arm of the sofa beside her. Bob stood by the window, a solid figure silhouetted against the daylight outside. Both of them looked much as Dot felt, and for similar reasons. They had talked things over between themselves – they had this advantage which Dot did not enjoy – and come to the conclusion that the only thing to do was remember their manners and play it by ear; Dot must set the tone. Although both of them had some very unfriendly memories of their previous encounters, their daughter Cheryl had made it clear that things must be different around here. With goodwill, they would.

Goodwill on both sides, that is.

Dot took in the scene, completed by the sleeping baby in his pushchair beside Marilyn, and took a deep breath. 'How nice to see you both again,' she said, somewhat inaccurately, 'and on such a happy occasion, too.' And she crossed the room to place her cheek briefly against Marilyn's in greeting, before stepping back to look at her. 'What have you been doing to yourself? Did you have a fall?'

Stupid question. What else? Dot felt inept, not a familiar feeling for her. Marilyn gave a rueful laugh. 'I tripped over a rug, so silly of me! They thought I'd broken it –' she gestured towards her ankle – 'but it turns out to be only a very bad sprain. Bad enough.'

'I'm so sorry, it must be painful.'

'It's not too awful, so long as I keep off it,' said Marilyn. 'Just inconvenient, and now of all times.' The sprained ankle had bridged a difficult moment. Bob came forward into the centre of the room and held out his hand.

'Dorothy, good to see you, did you have a good journey?' They shook hands. Debbie, seeing that there was to be no bloodshed, at least for now, took the opportunity to get everything over at once.

'Sit down, Mum, take a break after your drive, and I'll make us a cup of tea and after that I'll take your case up. You're upstairs this time – same front room, even better view, but I'm afraid it will mean sharing the bathroom with Mike, Marilyn can't make it up the spiral stairs.'

'Except on my bum,' said Marilyn. She made a face. 'I feel so stupid.'

Dot wasn't sure she wished to share a bathroom with a strange man, but she put a good face on it. She smiled at Debbie as if she didn't mind. 'That will no doubt be a new twist on "sleeping in your own bed",' she observed, and Debbie laughed. 'At least you can be sure it'll be comfortable,' she said.

There was no sign of Cheryl's brother, Dot had noticed, and neither did he appear while they drank their tea and ate slices of a really rather delicious cake, for which, no doubt, her son-in-law was responsible. The brother was recently discharged from the army, somebody had mentioned it at Christmas, which could mean anything from an uncouth squaddie to an officer, although she feared, not the officer. She asked after him.

'I'm told your younger son is staying here with us too,' she said. 'Just out of the army, I understand, that must be a relief for you.' She had met neither of Cheryl's brothers, although she had met her sister and her sister-in-law at Oliver's wedding. No doubt that would change this weekend.

'Yes,' Marilyn answered happily. 'It's so lovely to have him back at home and not have to worry about him. He'll be along later, he went down to Debbie's sailing school to lend a hand with the boats – he likes to be busy, you know, after such an active life.'

There was a brief, noisy interruption here, as the baby woke up and began to cry loudly for attention. Debbie got to her feet with a brief apology. 'He's hungry. If you excuse me a moment, I'll take him up and see to him, and when he comes back he'll be in a better mood to say hullo to his Grandma – won't you my pet?' This last to the squalling baby; young as he was, he was adept at making his wishes known. It was probably safe to leave them, she decided, and she couldn't really feed Daniel in front of Bob. They all seemed to be getting on quite well, but she crossed her fingers all the same as she climbed the stairs.

Back round the fire, Dot picked up the conversation where it had left off. 'And what is he – your son – planning to do now that he is a civilian again? Will he be settling near your home so that you can see something of him? – I'm sorry, I don't know if he is married or not.'

'Never had the time,' grunted Bob, as if he disapproved.

'Sadly, no,' said Marilyn, although whether about the marriage, or lack of it, or the settling near home wasn't clear. 'He was offered a job by someone in the regiment – one of the officers – who was discharged at the same time and buying a business, so he'll be living in Devon for a while.' She sighed. 'It would have been nice if he'd been nearer, but at least it's on the way to Cheryl.'

It was so strange to find herself having a civilised conversation with Marilyn, although perhaps not Bob quite yet, that Dot found herself saying, as if she really wanted to know, 'So what is this business to be?'

Bob, unexpectedly, was the one who answered. 'It's a garage business. They were REME, our Mike is a fully qualified mechanical engineer. There's four of them, this Captain Anstruther who bought the place – on its last legs, from what Mike was telling us – then Mike, to be in charge of the workshop, and two others under him. All ex-army. They take over middle of next week, so it's worked out well with the christenings and Marrie's ankle an' all.'

It was the longest speech Dot had ever heard Bob make. 'It sounds very exciting,' she offered.

'One thing you can say for the army, it gives a man a trade,' said Bob. The burst of loquacity seemed to have exhausted his energies, and he relapsed once more into a watchful silence. Marilyn said, sombrely, 'At least he came back safe. There was plenty that didn't.'

Dot felt it necessary to change the subject. She said, brightly, 'My first husband's family live in Devon. I wonder if it is anywhere near to them?'

'It's in a village called Waldren Stavey,' Marilyn offered. Dot said, 'My first husband's children live under Stavey Tor. I wonder if he will meet them?'

'Perhaps they take their cars to the garage,' said Marilyn. 'That would be a coincidence,' and Dot said no, probably not, since Henry's daughter Isobel's husband was also something in the mechanical line. 'Agricultural machinery, I believe,' she added. 'I daresay he can do cars as well, for the family. I remember he was always very handy with his toolbox.'

Dot had subconsciously heard the key in the front door during this exchange, and assumed it would be Mawgan returning home; she was therefore startled when a strange voice joined the conversation.

'That'd be George Ballantyne? We've met up with him already, and his daughter. Small world, isn't it?'

Dot turned swiftly, to see a strange young man approaching her, hand held out. He grinned at her obvious astonishment. 'Sorry, did I make you jump? I'm Michael, the black sheep of the family. Mike.' His hand, strong and friendly, engulfed hers. 'Pleased to meet you, Mrs Nankervis.'

He was not, Dot considered, exactly good-looking, but possibly with a modification to the bristly, bright red pelt covering his head he might be. He had a moustache, too, that looked as if it had escaped from her favourite Carl's "designer stubble" except for being red rather than black. Green eyes like Marilyn's, the red hair was hers too. Very like Cheryl, and her sister Tracy, a strong family resemblance particularly when he smiled, as he was doing now. 'How do you do?' she said, 'I have heard a lot about you!'

'No good, I daresay.' He released her hand.

She smiled back at him, recognising that no response was required. 'So, which of my grand-daughters is it you have met? Alice, or Elizabeth?'

She saw his eyes widen in surprise, although why he should be surprised she didn't understand. Then he grinned. 'Both of them, actually. But mainly Liz.' He sat down beside his mother. 'How're you doing, Mum?'

'Bored,' said Marilyn, with a grimace. 'I don't suppose you are.'

'No, I had a great afternoon! Anyway, you had a baby to play with.'

'He slept,' said Marilyn. 'They do, you know, at that age. If you're lucky,' she added, under her breath. She found herself exchanging a smile with Dot; that had to be a first.

'Not what Oliver was saying, about young Zoë,' Mike said.

'You've met Oliver, have you?' Dot asked, trying to keep a grim note out of her voice. Whatever her relations with her daughters had become, her stepson was still a thorn in her side. She thought that Michael Wainwright had picked up on it, but he only said, 'We met at New Year. An amazing man. He took me up to see his studio today.'

Bob grunted again, and Dot recalled that he always had been a grunter. 'Doesn't sound as if you did much work, then.'

'Oh, I did quite a bit. This was after we'd finished.'

'*Oliver* was helping with Deborah's boats?' asked Dot, unable to believe it.

'Certainly was. Oliver is very handy with a paintbrush, obviously. Knows a bit about rigging too, he's a good man on the job.'

'I thought Oliver had foresworn anything to do with boats for ever and ever, amen,' said Dot, before she could stop herself. Mike gave her a steady look, what had he heard in that brief statement?

'Apparently not,' he said.

'Then I'm very glad to hear it,' said Dot, briskly. She got to her feet. 'Since Deborah is busy, I think we should clear away the tea things, and then I shall wash up. You can help, young man.'

Mike leapt obediently to his feet. 'Ma'am! And then I'll take your case upstairs for you. I see that Deb left it for people to trip over.'

'Deborah has her hands full,' Dot told him. She wondered why, in present company, she felt the need to revert to "Deborah". She had been doing quite well with "Debbie" lately. Considering this, as she carried the teapot through ahead of Mike with the tray, she came to the conclusion that it was because among the Wainwrights she still felt a need to assert herself. In fact, she felt ill at ease in spite of all her good resolutions. She was aware of a sudden desperate need to be on her own for a moment, so she sent Mike away when everything was cleared.

'I can get this into the machine. You go and move that suitcase before someone really does trip over it,' she told him, and was relieved to see him go. It had put her out of her stride, for some reason, to learn that he was on "Liz" terms with Elizabeth.

Debbie meanwhile, safely upstairs on her new, her mother's old, big sofa, and unaware of unsuspected connections, employed the time while Daniel fed himself into a stupor by ringing her sister; she had a lot to tell her. Babies, she decided, as she punched in the number on her mobile with one hand while holding it, and cradling her son with the other, were great for teaching you to multitask; they were great altogether. She wouldn't mind a couple more sometime, so long as they didn't stop her working. The ringing tone in her ear stopped, and her sister's voice said, 'Hullo?'

'Suse! It's me.'

'I know. Has Mother arrived safely?'

'She most certainly has! Suse, you wouldn't *believe*! I don't know who's taken her in hand, but she looks *stunning*! I had to look twice before I believed it was her!'

'In what way, particularly?' asked Susan, curiously.

'New hair, all soft and loose and streaky, it suits her. Decent clothes for once, nice trousers and a sweatshirt, and a silk shirt under it, fabulous colours too. Eyebrows, she never seemed to have any. She's darkened her lashes, used make-up on her eyes, done it well, too. She looks years younger. And ... happier, somehow ...' her enthusiasm faltered on the last words. Susan said, cynically, 'Well, I hope it isn't all for Jerry's benefit. He's never going back.'

'I think she knows that.'

'I hope she does,' said Susan, again, and then added unexpectedly, 'He's put her through enough over the years. It's time she got herself free of him.'

'Perhaps it's the new house,' said Debbie, but doubtfully now.

'I hope so. Or the new plans she has to go with it.'

'That's an awful lot of hope you just handed out,' said Debbie.

'Don't you feel she needs it? She's left it awfully late to get herself a life.'

'She's got the guts to do it,' said Debbie and Susan said, for the fourth time, 'I hope so.' There was a pause, while they both thought that Susan was very like their mother, and that she had found the guts. Then Debbie heard someone on the stairs, and changed the subject.

It was only Mike with the suitcase, but as it happened Dot wasn't far behind him. She paused at the top, looking approvingly at her familiar suite in its new environment. It looked right up here, she decided, this was a lovely room. Spacious, and empty, and with that stupendous view over the water. She hoped Deborah had no intentions of adding any more furniture; the suite, the coffee table, and the built-in bookcase were just right. Debbie held out the mobile.

'Susan,' she said. 'Say hullo. She was asking if you were here.'

Dot had a quick chat with Susan, and then sat for a few moments beside Debbie and the increasingly somnolent baby. 'He's a very good baby,' she observed, and Debbie said cynically, 'At present. Give him time, look who his father is after all.' They exchanged a smile, and Dot was surprised at how readily it came. She must watch this, she would begin to approve of him! She said, 'It's all very well now, Deb – Debbie, but how will you manage when your sailing school opens again next month?'

Debbie took a deep breath. Her mother wasn't going to approve, but it had to be faced. 'Oh, that's all organised,' she said, lightly.

'Yes?' Dot prompted.

'Yes. I shall go out with the boats in the mornings, while Chel is working at the Fish, and Gosia will look after both babies down at the sailing school. She'll keep them until lunch time, and if they're asleep she'll help prepare the lunches for our students – much as would be the case if they were at home with us, we'd do things while they slept.'

'Zoë won't be doing too much sleeping soon. She's six months old! Nor Daniel, either, before your season comes to an end.' She had not, Debbie noticed, risen to the bait of Gosia's name. A great step forward. She said, 'Then she'll play with them or take them out for a walk, and Mrs Phil, who is our stewardess, will manage. The babies will be the first priority.'

'And in the afternoons?' asked Dot, trying not to sound censorious.

'In the afternoons I'll take over the hire boats from Roger, and Daniel will sleep in his pram outside where I can keep an eye on him. We don't get that many people hiring, I shall have plenty of time for him. And if I'm in the office instead, he can still be with me and I shall put him on the floor to play when he's awake.'

'And Zoë? I hate to sound inquisitive, Deborah, but they *are* my grandchildren. With you and Cheryl so wrapped up in your work, I would like to be sure they are adequately looked after.'

Debbie shot her a quick grin. Daniel had finished his tea, his eyes had closed and he was peacefully asleep. She eased him into a more comfortable position and said, 'Don't worry so Mum, Chel and I want to be sure too. Chel will have Zoë herself after lunch, she only works mornings at the pub, and if she does have to be down there for any reason, then Zoë will go with her. And effectively, I shall have Daniel. It's only the mornings, and sometimes in the evenings, we need to cover.'

'Well, it all sounds very organised, but I hope it works in practice,' said Dot, severely. She rose to her feet. 'I shall go and unpack, and maybe have a little rest for an hour I think. Please make my apologies to Marilyn and Bob. And Michael,' she added.

The bedroom was oddly familiar with the twin beds, the chest and the bedside tables from her own house. Mike had placed her case on a collapsible stand at the foot of the bed, which was not hers but, Dot conceded, a helpful idea. She opened it, but before she started to unpack walked to the window and stood looking out at the view with eyes that hardly took it in. She had thought that this weekend would be an ordeal, but so far it had been like any other visit to family or friends. Marilyn and Bob hadn't been exactly warm, but they had been polite; one could build on that, and Michael seemed a pleasant young man: a strange coincidence that he should have met Elizabeth, or perhaps not so strange in the context of village life. Dot was more used to town life, of course, but she would have to accustom herself to a smaller arena when she moved. Was she looking forward to it, or had she let Benita talk her into it because she wanted to help her friends? She found she wasn't entirely certain. Certainly, she had to do something with her life, but she had no confidence in Benita's motives; belief in other people, she was only now realising, was something that she had never learned and if she did Benita an injustice, she was sorry but she couldn't help it, she had been disappointed too many times. Could you ever go back, she found herself wondering, to your lost dreams and ambitions and build simple contentment from them? She had no idea, but she would no doubt discover the answer.

Liz drove to Cornwall the following afternoon, and if she had any qualms about leaving an almost complete stranger in charge of her home, her cat and her computer, she did her best to smother them. She couldn't be a prisoner, even if that was what Paul intended. To be fair, she had decided, he probably hadn't thought it through, all he wanted was to create a situation, possibly so that she would turn to him for help, although if that was the case he must think she was really stupid. Perhaps he *did* think she was really stupid? Or it could be just that he wanted to make her pay for dumping him, and she hoped that was more likely.

But the more distance she put between herself and Waldren Stavey, the more uneasy she began to feel. If Paul was just trying to prove a point, he wouldn't physically hurt her, she told herself, but she didn't seem to be listening. She found she was holding an argument with herself.

He had done no good to her flat – if that was down to him, who knew?

Those horrible emails could simply be unpleasant spam.

She didn't know anyone else who had received things like that, but then again, she hadn't asked either.

Mark Jones would have heard about it if somebody was sending them out randomly. He was that kind.

There was nothing she or anyone else could do about it unless Paul came out into the open. If it was him. Maybe he would just get tired of it. If it was him. Maybe the police would track him down. If it was him.

She tried to concentrate on her driving, but her subconscious persisted in switching onto autopilot, allowing her conscious thoughts to continue to range free. She even wondered at one point if she should have come away from home at all, but that was ridiculous. Her thoughts came full circle. She couldn't be a prisoner. And before she reached St Erbyn, she must manage to put it out of her mind or she would cast a blight over the whole weekend!

There was not, she found on arrival, much chance of that! Susan's house, already accustomed to various children trailing in and out and making themselves at home, had been invaded by Chel's sister Tracy, husband Tom, and their two children Micky and Candy. There was simply no room for anything else, Liz realised it the instant she stepped through the door. Certainly not introspection.

'I'm afraid it's a complete madhouse,' Susan told her, as she greeted her with a hug. 'Lovely to see you, did you have a good journey? I hope it was an easy one, you're going to need all your strength here!'

A strange, red-headed child of about Seb's age appeared on the stairs. 'Auntie Susan, can we have some Coke?'

'Please!' shouted someone from the direction of the kitchen, 'And no, it's nearly tea time. Go away Candy! Go and annoy Annabel and Kayleigh!' The child on the stairs raised her eyes to the ceiling in despair of adults, but obediently vanished upwards. Susan looked at Liz and lifted her shoulders, spreading her hands in a gesture of helpless defeat.

'Come into the kitchen and meet Tracy. Then you can go upstairs, you're in the small back room I'm afraid. We have a house full.'

'I like the small back room,' said Liz, following into the kitchen. 'I like the view of the creek. Hullo,' she added, to the strange woman cutting bread by the stove. 'You must be Chel's sister Tracy.'

'And you must be Liz.' Tracy put down the knife and held out her hand. 'Sorry, I'm a bit buttery. We thought we'd feed the children and then have a suitably grown-up dinner later on. Not, alas, when they've gone to bed, but they might at least go upstairs.'

'And after that,' said Susan, rattling plates onto the worktop, 'we thought we'd escape to the Fish for a while. Gemma next door has said she'll babysit, she must be mad but if we send Kayleigh and Ben home before we go, she might just survive.'

'Rather her than me,' said Tracy cheerfully. 'They're all over-excited, and Candy and Micky are tired from the journey as well. Lovely!'

Funny, Liz found herself thinking, how when you heard an unusual name once, you tripped over it everywhere. Sergeant Mike had a niece called Candy, he had mentioned her – the first time they met? The second? She said, 'Are any of the others joining us?'

'Not Chel and Oliver, Mum and Dad are going down there for the evening, Richie and Louise are there. We thought we might ring Debbie and ask her if she wanted to join us – she's got Susan's Mum to look after Daniel, and Susan says she doesn't get out much. I expect Mike will come with her, he isn't going to the creek, too many babies!' She paused, 'Well, he'll come whether she comes or not, actually.'

Another name that was following her around. A red-headed boy stuck his head round the door, but before he could speak, Susan said, 'Ah, Micky, the very person we need! There's a bag in the middle of the hall, could you take it up to the back bedroom for Liz, please?'

'I was just –'

'– and then,' his mother interrupted, 'you can call them all down. Tea's about to go on the table.' The boy vanished.

'You will notice,' said Tracy, taking sausages from under the grill and slapping them onto the plates with a practised hand, 'that my husband Tom and Susan's lovely bloke Carl are conspicuous by their absence.'

'I had noticed,' said Liz, grinning. 'Where are they?'

'They found it vitally necessary to go and move furniture around at the sailing school,' Susan told her. 'The baptismal feast after the christening is being held there, didn't Debbie tell you? It's big enough to hold everyone, and it's neutral ground, Deb and Oliver both have connections – although Oliver's are a bit tenuous! Mrs Phil, Gosia and the Fish are doing all the food, all we have to do is turn up and celebrate.'

A sense of occasion was beginning to take hold of Liz, she felt better every minute. 'It all sounds great.' She paused. 'Is that elephants on the stairs?'

'Just children. Six of them, but at least we haven't got Damien today.'

Liz felt her astonishment was written all over her face. 'Damien! Do you mean he comes too?'

'When he feels like it, he's very protective towards Annabel. Ben and Seb are a bit young for him, but he mooches around occasionally and teaches them things they'd be better not knowing, I daresay, and they look up and worship – unfortunately. We put up with it for the moment, because he and Kayleigh saved Annabel's life – her school life anyway – and of course, he's Ben's cousin.'

'It might do him good, rather than them bad,' Liz offered, by way of consolation, and Susan laughed. 'It *might*. Somehow I doubt it, Damien is a hard case –' She broke off as the crashing on the stairs stopped and a stream of children came through the kitchen door, talking at the tops of their voices and heading determinedly for the table. She grabbed Annabel in passing. 'Where's Loki?'

'In the filing basket,' said Annabel, undeflected. They all sat down, with much scraping of chairs. Susan looked at Liz, and said, with sympathy, 'I should go and unpack, if I was you, Liz. I'll ring Debbie in a minute.'

Liz made her escape as soon as she could get through the door and ran up the stairs that she fancied were still shaking from the recent stampede. She found she was laughing as she went into the small back bedroom; remembering the defensive Susan whom she had first met, it seemed incredible that her house should have become the meeting place for a hoard of unruly village children – well, three anyway, but Damien was a hoard in himself and Kayleigh was ... well, *loud* was the first word that came into her head. She was about to pick up her bag from the floor, still laughing, when she realised that "Loki" was not, as she had subconsciously assumed, a book, but a small black kitten, and he was no longer in the filing basket, which was a strange place for a kitten anyway. Micky had left her door open, and he was now in the middle of her pillow, making himself at home. She picked him up and cuddled him, purring, under her chin.

'You darling! Where did you come from?' Still cuddling him, she abandoned her intentions of unpacking and lay on the bed with the kitten sitting on top of her. The problems at home seemed at last to be a galaxy away, Mark Jones could look after them for a while, she judged him perfectly capable. Tonight, she would go out with friends and put the whole thing out of her mind. And if Paul had the temerity to turn up in either place, someone would see to him for her. She closed her eyes blissfully, she hadn't realised how stressed out she had allowed herself to become. Damn Paul! He wasn't going to spoil her life!

After a while, she heard male voices in the garden below. The kitten had stopped kneading her breast in ecstasy and fallen asleep; she laid him gently aside and got up to look out of the window. Carl, a strange man who must be Tom Harrison, and Clinker were coming up from the foreshore, the cavalry had arrived at last, time to get herself organised. She started unpacking, but the fact that Loki then woke up and wanted to help didn't make the job easy. He finally settled in an open drawer, on a warm woolly sweater, and she left him there while she finished.

Debbie, consulted, expressed pleasure at the idea of a drink somewhere other than in the house. 'Even if it's only lemonade, I don't seem to have had a night out for ages. I'll just ask Mum if she minds being left on her own for a bit. It does seem a bit unfair when she's come all this way to be with us.'

Dot expressed her willingness to be left to babysit. 'I shall watch the television, or read a book, and be quite happy. You young things go and enjoy yourselves, you deserve a treat.' In a pub? Debbie wondered, but her mother was so full of anomalies this weekend, she found herself less startled than she would have been three months ago. There was such a lot she wanted to tell Susan, it would take all evening! She said, 'We won't be late, anyway,' and passed the confirmation on to her sister.

'About half past eight then, if that suits you,' said Susan, and rang off. Dot returned her attention to the magazine she had been reading, merely saying, 'Michael will look after you,' as if Debbie needed looking after anywhere, let alone in a pub that belonged to her own husband.

When Mike came in later on, Debbie informed him of the treat ahead. 'Susan and Carl, you've not met them yet, and your sister and Tom, and Liz, who is going to be Daniel's godmother. Liz is Susan's niece.'

A curious look crossed his face – Debbie found it curious. He said, 'Is she indeed? I shall look forward to meeting her – presumably she's above the age of consent if she's coming too?'

'Good heavens yes, she's older than Suse! Our family is a real muddle, but you'll get used to it – Susan and I are half-sisters. Susan's father was Mum's first husband and Liz's grandfather.' She watched his expression become bemused. 'Don't try to work it out.'

Mike said, as if he was testing a theory, 'So your Daniel and your sister's niece Liz aren't actually cousins?'

'Not really,' said Debbie, and was surprised when he laughed outright.

But of course, all became clear when they arrived at the Fish that evening and Liz nearly choked on her drink when she saw him. Between bouts of indignant coughing, she managed to say, 'What are you doing here? You said you were going to Suffolk!' Mike kindly removed the glass from her unsteady hand and patted her on the back.

'I did go to Suffolk. And you never said you were coming to Cornwall either.'

Debbie looked at them both in surprise, nor was she alone. 'Do you two know each other?'

'We've met a couple of times,' said Liz casually.

'Yes,' said Mike, simultaneously, meeting her eyes. She hadn't noticed before that his were green. Looking from him to Tracy, she realised why she had kept thinking she had seen him before.

'You're Chel's brother,' she said.

'And you're Oliver's stepmother's granddaughter,' said Mike. 'That makes us family, so you can stop scowling at me.'

'I thought you'd abandoned me to my fate,' Liz accused him, but she did it with a smile.

'Never! Would I? Only my mother had an accident and Dad had to be in the shop, so they summoned up the reserve – I was the only one at a temporary loose end. So I couldn't come back myself, but I sent reinforcements, I hope they arrived.'

'They did, thank you.' She turned to Susan, who was nearest. 'He's going to work at the garage. We met one lunchtime in the pub. I had no idea who he was.'

Mike, too, turned his attention to Susan. 'So you're "Auntie Sue" – well, if I had met you without Liz here, I would have had no idea who *you* were either, so that makes us square. I had quite a different picture in my mind ...' They all laughed, and the conversation began to divide naturally into groups that were basically male and female. The men stayed at the bar, but Debbie firmly led the way to a table near the fire, saying, 'I feel as if I've been on my feet since dawn. Let's be comfortable.'

'Bit of a reality check, being a mum, is it?' asked Tracy, and Debbie laughed before taking the cue and segueing easily into what was foremost in her mind.

'And talking of mums,' she said, 'what did you make of *our* mum this morning, Suse?'

Susan took a minute before she replied, because if she told the truth, she wasn't sure of the answer. Finally, she settled on, 'She looks great,' which was no answer at all. She exchanged a helpless look with her sister. It isn't easy to absorb a sudden transformation in somebody who has been part of your life since birth. Debbie put this into words. 'She looks great, but she doesn't look like Mum.'

Liz saw where this was going, and had opened her mouth to speak when Tracy forestalled her. 'And a good thing too!' she said briskly. 'The last time I saw her – which was also the first time come to think – at Cheryl and Oliver's wedding, she looked as if she'd been breakfasting on iron bars! Sorry girls, but she did. She looks ten years younger now.'

Susan shook her head, not so much in denial as confusion. 'She's always been so positive. Now ... well, she isn't. She's changed on the outside, but she doesn't seem to have worked out how to do the same inside. I'm not sure what I'm trying to say.'

'She isn't at home with herself,' said Debbie, putting it in a nutshell. 'Did she show you the photos she took of this house she's buying?'

'Yes. That doesn't look quite like Mum either.'

'Now come on,' said Liz. 'Have you thought that maybe where she's living *now* isn't "quite like Mum", and what you see in those pictures *is*? It's all her own choice, remember. No input from Jerry, no need to think about you lot. Just her.'

Debbie said, with unrecognised percipience that, had she known it, spoke volumes on her understanding for her difficult mother, 'I just think she isn't telling us everything.'

'So, why should she?' asked Tracy, reasonably. 'Do you tell her everything?'

Liz asked, 'About what?'

'About the house,' Susan replied immediately. 'There are no details – it wasn't on the market, her new friend Benita Vachell knows the sellers. We only know what she chooses to tell us, or what we see in the photos she chooses to show us.'

'And we know Benita Vachell hardly at all.' Debbie put in. Both Tracy and Liz looked at her in a way that made her want to wriggle in her chair.

'It isn't as if you two are there to help her,' Tracy pointed out.

'I know, I know,' said Debbie. 'We both of us sound as if we're jealous. We're not. But Mum has always had Dad to look after her –'

'Hold that, right there,' interrupted Liz indignantly. 'Your mother is a grown woman, she's been round the block twice – she doesn't need anyone to look after her, she's perfectly capable of looking after herself!'

'I didn't mean it quite like that,' said Debbie, helplessly.

'Look,' said Liz. 'If you don't like Benita Vachell, whoever she is, helping your mum, then go home and do it yourselves!' She looked from Susan to Debbie. 'Yes, I see, you're both too busy with your own affairs. In that case, let her be busy with hers, and stop looking for trouble! What makes you think she's helpless anyway? She looks to me like a person who's perfectly capable of running her own life. All that's the matter with her, if you ask me, is that she hasn't worked out what to do with it now she's got it back.'

'She isn't happy,' said Susan.

'Ah,' said Liz. 'That's different, and maybe true. She certainly wasn't entirely happy when I met her last month. But think of this; she can't go back, and she hasn't yet found a way forward – that you know of. Would that make you happy?'

'With blonde streaks and eye shadow, and a whole new wardrobe?' Debbie demanded.

'Really?' Liz looked interested. 'Well, good for her! You said yourself just now, Susan, that she looks great. What you're really saying is she doesn't look like a mum any more, not just yours but anybody's, and why should she? You both made it quite clear to her that you don't need her in that role.'

'We're grown up too,' said Susan, quietly. 'She can't dictate to us as if we were still children.'

'And neither can you dictate to her,' said Liz firmly, caught Susan's eye, and they both smiled ruefully. 'Sorry. I shouldn't have said that.'

'You're very defensive about her,' Debbie accused, still contentiously, but Liz had abandoned the fight. She spread her hands in disclaimer.

'Not about her. Not really, she can look after herself. I suppose I'm feeling guilty at the way my family treated her, as well as everyone else. I liked her, when I met her, she's like a Jack Russell terrier – all bark and threats and don't-you-mess-with-me, but wanting to be loved all the same even when she bites the postman. She needs you to be supportive, she needs us. Let's not any of us let her down.'

Debbie looked down at her hands without speaking, because it could be argued that she, of all of them here, had let her mother down. She and her father both, worse than anyone. She fidgeted. Although

Susan had wondered, it occurred to Debbie for the first time that maybe they weren't alone. That it was an ongoing battle that their mother fought, and Jenny Carruthers and her coven of *un*charitable witches were only the tip of an iceberg that hid deep, deep in the ocean. She thought all these things, but what she said was, 'So what you're actually saying is, we should be grateful to Benita Vachell.'

'Exactly that,' said Liz, and to her relief, Debbie smiled.

'Truce, then? Actually, I liked Benita.'

Tracy said, 'What it amounts to really is that it's just as hard, though more unusual, to see your mother growing away from you as it is to see your children doing it,' and both Debbie and Susan went very quiet.

'It's like when you write a book,' said Liz. 'When you're in charge, you can show how it is from both sides. But in real life, you only see people from one side. The outside, and only what they care to show you even then. Not even that; people seldom act, but they do *react*. And it's what they react *to* that makes them behave the way they do.'

'That,' said Tracy, picking up her glass, 'is too profound for a night out in a pub. And here come the men at last! It's our lucky night!'

The arrival of Carl, Tom and Mike brought to an end a discussion that had already gone far enough. Ordering fresh drinks and then shifting up to make room for everyone created a natural diversion, and talk became fragmented, several different conversations taking the place of one. Mike had slipped into a seat beside Liz, of design; he wanted to know that all was well with the arrangements he had set in place for her. He asked, 'Mark found you all right, then?'

'Yes thank you. And thank you for sending him. I'm not sure I could have come away without him there.'

Mike sat up alertly. 'Why, has something else happened?'

'You could say that.' Liz twirled her glass round and round on the table in front of her. 'He sorted out a little computer problem I was having.'

'He's good with computers,' Mike agreed. He looked at her carefully. 'So, what happened? A virus or something? You might as well tell me, for he will.'

'Even though it's my business?' asked Liz, not sure if she liked this. He laughed.

'I was his senior NCO. Old habits die hard.'

Conceding, but only to herself, that she would have told him anyway if Mark hadn't, Liz told him about the nasty emails, and what Mark had said. She found herself telling him about the first one, that had turned her stomach and made her throw up in the bathroom. He looked grave, and a little shaken, which in its turn, shook Liz more than she was shaken already.

'He's right you know, you should tell the police. That's one nasty stalker you have there.'

'They wouldn't take any notice.'

'They would. Particularly if you told them what happened to your flat.'

'And a fat lot of notice they're taking of that! They just say I left the window open, even though Richard agrees that I didn't!'

'That doesn't necessarily mean that they haven't taken notice.' When Liz was silent, he went on, 'Did you tell them about this Paul?'

'They didn't ask. And anyway, they had made their minds up.'

'Show them those emails, and they may ask. In fact, I'd take a bet that they will.'

'I just feel ... it would make a lot of trouble. I don't think Paul would actually hurt me.'

'Don't you, indeed. After what happened in London?'

Once again, Liz was left without words. Before she had a chance to muster her arguments, Tom interrupted.

'Another beer, Mike? Liz?' He gathered up their empty glasses. 'Deb says she has to go home soon, or his nibs will be awake and yelling, so we need to get one in quick.'

'Sorry Mike,' said Debbie, smiling at him. 'It comes of going out with a mobile milk bar. I can't leave my poor mother with the fallout, it wouldn't be fair!'

If Mike had been going to say anything else, the moment for it had gone, and Liz was relieved. Whatever old loyalties made her so reluctant to indict Paul, she didn't wish to explore them here, she wasn't even certain that she could identify them. Certainly not residual love, love as such had never entered into their relationship. She wanted to persuade herself that he would get over his chagrin at being dumped without police intervention, and surely it was most likely? He wanted to teach her a lesson; when he felt she had learned, he would stop. Perhaps he had already stopped when the only reaction he had got was that his emails came back to him.

She did hope so.

For the remainder of the evening, up until the moment when Debbie and Mike had to leave, the conversation was more general. Liz was curious about the acquisition of Loki, she said she had never seen Susan as a cat person.

'It was a con job on Kayleigh's part,' Susan informed her. 'She told Annabel he was going to be drowned if he didn't find a home. He was far too old to drown.'

'But you fell for it anyway?' said Mike, grinning.

'I fell for Annabel's pleading, she needs something to love. And he's a nice little cat.'

Carl put in, 'When he gets a nuisance, we just file him.'

'I'm surprised Clink hasn't eaten him yet,' Debbie observed, much as Seb had. Susan shook her head. 'Clink likes him. Loki makes him feel protective, it's very sweet. Loki sleeps between his great big paws in the evenings.'

'You *file* him?' Tom asked, curiously and Susan explained, amid laughter. 'We've lined the filing basket with an old towel. Carl uses a cardboard box instead, but he has to put it somewhere else.'

Debbie looked at her watch soon after and said that she must leave. 'I'm up to the gills with fruit juice anyway. I'm sorry to drag Mike away, but it's a long way to walk – for either of us -and it's raining too, judging from those people who just came in.'

Mike and Debbie left on their mercy mission and Susan moved into the seat beside her niece. 'You seem to be on very cosy terms with Chel's brother,' she said. 'Why didn't you say?'

'I didn't know he was Chel's brother, that's why,' Liz told her. 'We met in the pub – we told you that – when they came to look at the garage.'

'This is Ole Jarge's garage, that you were on about before?' said Susan, checking.

'Thank goodness. Yes.'

'So, he'll be living in your village?' said Susan, and laughed. Liz gave her a cold look.

'Don't you go getting any ideas, Auntie Sue,' she said. 'We met in the pub, is all. And then we met again and he took me for a drink because I was the only person he knew. That's it!'

Susan gave her what could only be described as a sly look from under her eyelashes. 'If you say so. I just can't help remembering what Richard said at Christmas. I think it was Richard, anyway.'

'And what was that?' asked Liz, who had forgotten.

'Something about, relationships in our family couldn't get more complicated if they tried,' said Susan, and Liz said, 'No chance! No chance! He's an ex-army sergeant with a ginger moustache, for goodness' sake!'

'Really,' said Susan, and added wickedly, 'I do hope you had your fingers crossed when you said that.'

'Huh,' said Liz. 'No way, I promise you! He's OK, I grant you that, but I assure you, he doesn't make my heart miss a beat!'

She kept to herself, as she knew, of course, that a good romantic heroine should, the swift stab of ... well, something, never mind what, that had shot through her when she saw Sergeant Mike, ginger moustache and all, leaving the pub with his arm companionably round beautiful blonde Debbie's shoulders, and the two of them laughing at some joke between them.

XXIII

It didn't rain for the christening. The sun shone from a cloudless sky and the air outside was touched with the faint but un-missable breath of spring, a perfect day for a perfect occasion, said Marilyn, over breakfast, although Dot, getting changed into her Sunday best to go to the church, wasn't convinced. Yes, the weather was perfect, yes the occasion was delightful, but she had to run the gamut of Helen and Jerry – and Nonie Fingall – and there was something she had to say to Jerry that didn't exactly suit the day. If she ever saw him at any other time, she would have saved it, but she didn't these days, and it had become imperative to sort the matter out. She felt as if she was stuck in a time warp until she had, and although, of course, she could have written to him, she didn't wish to do so on such a personal subject. Jerry hadn't been the best husband in the world, but he deserved better than that.

Even so, as she pulled the elegant black dress over her head and smoothed it over her hips, she felt a certain satisfaction. The dress really did things for her. She did a twirl in front of the long mirror inside the wardrobe door, liking what she saw; Benita, at least about this, had been absolutely right. She turned back to the dressing table and picked up her hat – or rather, a small black fluff of feathers and ribbon called, according to the shop where she had bought it, a fascinator; in spite of Benita saying that people were more informal these days, she knew she wouldn't feel right in a church without something on her head. It nestled like a baby bird in the blonde waves of her restyled hair, held in place with a clip; a very expensive baby bird, probably something mythical and rare, such as a phoenix, as in Debbie's sailing school. Appropriate enough, when she felt herself to be rising from the ashes of a past that had run its time.

Debbie had come into her head quite naturally that time. She was improving.

Dot flicked her hair into place and turned to the bed to slip on her jacket. She picked up her bag and the shoes with killer heels; she wasn't running the risk of going tail over top down that spiral staircase! Then she took one last satisfied glance in the long mirror, closed the wardrobe, and left the room to face the waiting day. Safely at the foot of the stairs, she put on the shoes, smoothed the lapels of the jacket and checked that the antique sapphire and diamond brooch Henry had given her on their marriage was securely clipped in place, its old-fashioned safety chain properly fastened. The rest of the party were assembled in the sitting room, she could hear their talk and laughter. She drew a deep breath and walked through the door.

Because she was the last to arrive so that they were all waiting, they all turned and looked at her. She saw Debbie's jaw drop and had time to feel a glow of satisfaction before, to her astonishment, Bob and Mike began to applaud, and Marilyn smiled and said, 'Dorothy, you look marvellous! Fit for a wedding!'

And so she did, Debbie thought, closing her mouth so that she could smile with it – her hands were too full of Daniel to clap. Dot couldn't know, of course, that before she appeared they had discussed how difficult the day was likely to be for her, and resolved to support her in any way they could, but that had become immaterial when she had hoisted her battle flag this high! There had been incipient signs of it all weekend, but Debbie hadn't realised that she had thrown away her old image of – it had to be faced – expensive upholstery, with such finality. She had never realised that her mother was such a handsome woman, she had always just been Mum.

Mawgan hadn't clapped either, but he was looking at her with critical appreciation, He hadn't seen that much of Dot over the weekend, nor she of him, since his restaurant was especially busy on Friday and Saturday nights, although signs of him were apparent in a boned and stuffed wedge of salmon left ready in the fridge with precise instructions for its cooking skewered to its scaly flank, and a rich beef casserole waiting its turn on the shelf below. Debbie, following instructions to the letter, had managed to produce two excellent meals, although Dot had considered her vegetables just a little bit too far on the *al dente* side, which wouldn't have mattered so much if that hadn't also included the potatoes. But he was here now, sharp Italian suiting and all, ready to go to the church with the rest of them.

It was very peculiar, she reflected as they all went outside to the cars, how clothes altered one's attitude, peculiar and rather shaming. Dressed like this, knowing that she looked elegant and fashionable, made her feel like a different person, one who could take her place with confidence and not feel that she had to assert herself, for her appearance was already doing that for her. Of course, there was no telling how it would work with Helen Macken and Jerry.

Debbie and Mawgan were planning to leave their car at the sailing school and continue to the church on foot, with Daniel hopefully sleeping in his pushchair, so Dot travelled with the Wainwrights; the killer heels would never make the distance, as Marilyn pointed out. Or at least, she said, 'You don't want to ruin those beautiful shoes,' which was a polite way of saying the same thing. So that Dot arrived at the church with no family support, but only the debatable backing of Bob, Marilyn and Michael, which left her feeling vulnerable, and hating herself for it. She therefore walked up from the lych gate in a defiant frame of mind, which simply went to prove that fashion wasn't even skin deep after all. From her point of view, it was unfortunate that Jerry and Helen, together with Anona Fingall and a swarthy, dark, good-looking man who must be Anona's Greek husband, were standing outside in the sunshine.

Helen spotted Dot first, her antennae were very finely tuned where Dot was concerned. For a second, she didn't recognise her. When she did, she muttered darkly in Nonie's ear, 'Look who's here, all done up like a dog's dinner!'

'Sssh,' said Nonie. 'She'll hear you. Anyway, she looks pretty good to me, and good for her!'

'You would say that,' said Helen, unreasonably. 'You always took her part.' Which was unfair, she knew as she said it. She compounded the error by continuing, 'Just so long as it isn't all for Jerry's benefit, because she's wasting her time!' And even while she was speaking, Jerry stepped away from her to go and greet his wife and Nonie hissed, 'Go with him – and be pleasant, Helen, please!' and she gave her friend a push as she said it.

Helen followed Jerry down the path. Truth to tell, she was in as much confusion as Dot on this, rather complicated, occasion. Oliver and Debbie hadn't thought it through, she decided now. At christenings, doting grandparents sat together and ... well, doted. It was part of the tradition. Only this time, Dot was Daniel's grandmother, she was Zoë's, and Jerry was grandfather to both of them, and she and Dot couldn't stand each other, each one of them having played the woman scorned to the other. It was this ambivalence, as much as anything, that was making her edgy. He could hardly sit between the two of them, after all, so how should they play it? How *could* they play it, indeed?

With dignity, her common sense answered her. She reached Dot a step behind Jerry, just as he bent to give his estranged wife a peck on the cheek, and stepping forward, gave her a peck on the other. Not exactly turning the other cheek, but close. 'Dot,' she said. 'How are you?'

'Thank you, I'm very well. And you?' Dot sounded, and felt, brittle. Jerry thought that if anyone had been handy with a knife, they could have cut the atmosphere into chunks. He said, 'You're looking very smart today, Dorothy,' and felt like an idiot. Fortunately, before any of them could stumble any deeper into the mire, Annabel and Sebastian came racing through the lych gate and flung themselves on their assorted grandparents, and Susan and Carl followed close behind. Unlike Debbie and Oliver, Susan had worked out that this had only been a good idea in some respects, and she swiftly circumvented any awkwardness by greeting Jerry and Helen and sweeping Dot off in the wake of the children. Carl slipped his arm through Dot's, saying comfortably, 'You stick with us, Dorothy, when Susie goes off to be a godmother, I'll need moral support with those two hooligans,' and the situation was smoothly resolved. Jerry and Helen were left looking at each other. Each of them was uneasily aware that they had never seen Dot look better, even in her younger days, and each of them was wondering what it meant. They walked back to Nonie and Theo without exchanging confidences, and Nonie greeted them with a sardonic look. 'Well, you never expected it to be easy, did you?' she asked, and Jerry said hurriedly, before Helen had a chance to say anything, 'Should we go inside, do you think, and find ourselves a pew?'

The congregation that morning was the biggest the little church had seen since Christmas; not only the Nankervises and the Wainwrights, but also the Angwins from St Austell and other friends on Mawgan's side; Dot noticed immediately the slight, dark young man who had been so full of himself as best man at Deborah's wedding, this time with a very fancy blonde beside him, and the couple she had taken to be Mawgan's parents sitting with a dark girl who had been one of Debbie's bridesmaids and a young man who might possibly be a husband, boyfriend, or simply a family friend. Among the other strangers, she had no way of telling who were the

451

normal congregation and who the guests invited for the christening, but which ever way it went, she thought it was good to see so many people in church. She wondered if the church in Shearwater had a good congregation, and if she would she fit in there; she had never been inside it, perhaps she should make a visit on her return home. It was historic, and reputed to be beautiful, and the members of its congregation held the potential to be her future friends. Or even, as Benita had so perceptibly predicted, her enemies, but this time she hoped to achieve more of the former. She had experienced enough contention, she was battle-weary to a degree she had never noticed while the fight was on. Well, Jenny Carruthers and Helen Macken between them had ended all that, and quite possibly done her an unintentional favour. The thought was satisfying but more than that, it was unexpectedly comforting.

This pretty village on the river was her children's place, where she would always have a welcome but never have a home. Jerry's place now, the one that held his heart, was presumably St Ives, where Helen lived these days, and Helen's place was near her old friend and among the artists who were her natural peers, all of them returning to the loyalties with which they had begun. Her place had yet to be established. Perhaps Shearwater was that place, or she could make it so. And then, because Dot would always be Dot, she thought, and Ernest is a Vachell, and Benita will know them all and the Ravenscourts too, and Jenny Carruthers and her set can put that on their needles and knit it!

Christenings as part of a church service are not private family occasions, and Dot was surprised how many of the congregation shifted themselves discreetly into the background and stayed for the ceremony. She noticed those two children who seemed to haunt Susan's house, presumably with their own parents for once, and the woman she had met behind the counter in the village shop when she had been in with Deborah one day, and wondered if she would ever achieve similar popularity. She wasn't sure she was sufficiently outgoing so she would need to make her mark in other ways. Being useful, no doubt, her usual option, although next time she resolved that she wouldn't let that turn into being used.

Zoë Eleni Nankervis and Daniel Philip Angwin both behaved as babies generally behave at christenings and yelled blue murder, Zoë louder than Daniel, but that was to be expected and not only because she was six months older, you only had to look at who her father was. Susan and Michael stood as godparents to Zoë, very suitable, and Elizabeth and a strange man, some friend or relative of Mawgan's presumably, accepted that privilege on behalf of Daniel. The vicar didn't drop anybody, and everyone smiled and looked happy, as if the stony paths that had led to this happy day were all forgotten. Dot, knowing where at least some of those paths had meandered, wondered if such things ever were, and doubted it, and looking across the font, found herself meeting the eyes of the woman she took to be Mawgan's mother. They had never spoken, never even met, and that must be rectified now. She smiled, and Cally Angwin returned the smile a little doubtfully. Now there was a woman who would never put the past behind her, Dot found herself thinking, and wondered what it would be like to live with such grief; a son in prison, a daughter missing. Perhaps she herself hadn't so much to burden her after all.

Although the sun was shining, it was still only mid-March, too cold to hang about outside the church. The party moved on after only a brief exchange of civilities with those from the village who had stayed for the ceremony and made its way on foot or by car to the sailing school. Since most had parked their cars up there and walked to the church, this really meant only a couple of cars moving off, including the Wainwrights' conveying Marilyn's ankle and Dot's shoes, and driven this time by Bob, and another car conveying three elderly people who seemed to belong with the Angwins. The rest of the party formed a cheerful procession with an assortment of children dancing ahead to the accompaniment of adult shouts to keep in to the side of the road, please, Micky, Nicky, Annabel, and *Candy*, if you can't do as you're told you can come and hold my hand! One more car slid in beside the first two as they squeezed into the parking area; Oliver and Chel, with Zoë, still disapproving of her unexpected wash at the top of her voice, in the back.

'We're the vanguard, dispatched to welcome you in,' Chel told them as they climbed out of the car, and everyone smiled pleasantly and nobody mentioned that they had been elected for the job because Oliver would have found the walk from the church hard going, although they were all aware of it. Oliver had moved away to assist Mawgan's two grandmothers to alight from their car, no doubt he was aware of the subtext too, Dot thought, and felt something she had never expected to feel for her difficult stepson; compassion. Because he rejected pity, managed his life within his limitations, and would never talk about the event that had left him disabled, it was easy to forget about it – which of course was what he intended. You could say what you liked about Oliver, Dot decided, and she often had, but he had great fortitude, and you had to admire him for that. Even more for that than for the God-given gift bequeathed to him by his talented mother, or for going single-handed round the world in that boat.

The small advance party moved round to the front of the building, where an easier flight of steps than the one from the car park led up to the balcony, and from thence into the main room – clubroom, lecture room, bar, whatever it was needed for at the time – where the christening party was to be held. Some spare chairs and tables borrowed from the Fish had augmented the seating to accommodate the large party and Phil and his wife, who must have sneaked out of the church the instant the ceremony was over, were respectively behind the bar and setting the final touches to the buffet laid out at the end of the fortunately spacious room, planned by Debbie with just such occasions in mind when the place was first built. A spectacular cake on a stand, iced in four squares of pink and blue and decorated at the edges with tiny trains and teddy bears, took centre stage on the buffet table. All the grandmothers present admired it with sentimental sighs. Bob, Oliver and Garfie Angwin headed straight for the bar.

Chel settled her own mother in a comfortable position with her foot resting on a stool they had brought with them, while Dot saw to the Angwin great-grandmothers, two women who could not have been more different, the one tall and upright, the other round and merry, with a Cornish accent that, when added to the effects of what must have been quite a severe stroke, was almost unintelligible. Fortunately the taller of the two was able to introduce them both, stiffly formal; herself Mrs Rowe, her companion Mrs Angwin. Dot introduced herself in turn, and when Chel came over to join them and welcome the two old ladies, it dawned on her that Chel had never met them before either, so that more introductions had to be made. Mrs Angwin, visibly melting towards Chel at least, nodded towards the bar, and said, 'Brother?' and when Chel, making a swift and fortunately accurate deduction, said yes, nodded again, and said, 'Very ... *pretty* family,' and smiled. 'Son?' she then asked Dot, who disclaimed and said Oliver was her stepson, which didn't seem to go down well, and then Garfie came over with a tray of wineglasses and Chel and Dot retired to the bar with their wine in what was an unprecedented accord.

'I fear,' said Dot, 'that there is a class divide at this gathering. I sensed disapproval coming from Mrs Rowe like heat from a fire!'

'I think it was your lovely hat thing,' said Chel, smiling. 'It's very flighty,' and neither of them said that it was more probably because of Dot's public repudiation of the wedding of their mutual grandson to Dot's daughter. How many pitfalls had she dug in her life? Dot wondered. How many more would she topple into before she had it reorganised?

It was neither the first nor the last pitfall that awaited her over this weekend.

The next one came out of the blue. Her son-in-law appeared at her side after a while, a glass of beer in his hand and purpose in his eye. 'All right then?' he asked her, and without waiting for a reply, continued, 'I got to thank you for that report you sent me, it come in useful, give me a good idea of what's going on there.'

'It was no trouble,' said Dot, more stiffly than she had intended. She went on, 'I enjoyed the experience, if I am to be honest. I had never been inside such a place before.'

Mawgan grinned at that. 'Sounded as if that might be a good thing,' he observed.

'And are you going to proceed further, or has it put you off completely?' asked Dot, and was astonished when he replied, 'I'm coming up to give it a look over on Wednesday. Wondered if you'd let me give you lunch, if I decide to go ahead I'd like a word with you.'

'With me?' asked Dot, her mind reeling. What had he in mind? A lecture on how to treat her own daughter or ... well, what? Her previous experience of words with him covered a wide field and left it open for infinite speculation. He appeared to take her acceptance of his invitation as read, for he said, 'I'm seeing the place at ten, pick you up around one be all right?' and before she had formed a suitable reply, someone attracted his attention and she was left momentarily alone, and a sitting cuck for the next ambush. There was a moment's breathing space.

Liz was feeling as if the disc in her bag was burning a hole through the leather. The more she thought about it, the more she began to feel it was a liberty to ask Jerry to take charge of it for her, only she couldn't think of anyone else. She hadn't dealt with a solicitor since she bought the cottage, and in any case she didn't want to use one recommended by her family for reasons of confidentiality – not that any solicitor would betray her affairs to them, perish the thought, but she seemed to have this deep-seated instinct to keep the behaviour of the abominable Paul from people who were, it had to be faced, old family friends. Jerry, on the other hand – "the solicitor" in family lore – was a stranger that, paradoxically, she was certain she could trust although she had never met him before. Her grandfather had trusted him, and whatever the outcome, he had stuck to the letter of the arrangement between them, serving his late client's interests and not allowing Carol to derail him. It was all she had to go on. He was a stranger, but at the same time, he wasn't. And he was Susan's stepfather, and she had respect for Susan's opinions.

Although come to think of it, Susan's opinion of Jerry Nankervis was a bit equivocal in places.

Liz pulled herself together. She was trying to mend that fence, not knock another hole in it. And she either meant to trust Jerry or she didn't, and if she didn't ... well, she could put the thing in the bank, she supposed, but she felt an obscure need to have a more personal second in her corner if it ever came to a fight. She smothered a sigh. Paul had really got to her, as no doubt he had meant to do, and there was Jerry just heading for the bar on his own, there would never be a better moment.

Jerry knew who Liz was, of course, but he was nonetheless surprised to find her stepping into his path, smiling and holding out her hand, as he made his way across the room through the cheerful crowd. 'Mr Nankervis – we've never met, but I'm Henry Worthington's granddaughter, Elizabeth Ballantyne. I expect you know that.'

Jerry transferred the empty glasses he held to his left hand and used his right to clasp the one outstretched to him. He said the only thing that came into his head. 'Your grandfather was a very dear friend. I'm happy to meet you –' He nearly added "after all these years" but stopped himself in time. He expected her to smile and pass on, but she didn't. She retained his hand as if to prevent his escape and said, 'I know that, and it's because I know it that I'd like to ask you ... well, a favour I suppose, if you don't think it's cheek. You don't have to do it.'

Jerry paused. He put the glasses down on a nearby table and considered the woman in front of him. He couldn't imagine what she could possibly want with him, and asked the obvious question. 'Is this business, or personal?'

'Bit of both, really.' Liz hesitated. The further she got into this, the more outrageous it began to seem. Too late to stop now. She said, 'There's something I need to put with a solicitor. I thought of you, because ... because ... I shouldn't be asking, should I?'

'I don't see why not,' said Jerry. He smiled at her. 'You're my stepdaughter's niece, that almost makes us family, doesn't it? Would you like to sit down here –' he indicated the temporarily unused table – 'and tell me about it?'

They sat, and Jerry pushed the glasses he had deposited aside, and when Liz didn't immediately say anything, he asked, 'So what is it that you want me to look after for you?'

It made it easy. Grateful to him, she opened her bag, groped in its depths for a moment, and laid the CD in its transparent plastic envelope on the table between them. She had written on it Ladybird, *Ladybird, Chapters 1-12 © Elizabeth Ballantyne* and then the date. Jerry picked it up and looked at it, then laid it down again. He studied her carefully.

'Do I take it that I should mug up on copyright law and plagiarism?' he asked carefully, but Liz shook her head.

'I do hope not. It's just a precaution. If you could sign it and date it, and then keep it for me in a drawer or something just in case ...' She looked down at the disc, fiddling with it to avoid looking at him, wondering how much she ought to tell him, but only said, 'A business arrangement, naturally.'

Jerry felt in his pocket for a pen. 'Then perhaps, if there's a "just in case" involved, we should have a witness to my signature.' He beckoned to Mawgan's friend from the wedding who was just brushing past on his way to the bar, with no idea of whom he was accosting. 'Can you give us a second, just to witness a signature? Would you mind?'

The man paused, surprised, but then, his life was full of surprising things. He said, 'Of course,' and when Jerry had written *J.L. Nankervis, solicitor*, and the date, he added below, with a flourish,

Connor Delaney, Radio DJ and TV Presenter, and again, the date. He handed Jerry back his pen and flashed Liz his beguiling Irish smile. 'That'll be worth a fortune on *The Antiques Roadshow* in fifty years time,' he observed. 'You and me both, and don't tell me, a story behind it?' He moved away without questions and Jerry and Liz looked at each other. Jerry picked up the disc and slipped it into his pocket.

'Anything you want to add to that – just for the record? As our friend just said, there's a story behind it, isn't there?'

'Not really a story,' said Liz. She realised she couldn't in fairness leave it there, neither could she burden him with everything, not at a party. So she said, 'Someone who thinks he owes me a grudge got access to my computer when I wasn't around. I just felt it might be a good thing to stop up the holes.'

'And that's it?' asked Jerry.

'Pretty much.' She saw Dot hovering out of the corner of her eye and rose to her feet. 'You'll be needing to send me an account. I've put an address label on the back, if you look – but Susan knows it anyway. I don't suppose anything will happen, but thank you. It makes me feel safer.'

'I take it that you've taken precautions that it doesn't happen again?' said Jerry and Liz assured him that yes, she had, and turned to Dot, but it turned out it was Jerry that Dot wanted. She slid into Liz's vacated chair before Jerry had a chance to escape, so that he was trapped where he was, conscious of Helen and Nonie watching him from across the room and feeling mildly irritated. 'Dot, this is neither the time nor –' he began but she cut him short.

'It seems to be the only time and the only place that I'm going to be offered,' she pointed out. 'I'm certainly not going to pay to speak to you in your office! This won't take long, Jerry. We can go into the details by letter, but I felt I owed it to you to say it face to face. I'm going to start proceedings for a divorce.' And then, because it was an absurd thing to be saying on such a very family occasion as a double christening, she felt a smile start creeping across her face at the expression on his.

'Good God!' said Jerry, shocked into incoherence.

On the other side of the room, Helen nudged her friend and scowled. 'Just look at her – flaunting her new image and smirking at him – the utter cow! Can't she just leave him alone? She *haunts* me for ever and ever amen!'

Nonie viewed the encounter with a less prejudiced and more judicial eye. 'It doesn't look as if she's flaunting herself to me,' she said, 'although I'll allow you the smirk – but it looks to me more as if she's laughing at him.'

'So what's the difference?' Helen demanded. She knew she was showing herself up, but she couldn't seem to help it. Dot had always had the same effect on her, and particularly now, when she was looking so ... well, different. Like someone who might have been a serious threat if she'd taken the same trouble in the past, before she herself met Jerry.

'Every difference,' said Nonie. 'She's scoring a point off him, if you ask me –'

'– and he's not liking it!' Helen interrupted, and Nonie said mildly, 'Would you?' Helen muttered something inaudible, and Nonie said, 'Just put your hackles down, or you'll be handing her a point that I, personally, don't think she's after. Come and coo at your granddaughter and leave them to it. You'll start attracting attention.' And she led Helen away to where Zoë lay grumbling quietly in her pushchair because, just for a moment, she wasn't the centre of anyone's attention.

Back at the table, Dot gave Jerry a moment to recover from his astonishment, and continued calmly, 'I shall be completing on the house sale in six weeks time; we originally paid for it between us, so I shall divide the money accordingly and have the money transferred to your account. The rest is simply paperwork. I trust that is to your satisfaction.'

'No Dot. There's no need for that. You keep the –'

Dot said, with steady determination, 'I don't want your money Jerry. I neither want nor need anything from you except that which you can't take from me. Our daughter. Our grandchild. And, I suppose, courtesy from both you and Helen when we have to meet, as no doubt we will from time to time.' She relented a little at his expression. 'We should never have married, Jerry. We both know it. And while I can't regret it because of Deborah and little Daniel, it was still wrong. Marry Helen again. You should never have let her get away with divorcing you.'

'She won't have me,' said Jerry, before he could stop himself, and Dot laughed outright. She got to her feet. 'Then good for Helen,' she said, and walked calmly away from him into a life of which, he realised, he knew nothing at all and possibly never would. Just for a moment, he felt ... no, not remorse. Something probably closer to resentment, but he didn't study it closely. He rose to his feet in his turn, gathered up the glasses and Liz's CD, and continued his interrupted journey to the bar.

Once served, he carried the filled glasses back to the table where Helen, Nonie and Zoë awaited him. Helen greeted him with a chilly look. 'I see Dot pinned you down yet again,' she said, confrontationally. Jerry put the tray with the drinks down carefully and wondered where Theo had got to; he felt he needed a little masculine support. He took the CD Liz had given him from his pocket and held it out.

'Can you look after this, just until we get home? Elizabeth asked me to keep it for her.' Helen took the disc and slipped it into her bag without removing her eyes from his face.

'What did she want? Dot, not Liz.'

Jerry looked at her consideringly. Dot had always fired Helen up to explosion point, simply by being Dot, but at least this time she had probably struck the right note. He said, 'She wants a divorce, apparently,' and waited to watch her reaction. Helen snorted.

'I thought she didn't believe in it! Although it didn't stop her marrying *you*, and I would have thought that would have classed as bigamy in her book!'

'She never can do the right thing by you, can she?' said Jerry, and Helen said, 'No.'

'Come on, you two,' said Nonie, before Jerry could react. 'This is a happy, family occasion! Don't start a fight, Helen, particularly when you've apparently won it already.'

Helen gave a reluctant smile. 'She always presses the right buttons for me,' she said. 'Sorry Jerry. That's good news, I should have been more generous.'

'And don't say "yes, you should," said Nonie quickly, forestalling almost those very words on Jerry's lips, and all of them, thankfully, laughed.

Dot saw the three of them laughing together, and Helen cuddling the baby, and a small, cold, lonely wind seemed to blow through her. She had thought at one time that they were all friends, but she saw now that she had been wrong. Jerry had pitied her, Nonie had put up with her, Helen had resented her; why was it so obvious now? Only Henry's family had extended real friendship to her for his sake, and Carol Worthington QC had put a stop to that – not that she had been a QC at the time, and perhaps experience had taught her, as it was now teaching Dot herself, to be more pliant in her views. So, she had hung on to the shadow and released the substance, and whatever Elizabeth tried to tell her that was different, that was how it would remain.

One of the doors onto the balcony had been left open to allow fresh air and the spring sunshine into the crowded room, she made her way towards the opening. Fresh air, and five minutes on her own, would be very welcome right at this minute.

Only, she saw as she stepped outside, she wouldn't be on her own. There was already somebody there on the balcony. Cally Angwin sat there on a folding chair, a pushchair beside her and Daniel, wrapped in a warm shawl, cradled in her arms asleep, her eyes on the view of the river and her thoughts a million miles away. So still was she, and so intent, that Dot took a step back to leave her alone as she so patently wished to be, but Cally heard the movement and turned her head. She smiled, and if the smile was hesitant at least it was there.

'Mrs Nankervis, how nice. Come and sit with me – we haven't had a chance to be introduced yet in all this crowd, I'm Mawgan's mother.' She held out the hand that wasn't needed for the baby. 'Fetch another chair – they're over there.' She nodded to a stack of chairs against the wall. Dot fetched one and unfolded it and sat down. She returned the smile, although she felt decidedly awkward. Mawgan's mother must be well aware of her reaction to his marriage with her own daughter. Cally said, looking down at the baby, 'He was grizzling and getting so hot in there, I brought him out for a breath of air. Isn't he a darling, our little grandson?'

For a moment Dot thought that she meant "our" in the sense of "my family's", but then she realised that Cally meant it in the sense of the two of them, the grandmothers.

'He's the image of his father,' she said, and Cally laughed.

'The Angwin genes are indestructible. Of all my children, Allison is the one most like me, and even she you couldn't mistake for anyone's child but Pip's.'

Dot could think of no sensible response to this, and a brief, uncomfortable silence fell between them. Cally broke it, looking down at the child and not at Dot. 'You didn't come to the wedding.'

'I was at the wedding itself,' Dot said, carefully. 'I didn't attend the reception.'

'I didn't see you. I'm sorry.'

'I was at the back,' said Dot. Cally said nothing, and Dot continued, not certain if explaining would be wise or not but feeling constrained to do so. 'Deborah and I disagreed over her engagement. It was at a bad time for me, I think now I may have overreacted.'

Cally said nothing for a moment, thinking this over. Then she heaved a heavy sigh. 'I can't blame you, of course. It must have looked dreadful to you.'

'I think perhaps it is a mistake always to judge by how things look,' said Dot, with belated wisdom.

'You were a stranger,' Cally excused her. 'When even his own father couldn't come to terms with what had happened –' she broke off abruptly, and Dot said gently, 'It must have been a very bad time for you all.'

Cally said, explaining where she was no more certain than Dot that explanations were the best way, 'They had always been at loggerheads – Mawgan and Pip. When Mawgan didn't want to go into the business they fell out, big time. Pip thought cooking was women's work, he made it very clear he despised Mawgan for wanting to make it a career. He blamed my mother, she taught him to love it when he was a child, so they fell out too. Nothing was ever the same after that, so when ... when our son-in-law died ... then there was no firm ground to stand on. The family went to pieces.'

'It must have been very hard,' said Dot, trying to imagine it, but imagination had never been her strong point and she failed.

'It was dreadful.' Cally raised her head to stare across at the river with eyes that didn't see it. 'We were torn in two – did we believe Mawgan, or did we believe Cressida, and Mawgan was the stronger of the two so ... as we couldn't have it both ways ... we supported Cress.'

462

'And are things better now?' asked Dot. Cally shook her head, not so much in negation as in despair.

'Some things are. They began to get better the moment Debbie came into our house ... she's very special, but you know that of course. She brought sanity with her, she took away all the argument and bitterness, she gave us all hope ... without her, I think we would have blown apart under the strain.'

'I'm happy to hear it,' said Dot, helplessly. Cally turned her head to look at her, her eyes focussing now.

'You should be very proud.'

'So what exactly did she do?' asked Dot, curiously, after a pause.

'She worked a miracle. She made Pip and my father-in-law see that they had no right to Mawgan's life just because of the business, she pointed out that although he was the only son, he wasn't the only child. She told them that girls could run a business just as well as boys, and there was a daughter ready in the wings only waiting the chance to take over. She made them see that that was possible. And they did it ... in the end ... and it's worked out wonderfully. And now Allison has got engaged to the electrician who sub-contracts for them, and the business will go on with the two of them when Pip retires ... and so God's in his heaven, and all should be right with the world,' she finished bitterly.

'But it isn't,' said Dot, quietly. 'Well, nobody gets everything. You can't expect that.'

'I don't,' said Cally. 'I'm not a fool. But I have to live with the fact that my son will never be as he was, he's been through too much. There's a wedge been driven through our family, and the ... the *joy* has gone out of him. He's making a good living, he's a celebrity, the whole country outside Cornwall likes him, he has a lovely wife and now this little boy ... but the Mawgan we knew has gone for good. This one you see now is somebody different.'

'Everybody grows up,' said Dot. There seemed nothing else to say.

'Debbie is the best thing that could have happened to him,' said Cally, soberly, 'she gave him back the sun.' She looked down at the child in her arms. 'And this little boy. There'll be others. A future.'

A silence fell. Dot was almost afraid to speak, fearing that her usual bull-in-a-china-shop approach would be out of place. But the question had to be asked, it would look worse if it wasn't. 'And your other daughter?' she asked. 'Cressida? What has become of her? I don't see her here today, do I?'

There was a long, long pause, and then Cally said, in a voice so low that Dot had to strain to hear it, 'We don't know,' and even Dot couldn't miss the terrible grief behind the words. She sat up straight.

'What do you mean by that, exactly? If she is missing, you should inform the police.'

Cally shook her head, but not, it appeared, in denial. 'Oh, we've done that,' she said. 'But she's of age, they say there's no reason –' Her voice broke, and she went on unevenly, '– only that she lied and lied and sent her brother to prison, and even if we could tell them that, it would only be reason enough for her to have run away. So they're not really looking ...' Tears had come into her eyes and begun to run down her face. Dot held out her arms.

'Give me the baby. Find a hankie, take five minutes. Then tell me properly.' She took the sleeping Daniel into her arms and Cally fumbled in her bag for a tissue. She wiped it across her face and blew her nose hard.

'Sorry. I'm making an exhibition of myself. But on a day like this – well, she should be here. Or if, like Anna, she couldn't be, then she should have sent a card and a gift. There shouldn't be this ... this nothingness. She doesn't even know –' Her voice broke again, and she bit her lip, hard. Dot didn't speak, and after a few minutes, she went on unsteadily. 'If we had been honest, if we had faced up to the truth, *then* they might have looked properly. If we had admitted that Cress was ... well, different, and got help for her, then none of this would ever have happened. She wouldn't have married Mike Stanley, she wouldn't have lost her way, he wouldn't be dead ... Mawgan would be whole. But we didn't, and now they're all lost. We didn't want to know. Only Allison, and I told her she was jealous because she had been the baby for so long and Cress ... and she was right all along!' She ended on a howl and buried her face in her hands.

When Cally had had a few minutes to recover herself, Dot said quietly, 'None of us get it right all the time, we all tend to bury our heads, you know.' Susan came into her mind as she spoke, she hadn't wanted to know about Susan and look where that had got them all? Of course, the problems were diametrically opposed; Susan had been too bright for her mother's plan for her, Cressida apparently not bright enough. She made a face at herself at this dismissive conclusion, but it made no difference in the end, she and Cally had both got it wrong. It was only the end result that was different, because Susan, ultimately, could fend for herself. She said, 'When did you last hear from her?'

Cally sat up, conscious that she was being guilty of a monumental social crime, but it was done now, she might as well finish the job. So she said, unsteadily, 'She worked in a café in Falmouth. She rang home occasionally, but she didn't come, she said she was trying to stand on her own feet. We thought ... we thought that she was there because she was hoping to make it up with Mawgan ... but she never got in touch with him. He knew she was there. He didn't, either.'

'And then? What happened to her?'

'She walked out one day and never came back. She took all her things from where she had a room, and just ... vanished. The girl she worked with said she had gone with a man, some friend of Mike's, and that's why the police aren't really taking much notice. But if she had done that, she would have told us. She *would*!' She sounded as if she was trying to convince herself. Dot looked at her seriously, and for a moment said nothing. 'I'm sorry,' said Cally, and gave another scrub at her face. 'It's just that all this – the christening, and everyone here and happy – it just hit me. I'm making a fool of myself, aren't I? What must you think of me?'

Some other people had come out into the sunshine, they were talking and laughing at the far end of the balcony, leaning over and looking at the river. Dot spoke carefully, so that she wouldn't be overheard. 'There are other ways than through the police of tracing missing persons. Have you thought of a private detective?'

'I wouldn't know where to begin,' said Cally, on a note of panic. 'And how would you know you could trust them? And Pip would never hear of it, I know.'

'As to your first two points,' Dot said, 'I can give you the name of a man whose trustworthiness I can guarantee.' She didn't add that the man she had in mind had a flying start on the problem, since she had already employed him herself to look into Mawgan's affairs. She was a little ashamed of that now, to tell the truth, although at the time it had seemed the only thing to do. 'As to the last, that would be for you to sort out with your husband. But it might be a line to follow.'

'It's been two years,' said Cally, desolately. 'That's what I can't live with. Because I can't believe my little girl would stay away for that long and not send so much as a postcard unless she was ...' she took a deep breath, and left the sentence unfinished. Dot reached out and took her hand, wordlessly. There was really nothing more to be said.

After a while, Cally pulled herself together. She removed her hand and smiled at Dot, a little shakily. 'I'm sorry. I'm making a fool of myself, aren't I? Spoiling your day.'

'I think you needed to say that to someone. Didn't you?'

'Yes.' Cally paused, hesitated, and then managed a smile. 'I can see where Debbie gets it from.'

'Gets what from?' asked Dot, momentarily bewildered, and Cally said, quite seriously, 'The gifts of understanding and kindness,' and Dot was lost for words. It didn't sound like herself. If she had such gifts, which she doubted, she had misapplied them.

Cally began to ready the pushchair for the replacement of the baby, it meant she didn't have to look at Dot. She hadn't expected to like her, if she was honest, but she had found someone very different from what she had been led to expect, and she felt, obscurely, that she owed her something for prejudging her. She spoke with a laugh in her voice that was as much a reaction from the scene just passed as genuine amusement. 'And if you really want to know,' she said, 'my mother's attitude when I wanted to marry Pip was exactly the same as yours – she was utterly horrified and really, with far less reason. So there can be no hard feelings, on our side at least.' She held out her arms for the baby and their eyes met. Dot felt uncomfortable.

'I think I am getting to know your son,' was the best she could manage, and Cally said, 'If you are, then you're the first!' She looked up, past Dot. 'Hullo Debbie, looking for the boy? He's not been kidnapped, he's here.'

'No,' Debbie said. She thought there was a lingering atmosphere and felt uncomfortable. This juxtaposition of grandmothers didn't seem exactly desirable, which was why she had come outside – to prevent bloodshed, maybe, only there didn't seem to be any. She noted that Cally had been crying, but they seemed on good terms. She wondered, but didn't ask. Instead, she said, 'If you don't hurry up, there'll be no food left. Go and get something while there's yet time, I'll look after his nibs, he'll be yelling for his own grub any minute now..' She turned the pushchair round to face her, cradling the baby in her other arm, and smiled at them both. 'You can set your clock by him.'

Dot took Cally's arm. 'I think we have been dismissed,' she said. 'Come along, something to eat will make us both feel better.'

Debbie watched them go, her chin resting speculatively on her son's downy head. Whatever had gone on between those two, it hadn't been the Night of the Long Knives as might have been expected with the history between them. In fact, they looked to have reached some understanding that seemed, against all odds, to have broken through a reserve in Cally that Debbie had begun to suspect was slowly destroying her from within. There were no guesses as to what that might be about, although how Dot had worked her miracle was a different question. Then the baby she cradled began to grumble and she headed off for the privacy of the office to attend to him.

The christening party began to look as if it would go on for ever. The cake was cut and eaten, a toast was drunk, but there was still no sign of anyone actually leaving, they were having too good a time. Eventually, it was Garfie Angwin who rose reluctantly to his feet and broke up the party. 'Time to get my two ladies on the way home,' he said. Cally looked at her watch.

'And we should be leaving too.' She looked around. 'Where's Allison got to?'

Allison was by the bar with her brother, her sister-in-law, and her new *fiancé* and had to be dragged away with promises called over her shoulder to be right back, to say a proper goodbye to her grandparents. Susan looked at Dot. 'How about you, Mum? Ready to leave? I think Chel's parents are just about on the wing.'

'I think perhaps we should,' said Dot, but regretfully. 'Those children are getting a little wild.' She would be away first thing in the morning, and was reluctant to say goodbye to them. Susan looked at her with unexpected sympathy.

'You can come back, Mum. Any time you want. If Deb is tied up, you can stay with me. Carl is away a lot of the time in the summer, we'll be glad of the company.'

'It doesn't seem right,' said Dot, discontentedly, referring to Carl's unavoidable absences rather than staying with Susan. 'Can you not arrange things more sensibly, Susan? Those children need a man to help you control them. Under the influence of that Kayleigh, Annabel is getting quite out of hand sometimes.'

To her surprise, Susan took this without pokering up as she usually did. 'Oh, it's all in hand Mum. We know that too. And don't worry about Kayleigh, she's OK when you get to know her. Annabel needs knocking off her perch, she was a bit too much the little lady.'

'She certainly isn't now,' said Dot, darkly, and then Cally came over with Pip to say goodbye before Candy's pernicious influence could join Kayleigh's in her condemnation. Cally kissed Dot's cheek with real affection.

'It's been so good to meet you at last, Mrs Nankervis –'

'Dorothy,' said Dot, returning the friendly embrace.

'Dorothy. And I'm Cally. We'll see each other again, I'm sure, next time you're here you must get Debbie to bring you over. And I'll think about what you said, and talk to Pip about it.'

Then Pip came forward to shake hands, and there was a further drift towards the balcony and the stairs.

Susan began to round up her family, retrieving Carl from behind the bar, where he and Roger were relieving Phil and his wife so that they could eat something. Roger came with him, his arm around Gosia, to say goodbye to them all. Dot and Gosia, who had managed to evade each other all afternoon without, they both hoped, making it obvious, found themselves eyeball to eyeball. Dot recovered her poise first. 'Maria,' she said. 'How nice to see you again. Congratulations on your engagement, my dear.' And she smiled at Roger. 'And when is the wedding to be?'

'October, when the season's finished.' His answering smile held reserve, Dot hadn't been too good a friend to Gosia in the past, when she had worked for Susan and Tom. But it was Gosia who added what Roger had no intention of saying. 'We hope you will come, Mrs Nankervis. It would be good to be friends.' Which was being too direct for Dot, who immediately backed off.

'That's very kind of you, Maria,' she said, which committed nobody. 'Shall we see nearer the time?'

'Gosia,' said Roger.

Dot could feel his confrontational attitude encouraging her own to rear its ugly head and turned away with a vague nod to make her way over to Marilyn and Bob. The party was coming to an end rapidly now.

Mike caught at Liz's arm before she finally escaped through the door after Susan and the children. 'You off home tomorrow?' he asked.

'Yes. I shall leave early, to avoid the traffic. And your friend will probably want to get away and be about his own affairs.'

'Yes, there's things we need to sort out before Wednesday. Look, I'm off first thing tomorrow too, getting the parents back to Suffolk, I won't be back in Devon until late. But I'll try to get to see you Tuesday sometime, if that's OK? Just to make sure all's well.'

Liz could have said there was no need, she would be fine, but she didn't. 'That would be nice of you,' she said, instead.

'Oh, I am very nice,' he said. His eyes, green and amused, met hers. 'If I had a glass in my hand, I'd drink to Tuesday, but I haven't. So, see you then.' He gave her shoulder a quick squeeze and vanished into the diminishing crowd.

Susan, Carl and the children had already disappeared down the staircase from the balcony, and Tracy and Tom and their two were off to Creekside with Chel and Oliver. Liz paused, momentarily alone, a quick smile rising unbidden to her lips, and then followed her aunt's family down to ground level.

She had not, she realised, given Paul one serious thought all day apart from her brief talk with Jerry. Perhaps that would change tomorrow, of course. It was disconcerting to realise that she almost hoped it would.

469

XXIV

Monday, Tuesday, Wednesday ...

Liz planned to leave for home after breakfast on Monday morning; Tom, Tracy and their children had left around seven o'clock the night before to be home for work and school the next day, so the kitchen was eerily quiet as she and Susan shared coffee and toast. Carl was already away to the sailing school working on his boat, Annabel and Sebastian at school themselves. Only the kitten, Loki, sat on the table and watched each mouthful disappear, and Clinker lay under their feet.

'It's been a good weekend,' said Liz.

'Yes.' There was a reservation in Susan's voice that Liz didn't understand, and decided not to follow up. Instead, she said, 'If you let that kitten sit on the table because he's little and cute, in a month or two he'll be twice the size, a feline teenager and a complete menace.'

'You speak from experience?' Susan scooped up the kitten and held him cuddled under her chin. He had already grown appreciably. Liz made a grimace.

'I do. And anyway, it's unhygienic.' This ignoring the fact that her own cat sat on the kitchen table whenever he felt like it, although not necessarily with her goodwill.

Susan put the kitten down on the floor, where he mewed pathetically. She felt like making the same noise herself. It wasn't simply that the lovely weekend was over and everyone leaving for home, it went deeper than that and she was ashamed of where it began; with all the gifts of furniture, china, and household goods heaped on her little sister while she received nothing, not even the offer of a spare Dresden shepherdess – which she would in any case have refused. You couldn't say that sort of thing even to your dearest friend. She couldn't even say it to Carl, who come to think probably was her dearest friend. He would say something comforting that would completely miss the point, and in any case she couldn't bring herself to let herself down in front of him. Certainly not after their last confrontation – if you could dignify it by the name – which was still unresolved between them.

Liz munched toast for a minute, knowing something was eating Susan and unsure what was the right thing to say. Looking for the most unprovocative subject, she unwittingly hit on one of the more provocative. 'Your mother looked fabulous, I thought. She's a handsome woman when she takes the trouble, let's hope she goes on doing it now she's got started.'

Susan didn't want to discuss Dot. Her mother's transformation at the instigation of Benita Vachell had made her feel guilty, as well as resentful. She and Deb could have done that years ago if they had tried – or then again, perhaps they couldn't. Dot had been different lately, and why was that? Susan didn't even want to think about it. She turned the tables neatly.

'Odd, wasn't it, you knowing Chel's brother and not knowing you did? Like something that happens in one of your books.'

Liz was indignant. 'I'd never write anything so trite!' she retorted, and Susan raised her eyebrows.

'Life is triter than fiction? That's a new one! You seemed to get on very well together.' It was half a question. Liz rose to the challenge.

'Never! Don't go getting ideas, he has a ginger moustache.'

'He could shave it off,' offered Susan. It wasn't lost on Liz that in teasing her, Susan was relaxing, and it made her wonder. She snorted.

'He'd still be an ex-soldier with red hair,' she said. 'Anyway, the *possibility* of a ginger moustache would always be there, haunting me. I'd wake up every morning and see its ghost –' she broke off, and hurriedly reached for her coffee, burying her face in the mug.

'You'll say that once too often,' Susan warned her, and then a wicked grin appeared on her face. 'I see you've thought about it, though.'

Had she? Liz thought about it now, and found to her horror that the idea wasn't as repulsive as she was making out. She liked Mike Wainwright, had liked him from the start in spite of her protestations, and he seemed to like her too. It was a relief, in a way, to discover that Paul Attwood hadn't put her off men for life, but of course it could simply be a desperate reaction to her new single state. What was the word for that? – *transitional*.

Face it Elizabeth. You've been technically single for years. Paul was only ever in love with himself.

'Well?' said Susan, pleased to be carrying the war into the enemy's camp with such resounding success; Liz's face spoke volumes, each one a romantic novel.

'It's early days,' she said, which neatly begged every question on the list. Susan, who had merely been teasing to escape an awkward subject, began to wonder in earnest. She looked at Liz more closely.

'Don't peer at me like that,' said Liz. 'There's nothing – nothing at all – except that he helped me find a cat-sitter.' Who had turned out to be rather more than that. Almost, then, she told Susan about the horrible emails, but what was the point really? She'd only say *I told you so*, and they'd been stopped now anyway. She put down her mug and looked at her watch. 'And I'd better be off home and let him get away, he's got a job to do, and so have I. Do you want help with the washing up?'

'It'll go in the machine. You get off.'

When Liz had gone, the house seemed emptier than ever. A prey to her own miserable thoughts, Susan stacked the washing up machine, wiped down the worktops, and then stared out of the window. She wouldn't have felt so bad if her resentment hadn't been so small-minded. Deb, though, had always been the favourite. Deb and Oliver, Jerry's children. Of course, Mum hadn't showered Oliver with gifts either, but then he and Chel didn't need furniture, did they? If they had ...

Neither do you need it. What's the matter with you? I thought you'd got over this pointless sibling envy! Mum needed to downsize, Deb needed chairs and beds, even if not the teacups, and that's all there is to it. Snap out of it, for heaven's sake!

You upset Carl, too.

What's with this *too*? The only person you've upset seems to be you!

I wish this was a college day. I hate the emptiness when people go away. Liz was right, it was a lovely weekend, that always makes it worse when they go.

Susan turned away from the view outside and was about to take herself in hand and go to commune with her computer when the doorbell rang. For a moment, she hesitated about answering it. She wasn't in the mood for company, and she had work to do, but upbringing prevailed. You couldn't lurk out of sight if people were ringing your bell, and she went down the passage and opened the front door. Dot stood on the step.

'Susan dear, I'm so glad I've found you at home. Deborah said she didn't think you went to college this morning. May I come in?'

Susan closed her mouth, which had opened in surprise, and held the door open. 'Of course. Would you like coffee?'

'No thank you.' Dot came in briskly, and Susan closed the door behind her. 'I'm on my way home, it would only be a nuisance. I've been trying to find an opportunity to talk to you all weekend, but it's been so busy there never seemed a suitable moment for what I wanted to say.'

'Well ... come into the conservatory, we can talk there and look at the garden ... not that there's much to look at in March, but –'

'Susan, you're waffling,' said Dot, severely. 'Have I interrupted you in your studying? I'm sorry if so, but this was the last chance before I leave.'

'No ... no. Liz has only just left, too'.

They went into the conservatory and sat down. Dot said, 'What a delightful young woman Elizabeth is. You know she offered to come and help me with the move?'

Liz too. Susan also ran. Susan made herself smile. 'Did she? That was nice of her. Of course, if it's at the right time I can do it, but it might be in the middle of exams.'

'It seems so strange for you to be sitting exams at your age,' said Dot, with obvious disapproval. She fumbled in her bag and removed a small object, holding it in her hand. 'Susan dear, I was clearing out my dressing table drawer the other day and I found this right at the back. I had almost forgotten about it.' She looked down at the item cupped in her hands, and added, so softly that Susan almost didn't hear, 'I think I wanted to.' She met Susan's eyes, and held out her hand. 'I want you to have it. Take it.'

Susan looked at the small velvet ring box sitting on her mother's palm, and then at Dot. She hesitated and then took it in her own hand.

'Open it,' said Dot, and watched as Susan lifted the lid and caught her breath.

'Mother – it's beautiful! Where did it come from? I've never seen you wear it, never seen it before at all.' She took the big topaz out of its box to study it better. It was set in a ring – silver or possibly white gold – and of an unusually deep golden yellow. It looked as if it had never been worn at all, brand new and sparkling.

Dot spoke quietly. 'Your father gave it to me. I had a lot of trouble conceiving the first time, so that when I finally managed it, it was a cause for celebration. He knew I loved topaz, he bought it for me when he was on a trip to Paris and brought it back as a surprise. I loved it and wore it always for a while. Every time I looked at it, I was reminded of how kind he was and how thoughtful and it made me feel ... wanted, I think. I didn't often feel wanted in those days.' She spoke bitterly, and then bit her lip and looked at Susan. 'Forget I said that. I abhor self-pity.'

'But I've never seen you wear it,' said Susan, for the second time, and then said, 'Oh,' as she remembered.

'No. Henry died before he even saw you, and after that, somehow I didn't have the heart. But you will. I would like you to have it, and so would he, if he were here. So take it and enjoy it.' She felt in her bag again and took out an envelope and laid it on the small table between them. 'I had it valued for you, you must have it insured. But wear it, and enjoy it, and think of your father. He would have loved you.'

'That's what Isobel says,' said Susan. She slipped the ring onto her finger and held out her hand to admire it better. 'I don't know how to say thank you. It's a wonderful gift, and I shall treasure it always.'

Dot had risen to her feet. She said, reverting to type in self-defence, 'And if you ever get around to marrying your friend Carl, it will make a nice engagement ring for you.'

'So it would,' said Susan, although she thought – and even to think it was a step forward she was reluctant to take – that Carl would wish to provide his own ring. She set the box and envelope aside and rose to hug her mother. 'Thank you, thank you, thank you.'

'Just take care of it,' said Dot, returning the hug. 'You're a good daughter, Susan. Never think I don't know. I know you feel I often favour Deborah, but you are my dear, good girl. And now, I must be on my way. I shall be busy for the next few weeks, sorting everything out. The new house is much smaller in every way than the present one.'

474

'However will you choose?' Susan asked, still shaken by that brief scene, escorting her mother to the door. 'All your lovely things, won't it be impossible?'

Dot smiled. 'I have worked it out, what furniture I shall take and what it will accommodate. As for the rest, I shall pack all my favourite things in descending order until I have reached saturation point, and then you and Deborah and Cheryl can choose what you would like from the rest, and the remainder will go to auction. One cannot be sentimental about these things. And now, I really must go. I wish I could stay longer, but it is a long drive.'

They kissed, and Susan stood on the step and waved as her mother drove away. She went back indoors somewhat bemused and stood for a moment looking at the beautiful ring on her finger. Then she picked up the envelope and opened it and read its contents and her eyes became circular with shock. Whew! So much for a load of second-hand furniture! And there she'd been, beating her breast over it. White gold, then! But far more valuable, she realised, was the warmth that her mother's gesture had left behind it, and she remembered what she had said.

It made me feel wanted. Well, here it was, doing the same thing again.

Not for the first time since she had begun to learn about him, Susan felt a stab of regret that she had never had the chance to know her father, so poignant that it made tears start to her eyes. Then she blinked, and pulled herself together. She picked up the ring box and the valuation and headed once more for her computer. Ringing the insurance company, which she had better do first, would stop her drowning in sentiment, and then she had some archaeology to study. As for any other implications of Mum's visit, she would consider them later on.

It looked as if she might get that spare shepherdess after all.

She was unaware that, although she still addressed her mother as "Mother", she had for some time been thinking of her as "Mum" as Debbie did, but sitting at her computer now, looking at the topaz on her finger, she did feel, for the first time, the start of a crack in the invisible wall that each of them had helped to erect over time.

*

Liz headed for home in a light-hearted mood, but as she drew nearer to the border between Cornwall and Devon this mood unaccountably darkened. It wasn't that she didn't want to go home, it was more a matter of what she might find when she got there.

Probably not Mark Jones: if he had any sense he would realise there was no reason to wait, and be off about his own business. In spite of what she had said to Susan, Liz believed that this would be what happened. Tib would be there, trying to convince her that he hadn't been fed. Two days' post too. It was the idea of the post, she discovered at this point, that was bugging her. Paul had not so far written her anonymous letters, if you discounted the emails, but when other avenues were sealed against him, who knew what he might do? She really, really didn't want to be reduced to being scared of opening her own letters! Particularly since she tended to get such a lot of them. Even fan mail forwarded by her publisher wouldn't be one hundred per cent safe, since Paul knew the ropes as well as she did herself.

She had almost succeeded in convincing herself that she was being ridiculous when she turned into the village street and saw Mark Jones's motor bike still parked outside her cottage after all. Her spirits immediately plummeted again, because surely he had things of his own to attend to. She pulled into her parking slot, and as she got out of the car he appeared at her door so he had been watching for her.

'Hullo.' He took her bag from her hand and stood aside for her to enter the house before him. 'Good weekend?'

'Lovely, yes, thank you. Everything all right here?' She spoke casually, as if pretending she hadn't feared something might happen would make anything that possibly had happened un-happen ... she wasn't sure where that slightly convoluted line of reasoning was going, and abandoned it. Mark had placed her bag at the foot of the stairs and was heading through her study to the kitchen. She followed him.

'Want a coffee while I make my report?' he asked her, with a smile that ought to have made her feel better, but didn't. 'I was just making one while I waited for you.' He lifted the steaming kettle and held it up temptingly. Liz shook her head.

'I had one earlier, before I left. I'll leave it till later.' She pulled out a chair and sat down, her elbows leaning on the table, saying, 'You really didn't need to wait around for me.' Mark poured water into a mug and came and sat opposite.

'I thought I'd better check with you, although it was a quiet weekend on the whole. I cleaned out your computer, checked everything out, did a bit of springcleaning for you – you should defrag more often, you were clagged up like a blocked drain in there. I take it you know how?'

'I just forget,' Liz confessed. 'When everything begins to slow down almost to a stop, *then* I remember. Did you find anything – apart from clag, that is?'

'Only what should be there. No nasties. Only ...' He hesitated, and her heart sank.

'Only what? You said it was all quiet.'

'Well ... it's probably nothing. Nothing to do with your computer this time. No prowlers. Only, while I was working at it your telephone rang.'

'It does that,' said Liz. She paused. 'Did you answer it?'

'It'd rung several times actually, and I left it for the answering machine to pick up – you've got four messages by the way – but this time I was concentrating on something else and I picked it up without thinking. I said "Hullo".'

'And?' asked Liz, when he didn't immediately continue.

'And nothing, really. Someone said "Oh!" and slammed the phone down.'

'Male or female?' asked Liz. Her heart sank. Mark said, 'Male,' and a silence fell between them, full of unspoken thoughts. Finally he went on, as if it might comfort her, 'Could just have been a wrong number, you'd be amazed how many people just hang up. There was nothing else, I told you, nobody hanging about outside or anything, just an ordinary weekend.'

'I'd better listen to the messages,' said Liz, without enthusiasm, but Mark assured her they were nothing.

'Sorry, but I couldn't help hearing them. Someone called Beck rang twice –'

'My agent,' said Liz. 'I'll ring her back.'

'A couple of others. Both women.'

'Story of my life,' said Liz, on a sigh.

'And there were some that didn't leave messages. Not everybody does.'

Liz didn't want to discuss phone calls any more. She said, 'Did the cat behave himself?'

'Mostly. He brought me a present; the biggest rat I've ever seen. I pitched it over the wall into your neighbours' shrubs.'

'They'll appreciate that.'

'They won't even see it. Some fox will carry it off.' Mark finished his coffee and carried his mug to the sink, washing it out meticulously. Liz had already noticed that the kitchen was sparkling clean, she had wondered if she would return to a bachelor tip. She now saw that she had done him an injustice. 'I put the sheets and towel into the machine, but I haven't turned it on. It isn't full, I thought you might have something else after the weekend.'

'You are virtuous!'

'The army trains you well. Anyway, Sarge would put me on a charge if I left you a mess.' He grinned at her, disarmingly. 'I'll be away then. You know where to find me if you have any more computer problems.' He paused. 'The steak was great. Thanks.'

'My uncle reared it. Do you want to know its name?'

'I think I'd rather not be introduced to my dinner – even retrospectively.' They parted on a laugh, and Liz went back indoors. She heard the bike start up and the diminishing roar of its departure. The house felt all of a sudden very quiet. She looked at her bag waiting at the foot of the narrow stairs and decided that it could go on waiting for a bit. Then she peered round the door of her living room, but there was only Tib, curled comfortably in the best chair and reluctant to bestir himself to say hullo. There remained only her study. She went in and sat at her computer, and looked at the yellow light on her landline phone that told her that messages awaited her attention. With a sigh, she pressed the button and prepared to listen. Even a recorded voice was better than no voice at all.

Rebecca Studley had rung twice, once about a talk Liz was supposed to be giving at a writers' congress in May, once to ask her to ring back. Alice had rung, apparently to say merely *sorry, I forgot you were away*, and the last message was from the agents handling the sale of her flat, again asking her to ring back. Perhaps they had sold it, she wondered listlessly, although it was unlikely given the state it was currently in. She had to start somewhere, so she dialled Beck's number.

After a brief chat with her agent, she went on to the estate agents, who wanted to know when her flat would be back on the market as they had someone who might be interested. Since her insurers were dragging their feet, she could only promise to let them know and after that there remained only Alice, who was out and didn't reply. She sat there for some while when she finally put down the phone, staring at the blank screen of her monitor and wondering what on earth was the matter with her. Then she looked at her watch. Then she made a cup of coffee and forgot to drink it. Finally, irritated with herself, she checked her fridge and went out to visit the shop in the hopes that the fresh air might clear her head.

It didn't. In fact, an animated chat with Mrs Pinkerton about the imminent takeover of Ole Jarge's garage made her more distrait than before. It was strange that a novelist such as herself should fail to recognise her symptoms; she put it down to the let-down feeling that you get after a holiday and told herself to snap out of it and get on with some work. She made herself walk home a lot more briskly than she had set out, put away her shopping, and then carried her abandoned bag upstairs, where she stood for some time at the back window of her bedroom, staring out on the garden and the distant moor. In the end, it was the ringing of the telephone downstairs that brought her back to her surroundings. Without really giving it much thought, she ran down and caught the call just as the answering machine clicked in.

'Hullo?'

There was a silence. She thought she could hear somebody breathing, but wasn't sure. Then whoever it was put their end down with a click and she was left standing with her own phone in her hand.

Number withheld. Well, there was a surprise!

Liz put the phone down very carefully, as if it might explode if she didn't. Of course, she told herself, Mark Jones had been quite right. People dialling wrong numbers often did just put the phone down when a stranger answered. Or if not *often*, they did do it. But if it was the same person who had rung her and got Mark, then ... well, this time he had got her, hadn't he? Or she?

If it was Paul, and of course it didn't have to be, what would he have thought when a man answered?

It could have been four different people who rang and left no message.

She pulled herself together and went back upstairs to unpack, carrying her washing downstairs and pushing it into the machine with the sheets from Mark's bed. Tib, hearing her moving about in the kitchen, came prowling in and stared meaningfully at his food bowl and she picked him up to cuddle him, purring, in her arms. Then she put him down, opened a tin of sardines and flicked one into the bowl, and he sniffed at it, whisked his tail and dived out through the cat flap. A cat thing, but she could always have them for lunch. She put the rest of the tin into the fridge and went into her study, sat down at her desk and began to open her post. There was nothing untoward in it. No anonymous letters, no letter bombs, not even, as it happened, any bills. Most of it was headed to the bin. Liz gathered this junk mail into a neat pile but didn't move to dispose of it. The silence in the house pressed against her ears.

This would be what he would want, if it was Paul, of course. To turn her home into a place of fear. She thought of Tib, so little and vulnerable and loved. She thought of fire. She thought that no, Paul wouldn't, and then thought that she had never thought he would send her foul emails either and felt sick.

It didn't have to be him. She was only assuming that it was because of the flat.

But if it wasn't, then that scenario was almost worse.

A disgruntled reader, someone who felt that what she wrote had in some way injured them, that could be it. Except that the sort of thing she wrote was unlikely to injure anyone, and how would they know where to find her anyway? Some complete nutter then, who felt themselves passed over at some book-signing or talk, and had followed her home. She couldn't recall anything like that, but then she wouldn't, would she, if you took into account that the only reason she might ignore someone was if she hadn't seen them in the first place? But to go down that road was to enter the realms of real nightmare, and on the whole she thought she preferred to believe it was Paul, getting his own back in a stupid revenge.

There was no point in this. In a swift, decisive movement Liz got to her feet and walked briskly through the kitchen to the back door. Just outside, a small lean-to shed against the wall housed her recycling bins. She dumped the junk into the appropriate container, returned indoors and poured her undrunk cold coffee from earlier down the sink and washed the mug. The she went back into her study and sat down once more at her desk and switched on the computer; at least she was sure now that wouldn't attack her! She was waiting for everything to boot up when her phone rang again, and this time she looked at the caller ID before she picked it up.

'Alice! How's things?'

'Boring,' Alice told her. 'Can I invite myself to lunch? Gil is off somewhere with the van, and the kids are at school, I can sneak a couple of hours. I want to hear all about your weekend.'

'It's only sardines, and the cat has had some of those.'

'Wonderful! Meet me for a sandwich at the Three Bears?'

Remembering the last time she had lunched with her sister at the Three Bells made Liz smile, although there was nobody to see her. But of course, she added in her mind, he wouldn't be there today. He was on his way to Suffolk, or maybe by this time, on his way back.

'Why not?' she agreed. 'I'm all up in the air anyway, with only just having got back. Maybe after lunch and a good gossip I shall be able to concentrate better.'

It sounded plausible, and for the next hour even just the idea of it worked. She edited the last chapter she had written to remind herself of where she had got to and to get the feel of the book again after her weekend off, then shut down and prepared to meet Alice. She wouldn't tell her sister about the phone calls; like the emails, the family would probably not fully understand about them and would make all kinds of practical and unacceptable suggestions, such as "come home until whoever it is gets tired of it" or "You should tell the police". Tell the police what, exactly?

She could show the police the print-out Mark had made, but some ridiculous residual loyalty to Paul was preventing her. She would, prefer to resolve the problem without actually ruining him – which wasn't to say that he deserved the consideration.

No immediate solution there. She locked up the cottage with a certain amount of relief and headed off to the Three Bells. She had at least one piece of news that would deflect Alice from anything else. When they were settled in an inglenook with iced tonic water and generously filled cheese and pickle sandwiches, she produced it like a rabbit from a hat.

'Guess what,' she said. 'You never will!'

'Guess about what subject?' asked Alice, in her best elder sister voice. Liz smiled, unaware of how that made her look, and Alice narrowed her eyes. Cat at the cream time, eh? 'Come on, give,' she commanded, and Liz said, 'Sergeant Ginger Moustache, remember him? Turns out he's Chel's brother. I ran into him again at the christening.'

Alice took a minute to digest this gem. 'Well well,' she said, eventually, unable to think of anything cleverer. Liz's smile deepened into an outright grin.

'Bit of a facer, isn't it? I never knew her name was Wainwright before she married Oliver, or I might even have guessed it. They're very alike. The other sister, Tracy, even more so. They've all got that bright red hair – only the oldest brother has dark hair instead. The rest take after their mum, even the kids – Tracy's kids, that is, and Richie's. Zoë looks as if she's going to be dark like her dad.'

Alice, who had known Liz all her life, realised that she was evading some issue a sister could only guess at, and decided to let her do it. Her guess, she was sure, was a good one, and time would tell. So she entered on a discussion of all the details of the occasion just passed, and asked particularly after Dot.

'She'd done something to herself,' Liz told her. 'She looked ten years younger and miles more attractive, being single again seems to suit her.' She paused. 'She's going to divorce the solicitor, apparently. She told him so at the christening Deb says, what style!'

'Well, good for her. She's best shut of him completely from what Susan says. Do you think her new image is because she's got a better iron in the fire?'

'I don't think she's either bought the iron or laid the fire,' said Liz, with passing regret for it was a nice idea. 'I think she's just reinventing herself for a better life, and good luck to her! The only person who looked put-out about it was the solicitor's ex-wife.'

'The sculptress woman? What's she like?'

'Stunningly beautiful, even at her age,' said Liz.

'No insecurity there, then.'

'Far from it. I got the feeling there's a lot more to it, but hey, who cares? Our almost-grandmother has got away, and good luck to her, I say!'

'Is there such a thing as a stepgrandmother?' Alice wondered, not by any means the first to do so.

'Wouldn't that be a grandstepmother?' Liz offered.

'Whatever it is, I'd love to meet her,' said Alice, and Liz said, 'I'm working on it.'

Talking to Alice and eating lunch in the jovial atmosphere of the pub put Liz in a good mood to go home and tackle her new book in earnest. She shut down her computer when the light began to fade, took off her glasses and rubbed her tired eyes. Driving home this morning, working half the day, they needed a rest. She decided to get herself some dinner – not sardines on toast – and chill out in front of the telly for the evening if there was anything on. If there wasn't, she'd watch a favourite film on DVD and if Tib wasn't otherwise engaged slaughtering some innocent creature outside he would no doubt come and join her. Once, only a short while ago, the contemplation of such an evening would have pleased her, tonight it seemed to lack something.

Susan's mad household over the weekend, she decided. People and laughter and children under foot; it would take a while to settle back into her pleasant little rut. That's all it was. And she went to peer into her freezer for something easy and delicious to cook and felt quite relaxed and at peace. She would have an early night, and tomorrow she would wake up fresh and rested and all the goblins would have gone away.

Early on Tuesday, she was woken from a deep sleep by the ringing of her mobile on the bedside table. Groping for it in the dark, only half-awake, she wondered what time it was and why someone should ring her at this hour; in her somnolent and bewildered state she only thought of some emergency and answered the ring without thinking beyond that.

'Hullo?'

There was a short silence. During it, her eyes focussed on the illuminated face of her clock: it was 2 a.m. She was still absorbing this information when the voice began in her ear. It was no more than a hoarse whisper, toneless and unidentifiable.

I'm out there watching you,' it said. You can't see me, but I see you, lying there in your bed with your – At which point Liz turned

off her phone in a reflex action and dropped it onto the quilt. She
was out of bed and at the front window in a flash, peering out into
the moonlit night, up and down the street, her heart thumping wildly.
There was nobody in sight. She looked at the other window, at the
opposite end of the room, but there could be nobody in the garden,
it was completely fenced in and private, not even a gate, for it backed
onto the garden of the house lower down the slope and to either side
there were neighbours all along the street to the far ends. Her mind
worked this out even while the rest of her thoughts panicked.

After a while, shaking not only from the cold, she climbed back
into bed and pulled the quilt up round her neck. A small thud
announced the arrival of her mobile on the floor, and she left it there.
She lay where she was, unsleeping, until the dawn came and light grew
in the two windows of the room, and she thought, *I can't live here
alone with this, I shall have to go home or go somewhere different
if it's going to go on*, and was furious and resentful that this would
be to let Paul win, while knowing that here on her own she would
never feel comfortable again.

Blessedly, full daylight brought the return of both her sanity
and her courage. Liz, sitting at the table with a cup of coffee while
Tib crunched his way through a bowl of cat biscuits, realised that
there was a third alternative to the two panic-generated ultimate
responses of the early hours, encapsulated in the original premise. If
she couldn't live here alone – if she was afraid to do so, and she was
ashamed to realise that she probably was – and she didn't want to be
driven out, then she would have to call up some reinforcements. One
reinforcement, that is to say. On the face of it, the idea held some
interesting risks of its own.

She only wanted his protection, she told herself, she wasn't after
his body. He knew most of the story anyway, and he had turned up
trumps in the first instance. If she told him the whole thing ...

It occurred to her that *he* might be after *her* body, and for the first
time she wondered how she would feel about that. Nothing like as
bad as she felt about being whispered at in a pornographic manner
at two in the morning in an empty house, she realised. And he was
Chel's brother. It was almost a reference. It made him a friend, surely.

Still in two minds about her interesting idea, she made a piece of toast and carried it into her study, where she sat at her computer crunching it and thinking about the mess she appeared to have got herself into. If she chose to inform the police, as she should do, how would they trace the call? She had an idea that to do so, she would have to keep whoever it was talking for a while, and the idea was totally repulsive. Paul – if it was Paul, as it almost certainly was since he had used her mobile number this last time – wouldn't use his own phone, he could be using any phone in the whole of London and he was far too fly to use the same one twice. He was also, she suspected, far too fly to allow himself to be beguiled into talking too long.

He knew, too, that she usually had her mobile on the bedside table at night. The evidence against him was stacking up, but it wasn't irrefutable. That word *almost* still remained.

She thought of confronting him, and shuddered at the bare idea of how he would react. A suit for slander might be the least of it, and since she had no absolute proof of anything at all, could prove expensive in every way. Likelihood wasn't enough; she could, quite easily, destroy herself rather than him and she would prefer to destroy neither of them.

She swallowed the last piece of toast and licked the marmalade off her fingers, and as she did so, she saw a truck pulling up on the other side of the road. It wasn't one she had seen around before, and it seemed to be empty so it wasn't delivering anything, but then again no, it wouldn't be, for the driver was jumping down into the road, and he was a red-headed man of medium height and build with a ginger moustache. The Mounties, to use a popular cliché, which of course a reputable writer would never do, had arrived. She got up and went to open the door.

'Good morning,' he called as he crossed the street towards her. 'Not too early for you, am I? Only I have to be up the road at the garage by ten to check things through with the Captain and Mr Pryor before tomorrow's handover.'

'Not at all, I've been up for ages. Come in, have you time for a coffee?'

Mike glanced at his watch as he came through the door. 'Just a quick one then. How's things?'

Liz led the way into the kitchen and picked up the kettle before she answered, 'Not brilliant. Have you seen your mate Mark?'

Mike pulled out a chair and sat down, uninvited, leaning his elbows on the table. 'He said he thought you might be getting some funny phone calls, but he wasn't sure.'

'He can be sure now.' She switched the kettle on and sat down opposite to him. 'I had a ... well, it's not fair to call it a dirty phone call, it didn't get that far – in the middle of the night.'

'But it was shaping up that way?'

'Probably. Yes.' She hesitated. 'It made me feel ... oh, I don't know. Threatened? Invaded? Not good, anyway.'

'Your friend Paul, do you think?'

'Well, there are other nutters around, but it seems a bit of a coincidence on top of everything else wouldn't you say?' She shivered. 'He said he was outside, but I looked and there was nobody there.'

'You can say you're anywhere you like on the phone,' Mike pointed out.

'Yes. If it was Paul, on a Tuesday he was probably in London. But whoever it was used my mobile number, for what that's worth.'

Mike said nothing for a few moments, he appeared to he engrossed in a study of his nails, his fingertips curled over the better to scan them. He said, 'That can't have been nice, here on your own. Is there anyone who you could ask to come and stop with you for a bit – just until it blows over?'

'And what a fool I should look!' Liz retorted, momentarily stung. The kettle boiled and she got up to make the coffee. With her back to him, she said, 'Actually, I was thinking about that. Did you ever find somewhere to stay?'

'Checked out a few B&B's, but it would be expensive all things considered, and only be until Easter anyway. I'm in one now, it's not ideal.' He tilted back his chair on its legs and looked at her back thoughtfully. 'Mark and Ted found themselves a caravan to rent in a farmyard. There's room for three of us if we take a deep breath and squash up.'

'Not ideal either then,' said Liz.

'No.'

She carried the mugs over to the table and pushed the sugar in his direction as she sat down. There was only one way to do this, head-on. She said, 'I don't suppose you'd consider my spare room?'

'As a temporary measure, you mean?'

'It's not as if we're really strangers,' Liz went on, justifying herself. 'You're Chel's brother, I've known Chel ... well, for a while anyway. And she's Susan's sister-in-law.'

'That makes me nothing at all,' Mike pointed out. He looked at her seriously. 'It may not happen again.'

'It may not,' Liz agreed. 'The emails did though. Just maybe for a night or two, to see what develops? I do a good breakfast, when I try.'

'You have family round here,' said Mike.

'Yes. But if I told them, they'd start fussing and insisting I went to them until it blew over, and I wouldn't want to do that. This is my home, why should I be driven out of it?'

There was a silence. Mike looked down at his mug, turning it round and round between his hands apparently lost in thought. After a while Liz said, 'Don't worry, forget I asked. It was cheek really.'

He looked up then with a sudden smile that for some reason made her stomach feel as if it had just dropped out onto the floor. 'No it wasn't. I was just thinking.' He didn't say what he had been thinking about. Instead, he lifted the mug and drank from it, putting it back on the table with care. 'OK then. It's got to be a lot better than slumming in that caravan with those two yobbos. Bed and breakfast, and I can get my evening meal at the pub. But we must arrange a proper rent.' Although, he found himself thinking, that wouldn't change anything, and he wondered if he really knew what he was doing, and if he did, if it was even a wise thing to do.

'No,' Liz said. 'No rent. Why should you pay me, if you're only here for my convenience and peace of mind?'

Mike felt unreasonably that to pay her would be to protect her from the unruly thoughts beginning to occupy the very back of his mind. *Beginning*? They had been there since that first meeting in the pub. Nothing overt, just there. She was an attractive, intelligent woman, and it was a long time since he had met one of those.

'No, you must let me,' he said. 'At least for food. I eat like a horse, you've no idea.'

Liz recognised a need for compromise, or she might lose her guard dog before she fairly had him. 'All right then. You share the bill for the bacon and eggs.' She raised her own mug in a toast. 'Here's to our partnership, and down with Paul Attwood!'

'Definitely down with him,' said Mike, clicking his own mug against hers. 'When d'you want me to move in?'

'Now?' said Liz. 'Bring your stuff over tonight, why don't you? Oh – perhaps I ought to show you the room first. You might find it a bit girlie.'

Mike glanced at his watch, and swallowed the rest of his coffee hurriedly. 'I'll take it on trust, I have to go. You'll be OK in daylight?'

'Of course.' They both got to their feet together, which brought them nose to nose. Mike said, 'Don't answer any numbers you don't know.'

'No,' Liz agreed, unexpectedly short of breath.

In the brief pause that followed, Tib came pushing through his cat flap and jumped between them onto the table, and whatever the moment might have been shattered before it fairly began. Mike gave Liz a brief, brotherly kiss on the cheek and turned for the door. 'See you later then.'

'Yes,' said Liz, wondering where the bulk of her vocabulary had got to, and when he had gone, stood there in the kitchen with her hand against her cheek, staring down at her purring cat just like one of her own heroines. Tib stared back, his golden eyes enigmatic.

'He's been in the army for years,' Liz told him. Tib looked unimpressed, and she pushed the point home. 'And he's got a ginger moustache.'

Tib flicked his tail and jumped down onto the floor. So what? his attitude seemed to say. Liz gathered up the mugs and carried them to the sink, telling herself that her unfamiliar reactions were simply the result of a sleepless night, her nerves were shot to bits. He wasn't going to impose, he had made that quite clear. A business arrangement between friends, that's all it was.

She found herself wondering what Alice would make of it, and on the whole, decided that she didn't want to hear. And she resolved to be using her contact lenses when he returned tonight. She should do so more often, she told herself, justifying. They had cost enough, she was just lazy about it. Really.

On Wednesday, Mawgan turned up on Dot's doorstep as promised, not exactly on time but not long afterwards, driving his outrageous red car and looking almost respectable in a suit; not his beautiful Armani number, but a good business suit just the same. His sartorial elegance in the line of business and social events always managed to take Dot by surprise; she knew as well as anyone that he could be as rough as rats when he tried – or perhaps, she found herself thinking now, that should be when he *wasn't* trying, and to her chagrin found herself, yet again, hiding a smile.

'Sorry I'm a bit late,' he apologised. 'It all took longer than I expected. What a mess!'

'And are you planning to go ahead with it?' asked Dot, with interest.

'I'll fill you in while we have lunch. Where would you like to eat? Deb says there's a good Italian restaurant in town, fancy that?'

'We would need to ring to be sure they have a table,' said Dot. 'At lunchtime, they just may have, in the evening it is impossible without booking weeks ahead.'

Mawgan extracted a small mobile phone from his breast pocket. 'Sounds promising. Number?'

Dot had often eaten at Mario's, and carried the number in her head. The table duly booked, she was ushered into the Porsche after some papers and a clipboard had been flung out of the way behind the seat, and they set off with barely time for Dot to powder her nose She wondered if Mario's receptionist had recognised the name *Angwin*, and realised just who was planning to pay them a visit. If they didn't know now, they soon would, and the thought gave her satisfaction. She wondered – hoped even – if Jenny Carruthers would be lunching there today.

Jenny wasn't, but Mario himself greeted them at the door, and he already knew about the Dock Inn and had put two and two together, although whether they yet added up to more than three-and-a-half, Dot had still to learn. He knew Dot well of course, and allowed himself a quick, private nod when he saw her with Mawgan, as if her presence had confirmed something that he had guessed for himself. 'Good afternoon, Mrs Nankervis.' He clasped Dot's hand warmly, and then extended his own to Mawgan. 'And Mr Angwin, I am so happy to meet you. You are coming to join us in this town, I hear.'

Mawgan took the outstretched hand and said, 'Maybe.'

'Welcome to my restaurant. You will see, we have no fear of competition, there is room for us both. Come.' Mario led them himself to their table and saw them settled, handing them the menus with a bow. 'Enjoy your meal. I will see you later.'

When he had bowed himself off stage, Mawgan and Dot exchanged a look over the tops of the menus. Mawgan was grinning. 'News gone ahead of us, you reckon?'

'Conjecture, at least,' said Dot. She laid her menu down. 'And what did you think of the Dock Inn? Are the newsmongers correct in their assumptions?'

'Tell you while we eat. There'll be less chance of being interrupted.' He glanced at the card he still held in his hand. 'This looks promising. Anything specially good you recommend?'

Dot said, 'The pork Milanese is Jerry's particular favourite, I prefer fish at this time of day.'

'Italians do like their food,' commented Mawgan, appreciatively, and as he spoke, something she had heard on the grapevine went *click* in Dot's memory, and she said, 'Did not you run a restaurant in Italy at one time yourself?'

'Certainly did,' said Mawgan, 'Or at least, I ran the kitchen. I was head chef – the restaurant wasn't mine.' He laid down the menu and Dot had time in the ensuing pause to reflect that it was a black mark against herself that she had even needed to ask, when her own daughter had been married to this man for two years. There was a great deal of ground to make up. Before she could put this in words, if she even intended to try, Mawgan spoke again, a complete change of subject that took her by surprise.

'I got to thank you, Mrs Nankervis,' he said. 'You was good to my Mum at the christening, she says. She was some upset, I b'lieve. Made a right fool of herself, according to her.'

'It was natural enough,' said Dot. 'Such a family occasion ...' She wondered, given the circumstances, if it was wise to continue, and then decided that it would be worse not to. He had brought the subject up himself, after all. She went on, 'It grieves her very much that there has been no word from your sister. Has nobody any idea of where she might have gone?'

Mawgan made a slight movement of his head that might have been meant as a negative. He said, 'She was in Falmouth, last anyone heard of her.' He took a breath and let it go again.

'You were going to say?' said Dot.

'Nothing.' No point in saying, to Deb's mum of all people, about his unsubstantiated misgivings – you couldn't even call them suspicion – over the fire at the old sailing school. No point even in admitting to himself that those same misgivings were at the bottom of his generosity towards Tim Howells, who had lost everything that night; his marriage, or what was left of it, his business and his reputation. It was something that couldn't be proved, and even the suspicion was probably down to his own guilty conscience. He should have realised about Cress, they all should have realised, even if it was hard to accept that your own sister, so still more your own child, was completely ... well, inadequate, let's say. But Deb's mum was waiting for him to say something, and so he said, 'Mum said you offered to put her in touch with a private detective.' Another delicate subject between them, as they both knew, but better than the other.

'Yes. I still will, if she would like me to.'

'I think she would,' said Mawgan, without looking at her. He began to play with the knife beside his place. 'It's the not knowing that's hardest. Whatever we found out, if we found out anything at all, has to be better than the nothing we have now. If she's lost, we can't seem to find her, if she's dead, we can't mourn her. What do they call it these days?'

'Closure,' said Dot, although her private opinion was that there could be no such thing. The waiter came to take their order, and when he had gone the discussion seemed to have gone with him. Dot merely said, 'I will find his card to give to your mother when you drive me home,' and Mawgan said, 'Thank you,' and that appeared to be that. Dot wanted to tell him that he shouldn't blame himself, but remembering other occasions when she had tried to interfere for what she felt was someone's own good, she didn't do so. They spoke about general things for a while; Daniel's progress, the coming spring with all it's opportunities for the Fish and the sailing school, Dot's coming move. When they seemed to have run out of small talk, Dot decided to take the bull by the horns, and wring an answer out of him this time.

'Now, tell me about the Dock Inn,' she said. Mawgan gave her a meditative look.

'It was well spotted,' he said, after a pause. 'It's a fine old building, good position, loads of potential. But you were right when you said it was a mess.'

'So, will you be making an offer for it?' asked Dot.

'Would you?' he countered. She thought for a moment, recognising that the question required a sensible answer. After a moment, she said, 'Yes. I think I would. For your particular purpose, I think it's probably ideal. That part of the town will develop along different lines alongside the decline of the fishing industry. I imagine it may become much sought after if the dock becomes a marina.'

'Do you think it will? Is there talk of it?'

'There is always talk,' said Dot. 'However, it seems the obvious future for it. The leisure industry is booming along this coast, and Embridge Harbour offers unusual advantages for shelter and security.'

'That's what I think, too,' said Mawgan.

'So?' Dot raised her eyebrows in a query.

'So yes, I think I'll make 'em an offer. Which is why I wanted to talk to you particular.'

All sorts of things went through Dot's head when he said that, principal among them *he's going to ask for a loan* and a pang of accompanying disappointment. She had begun to think better of him, even if reluctantly. But she was wrong.

'Thing is,' he went on, 'there's a lot needs doing, and it needs to be done right. I can't be here all the time, I got other fish to fry as you know. Howells can oversee the start, report back to me and I can come up if there's any snags, but when he goes to Italy –'

'Italy?' Dot interrupted, startled.

'Yeah. He's going out to work under Luigi for six months, give or take, soon as he's got his bits of paper. Learn the business on the shop floor. Time we can open, round about Christmas I reckon, he'll be ready to take the reins. He's not stupid, Howells. Not all-round stupid, leastways.'

'You've been very good to him,' said Dot, giving credit where it was due.

'Somebody had to be,' said Mawgan. There was a short pause, while they both thought about that, then he went on, 'So I want to ask a favour. It sounds cheek, but I think you might like it.'

492

At that point they were interrupted by the arrival of the food, and when the waiter had finished setting it out, pouring wine, and asking if everything was to their satisfaction, Dot picked up the thread where it had been dropped. Her curiosity was aroused, what could he possibly want from her? 'So what is this favour you want to ask of me?'

Mawgan took a reflective mouthful of his lunch before he answered, then he said, 'By that time, hopefully most of the major building work will be done so long as there's no problems with the sale, and it'll be down to decorating and installing new equipment. You should be finished moving into your new place by then, I thought as you might have time to organise the job.'

'Me?' asked Dot, taken by surprise. He smiled at her.

'Why not you? I seen the job you made of your own place, you got a good eye. I haven't got that, me, I'd just slap a bit of paint around and leave it at that, but I reckon you know enough about interior design and old buildings to oversee a good restoration job. Deb agrees with me, and she tells me you're pretty hot on this heritage lark. I'd like to bring the old place back to its glory days, what d'you think? As a proper business arrangement, o' course.'

Several things went through Dot's head as he waited for her reply. First of all, that he knew what he was talking about, he had done an apprenticeship in the building trade and he was nobody's fool. Second, time might hang heavy on her hands once she had her life reorganised to her satisfaction, and it would take a while for new contacts and interests to fill the void. And last of all, it would be a project after her own heart and she could feel her enthusiasm rising to meet the challenge. What she didn't know, she would enjoy finding out. There would be time while the repair work went on, and the transformation of the old inn from run-down drinking hole to top-notch public house and restaurant would give her immense personal satisfaction. She hadn't had a lot of that in her life, it had been snatched away early.

Mawgan was watching all these different ideas and emotions chase across her face. He said, 'I see you quite like the idea. That's good, because I can't think of anyone better to take it on.'

'I'm sure you could find someone ...' Dot began, automatically putting herself down as she immediately realised. She covered the moment by taking a sip of wine.

'I daresay I could, 's good anyway, but I'm asking you,' said Mawgan. 'Do you want the job, or not?'

'I should love it,' Dot admitted. 'But –'

'Good. Then it's yours.'

'I've not done anything quite like it before,' said Dot.

'Even better. Let's be original.' He raised his own glass. 'Here's to our partnership. It's not before time.'

'And when it's all done,' said Dot, with satisfaction, 'you and Debbie and Daniel will have a perfect reason to come to Embridge. You can stay in that flat –'

'Hardly,' said Mawgan. 'Howells'll be living in that. And anyway, Deb'd kill me if I even suggested it. We'll stay with you, of course. If you want us, that is.'

'Of course I shall want you,' said Dot, and added, to make her intention quite clear, '*All* of you. I shall love having you.'

'Sounds like more'n I deserve,' said Mawgan. Dot decided to leave that alleyway unexplored, a lot of things that had occurred in the last quarter of an hour were more than she deserved, too. She said, 'I shall enjoy working with you, I'm sure.'

'That's good then.' They ate for a while in silence, and then Mawgan said, hesitantly, 'Deb tells me you're going to divorce Jerry. Is that what you want?'

Dot met his eyes across the table, and was surprised to see that he looked slightly uncomfortable. She said, 'It's what you advised.'

Mawgan pulled an expressive face. 'Seems to me I'm going to have to be a bit careful how I go handing out advice these days,' he said. 'Look what I done to Annabel, trying to set her right at school, telling Damien Tregear what he should do, and now you too. You twice. Why don't I never learn to keep my mouth shut?'

'Generally speaking, your advice appears to be excellent,' Dot replied tranquilly. She took another mouthful of her sea bass. 'As for Jerry, what point would there be in continuing in the name of a marriage that was most definitely over? I find,' she went on, amazed to realise that it was true, 'that less and less these days do I care about the outward appearance of things. And that, my dear Mawgan, goes for Kayleigh Tregear as well – I presume that Kayleigh is to whom

494

you were referring just now? No, she is not the friend I would have chosen for my granddaughter, but it seems to me that she is both loyal and protective and, if I believe Susan, that she saved Annabel from a very bad time at school. Annabel,' she continued reflectively, 'was bound to come to grief at that school, I am only surprised that Susan couldn't see it from the first. Sebastian, as it turns out, is quite different.'

'Seb is more careful – or luckier maybe – in his choice of friends,' said Mawgan bluntly. 'He's not so full of himself, neither.'

'That may be so. Annabel, I fear, has learned from my example, she chooses for the wrong reasons and then lives up to them.'

'That's very honest,' said Mawgan.

'And does that surprise you?' When he looked confused and didn't answer, she went on, 'I may be stubborn, misguided and tactless, Mawgan, but I am not stupid. I realise that my troubles are largely self-inflicted, and I hope I am not too proud to learn from it.'

'Well, we all hope that – for ourselves,' Mawgan finished hurriedly.

'For each other, too, Mawgan. That party that Susan and Debbie planned for me at Christmas was a turning point for me, just as I believe that your meeting with Deborah was for you. One should never reject such a second chance.'

Mawgan had spoken before he had fairly thought. 'Oh, it wasn't Deb and Susan thought of that,' he said. Dot looked at him for a moment, her face expressionless. Then,

'Who, then? It wasn't you – it was fairly apparent that you wished yourself elsewhere, at least to begin with. Carl?' She had a soft spot for Carl, and would like to have believed it. But –

'No,' said Mawgan. 'No, it wasn't Carl.'

'Who, then?'

'Oliver,' said Mawgan.

Dot sat very still, her fork suspended in mid air. A dozen emotions chased themselves across her face, all of them unidentifiable, probably even to herself who felt them. She felt unreasonably shaken. Oliver ... Oliver who had made her married life with Jerry such a misery, Oliver who had behaved always as if he hated her, Oliver who had nothing good to say about her and whom she had always misunderstood ...

Oliver had planned that wonderful party that had given her back her beloved daughters when she had thought them lost to her, and by her own fault. Oliver had given her this second chance. *Oliver* ...

'Well, you have surprised me,' she managed at last. Mawgan didn't pretend to misunderstand.

'I think it was his way of saying he was sorry,' he said. 'Like he told me it had to be mine. And he has no idea of exactly how much I've got to be sorry for.'

'And are you? Sorry?'

'Difficult one, that.' Mawgan thought for a minute. 'OK then, try it like this. For what I done because of what you done, no, I'm not sorry. For having done it quite that way, yes I prob'ly am.'

'That's generous,' said Dot, thinking about it. 'I think I feel somewhat the same, indeed. For what I did in the light of what I thought I knew, no, I'm not sorry either. But that I stooped so low as to do it without enquiring further, yes for that I shall always have regrets. I am profoundly ashamed, to be truthful.'

'Both of us was trying to protect Deb,' said Mawgan, and gave a rueful laugh. 'Who don't need it. Deb more'n any of us knows exactly what she's doing.' He picked up the wine bottle and held it over her glass, his head cocked enquiringly. She nodded, laying down her fork.

'That's lovely.' She picked up the refilled glass and took a sip. 'I feel considerably better for this little chat. And thank you.'

'For what, particular?' he asked, surprised.

'I think ...' said Dot, trying to work it out for he deserved an answer, 'I think, for what you tell me concerning Oliver. And for your offer of an immediate goal in a life that seems to be dissolving around me and has yet to regenerate itself. I will not say for forgiveness, for I believe that is something that neither one of us feels.' She looked at him, and was interested to note that he could meet her eyes without flinching. 'You have hidden depths, Mr Angwin.'

'That makes two of us then.' He touched his glass against hers. 'Here's to better times, Mrs Nankervis.'

Dot swallowed. The words stuck in her throat, but she got them out. 'Call me Dorothy. Please.' Mawgan hesitated only fractionally, but she saw it anyway. Some things are beyond invisibly mending, she reflected sadly. Cobbled together was the best they were going to manage.

'OK,' he said, finally. 'To our better times, Dorothy. And may our partnership be a howling success!' And Dot smiled, and said, 'With two such determined and ruthless protagonists as ourselves, I am sure that it will be, Mawgan. And you may consider my part in it as the wedding present that I never gave to you.' She saw that her last words had achieved something that most people had come to consider impossible; she had silenced Mawgan Angwin, and hid a quiet, satisfied smile.

XXV

Over the next eight or ten weeks that led up to Dot's moving day, a great many small things happened, straws that merely blew in the wind, and one or two seminal ones.

Liz's new lodger, for instance, fitted into her life with barely a ripple. He arrived on the evening of the day on which they had made their agreement, moved a big holdall, a laptop and a large camera bag into her spare room, had a shower and a badly needed change of clothes and took her out to dinner at the pub to celebrate their new association. His two friends turned up later on, and she left him there and walked home to settle down with Tib and the telly. When he returned home later, he went off to his room with her mobile and, presumably, went to bed. There was no sound when she went upstairs later, but the thought that he was there, and that he would field any unpleasant phone calls during the night, allowed her to sleep soundly, Tib curled into her back until some time in the early dawn, when he was off about his own business in the quiet garden.

All three of them met again at eight o'clock over coffee for Liz, cat biscuits for Tib, and a large breakfast for Mike. There had been no calls in the night, he reported, and by eight-thirty he was gone and didn't return until after six o'clock. After a shower he went off to join his friends again, taking the spare door key with him, and Liz didn't see him again until he put his head round the sitting room door to say goodnight. The same pattern was repeated over the next few nights, and Liz tried not to feel disappointed. After all, she had only asked him to be her lodger, and that was all that he had agreed.

There had been no more phone calls. She wondered if Paul knew she had a watchdog in the house, and found the thought, which should have comforted her, made her uneasy.

Explaining Mike to her family, on the other hand, was unexpectedly easy, suspiciously so indeed, which on present form was likely to prove a disappointment for them.

'I've taken a lodger,' she told her mother. 'He's working at the garage, and needed a temporary room.'

'A man?' Isobel asked, doubtfully. 'Is that wise, Liz? After all ...'

'Mum, don't be so dated,' Liz told her. 'Anyway, it isn't what you think, I didn't just pick him off the street. He's Susan's sister-in-law's brother, and practically family.

'In that case,' said Isobel, more happily, 'you had better bring him over some time. He and your dad would have something to talk about, which would make a change from Paul. How is Paul these days? We don't seem to hear so much about him.'

'Don't get ideas,' said Liz, ignoring the question about Paul. 'It's a temporary business arrangement, is all.'

'If he's practically Susan's brother-in-law, he's practically mine as well,' Isobel pointed out. 'Anyway, he's a newcomer here. He'd like to meet people, I daresay. And he's met your Dad already, I believe.'

'I'll run it past him,' said Liz.

Alice's reaction was more predictable. 'You sneaky bugger, you!' she exclaimed when Liz told her. 'Have you told Mum? What did she say?'

'She invited him to lunch on Sunday,' said Liz.

'And is he going to come?'

'I haven't asked him yet.' Liz eyed her sister coldly. 'And nobody has asked you, either, so less of the "come".'

'What did he say when he found you knew his sister?' Alice asked, dismissing the last comment as frivolous. She would be asked, they both knew it, her whole family would be if Sergeant Mike accepted the invitation. They might not go, though, she thought immediately afterwards. They wouldn't want to scare him off. Paul might creep back in.

'I don't *know* her.' Liz denied. 'I've met her about twice, is all, because of Auntie Sue. I don't know her well enough to call her a friend, or not as I define one.'

'You like her, though, don't you?'

'Yes. But that's as far as it goes.'

'You can improve on that, though,' said Alice, cheerfully.

'Ginger moustache,' Liz reminded her, knowing it was pointless. 'Ginger hair. Army background. An NCO, which is even worse if anything. Red-headed bully boy!'

'And yet, you've invited him into your home,' Alice said, thoughtfully, and Liz said, as she had said to Isobel, 'Don't go getting ideas.'

When she gave her mother's invitation to Mike, to her surprise he seemed quite pleased.

'That's kind of her,' he said. 'I'm getting a bit sick of the bar menu down the road, to be honest.'

'You could always try the restaurant,' Liz pointed out, and he laughed.

'Every night? I'm not *that* well paid!'

This hadn't occurred to Liz before, she realised that it should have. She said, 'You don't have to go out *every* night, you know. I can as easily cook for two as one, and it'd be nice to have company over the telly now and then.'

There was a silence, as each of them looked at the other, and both of them knew that Liz's invitation, and his possible acceptance, would constitute a change in their relationship that might lead ... well, anywhere, if they were being honest. Finally, Mike said, 'That would be nice. Now and then, I don't want to encroach.'

'You wouldn't be,' Liz told him.

'Right, then. Thank you.'

'And do I tell Mum we'll be there on Sunday?'

'It would be rude to refuse, wouldn't it? Yes, I'd like that. Thank her, too, will you?'

'If she asks Alice and Gil & Co. as well, you might live to regret it,' Liz warned him, and he laughed.

'You forget I'm Candy's uncle.'

When it came down to it, Alice found herself unable to resist the expected invitation. It was asking too much of her kind intentions, so that when Mike arrived at the house with Liz he found it overflowing with energetic children in an all too familiar way that had the effect of making him feel immediately at home, which had been one of the arguments that Isobel had used to change Alice's mind.

'We don't want him to feel that we're looking him over, like a prize bull at a show,' Isobel had said. 'A family lunch with the twins and William there to make it completely informal will be far, far better, so please don't let me down, Alice.'

'Put like that, how can I refuse?' Alice said. 'Did Liz make you think there was ... well, anything going on there?'

'Such as what?' asked Isobel briskly dismissive, but immediately spoiled it, by saying, 'You've met him, haven't you Alice? What do you think?' But sisterly loyalty prevented Alice from saying more than, 'He'd be a great improvement on Paul, but don't get your hopes up. I think it's a case of "just good friends",' and wondered if she believed it.

Liz had wondered if Mike had accepted the invitation simply out of politeness, or because he had nothing better to do and it was a free meal. She had forgotten, if she had ever really considered it, that he came from a large family himself and so failed to take into account that he had probably missed them over the years of his absence. He came with her to Isobel's Sunday lunch in the mood to be pleased, and therefore succeeded in pleasing with no effort at all. There was only one rocky moment, when Lulu asked, in all innocence, 'Mike, are you Auntie Liz's new boyfriend?'

Liz went scarlet. Alice grinned appreciatively. Isobel was about to shush her granddaughter, but Mike said peacefully, 'No. But I'm working on it.'

'Good,' said Lulu, nodding her satisfaction. 'You're much, much nicer than Paul. Almost as good as Carl.'

Isobel found her voice. 'That'll do, Lu,' she said. Lulu, knowing perfectly well that she had spoken out of turn, said airily, 'I just wanted to know,' and since everyone else round the table had wanted to know too, that rather put a stopper on the discussion. George stepped in hurriedly with a query as to how things were going at the garage, and the moment was glossed over.

When lunch was finished with no more unfortunate social bellyflops, the three children were sent off to take the dogs – there were two of them – for a walk while the grown-ups had a peaceful cup of coffee.

'Sorry about Lulu,' Isobel murmured to Mike, under cover of a more general conversation. 'She really shouldn't have said that.'

'Don't worry about it, I didn't mind,' Mike said, and Isobel added, before she could stop herself, 'And are you? Working on it, that is?'

'I like the idea,' Mike told her, 'but I haven't yet put it into practice.' He glanced across the room to Liz, giggling with her sister over some joke. She was looking particularly fetching today, he thought. She had put in her contact lenses for the occasion, and without her rather severe glasses she looked far more the merry Liz that he had seen and begun to appreciate over the christening weekend. No stress, he concluded, and not for the first time wondered about the absent, but determined not to be forgotten, Paul. He would have liked to ask Isobel about him, but he was hardly on those terms either with Liz or her family. He was wondering how he could put such a question without raising others, best left unasked, when George engaged his attention and their common interest kept Mike occupied until Gil announced that he had business to attend to even if the rest of them had time to loll around all afternoon, and the party broke up.

Mike drove Liz's Mercedes back to the village, and Liz sat beside him in a pensive silence that he didn't disturb. It was only when they drew up outside the cottage that she asked him, exactly as her mother had, 'And are you?'

'Am I what?' asked Mike, surprised.

'Working on it. Working on me. Don't play the innocent, Michael Wainwright, you know perfectly well what I'm talking about.'

'Oh. That.' Mike looked at her, rubbing the end of his nose thoughtfully. 'Well, I don't know how you feel, but we seem to get on all right. I realise you're on the rebound, so nothing serious of course. Just friends who maybe go around together a bit?'

Was she on the rebound? Liz wondered, and rather thought not. However she didn't say so. Instead, she said, 'Well, I suppose, until we've sorted out Paul, or until you meet some other girl, it would pass the time ...'

'...since we're sharing the same house,' said Mike, in a reasonable tone of voice that made her look at him suspiciously. His eyes gleamed green and wicked.

'You,' Liz told him, 'are taking the mick, Mick!'

'But alas,' said Mike despondently, 'it's *only* the same house we share.'

'Back in your basket,' Liz told him. She opened her door, feeling in her pocket for the keys. 'Are you coming in, or are you spending the rest of the afternoon there?'

He hesitated. 'Look, Liz. Joking apart, I don't want to crowd you, my brown-eyed girl. I can amuse myself, you know.'

'I bet you can.' She paused. '*What* did you just call me?'

'It's a song,' he explained. 'It just fits you. Listen, it's a lovely afternoon, and we've eaten a huge lunch. How d'you fancy a walk up to the tor to work it off?'

'Cheap date, cheapskate,' Liz told him. She looked up at the blue sky arching above them and felt the cool breeze on her cheek promising spring. The birds were beginning to argue about nesting sites, the sun was shining, what a dreadful cliché, to be sure; he seemed to generate them. But it was a good idea. 'I'll have to change my shoes.' she said.

'I'll fetch my camera while you do it.' They exchanged a smile. OK, Liz thought, just friends then, I can live with that. She would make him keep to it, and see what happened next. He was a great deal too full of himself, ex-Sergeant Michael Wainwright. She recalled that she had meant to do a bit of work when they got back from lunch and a bubble of laughter rose in her throat, so much for not encroaching! She didn't tell him so, however.

The wind had more bite to it than it had seemed as they sat outside the cottage, their walk up to the tor was brisk, although Mike did pause once or twice to take photos.

'You do a lot of photography?' Liz asked him, shivering when they paused in the chill breeze that whistled round them as they breasted the hill.

'Quite a bit. Only as a hobby though.' He noticed her shiver and plunged a hand into the pocket of his padded camouflage jacket. 'Here – take this. Keep the top of your head warm and the rest of you will be warmer.'

"This" was a khaki knitted hat. Liz put it on and pulled it over her ears and down to her eyebrows, grinning at him, and he lifted the camera he was still holding and took a picture before she had time to react.

'Brilliant,' he said, reviewing it on the little screen. 'Come on then, up we go.' He tucked the camera back into its bag and took her arm. 'Last one to the top's a sissy!'

They arrived back at the cottage in the early dusk, for the clocks had yet to go forward, and Liz dumped her coat in the hall and headed for the kitchen. 'Time to put the kettle on. Or better still, open a bottle. Red or white or beer?'

'Beer? You have beer?' He followed her through the study and flung his own coat over the back of a kitchen chair.

'Paul did,' Liz said, and right on cue, her mobile rang. She picked it up without thinking and said 'Hullo.'

The same heavy breathing. The same whispering voice. Without speaking, she handed it to Mike and he put it to his ear. She watched his laughing face darken as he listened. After a minute he switched it off and looked at her, all laughter gone.

'Shit,' he said. 'Was that him? For sure, I mean?'

'I think so,' said Liz. 'It has to be, doesn't it? Who else would bother?'

'That's the sort of thing you had in the middle of the night?' Liz nodded dumbly. 'Shit,' he said again. 'No wonder it unsettled you. It's bad enough in daylight, with company.'

'You thought I was making a fuss about nothing, didn't you?' Liz accused, but he shook his head.

'Not after seeing those pictures. Mark had printed them off, did you know? He found them in the bowels of your computer. Come to think, *bowels* is just the right place for them.' He paused, looking at her seriously. 'We have to stop him, Liz, this is downright sick. Are you sure you don't want to go to the police?'

'What good would it do? You check, if you don't believe me, the number will be withheld.'

Mike did check, but he knew she would be right. He said, 'The police have facilities that we don't, Liz. You should tell them.'

'He's not daft enough to be using his own phone. My guess is a different call box every time.'

'You don't write thrillers, do you?' He raised an eyebrow. A ginger eyebrow, Liz reminded herself firmly.

'No.' She went to the fridge and took out a can of beer and a half-empty bottle of Merlot. The pleasant day that they had spent, the family lunch, the companionable walk to the tor, had gone abruptly into the past. 'What am I going to do about him?' she asked miserably. 'I can't live like this for ever Mike. I can't!'

'You could change your phone number. Buy a new simcard. Like you did with your email.'

'I could. But that feels like giving in to him, and he'd like that. After all, I do have the option of hanging up on him.'

'He'll get tired of it eventually.' But he sounded doubtful. Liz handed him the can and reached for a glass, but paused with it in her hand. A wave of panic, totally at variance with her brave words, swept through her. 'Tib – where's Tib? He isn't here!' The glass rattled onto the table against the wine bottle and she ran to the back door, pulling it open and calling. There was no sign of the cat, but then cats are not good at coming when they're called. She ran out into the garden and began to search in increasing panic, looking for what, she wasn't sure. A striped furry body perhaps, friendly purr silenced for ever in order to make her sorry, but she couldn't even put that into thought, never mind words. After a few minutes Mike followed her. He put his arms around her.

'It's all right Liz. He's snoring in the chair in your sitting room.'

'Oh God!' She turned to him and buried her face against him. 'Oh Mike, I'm sorry, I'm so sorry, what a fool! Only, I thought ...'

'He's really got you going, hasn't he?' said Mike angrily.

'Over a cat – just a cat. What's the matter with me?' Liz tried to pull herself together, but that moment of blind panic had left her shaking harder than the wind on the tor.

'You love him,' said Mike. 'It's not stupid, Liz. You love Tib, and Paul hurt him.' He tightened his arms and then let her go. 'We'll get him one way or another. Come on, let's have that drink.' And when they did catch up with Paul Attwood, he thought, as they went back into the warm kitchen, he would strangle the bastard with his bare hands and string him up for the crows!

At around the same time, Tom Casson made a serious tactical misjudgement. He had rung Susan, contrite and apologetic and pleading for a second chance, earnestly promising reformation in the future, and received for his pains a categorical repulse.

'You must think I'm stupid!' she had told him, roundly. 'You forget, I've heard it all before and I know exactly what it's worth!'

'No Susan, listen, please! This time it's different!'

'Oh? In what way, for instance?'

Tom's voice assumed a note of desperation. 'I've learned my lesson, I promise – what Lorraine has done has –'

'What *Lorraine* has done?' Susan interrupted, furiously. 'The way I hear it, *you* got the sack for harassment, and Lorraine did exactly what I did, she found it the final straw and she dumped you. And are you now saying you didn't deserve it?'

'I couldn't seem to find my way with you gone,' he pleaded. 'We had good times Susan, you know we did. And you always stood by me, you weren't like Lorraine. I must have been bewitched.'

'I stood by my children. Not you,' Susan told him, and forbore only with a heroic effort to remind him that if he hadn't so rudely interrupted her, she would have told him she was leaving him before he told her the same.

'Then stand by them now. They need their own Daddy, not some lusty young stud. And I need them. I never realised how much I would miss them.'

'You haven't missed them enough to contact them. Not even a postcard, Tom, since Christmas! And how much trouble is it to just pick up the phone and ask them how they're doing? Annabel cries herself to sleep over you, did you know that? She thinks you don't love them.' Tom was silent, and she went on, 'No, Tom. All you want is your nice comfortable life back, with me picking up all the bills and you doing exactly what you please. Go and live with mummy and daddy, they might just stand for it. It's about your mark!'

'They don't want me to,' said Tom sullenly, and Susan laughed. She bit her lip immediately afterwards, but the laugh was still there, trembling over the wire. Tom said, 'You might at least ask them how they feel about it – the children. It's about them as well as you, as you keep on telling me. It's about their welfare and happiness, as well as your sexual gratification. If Annabel cries –'

Susan bit down hard on a justifiable retort as to just *whose* gratification was he referring to? that would have precipitated a flaming row with which she couldn't be bothered. She said, 'Annabel's learning. The tears get less and less. They're settling down, Tom, in almost every way they've never been so happy, and if they've learned lessons no child needs to learn at least they don't need or deserve revision. Leave them alone, you've done enough damage.'

'I love you all,' cried Tom, playing his ace with a break in his voice. 'I didn't realise. I've been a fool, I admit that, but I'm the children's father and I miss you all. I'm sorry to the bottom of my heart. Surely all that counts for something?'

'Nothing whatever, believe me,' Susan told him. 'And you certainly didn't seem to realise you were the children's father in the past! Go learn to stand on your own feet, Thomas.' And she put the phone down. He heard the click and his heart sank, self-pity obliterating even his resentment at the way she had twisted his own words round to attack him. No job, no income, no welcome anywhere. He conveniently ignored the settlement he had received from the sale of the matrimonial home, which he should have known, as an accountant, was sufficient, if cannily invested, to keep him the rest of his life without his ever needing to find another job, even if he bought himself a small flat with part of it, and felt desperately ill-used. There had been nothing in it, nothing in any of it, he loved his family, he told himself, and as for that bitch at the office, she had too high an opinion of herself and a very malicious imagination! He couldn't help what he was, could he? Any more than Susan could help what *she* was. If she had loved him, she would have forgiven him, but no, she was too busy being clever!

He failed to draw from this the obvious conclusion, she hadn't loved him. Instead, he thought of the one ally that he could be sure of, the person who had supported him nobly throughout his abortive custody battle for the children and could be trusted to support him now, even if his own parents had let him down. He went to visit his ex-mother-in-law.

He had failed also to notice what was happening around him to other people. When Dot had encouraged him in his custody battle, she had been desperately afraid of losing everything: her children, her grandchildren, the lot. She had since learned that her fears had been groundless, people who really care for you aren't that easy to lose, however much you may deserve it. She was bitterly ashamed of how she had misjudged them all – including Oliver as it had turned out – and she was therefore far from overjoyed to find Tom on her doorstep with his burden of self-inflicted woes when she had so many better things to attend to. Her invitation to come in was grudging, and she didn't offer him coffee.

They sat in the denuded drawing-room, among boxes that Dot had been carefully packing with her precious china and glass from the cabinet when the doorbell interrupted her, and she said, 'So what may I do for you, Tom?' in a tone of voice that should have warned him. Dot had had a bellyful of Tom lately both from Sally and from Ingrid, who was frankly disgusted with him; her sympathy and patience were alike exhausted.

Tom had decided on a disarmingly rueful openness as being his best weapon. He said, 'Dorothy, I need your advice,' in the manner of one laying all his cards on the table.

'In what way, exactly?' Dot asked him. 'It seems to me that your troubles are all of your own making, and the only person who can help you is yourself, Tom. But tell me, if you feel differently. I will of course advise you if I can.' She sounded tepid, even to her own ears, but Tom was so self-absorbed that he didn't even notice.

'I've made a terrible mess of everything,' he confided. Dot couldn't disagree with him, so she said nothing, and he went on, 'I don't know what came over me!' He waited for her to say something sympathetic and comforting, but instead she said, 'Sexual desire came over you, Tom, which you had not the strength to resist, and as you well know,' and felt that she had really been rather restrained in her answer.

'I can't help the way I am,' Tom protested. 'I like women – they like me. What am I supposed to do? There was never anything in it, nothing serious, just a bit of fun. I was married to Susan, I loved her, I loved my children! She made too much of it.'

'If you really did love her, then you had a very individual way of showing it,' Dot told him roundly. 'I understand you had already asked Lorraine to marry you before Susan even told you she was going to leave you.' She added, because she couldn't resist it, 'And what you were meant to do, Tom, since apparently you cannot work it out for yourself, was to keep your hands to yourself and your equipment in your trousers.' Oops! That hadn't come out of her mouth quite the way she had it arranged in her head. Tom looked stunned. Since she found herself with the advantage, Dot followed it up with, 'And please don't give me any rubbish about Susan being frigid. Firstly, she is not, and never was, and secondly, if that was the case, why are you here now? I am assuming you want me to intercede with her on your behalf, now that you have lost your job and Lorraine has had the sense to give you your marching orders.'

'It was a mutual deci –'

'My understanding is that she threw you out and threw your possessions after you,' Dot interrupted smoothly. Tom said lamely, 'Anyone can make mistakes. I'm only human.'

'Apparently,' said Dot, with a look that made him feel about six inches high. There was a pause, during which Dot rose to her feet and resumed her packing. Tom sat there, wondering where to take his argument next. He had a feeling that there was no point in claiming that he had been unfairly dismissed and that the woman had made too much out of nothing; judgement would have already been passed on that one thanks to Ingrid Hetherington, a cow if ever he met one. Even so, he felt impelled to continue on his chosen path with much the same recklessness as one who drives through a red light in heavy traffic. There was only one viable shot in his locker that he could see. He loaded it into the barrel.

'Susan says that Annabel cries herself to sleep every night. I can't bear that Dorothy, she's my little girl. I want to make amends. I want to be a proper father again. I'll swear on the bible if you want, there'll be no more affairs. I'll do anything, just tell me what. Please. Annabel ...'

Dot put down the dish she was holding, with great care. She turned to him again.

'I am hearing a lot of the personal pronoun, Tom,' she said. 'A whole catalogue of self-justification and oh, poor misunderstood me. However, I hear no penitence for the humiliation you inflicted on Susan, over years I understand. And as for being a proper father, to my present knowledge you were never that, and nor do I hear mention of Sebastian in your pleas now, I presume because his attitude cannot be turned to your advantage. I understand that you may arrange to see them both at any time you wish. You have been unemployed for almost four weeks now, Tom. How many trips have you made to Cornwall in that time?' Tom said nothing, and she went on, 'It doesn't become you to use Annabel's distress as a weapon. Those children are happier, and far better off, than they have ever been.'

'It isn't suitable, Carl Colenso living with them, you must see that. Susan isn't even planning to marry him – and if you're criticising me, what about her? At least I never flaunted my affairs under the noses of my children!'

Dot gave him a long, cold look. 'Shall we consider all of that unsaid, Tom?'

'What's sauce for the goose –' he began, and then stopped, reddening.

'Let me give you some advice, since you say you came here to ask for it,' Dot said to him. 'Stop feeling sorry for yourself, your wounds are all self-inflicted. Find yourself somewhere to live, find yourself another job. Keep your hands off married women and safely in your pockets. Try to resist telling malicious lies about either my daughter or Lorraine, or on any other subject that may seem expedient. Make an effort to make your parents proud of you, your behaviour has caused them deep distress. And rather than using your spurious affection for your children to achieve your own ends, show them some genuine affection. Visit them. Take them on outings. Send them postcards to tell *them* you love them still, because it seems to me that you only tell the rest of us. Make yourself take on the semblance of a man. And if you value your skin, do nothing to damage the relationship they have with Carl, who is a better father to them than you have any hope of ever being.'

'Ho!' said Tom, rising to his feet. 'I'm not afraid of that toyboy!'

Dot looked him over in a considering way that made his palms sweat. 'Oh,' she said gently, 'I wasn't referring to Carl. I was referring to myself.'

Tom turned on his heel, and made for the door. There he paused, and flung back over his shoulder, 'All right, feel that way about it, I can see he's got your vote. But remember this, while you believe the sun shines out of his arse – ocean racing is a rough, dirty business and he was very, very good at it! And it's *my* children involved here!' The door slammed behind him and the plates remaining in the cabinet rattled in sympathy. A moment later the front door slammed too. Dot stood for a moment, listening, and then dusted her palms together and continued her packing. She had been wanting to say all of that for quite a long time, she realised. It was a few minutes before she realised exactly why it gave her such satisfaction, and when she did, she allowed herself a quiet smile.

It was the first time for a long time, possibly ever, that she had launched her ammunition at the correct target and she had done it in defence of her own – her own child, grandchildren, friends. And

510

if there had also been an element of revenge there, then for once she felt that she was entitled. His cavalier treatment of Henry's daughter was unforgivable.

Sally was a good friend, she reflected as she wrapped the next precious ornament in bubblewrap, and she was fond of her, but Irwin was right, she had spoiled her only child. She, and all those silly women who had been bedazzled by his good looks and selfishly ignored the fact that he was a married man. She thought about the self-justifying panegyric on the subject of Thomas Casson to which she had just been forced to listen and reflected, with grief, that she herself had fallen for his specious charm too when she singled him out for Susan all those years ago.

Maybe he would take her advice to heart, more probably he wouldn't. For Sally's sake she would like to see him pull himself together, but Susan was well out of it. If it wasn't for the existence of Annabel and Sebastian, she would feel deeply responsible for what she had done to Susan. As she did feel deeply responsible for what she had done to Helen, she thought now, for hadn't she been just the same as those silly women who pursued Tom? Wrap it up how she would, she had wanted Jerry for herself, if not actually in her bed, in her life. And she had got him in the end, and what joy had it brought any of them?

Deborah, she answered herself, and was that justification? But to that question she knew that there was no answer.

Easter Saturday, when the first of the sailing school's clients were due, signalled the start of a long and largely lonely summer to come. One more night, and then he's gone all week, every week, Susan thought desolately as she stared at her computer screen. Everyone was out except herself and Loki, the children and Carl down by the river and Clinker along with them. Saturday was supposed to be Carl's day off, she thought, with a touch of resentment. She had been looking forward to a last day together, but he had gone off immediately after breakfast, saying that this first week there was a lot to organise. At least it gave her a chance to put in some work on her degree.

Which she did, for quite some time. In fact, she managed to lose herself in how to identify Neolithic pottery quite successfully until Loki, considerably bigger and bolder by this time, leapt onto her desk and attempted to make himself at home on the printout of her current thesis. She dropped her hands from the keyboard and looked at him. He began to wash his paws, like all cats engaged in something they aren't supposed to be doing, refusing to meet her eyes directly.

'He spoils you,' she told him, without specifying who "he" might be since it was sufficiently obvious. 'You're going to miss him too, aren't you? Seven and a half months, Loki, think of it! Seven and a half months when he'll only be home a couple of nights a week, how will we bear it? I've got used to him around ...' She picked up the little cat and stroked him. 'Last summer, it was wonderful just to have him for that much. How spoiled I've got during the winter!' Loki, impatient of such sentimental rubbish, wriggled and slid through her hands to thump onto the floor. He gave her a reproachful look and jumped back onto her thesis where he began to settle down. Susan could have taken this chance to return to her studies, after all the substance of the thesis was stored on the computer and thus available to her without inviting further disturbance, but instead she found herself leaning her elbows on the table and staring blankly at the screen. It was impossible to concentrate; she was already missing Carl more than she would have thought possible. Realistically, she knew, he would never be around every day of every year, one or other of his different jobs would always take him away now and then; research, lecture tours, events that required his presence as a journalist, but at least some of those she would probably be able to go with him. That was fair enough, they weren't joined at the hip. But two miserable nights and one miserable day for the whole of a long, long summer looked unbearable in prospect. It would be very hard on the children, she wasn't sure if they had realised.

And me, and me, and me ...

And he wasn't even gone yet, so what did that make her? A sentimental, possessive twit, that's what!

At this point in her ever-more-negative thinking, the telephone rang and made her jump. Loki leapt off the desk, equally startled, and she picked it up in relief. Even a nuisance call would be an improvement on the last quarter of an hour. But it wasn't a nuisance call. It was Debbie.

'Suse?'

'Hi Deb. What can I do for you?'

'A good question. Can you meet us at the Fish for lunch?' That was unexpected, but probably better than continuing her plunge into gloom. Susan said, 'The children are supposed to be back here for that. If I bring them, I suppose.'

'No, it's not that sort of lunch, more of a business lunch really. Mrs Phil has offered to make them all a picnic and keep an eye on them while they eat it.'

'Business?' asked Susan, knitting her brows. 'I'm not involved in your business, Deb.'

'You'd be surprised,' her sister told her. 'We've had a very peculiar morning, Suse. Do you remember what we were talking about just before Christmas?'

Susan did, of course. 'About shore-based courses?' It had sounded wonderful at the time, now, faced with reality, it was more like something and nothing. She began to be a little ashamed of herself. 'You're definitely doing them, then?'

'Oh yes, they're in the brochure. There are one or two bookings, and we've picked out a boat and are getting a survey done as we speak. But that's not it ...' Debbie hesitated. 'A bloke came by this morning, asking if we had a job for him as an instructor for the summer.'

'Ideal,' said Susan.

'Well, possibly. It's one thing to ask. He heard about us through the sailing club, and dropped in on the off chance – he and his wife were down here at Easter, looking for a cottage. They live in London, but keep a holiday home and a boat along the south coast somewhere – Poole, or Lymington, one of those places – but she's a potter, and she wants to be in a place where things are ... well, craftier, I suppose, and he's had enough of commuting to work every day. Children all grown up and flown the nest, so they thought they'd sell up everything and come and live the good life here in Cornwall while they were still young enough to enjoy it.'

'Has he got the necessary bits of paper?' asked Susan, ever practical.

'He brought them with him. He's been involved with sail training schemes connected with his sailing club. He was going to sell the boat, but he said perhaps we could rent it off him. It's an idea, if we could afford to do it, but ... He seemed like a nice bloke,' she ended,

'So, did you snatch him up?' asked Susan.

'Not then and there, although we may if it all scans out. We sent him away and asked him to come back when we'd thought about it – we already have a possible instructor lined up for the new boat, so ... anyway, we had a cup of coffee in the office, and things got rather surreal from then on.'

'I think I can guess,' said Susan, slowly.

'Yes. You probably can. Only Carl won't commit himself until we've talked with you.'

'I see. Well ...' Somewhere in the background she heard the back door opening, and shutting again. Footsteps crossed the kitchen tiles, she knew whose they would be. 'All right Deb. So long as the children are looked after and fed, I'll meet you for lunch. What time?'

'Can you make it about 12.30? We'll have people start arriving this afternoon, we'll need to be back.'

'Fine. See you then.' She put the phone back on its rest, very carefully, and spun her chair round to face the door. Carl leaned in the doorway, watching her. He said, 'Sorry Susie. I didn't mean to put you on the spot. It's just the way it happened.' He pushed himself off the doorpost and came towards her. 'I didn't expect Deb to ring you quite so quickly.'

'It doesn't matter,' said Susan. She got to her feet and met him halfway, putting her arms around him and feeling his around her shoulders. She rested her head against his chest, breathing slowly. 'Do you really want to do this? You've enjoyed working for the sailing school.'

'That was then. This is now. And I want to be with you.'

'I want you to be with me, too. So, you're going for it?'

'If you're sure.'

'If *I'm* sure? It has nothing to do with me.'

'It has everything to do with you, as you very well know.'

Susan said, slowly, 'You are not Tom Casson. I believe in you. I'll back you every bit of the way, because I believe that you'll succeed but I don't care if you don't. And anyway,' she raised her face then and grinned at him, 'I saw the letter. If total strangers are prepared to gamble a six-figure sum on you, who am I to hold back? Go for it, I say!' Then, when he said nothing, she went on. 'That day when you first mentioned it, I was in a bad mood. I was resenting Tom because his idiotic behaviour had forced me into something I didn't want to do, even though I knew I had to, and I took it out on you. I'm sorry. I wasn't thinking properly. Money is not an issue between you and me. You don't depend on me, and I can't see that you ever will.'

She thought that he might say something modest and appreciative in reply, but he didn't. Instead, he said, 'It must be very hard, being a woman with money. You'd have to have the self-confidence of ... of that cat, to carry it off.'

'I was just unlucky. Debbie carries it off all right.'

'Debbie's situation is utterly different in every way,' said Carl. He glanced at his watch. 'Lunch, then?'

The subject was closed, and Susan was glad of it. She kissed him and was about to step back when to her surprise his grip tightened on her arms.

'Marry me, Susie. Not today, not tomorrow. When you're ready. Will you?' and Susan said, giving more ground than she would have believed that she dared, 'If I ever marry anyone again, Carl, it'll be you.'

There was a moment's pause before Carl nodded slowly. 'OK. I'll settle for that. Now come along, or we're going to be late.'

Debbie and Roger were already installed at a table by the window when they arrived at the Fish.

'We've ordered,' Debbie told them. 'Get yourselves organised and come and sit down.' She gave them a close look, but made no comment and Susan wondered if they looked as dizzy as she felt and stole a glance at Carl as they went up to the bar. He was much as usual, she decided, although perhaps a bit too much as usual for a man on the edge of a life-changing decision. He caught her look and grinned at her.

'Champagne?' he asked. 'No, perhaps better not. Deb might take it the wrong way.'

'A Stella, and a ham sandwich, and don't forget we're eating tonight.' The last meal, apart from breakfast tomorrow, that they would have together for a week. It felt less daunting than it had an hour ago.

'Go and join Deb and Roger. I'll bring it across.'

'I'll wait. Let's face them together.'

When they finally joined the others, Debbie immediately declared the meeting open, saying, 'There can't have been a *more* extraordinary general meeting in the history of general meetings. I take it you're *au fait* with developments, Suse?'

'Yes I am, but apart from saying that I'll agree with anything Carl agrees with you, I still don't see that it's any of my business. You and I discussed the possibility last year, Deb. I don't think there's anything to add to that.'

'Did you, indeed?' said Carl, raising an eyebrow.

'Only in general terms,' Debbie assured him. 'It was inevitable, eventually. What we didn't expect was the six-figure capital injection, or come to that, the contraction of the time scale brought about by our visitor this morning. Those two things change everything. And it does have something to do with you, Suse. You're the one that's going to notice more change than we do – after all, so far as we're concerned, when he was actually working, he was never here.'

'I know the feeling,' Susan agreed, meaning something rather different. Debbie sighed, perhaps with fellow feeling. She said, 'Since we're already a limited company, it's simply a matter of doing the paperwork, and since Dad is our solicitor, and Val Harries is our accountant, there's no problems there. It's just a matter of the timing, and that rather depends on our friend this morning.'

'He said he could he down here by Whitsun, if he left his wife to clear up in London,' said Roger.

'Had he asked her?' asked Susan, curiously.

'Since he must have realised we'd need him at the beginning of the season if we needed him at all, I imagine so,' Debbie answered her.

'If we use his boat, and he doesn't therefore need to sell it to finance his new lifestyle, then he can live on it,' Carl pointed out. 'I did, after all.'

'We never paid you rent for yours,' said Debbie, half-regretfully.

'But I'm a director. *Hierax* was my stake in the business.'

'It seems a bit like dumping you when we've no further need of you,' said Debbie. 'Do you mind? We are rather jumping at the chance, but it isn't like *that*.'

'Believe me, I need to be dumped. This is my big opportunity. I can't afford to screw it up, there are too many writers about at least as good as me, and some much better.'

'It seems such a long way from where we all began.' Debbie spoke wistfully.

'It's called success,' Carl told her. Susan looked at Roger.

'How about you, Roj? You're being very quiet. Are you happy about it all?'

For a minute, Roger said nothing. He looked at his hands, clasped around his glass, and seemed to be choosing his words. Denise, the barmaid, arrived with their lunches and had gone again before he found the ones he was searching for.

'I'm not sure how I feel, to be honest – and I may as well be. I can't put money into the business, I feel like a bit of an also-ran. The junior director, hardly qualifying for the title.'

'The place wouldn't run without you,' said Debbie, quietly. 'We started it together, the three of us. All of us put in equal time and effort to make it a success. Carl is withdrawing most of that time, and putting in capital to keep his seat on the board. You don't have to do that. It's his circumstances that are changing. Not yours.'

'I know. I can't help the way I feel.'

Carl shifted in his chair. He said, 'Roger, I'm about to make a confession that's probably, by this time, sufficiently obvious anyway. Right from the start I never had the same involvement as you. I was in it because it was opportune, and right then I needed the money. I never intended to stay for more than the first season, but I got hooked, and one of the things that's hooked me is the commitment of you and Deb, it's compelling. I don't want to let you both down now because things are working out for me, and that's what I'd do if I just walked away and burdened the business with more expense when it's really starting to take off. I've got to put the money somewhere, it can't just sit around doing nothing. I choose to invest it in you two, and in the bridge that carried me across. I've never had your loyalty to the business – for goodness' sake, I walked out once before and left you stranded! Maybe this is my apology.' He paused. 'Shit, I didn't mean to say half of that.'

Debbie said, 'You're the kingpin, Roj. We built the whole thing round your input, you and I. If you don't realise that, I'm telling you now.'

Roger rose to his feet abruptly. 'Another round, everyone? I'm going to get another beer anyway.' He gathered up the empty glasses and headed off. Carl made a movement as if to follow, but Susan put a hand on his arm.

'No, wait Carl. He wants five minutes to himself. And I want to say something. Not that it's any of my business, so shoot me down if you want. Just remember you invited me to sit in on this meeting while you do it.'

Debbie and Carl looked at her, and she stared back defiantly. Finally, Debbie nodded. 'OK, go ahead. What do you want to say?'

'Just this,' said Susan. There was no time to mess about. 'What you both just said to Roger is perfectly true. And although I know that he's drawn money from the business as salary for the work and commitment he gives, have you ever given him a bonus?'

'Well ... no,' said Debbie. 'There's never been enough money around these first couple of years, and it never occurred to me – to any of us. We've none of us had anything extra, it's all gone back in.' She exchanged a glance with Carl and swiftly lowered her eyes to her half-eaten sandwich.

'Then do it now. Or not right now, when you've had a chat with Val and Dad and the dust has had time to settle. And award it in shares, he's worked for them. He has as much of a right to them as Carl has for the shares *he's* worked for in his own interests.'

'She's right, Deb,' said Carl. 'I'm in favour, anyway.'

'I should have done it right at the start,' said Debbie, in tones of mortification. 'God, I am a self-centred cow! There's something else too that I didn't see at the time, and I could kick myself for – isn't there, Carl?'

'Me?' asked Carl. 'I've got no quarrel with you, Deb.'

'Then you should have. It never entered my head until Christmas, listening to people at the club. It's been haunting my sleep since, how could I have been so crass? All that time and effort I spent on persuading Oliver to teach navigation in the winter – it was you I should have been asking, wasn't it?'

'Think nothing of it, Deb,' Carl disclaimed.. 'I'm not nursing a grudge, and anyway, I think you did the right thing – Oliver's is a name everyone knows, he's a charismatic person with a romantic history that draws them in, and he knows his subject as well as I do. As for me, everyone's heard of *Orb*, but it's Larsen who has the glory. Who's heard of Carl Colenso? Apart from ocean racing buffs, and how many of them come to your classes?'

'That's hardly the point,' objected Debbie. 'I should have at least consulted you. The truth is, I had no idea what I had on my team – no real idea, to be honest, what ocean racing really involved, or what a tactician actually *did*. You were the navigator, weren't you?' Carl said nothing, and she went on, 'And the damn boat's a legend! I don't know where to put myself for embarrassment, and that's the truth.'

'Just brush up on your interview skills before you tackle Toby Bennetts,' Carl suggested, grinning.

'Well yes, there's that of course – but I never really interviewed you, did I? You just drifted into our plans, and it was nearly a year before I even knew you'd so much as set foot on an ocean racer, and I'm gutted! You're as much a professional as Oliver. More so, probably.'

'Ex. And look at it this way. I could have told you.'

Roger came back, the four refilled glasses balanced between his spread hands. He set the cluster gently down on the table and resumed his seat. Debbie turned to Susan.

'Did *you* realise what a hard man you'd thrown in your lot with?'

'I realised he was a very good sailor,' said Susan, feeling it to be inadequate. Like Debbie, she had never given it particular thought. She did now.

'*A very good sailor*,' Debbie repeated. 'That makes two of us, then. I'm really looking forward to reading his book when it comes out in – what, June?'

Susan had read it in manuscript form. She wondered now, and for the first time, how much of its gut-wrenching tension was down to imagination and how much was personal experience. She had thought of it as a brilliant, imaginative and fast-moving thriller, but was it also partly autobiographical? Not the skulduggery that underlay the plot, of course, but maybe some of the skulduggery that defined its setting? She looked at Carl with new eyes.

'I think I always thought of ocean racing as sort of glorified yacht racing, with pay but without the home comforts,' she apologised.

'A very fair description.' He was laughing at her now – at both her and Debbie. Roger looked from one to the other of them and raised his eyebrows.

'Domestic yachtsmen, that's us,' said Debbie, with a shake of her head. 'Aggressive, competitive and pitiless, that's you.'

'You're good at what you do. You never even wanted to be in competitive yacht racing once you'd moved on from dinghies.'

'Was your father – competitive, I mean?' asked Susan.

'Where do you think I learned? Oh, he didn't do the big races, never enough money for one thing. But anything he could qualify for, and find the time to sail in. Double-handers mainly, he only had a small boat.'

'And you crewed for him,' said Debbie, stating a fact.

'Mostly. Yes.'

Debbie swallowed the last of her sandwich, finished her drink, and got to her feet, looking at her watch as she did so. 'Well, this *has* been an interesting day,' she said. 'Now, I'd better go and rescue Gosia from my child, she'll be demanding overtime at this rate! Roj, when you get back, can you ring that Bennetts man and ask him to come over tomorrow sometime? Lunchtime would be best. You'll find his number on my desk.' She left, and the three remaining were left looking at each other.

'Do you ever feel you want to go back to it – to racing?' asked Roger, casually.

'No. It was good while it lasted, but my father's dream rather than my own. He liked that I lived it for him, but then he died.' Carl spoke without sentiment, but he lifted his glass and took a good swallow. It hid his face, Susan noticed, and it was she who asked, 'But don't you miss it? The excitement and the glamour and all the rest of it?'

'I'm only a simple Cornish lad. And I didn't really like some of the people – not the ones I sailed with, I don't mean. The money men. The sponsors. You've got to be a real enthusiast to go risking life and limb for somebody you don't even like.' He put down the now half-empty glass with a bang. 'So if you're asking if I'm going to go roaring off round the globe yet again, the answer is probably no. Been there, done that. But I dare say I may cover the odd major event to keep the wolf from the door in the general course of my resumed career as writer and journalist.'

Susan, feeling momentarily as if she had thrown in her lot with a complete stranger, said the first thing that came into her head. 'Can I come too – not always, obviously, just now and then?' and saw the pain die out of his face with thankfulness. She knew already that Carl and his father had been close, she hadn't realised quite how close until this afternoon. 'Well?' she said.

'Sorry Susie.' He gave her an apologetic look. 'I didn't mean to start ranting. Of course you can. From the sounds of it, it will widen your horizons considerably. I'm surprised at you and Deb!'

'Oh, our racing was always at club level, very gentlemanly, give or take the odd dinghy championship,' said Susan, and they all laughed. Roger picked up the last pickled onion from his ploughman's lunch, crunched it, and licked his fingers.

'Better go then, I suppose, duty calls. And the punters will start appearing before you can turn round. Are you coming back over, Carl?'

'In a minute. You go ahead.' Then, when Roger had gone, with a cheery wave as he went through the door, he looked at Susan.

'All right, Susie? I didn't mean to open such a can of worms with my well-intentioned strategy.'

'You must have known you'd start *something*. I felt sorry for Roger.'

'I never gave his position a thought. Your suggestion was great, by the way.'

'Thank you.' She picked up her wineglass and held it before her, looking at him over the rim. 'You are a dark horse, aren't you? And I never guessed, never even gave it a thought.'

'Oliver knew. Does it make a difference?'

'Nah. Should it? It doesn't make you someone else, it simply means I know more about you.'

'Good, then.'

Susan set down her empty glass. 'Come on, we'd better go. I'll walk up with you and round up the children, you won't want them underfoot this afternoon.'

Hand in hand, they strolled back along the foreshore to the sailing school. 'Just like one of Liz's novels,' said Susan, happily.

'I'm sure Liz would just love to hear you say so.'

A few steps crunched underfoot in silence, then Susan asked, 'How's Deb managing, with the baby and everything?' and Carl smothered a laugh.

'Much as you'd expect. Dumps him in his pushchair while he'll cooperate, and when he starts acting up, puts him into one of those sling things and hangs him round her neck like a necklace, and just carries on as usual.'

'She's far more laid back than I ever was,' Susan admitted, on a sigh. 'I had what felt like a running battle with both of mine right from day one. If we hadn't had a nanny, they'd have been out of the window, crash, finish!'

'Just wait until he starts teething,' advised Carl. He released her hand to slip his arm around her shoulders. 'Anyway, you're not Deb. Never were, never will be. And Annabel and Seb are a credit to you.'

'A credit to somebody, anyway. Not sure it's actually me. Gosia, probably.'

'Giss on,' said Carl. 'Stop putting yourself down. I've told you about that before.'

More shingle crunched beneath their feet. Susan said, 'How long, do you think? Before you come ashore.'

'A month, maybe. But there's only one booking for the yachts the week after next, and Phil will take that one. And at the beginning of June, I'd have to have had a week off anyway, for the book launch. There's a big party organised, hope you've got your posh frock ready.'

'A different life,' said Susan, thinking about it.

'Just goes to prove something,' said Carl, contentedly, as the sailing school came into view round the curve of the foreshore.'

'Like what?' asked Susan.

'Black cats are lucky,' said Carl.

XXVI

Dot took her commission to oversee the restoration of the Dock Inn seriously, not simply to help Mawgan, whom she knew would have been able to find someone else for the job quite easily had she refused it, but because it appealed to her. After the completion date, when the builders had been in for a week, she rang Tim Howells and arranged to go with him on one of his visits of inspection so that she could take a series of photographs to study and compare with heritage magazine illustrations of similar properties of the same era. She was anxious to get things absolutely right, and this would take time, she knew; time better spent before the renovation work started, while the builders were still in destruct mode, so that progress could continue unchecked. She was surprised at how much had already been done; the whole of the inside was stripped to its bare bones, and the workmen were carrying the debris out to three big skips in the car park. She had advised this herself – there were few of the original fixtures and fittings surviving and the woodworm had affected everything – and was flattered to find that she had been taken at her word. 'We should take a tour round some of the reclamation yards,' she told Tim.

'We?'

'You're the manager of this project, I understand.'

'That's true, for the moment anyway. But Mawgan will want some say in everything.'

'We can place a deposit on anything we think may be suitable, and he can review it when he comes to check on progress. I know he is planning regular visits.'

'Doesn't trust us, maybe,' said Tim, trying not to resent it.

'And why should he?' asked Dot. 'He knows nothing of our expertise in this field, although I assume, with his background, he has plenty of his own. It is up to us to show him of what we are capable.'

'You know there's been a television crew round, filming?'

'Mawgan did mention that they would be here from time to time, yes. Making another series, I understand.'

'You and I are going to be in it.' He grinned at her. 'You anyway, I shall be in Italy. But you could probably start up a good business on the publicity from it! If we get it right, that is.' He meant it as a joke, but to her amazement it struck a chord that reverberated deep within some personal space where she hadn't visited for a while now. *Find out what makes you happy ... then get on and do it ...* Well, it was early days.

Their inspection over, and Dot's pictures duly taken, Tim drove Dot back to her by this time rather decimated house, and she made him coffee while they talked over their future strategy. Dot fetched yellow pages from the hall and looked up reclamation yards, they made notes.

'They've got some good reclaimed timber to replace the beams that have gone too far already,' said Tim. 'It's a wonder the whole thing hadn't fallen down.'

'It was a crying shame to let such a lovely old building go to rack and ruin,' said Dot. She repeated a remark she had made once before, 'It is part of the town's history. I cannot imagine what the council were thinking of even to consider knocking it down.'

'Pound signs,' said Tim, and Dot nodded her head in agreement.

'Greed, yes.' There was a short silence, then, 'Tell me, Tim,' said Dot. 'You're a sailing man. What do you know about ocean racing?'

'Me?' Tim stopped himself saying "sod all" by a whisker, and said instead, 'Nothing at all. Or better, what I do know makes me glad I never did any. I did the Fastnet once. That was enough.'

'Only someone was giving me the idea only the other day that it was a very rough, cut-throat kind of sport.'

'Fair enough, I suppose. At that level, you can't stand aside politely for the other fellow. You hustle through.'

'That's the impression I received.'

Tim wasn't stupid. He said, 'You're thinking of Carl Colenso. I wouldn't worry. I only met him a couple of times apart from that night at the club, but he seemed a good bloke, stepped in to help us out of a hole when we were complete strangers to him. Everybody is a bit different when they're engaged in competitive sport, it doesn't mean they're like it all the time. You couldn't carry on like that in real life.'

'True,' said Dot, thinking of her own days in competitive sport. For the first time in years, the memory made her smile. 'At least, I suppose, I may depend on his having the steel to defend my daughter against unpleasantness?'

'I would certainly think so.'

'Then I am happy to have your confirmation of my own opinion. I find, these days, that I am very aware of my own ignorance of the world in which other people seem to live. I have made some serious misjudgements of late, and Susan is very dear to me.'

Tim looked at her in sympathy, he had made one or two of those himself. One in particular: the same one that Deb's mum was probably thinking of as she spoke. He said the first thing that came into his head. 'We just have to get on with it as best we can, I suppose,' and thought as he said it how trite it sounded, and how easy it was to say and often how hard to do.

When he left, Dot sat for a while in the quiet and increasingly bare house, thinking about what she had to do next. She was, by this time, living in her drawing room, its depleted furnishings supplemented by a new, smaller dining room table and matching chairs, and the sideboard that she had decided to keep; the by this time unfurnished dining room was stacked with boxes and pictures waiting for the removal men. Three of the bedrooms upstairs were empty, cleaned and ready for the new owners, and all the surplus furniture that the children hadn't been able to use was gone to the saleroom yesterday; the few pieces that Susan, Debbie or Cheryl had asked for were in the hall waiting for the carrier to Cornwall. The resulting emptiness, although sitting here she couldn't actually see it, seemed to have got inside her head. It was very lonely there.

This had not, she found herself thinking, been a very happy house. Oliver, Susan and Debbie had passed their turbulent, and for at least two of them unhappy, teenage years here, the last illusion of her marriage to Jerry had finally foundered and died here, she had made some appalling mistakes while living here. For all these reasons she had thought that she would be able to leave it without emotion but that wasn't turning out to be the case. It was taking all her courage, to step away from her past and start afresh, and she wasn't certain any more that she could do it on her own. Of course, Leanne was coming over to help, and her husband Darren had promised his services to do all the man things involved in a big move, Benita, too, had promised be there to lend a hand, but she would have liked the support of her own family as she took this huge step into the unknown. The fact that none of them would be there seemed to underline the mess she had made of her life so far. Loneliness, as she felt it now, would make a suitable epitaph for her time here.

After a while, she picked up the phone and dialled a familiar number. If you didn't ask, she told herself, you didn't get, and even if she could already guess the answer it would be good to hear her daughter's voice.

'Susan,' she said, when the phone at the other end was picked up. 'How are you, dear?'

'Fine. How's the move going?' Susan's voice held circumspection, probably she had guessed what was the reason for this call. Dot decided, on impulse, not to satisfy her expectations. She could do this on her own! She replied, 'It's going well, thank you Susan. I complete on Haymans tomorrow, and then there's ten days to allow me to get the carpets cleaned and to hang my new curtains, and I complete here on Thursday week and the removal men will be here at eight o'clock that day. I would have preferred sooner, but the holiday will intervene and hold us up. I'm looking forward to the move, it will be good to get out into the countryside.'

Susan had never seen her mother as a country person, and she would have nobody living close that she knew; she saw through this cheerful smoke screen and was sorry. But it couldn't be done, she had children to look after and significant exams coming up.

'It'll be hard work on your own. Why don't you take Liz up on her offer to help? She meant it, you know.'

'Elizabeth has her own work to do. Leanne and Darren and Mrs Adams will be helping me, I shall manage very well.'

'That's not the same as having someone around to share the fun – it *will* be fun, you know, if you have time to draw breath that is. Ask her. She can only say no.'

It occurred to Dot that if Liz did say no, she would find it hard to bear. Anyway, she couldn't ask the Worthingtons for favours, not after the way they had behaved over Henry's will. So she changed the subject, asking after the children and Carl.

'Carl's off sailing, but it's to be his last scheduled trip,' Susan said, her happiness ringing in her voice so that Dot felt a pang of jealousy. 'Seb and *Swallow* are entered in the eleven and under race at the Bank Holiday regatta Deb and Roger have arranged next weekend. He's fancied to win, it's a shame you'll be too tied up with moving to come and cheer, but I'll make a film of it and send you a copy. Carl's got all the gear to make a DVD for you.'

'That will be nice,' said Dot. She had given up protesting that Seb was too young and silly for such activities; Seb had changed, and so had her opinion of his father's opinions, she found she now preferred her own. She said, 'Have you heard any more from Tom?' and Susan said, 'No. And I'd better not. He sent the children a postcard and said he was buying a flat.'

'That sounds very much as if he has given up hope of a reconciliation,' said Dot, with satisfaction. Sally had already told her that this was the case, with some relief in Dot's opinion, but Dot was pleased with this confirmation. Good to know that her own advice could carry as much weight as ... well, as other people's.

Dot chatted on for a while, detailing her plans for the coming move, but when she had rung off, Susan sat for a while looking at the phone and thinking. In the past, she would never have dreamed of overruling her mother's expressed wish, but times had changed, or at least, they were changing. The fact that Dot hadn't asked, but merely hinted, for her own assistance weighed in the balance too; it implied that she expected a refusal but didn't want to hear one. After a few minutes, she reached out and picked up the phone again, and she, too, dialled a familiar number.

Liz's life had by now changed out of all recognition. She was so accustomed to living on her own that at first it had seemed strange to have another person permanently in the house, but she had very soon become used to it. Mike Wainwright was a very easy house guest – if you could call someone a guest who paid for their keep, that is. He was out most of the day from Monday to Saturday leaving her free to work in peace, and returning usually after six o'clock to have a shower, share dinner, and if he didn't go down to the pub with his mates, to settle down with her in the sitting room to watch television, to read or to talk as they felt inclined. Since that family lunch, it became their regular habit on Sundays as the weather improved to take a picnic and walk together up to the tor, or over the moors, returning to the house pleasantly tired to clean up and go down to the pub for dinner. They became friends long before they became lovers.

Occasionally, they went to the farm or to Liz's parents' home for a meal in the evening. George liked Mike, they had a lot in common, but if he had any ideas in his head about a future son-in-law in his own line of business, he didn't voice them. Alice, predictably, was slightly more vocal on the subject.

'So, have you got the gorgeous grenadier out of the spare bed and into your own yet?' she asked, over coffee in the pub. They had met in the shop, Liz began to wish that they hadn't.

'What makes you think that I want him there?' she asked.

'If you don't, you need to see a doctor,' Alice told her. 'If you don't know it, I'm telling you now – he's the best thing that ever came into your life!'

'We're friends. That's all.'

'Ho!'

'Anyway,' said Liz – unwisely, as it turned out, 'what makes you feel that Mum and Dad would want an oily garage mechanic as a prospective son-in-law?'

'What makes you feel that they wouldn't?' Alice asked. 'Dad says his prayers every night, in case you haven't noticed, and it has very little to do with the vast improvement on Paul.'

'I –'

'Dad was an "oily garage mechanic" himself, in case you hadn't noticed, for all he's gone a bit executive these days. Soldier boy is a gift from the gods.' Liz was silent. Alice pushed home her advantage, in a way that only an older sister would dare. 'I see you've thought about it.'

'No,' said Liz, defensively.

'Then why did you say what you did? *I* never said anything about marrying him.'

Altogether, not the most satisfactory coffee break the sisters had ever enjoyed together, but when she was home again, sitting in front of her computer, Liz found her thoughts straying away from the doings of her current heroine and concentrating rather too hard on her own doings.

Ex-sergeant Michael Wainwright was her best friend, her daily companion. He by this time simply turned off the mobile phone at night since there seemed nothing to be gained by leaving it on, but he stood to protect her against any further threats, that had so far not materialised. They could walk and talk together for hours, laugh at the same jokes, enjoy the same programmes on the television, that is if you discounted rugby matches. They could even share the kitchen, cooking their evening meal together in amicable companionship. Did all of that mean that she loved him?

Liz thought now that perhaps it did, although it hadn't occurred to her before. Some novelist you are, she told herself wryly. You never even saw it coming.

What she felt was so different from the purely sexual passion that she had enjoyed with Paul that she simply hadn't recognised it. That was sad! The relationship with Paul had been competitive, lustful and heady and in the finish, both destructive and transient. This one had a feeling of solidity about it, something that could last and last, built on strong foundations that could hold far into the future. It could break her heart.

For there to be the traditional happy ending, it was a river that had to flow both ways.

Mike was in a difficult position, of course. He had come under her roof to protect her, he wouldn't now take try to advantage of her. From his point of view, perhaps *couldn't* would be more accurate. He was connected, however tenuously, with her family, he was in a position of trust. He was a newcomer here, on probation in a village where her own family had lived for generations. If they were ever to be more than friends, he either had to move out so they could start level or she had to make the first move herself. That might take some courage. Suppose that he didn't feel the same way? Perhaps, when the persecution from Paul finally ceased he was planning to move on, and without a backward look. Perhaps it had already ceased. There were no more daytime calls, none at night. She found herself, bizarrely, hoping that Paul would find a new way to persecute her while at the same time feeling apprehension as to what that might be.

So she let the golden days of that spring slip by, working during the day in her empty house, curled up alongside her lodger on the sofa in the evenings, his arm companionably round her shoulders as they laughed together over some sitcom, walking the moors with him at the weekend with the sweet wind in their faces and the sun warm on their skin, until the weekend came when she had to go up country to address the Congress of writers on the subject of how to write a genre novel and remain original. If she had succeeded in that herself: if she was honest, she was never entirely sure. If she made out to be so, she was even less sure that other professional writers would find her credible as a speaker, but perhaps that was her own cynicism speaking. On the other hand, they must have thought she held the key to the secret to have asked her to speak in the first place.

She began to feel cross with herself. She had so many ambivalent feelings on so many subjects these days, she was getting on her own nerves never mind her sister's! The only good thing that had happened lately was that the London flat, with all its mixed memories, had sold almost as soon as it went back on the market. One problem solved. An awful lot seemed to remain.

She left for the Congress, still in ignorance as to Mike's feelings towards her, leaving him, had she but realised, in exactly the same state about her. When she came back, he told himself as he watched her drive past the garage on her way up-country on the Friday morning, when she came back he would tell her that it was time for him move out. The appalling Paul had apparently ceased his persecution, there was no more reason for him to stay. If he left, perhaps this inhibiting lodger/landlady thing would get up and go away too and they could have a sensible relationship. He had been too well brought up, he thought gloomily; he could no more take advantage of a woman whose house he was paying to share, right under the eyes of her family, than he could fly to the moon. And not just her family. He was aware that his own were giving them equal attention because Susan was Cheryl's sister-in-law as well as Liz's aunt, a chain of relationships that under any other circumstances would be risible.

Not these circumstances, however. It made what should have been a private voyage of discovery between two people into a box-office draw on a public stage!

Families. Couldn't live with 'em, couldn't live without 'em. They meant so well, too.

And then, early on Sunday evening, Liz arrived home, and everything changed.

The Congress had gone well. Liz wasn't sure that she had convinced anyone, but she had certainly made them laugh and she

530

had met some interesting people. Her fellow speakers had been entertaining and the food in the selected venue had been excellent. She had missed Mike and Tib, but in the pleasure of mixing with her own kind and sharing experiences and ideas she had also quite often forgotten them, or almost. She drove home and parked outside the cottage with more sense of homecoming than she realised she had ever had. She carried her bag indoors and set it down in the passage. The sound of the radio and a pleasant smell of cooking wafted from the kitchen, she followed her nose.

Mike looked up from the stove when he heard her footsteps, a smile of welcome on his face. 'You're back! Did you have a good weekend?' He stepped towards her and planted a swift, brotherly kiss on her cheek before stepping back to the stove as if he was afraid she might bite him. 'I'm just making a stew. I didn't know what time you'd be back.'

Squashing down a slight feeling of disappointment, Liz said, 'I smelt it as soon as I came in. It smells wonderful, and I'm starving!'

'Well good. It's almost ready, by the time you've unpacked and checked your post it'll be fit to go on the table. We can talk properly then, and you can tell me all about your lecture.'

'That'll be thrilling for you! All right, I won't be long.' She vanished, and Mike picked up the pan of potatoes standing ready on the worktop and put them on the stove. He began to set the table, humming along with the music on the radio; the house felt indefinably different now that she was back.

He heard her come downstairs and into her study, and the squeak of her chair as she sat down. There was a whole pile of letters from the weekend, a couple of books from Amazon and a square parcel wrapped in black plastic, they would keep her busy for the time it took the potatoes to finish cooking, and they could sit down together like – well, like a couple. He contemplated the idea, and found it pleasant.

The radio had moved on from music to chat, he wasn't interested in listening to that. He turned it off.

In the silence, there was the sound of scrumpling paper from the next room, and the click of a drawer opening and shutting. Liz was humming too; he liked hearing her, it was a happy sound, like the buzzing of contented bees. There was the splitting sound of tearing plastic.

The humming stopped abruptly, breaking off in a tiny, whimpering cry. A horrible smell came seeping in over the savoury smell of stew, one he had smelt before all too often. It had no business here. Mike ran, almost tripping over the step up to the study in his haste.

Liz sat at her desk, her face white with shock, the wrappings of the square parcel at her feet and a cardboard box open in her hands. The foul smell of putrefaction hung in the air, solid as a wall. Mike moved without thought, snatched the box from her hands, banged on the lid, gathered up the wrappings and headed for the back door with it. He called over his shoulder, 'Open the windows,' but when he came back five minutes later, she hadn't moved. He opened the study window himself, and then pulled her to her feet and into his arms. For a minute, neither of them said anything, then Liz spoke in a whisper so small that he hardly heard her. 'Did you see?'

'Yes,' said Mike. He had looked, and he was cold with rage against someone who could do such a vile thing. Liz said, 'A kitten. A little kitten, tabby and white just like Tib. Dead. Suffocated. How *could* he?'

A good question, Mike thought, but didn't try to answer it. Liz began to cry, without sound, the tears running down into his shirt, and unable to think of a word to say, he held her close and thought black and evil thoughts of what he would do to Paul Attwood if he ever caught up with him. After a while, Liz raised her head and sniffed. 'Sorry,' she said. 'It was just ... the shock. And he was so small and sweet ... and it was such a cruel thing to do ...' Her face was tilted up to his, her eyes still swimming with tears. It seemed the most natural thing in the world to kiss her. It wasn't in the least brotherly. After a moment, her arms came round him too. He waited a few minutes, then kissed her again, more gently this time, and put her away from him.

'Go and wash your face,' he said. 'I'll pour you a drink and leave it on the table, and I'll go out and bury him. It won't take me long.'

'Somewhere nice,' said Liz, sniffing. 'Poor little thing ... bury him under the smokebush, and put one of those flagstones in the shed on top so that nothing ... nothing ...' She put her hands over her face. Mike squeezed her shoulder sympathetically.

'Come on sweetheart. Don't break your heart. Please.'

She shook her head without speaking, turned away and headed

for the hall. He watched her go, and then returned to the kitchen. He turned down the heat under the potatoes, poured a good dollop of Liz's cooking brandy into a glass, and flung the kitchen window wide. The dreadful smell seemed to be everywhere. He left the back door open when he went out to the shed for a spade and a flagstone. He had a feeling that the smokebush was the red thing halfway down the garden, he hadn't liked to ask. He set about his grim task with rage in his heart. After a while, Tib appeared on top of the neighbours' fence and sat watching him. Mike looked at him.

'You could make yourself useful, and go indoors and comfort her while I see to this,' he told him. Tib whisked his tail and began to wash a paw. After a few moments he jumped down and strolled off down the garden, not liking the smell that hung around. Mike made a face at his retreating rear end.

Sexton's duty completed, he returned the spade to the shed and stuffed the wrapping from the parcel into a plastic bag which he put onto a shelf before he went indoors. Liz was sitting at the table, the glass of brandy between her hands and her face sombre. He ran the tap and reached for the soap, speaking without looking at her.

'If it helps, it wasn't alive when it went into that box. It'd been hit by something from the looks of it, I imagine it died instantly. It was still a very unpleasant thing to do, but it would have been roadkill, a snap decision when he saw it so conveniently somewhere probably, not quite as horrible as you thought.'

'Thank you,' said Liz, without looking up. He finished washing his hands and came and sat opposite to her at the table. 'Drink your brandy. It'll help you get your balance.'

She picked up the glass, but didn't drink from it. She said, 'The very first email he sent, that was a tabby cat too.' She twirled the glass in her fingers, still not meeting his eyes, and then set it down, untouched. Mike reached across the table and covered one of her hands with his; she turned her own beneath it and clutched his fingers, hard. After a while, she spoke again. 'I find it so hard to understand. Why should he persecute me? We were friends, we had some good times. They just came to an end, but that happens to everyone sometime or other. Why try to make my life a misery?'

'As a guess, because someone is making *his* a misery, and he's taking it out on you,' Mike suggested.

'I thought he'd given up,' said Liz, unhappily. Mike had too. He recognised that the unspeakable Paul had probably seized an opportunity, but what sort of feelings would he need to have towards Liz to do so?

'Perhaps he has, now,' he said. It was hardly comforting. He picked up the brandy glass and put it back into her free hand, and this time she did take a small sip from it. The colour was coming back into her cheeks, she took a second sip and straightened her shoulders, but he noticed that she didn't let go of his hand.

'He must really hate me,' she said unhappily.

'He must hate pretty well everyone to behave like he's doing. But I love you.' Rushing in where angels feared to tread, he told himself, and what a moment to choose. But it seemed such an easy cue.

Liz had just raised the glass to take another sip, she choked on it and put the glass down hastily, covering her mouth with her freed hand. She looked at him, round-eyed, over her fingers and when she had got her breath, said, somewhat muffled, 'What did you say?'

In for a penny, in for a pound. 'I said, I love you. You are the sweetest breath of air in my life for the last sixteen years.' He realised that he could have chosen his words better under the circumstances and bit his lip. Liz's face softened, she lowered her hand. 'Well, good,' she said.

'Good, why?'

'Because I love you, too.' As simple as that. They leaned towards each other across the table and exchanged a kiss that went on for a while. Then Liz began to feel the edge of the table digging uncomfortably into her ribs and sat back. 'This is ridiculous,' she said.

'It'll cause a bit of a flutter in the dovecotes,' said Mike. He grinned at her, ruefully. 'Will you marry me anyway, and take the flak?'

'Quite possibly. But only if we can slip off and do it somewhere quietly, where nobody knows us.'

'Gretna Green, you mean? I don't think you can do that these days. And anyway, they'd all be awfully disappointed, it'd be mean.' He leaned forward again, and then drew back and got to his feet instead. 'Damn this table! Let's go to the pub and celebrate.' It didn't seem the moment to suggest anything more intimate which was a pity, but Liz needed time, he could see that.

'What about dinner?' After all the trouble you've taken, too!' Then Liz went on, more soberly. 'We can drink a toast to that poor little cat, at least his short life achieved something. Don't deny it, we'd have been tippy-toeing round each other for ever, caught in the spotlight, without this.'

Mike got to his feet. He crossed to the stove and prodded the potatoes, drained them into the sink and tipped them into a dish. He was thinking, soberly, that this wouldn't be quite what Paul had in mind when he sent his terrible gift, but how much he would like to repay him for that anyway, but what he said was, 'All this'll keep in the oven if I cover it. Close the windows while I see to it.'

The simple request brought back into the foreground the reasons why the windows were wide open in the first place. The smell had gone by this time, the memory of its cause, Liz thought, would stay with her for a long time. It would be good to be out of the house for a while; when they came back, perhaps it would feel different. Right this minute, she didn't want to be here; how wise of Mike to see it.

But they were fated not to escape quite so easily. While Liz was still closing the windows, the phone rang. 'Liz!' said Susan, when her niece picked up the phone. 'I've been trying to get hold of you for three days!'

'I've been away,' Liz explained. 'I had to give a talk in Cheltenham. You should have left a message.'

'Too complicated. Anyway, I needed to talk to you.'

'OK, I'm here now. So what can I do for you?'

Susan told her. When she had finished, Liz said, 'I'll give her a ring. See what she feels about it.'

'But you'd go, if she wanted?'

'Yes,' said Liz. She didn't feel she could say anything else. She said goodbye to Susan and went slowly into the kitchen. 'That was Susan.'

'I gathered. You look downcast, what did she want?'

'Let's get down to the Three Bears, and I'll tell you.'

It was still a bit early for the pub, so they had it almost to themselves. Mike bought two beers and carried them over to the table by the open window where Liz sat, staring pensively at her hands.

'If you wanted to give this pub a nickname,' he said, as he sat, 'It should have been the Three Beers, not the Three Bears. So, what's the problem?' He pushed her glass across. 'Drink up, you never finished that brandy. You need the alcohol, it'll do you good.'

'It's not exactly a problem,' said Liz. She took an obedient swallow of her lager. 'It's just that I offered to help Auntie Sue's mum, who is sort-of my grandmother, move house, and Susan wants me to cash in the chips. She can't go, it's the launch of Carl's book the same time, and Deb can't, obviously.'

Mike looked at her thoughtfully. 'I see. Is this imminent?'

'She moves at the end of next week – sort of straddled over the bank holiday.'

'Did she accept your offer? I mean, if she asked Susan not you, does she want you?'

'Who knows? There's history with the family – my Aunt Carol caused a bit of a buzz over my grandfather's will when he died, and it left a bad taste behind. She might not feel she *could* ask, or she might not want to.'

'Only one way to find out.'

'Yes. Only it'd mean being away for a week, at least, and I don't want to be.' Mike said nothing, and she went on, 'I know it's pathetic, I'll be back before you know it ... an hour ago I would have gone without a second thought. Now, I don't want to leave you.' She made a face. 'How stupid can you get?'

'I won't run away while you're gone,' he said, smiling at her. She shook her head.

'I never imagined you would. It's not you, it's me. Take no notice, it's been a trying day.' They drank in silence for a few minutes, each of them thinking their own thoughts, then Mike drained his glass and held out his hand for Liz's. 'Another one? Hang in there, I'll be back. I think I've just had an idea –' He was gone before she could question him, and as she waited for him to return, she wondered at how her life could change so dramatically so quickly. It was partly the shock, she realised, that had precipitated things. But this had been waiting to happen since the day he moved in, and probably before that.

So much for prejudice. An army background made a man resourceful, and perhaps she could persuade him to shave the ginger

536

moustache. Or perhaps she wouldn't bother to try; it not only grew on him, she discovered it was starting to grow on her, too.

He slid back into the chair in front of her and pushed her refilled glass across. 'What I was thinking,' he said. 'Why don't I come with you? I'm sure Dorothy could use a man about the place, and there must be somewhere close I could stay.'

'You've got your job,' said Liz, but liking the idea.

'I can scrape a week's holiday, I daresay. And Mark will sleep in the cottage and look after the cat if we ask him, glad to get out of that van I wouldn't wonder. Run it past her, see what she thinks.'

There would be only one thing she would like better, Liz thought, that they could stay somewhere together. But that was a non-starter, Dot would want her company in the house. That was the whole point of her going at all.

'I'll give her a ring when we get back, while you finish off the dinner. But are you sure you can have the time?'

'Pretty sure. I'll find out tomorrow. Just mention it as a possibility, see what comes back.'

'I don't know what she'll say, mind. I don't know her very well at all, although I think I'd like to. The family would like to bury the whole disagreement under the chestnut tree, but you can't force it.'

'From the tales I've heard, and what I saw at the christening come to that, she can be a bit spiky,' said Mike, tentatively.

'Yeah ... she can. But I think a lot of it is defensive, and you could as well blame a cornered rat for having a nip at you. She's not a particularly happy woman.'

'And you plan to make her happier?'

'I don't see why I shouldn't try. Even Aunt Carol admits that a lot of the original argument was her fault, not Dorothy's. And I loved my Grandad so Mum says – not that I remember.'

'Fair enough. Let's see what we can do, then.'

They finished their drinks and walked back to the cottage, and while Mike returned to the kitchen to see to the meal, Liz sat at her desk and took out the number that Susan had given her. Mike was quite domesticated; she wondered idly if it was the army or his family background that made him so, before realising that she was putting off something she was nervous about doing and picked up the phone.

Dot sounded surprised to hear her voice but not, Liz thought, entirely displeased.

'Elizabeth! What a nice surprise. What may I do for you?'

'I think it may be more what I can do for you,' said Liz. 'You must be close to your moving day, I'm ringing to see if you want to take me up on my offer of help. There must be an awful lot to do on your own, and I know Susan and Deb are tied up.'

'That's very nice of you, to think of it,' said Dot, sounding taken aback. 'I really don't know that I can ask it of you.' She wanted to, Liz heard it in her voice.

'It won't be a problem. I can bring my laptop and still go on working between times. It'll be a bit grim, won't it, doing the job on your own? You've been there for a long time –'

'– through good times and bad?' Dot finished for her. 'Well yes, I daresay it may be a sad occasion in some ways, but since I shall be going to somewhere very beautiful and far more suitable, I shall manage.'

'But you don't have to do it on your own.'

'I shall have help, of course. Leanne and her husband have offered their services. Darren will drive the van for me and Leanne –'

'Van?' Liz interrupted, not able to stop herself.

'I plan to hire one to transport my precious things the day before the move. I wouldn't trust the removal men to do it.'

Liz's brain went into overdrive. This was a gift from Valhalla. She said, 'Don't be in a hurry. I might be able to help you with that.'

'You have a van?' asked Dot, surprised.

'Not exactly. But Mike, my ... my lodger, I suppose, has a truck – you know, you met him at the christening. He's said he'll come with me and lend a hand with the heavy stuff if he can get the time off, and if you need it.'

Dot allowed a pause for thought. So Elizabeth's lodger, as she thought Susan might have mentioned actually, was Cheryl's brother. The pair of them, Elizabeth and Michael, were family in a way. To have family around her, even at second hand, or even third, would be a relief, if she was honest. She had been feeling rather alone as the house became emptier, even though her proven friends, Ingrid and Sally and Bennie, and even Marie Law, had been very supportive. She said, 'I don't wish to put upon you both.'

'You won't,' said Liz, firmly. 'We'd like to help. I'll come anyway, if that's all right, and Mike will let us know tomorrow if he can get the time. You won't have to put him up,' she added hastily. 'He'll stay somewhere local.'

'No he will not. If he is coming to help me, the least I can do is to give him a bed,' said Dot. She paused. Of late, particularly since her assessment of Carl, and of his relationship with Susan, her views on the manners and morals of modern young people had undergone a very slight change. She said, 'Would that be two rooms needed, Elizabeth, or one?'

Liz went scarlet to the tips of her ears, although Dot couldn't see it. She swallowed.

'Er ... one would be fine, if that's all right. Save on the sheets,' she added, lamely, and could have kicked herself.

'You just let me know then, how many of you will be coming,' said Dot, as if Liz was bringing an army rather than one ex-soldier. Liz promised she would ring tomorrow evening, and they said goodbye. Liz put down her phone and went thoughtfully into the kitchen. She had gone out on a limb, she realised, and now she had to be careful not to saw off the branch she was sitting on.

Mike was just dishing up. He looked up as she came in. 'So? What did she say?'

'She was pleased, I think – about me offering. And she was quite interested in the idea of you when I mentioned you had a truck – she was going to hire a van. She said she'd put you up if you can come,' she added, casually. She pulled out a chair and sat down. Now or never. 'She asked if she should make up one bed or two.'

'And you said?' Mike put the plates on the table and sat down opposite to her. He was grinning, she saw.

'Didn't seem any point in her making up two.'

The grin broadened happily, but what he said was, 'You won't mind grinding along all that way in a truck?'

'It's quite a new truck,' said Liz, hanging on to her dignity. 'I'm sure I shall manage.'

'You get a good view,' he offered. They began to eat, but after a few bites, Liz laid down her knife and fork. She had gone rather white.

'I'm sorry Mike. It's a lovely stew, but I can't ... I think it's the smell, although it's a lovely smell ... and I keep thinking ...'

Mike gave her a steady look. He realised that this wasn't just about the dead kitten, grim though that had been, it was about feeling hated so much by someone she had presumably rather liked, and he sympathised. He was hungry, however, and not predisposed by his army training to be soft, nor did he feel that softness and sympathy were what she wanted now. So he said, 'Go and watch the News. I'll finish mine and clear up and come and join you.'

'Thank you,' said Liz, and got up and left.

Something, Mike thought as he finished his stew, would have to be done about Paul, although he was damned if he knew what. What he would *like* to do was more likely to land himself in trouble than Paul Attwood, although it would give him immense satisfaction. The trouble was that there was nothing they could prove. He had kept the parcel wrapping, but he was pretty sure that there would be no fingerprints on it beyond his own and Liz's, and probably the postman's. There were no flies on this Paul.

He finished his meal, and carried the plate to the sink. The clink of crockery brought Tib through the cat flap like a missile, and he scooped the cat up and addressed him severely. 'So, where were you when you were needed?' he asked. Tib wriggled and tried to jump down, and Mike carried the squirming animal through to the sitting room and dumped him on Liz's lap.

'Here – cuddle this. I won't be a moment.' A little to his surprise, the cat didn't immediately jump off and streak for the door, which he thought he might have done in Tib's place. He left the two of them smooching together and returned to the washing up, covering Liz's almost untouched plate with foil and placing it in the fridge. Very domesticated, he thought, pulling a rueful face. Mum would be proud of me.

Back in the sitting room, Liz and the cat were curled up comfortably together. A little colour had come back into her cheeks, he was glad to see, and she looked up as he came in, saying, 'Sorry about that. I never thought I was such a fool.'

'Think nothing of it. As you said earlier, it's been a trying day.' He sat down and put his arm around her, feeling the warmth of her nestling into his shoulder and the warmth of the cat on his thigh. He made a rueful face. 'Love me, love my cat, I see.'

'Of course. Do you really want to marry such a stupid woman?'

'Very much. Shall we go for it?'

'I always thought I was an intelligent, creative, natural loner. You've turned me into melted butter.'

'I'll take that as a yes, then, shall I?'

'Please.'

The News was over, a popular sitcom was now filling the screen. The three of them settled down in front of it, although none of them was seeing it. Tib was fast asleep, Mike, Liz thought as she stole a glance at him, was miles away; somewhere dark and stony from the set of his mouth. Her own thoughts were scattering like frightened birds: emails she had weathered, abusive phone calls Mike had fielded for her, but dead animals in the post were another thing altogether. How much Paul must have come to resent her! It came into her head that to do this to her he could never have liked her that much in the first place, just made use of her. Well, everyone had been telling her that for some time, she had simply chosen not to listen.

"The sex was good", she remembered saying. How pathetic! She shut her eyes as if by doing so she could shut out the sight of that sad singleton that in spite of her protestations she realised she had always been. Paul had never been a partner. Paul had been in it strictly for himself, and she had been the only one who failed to notice it. After a while, reaction set in and her eyes stayed shut; there is only so much drama one person can take in one day, on or off the television. The sitcom came to an end and changed to a documentary on marketing practices, a subject on which Mike had only a peripheral interest. He looked at his two companions and saw that they were both fast asleep. He gave Liz a nudge. 'Oy you. If you're that tired, why don't you take yourself to bed?'

Because she was half-asleep, Liz answered without thinking. 'I don't want to be alone.'

'You don't have to be,' he suggested. Liz sat up straight.

'What?' She sounded bewildered, remarkably so since she was a novelist who wrote this kind of scene as a habit. He grinned at her.

'You could take your cat up with you.'

They both looked down at the gently snoring cat. Liz said, 'You can't rely on him. He goes out on the tiles with other women as soon as the moon comes up.'

'Other women?'

'The cat from two doors down actually. Neither of them has anything to boast about, but they get on. She keeps him under her paw.'

'Sounds about right. Well then, failing Tibbles, how would you feel about me?'

She looked at him, a considering expression on her face. His eyes gleamed green in the lamplight and her heart began to flutter treacherously. 'It could save on the laundry,' she said.

He nodded solemnly. 'And you could have your friends to stay again.'

'A big plus.'

Mike rose to his feet, and the cat jumped to the ground as Liz reached for the remote. The documentary hiccupped to a blank screen. Tib marched towards the kitchen, tail up, and Liz looked apologetically between his departing rump and Mike's face. 'Just let me feed the cat.'

'Better shut the kitchen door. We don't want to make him jealous.'

I should change the sheets, Liz found herself thinking, as she tipped cat biscuits into Tib's bowl, only it would look a bit calculating to do it now, and to do it earlier might have looked a bit previous. Tomorrow ... tomorrow was an empty page that waited to be written on. Today needed a row of neat little stars to mark its indelible and overdue end.

Liz went upstairs smiling to search for those stars.

XXVII

When she replaced her phone after Liz's call, Dot stood in her denuded hallway in an unusually ambivalent frame of mind for her; the open-handed way in which Liz had offered her time, her services, and her friend's truck, was unfamiliar territory although she wasn't quite certain why, except that it made her vaguely uncomfortable, but thankfully, there was work to be done to take her mind off it; two days' unbroken sunshine meant that her tubs needed watering. She went purposefully through the house and out into the garden, but the unfamiliar mood came with her. It reminded her a little of how she had felt after Debbie and Susan had visited before Christmas, but it had a sweeter feel. There was no ultimatum here, no last-ditch attempt to negotiate peace. It had come straight from the heart, out of simple kindness, if not affection, and a genuine wish to help her through what could be a difficult time. Something she hadn't deserved.

As it might be difficult, Dot thought now. She hadn't necessarily been happy in this house, but it had been part of her life for a long time now. A lifeline, she now appreciated; the house had been a fixed point in a shifting wilderness of quicksands. Its prestigious position, handsome exterior and luxurious interior had given her credibility, what she had compensating her for what she had not. It had provided a platform from which to conduct the activities that had filled her days and made up her life – barren activities, as she now accepted. Charity that didn't come from the heart was an empty tin can, held out as much for praise as donations. Charity that came from a wish to be first among equals was an insult to the recipients, and the person who had failed to recognise it was a stranger she pitied but no longer understood.

Her despised son-in-law was the only person who seemed fully to understand that her involvement with good works had helped her to define herself, giving her position in a world that had, on the whole largely ignored her since the day she left school and ceased to be the famous Dee Shipham, Captain of Games and putative future tennis ace. At home, of course, she had never mattered much – neither in her parents' house, where she was mainly a duty rather than a joy, nor in Jerry's, where she wasn't Helen. The brief and potentially happy period of her marriage to Henry she had wilfully spoiled for herself.

Now it seemed as if that transient, largely undervalued and far too brief period of happiness was seeking her out again, almost as if Henry was reaching to her from wherever he was to help her to build herself another life that, this time, would be worth something. Dot wasn't given to being fanciful, but the fact that Henry's granddaughter, who owed her nothing, had come forward of her own free will to offer help when she saw it would be needed was both heart-warming and extraordinary. She hadn't even had to be asked. She had offered originally quite spontaneously, and if Susan had prompted her this time, then that was because otherwise Elizabeth wouldn't have known that now was the moment.

The same with Mawgan. She hadn't said to him that she was desperate for something occupy her empty days, but all the same he had quietly given it to her. First with uncannily apposite suggestions about moving house and finding something fulfilling to do, second by supplying that something. The Dock Inn wasn't just a lifeline that occupied her time, it was a door opening onto a new world, new dreams, new ambitions. New talents, too, or perhaps they had always been there, unrecognised.

Mawgan had been down once more since his first visit, to inspect the building work and go through her ideas; he had seemed impressed, and on a whistle-stop tour of the reclamation yard at the back of town, which had been accompanied, embarrassingly, by a TV unit, had given approval to several of her finds, including a complete bar counter that had been rescued from a fire in an old pub somewhere north of Embridge, and would make a perfect replacement for the worm-eaten disaster recently chucked into a skip as irredeemable. He had taken her to lunch at Mario's again, this time without the followers, and Mario himself had sat at their table for ten minutes, talking enthusiastically in a polyglot mixture of English and Italian which had finally, when he realised he was understood, moved on into pure Italian, in which Dot was interested, but not altogether surprised by this time, to find Mawgan was fluent. Tim had joined them for coffee, at which point Mario had left, clapping Mawgan on the shoulder and shaking hands with Dot with a beaming smile. Mawgan watched him go with an odd expression on his face. Dot had said, 'He seems very friendly,' half as a question, and Mawgan had laughed, and said, 'Never underestimate the competition, Dorothy.' He had hidden depths, her son-in-law. Still very *arriviste* in Dot's opinion, but she was coming round to his good points.

Tim would be gone to Italy in a fortnight, and she would be in sole charge here in Embridge. She found her spirits lifting at the thought. While she was sufficiently self-aware to realise that some of the pride she would take in the work was in order to impress and to put the noses of her fair-weather friends of the past out of joint, she knew that it was also important for another reason. She needed to do a good job to prove something, not just to the world in general, but to herself. Well, "know thyself" was a familiar saying. She would learn.

But how green with bile and envy they would all be, if she appeared on the television!

She had enjoyed that business meeting at Mario's, the feeling that she was a valued contributor to a constructive discussion, at least until they had changed language, and again when Tim arrived. The project would be all hers when Tim had gone. She had wondered if Mawgan would import a substitute, but he made no move to do so. Indeed, he said, on leaving, 'Take care of it all now, Dorothy, and keep in touch. It's in your hands when Tim's gone.'

She thought about that as she hosed the tubs of flowers. It felt good.

Liz rang on Monday evening, to say that Mike had the time off from Sunday to Sunday, inclusive of the Bank Holiday and Dot's moving date. 'We'll come down in the evening the day before, if that's OK,' she said. 'That way we'll be with you for the maximum amount of time to give the maximum amount of help. Mike finishes at five on Saturday, we'll be leaving here around six, I expect. We'll stop somewhere for a meal on the way, it'll take us about three hours to get to you, maybe more in the truck.'

'That will be lovely,' said Dot. 'I shall be busy packing the last of my things, the books and ornaments I left out to make the place look furnished, and the kitchen things – and pictures of course. I shall be glad of a tall man for that!'

'He's not that tall,' said Liz, laughing. 'You need someone like Oliver, or a good stepladder.'

'I'll get out the stepladder,' said Dot, and ventured on a modest joke. 'It will be less argumentative.' She was looking forward to Saturday as she replaced the phone. It would be pleasant to have company, but in the meantime, there were other things to look forward to.

On Monday morning, she completed on Haymans and that afternoon, drove herself over to Shearwater to inspect her new property. She arrived just as the last furniture van was leaving, and the departing family was preparing to get into their car and drive away. When Dot drove through the gates, Bennie's friend Viv Tarrant came over to speak to her as her husband and two young sons loaded the last suitcases.

'I'm so glad we've seen you! I left you a note, on the kitchen table. We can't find the cats.'

'Oh dear, how tiresome for you,' said Dot, while thinking that surely anyone with any sense would have had them in the cattery waiting transit – to France, she believed – days ago.

'The boys are very upset – but we have to catch the ferry at Portsmouth this evening, and we can't hang around. Do you think you could you catch them when they come back, and take them to the vet for me? We should be so grateful. We have homes lined up for them, the vet will see to it, she's arranging it all.'

So they weren't planning to take these cats with them. Poor things, no wonder they ran! Dot could empathise with the poor, unwanted animals, particularly as a rather smug-looking dog was watching out of the car window. She said, 'You've left the vet's telephone number?'

'Of course. And some catfood, they'll be hungry, poor darlings. We really should be so grateful.' That was the second time she had said that. Dot wasn't an animal lover, but there was really nothing that she could say but, 'I'll catch them if they come back, of course.' Viv looked relieved.

'They can get in through the cat flap. Thank you so much. Now we must really dash, or we'll be late for the boat – enjoy Haymans, it's a lovely place! We're sorry to be leaving.' They were gone in a swirl of gravel, waving as they went. Dot stood on the drive, looking around her. How many cats, she wondered. That hadn't been mentioned. She imagined she could feel a dozen baleful eyes watching her from the ornamental shrubs – camellias, she thought – lining the wall between the house and the adjoining cottage. She really didn't like domestic pets, although Deborah, she remembered, had once had a rabbit that lived most of its time in a run in the garden, but seemed to enjoy watching golf on the television from Deborah's lap.

She was just putting her key into the lock when another car turned in through the gates. For one wild, wonderful moment she thought that it was the family coming back for one more attempt to find their cats, but it was Bennie. She parked alongside Dot's car and stepped out onto the drive. 'I thought I might find you here. I rang you and there was no reply, and I know if it was me I couldn't resist.'

Dot had the front door open, she smiled at her friend. 'Benita, how lovely. I was just going to have a look round to see how they've left the place.'

'Great! Let's have a good old nosy!'

'They have left their cats behind,' said Dot, leading the way into the hall. 'It seems that the animals ran away and hid. How many of them, history does not relate.'

'Are they coming back for them?'

'Apparently not. I have to catch them and take them to the vet.' Disapproval was heavy in her voice. Bennie sympathised with that, more on the cats' behalf than Dot's. She said, 'You could keep them. They're nice cats. They'd be company for you.'

'I think not.'

They stood in the square entrance hall and looked around them. It was a satisfying space, stone flags under foot, a big, handsome fireplace and a wide window onto the porch, with a wooden bench beneath. A graceful staircase wound upwards and six doors opened off from either side and at the back. Scraps of paper and whisps of straw blew about in the breeze from the open door. 'Let's start with the kitchen,' Bennie suggested. 'If the cats are around, that's where they'll be. I expect, although after all the upheaval there must have been today, they could be miles away.'

There were no cats in the kitchen. A tiled floor showed signs of muddy boots traipsing to and fro, and a couple of drawers of the, thankfully modern, units were left open, and a cupboard. The red four-oven Aga sat in its alcove, cold and slightly greasy-looking with an igloo-shaped cat basket alongside. Dot closed the drawers after peering inside them. 'The place will need a good clean,' she said, with a sniff.

'Moving is like that,' said Benny. 'You never know how much subversive grime has accumulated in dark corners until you leave the place bare, however clean you think you are. Your Leanne and her mother will soon sort it for you.' She walked across to the far worktop where two metal bowls and a bag of catfood sat on top of a sheet of paper. She picked the paper up and handed it to Dot. 'Here, they've left you a note. Vet's address and that.'

Dot took the sheet of paper. It was quite long, for a note.

Dear Mrs Nankervis,

I'm so sorry, but we couldn't catch the cats, the removal men left the conservatory door open and they slipped out when no one was looking. They'll come back, when all the large men with large boots have gone away, would you mind very much shutting them in somewhere and ringing the vet? She will come and collect them, the cat basket is out in the garage. I have left food, they may just sneak in and out for a few days but the food will bring them back in the end, I hope, if you could feed them for us.

There are two of them, Fatso and Secret Sam. You will know which is which!

I do apologise for putting you to this trouble. We should have got them away days ago, but the boys do love them so. We'd have taken them, but they'd have hated the journey and we'll be in rented accommodation at first.

Enjoy Haymans.

There was a signature, and the vet's telephone number scrawled below it. Dot laid it down on the worktop without comment and turned away. That last bit sounded to her like an excuse, but it wasn't her business. She said, 'Shall we look at the rest of the house? A place always looks so different with someone else's furniture.'

The conservatory opened off from the kitchen, glass panelled french doors, put where the window had been, leading to a big room with a bay window facing across the garden to the downland. It would get plenty of sun, Dot saw with satisfaction; plants would love it, and it would make a pleasant place to sit on summer evenings, and since the back door with the cat flap opened to the side, beside the Aga, it was not subject to invasion by cats at night – although, of course, the cats would be gone soon. The french doors let plenty of light through to the kitchen, which had another small window beside the back door, opening onto a small back porch, that could be left ajar for air in the wintertime. Dot nodded her approval.

When they had made a thorough inspection of the kitchen and its adjoining scullery with its big walk-in larder, they returned to the hall. The door beside the fireplace led into what had been the dining room; there was a serving hatch through to the kitchen. It was a pleasant room, beautifully proportioned, with a polished board floor; the long green velvet curtains had been left at the windows by arrangement. Dot stood in the middle and spun slowly round, mentally arranging her furniture. It still had the original Georgian ceiling with its elaborate plasterwork, and another good period fireplace. She could give splendid dinner parties for her friends here, it was just the right size.

The room on the opposite side of the hall was the drawing room. Another handsome fireplace, another beautiful original ceiling. Dot hadn't wanted the curtains so the windows were bare, and the carpet was going too just as soon as it could be arranged, but it had promise.

From the drawing room, the hall narrowed to allow for the staircase, and a short L-section led off to the right with one door to the left, which led to a cloakroom, and one straight ahead, with enough space opposite the cloakroom for a chest for boots and shoes, and hooks for coats. The second door led into a smaller room at the back of the house, to Dot's newly readjusted thinking the most satisfactory room of all. It, too, had a fireplace, and a big window that looked out over the garden. She would have her desk there, and a big, comfortable armchair by the fire. Her favourite books on the shelves fixed to the wall, and perhaps a television, and her most treasured ornaments arranged on the mantelpiece. Family photographs? Yes, those too. Oliver's Christmas present picture would hang over the fireplace. When she was on her own, it would be her own private space, she wouldn't be lonely in this room. She had picked out carpets and curtains for her sanctuary, which would be laid and hung when the walls had been painted this week. At present they were a very dark, gloomy red, like dried blood, she planned on a warm buttery cream to make the room look bigger. 'Magnolia', Bennie had said, laughing at her, 'Really, Dorothy!' Well, let her laugh. With the white ceiling and the dark wood of her furnishings, it would look splendid! And anyway, it wasn't magnolia. It called itself "Honeycomb White", and Dot, thinking of it now, suppressed a smile. From somewhere, just lately, she suspected that she was resurrecting a mild sense of humour. She wasn't sure why it should make her feel better about life in general.

The last door from the hall led into a red tiled enclosed porch, with one door to the outside and another, under the stairs, to the cellar. The boiler lived down there, and a splendid wine rack, about the stocking of which Dot intended to consult her son-in-law. Another step forward.

'Let's go upstairs,' said Bennie, when they had peered down the cellar steps and decided not to bother. They knew what was down there, after all; not a lot at present.

There was a stained glass window on the half-landing that spilled coloured light over the banisters and onto the flagstones below when the sun shone through it, and upstairs, there were four bedrooms, two large ones, en-suite, at the front – the commodious en-suite bathrooms and some walk-in wardrobes having been created from what had originally been a slightly smaller fifth bedroom in the middle, possibly a dressing room – and a large family bathroom at the back, with a huge airing cupboard along one wall and a centre bath on a little raised platform. A considerably more modern shower had been tucked into the corner behind the door, with what Dot considered to be a quite lethal array of nozzles, it looked as if it might easily blast an unprepared occupant halfway across the room! Even in here, as in all the other upstairs rooms, there was a small but elegant iron fireplace underlining the age of the place, and the same beautiful cornice, although less elaborate than downstairs. Even the separate lavatory – a feature which Dot greatly appreciated – had this. On either side of the bathroom and the stairwell was a smaller bedroom, but still a good size, each with its own hand basin. Dot walked across to the window of the left hand one, slightly the bigger of the two, and leaned on the window sill, looking out in satisfaction at the view of the garden, the very top of the wire tennis-court enclosure beyond the low-growing shrubs, and the downs lifting to the horizon behind the fields beyond. 'This will be my room,' she said, and heard the contentment in her own voice. Like the purr of a cat, she found herself thinking, and fleetingly wondered where they were, Fatso and Secret Sam.

'Really?' Bennie sounded surprised. 'I would have thought you would have chosen one of the big ones at the front, with the en-suite bathrooms.'

'I like this one,' said Dot. 'What do I need with a huge room to myself? I'd rattle round in it like a pea in a can! And there will be only me here, most of the time; I shan't need to share the bathroom often. If at all, for the house will only be full when the family are here, and the children can share a bathroom, or use their parents'.' She was thinking of Carl as a parent to Annabel and Sebastian, she realised. If only he was!

'What are you going to do with the attics?' Bennie asked, for there were two tiny dormer rooms up a narrow flight of stairs, probably servants' rooms originally, and used by the previous owners for storing things. But Dot wasn't listening, she was looking out of the window at the view, lost in it Bennie thought, and no wonder after looking out on streets and houses for so long!

The field behind the house, Dot was pleased to see, was newly mown, long swathes of grass drying in the sun and its thistles and docks that had threatened her garden now banished, hopefully for good. There was a man in the field; it was too far to see him clearly, but he was a tall man, hatless with dark hair, and a black and white dog at his heels. He was walking along the hedgerow as if it interested him. The man wore blue jeans and a check shirt, and in spite of his heavy boots, didn't look precisely like her idea of a farmer. She found herself wondering for the first time exactly which of Ernest's many cousins had taken over the lease of the land. She should have asked; he, whoever he was, would be her neighbour, or perhaps she didn't need to ask now. Life in Shearwater might turn out to be more interesting than she had imagined. She turned to Bennie.

'You said that one of Ernest's relatives had taken over the farmland,' she said. Bennie gave her a serious look, but simply answered, 'Yes.' Dot looked out of the window again, and Bennie followed her gaze. The man was crossing the field to the far gate now, with the long, easy stride of a born countryman, the dog trotting alongside. Bennie sighed inwardly. You never knew how Dot would react, she was, or had been, a bit of a social climber and sides had definitely been taken in the battle between the influential, but not necessarily universally liked, Mary Vachell-Chillingworth and her only child, Francis. But Dot asked no further questions, and finally turned away from the window. 'Let us go and look at the garden,' she said.

The garden, although Dot peered suspiciously round it, was catless, or at least, appeared to be. They made a brief, and in Dot's case proprietorial, inspection of the flower beds, peeped into the potting shed behind the garage, but didn't go down to the tennis court. Then Bennie suggested going back to the farm for a cup of tea, and Dot put down two bowls of cat biscuits beside a water bowl on the floor, locked up carefully and returned to her car. She would have liked to stay longer, but she had wanted to be on her own if she was honest. It was good of Bennie to come, good to have friends, but she had wished to savour her house and her future there in private. Tomorrow, she could come again. Alone.

She could feed the cats while she was here.

And on Saturday evening, Elizabeth, and Cheryl's brother Michael, would be with her, and she didn't know quite why it was, but she had a feeling that after that she would never be as lonely again.

Liz and Mike arrived shortly after ten o'clock on Saturday evening, and Dot's eyes lit up when she saw the truck gleaming under the outside light. It would be just the thing for transporting her tubs of flowers, she saw at once, and tomorrow was Sunday, the next day a Bank Holiday, and Darren could give Michael a hand while she and Elizabeth packed things, and Leanne worked on perfecting Haymans ready for the move. Mrs Adams would look after the children – Leanne and Darren had two, of primary school age so they would be nicely out of the way for the move itself – or they could play in the garden. Perfect! She greeted her guests warmly, everything neatly organised in her head, and found herself smiling, not only for them but at herself. There she went again! Bossing everyone around.

'Now come on in – that's right Michael, bring the cases – I apologise for the mess, it all looks a bit. bare.' She gave Liz a hug and a kiss on the cheek and led the way indoors.

'Goodness!' said Liz, looking around her. 'I see what you mean.' "Bare" she thought, wasn't quite the right word. There were plenty of things in the entry hall, they just weren't furniture.

'Mind you don't trip on the boxes,' Dot warned her. 'Now, I'll show you your room, and you can sort yourselves out while I make us all a nice cup of tea. Come down when you're ready.' She led the way upstairs.

It was a good feeling, having them here, she decided as she put the kettle on. The quiet, lonely house seemed suddenly full of life the moment they came across the threshold and she resolved then and there that she would see that in the future Haymans had plenty of people coming and going and actively encourage casual visitors, something that she had never done in the past. Why not? she asked herself now, and knew that it all came down to lack of confidence again. She had thought that they might pity her, once she had got through the stage of believing that they might envy her, although that change was of recent date. She had never been like that in what she had recently fallen into the way of thinking of as "the Dee days". She thought now that then she had the confidence generated by outstanding talent, something that had been steadily eroded since, first by her parents and the arbitrary blasting of her ambition, then by Helen and her beauty that had taken Jerry from her. She knew now that Jerry was right all along when he had claimed they had only been friends, but she had been so innocent, and face up to it, so determined to escape her situation. Her belief in the mythical "Mr Right", fostered by her upbringing, and her trust in the equally mythical reality of Happy Ever After had alike betrayed her. She hoped that she was wiser now.

Or maybe, for "determined", she should substitute "desperate".

Over the tea, she outlined to her guests her plans for tomorrow. 'If we get the garden cleared immediately we have had breakfast, we should be ready to leave for Shearwater by mid morning. There are some boxes that can make up the load, things that can be unpacked and put away, out of the way, such as linen, and most of the kitchen equipment, I have kept just what we need here. Some books. If I supervise the garden, Elizabeth could be packing them – if you wouldn't mind, dear? They are all my favourites, still in the bookcase there.' She nodded towards it. 'They used to be in the hall, but I find them company, isn't that silly?'

'Not in the least,' said Liz. 'And I don't mind packing them, it's what we're here for.'

'And then,' said Dot, unaware of the deep contentment in her voice and face, 'we can all go over to Haymans and put everything away in its place. We can take a picnic, or perhaps you would like to lunch in the Ravenscourt Arms, I believe they have a very good carvery there, and it will be Sunday after all. And then we can come back here refreshed, for another load.' The more they took over there, she already realised, the more she would feel the place was really hers, but she didn't say that, not exactly. She said, 'If we can take as much as possible over there in advance, and put it away – clothes in the wardrobes, books on the built-in shelves, curtains hung ready – it will be so much easier on the day.'

'You're really looking forward to that house, aren't you?' said Liz, smiling at her, and Dot had to admit that yes, she was.

They all retired to bed after that, Dot saying that there was a lot to do tomorrow and that Liz and Mike had had a long day today, and when they were alone, Liz said to Mike, 'You didn't have a lot to say this evening. Tired?'

'A bit. But I was thinking too.'

'Thinking what?'

'Actually, about how you would feel, leaving your home for a new one.'

Liz considered this, and thought that she should have done so before. She said, 'I don't know. I suppose, if we get married, I shall have to.'

'What's with this *if*? You're not having second thoughts?'

Liz looked at him, and her lips curved into an involuntary smile. 'No.' She allowed the smile to change to a slight frown. 'I just hadn't thought it through. But it's OK. You're better than a house.'

'We won't have to do anything immediately, but your place is all right for one, a bit cramped for two. We'll never fit my stuff into it.'

Liz laughed out loud, a happy sound.

'What's the joke?'

'For some reason, I hadn't thought of you as having stuff. I imagined you as a bit of a rolling stone.'

Mike stretched luxuriously and reached for her, drawing her close. 'The accumulated clutter of over thirty years of living is taking up space in my parents' loft as we speak.'

'Even your first teddy bear?' asked Liz, snuggling.

'Quite possibly, knowing my mother. And talking of mothers, when are we going to come clean to everyone?'

'Clean?' asked Liz, surprised.

'Technically, we're engaged – remember?'

'So we are,' said Liz. She had enjoyed their week of private joy, but he was right. They had to tell everyone eventually, and since she saw no likelihood of their decision changing, it might as well be now. So she said, 'We'll tell Dorothy while we're here, and the rest of them when we get back.'

'Good.' He released her gently, but keeping close. 'We'll buy a ring in Embridge, and you can flash it at them all when we get back. Now will you finish in the bathroom, so we can go to bed?' Before she could answer his mouth covered hers, and it was impossible to speak, but that didn't stop her thinking what a world of difference there was between good sex and real love, and what a barren life Paul was going to have if he didn't wise up.

In the morning, there was no time for such thoughts, which had in any case evaporated in the pleasure of what had almost immediately followed them. 'Darren promised he would be here soon after ten,' Dot said, briskly slapping toast into a rack and giving it to Liz to put on the breakfast bar – a facility that Dot had seldom used, being brought up to sit at the dining room table for her meals. 'We have plenty of time to get breakfast out of the way, and then I can show Michael what needs to be loaded to take to Shearwater.'

'I can wash up while you do it,' Liz offered helpfully, and Dot smiled approval and said, 'That will be very kind, Elizabeth dear. The machine is over there.' Of course.

By the time that Darren roared in on his motor bike, Mike had moved most of the tubs round to the front with the help of a porter's barrow that Dot kept for moving bags of compost around the garden, and Liz had been provided with two large cardboard boxes and an introduction to the bookcase: she began on her allotted task at once so that it would be done by the time the men had loaded the truck and were ready for the fillers. Dot bustled off with a magic marker in her hand to mark more boxes she wished to take with them, leaving Liz to it, but when she returned one box was only half-full with books and Liz, as she should have guessed, was dipping through the next one that should have been joining them. She looked up as Dot came into the room. 'You've got some brilliant books here – quite old, some of them. A whole set of Arthur Ransome, some of them are first editions, did you realise?'

Dot had never given it a thought: she said, with some severity, 'You are meant to be packing them, Elizabeth, not reading them.'

Liz closed the book hurriedly and placed it in the box. 'Sorry. I can never resist a book.' She added, casually, 'Who was Dee Shipham? You seem to have several that belonged to her, was she a friend?'

Dot stopped in her tracks. Dee Shipham was her lost *alter ego*, the clear mirror image of her distorted self; just lately she had shown too many signs of stirring in her grave. Haymans had started it. Now Liz. She said, 'I was Dee Shipham. Dee is what they called me at school, Shipham was my maiden name. Those Arthur Ransome books date back to my childhood, I kept them for the children, and then later for my grandchildren.'

'It shows,' said Liz appreciatively. 'All of them, right down from Oliver to Seb, have this passion for boats and sailing. All your fault, then.'

Dot had never thought so, but now she came to consider perhaps Liz was right. She found that she quite liked the idea, even if it had been unintentional. Another Dee thing, like tennis, and leadership skills, too long packed away in mothballs.

Liz was saying, 'I like Dee. It suits you much better than Dot, Dot is old fashioned and stuffy. Grannie Dee – it sounds just right.' She looked up at Dot, standing there with her pretty blonde hair unusually tousled after her spell in the garden, in her T-shirt and jeans that she had put on for working, that were so unlike her usual style, and was oddly reminded of a moth she had once watched emerging from its chrysalis.

Dot said, sadly, 'I am old fashioned and stuffy, I know that. And Dee is long gone, whoever she was.'

'She's you,' said Liz firmly. 'She's still you, in there somewhere.' She took another book from the shelf and placed it in the box with its fellows, wondering if she dared ask Dot if she would let her buy her a new tennis racquet to go with her tennis court, and not quite finding the courage. Dot felt a need to assert herself.

'You need to work quicker than that, Elizabeth, or we shall all be waiting for you,' she said firmly, and left the room more briskly than was strictly necessary.

Not too long after that, the truck was fully loaded and ready to leave for Haymans, and Dot locked up and took Liz out to the garage, where her own car waited. 'They will come after us,' she said as they got into it. 'Darren knows the way, but we shall be faster, of course. You may explore the house while I direct the unloading, see what you think of it.'

Liz settled into her seat, accepting that on this trip, at least, she was little better than supercargo. She wouldn't be much good at lifting boxes and tubs, and she didn't know where anything went until she was told, useless! But she would enjoy exploring the house on her own, she liked looking at houses. Thinking of this made her think of what Mike had said last night. Looking at houses with him might be even more fun, and she wondered what sort of a home he had in mind, and more importantly, how much they would be able to spend. There were some lovely houses in Waldren Stavey, but she didn't think a professional soldier would have salted that much money away in spite of the investments he had mentioned, and she had already realised that he had no intention of battening on her. But knowing Mike, he had it worked out, and eventually he would tell her – half shares would be good, and if they did need a mortgage to cover his half, he had a good job and would be able to pay it. That would work for both of them, and she wouldn't argue over it.

When they reached Haymans, Liz was despatched as per schedule to take her feeble female self on a tour of the house while Dot gave orders and Mike and Darren hefted things about. Dot spent some time outside, indicating the positioning of her tubs around her new patio, and then showing her helpers the rooms into which she wished the boxes to be placed. That done, she left them to get on with it and went to the kitchen to feed the cats, of whose presence, as she had come to expect, there was no indication but empty bowls. Their appetites were good, that was a hopeful sign. They hadn't run away completely and with Liz's help, perhaps she could catch them and get them to the vet and off her conscience. Liz seemed to like cats.

That done, there was nothing she could usefully do until the men brought in the boxes for the kitchen. She walked to the double doors to the conservatory and pushed them open, and a wave of warm air surged out to meet her. Really, it wouldn't hurt to open the french windows to the patio and some of the others too, to let in some fresh air. She walked round doing this, making a mental note to close them when they left later on, and then stood and looked round her, leaning back with her hands propped on a window sill, unaware that it was a pose that belonged more to Dee, happy in her own achievements and stirring in her grave only an hour ago, rather than to uptight Dot. It was a big conservatory. The people who had lived here had used it as an extension to the kitchen to make a family living space where the boys could play and run in and out of the garden without tramping their dirt everywhere, and Benita had told her that they had seldom used the two main reception rooms unless they had guests. It would work the same for her. Annabel and Seb were rather older than the boys of course, but when little Daniel was bigger it would be ideal, she could cook and look after the family's needs and still keep her eye on him. Because they would come, Debbie and Mawgan and Daniel, not only for the Dock Inn, she was beginning to accept, but for herself. They would really love this house, all of them. Oliver too, and Cheryl and Zoë, they would like it here if they ever came, and she was coming to believe that perhaps they might if she asked them. Out of duty maybe, to start with, but later because they would want to. Susan, of course, had always come, and now she was hopefully shot of Tom Casson, more willingly than ever before, and her nice Carl too. With a feeling of deep satisfaction, Dot returned to the kitchen to switch on the kettle; there were decent mugs in the top of one of the boxes, although she would never use one herself, naturally, and the men would be glad of a drink. Milk and sugar and teabags that she had left in the built-in fridge for the workmen's use, they had provided their own mugs. She dug into a box for the teapot, left handily on the top.

Liz came into the kitchen while Dot was setting out the retrieved mugs, looking about her with interest. She saw the cat bowls by the door, with the scattering of cat biscuits, and asked, 'Any sign of them yet?'

'I have not really been here to see. I asked the workmen to put that food that the Tarrants left for them into the bowls every evening when they leave, and when I have come over the next day to check on the work it has gone, so I assume that they are still about, but I haven't seen them.'

'Poor things,' said Liz. 'Why don't you keep them? I'm sure they'd prefer that to being split up and parcelled out to strange people in strange places.'

558

Dot's reply was less dismissive than her reply to Bennie had been. 'I have no experience with cats,' she said.

'Cats are no trouble. They pretty much do their own thing. And it's like something I read somewhere once, *another heart beating in the house*. I don't know who said it, but it's true. It makes a house into a home.'

'I expect you were brought up with animals,' said Dot. 'I was not.'

Liz made no comment on this. She walked to the conservatory doors and looked through, and then said the same thing that Dot had thought when she first saw it. 'How odd, having this opening off from the kitchen. You'd have thought they'd take it from a reception room.'

'The only reception room at the back is the small one by the cloakroom,' said Dot, thinking *my* room, I'm glad they didn't. 'This is the more open side of the garden, and it was practical too. They used it as a family room, and they could all be together even when the mother was working in the kitchen. They ate in there too, there is room to put a table and chairs at this end.'

'This is a lovely workspace,' said Liz, turning her attention to the kitchen.

'It is certainly very pleasant,' said Dot, 'It has fortunately been modernised with great sympathy, in keeping with the house without being old-fashioned.' She put the bag of catfood into the cupboard and looked at her watch. 'There's no time to unpack anything before lunch, shall we go and look at the garden while the kettle boils?'

'I'd love to,' said Liz, thinking of the tennis court. Unaware that she had an ally in Ingrid, she was determined to push Dot into taking up tennis again, one way or another. They went outside and Dot took her on a guided tour of the vegetable patch, the patio, the rockery, and the lawns, but made no move to go down through the shrubs to the bottom of the garden. Eventually, Liz felt constrained to say, 'What about the tennis court? Can we see that?'

'If you wish,' said Dot, with no obvious show of reluctance, but Liz still wondered why she had needed to ask. She followed Dot down the path through the shrubbery, and almost ran into her when Dot stopped abruptly. 'What on earth,' Dot said, 'is *that*?'

There was a face peeping out from under a hydrangea, a broad, furry face, with generous tufts of silky-looking brown and white hair on either cheek, long whiskers, and two tufted ears on top. Wide green eyes and a pink nose completed what was, on the whole, a good-natured impression. The eyes looked at them for a moment, blinked once and then the head quietly withdrew. There was a slight rustle in the leaves, then nothing.

'A cat,' said Liz, helpfully.

'But it was *huge*! No cat was ever that big.'

Liz suppressed a grin. 'I imagine that was Fatso. From the looks of him, he's a Maine Coon, or he's got some Maine Coon genes.'

'What on earth is a Maine Coon?'

'A very large type of cat, it comes from America. Long silky hair and a broad back you could serve tea on. Enormous paws. Likes water.' Liz leaned forward and parted the leaves gently. There was nothing there – nothing alive that is. 'There – see?'

Dot looked. There was a patch of soft earth under the bush, and right in the centre of it, a pawprint. She drew a breath.

'That's never a cat made that!'

'I promise you, it is.'

'Then I dread to think what Secret Sam will be like.'

'He may be another the same,' said Liz, laughing. 'Although, I imagine him more as slinky and black, with laid back ears and his tail carried low, ready for a fight. We shall see.'

'Hmm,' said Dot. She moved on down the path, and Liz followed, curious to see what lay at the end.

The tennis court was a hard court. It stood, surrounded by its wire cage to stop balls flying all over Dorset, in the corner of a rectangle, the remainder of which was an L-shaped patio area with a small stone shed tucked into one corner by the shrubbery. There was a brick-built barbecue in another corner overlooking the fields, with a cupboard beneath to hold a gas bottle. Liz looked round her approvingly. 'You want to bring some of your tubs of flowers down here, to soften the edges,' she said. 'It would be a wonderful place to hold a tennis party!'

'Yes,' said Dot, but shortly. She walked to the wall that overlooked the fields and stood there, looking out. There were no farmers and no dogs to be seen this morning. After a moment, Liz came to stand

560

beside her, slipping her arm through Dot's companionably.

'You should take full advantage of it all,' she said, gently. 'You really should. This lovely court ...'

'The children will no doubt enjoy it,' said Dot, in a tight voice that gave too much away.

'You too,' said Liz. She said what Ingrid had said. 'Join the local tennis club. Get your hand in again. It'll all come back to you.'

'I suppose your parents told you,' said Dot, not looking at her.

'Yes.'

Dot said, in a meditative tone of voice, 'There are no sadder words in the English language than "too late", Elizabeth. And that is not original, but it is still true.' She looked at her watch again, forestalling any response. 'And now if you have seen all you want, those men must have finished unloading by now and they will be thirsty. We should go and make that tea.' She turned and without looking at Liz, headed for the path with a firm step, and Liz, perforce, had to follow meekly. But the subject wasn't closed, she was resolved on that.

She wondered idly, as they walked back up the garden, where Dot had acquired her stilted manner of speaking, she sounded like her own grandmother half the time. It didn't go with her changed outer shell, with the windblown blonde curls, the jeans and shirt, the robust build. There was somebody else – Dee Shipham? – in there somewhere. She had to come out, even if the process was painful. She wondered how far it would be politic to push – or pull.

They drank tea in the kitchen, and then Darren wanted to get back to Embridge so that he could spend the afternoon with Leanne and their two little girls, so Mike gave him the keys to the truck and he drove off back to town. The three remaining took themselves to the Ravenscourt Arms and its Sunday carvery. There, it soon became apparent that Liz wasn't the only one on a mission. When they were seated at a table by the window, with their plates of Sunday roast in front of them, Dot waded right in.

'And are you two planning to marry, or are you going to be like Susan and Carl and simply cohabit?' she asked them, straight out. Liz and Mike exchanged a complicit glance; Mike raised his eyebrows, and Liz gave a slight nod. Why not, after all? Dot hadn't often been the first recipient of a confidence, so far as she was aware.

'Funny you should ask that,' Mike said, easily. He stuck his fork into a crisp roast potato and held it suspended above his plate, smiling at Dot. 'The only thing that's stopping us from announcing our engagement is that I haven't had time yet to buy Liz a ring. I hoped we might squeeze a half hour this week, there must be a good jeweller in your town. Then we can go home and flash it about and surprise them.'

Dot turned faintly pink, understanding the ... well, the honour really, she supposed, that had been done her. She said, 'There is an excellent jeweller in Embridge, we can certainly make time to visit him. In fact, by Wednesday afternoon, I suspect that we shall be driven into the town by hunger and the lack of anything left to cook with.'

'As bad as that?' Mike asked, laughing, but Dot nodded her head.

'I imagine so. I think it will be a good idea to get as much as possible over here and put away before the big move. That can include all the kitchen utensils and a lot of the everyday china. My clothes can go in one of the walk-in wardrobes, I can move them into my own room at my leisure later on. And all the gardening equipment, the mower and the hoses and implements, can go in the shed by the garage. The contents of the garage, too, if we have the time. It will all make the moving day so much easier, since you and your truck are here to help.'

'I knew I'd come in useful one day,' said Mike, in a satisfied voice. Dot smiled at him, a more open smile than she had smiled for a long time. She said, 'And let me be the first to congratulate you on your engagement. I think you will be very well suited.'

'How can you say that?' asked Liz, curiously. 'I love him, of course, but he's in-your-face practical, covered in grease and oil, and I'm spaced-out creative.'

Dot looked from one to the other, indulgently, and spoke without thinking from instinct that she had forgotten she had ever had. 'You speak the same language,' she said, and for a moment was consumed by envy so that she could have cried.

XXVIII

The next few days followed the master plan laid down by Dot and circumstances. Everything that could be moved with the truck and put away at Haymans was loaded, transported and stowed. At the Embridge end, Ingrid, Sally and Marie Law had all turned up at one time or another to offer assistance with packing; in Shearwater, Bennie appeared on the doorstep to help with the unpacking. Leanne and her mother cleaned energetically in the wake of the exodus. Certain areas of the Embridge house, most notably the kitchen, became emptier and emptier, and by Wednesday there was nothing left in the kitchen at all but a frying pan, three plates, three cups, three saucers, three sets of cutlery and one bread knife, together with a basket to put them in when they were finished with. In the spring-cleaned fridge, which was staying as part of the fixtures and fittings, reposed a packet of rolls, an airtight box with bacon in it, half a dozen eggs in an egg box and four apples, plus half a bottle of milk for the instant coffee, which stood on a shelf with a packet of cereal and a pot of marmalade beside it.

'Your grandmother is a fantastic organiser,' Mike told Liz, appreciatively. 'Everything organised for a quick getaway: feed the troops, scram! Us too. Organised, I mean. I don't want to get away.'

They had been ordered to be ready to leave for lunch, followed by a visit to the jeweller favoured by Dot, just as soon as they had washed their hands and brushed their hair. All the work was done that could be done, an afternoon seeing the town and perhaps taking a quick look at the Dock Inn was the plan for the rest of the day, followed by dinner with Ingrid and Alex when, Dot said, they had all had time for a shower and change of clothes. 'And then, an early night,' she told them firmly. 'It's going to be a long day tomorrow, and the removal men will be here at eight o'clock sharp.'

Liz had wondered if Dot would accompany them to the jeweller, but she didn't. She dropped them in the town square after they had lunched at a pleasant country restaurant on the outskirts, pointed out the shop, and then said she would go and take a look at progress at the pub and meet them for a cup of tea at Borden's later on. She pointed out Borden's, although they could hardly miss it. When she had driven away, they walked across and looked in the jeweller's window.

'This feels a bit like a dream,' Liz said, on a sigh. 'Something that's happening to somebody else – you know?'

'Not changing your mind, I hope.'

'Certainly not. But whether we admit it or not, choosing a ring is something that most women dream about from the time they first recognise the potential of boys. And although I always said I didn't care about marrying, I find now I'm as soppy as a heroine in the very worst kind of romantic novel.'

'Been crying wolf?' asked Mike, grinning down at her. 'Well, here he is. Let's go inside.'

The manager had seen the car that dropped them off through the window, he greeted them with flattering deference, in spite of their slightly scruffy appearance. Half the town, it seemed, knew that Dot was moving, and slightly to Liz's surprise after Dot's public fall from grace, the jeweller at least was sorry. 'A great lady, Mrs Nankervis,' he said. 'She's done a lot of good in this town. Now, what may I do for you?'

He seemed not at all scornful of their modest requirement, producing a tray of moderately priced rings with murmured congratulations and none of the looking down his nose that Liz had half expected in such a posh shop. After some debate, Liz picked out a pretty emerald flanked with small diamonds that coincidentally, conveniently fitted perfectly. She found she didn't want to wait for something to be altered, and was ashamed of herself. 'Because it's the colour of your eyes,' she told Mike, sentimentally, and then blushed scarlet. 'Oh, God and the saints preserve me from ever putting that crumby line in a book!'

'I thought it was meant to be my line, anyway,' Mike told her. Liz regained her composure.

'There are no precious or semi-precious stones the colour of cough syrup,' she told him.

'More like HP Sauce,' Mike suggested. He held out the ring to the jeweller. 'The lady likes this one. That's good enough for me.'

The ring was put in a box, and Mike produced a credit card, then they left the shop and crossed the square to Borden's. They sat at a table by the window in the top-floor restaurant, as instructed, to wait for Dot.

'What an amazing view,' said Liz, looking down out of the window at the town square below, unexpectedly embarrassed by the last half hour's work, and Mike, said, 'Yes.' She turned her head and found he was looking, not at the view, but straight at her, and for the second time in twenty minutes, turned scarlet. He held the ring box in his fingers, and now he had her attention he flicked it open and set it on the table between them, picking the ring out carefully. 'Give me your hand – no, the other one, stupid!' He slid the ring onto her finger and closed her hand in his, warmly. They sat there in the sun, hands clasped, without speaking, each of them feeling that a long journey had ended in homecoming. If only, Liz found herself thinking, they could finally sort out Paul. He was a loose thread that could well unravel the whole tapestry of her contentment. She was still having nightmares about his last unwanted gift.

Dot joined them soon after, admired the ring and kissed them both affectionately. 'This week would have been hard and rather lonely without you,' she said. 'I'm so glad the pair of you came, although it has been an odd sort of holiday for you both. I'm working you very hard.'

'Your friends are rallying round too,' Liz reminded her.

'Friends are not the same as family,' said Dot, smiling at them. Liz said, carefully for she wasn't certain if this was the moment, or if there would ever be one, 'Why don't you come to visit us when you're settled? Meet the rest of the family, they'd like that.'

Dot's face shut, there was no other description for it. She said 'Yes, you said that before Elizabeth. I think that book is closed, don't you agree? We have all got on very well without each other all these years.'

'But you haven't,' said Liz. Dot didn't reply, she picked up the printed menu on the table.

'Shall we order tea?' she asked.

Liz didn't push her point, but she had caught something in Dot's expression that made her think that she had made a dent in her armour. It emboldened her, when they had drunk their tea and were on their way back to the car, to try a different attack on the fortress of Dot's defences, and this time it was an even more daring one.

She had spotted the shop when they left the jeweller. "Windward Sports" it announced itself, with a window full of sports equipment and sweatshirts carrying sporty logos. She took her courage in both hands as they came up to it.

'Will you let us buy you a house-warming present, Grannie Dee?'

Dot hadn't noticed the proximity of the shop, not doing so was a well-established habit. She smiled at Liz and said, 'That's very sweet of you Elizabeth, but I don't think there is really anything I need, do you?'

'Well, actually there is,' said Liz, firmly. She took Dot's arm. 'It's a terrible shame to waste that lovely court. Let us buy you a new racquet – *two* new racquets, so that you have one for a friend if you need it. You'll have such fun, and it'll soon come back to you.' She caught Mike's eye over Dot's shoulder. Mike, of course, had no idea of Dot's lost dream, he looked, if anything, surprised, but he said nothing. 'Come on. Let's go inside.'

There were no shops in the centre of Embridge which weren't very expensive, the rents saw to that. Dot found herself propelled through the door of this one before she had managed to find a word to say, and Liz was explaining their errand to the assistant before she could be stopped.

It was a curious feeling. As if something in her head – or her heart, or her stomach, Dot wasn't sure which – that had been frozen into silence was now thawing and finding a voice. She wasn't sure, just for a humiliating moment, if she could stop herself crying out, or even just crying, which would be worse, but a lifetime of hiding her feelings came to her aid. She picked up the racquet that the assistant was showing them with a nonchalance that covered a maelstrom of mixed emotions. It slid into her grip like the hand of an old friend and she hefted it thoughtfully. Racquets had changed since she last played; long gone was the wooden frame and the wooden press that kept it from warping, but the principle remained, and a contradictory unfamiliar familiarity. 'It feels a bit heavy,' she said, in a voice whose normality astonished her. 'Do you have a lighter one, with perhaps a slimmer grip?'

The second one was better – much better. She tossed it in her hand, thinking that she would certainly need a refresher course of some kind for this new technology would have changed the game she knew, subtly maybe but inevitably, and the assistant said, 'If you stand back a little, madam, there's room to try a small swing. Just pull your arm back and swing it forward, try the balance, see how it feels for you.' His accompanying smile was a little patronising: poor old bird, you could almost see him thinking, what does she want with a racquet like that? and Dot tried to ignore him. She stepped back and took a swing, imagining the small white ball flying towards her, and hit it amidships with a thump that she almost felt. It was good – not entirely familiar, but good all the same, she was going to enjoy this after all. She didn't realise that she was smiling.

'You can see you've done that before,' said Liz. Dot looked at the racquet in her hand with what she feared was close to complacence, but she didn't care. Dot had come a long way in the past few months and was beginning to know, and even to laugh at, her own failings. She tried a couple more racquets with increasing confidence, came back to the second one and felt that she had been reunited with a friend. She said, 'This one,' and Liz said, 'And what about the spare?'

'You really shouldn't,' Dot began, 'I can perfec –' She got no further.

'Yes I should. Choose, and don't argue!' and Mike thought, but wasn't absolutely certain, that he heard her mutter afterwards, 'Time somebody did.'

They left the shop with Mike carrying the two racquets in their zipped covers, together with a box of tennis balls, in a plastic bag which Dot felt was rather mundane when they represented so much. She must buy herself a proper sports bag, and then she found that she was blinking back tears and stepped out for the car park with a briskness that made Liz protest. She wished afterwards that she hadn't, but Dot only said, 'We haven't much time if we're going out this evening, I still have to drive back to Shearwater to feed the cats. The carpet layers finished this morning.' It might have sounded like the ultimate *non sequitur,* had Dot not mentioned her arrangement with the workmen. Dot was a great organiser, Liz appreciated, Mike was quite right. She hoped that Fatso and Secret Sam appreciated it all.

She would really have to re-christen Fatso, if she decided to keep them that was, it was a terrible name to give a beautiful animal. That was small boys for you, of course. Liz hoped she would keep them, both for their sake and for her own. Cats would be the perfect companions for Dot; like her, they kept themselves private, although admittedly with a very slightly less touch-me-not exterior, and they would miss each other if they were separated and given to strangers. If Fatso really was a Maine Coon, he might even, horror of horrors, fall into the hands of someone who would want to show him, a truly awful fate for an animal that had been a child's beloved pet.

Mike and Liz were interested to see the Dock Inn, so Dot drove out to Shearwater that way. Since it was covered in scaffolding, where the men were now repairing and renovating the outside, there wasn't much to see, but Dot was able to tell them that the building dated back to at least the seventeenth century. 'Records show that it was certainly there by 1649,' she informed them. 'It is an interesting old building, a landmark. It would have been a crime to knock it down!'

'Were they going to?' asked Mike, with interest, and Liz, remembering what Dot had said on their first meeting, added, 'How old is your own house, Grannie Dee? Haymans I mean – not the one you're moving out of.'

'About two hundred years,' said Dot, with satisfaction. 'It was built during the reign of George III as a small manor house with the farm attached. One of the Ravenscourt daughters married the original Hayman, and the property remained in the family for one hundred and sixty years. The farm buildings are largely gone now, but the garage and garden shed are part of the original stable, and the tennis court and its patio are based on the foundations of a barn and a dairy, so Benita tells me.'

'So you got your history,' said Liz, smiling, and Dot agreed that yes, she had.

Yet again, there was no sign of the cats beyond two nearly empty bowls, and a dead mouse which Mike disposed of. 'A gift from the feline Welcome Wagon,' said Liz, grinning, and Dot looked down her nose. She didn't say, however, that they needn't have bothered, and Liz took this as a positive sign. The phantom cats were making their presence felt; Dot would soon begin to think of them as a part of Haymans if she wasn't careful.

The dinner that followed with Alex and Ingrid was informal, a simple barbecue in the sunlit evening garden, relaxing under big umbrellas in comfortable garden chairs. 'As far away as you can possibly get from moving house,' said Alex, pouring wine. 'Relax in the sunshine, eat, drink and be lazy.'

Dot accepting a glass with a smile that for a second, Alex found strangely unfamiliar, said, 'It was a lovely idea of yours, Alex. I don't know what we would have done back at the house. We're down to subsistence rations for breakfast, before we pack the frying pan into the car.'

Liz noted the apostrophes and the touch of humour, and took heart; the times, they were a-changing, if only slowly. The tennis racquets seemed to have struck a chord, the music was merrier now. Alex, too, seemed to notice something new.

'You sound as if you're looking forward to it,' he said. Ingrid, approaching across the lawn with a bowl of coleslaw, said, 'Of course she is, it's a dream come true – isn't it, Dot? You always wanted an older house.'

'Then why on earth didn't you tell Jerry?' asked Alex, surprised, and Dot, who didn't really know why now that she came to consider it, except that they hadn't really discussed things like that and she was so besotted she let Jerry get away with it, changed the subject by asking, 'Has Susan told you about Sebastian's success in the regatta at the weekend?'

'She certainly has,' said Alex. He distributed the last wineglass to Mike and returned to the barbecue, but he was still close enough to continue with the conversation. 'Wiped the floor with them all, from what Susan says. Apparently Carl gave him some hints. Advanced tactics that he followed to the letter, and blew the twelve and under fleet out of the water! Sent them all into a panic by yelling "starboard" at every chance he got and pinching everyone's wind! Taking an unfair advantage, is what I call it!'

'Sebastian has turned out to have hidden depths, once he was away from his father,' said Dot, with approval. 'Carl says he should have a different boat next year. A Laser, I think he said. Something like that. He shows real promise, Susan tells me, although I am not quite sure of what, exactly.'

'They'll never part him from his beloved *Swallow*!' exclaimed Liz.

'Susan says that he's a smart little helmsman, and should be encouraged,' said Alex, sounding pleased. 'Time things looked up for that little family. I'm glad for them.'

'And Annabel has her horses,' said Ingrid. She flung herself into an empty chair and linked her hands behind her head. 'You should have a pony for her to ride here, Dot. Your friend Bennie would look after it for her, and her own children would exercise it.'

Dot said, for it was something that she had been considering for some time now, 'What Annabel needs is a pony of her own in Cornwall. It isn't enough for her to have one in Devon, or even here, she needs one where she can learn to look after it herself, and ride it every day. What they need is a horsebox, not another pony.'

'I'm sure Carl would be up for it,' said Alex, who had liked what he had seen of him. 'Come to that, it isn't beyond Susan to tow a horsebox.'

'If Sebastian is to have a Laser, then I think it should be looked into,' said Dot firmly. 'It seems to me that they are all so sailing-minded down there that Annabel's interests get sidelined half the time. I shall mention it to Susan and Carl, the next time I see them.'

There was a pause, while Ingrid and Alex thought about the conjunction of Susan and Carl, then Alex said, 'All right is she, your Susan? Everything working out for her as it should?'

'She seems so. Indeed, she is quite unfamiliar these days. So happy …' Dot listened to what she had just said, and Ingrid, watching her, said quietly, 'Not only Susan, it seems to me. You've come alive, Dot. Moving house, or the Dock Inn, something has lit you up from inside.'

'A little of both, maybe,' said Dot, smiling. She added, because Ingrid deserved it, 'Elizabeth gave me a present this afternoon.'

'Oh?' Ingrid looked enquiring.

'Two tennis racquets,' said Liz, and Alex looked at her with approval. 'Good girl! And are you going to use them, Dorothy?'

'Just as soon as I am settled, I shall make enquiries about membership of the tennis club,' said Dot, taking the plunge, and Alex said, 'Attagirl!'

The apostrophes had vanished again, Liz noted, but Dot seemed to find talking about tennis inhibiting. Perhaps not surprising. Liz hoped that she would find that she could still play when she put it to the test, although, given her history, it would be surprising if she couldn't. Dot changed the subject firmly. Enough was enough. 'And you, Alex? How are things going with Valentine Harries? Is he everything you hoped for?'

570

'He's good. Solid gold. He's taking a load off my shoulders, and people trust him, and like him too. Best day's work I ever did, taking him on. Here, these steaks are ready – plates, Ingrid, please!'

Dot gave a sigh, not exactly of satisfaction but more, perhaps, of regret for times past. 'It seems that we are all a great deal better off without Tom Casson,' she said.

'And what about your own protégé?' Ingrid asked, pulling out the chairs around the garden table. 'Come and sit here, all of you. Grub's up!'

Everyone obediently rose to their feet and took their places, and Dot said, 'Not my protégé, my son-in-law's. He is responding to treatment, I'm glad to say. He has had a rough time. I believe, by the time he returns from Italy in the autumn, you will see a great change in him.'

'And has he got over Debbie, do you think?' Ingrid asked. Dot thought before she replied. She had a certain fellow feeling with Tim over Debbie; the situation reminded her very much of her own with Jerry, so that she answered soberly and, Liz thought, listening, from the heart.

'I believe that one never entirely gets over such things. But he will survive. Mawgan says that the best thing that could happen to him is that he meets a beautiful Italian waitress and brings her home to help him at the Dock Inn. But Mawgan would say anything.'

'And that would cure him, do you think?' asked Alex, raising his eyebrows.

'I doubt it. But it would console him.'

Ingrid looked at her. She asked, 'What did Deb say, when she heard what her husband had done?'

'Over Tim? She was deeply touched.' Dot paused, wondering how much she should say, for Debbie had been more than touched, when she spoke to her mother about it she had been practically in tears. 'For he doesn't owe Tim anything,' she had said. 'Tim was quite horrible to him, and caused him no end of grief. I can't believe that he could now be so generous!'

'You care about Tim still,' Dot had said, and Debbie had answered simply, 'We almost loved each other. We've been friends for a long time. So yes.'

She said none of that now, however. 'They were friends,' was all that she permitted herself.

There was a pause in the conversation here, as everyone passed around the salad and started to eat. Then Ingrid said, 'The word on the street, Dot, is that your friend Jenny Carruthers is not a happy bunny. A rumour is going around that they're filming another series with Mawgan and featuring the renaissance of the Dock Inn, and that you're to be in it. Is that true?'

'I believe I may feature in one episode,' admitted Dot, trying not to sound smug. 'Possibly more. It depends how it works out, apparently, when they have finished filming. It will be, after all, primarily a cookery programme: the Inn, and the work taking place there, is merely the background.'

'Goody goody, if you're there at all,' said Ingrid. 'I like to see the enemy eating dust! Some people have been saying that they miss you on all those committees, and you should be invited back. Although where that would leave Jenny, I hate to think.'

'Where she deserves to be?' Alex suggested. 'Would you go back, Dorothy – after all that's happened?'

'No,' said Dot.

'That was very unequivocal.' He smiled at her. 'Found something better to do? Good! Henry would be pleased.'

Dot said, enlarging on her brief negative, 'I was edged off those committees for all the wrong reasons, and I would be invited back for the same. My private life is no concern of theirs. And yes, I have found something better to do. Several things, indeed.'

'Well, good for you.'

Sitting here among Henry's friends and family, Dot was unexpectedly swept with such a longing for his affection, kindness and understanding that she was unable to speak for a minute. Perhaps reading something of this in her face, Alex turned his attention to the other guests.

'So tell us about you, Michael,' he said. 'You're being very quiet. Dorothy tells us you're Cheryl's brother, that's a bit of a coincidence with you engaged to Liz, here.'

'Not really, when you think about it,' Mike denied. 'It's how people meet – someone knows someone, and meets someone else through them ... coincidences like that are happening all the time.' He flashed a sudden grin at his host. 'And the reason I'm being quiet is that I'm gathering information. This is all new ground to me.'

'The only real coincidence is that he showed up in Waldren Stavey,' Liz put in, 'and as none of us had any idea who he was, nor he who *we* were, you wonder how many undiscovered coincidences like that happen every day. It's only the christening that blew the gaff. Without that, we'd quite possibly never have known.'

'Yes, you would,' said Mike. 'You'd have known the instant Susan came to stay – which she does frequently, I understand. Or Cheryl would have realised when I told her your name – or all would have been revealed at the wedding; that would have been unlikely, but interesting.'

'Ooh, yes,' Liz contemplated such a situation, round-eyed, and being a writer, wondering if she could work it into a plot. It would require a great many coincidences and omissions, a lot more complicated than those that had brought her and Mike together, but it could be done – at least, in her sort of fiction it could probably be done. She came to the conclusion that it might be a bit unbelievable. Truth was stranger than fiction, yes, but on the whole, truth got away with it better.

Alex was asking Mike about his job, and when he heard what it was, he laughed. 'Liz's father will be pleased. How did he take your engagement? Dancing on the roof, I would imagine.'

'He doesn't know yet. We're breaking it to them when we get back,' said Mike, and Liz said, 'You know my father?' in amazement.

Alex looked at her. He said, 'Well, of course I do. Your grandfather was my friend as well as my client. If nothing else, I would have met him at the funeral, but as it happens I knew him – knew all of them – long before that. I've stayed on the farm in the days when it belonged to your grandmother's family.'

'Did you know my grandmother too?' asked Liz.

'Only briefly. She was a great lady.' He smiled at her. 'I remember you when you were a baby.'

The interval had allowed Dot to regain her balance, and the rest of the evening passed pleasantly. They didn't stay late, leaving as the sun went down to get an early night before the big move the next day, and when the guests had gone, and they were clearing up, Ingrid remarked, 'I thought Dot was different tonight. This move has given her a new lease of life.'

'Has given her a life, you mean,' Alex amended. 'The promise of one, at least. And I think it's quite as much Liz and Mike as the move.'

'Do you think she'll make contact with Henry's children again, because of it?' Ingrid speculated, and Alex shook his head and replied, 'Anybody's guess.'

The following day, by contrast to the evening, was very far from peaceful. It began early, with a quick breakfast and the final clearing of the kitchen to allow Leanne and her cleaning equipment to move in. 'We can shut the door on that room,' said Dot, with satisfaction, and went on to enumerate further no-go areas for the removal men, when they arrived – any minute now, if they were up to schedule. She glanced at her watch, and then out of the window. 'And here they are, right on time!' and neither Liz nor Mike said, although they both thought, that the removers probably didn't dare to be otherwise.

Liz recalled having heard somewhere that moving house was one of the three most traumatic experiences a person would experience during their lifetime, up there with bereavement and divorce, and by the time the day was over she could believe it. She and Leanne had been deputed to see the furniture out of the old house, while Dot and Mike went in the truck to Shearwater to supervise its installation in the new, Dot hopping aboard with a nonchalance that would have amazed her old associates. Working alongside Leanne, Liz naturally got on good terms with her, as armed with a detailed list of instructions and Dot's authority, they bullied and persuaded the men into loading up the big removal van in the order that Dot had specified and saw them on their way with the first load. Leanne shut the front door on their departure and wiped a dramatic hand across her brow.

'Phew! Reckon you and me got the dirty end of the stick here! If they said once more as it wasn't the best way to do it, I was going to hit 'em with me umbrella! Fancy a cuppa? We've a bit until they get back and my mum gave me sandwiches and a thermos, there's plenty for two if you don't mind drinking out the screw cap.'

By this time, Liz would have killed for a cup of tea and drunk it out of a flowerpot if need be, so the two of them settled comfortably at the breakfast bar in the clean and empty kitchen and shared Leanne's lunch. Mrs Adams had generous ideas on the subject, and there was plenty for two. While they ate, they talked. 'She's a good lady, Mrs N,' Leanne confided over the tea and sandwiches. 'I know as there's those that think she's a stuck-up snob, but she's been good to us, giving us that cottage and everything, and a chance of a better life for the kids than they'd get on a council estate.'

'Cottage?' asked Liz, at a loss. Leanne looked surprised.

'Di'n't she show it you? No, p'raps she wouldn't of, there's people in it I b'lieve. It's part of the new house, it goes with the property. It's a holiday let, and it had bookings when Mrs N bought the place, but she says she's not taking any more after the last one already booked, middle of September that is. Then she'll clear it out and me and Darren can move in with the kids. My mum's really made up about it. She thinks Mrs N is like some kind of saint.'

'Goodness,' said Liz, unable to think of anything better. She had no idea where Leanne and Darren lived, and although she had a vague recollection of a cottage adjoining Haymans, she had no idea about that either. She hadn't even realised that it was part of the property. Fortunately, Leanne was ready to tell her.

'She says as we can have it for what she calls a "peppercorn" rent, which means next to no rent at all, just for the legal thing. And I go on working for her, so many hours for the cottage, and the rest and stuff like helping with parties or extra jobs and that, counts as overtime, so I get money for that. And Darren gives her a hand with the garden evenings and weekends when she needs it, and o' course he'll still have his job and we don't have to pay no rent out o' that, so we'll be better off than we've ever been. And the kids can go to school in Shearwater in the autumn, and that's a good little school.'

'It sounds ideal,' said Liz.

'It'll be grand. And Mrs N says we can decorate it how we like, soon as the last visitors is gone. It's got a little garden where the kids can play, and no busy road for them to run on. Just fields all round, and a lane where they can ride their bikes. Bliss!' She closed her eyes to think about it, and then opened them again and gave Liz a fierce glare. 'So anyone as says as she's a stuck-up cow, they've got me to reckon with!'

'Don't blame me,' said Liz, pacifically. 'I think she's a star. She's just been a bit eclipsed lately.'

Leanne gave her a dark look. 'My mum says as the way as she was treated by that solicitor is a crying shame! Not that I knew 'im much, he was mostly before my time, but she was dead upset when he upped and left her, that I do know. Not that she ever let on, but you could tell. My mum said as she'd of liked to take her in her arms and hug her to comfort her, but you don't do stuff like that with Mrs N.'

But this was getting too close to the bone for Liz, and she changed the subject tactfully, asking Leanne about where she and Darren and the children lived at present, which turned out to be in a council house on an estate at the edge of town, and within four doors of her parents.

'Bit rough it is,' said Leanne, musingly. 'Not that it's as bad as some, I grew up there and I had a good enough time. But you want more for your kids, don't you? A cottage in the country has been our dream, I never thought as we'd have the luck ...' she tailed off, and Liz saw, to her surprise, that her eyes had filled with tears. She dashed them away angrily. 'Look at me! What a silly fool! Only it's so good I c'n hardly believe it, and September feeling like a century off.'

'Won't your mother miss you all?' Liz asked, but Leanne shook her head.

'She's got Dad, and all her friends, and we won't be so far away. She'll be glad to not have all the child minding come the holdiays, not that she minded like, but it stopped her doing things. Right next door like that, we'll not have to worry.' The tea was all gone, she screwed the cap back on the thermos and dropped it into her bag. 'Now, I suppose, I'd better get on with them bathrooms, or those men'll be back before you know it.'

Liz sighed inwardly, but there was no help for it. 'Give me the vacuum cleaner, and I'll go round the bedrooms then.'

The seemingly endless day went on; at one end, Liz and Leanne directed the men loading up the removal van, set about the cleaning when they were gone, and accepted another cup of tea, this time from one of Dot's neighbours and accompanied by home-made cake. By six o'clock, the house, garage, and garden shed were all empty and swept out and Leanne was going round the skirting boards with a damp cloth, and Liz preparing to drive Dot's car to Shearwater. She said goodbye to Leanne.

'I'll see you again before the year is out,' she promised.

'I'll be over Monday, but I expect you'll be gone by then,' said Leanne, smiling. In a bizarre way, they had enjoyed their day together.

'We're leaving at five a.m., so unless you work very unsocial hours, I expect so too,' said Liz. 'We were going to back on Sunday, but ... well, I think my grandmother would like it if we stayed over, so we shall.'

'Is she really your grandmother?' asked Leanne. 'She looks too young.' She corrected herself. 'These days, she does.'

'What you really mean is, I look too old,' Liz told her. 'She was married to my grandfather. I suppose that makes her my grandmother, sort of.'

Liz climbed into the car and drove off, waving, and found her way through the lanes to Shearwater. Here, the house was in a state of organisation that surprised her, their work over the past few days had certainly paid off. The furniture was in the right rooms, if not necessarily in its final position, and the kitchen and conservatory were tidy and habitable – the conservatory furniture all being new, and delivered the previous day – and there was a wonderful smell of beef casserole pervading the hall as Liz stepped inside.

'Dee's friend Benita dropped it off,' Mike told her, gathering her into a warm hug. 'I've missed you. How was your day?'

'Frenetic,' said Liz. She took time out to receive his kiss properly and then looked around her. In the space of one day, and with very few of her personal possessions as yet on display, Dot had managed to create a surprisingly strong impression of home, and the delicious scent of the casserole was only part of it. She was still taking this in when Dot herself appeared from the kitchen to greet her.

'Elizabeth! My goodness, you look tired, I didn't realise you would be here so late! What have you been doing all this time?'

'Just clearing up the mess,' said Liz. 'You'd be amazed, the way the place looked after the men had gone, and Leanne and I thought we'd do it now, then nobody has to go back and do it tomorrow.' She felt in the pocket of her jeans. 'Here's the keys. Leanne's going to pull the door shut behind her when she leaves.'

Dot accepted the keys almost with reluctance, and put them hurriedly down on the hall table. 'That was very kind of you both, I'll take them to the solicitors tomorrow.' Liz had an impression that she only just resisted wiping her fingers. Had she really been so unhappy in that house? No way of asking, and no time to wonder either, for Dot went on, 'There's time before our dinner for you to have a nice shower and freshen up, you'll feel better then. Michael will show you where you're sleeping. Now I'll just go and see to the potatoes – lovely new ones off the farm, only dug today! Imagine!'

She bustled off, and Mike took Liz upstairs. Dot had given them one of the front bedrooms and the bed was made up with clean sheets all ready. Liz looked at it longingly, after the day she had just had she felt hot, sticky and tired to the bone. Mike saw her look and grinned.

'No, you can't. Go and clean up and then come downstairs. We'll indent for an early night after dinner.' He held out his arms and Liz fell into them and stayed there, leaning heavily against him, her eyes closed and enjoying the contact. He smelled of shower gel and fresh linen and after a moment or two, envious, she pushed herself away.

'I'll get into the shower then.' Her bag was sitting on a stand by the wall, she opened it and took out clean clothes, throwing them onto the bed. 'You go and help Grannie Dee, or we'll get sidetracked. Off you go!'

The shower was bliss, lovely hot water and soft, warm towels to follow, and Liz, feeling revived, went back downstairs and made her way to the kitchen. There was a table in the conservatory as well as the one in the kitchen, and it was on this that Mike was laying the cutlery while Dot prodded potatoes on the gas hob that formed part of the worktop surface, for the Aga was out at the beginning of June; an oven similarly occupied the space beneath. The kitchen was thoughtfully laid out; up to date without being more anachronistic than could be avoided.

'I thought we'd eat in the conservatory, it's such a lovely evening and all the doors are open. You go and take the weight off your feet, Elizabeth, this won't be a moment. Benita brought it all ready, vegetables in it as well, there's really nothing for you to do. Michael, you'll find the glasses in that cupboard.' She pointed. Liz went obediently through into the conservatory and flopped into one of the new cushioned chairs by the open doors, feeling the stress of the day ebbing through her tired limbs, enjoying the moment's peace. Outside in the garden, in the early dusk, she thought she saw a sleek shape skimming along beneath the hedge between the house and the cottage, but she couldn't be sure. If she was right, Secret Sam was definitely black, and also curious as to what was going on. She wondered if he would pluck up courage to investigate closer, but he simply vanished into the gloom beneath the camellias.

Of course, he – it – could be Secret Samantha. Time would tell. She removed her glasses and rubbed her tired eyes. What a day, and when she married Mike they would be doing it all over again! She lay back with a happy sigh and thought about it.

Mike appeared at her elbow, holding out a champagne flute sparkling with pale golden wine. 'Celebration time. Drink up, it'll revive you.'

'Just sitting here is reviving me, but thank you, that's the perfect cherry on top. This is a lovely house – a lovely feel to it.'

'And a lovely dinner, just going on the table. Up you get!'

Dinner was as tasty as it had smelled, beef casserole and new potatoes, and a bowl of crisp green salad, followed by fat home-made cheese scones with stilton and a bunch of cool green grapes.

'All grown on the farm,' Dot told them. 'Even the cow, I understand. Benita is a good friend. Of course, I bought the grapes and the Stilton, but Benita tells me they make the cheese that went into the scones.'

'What a wonderful Welcome Home dinner,' said Liz.

'What a wonderful welcome home altogether,' said Dot.

The next morning, Dot woke early when the sun peeked between her curtains and sat up with an unusual surge of anticipation as she contemplated the day ahead. Looking at the clock on her bedside table, she saw that it was only half past six, but it was impossible to stay in bed when there was so much that she wanted to do. She got up quietly, washed and dressed and stole downstairs; there was no sound from the occupied spare bedroom. Such pleasant young people, she thought. They deserved a lie in, she would get breakfast later – much later. They were only just engaged, after all, and she had been working them very hard. She smiled indulgently, amazed at how far she had come from her rigid disapproval of the past.

The kitchen was quiet, empty and full of early morning light. Dot switched on the coffee maker and reached down a cup and saucer before pushing open the doors into the conservatory; it was early yet to open the french doors to the patio but she unlocked a couple of windows and pushed them wide before returning to the kitchen.

The cat bowls were almost empty. She picked them up along with the water bowl, threw away the old food and washed them before taking the cat biscuits from the cupboard. She had replaced the fresh water on the floor and was just about to fill the food bowls when a small voice around the level of her knee said 'M'rowp?'

Dot looked down hurriedly, and saw with relief that her unexpected morning companion was the normal size for his species. Liz had been right about some things; he was completely black, and very sleek and handsome, but there was nothing furtive or slinky about him, he had all the confidence of an animal who knew that he belonged here, and was happy to see things returning to normal. When he saw her looking at him he butted her calf with his hard little head.

'Well, good morning,' said Dot. 'You must be Secret Sam.' She put one of the bowls down on the floor gently, but instead of going for the food he rubbed at her hand and began to purr. Dot wasn't used to animals, apart from Susan's large, smelly dog, but she laid a tentative hand on his head and stroked him. His short fur was soft and warm and somehow comforting, and a strange, unbidden thought came into her head. She pushed it aside and gave him a severe look. 'Don't you try your wiles on me,' she told him. 'You're off to pastures new this morning, and don't you forget it.' She stood up straight and looked around her. She hadn't heard the cat flap, he must have been in the cat igloo by the Aga. She was almost afraid to look inside, but it was empty anyway. The enormous Fatso was still out on the tiles. Good.

Even as she thought this, there was a thud from the conservatory as a huge tabby cat landed on the windowsill, miaowing loudly. Another thud as he hit the floor and walked cautiously towards the kitchen door. He and Dot looked at each other suspiciously. He was everything Liz had said he would be; big fat paws, broad back, plumy tail, long silky fur and the big, good-natured face that she had already encountered. He was like a child's teddy bear come to life, but for all his size, not as brave as his smaller companion. He hesitated on the threshold, his eyes on the food bowl Dot still held, unsure whether he was more hungry or more scared of a stranger. Finally, the sight of Secret Sam crunching happily on his breakfast became too much for him and he sidled in as Dot put the second bowl down beside the first. Even so, he wouldn't go near it until she had moved away.

'You big softy,' she told him, as she poured her coffee, and tried to keep affection out of her voice as she said it. After all, she didn't even know the animal. She carried her coffee into the conservatory and sat in one of the armchairs, and after a moment Secret Sam came to join her, leaping onto the matching sofa and settling himself down. Dot found herself thinking that she would have to buy a nice throw to protect the new cushions, and stopped herself immediately. She didn't want cats. She *definitely* didn't want cats. Fatso – terrible name! – was more cautious, as before. He didn't go so far as to escape unseen via the cat flap, but he slithered past her as quickly as possible and disappeared through the window again. He didn't go away, however. He settled himself in a patch of early sunlight on the patio and began to have a wash. Dot got a distinct impression that they both were happy to see someone living here again. After a while, she got up and opened the patio doors. Fatso didn't exactly run off, but he got up and strolled away. Secret Sam didn't move at all.

By the time that Mike appeared at half past seven, instead of the unpacking she had intended to continue, Dot had done some thinking. Cats didn't need to be taken for walks, they saw to all that for themselves, they didn't leave revolting little parcels all over the lawn and if she wanted to go away they would be fine if somebody would feed them, a neighbour perhaps, when she knew them, or Bennie, although it was several miles for her to travel. They didn't paw at you with muddy feet, or jump up and knock you over, or smell. Neither did they bark noisily every time someone came to the door. These two appeared to be clean and quiet, and if they brought in the odd mouse or worse, bird, perhaps it was a small price to pay for their company. Secret Sam, although fast asleep, was definitely company.

'Hullo,' said Mike, coming to the door. 'I see you've found a friend. Or has a friend found you? Has the other one been in yet?'

'He came and went,' Dot told him. 'He is absolutely huge! Liz says he is something called a Maine Coon. But I can't have a cat called *Fatso*!'

'The Great Catsby?' Mike suggested. 'Then you could call him Catso for short, and he wouldn't even know you'd changed his name.'

'I am not keeping them,' said Dot, repressively, as much to convince herself as Mike. 'There is coffee in the jug, help yourself. Is Elizabeth getting up?'

'She's in the shower.' Mike fetched a cup and filled it and went to sit beside Secret Sam, who raised his head, yawned pinkly revealing a set of excellent teeth, and went back to sleep.

'Then I shall start breakfast in a moment.'

'That sounds good.' Mike leaned back and stretched out his legs luxuriously. 'So what's the plan for today?'

'If you can carry the boxes we put upstairs into their labelled rooms, then Elizabeth and I can unpack them,' said Dot. 'And while we do that, perhaps you wouldn't mind taking the keys into town and giving them to the solicitors? I will tell you where to find them. Jerry will be there, I daresay, give them to him. Completion is at midday, so they must be delivered before then.'

'You don't want to go and check that all's OK back at your old place?'

'No,' said Dot, with finality. Truth to tell, she never wanted to see the house again, which surprised her a little. She hadn't realised, until she got away, how unhappy she had been there, it had sneaked up on her insidiously, over a long time. She added, 'And if I make a list, perhaps you could slip out to the Farmer's Market if I give you directions.'

After breakfast, Mike duly brought the boxes down to their final destinations and drove off with two lots of written instructions and a set of keys, and Liz and Dot repaired to Dot's sitting room, top of Dot's "to do" list for some reason that she hesitated to define, for it would have been more sensible to start with the drawing room, where they could all three of them sit in comfort. In her own room, there were only two comfortable armchairs beside the fireplace, although the bigger of the two windows, the one overlooking the garden, had a cushioned window seat. Behind the door there were the two shelves of books up on the wall, and beneath them a table on which already stood a large flowering plant. On the other side of the door, the narrower wall accommodated a glass fronted corner cupboard, at present empty. Opposite to the door there was another, smaller window with no window seat, with Dot's desk beneath it, and against the wall by the fireplace a cabinet that bore a sophisticated music centre on its top, and was destined to hold CDs and DVDs, at present packed in one of the boxes on the hearthrug. The television set, with the DVD player, was opposite to the chairs by the fire. A small coffee table waiting to have room on the rug and a footstool completed the tally. Dot looked around her with satisfaction. 'Let's get started,' she said.

Oliver's picture already hung above the fireplace; a blind had been fitted to the big window that could be pulled down on bright days so that it shouldn't fade in the sun, but the boxes were filled with other treasures. Not just the CDs, mostly classical, which Liz was deputed to arrange in alphabetical order on the top shelf of the low cabinet with the DVDs below, but treasured ornaments chosen to go into the corner cupboard which Dot arranged herself, and family photographs, a clock, and two tall vases for the mantelpiece. Two other pictures were to be hung either side of the big window, and a big ornamental plate above the music centre, and Liz was interested to note that Dot was very handy with a hammer; she had wondered if her grandmother would wait for Mike, but no. There was absolutely no feminine helplessness about Dot.

The last picture in place, Dot folded the boxes and stood back to admire the effect. She gave a deep sigh of pleasure. 'I think we've earned a short break, Elizabeth. Shall we make ourselves a cup of coffee and drink it in comfort, in here?'

'Should we do a little more first, do you think?' asked Liz, for it was only just after ten, but Dot said, with uncharacteristic sentiment, 'I want to sit in here and feel that it's mine.'

A little to her surprise, Liz seemed to understand. She said, 'Let's do that, then. Give me those boxes, I'll put them out in the garden shed for now while you work the machine.'

Secret Sam was still curled up on the sofa in the conservatory, Liz fancied he was relieved to have things getting back to normal. She gave him a thoughtful look as she headed for the back door. 'Are you going to ring the vet, now that they've come back?' she asked, and Dot said, as if absent-mindedly, 'Soon.'

They carried their coffee back into the finished room and settled into the armchairs. Dot looked around her with satisfaction, it really looked very nice indeed.

'This is Dee's room,' said Liz, watching her. 'I can see you'll be spending a lot of time here.'

Since this was what Dot had planned, she couldn't argue, even had she wanted to. She said, 'It will be friendlier when there is just me. I find sitting on my own in a large room is not ...'She hesitated, and then finished, '... really comfortable,' on a surprised note, as if she had made a discovery.

Liz looked at her in surprise too, and made a discovery of her own. The reason she loved her tiny cottage was because it was *comfortable*, just as Dot said. Had it been any bigger, living there on her own she might have felt lonely, as Dot obviously had. With Mike to live with her, it would be different. They would make their own place, the cottage was her personal refuge and it was time to let it go. She looked at her engagement ring and felt her heart warm.

They had left the door ajar for air when they came in, now Dot watched it pushed wider, apparently by some unseen agency, and a moment later Secret Sam appeared round the back of Liz's chair. He had a good look round, peering under the furnishings as if he expected to find some lurking terror, then, apparently satisfied that all was well, jumped onto the window seat and settled down. Liz said, 'He's really at home, isn't he?'

'It was his home,' said Dot. Liz made no comment.

They moved into the drawing room next, hanging pictures and arranging the china cabinet, shifting the lighter furnishings around until they had it to Dot's taste, and were about to move back to the kitchen to see about some lunch when two things happened together; Mike returned with the shopping from the market and the phone rang. Dot picked up the extension on the kitchen worktop. 'Hullo?'

'Mrs Nankervis! It's Viv Tarrant here. How are you settling in?'

Dot said, 'We're getting straight, thank you. And you?'

'I don't think we're ever going to be straight again! The accommodation is all right, I suppose, but we can't wait to get into the farmhouse and have our own things round us. Only there is so much to be done, and the French workmen are so ... well, *French*, I suppose.' She laughed. 'But that isn't why I'm ringing.' She paused.

'So how may I help you?' asked Dot, prompting.

'Well, it's the cats,' said Viv, apologetically. 'The boys were very upset when we had to leave them running loose, it was bad enough having to leave them at all, but not knowing where they were ... that was cruel. They loved them, you know, it just wasn't practical to bring them, it wouldn't have been kind to them, they wouldn't have understood. Timmy and Ed had them for their birthdays as kittens, you know, a couple of years back. I hated having to give them away, but if they went to good homes ... But anyway, what I wanted to know is, have they turned up safely, and have you been able to get them to the vet? Timmy can't sleep at night, and he cries ... for two pins, I'd come back and get them and be blowed to it!' She hesitated. 'That must sound like a load of excuses.'

'No,' said Dot. 'It would have been different had you moved straight into your own house, of course.' She found that she felt sorry now, not just for the cats but for the two boys as well. Not to mention the parents who had had to make the difficult decision. She said, 'They have both turned up safe and sound. In fact, they hadn't gone far, they have been around ever since you left, although we could only tell by the empty food bowls until this morning. They had not lost their appetites,' she added, dryly.

'And have you managed to catch them and get them away to safety?' asked Viv. 'I think the boys would be a bit happier if they knew for certain.'

There was a long pause. Liz, who had been listening to Dot's end of the conversation with interest, watched Dot's face now with even more interest. A whole range of emotions flashed across it before she spoke, from outright denial to resignation. Finally, she said, 'Actually, Mrs Tarrant, I have not attempted to catch them yet. I have been thinking. This is their home, they are happy here and they are used to each other's company. I wondered, if you have no objection that is, if I might keep them. I do not wish to overset any arrangements you have made, of course.' She saw out of the corner of her eye Liz raise clenched fists to the ceiling in jubilation, and smiled at her.

'*Keep* them?' asked Viv, in amazement. Nothing she had ever heard about the notorious Dorothy Nankervis had prepared her for this. 'But that would be marvellous! But do you really want to bother with them?'

'It would be no bother,' said Dot, relieved now that the decision had practically made itself. 'They will be company, and they seem to be no trouble. And when you come back to visit your friends here, the boys may come to see them.'

'That would be ...' Viv seemed lost for words, and ended lamely by repeating, '*marvellous*. They'll be so pleased.'

Dot, unsure whether that last bit referred to the boys or to the cats, or both, said, 'And when you are settled in, you must find them two new kittens. But please, do try to discourage them from naming them things like "Fatso".'

'I know just what you mean,' said Viv sympathetically. 'I'll ring the vet then, and tell her the deal's off. She won't mind, there's always cats needing homes it seems, and not enough homes to go round. And I don't know how to thank you enough.'

'It will be a pleasure,' said Dot, and found that she meant it. She put the phone down after a few pleasantries, and met Liz's eyes defiantly. 'It was the best thing,' she said defensively. 'Poor things! And those two boys have been very upset, they will be happier now.'

'You're going to have to buy some more catfood then,' said Liz, smiling at her. 'The bag is almost empty.'

'You may go to the shop in the village this afternoon, if you will,' said Dot. The die now being cast, she moved on to the next thing. 'Now Michael, did you get that loaf?'

The remainder of the day passed in arranging the dining room, and then Dot sent her helpers off to the Ravenscourt Arms for an hour with each other while she prepared dinner. Liz offered to help her, but Dot shook her head.

'No, Elizabeth, you and Michael have been very good, but it's been a strange holiday for you both when you are only just engaged. You go out and have a little time for each other. I shall enjoy being on my own for a little while, too. I need to feel ...' She hesitated, because what she wanted to say was not only unlike her, but could be misconstrued. But Liz nodded her head, fully understanding. 'As if you belong here,' she said.

'That's it exactly! And tomorrow, there will be nothing that you can do, only small finishing touches that I need to attend to myself, and you must take the day for yourselves. I shall book a table at Mario's for the two of you for dinner, and I shall drive you there. You may take a taxi back, then you can enjoy a nice bottle of wine together. And before you say that it will be too expensive, this is my treat. My thank you, if you wish to see it that way.'

586

'I shall feel dreadful, leaving you all on your own,' objected Liz, but Dot patted her shoulder and smiled.

'You need not. I shall enjoy the time alone after the week we have had, and on Sunday it will be your last day, and we can do something together then. Benita and Ernest are coming to dinner then, my first guests. If it salves your conscience, you may help me to prepare for that.'

Unexpectedly, Liz put her arms round her and hugged her. 'You know what, Grannie Dee? Under that prickly exterior of yours, you're as soft as that cat of yours.'

'Catso, you are referring to, I take it? I feel that Secret Sam has his own agenda.'

'Catso?'

'I really cannot call the poor animal "Fatso". Now off you go, the pair of you, and enjoy yourselves. Dinner will be on the table at seven.' It was an order, and Liz meekly obeyed, collecting Mike on the way. When they were gone and the door had clunked shut behind them, Dot gave a sigh of pleasure, not so much at their departure as for having her house to herself for a while. She had been here for twenty-four hours, she reflected as she took vegetables from the fridge, and already it felt more like home than anywhere she had ever lived, even in the Henry days, for although she had been happy then, their home had been Henry's before she moved in, full of his past life, so never really her territory. Looking into the unknown future, she found it promising more than she had ever had. A return, however belated and after-the-fair, to the game she had loved, good friends, the company of her cats. *Her* cats. What a strange thought.

Right on cue, Secret Sam came padding through the kitchen on his way to the cat flap. She watched him with affection. What a wonderful feeling it was to be looking forward to tomorrow.

Driving home through the dawn on Monday morning, Liz said to Mike, 'So what do you make of my grandmother?'

'She doesn't in the slightest resemble what I had been led to expect,' Mike replied. 'She didn't at the christening, come to that.'

'She didn't resemble herself the first time I met her, either' Liz agreed. She hesitated, searching for a word and found one. 'She was *joyous.* Like someone released from a long prison sentence, not quite sure how to handle it, but full of hope.'

'She'll handle it,' said Mike, with confidence. 'Did you persuade her to come to Waldren Stavey? I heard you both talking earnestly while I loaded the truck.'

'*Loaded*,' said Liz, grinning at him. 'I love that word! Two bags? Hardly a truckload!'

'Don't split hairs. Did you?'

'I don't know. She said she might. It was an advance on outright "No", that's all.'

There was a long silence, while they both thought about that. Finally, Mike said, 'So, what happened? Do I get to know?'

'I can't tell you exactly. I was only about two at the time. But I know that she never wrote or spoke to them again.'

'And them?'

'They tried for a while, so Mum says. But Aunt Carol had said, or done, something that she apparently found unforgivable, and in the end they gave up.'

'She's never said anything to you – Dee that is, not your aunt?'

'No,' said Liz. She yawned. 'I only know from the family that it was something about my grandfather's will, and they weren't necessarily on Aunt Carol's side. Will you ever forgive me if I go back to sleep?' She closed her eyes and Mike drove on, the radio turned low and his attention already switched from last week to today. There was a busy time ahead of them; back to work first, and when the day was over, the prospect of informing their respective families of their future plans. Aware of Liz, sleeping peacefully by his side, he smiled at an oncoming car and allowed himself to feel optimistic. He had wondered how being a civilian would work out after the past eventful years in the tight comradeship of army life, but now he had the answer.

All right.

XXIX

The news of their engagement, made public that evening on a visit to Liz's parents, met with approval, and a certain amount of relief that the ghost of Paul Attwood was finally laid – for her family, at least. Although the week of their absence had, according to Mark Jones, passed without incident Liz didn't deduce from this that Paul had finally gone from her life; instinct told her otherwise, this would be just a lull. After his last effort, she genuinely dreaded what he might come up with next.

Isobel was on the phone to Alice straight away. 'Get round here at once, it's a mega celebration!' she ordered, jubilant. 'No excuses, bring the children too!' She put down the phone and gave her younger daughter the second big hug of the evening. 'I'm so thrilled! I thought you were going to hang about for ever until the juices ran dry!'

'Thanks Mum,' said Liz, making a rueful face. 'It's just that Mr Right was otherwise engaged.'

'And now he's engaged to *you*,' said Isobel, with deep satisfaction.

George's view was more practical. While they waited for Alice and Gil and their children to arrive, and Isobel and Liz were engaged in women's talk about weddings – "not thought that far yet" being Liz's main contribution – he drew Mike aside and said to him, 'Tell me, Mike, what's your commitment to Anstruther? Obviously you'll have to stay with him for a while, but is there a partnership or anything? Would you be able, or willing, to change horses?'

'No partnership.' Mike shook his head. 'I agreed to stay for a couple of years, until he'd got established. To be fair, I never saw garage foreman as a final ambition, and he knows it.'

George nodded his satisfaction. 'So, if you were offered a management position in an up and coming farm machinery dealership a couple of years from now, *you* wouldn't be unwilling and *I* wouldn't make an enemy of Anstruther?'

'So long as I still got my hands dirty. I'm no good at sitting behind a desk.'

'Oh, you'd get dirty, all right. Nothing like a good farm tractor for that. Interested, then?'

'Very much so.'

'I always wanted a son to hand the business on to,' said George, with deep satisfaction. 'So, what did I get? Two daughters and a gardener! Of course, you never know about William. Let's open a bottle of wine.'

Alice and Gil arrived soon after with William and the twins, having already worked out why they had been summoned and ready with their congratulations.

'So what's happened to your objections to the military?' Alice asked, grinning, and Liz muttered something and looked at her feet. 'And ginger moustaches?' Alice pursued relentlessly, and Mike, who was close enough to hear, looked interested.

'She doesn't like my moustache?' he asked.

'I love it!' said Liz firmly. 'One should always be ready to be flexible. I'm just glad he's not still a soldier, but there's all sorts of reasons for that, and at least one of them isn't prejudice.'

'And which one would that be?' asked Alice, teasing, and Liz didn't reply. She could not say, in this gathering of celebrants, that the thought of Mike engaged in fighting in Northern Ireland or Iraq, or Afghanistan, in all of which theatres of war he had served, gave her more grief even than the decomposing kitten, and she hadn't even known him at the time. Perhaps Alice understood, for she stopped her teasing and said, more soberly, 'I'm really glad for you, Liz, and I know you'll be happy. And Dad is over the moon! Does Auntie Sue know yet?'

'Probably, because Chel almost certainly does by this time. Mike rang his parents at lunchtime, and he reckons they'll be spreading the news like a flu epidemic!'

'How about our stepgrandmother? Does she know? You were with her all week.'

'Grannie Dee was the first to know,' said Liz.

'Who?' asked Alice, started, and Isobel, who had caught the last remark said, 'Dee? That's what Dad used to call her sometimes. Did she tell you?'

'It's what she was called at school,' Liz explained. 'I think she rather liked school. She was valued there.'

590

'That was a very perceptive thing to say,' Isobel observed, and Alice added, 'School isn't all bad. I quite liked it too.'

'I think she's the only person I know of whom it's true to say that her schooldays were the happiest days of her life, though,' Liz said, and added thoughtfully, 'So far, anyway.'

'And did you manage to persuade her to come and see us all?' asked Isobel, and Liz said what she had said to Mike. 'She didn't actually refuse.'

'Work on it. It's high time we all buried the hatchet. Even Carol thinks so.'

George, calling for a toast to the engaged couple, put a stop to the discussion to Liz's relief. She had every intention of working on Dot, she just wasn't wholly confident of succeeding.

'Can we be bridesmaids?' asked Lulu wrinkling her nose over the taste of her minute glass of wine. 'Us and Annabel, that would be nice, wouldn't it?'

'Wait and see. We might not have that sort of wedding,' Liz told her.

'Of course you will!' exclaimed Isobel. 'Mike's mother will agree with me, won't she Mike. You can't just slide off to a register office, or kiss a standing stone, or whatever you had in mind. Knowing you, it could be anything.'

'We thought we'd have one of those mass marriages,' Liz told her wickedly. You know. Several hundred couples, all chanting their vows together. They do them at the Glastonbury Music Festival, you get married for a year and a day. That's probably quite long enough!'

Lulu's eyes had gone completely circular, and Isobel said, laughing, 'Don't be silly, Liz!'

'Bridesmaids go in pairs – unfortunately,' Mike observed. 'This is a pity, because it means we have to include Candy – my niece,' he explained to Isobel. 'They're all the same age, more or less, someone would have to keep them in order.'

'I shall have Auntie Sue as a matron of honour in that case,' Liz decided, giving in to pressure, and Isobel looked relieved.

'That cuts out the standing stone then. Thank goodness.'

Discussing the inevitable wedding like this gave Liz a funny feeling in the pit of her stomach, it turned it from something that was comfortably in the future to something more imminent. She caught Mike's eye and was reassured. Although she wasn't going to get married in virginal white, whatever anybody said, and nobody, surely, could think it appropriate.

Liz rang Susan as soon as they returned to the cottage and, as expected, she already knew from Chel. 'I'd have told you earlier, but it only seemed fair to tell the family first,' Liz explained, and Susan said that she realised that.

'But I have to warn you,' she added, 'that Annabel is determined to be a bridesmaid. Did you want bridesmaids?'

'Katie and Lulu, too,' said Liz, resignedly. 'And Candy, probably. I didn't really want that kind of wedding but shucks, I can stand it!'

'It's only a day,' Susan comforted her. 'How does Mike feel about it?'

'Resigned, I think. He says he's survived worse.'

'I daresay he has,' said Susan, thinking about it, and Liz changed the subject; there was only so much wedding talk she could take in one day when she had barely worked herself up to being engaged.

'How's Seb, after his triumph?' she asked, and Susan replied dryly, 'The most popular boy in school right now.'

'Inevitable, but it won't last. Have you made a decision about the Laser?'

'That's a hard one. He won't be parted from *Swallow*, but Deb has come up with a possible answer. Carl put some money into the sailing school when he withdrew his services as an instructor, she reckons on putting part of it into a Laser fleet for schools to use, and Seb can practice on one of them. It would work, for a while anyway. But Roger still reckons he's the real deal, and Carl agrees with him. Oliver too. So we'll have to concentrate on that.'

'What about Annabel? Where will she come in?'

'Annabel's not much of a sailor. She likes it, but she thinks of it as a bit of a game. Make-believe, *Swallows & Amazons*. Not to be taken too seriously.'

'Grannie Dee – sorry, your mother – thinks you should get a horsebox, so that she can have her pony in Cornwall and just bring it with her when you come here.'

'Now that's a thought, perhaps we will. She'd be thrilled, that's a cert, she loves that little horse. Perhaps I'll have a word at the riding school she goes to, she can't keep it in the garden.' She paused. 'And how was my mother, do you think? Is she going to be happy in Shearwater?'

'She's already happy,' Liz told her. 'She opened out like a flower in the sun the moment she got there. But my God, she's some organiser! She had the whole move orchestrated like a battle plan! By Friday night, she had the last teaspoon in its appointed place!'

'Sounds about right,' Susan said, laughing. 'I just hope she doesn't find she's lonely.'

'She was lonely in Embridge, so what'd be new?' Liz asked, not laughing. 'But she's got company, anyway. The people she bought Haymans from left two cats.'

'Cats! But she doesn't like household pets! What's she going to do with them?'

'I should leave that to the cats,' Liz told her. 'They seem to think they're staying, and so does she. There's a black one called Secret Sam, he's already got her under his paw. The other one's a bit more cagey, but he'll come round. She'll love them in the end, you'll see.'

'This does not sound like my mother,' said Susan, unsure whether to be put out or pleased.

'This does not look like your mother,' said Liz. 'And a very good thing too. She wears jeans and a T-shirt like a normal person, and she's going to play tennis again.'

'Blimey!' said Susan, inelegantly.

'So watch this space.'

'I will. And did you persuade her to make up with the family?'

'I tried. I can't put it higher than that.'

'I hope she does,' said Susan, sober now.

'So do we all. But you can't push it. I sowed the seed, that'll have to do for now.' It was time to change the subject; Liz asked, 'So how did the book launch go? Did you enjoy it?'

Susan's hesitation was slight, but noticeable. Then she laughed, and said, 'It was interesting.'

'Useful word – interesting,' Liz agreed. 'Now tell me what you really thought. What did Carl think?'

'He hadn't expected the critics to be all over him like they were. And the publisher has put his book up for a rather prestigious prize, or has Paul told you that already?'

'Paul and I are no longer on those terms. He wasn't there, was he?' she added in trepidation. It hadn't occurred to that since Paul worked for Carl's publisher, he could well have been.

'No,' said Susan. She hesitated again, longer this time, as she wondered whether to pass on her impressions or not. Finally, she said, 'I got the idea that Paul isn't exactly flavour of the month, actually. I mean, I didn't go into it deeply, or anything, but I just wondered to Carl's agent if he was likely to be there, since he was the one who set the ball rolling originally even if his boss did cut him out, and she gave me a really odd look when she said that no, he wasn't, and changed the subject rather smartly.'

'Oh dear,' said Liz. Not that she cared about what happened to Paul any more, but he did seem to be taking things out on her just lately, and she didn't wish for anything else to be added to his tally of grudges, he would undoubtedly make it out to be her fault. 'Good for Carl,' she added, belatedly, and Susan laughed.

'He's not sure what's hit him. Everyone's predicting his book is going to be a terrific hit and a number one bestseller.'

'Oh, we're all that these days – if we sell at all,' Liz told her.

'Yes, I'd noticed that in the supermarket,' Susan told her. 'It seems to be tough at the top – no elbow room! And of course, in Carl's case, he has the advantage of being eminently hype-able. *Orb* is something of a legend, and since they finally tumbled to it, the publicity department is working that for all they can get.

'And how are you coping with having him under your feet all day?' asked Liz, for she had privately wondered if the pair of them might start getting on each other's nerves if there was no respite all summer long, but Susan only laughed again, happily.

'Well, he isn't, really. He spends some time a couple of days a week down at the sailing school, in the office, and every now and then he disappears for a couple of days to report on something. And it's great to be able to go sailing in *Hierax* whenever we want, and he takes the kids fishing in the little motor boat in the evenings sometimes, too. It's pretty much like having a normal husband at work, particularly when I'm at college. And the children are really blossoming, having a proper dad at last, even if he isn't – if you see what I mean.'

'Your mother thinks the world of him,' Liz told her.

'Really?' Susan sounded surprised, as well as pleased. 'I thought she thought he was too young.'

'She's learning to live with that,' Liz told her. 'And apparently she saw off your ex like an evil-tempered Rottweiler having a bad day, so you shouldn't have any more trouble *there*.'

'Did she tell you that?' asked Susan, interested.

'No. Her friend Ingrid did. Apparently his mother is very upset, but his father hung out the flags and said he hoped he'd learn from it. Don't quote me. That's hearsay. Did you know that your godfather knew my family?'

'Well ... he *is* my godfather, so you must see that it follows.'

'I never realised. Well, be honest, I never thought about it.'

'You live and learn. You keep working on her, if Uncle Alex is on your team, you might even succeed in making peace.'

'I'll try,' Liz promised, but thought that it would only happen if Dot herself wanted it. And so far, there was no sign that she did.

To start with, Dot was just a little lonely at Haymans, she admitted it. She was used to having her crow mates, Ingrid and Sally, within easy distance rather than seven miles away and she missed them. Of course, they were still there for her, but there seemed little point in moving out into the country to make a new life and then heading back for the town and the old life at the first hurdle. Benita was nearer, of course, but Benita had affairs of her own to attend to, with the farm and two teenage children, and what Dot had come to see as the mixed blessing of a husband. Dot was aware, too, that Benita was almost twenty years her junior and had other friends, more her age and of longer standing. She enjoyed her young friend, but had no intention of turning herself into a duty.

So, in spite of every attempt to keep herself busy, she found herself with far too much time for thinking, and far too many things to think about. It was as if her life had been cracked in half as neatly as an egg, and now the yolk of reality was spilling stickily all over everything.

One thing that she finally accepted was that Jerry had never loved her. She couldn't even recall him ever telling her that he did. They had come together because they were friends, no more, because they were each reacting to a grievous loss, Henry's death and Helen's defection, and because they each had a child who would be the better for two parents and a sibling. A marriage of convenience for the sake of the children, that was all they had ever had together. They should have known better, Dot thought now. Helen would have come round eventually, that was obvious by this time, and she herself might have met someone who would have been a better husband than Jerry had been capable of being, at least to her. She might even have learned not to be the complacent, social-climbing frump that she now realised she had allowed herself to become in order to fill an empty void, and long before Benita took her in hand. She couldn't help feeling that she had thrown her life away. If the old Dee was stirring now, it wasn't down to her.

One decision she did make, and set about putting into practice. She didn't wish to retain Jerry's name; it had never really been hers and she had no desire to share it with Helen, whom she had never liked very much, and who had liked her even less. She would revert legally to her first married name, the one to which she felt entitled. She wouldn't go back to unhappy Dot Shipham again, she would be Dee Worthington – and if indeed the old Dee still existed, Dot resolved to seek her out. She only hoped that Dee wasn't buried too deep for resurrection.

But it was all very well to make resolutions, all very well to tell herself that she would soon settle down and find herself a niche in Shearwater, it seemed almost impossible to bring herself to the point of going out to make contact with new people. Suppose they had heard about her through Jenny Carruthers and gave her the cold shoulder? And where did one start anyway? She had no idea, she had never had to make a start from cold before. She had made a couple of forays to the village shop and nobody had shown much interest, presumably taking her for a visitor, and she had been to church, where the vicar had been kind and she had seen not a soul that she knew, so that the intermittent visits of Leanne to do the housework were beginning to be something to which she looked forward. She began to wonder if she would be reduced for ever to the companionship of two cats, and fortunately managed to laugh at herself.

It was the daytime that was bad, the empty hours with nobody to talk to unless she picked up the phone hung heavy on her hands, but the evenings were subtly different. She had become used to spending evenings on her own in her big, beautiful house in Embridge, but Haymans had very quickly become a home, which she found to be an entirely different thing. She sat in her small, cosy room with her books, television and music, with the door ajar to allow her two new companions to drift in and out, and quite often Secret Sam came and curled on her lap, his purring warmth a great comfort, and she recognised a new contentment in herself. She had planned for, looked forward to, evenings like this, and the company of animals was turning out to be an unexpected bonus. Fatso, aka Catso, was more cautious, but he had got as far as settling down on the window seat, and eyeing up the empty armchair. He hadn't yet let her touch him, but he was working round to it. She found that she was getting fond of both of them, but it was only in the evening that they came and sat with her on these warm summer days. In the day, and she presumed the night as well, they were out seeing to their own feline affairs.

She would not keep phoning her daughters and her friends. This new singularity that had come upon her was a challenge that she was determined to beat for herself.

Then, on her third visit to the shop in quest of milk, bread and catfood, which had all run out together, everything changed. She was heading for the till with her basket when a woman accosted her. 'Hullo,' she said. 'You're Dorothy Nankervis, aren't you? Our children know each other, they sail together at Embridge Harbour, or they did at least, at one time. Your Debbie and my Penny are great mates – I've been meaning to call round and see you, but I thought I'd give you time to settle in first. Moving is hell, I know.' She paused, meeting Dot's blank surprise with a friendly smile. 'Sorry. We have met a couple of times, perhaps you don't remember – Valerie Harries.' She changed her own basket to her left hand and held out the right, and Dot clasped it with what she hesitated to call relief, but she had begun to wonder if she was invisible here.

'How very nice to meet with you,' she said.

'You too. How are you liking Shearwater?'

'I haven't yet had much to do with it,' Dot told her, 'so much to do...' She tailed off, because actually, she hadn't that much to do thanks to her own powers of organisation and Leanne's visits. Valerie seemed to take it at face value, however. She said, 'Oh, I do understand!' sympathetically. 'But you can't sit around among the packing cases for ever, you know. You must come round and have coffee and let me fill you in on Shearwater's social life.' She looked at her watch. 'Come now. Why not? My family are at work – those that still live at home.'

Dot hesitated. 'That's very kind of you ...'

'Ah, come on,' said her new friend, moving her towards the till. 'We'll pay for our shopping and then you can follow me home, if you've got a car with you, or I'll drive you if you haven't.'

'I haven't,' said Dot, and went on to over-explain. 'When I only need a few things I prefer to walk to keep fit –' She made a face at herself. 'Get fit, I should have said. Town life makes one lazy.'

'I can imagine,' said Valerie. 'You'll have to take up something, get yourself *really* fit – not that I'm saying you look *un*fit,' she added hastily. 'Do you play tennis? I know you've got that court out at Haymans.'

They had reached the till, which gave Dot a moment to gather her thoughts, but when they had both paid and were heading for the door, Valerie repeated her question. 'Do you play? Or do you plan to turn it into a swimming pool or something?'

Dot had her answer ready by this time. 'I used to play at one time,' she admitted. 'I was thinking of taking it up again, although I imagine I shall find myself very rusty.'

'Oh, great!' said her new friend. She opened the back of a car standing at the kerbside. 'Throw your bag in here. That's it.' She went round to the driver's side, and as she got in, went on, 'You must join the tennis club, if you're not a member already, that is. I'll propose you – we can play together in the mornings, when all the little worker bees are slaving. It's hell finding a partner at that time of day!' The car rocketed out into the road, and Dot thought how strange life could be: everything went wrong for years and years, and then suddenly the whole focus shifted and things fell over themselves to go right. Valerie said, 'I can't keep calling you Mrs Nankervis. Do you like Dorothy, or Dot, or what? I'm always Valerie, never Val, or I get mixed up with my son.'

'Actually,' said Dot, feeling the oddity of it for the first time, 'I prefer Dee. And it's Worthington rather than Nankervis. Jerry and I are getting a divorce, he has gone back to his first wife.' Might as well get it over. Everyone who didn't already know would know in the end.

Valerie-never-Val shot her a sympathetic glance. 'I had heard that. You must be gutted. I'm sorry.'

'Don't be,' said Dot – it would be a while before she felt like Dee again, whatever anyone called her. 'We married for all the wrong reasons, and all things considered we had a good run. But enough is enough. I have no regrets.'

Valerie nodded as if she understood, but she had to pull aside for a tractor at that point and didn't reply directly. Dot had an unusual feeling, as if the persona of Dee, so abruptly resumed, had brought luck along with her. She said, tentatively, 'So you are a member of the tennis club?'

'Have been for years.' The tractor was out of the way, Valerie pulled across and signalled a right turn. 'I'm not that good – but I enjoy a knock-up, and it's good exercise. And it's a great social life.'

Dot had never considered tennis to be simply "good exercise", but even a toe in the door was better than a closed one. She said, 'Someone mentioned that there was someone – a member or a professional, I didn't ask – who would give coaching.'

'There is.' Valerie completed her turn into what appeared to be a new executive estate. 'He even played at Wimbledon and stuff – but now he's too old for that he likes to keep his hand in. Now he *is* good. Unlike me.'

Although at that moment she was still sitting in the car, Dot had a sensation of sun on her skin, warming her. She gave an involuntary sigh of pleasure. 'That's wonderful,' she said.

Valerie turned into the driveway of a lush mock-Tudor mansion and parked in front of its porticoed front door. 'Come on in,' she said. 'We can talk over coffee.'

Dot, who had lived in similar houses all her married life – Jerry putting distance between himself and his old life with Helen, she now recognised – appreciated the house for what it was, the home of people who had arrived, set among other similar homes and therefore similar people. People of a type whom she had once called her friends, without ever being fully accepted. She liked Valerie Harries, and moreover intended to make use of her contacts, but she had a growing awareness of wanting something more in her life than a calculated social whirl. She didn't fit there, and it had made her ... well, *pompous* was, sadly, the first word that leapt to mind. The second, unfortunately, was *overbearing*. She needed to find her level, and wondered where it would be.

Alex and Ingrid, and Marie Law and the General, were not that kind of people. Why had she never thought to work out exactly what kind of people they were? About Sally and Irwin, she was no longer certain, but friends could be chosen from all circles. Even her son-in-law was turning out to be a friend of sorts.

They sat to have their coffee in a trendy but friendly "country" kitchen, for which Valerie apologised with a laugh in her eyes. 'It was here when we bought the house – part of the package, you know – and actually, when we had banished the corn dollies I began to rather like it. Even if it does rather remind me of a film set for the Deep South. Yours is a bit like it, I know, but it's based round something that's genuine, and that makes all the difference.' She sighed regretfully. 'I'd have loved that house, but there's no way we could afford it. You are lucky.'

If Dot felt quietly complacent, she managed for once to hide it successfully. She smiled, and said, 'Yes, I'm very fortunate. Now tell me about village life, what goes on here? I have never lived in the country before, you know.'

So Valerie told her all about the Gardening Club and the Friendship Club and the Amateur Dramatics Group, all of which she claimed would welcome Dot warmly, and ended her catalogue by saying, 'And of course, the WI. They meet tonight, why don't you come with me? I'll introduce you to some people, you'll soon make friends. There's a talk on pigs.'

Dot hesitated. She had never seen herself as a Jam & Jerusalem person, but perhaps she had been wrong. She ought at least to try it, she told herself; she had jumped to too many conclusions in her life already. So she accepted the invitation, although she could claim little interest in pigs, and that evening Valerie met her at the end of Haymans Lane at seven o'clock prompt, and they walked together to the Village Hall. Dot was guiltily surprised to find that she had a good time; the group welcomed her and she enjoyed the entertaining talk on preparing pigs for show, and over the tea and cake afterwards several people were nice to her and invited her to join in other activities. They weren't necessarily the kind of people among whom she had sought her friends in the past but if anything she felt ashamed about that, no doubt a change for the better. She left at the end of the evening in a relaxed and contented mood, feeling that she had made a real start on her new life and, more importantly, made some friends, and when she arrived home the light was flashing on her answering machine. She pressed the button and listened.

'Hi Grannie Dee, it's Liz. Hope you're out having a nice time! Can you ring me if you're not back too late? Or I can ring you tomorrow morning – 'bye now.' She had omitted to leave her number. Dot looked at her watch. It was only a quarter to ten, and in her experience Liz and Mike weren't early-to-bed people unless they had spent the day shifting furniture. She dialled 1471 and then 3 and listened to the phone ringing in Liz's study. When Liz picked up, she sounded pleased to hear her voice.

'Oh good, I'm glad you rang back! Have you had a nice evening?'

Dot said that she had been to a meeting of the WI and Liz said, 'That's good. You'll meet lots of village people there. Did you like it?' Dot murmured that she might even join, and Liz said, 'Good,' again. 'Now, look Grannie Dee, I want you to listen to me and not jump in like you always do. I've got an invitation for you.'

Dot was immediately suspicious, both of the tone of Liz's voice and of the invitation itself. 'Oh,' she said, and heard Liz's sigh all the way from Devon.

'There you go, you see. Always looking for trouble! Now stop it, you're a great person.' She paused, but really, the only way to deal with this was to wade in with both feet. 'Mum and Dad are giving a party to celebrate my engagement to Mike, and we all want you to come – no' – as she heard Dot draw a breath to speak – 'let me finish. It's to be a lunchtime barbecue at the farm, and everyone will be there – Susan and Carl and the children, and Chel and Oliver and the baby, people you know, to give you moral support. And everybody wants you there. Think about it, please Grannie Dee, before you say you won't.'

The idea of gaining moral support from Oliver was a new one, but the presence of Susan would be a plus, certainly. Dot supposed that Marilyn and Bob would be there too, and the other brother and sister and their families. The little girl with red hair – what was her name? Candy, that was it, she was a character! If not moral support exactly, they would provide familiarity, and at least she wouldn't have to face Jerry and Helen or Nonie Fingall. She made a concession.

'May I think about it? It would be quite an ordeal, as you know.'

'Only for five minutes,' Liz promised. 'Once the ice is broken, you'll be fine. Please come. We want you to, Mike too.'

'I'll think about it,' Dot repeated. 'I'll let you know.'

'Soon,' said Liz. 'And think positive. It's to be on Sunday week, write it in your diary. Underline it in some cheerful colour, not red.'

She had got further with her invitation than she had expected, Liz concluded as she said goodnight. Whether she would get any further yet, she wouldn't like to hazard a guess.

Dot went to the party, of course. She realised, after she had thought, that she didn't really have a choice, and perhaps, if Henry's family wanted to mend fences, it would be silly to turn her back on them, particularly for what seemed, at this distance and after so much had happened, to be a simple misunderstanding. She also discovered a little to her surprise that she didn't want to be left out, and as she would be staying with Liz and Mike, as Liz told her when she rang to accept, she would be able to escape if it all became too much when the party was over. In the intervening days, she kept her mind off it by playing a few games of tennis with Valerie down at the club, where she was now a temporary member pending election. Valerie was shocked – there was no other word – by their first encounter.

'I thought you said you needed lessons,' she accused, when, after she had won the first set by a whisker, Dot began to get her eye in and proceeded to wipe the floor with her.

'I do,' said Dot, forbearing to add that Valerie had been rather easy to beat. Valerie, reading the truth in her eye, laughed and said, 'Well, I'd hate to play against you after you've had them. Have you really not played since you left school?'

'Once or twice maybe, on holidays, when the children were young. Not seriously.'

602

'Playing against me is hardly serious,' said Valerie, with unabashed honesty. 'Lets go and have a coffee in the bar, and then you can get the details off the notice board and book a few sessions with Andy.'

Dot had enjoyed herself, and although drinking in bars wasn't her style, was quite happy to be persuaded. Hadn't been her style *in the past* she corrected herself, following her new friend off the court. If this was new-life time; it was starting to look promising. Perhaps even Elizabeth's engagement party wouldn't be as bad as she feared, although even had her imagination been less limited she would have been hard put to imagine what would actually happen in Devon. Not that it was exactly the party that caused the trouble ...

The day before Dot was due to set out from Embridge, Liz had a phone call from Cecy.

'I thought you ought to know,' she said, 'and I know that never means anything good, and it doesn't this time, either. It's about Paul.'

Liz's heart sank. The fact that Cecy hadn't preceded Paul's name with an epithet such as *plonker* she felt boded no good. 'What's he done now?' she asked.

'It isn't actually him that's done anything this time,' said Cecy. 'Nothing new, anyway. You remember what I told you about that flat of his that *isn't* his?'

'You said it belonged to some author with a bit on the side.'

'Yes. Well, the bit on the side's husband found out about it, and the shit has hit the fan. He isn't a happy bunny.'

'I can see that he might not be, but what has it to do with Paul?'

'Everything. Listen. The husband had apparently been suspicious for some time, and he had set a private detective on his wife, who had seen the author, who he then tracked back to London and found Paul caretaking while the author was having his jolly in the Malvern Hills, or wherever it was. He reported back to the husband – are you still with me?'

'Just about. Go on.'

'The husband hit the roof, beat up on his wife and stormed off to London and confronted the author, who tried to deny everything, so he – the husband this is – burst into the publisher's office – that's Paul's boss, you understand – demanding blood and raving about a conspiracy between a member of his – the publisher's – staff, that's

Paul of course, and the author that the publisher published ... am I making sense?'

'Let me guess,' said Liz, cynically. 'The publisher wasn't going to take issue with the author – do I know him, by the way?'

'Probably. Keep going, you're on the right lines.'

'Wasn't going to take issue with the author, then, because he brought money and prestige to the business, so he made a scapegoat of Paul to satisfy the husband's blood lust, and Paul is now out of a job without a roof over his head and no chance of a reference.'

'Bingo!'

'Oh dear,' said Liz. It was the only thing that came into her head.

'It's worse than that, even,' said Cecy, not without sympathy. 'Because the man's wife is planning to sue him for assault and divorce him pronto – he blacked her eye and broke her jaw, apparently – the author is trying to stitch Paul up for the benefit of the press, claiming that he was a procurer, or something, and he had no idea the woman was married – and even if nobody believes it, and I don't see how they can, it's enough to ruin him in publishing for evermore. Because, you see, it was through the publishers that they all met. At some party, the man is quite important in something, I don't know what. I can find out, if you want to know.'

'I don't,' said Liz.

'You may find you have to anyway. If the press get hold of it ...'

'Oh *God*,' said Liz, suddenly aghast. 'They won't try to drag me into it, will they?'

'That's the thing,' said Cecy. 'If Paul has no job, and no prospects and is running out of cash, he may try to blackmail you by threatening to involve you. After all, you did babysit on his homeless weekends.'

'Oh God!' exclaimed Liz, again. 'It's nothing to do with me!'

'You're as famous as the other man. So that won't save you,' Cecy pointed out. 'Scandal among the celebrities – the tabloids will think they've died and gone to heaven.'

'*Shit*!'

'The husband could go to prison,' said Cecy, which was no comfort.

'She was cheating on him,' said Liz.

'No excuse for beating her up,' Cecy pointed out.

'Well, I think it is,' said Liz, with vigour. 'Stupid cow!'

'The court is unlikely to agree with you.'

'Perhaps they'll settle.'

'Not from what I hear. Anyway, I just thought you should know – forewarned is forearmed, sort of thing. And I didn't think you'd want it thrown at you at the party tomorrow.'

'You're coming, then?'

'Of course.'

They said goodbye, and Liz was left sitting at her desk and staring at an empty screen.. Cecy did rather like being the bearer of bad news, often wildly exaggerated, but this sounded horribly authentic. It was just the sort of mess that cocky, manipulative Paul would get himself into. The only thing was, Liz found that in spite of all the nasty emails, her vandalised flat, and even the dead kitten, she even yet couldn't quite believe that Paul would destroy her reputation unless there was something in it for himself. Which there wouldn't be. He must see that, surely. Then she wondered if he knew about her engagement; that would give it a new twist, and her cousin wasn't exactly famous for her discretion.

She wondered about a lot of things, and wished that Mike wasn't up at the garage, so that she could discuss it with him. She had no inclination to discuss it with Alice, whose reaction might be comforting, but would almost certainly also be unhelpful, but Richard might have an angle on the problem. Since her flat had finally sold she had heard little from him, but no doubt he knew all the details, if not from Cecy from other sources; it might be worth having a quiet word tomorrow. He would be there at the party, she knew, although an engagement party seemed the wrong place to discuss the problems of an ex in any great detail.

And then she wondered about her Grannie Dee. Uninvolved, objective, and a long way, Liz believed, from stupid. She had handled the human backlash from enough world crises during her charitable career to know which way was up. And she would take no prisoners, that was certain. Perhaps it would be worth while to run the problem past her? After the party; she would have enough on her mind before that.

So Dot drove to Devon to help confront problems other than her own, and experienced a Sunday that she was going to find it hard to forget.

She arrived at Liz's cottage in time for mid-morning coffee. The party was to be at three o'clock, to allow those who had to travel back to Cornwall time to do so, since all available beds were taken by people who had come from further away – Marilyn and Bob, for instance, were to stay with Isobel and George, Tracy and Tom and the children at the farm, and Richie and Louise, who had left their toddlers with their maternal grandmother, with Alice and Gil. Richard and Cecy would go straight back to London after the celebration, their parents were booked into a local hotel.

'It's just a family do,' Liz assured Dot, which Dot wasn't sure was comforting, a few outsiders might have made it easier. 'How nice,' she said.

'Mum says they've waited a long time for this moment,' Liz told her, 'and anyway, they all love an excuse for a get-together. It's just a shame that the others can't be here too, but they all live too far away – although Tony did say he'd try.'

'Others?' asked Dot, faintly. It sounded as if there were quite enough people already.

'Margaret and Jill and John,' said Liz.

Dot remembered Margaret and John, Owen's children of course, but Tony and Jill were new to her, as also were Richard and Cecily who apparently were going to be present. She resisted an impulse to dash back to her car and make a run for it, then to her surprise, found it replaced by a feeling that she been away too long. There was no time to consider this, however, for Liz was off again.

'It's a good thing it's turned out fine, because they'd never have got all these people into the house – it's to be at the farm, did I tell you? Lots of space, and Uncle Owen cleared out the barn in case it rained, we can shut the children in there if they're a nuisance, and lose the key!'

'Which they will be,' Mike put in cheerfully. 'What, with Candy there? Not to mention your twins. It promises to be the party from hell.'

'Oh well,' said Liz. 'Family parties generally are.' She smiled at Dot. 'Didn't you find that when yours were growing up, too?'

Family parties hadn't figured largely in Dot's married life. Jerry's parents had resented her, for lovely Helen had been a favourite of theirs, and her own had refused to have him in the house, a divorced man who had presumed to marry their daughter. According to their rigid moral code, that was Living in Sin. It was a wonder they had still opened their doors to Dot herself and his children, although in retrospect that had been a duty more than a pleasure. Dot felt a chill, and for the second time in ten minutes wished she hadn't come.

'Let's take our coffee into the garden,' said Liz, but before she had got the mugs off their hooks – no cups, Dot noted resignedly, but she was coming to expect this now – there was a ring at the door and Mike went to open it. Liz, Dot noticed with interest, froze as if it might be someone she didn't want to see, but when a moment later a woman's voice came from the hall she saw her relax. Then Mike came back followed by the very last person Dot wanted to see.

'The lady says she's your aunt,' Mike told Liz. 'One more coffee.'

Liz picked up the kettle, looking disconcerted. 'Hullo Aunt Carol. What a lovely surprise.' She shot a quick glance at Dot and thought that, at this moment, she would make a rather good statue. A marble one.

Carol had steeled herself to this encounter, knowing her own culpability and realising that the afternoon's party would be a difficult occasion if she didn't. Even so, she didn't want an audience for what had to be said, so she smiled at Liz and said, 'Thank you, Liz, I'd love a coffee, but may Dorothy and I have five minutes in the garden before you bring it out?'

A garden was a good place for a statue. 'Of course,' Liz said. 'All right with you, Grannie Dee?'

Dot pulled herself together. 'I think that would be an excellent plan,' she agreed. Clear the air, get it over, however one cared to view it. She led the way through the back door, Carol following, and Liz and Mike looked at each other.

'We'll give them ten minutes and then we'll go and separate them,' said Liz. 'If they haven't killed each other, that is ...'

'I take it, the ladies are not exactly soulmates?' said Mike.

'Aunt Carol caused all the trouble,' Liz told him, shuddering. 'And Grannie Dee made it worse. This is about Act Five of a classic family feud that you're witnessing now.'

'Oops. Should I have let her in?'

'You'd hardly have been able to stop her,' Liz told him, dryly. 'Where my Aunt Carol wants to go, she goes.'

Out in the garden, the two women walked without speaking the length of Liz's rose bed, neither of them wanting to be still, neither of them wanting to speak first. Finally, Carol said, 'This is a fence-mending visit, Dorothy. Maybe I spoke out of turn, all those years ago, but I never meant to shut you out. Or Susan. I've come to say I'm sorry.'

Dot noted the *maybe*, but also recognised the spirit behind the short speech. She stopped walking, and Carol stopped beside her. 'Possibly I over-reacted,' she admitted. 'It was a difficult time, with Henry so recently gone and a child to bring up alone.'

'It was crass of me to jump in like that,' Carol agreed, and again Dot noted that she had admitted no other fault. But if this was an attempt to meet half way, well, a lot of water had gone under the bridge by this time, and since she had won that encounter thanks to Jerry, she could afford to be generous now. She said, 'It was all a very long time ago, as you said. And if we are being entirely honest, it was I who shut myself out, and I very much regret, in the light of recent events, that in doing so I also shut Susan away from her father's family.'

Carol seized on this with relief, it was a safe opening, and moreover, undeniably all Dorothy's doing even if the cause was her own responsibility. 'It was the best day ever when she turned up. She's a lovely young woman Dorothy. You've done a good job, her father would be proud. And her children are a great bonus, Isobel's crowd love having cousins their age around.'

Dot took a breath. The first hurdle over, and if nothing had actually been resolved, both she and Carol had made the effort. There was no point in mulling over the past anyway, it was too long ago. She decided to let Carol get away with it. She said, 'Susan should know her father's family, and the children should know their cousins. What's done is done, what's past is past. Shall we call it quits, Carol?'

'And shall we say friends, too?'

Dot smiled at her, and borrowed a word of Carol's own. 'Maybe,' she said.

Carol laughed. She linked her arm through Dot's and turned her round to face the cottage. 'Then we had better go and put Liz out of her misery. She's probably got poor Mike looking for a spade to dig a grave by this time.'

Dot thought that Carol had skated through that too easily, and that it was typical of Carol to do so, but she had had enough confrontation just lately. She looked around for a safe change of subject, and her eye fell on a beautiful smokebush, and a small slab beneath it. She said, before she had thought, 'It looks as if someone already has dug a grave.'

They both stopped to look. The small slab was crowned with a tiny bunch of wild flowers, freshly picked. They didn't know it, but Liz had placed them there that morning as a thank you to the little animal that had precipitated her engagement to Mike. She had known at the time that it was a pointless, sentimental gesture but she had done it anyway. She still felt bad about the kitten, although its untimely death hadn't been her doing. Now, Carol shook her head.

'That wouldn't hold both of us,' she said, but Dot thought that it looked like the grave of a loved pet and couldn't raise a smile. She had a different opinion, these days, of domestic pets.

Liz came out from the back door as they approached, a tray of mugs in her hands, and placed it on a table on the small paved terrace. 'Coffee up,' she said. 'Come and sit down. It's lovely out here, gets all the sun.'

The four of them sat sipping their coffee, making small talk that Liz considered a bit stilted, and she wondered what had gone before. Her guests seemed to be on reasonable terms, but you couldn't use the word *warm*. Then Tib strolled across to see if there were any pickings, tail held high, and Dot bent to stroke him. 'Is this your cat? He's very beautiful.'

Tib, who knew already he was beautiful, rubbed round her legs, purring loudly and leaving cat hairs on her new black trousers, and Liz said, idly, 'How are you getting on with your two? Have you made friends with Fatso/Catso yet?'

'We are on speaking terms,' said Dot. 'I wouldn't put it higher yet. And I call him Catto these days, "Catso" sounded too like one of those tiresome speed cameras. Catto has a good classical ring to it.'

'But you've all settled down together all right?'

Dot said something she would never have imagined herself saying. 'I really wouldn't be without them. They are great company, and no trouble.'

'Give them time,' Mike murmured.

Carol listened to this exchange in amazement. She wouldn't have associated Dot with domestic animals, very much the reverse remembering her reaction to muddy sheepdogs on the farm. She realised that Dot wasn't the person she had taken her for, and wondered when and how the change had taken place. She had always been such a little snob, now she was practically human. No fool though; she fully realised how little Dot had conceded in their recent exchange and, on the whole, admired her for it. But cats? That one really came out of left field!

How about the village? Are you making friends yet?' asked Liz.

'A few. One of them took me to the Women's Institute last week. They were all very friendly and invited me to join.'

'And will you?' asked Carol.

'I think so. It seems to me that if one lives in a village, then joining in is how one gets accepted.' Dot smiled at a pleasant memory. 'I learned some very interesting things about pigs.'

'The friend who took you, is she someone you already knew, or someone new?' Mike asked, and Dot replied tranquilly, 'She is new as a friend to me, I had barely met her up until now, but my children know hers over many years. We play tennis together,' and waited for the reaction.

'Really?' asked Liz, delighted. 'And are you enjoying it?'

'I am extremely rusty,' Dot admitted. 'It is very many years since I played. Fortunately,' she added thoughtfully, 'this doesn't matter to Valerie, who is what we used to call a "rabbit" at the game when I was at school. But it is very enjoyable, she is great fun to be with. She has helped me to arrange a refresher course at the tennis club.'

'And are you going to join?' Mike asked.

'I am simply awaiting the next committee meeting. Of course,' Dot added, venturing on a mild joke, 'they may blackball me.' As soon as she had said it, she realised that perhaps it wasn't such a joke after all. But Jenny Carruthers didn't play tennis, to her knowledge, and for most of the others, the nine day wonder of her social downfall would be old news by this time. Only Jenny, who had called herself Dot's "dear friend", seemed to be gleefully rejoicing now.

Carol had listened to this exchange with amazement. She said, 'Tennis always was your thing, wasn't it? I remember Ant's father saying.'

'That was a long time ago,' said Dot, again. Before Carol could say anything further – if she had been going to – they were interrupted by a man's voice calling in the house, and a moment later Ant himself appeared, searching for his wife. He looked relieved to see them all sitting there over coffee, Dot noted; maybe he had been expecting blood? She said, 'Good morning, Anthony,' and rose to receive his quick kiss on her cheek.

'Dorothy. Good to see you again, it's been too long. You're looking good!' He kissed Liz and shook hands with Mike. 'You must be Michael, congratulations, you've picked a winner.'

Liz offered coffee, but he shook his head, saying that he had only come to collect his wife and they were expected at the farm. 'I told Owen I'd give him a hand putting out the chairs, and I believe Carol has been co-opted too, for some arcane rite in the kitchen. We'll see you all this afternoon.' They left, smiling, and the atmosphere almost visibly relaxed.

'OK, Grannie Dee?' asked Liz, and Dot said yes, thank you. Better than expected, indeed, she thought as she spoke, and the afternoon might be less of a strain in the wake of Carol's peace mission. Even so, she wasn't wholly looking forward to it.

It was, she thought on looking back later, a surprising occasion altogether. From the moment that her stepdaughter Isobel came forward to enfold her in a welcoming hug and kiss her cheek, it had been obvious that she wasn't going to rake over the past, or at least not today. Owen, Sarah and George, too, all behaving as if nothing had ever happened, was disconcerting, although what else they could have done at a party was debatable, but the oddest thing of all was the juxtaposition of what she supposed was now Jerry's family with what she had now to consider as her own, with Susan in one camp and Oliver in the other in spite of the fact that they had grown up together, and Debbie and Mawgan absent altogether because technically they belonged in neither on this occasion. It brought home to her as nothing else could have done how fragmented the family had now become, and whose fault it mostly was.

Had always been. Admit it, she told herself. You should have left Jerry alone.

She had already realised, as had Jerry too, that there was no point in wishing that none of it had ever happened. Debbie was always there, for both of them, making that wish pointless, and the fact that she wasn't here today only pointed up the inevitable conclusion. Even so, it was hard, impossible even, not to be sorry for her own part in events, although she need not accept all the blame. Jerry had had a hand in it too, he should have been stronger. And Helen could have been less hysterical. And Oliver, relaxing on a sun lounger just over there, looking elegant and beautiful and slightly out of place, withdrawn and watchful as Secret Sam with a mood on him, he wasn't blameless either. He had deliberately set out to cause as much trouble as possible, and she wondered now if he felt the same compunction as the rest of them – presumably anyway, she couldn't answer for Helen – did.

Liz took Dot by the arm, and took her round the family, introducing her to all the grandchildren and great grandchildren that she hadn't already met – the twins and William, Owen and Sarah's second son Tony, who had made the effort after all, Cecy and Richard, and Gil – another stranger. Alice, Dot had already met, long ago, although she would never have recognised her after over thirty years.

'Why d'you call her Grannie Dee?' Katie asked, curiously. 'She's Grannie Dorothy.'

'She likes Dee better,' said Liz, and Isobel, who was near enough to overhear, explained, 'It's what you Grandad used to call her, Katie. Do you really like it better, Dorothy?'

'It seems to suit me better now that I'm a free woman,' said Dot. Might as well say it all, she decided. 'I plan to go back to your father's name once my divorce from Jerry is final. I feel I was happiest then.'

'He'd be pleased,' was all Isobel said, but she smiled as if she was a bit pleased too, and lightly touched Dot on the shoulder.

Chel, standing with Susan and Tracy for a moment's peace from an exuberant and over-excited Candy, watched them thoughtfully. She hadn't, of late, had a lot of time for observation, but today Zoë had been annexed by her maternal grandmother and she was thus undistracted. She thought Dot looked, not only younger and smarter, but subtly different in other ways too, and said so. 'Your mother looks like a different person, Suse. She feels like one too. She's giving off different vibes altogether from her usual stuffy criticism of everything and everyone.'

'*Your* mother still looks a bit cautious around her,' Susan observed, then added, 'I suppose she has reason.'

'Don't we all?' said Chel, but she said it without rancour.

'Can the leopard change his spots after all?' Tracy mused.

'She probably hasn't. The spots were there all the time, they must have been. It's a sobering thought, isn't it?'

'I don't see why,' said Tracy, but both Susan and Chel were silent for a moment. Then Susan said, 'I hope she'll be happy. It's a big wrench for her, starting a completely new life at her age. I suppose you expect to be pretty settled as you come up to sixty.'

'Do you think she'll get married a third time?' asked Tracy, idly, and Susan looked at Chel.

'Well? You're the one with the tarot cards.'

Chel actually hated the tarot, and in the past had found herself actively fearing it too, but she knew what Susan was asking and had no real answer ready. She hedged her bets. 'It's too early to say. I don't think so. Maybe when she's really found her feet she'll make a friend. It's no good asking me, I don't know her well enough.'

'But you think she's had enough of being married,' said Susan, shrewdly, and Chel agreed.

William, Micky and Seb had gone to sit at Oliver's feet in silent hero worship for someone who had actually sailed alone around the world, while he talked idly with George and Ant, but the four little girls had dragged Carl off to look at ponies and Tony and Richard had gone with them. Owen was busy with the barbecue, and with a whole lamb that was roasting on a spit alongside; a fragrant smell was hanging seductively in the air. Dot sat under the trees, chatting with Sarah. They looked as if they were enjoying themselves hugely.

'Playing "do you remember",' suggested Susan affectionately.

'More likely discussing how not to bring up children, with direct reference to my niece,' Chel said. 'I don't think any of them – any of the Worthingtons – want to remember the past, not today. That'll come later, when they're all friends again. Or perhaps it won't.'

'You think they will be friends?'

Chel made a gesture that took in the whole chattering crowd, the two families mingling happily, the laughter and smiles, the long table laden with food. 'What do you think? After this, there'll be no going back. The parameters will be set in stone.'

Owen let out a shout from the barbecue, 'Grub's up, come and get it!' and Liz, coming up to collect them, said, 'The lamb was called

Hoopla. The twins named it, as if you hadn't guessed.'

'Don't they mind us eating it?' Tracy asked, obediently following Liz to the table for plates. 'Candy'd freak out!'

'They've grown up on a farm, They take it for granted.'

'And who are the sausages made from?' asked Susan, eyeing up the barbecue, but Liz laughed.

'Not our pigs. Our neighbour's. He's a practical, unsentimental farmer. It was probably called 22A or something.'

'Let's call it Paul,' Cecy murmured in her ear, overhearing, and the laugh was wiped immediately from Liz's face. 'Shut up,' she said. 'Not here, Cec. Please.'

'He's vanished from his usual haunts,' said Cecy, airily, as if it didn't matter.

'Well, he'd better not be in mine!'

Owen's shout and the delectable scent of roasting meat had brought the pony admirers streaming back from the field. Cecy slipped away in the crowd, intent on getting her share before the boys got there, and Liz followed on more slowly, thoughtfully, a small cloud on her horizon.

For if Paul wasn't in London, where then was he most likely to be?

XXX

By half past seven, the party was beginning to break up, as those who had to get back to Cornwall or to London began to say their goodbyes and head for their cars. Under cover of the departures, Liz murmured to Mike, 'Do you think they'd be offended if we legged it, too? I think Grannie Dee has had enough. It must have been a bit of an ordeal for her, even though everyone was so nice.'

'Give it half an hour,' Mike suggested, as quietly. 'It'll look less pointed, and it is our engagement party after all. Then you can have a word with your mum and we'll beat it.'

'Unless,' Liz added, remembering belatedly that Mike didn't see that much of his own family, 'you want to stay longer? Your mum and dad ...'

'They'll understand,' Mike assured her. 'Anyway, I expect everyone will be glad to get home and put their feet up by then. It's been quite an afternoon, your aunt and uncle certainly know how to throw a party!'

'They host all the big ones,' Liz told him. 'They've got the space.'

'And the lambs. Hoopla was delicious.'

'How many do you think were here?'

'It felt like hundreds. I didn't count.'

'And all family, yours or mine. There's a solemn thought.' She turned to speak to Dot, who was approaching them across the grass. 'Hullo Gran – we thought we'd give it half an hour and then slope off if that's OK with you, or do you want to stop on a bit?'

'I think that enough is enough, thank you. It has been a lovely party but I feel I should like to get away soon. What a crowd!'

'We were just saying that,' said Liz, sympathetically. 'Such a shame that Deb and Mawgan couldn't make it, but I suppose they do have a living to earn.'

'They were asked?' asked Dot, both surprised and absurdly pleased.

'Of course they were.' Isobel had joined them in time to hear her. 'If I'm Susan's half-sister, and so is Debbie, then she must be part of the family because that has to make her my ... something, anyway, and I want to meet her. She sounds great fun.'

'Quarter-sister?' suggested Mike, with a lift of his brows, and they all laughed.

Liz seized the opportunity. 'Mum, we thought we'd slope off soon, take Grannie Dee out to the Three Bears for a stiff drink to chill her out after all this.'

'What a good idea.' Isobel smiled at Dot. 'You must be shattered, Dee, but never mind. It'll be easier next time – for all of us. It's just that breaking the ice bit that's hardest.'

'You have all been very kind, but I feel I need time to reflect.'

'Don't we all?' Isobel made a face. 'But you must come again soon, and next time you must stay with George and me. I mean that Dee. We all used to be friends, didn't we?'

Liz thought that Dot looked a little bewildered; perhaps she wasn't used to such easy forgiveness. Poor Grannie Dee, she found herself thinking, she doesn't seem to have had much luck with her life so far. We shall fix that!

'I'll look forward to it,' Dot was promising, making an effort to sound as if she meant it, and Liz noticed that the apostrophe had slipped back in. She smiled to herself.

The departure of what Carol referred to affectionately as "the yuppie crowd" threatened to bring the party into a more intimate mode; Tracy started to murmur about bedtime, which Candy and Micky ignored, and Alice and Gil had begun to gather up their own children and start on the round of goodbyes. Liz decided that it would be unfair to subject Dot to any more close encounters today, the one with Carol had been quite enough, and seized the opportunity to thank everyone for the lovely party and slide dexterously out in the wake of Gil and Alice.

'Did you enjoy yourself, Grannie Dee?' she asked, as they drove off in Gil's wake, and Dot murmured that it had been interesting. 'But I need time to evaluate it,' she added. 'It was too much at one time, and I'm sorry if I dragged you away, but I am grateful too.'

'I could see you were flagging a bit,' Liz told her. 'Never mind – we'll dump the car when we get back, and stroll up to the pub and have a nightcap. Unless you've had enough?'

Dot reflected that she had not had many invitations in her life to have a drink in a pub, and decided to live a little. She felt easy with Liz and Mike, as she hadn't so far done with Liz's family – her family too, how odd. She said, 'Thank you Elizabeth. That would make a pleasant end to a lovely day, so long as you won't mind if I slip away when I have had enough? I imagine you two have more stamina than I have!'

'Not sure about that today, but that'd be fine,' Liz told her. 'Are we leading you astray, Grannie Dee?'

'I daresay it is not before time,' Dot admitted.

They parked the car at the cottage and walked together up the street to the Three Bells. The shadows were gathering as the night closed in, and as they walked Liz remembered what Cecy had said, and felt the hairs on her neck prickle. It wouldn't be hard to imagine Paul, lurking in wait in those shadows, watching and planning... what? He didn't know about Mike presumably, so would he throw himself at her feet and beg to be taken back? Browbeat her? Blackmail her? Hit her, even? He had behaved as if he hated her, and it wasn't a comfortable thought that he might be out there now.

'You've gone very quiet, Elizabeth,' said Dot, when they had settled at a table, and Mike had gone up to the bar. 'Is anything the matter?'

Liz had intended to ask Dot's advice anyway, she recalled. Perhaps now wasn't the moment, but the opening was too good to pass by. She said, 'Actually, I have a bit of a problem.'

'Something Cecilia said to you at the party,' said Dot, nodding, and Liz looked at her in amazement.

'You don't miss much, do you, Grannie Dee?'

'I saw your face,' Dot told her. 'All the fun went out of it.' She paused. 'She's a mischievous young madam, that one. So what's wrong? Tell me.'

'Shall we wait for Mike?' Liz said. 'Not that he doesn't know all about it, of course, but we might as well. No point in saying things twice.' She fell silent, wondering how and where she would begin. Across the room, her elderly neighbour Tina and her even more elderly husband, Sid, were nodding and smiling at her. She had asked Tina's help, she remembered; in view of what happened later, she had certainly asked an inappropriate person. Paul had turned out unexpectedly nasty, she was glad Tina had never been called upon to confront him. She smiled back and waggled her fingers in a friendly way, and then Mike returned, placing the glasses on the table and drawing out a chair to sit down.

'You two look very serious,' he said. Liz gave herself a shake and brought her thoughts back to now. She said, 'I was about to share my problems with Grannie Dee. You never know, she's a woman of the world. She might have a new angle.'

'The only kind of angle that arsehole needs is an angle *grinder* scientifically applied to his backside,' Mike muttered, not too loudly and Liz shushed him and turned to Dot.

'It's to do with an old boyfriend,' she said. 'He's making a nuisance of himself, rather, and ... I'd better tell you it all.'

Dot listened to the sorry tale quietly, interjecting a question here and there when it became complicated, as when computers entered the stage. At the finish, she said, 'He sounds to me a very insecure person. People who try to impose their will by bullying so often are.' As who should know better than I? 'It's surely unlikely, however, that he will persist in the face of your engagement to Michael here.'

'I would like to think so,' said Mike, and added, after a pause. 'But I don't. I think it might even make him more aggressive.'

'But so far, nobody has told him?'

'Not so far as we know.' Liz paused. 'He's lost his job, of course, and Cecy said tonight that he had left London. Nobody knows where he's gone.'

'Then you should hope that it's back to his own family, wherever they are, and the chapter is closed,' Dot told her.

'He hasn't got a family – not like that. A few cousins, perhaps. Some girl called Ashley he goes about with sometimes, not serious. His mother is around somewhere, but they don't speak much, he wouldn't go there.'

'A sad case,' said Dot, shaking her head. 'And what a stupid man, if he valued his position, to abuse it so.'

'It wasn't so much the job he liked as the status he thought it gave him,' said Liz, cynically. Across the room, Sid and Tina were getting to their feet and coming over to speak to them. Liz introduced them to Dot and they shook hands, then said goodnight.

'Us old folks need our rest,' said Sid, winking, and steered his wife towards the door. Liz murmured, 'They were my first line of defence before Mike came on the scene. Seems a bit inadequate with what's happened since.'

'But none of it was hands-on unpleasantness,' Dot pointed out, considering. 'All from a distance, on this internet you all talk about so glibly, or in the mail. You must hope that this is the way it will continue, and that he'll become tired of taunting you. Unless, of course, he already has tired of it.'

'He didn't kick poor Tib at a distance,' said Liz rebelliously.

'Tib is small and furry and wouldn't fight,' Mike pointed out. 'Just about his mark, the slimeball!'

'You have met him?' Dot asked, and Mike said no, he hadn't, and it would be best for Paul if he never did. Dot shook her head but made no comment. Those such as Mike, who were secure in themselves, she had learned by experience didn't make allowances for the less fortunate. She didn't like the sound of Paul Attwood, but nevertheless she had a certain fellow feeling: she had made an admittedly less spectacular, but recognisably similar, hash of her own life to date.

'It's a horrible feeling – being stalked,' Liz admitted.

'I imagine it is. Have you considered informing the police?'

Liz sighed, becoming weary of it all. 'I don't want to cause more trouble for him.'

'He's causing it for himself,' Mike pointed out. 'What worries me is, suppose he comes in person, when I'm not there?'

Since this was also worrying Liz she made no comment, but Dot said, 'Perhaps you need to borrow a large, fierce dog. It would make you feel more secure, maybe.'

'The only dogs I know are all great softies,' Liz told her.

Mike gathered the empty glasses together and said, 'Another one, Dorothy? Then we can talk about something more cheerful.'

'Not for me,' said Dot, shaking her head and reaching for her handbag. 'As a matter of fact, what I would really like is a nice ... *mug*, of something soothing and hot to help me sleep. It has been a trying day. Would you be very offended if I returned to the cottage and made myself a cup of tea?'

'Of course not.' Liz felt in her pocket for the keys and laid them on the able. 'There's milk in the fridge, and I think there's some Horlicks in the cupboard above the stove, if you like that. I'm afraid it's one of my weaknesses when I'm feeling low.'

'Horlicks would be excellent.' Dot picked up the keys and stood up. 'I shall leave the front door on the latch, then if I have gone to bed when you get back, you won't be locked out.'

'We shan't be that late,' said Liz, smothering a yawn. She had taken off her woolly jacket when they came into the pub; she had put it on earlier as it became cooler in the farm field. Now she held it out to Dot. 'Here, wear this – it'll be cold outside.'

'It will be cold for you too.'

Liz smiled. 'I've got my love to keep me warm,' she said, snuggling against Mike's shoulder. Dot gave her an indulgent smile.

'Very well then. I shall be glad of it.'

It was completely dark now, with only a sliver of moon like a fingernail clipping above the church tower, and Waldren Stavey had no streetlights. Away from the lights of the bright, cheerful pub, the village was inadequately lit by the light coming from the rare uncurtained window along the street, a fleeting advantage that served only to make the night seem darker. Dot made her way with care along the short distance to Liz's cottage, running into parked cars and slipping into the rainwater gulley; it was impossible to hurry. Apart from herself and a prowling cat that she thought might be Tib, the street was deserted, although she did think she saw a shadow retreating into a narrow alley beside the churchyard on the other side. Then a door opened ahead of her and a bright shaft of light fell across the tarmac. A man emerged from the doorway, and in the fleeting glimpse she had of him Dot saw that it was Liz's neighbour Sid, off back to the pub for another pint or two having seen his wife home, no doubt. He closed the door behind him and switched on a torch, shining it up towards Dot's face, then quickly away as if satisfied with what he saw.

'Evening,' he said, as he passed. 'Dark old night, isn't it?' Dot wondered if he had recognised her, the greeting could have been as easily given to a stranger as an acquaintance. She said goodnight and passed on her way. Sid had given her her bearings, Liz's cottage would be the next one along; when the dazzle from the torchlight had died out of her eyes she would find it easily. There was a dim light from the tiny hall window beside the door, by its meagre glimmer Dot slipped the key into the lock and gave the door a push. She thought she heard a footstep, not Sid's, scraping on stones, but when she turned the street was empty. Thoughtfully, she went inside and closed the door.

Liz's story, and her obvious nerves on the subject, must be getting to her. She gave herself a shake and made her way to the kitchen, switching on the study light as she went. Why? She didn't need it to see her way, the strip light above the worktop had been left on to make the house seem occupied while they were out. Without bothering to turn on the centre light, Dot slipped off Liz's jacket before stepping over to the stove and opening the cupboard above it. Now, where was that Horlicks that Liz had mentioned? She moved aside tea and coffee searching for it, and found it at the back. She took it out and set it on the worktop, opened the fridge and took out the milk, and began a search for a small saucepan.

Sid, meanwhile, had made his way back to the pub, but when he got there he made no attempt to approach the bar. Instead, he made straight for Liz and Mike, now joined by Mark Jones and his mate and that Angie who worked up at the garage in the office.

'A word with you,' he said to Liz and then, when she looked up enquiringly. 'Private, like.' He ducked his head to her companions. 'Won't keep her. Just a bit of business.'

Liz followed him to the door, where he paused after a quick glance round to see that nobody was in earshot. 'Tina would have me come,' he said. 'I told her 'twas nought, but she said as you should ought to know. You remember, a while back, as you asked her to keep an eye for that bloke as used to stay with you one time? Dark chap, a bit flashy, fancied himself. She believed as he kicked your Tib, that time as he broke your door down.'

'I remember,' said Liz, heart sinking. 'She's not seen him, has she?'

'She says she has.' Sid sniffed. 'Made me come out again and tell you, she could of sworn she saw him in the street, just about opposite your house. Just standing there he was, she said, under that big tree by the churchyard wall. Dark's the inside of a cow out there it is, and Tina's eyesight none too good in daylight these days, and I didn't see nothing, but she insisted I come back and tell you. Kicked up such a fuss, said as she'd come herself if I didn't. So here I am, but

I wouldn't take too much notice if it was me. Just seeing things, she was, with the night so dark and owls flying.'

Liz hesitated. It was no good relying on elderly, short-sighed Tina for reliable evidence, but her sighting had come rather pat on the heels of Cecy's news. No good involving equally elderly Sid either, if Tina happened to be right. She said, 'All right Sid, we'll be careful, and thank you,' and then she remembered. Dot had gone on ahead, alone through the darkness, back to the cottage. Could she be mistaken for Liz herself in the dark? Surely not! But she was a woman on her own, and a woman on her own was what Paul would be expecting. It would never occur to someone as conceited as he that there might be a man on the case.

The door wouldn't be locked, Dot had said she would leave it on the latch. On swift feet, Liz made her way through the crowd and back to the table. 'I'm sorry everyone, we've got to go,' she said, forcing a smile. 'Are you ready, Mike? Sid just brought a message ...' she ended lamely. Mike caught her eye, read something therein if not the whole truth, and got to his feet. 'Sure. We can drink with this lot any time.'

'Lovely to see you anyway,' said Liz, heading for the door. Mark Jones looked at Mike.

'Think I might just walk along with you,' he said, rising. 'Be back in a while, folks.' They followed swiftly in Liz's wake.

Outside in the dark street, Liz waited impatiently.

'It's him, isn't it?' said Mike, taking her arm and moving her swiftly along, then as Mark produced a torch from his pocket and shone it ahead of them, 'Well thought, Corporal – don't trip on that dustbin, Liz!'

'I can see a dustbin when it's big enough!' said Liz, indignantly. 'I don't know Mike. Tina thinks she saw him by the churchyard wall. Sid says she didn't. But Grannie Dee will have left the door unlocked, and I thought ...' her voice tailed off. They hurried on.

'This'll be the email expert, I take it?' Mark said, and then, although he couldn't see Liz's quick nod, 'Thought so. We'll get him, don't you worry.'

The door of the cottage, when they reached it, was closed but unlatched, exactly as it should have been. All three of them made a push through together and in their haste nearly got jammed in the door: Mike forced his way through first, the other two tumbling after him. The study light was on, they made for it in a body. Mike, in the lead, stopped abruptly when he reached the door at the scene of carnage he beheld.

'Bloody hell!' he said.

The watcher by the churchyard wall hadn't been waiting long. He had driven past earlier in the day, seen Liz's car wasn't there and thought cynically, in Cornwall yet again, with her bloody mischief-making aunt! Typical bloody luck! But since it was Sunday evening, there was every chance that Liz would be back later on, and he made another quick reconnaissance at seven o'clock. Still no car. He would, he promised himself, have one more try and then ... well, he didn't know quite what he would do if she wasn't back then. Sleep in his car and wait for morning? Probably, he had run out of other options; with no job and no prospects he had to hang on to every penny, he couldn't afford to stop in even the cheapest of B&Bs because there was always the inexorable tomorrow to cope with. Desperation rose in his throat and nearly choked him. She must be back, she *must*! She owed him, she must help him now, there was nobody else. He would make her.

He returned again two hours later in the gathering dusk, and there was the car, parked outside. He sighed with relief. There was a light shining in the hall window, she was back at last! Shaking with reaction, he took his car to the small car park outside the village shop and walked back. Nobody answered his ring.

That was odd. If she had driven back from Cornwall, she was unlikely to have gone to the pub, but of course you never knew. She might have been meeting someone. The man who had answered the telephone, for instance; well, he would very much like to meet that man. His fists clenched; what had he been doing in Liz's house anyway? It was his territory.

Wherever she was, she would be back. He walked across the road and took up his station in the shadow of the great tree and the wall. He would wait, and he would see her come, and then, *then*, he would make her help him.

The darkness gathered until it was thick as smoke. He saw Tina and Sid come back from the pub and the light of their torch on the road, and stepped back out of range. Tina's head jerked up and round at the movement, had she seen him, or maybe heard the scuff of small stones along the bottom of the wall crunch under his shoe? He tensed, waiting, but they went into their own house without coming to investigate and he breathed again. Maybe she had seen the movement, but if so she must have dismissed it as a stray cat, or a wandering dog maybe. There was a cat over there, he thought it was Liz's Tib. Bloody animal! He hoped that Liz had appreciated his emails and his gift, although of late the emails had been homing back to him and he had been unable to reach her. Someone must have helped her there, she'd never have known what to do for herself. The man on the phone, no doubt. But the parcel must have reached her. He smiled as he imagined her reaction when she opened it. He knew his Liz, she would have been bitterly distressed, and serve her right, she should never have dumped him like that! Her cousin, that cocky little Cecily Worthington, had run into him in the street, and he could have sworn she was laughing as she passed. He didn't like Cecy, she had told his cousin Ash something that had set her against him. It had to be Cecy, she was the only acquaintance they shared. Ash might have been an option when Liz decided to move on; models could make good money, but she had changed towards him after that, there was only Liz left. He moved out again onto the street, not too far from the entrance to the alley, and waited, nursing his fury and resentment.

He saw Sid come out of his house again and stride off down the street, back towards the Three Bells, and coming the other way, yes, there was somebody else. A woman. Liz? The light of Sid's torch shone momentarily on a familiar jacket. Yes, Liz. Good.

Dot passed from the light into the darkness again without him getting more than that brief glimpse and came along the road towards him. He had no intention of confronting Liz in the open, he stepped back into the mouth of the alley. He watched her fumbling with the lock as if it was unfamiliar, a dark shape against the lighter wall. That coat made her look wide across the shoulders, she should give up wearing it, he thought critically, and the light from the window, just catching a curl of her hair, made it shine gold. He liked blondes, but Liz would have to do.

He was thinking this, and blowing on the coals of his resentment over Ash, who had been appropriately ash-blonde and rather pretty, and more biddable than Liz until she met Cecily, when Dot finally persuaded the door to open and slipped inside, so quickly that he had no time to cross the road to crowd in behind her. His lack of concentration for that single moment had cost him his chance. The door closed, but there was no sound of the key turning afterwards.

He glanced quickly up and down the street, but there was nobody there to see and he slipped across, quiet as a wraith, and tried the door cautiously. It opened under his hand and he slid through, closing it behind him carefully, carefully ... the click of the latch was so tiny he barely heard it himself; Liz, now moving about in the kitchen, would never hear it. He trod silently along the hall, through Liz's brightly lit study and came to the kitchen door. There was a woman by the stove, a small black saucepan in her hand, her back to him. She had discarded Liz's woolly coat, which hung over the back of a chair, and both her sturdy build and her blonde hair were totally unfamiliar. He spoke without consideration.

'Who the hell are you?' he asked, furious with disappointment. The woman at the stove visibly jumped and swung round, the small but heavy cast iron pan in her hand. Their eyes met for a startled second.

Dot saw a tall, unshaven, wild-eyed man with pure rage on his face starting towards her with upraised hands, the fingers curled to seize her and from his looks, to shake the living daylights out of her. Unbidden, her long buried *alter ego* Dee Shipham leapt from the concealment where she had been becoming increasingly restless and reacted with a smooth decision that Dot, so uptight and dignified, could never have achieved. Her hand holding the saucepan swung back and up, and forward in a perfect over-arm serve and smashed down towards Paul's head with equally violent intent in her own defence. Stepping hastily back out of range, his heel caught the small step, hardly worthy of the name, where the wooden floor of the study met the tiled floor of the kitchen and he staggered and sat down abruptly, so that the blow caught, not his head where it had been aimed, but his nose, glancing painfully off it, flying out of Dot's hand as it did so. Both Paul and the dropped pan landed with a crash.

Paul gave a moan of pain and clapped his hands to his nose, and Dot, breathing fast, bent to pick up the pan. With it safely back in her hand, she said, 'I might ask you the same question, young man.' She looked at the man sitting there with, blood oozing between his fingers, critically. He looked unshaven and unkempt, but not exactly down and out, his suit was rumpled but neither torn nor dirty. If he was a burglar, he was a burglar who had been expecting to see someone, see Liz. She felt a momentary disquiet; if he was expecting to see Liz, he might be a friend of hers. On the other hand, he might equally be that Paul she had just been hearing about. She hedged her bets. 'I'm sorry, you startled me. Are you hurt?' She reached out and switched on the main kitchen light to see him clearly.

'What do you bloody well think?' Paul mumbled, and made to get up, but a quiet hefting of the pan gave him pause. He sank back down to his safer position on the floor.

'And since you were so kind as to ask,' Dot continued, 'I am Elizabeth's grandmother. And who are you, may I ask in my turn?'

Paul scowled at her as the blood dripped down onto his shirt, assessing.

'That's a bloody lie, for a start!' he said. 'You're not old enough. You're not old enough to be her bloody mother!'

'Thank you for that compliment,' said Dot, 'and kindly do not swear at me. Your lack of choice in your epithets, although appropriate, is becoming monotonous.'

Paul gaped at her, swallowing blood and indignation in roughly equal quantities. Who had hit whom, he would like to know? Her reproof was surely way out of order!

Out in the hallway, footsteps and voices could now be heard. Totally unnerved, Paul turned his head not sure whether he should be protecting his front or his rear, to behold a very angry total stranger advancing on him with the same monotonous epithet on his lips, too.

'Bloody hell!' said the stranger, on beholding Paul's bloodied countenance, and paused in his tracks. Dot quietly placed her weapon on the kitchen table. She said, 'I am so glad you have come, Michael. This man walked into the house without either ringing the bell or invitation, and behaved in a highly threatening manner. He surprised me, and I am afraid that I may have injured him a little.'

Even in the stress of the moment, it occurred to Mike that only Liz's Grannie Dee could have made a speech like that at a moment such as this, and he almost laughed. Only *almost*, however. 'Get up,' he ordered the intruder, brusquely, and when he did not immediately obey, put his hands under the man's shoulders and lifted him to his feet, not gently. Paul staggered, dripping blood, and Mike put out a foot and hooked a chair from beneath the kitchen table, dropping his burden onto it without ceremony.

Dot went quietly across to the kitchen roll on the wall beside the stove and pulled off several sheets, handing them to Paul. 'Put your head back,' she ordered as she did so. 'It will stop in a minute. It was barely a tap, you know, but noses are always so vulnerable.'

Paul made a muffled objection, but surprisingly, did as he was told. Liz and Mark appeared in the doorway behind Mike.

'Is this him?' Mike asked, and Liz nodded, wide-eyed. 'What happened to him?'

'Your bloody grandmother assaulted me,' Paul mumbled through the wad of paper. He added accusingly, 'I didn't even know you *had* a grandmother!'

Mark, seeing that his physical assistance wasn't going to be required, picked up the kettle and carried it to the sink to fill it. A nice cup of tea, he decided after a quick look at the protagonists, might work wonders. But Dot was quietly pouring milk into her saucepan and, 'Not for me, thank you,' she murmured. 'Would anyone else prefer Horlicks, while I am making it?'

Paul's nose, he estimated, had almost stopped bleeding, and he cautiously lowered his head, scowling at Dot over the wad. 'I could sue you for assault,' he said, accusingly.

'Oh, I wouldn't do that,' said Dot, tranquilly. 'My husband is a very, very good solicitor. He would know exactly how to present a convincing defence. After all, *you* were going to assault *me*, were you not? That makes it reasonable force, you know. And you had entered the house without invitation, knowing, as you must have done, that you were not welcome here.' It was stretching a point to call Jerry her husband, since their divorce petition was due to be heard in court the following week, but the rest of the speech was possibly true, although with the state of the law these days she wouldn't put serious money on it, and even if it wasn't it sounded convincing. It certainly seemed to carry weight with Paul, who was visibly recalling how Liz had changed the locks to keep him out. His scowl deepened. He gave his ill-treated nose a last cautious wipe and held out the scrumpled, blood soaked paper for someone else to dispose of; Dot picked it out of his hand with her fingertips and dropped it into the bin, kindly handing him a fresh sheet afterwards. 'Just in case,' she said.

The whole situation was becoming surreal, Liz decided. She pulled out another chair so that she could sit and see Paul at the same time. Her tone, when she spoke, was confrontational.

'So what are you doing here anyway?' she demanded, not in a friendly way. 'I told you we were finished.'

There was a pause, while Paul tried to think of a way to word his reply. He hadn't reckoned on presenting his case before a jury of inimical bystanders, at least two of whom had demonstrated their willingness to administer physical violence. It cramped his style. In the end he just muttered, like a sulky child, 'I wanted to talk to you.'

'OK, here I am. What did you want to talk to me about?'

'Look, couldn't we go somewhere private?' Paul asked, and Liz answered firmly, 'I go nowhere alone with you, Paul. Not after the way you've been behaving.'

Paul assumed a look of injured innocence and bleated, 'Why, what have I done?'

'You know very well,' Liz told him. 'Now, what do you want? Tell me, and then you can get out, and we can go to bed.' She wished immediately that she had worded that differently, caught Mike's eye, and blushed. Paul caught the look and the blush and his heart sank. It made him become confrontational.

'You owe me, Liz,' he blustered.

'I most certainly do not! If anything, the boot is on the other foot, after what you did to my flat!'

'What *I* did?' Paul asked innocently, widening his eyes. 'I have no idea what you're talking about.'

'I dumped you, so you sent someone to wreck it,' Liz accused. Paul shook his head.

'Not me, Liz. Whatever gave you that idea?' He sounded hurt. Liz, knowing that she was on unsafe ground with that one, however sure she was in her own mind, changed tack.

'And all those horrible emails you sent me,' she said accusingly. 'I suppose you're going to deny that, too!'

'I have no idea what you're talking about,' Paul said, but his voice lacked the conviction it should have had. Over by the worktop, where he was quietly pouring hot water into mugs, Mark said, 'It's possible to trace where those really came from, you know.' He turned towards Paul, a mug in his hand. 'Milk? Sugar?'

'Plenty of sugar,' said Dot, briskly. 'The man is in shock.' She narrowed her eyes. 'Not just over this, I suspect.'

Paul muttered something that might have been thanks, or then again, might not, and Liz went on, 'And you sent me a dead tabby kitten in a box. What sort of horrible man does that, Paul?'

'I did not!' denied Paul, and Mike remarked, half to himself. 'I expect your fingerprints are on the wrapping.'

Paul stared at him, the wind knocked completely out of his sails. 'I wore –' he began, and then stopped, horrified, and realising that he had cut the ground from beneath his own feet. He fell silent. Mark spooned sugar into the mug, stirred it, and handed it to him.

'Get that down you, and talk some sense,' he said. 'We know what you are: despicable. Now tell Liz why you came here tonight, and then get out like she told you.'

Paul looked around at the four unsympathetic faces staring at him, and realised that he could expect no quarter here. He muttered, 'It doesn't matter. It was nothing.'

'Oh yes it does,' said the sparky blonde woman who called herself Liz's grandmother. 'If we don't have it out of you now, you will come back when she is alone and try to bully her. So say what you came to say, and let us be done with it.'

'It doesn't matter,' Paul repeated more loudly. He put his mug of tea down on the table, it was too hot to drink anyway, and tried to get to his feet, but the red haired man with the moustache pushed him back, not gently.

'Get on with it,' he said. He had strong hands, and a nasty way of using them. Paul looked up into his face and saw granite. There was no way out. He said, sullenly, 'I wanted her help.'

The sad little grave under the smokebush in the garden came into Liz's head, and choked her. She said, unevenly, 'Why on earth should I help *you*?'

'Because you helped me get into this mess,' said Paul.

'I most certainly did not!' Liz cried, and Mike said, 'Get into what, exactly?' in a voice like cold steel. Paul shifted on the chair, uncomfortably.

'We had this scam going ...' he said, and felt the atmosphere drop several degrees. He added hastily, 'Me and this bloke, one of our authors, it was important to please him. He's good, the very best, he could have taken his business elsewhere if I'd refused... it was all in the firm's interests, it's not fair...' He tailed off, glancing shiftily around the circle. Four pairs of eyes stared uncompromisingly back at him.

'Please do continue,' said Dot. 'This is very interesting.'

'He had this flat,' said Paul, squirming on his seat. 'He had a lot of valuable stuff in it. He couldn't leave it all week, it could have been broken into.' He sounded defensive, even to himself.

'And how would that have concerned you?' asked Dot. Paul was beginning to dislike her intensely, by no means the first person to do so had he but known it. He blurted out. 'He wanted me to caretake for him. He might have taken his work somewhere else. It wasn't a crime, was it?'

'Of course not,' said Dot. 'Although it would be interesting to hear why this man couldn't look after his own flat.' She narrowed her eyes. 'So tell us, how does Elizabeth come into it?'

'If I was going to do it, I needed somewhere to go at weekends,' said Paul, sulkily, then looked up in defiance. 'She helped me. You know you did, Liz. You let me stay with you from Friday evening until Monday morning, every week.'

'I think "let" is the wrong word,' said Liz. 'When I tried to go somewhere on my own, you followed me, and then the next time you broke into my house. And I never knew about your arrangement, and you daren't say that I did!'

'I've lost my job over it,' Paul muttered. 'You can't lose yours, you're self-employed, lucky you! But I could tell your publisher, and they wouldn't renew your contract –'

'That,' said Dot, 'is blackmail, and before witnesses too! What a very silly man you are, Mr Attwood. You know perfectly well that Elizabeth had no idea of what you were up to.'

'She must have had some idea,' Paul retorted, nastily. 'Why else would I want to spend every weekend with her?'

'Because I paid for everything,' said Liz, coldly furious. 'What are you trying to imply, Paul? It was you who wouldn't push off when I gave you the hint!'

'Shall we return to the point at issue,' said Dot, firmly. 'Mr Attwood, perhaps you would be good enough to tell us how this seemingly innocent arrangement came to cost you your job?'

She knows perfectly well, Paul thought viciously, the bitch! They all do! That bloody Cecily! He glared at her. Dot met his glare, unimpressed. 'We are all waiting to hear your explanation,' she reminded him.

'It's none of your business,' he told her, shortly. Dot smiled on him forgivingly.

'No, it is not. But it is very much Elizabeth's, since you are trying to implicate her in your problems, and all of us here have *her* interests very much at heart.'

'And don't care a toss about me!' Paul retorted. It rang a familiar bell, and Dot sighed inwardly. Another one. She had thought – hoped – Tom Casson might have been a one-off, at least in her immediate family. Wrong, obviously.

Mike had so far left the conduct of the interrogation to Dot, who was doing rather well with it, now he took a hand. 'I don't actually see why we should care a toss about you,' he said. 'Your behaviour is beyond belief, and why, after all the grief you've caused her lately, you feel that Liz owes you anything I totally fail to understand.'

'And I totally fail to understand why you consider it your business!' retaliated Paul.

'It's very much my business, since she's going to marry me.'

In the silence that followed this announcement, you could have heard a pin drop. Paul pulled himself together after a moment, and said unpleasantly, 'Then I hope you're prepared for the consequences when everyone gets to hear how she aided and abetted one of her friends to seduce another man's wife!'

'Don't be obscene!' said Mike, angrily. 'Of course she didn't!'

'How else would you interpret it?' Paul met his look impudently. 'She did. You can't argue with it.'

Mike began to speak, hotly, but Dot interrupted. 'No Michael, leave this to me.' She looked at Paul as if he had crawled out from beneath a particularly slimy stone. 'What Elizabeth did, young man, was to offer friendship, not to this author that *you*, not she, aided and abetted in his disgraceful behaviour, but to you yourself, and if this is the way that you repay her, you should be thoroughly ashamed! *You* made shameless use of her, and that is the truth. *She* knew nothing about it, and I think you would be very ill advised to put it about that she did, unless you want to find yourself in court for slander. I would have thought your situation was bad enough without that added.'

'It isn't slander. Everyone knows she did it. And she's to get away with it, is she, while I've lost everything? I've lost my place to live, my friends, my job –'

'You can get another job. You are not stupid or incapacitated.' Dot wasn't so certain about "stupid" but she decided not to pour oil on the flames. 'Don't be so negative. You are young, fit, presumably capable of fending for yourself. Stop being sorry for yourself, and trying to drag innocent people into your troubles!'

'My boss told me he'd see I never worked in publishing again! Which is hardly fair when he will continue to publish the real offender!'

'That is life, my dear Mr Attwood. It is seldom fair. If you cannot work in publishing, work in something else. There must be plenty of other things you can do. Stack shelves in a supermarket if all else fails, there is always work somewhere for those willing to do it.'

'*Stack shelves in a supermarket?*' Paul echoed, as if she had suggested cleaning out sewers. Dot smiled at him kindly, what an irritating woman she was!

'It is at least more honest than procuring, or cadging off your friends,' she told him.

'*Procuring?*'

'I believe that is what the courts would call it. Enabling a man to cheat with someone else's wife is not a nice thing to do.'

'*Courts?*' asked Paul, disbelieving.

'Oh yes. If you persist in blackmailing my granddaughter, I promise you that is where it will end. I remind you, once again, of my husband's profession, he would have all the big guns trained against you.' She continued, piling on the agony, 'My daughter-in-law, too, is a lawyer, a QC in fact. I'm sure she would be happy to act for her niece.'

Paul stumbled to his feet. He knew when he was up against titanium. 'I'm going,' he said. 'You're all dead against me, I can see. I hope you can live with yourself, Liz, now you see what you've done to me!' He lurched towards the door, and Mike took his arm in a firm grip.

'I'll see you out,' he said.

There was silence in the kitchen when they had gone. Dot picked up the untouched mug of tea from the table and quietly poured it away down the sink, neither of the other two moved. Then Mike came back, grinning evilly to himself, and Liz asked accusingly, 'What did you do?'

'Tripped him into a huge pile of doggy-do that a wandering alsatian with a big appetite and an excellent digestive system had just dumped in the road outside,' said Mike, with satisfaction. 'Sometimes, life is just too generous with its gifts to be refused.'

'Poor Paul,' said Liz, guiltily.

'Don't be sorry for him, he's an arsehole.' He looked at Dot. 'You did brilliantly, Dorothy. Were all those things you said true, by any chance?'

Dot sipped her Horlicks thoughtfully, it was really very good, she hadn't drunk it for years and she resolved to get some on her next visit to the village shop. After a pause, she replied, 'I really have no idea, Michael. But then, neither has he. And I am very sure he will not ask.'

'I never expected to pity him,' said Liz, miserably. She felt torn both ways, grateful to Dorothy for dealing with Paul so expeditiously, sorry for Paul for the barren future he had wished on himself. Dot watched her for a minute, then said, 'Don't be sorry, Elizabeth. Men like that, flashily good looking and with no discernible moral sense, will always find a way to survive. You are not responsible for him, forget him now, he will not trouble you again.'

Liz said, half in despair, 'He didn't even blink when Mike told him we were engaged. Anything he felt was for the hole he had dug for himself, he didn't even care about me, he just wanted to pull me in with him.'

'And I doubt very much if he ever did care.'

'I should love to come across him stacking shelves,' Mark remarked, and Dot shook her head at him.

'He will never do anything so straightforward. Once he has ceased to feel sorry for himself, he'll find himself another silly, gullible woman, forgive me Elizabeth, and re-establish himself in a new image. He is not the kind to choose an honest path.'

'How could I ever have fallen for his line?' Liz marvelled.

'That, we shall none of us ever know,' said Mike. He put his arm round her shoulders and gave her a hug. 'He's gone, sweetheart, and Dorothy is right, he won't be back. Once the easy option becomes the difficult option, men like him vanish like smoke in the wind. They're all mouth – and if he does come back,' he added, 'I shall flatten him. And he knows it. Which makes his final departure doubly certain. I just hope he remembers to change his smart suit before he goes out on the catch.'

Mark went over to the sink and rinsed his empty mug under the tap, setting it carefully on the draining board. 'It seems as if my services won't be required after all,' he said. 'I'll take myself back to the pub, and wish you a very good night.'

'Give him a moment to get away,' said Mike, watching him.

'I won't hurt him,' said Mark. He moved to the kitchen door. 'Maybe just give him a memento to remember us by.'

'Leave him,' said Liz. 'You've been great, Mark, a good friend. But leave him.'

'Dorothy has already annihilated him,' added Mike. 'And I dropped him in the shit. Enough is enough.' Mark looked at him for a brief moment, then nodded his head, sharply.

'OK. If he leaves me alone, I'll leave him. But I daresay he's gone by now. Goodnight, all.'

He was gone. Dot gathered up the last of the cups and placed them in the sink. 'I think I shall go to bed, and leave you two on your own,' she said. 'It has been a tiring day, and I have a long drive tomorrow.'

'You've been a star.' Liz detached herself from Mike and went to put her arms around Dot, hugging her. 'You were magnificent, and I love you for it.'

'I'm happy to have been of use. But how you came to be mixed up with such an objectionable man, I shall never understand, and for such a long time, too. What were you thinking of, Elizabeth?'

'He wasn't objectionable until quite recently,' Liz said, feeling that she had to defend Paul, for it was true, he had been good company until – well, she supposed until his life began to fall apart.

'Cornered rat syndrome,' said Mike, thinking along similar lines, but Dot was sceptical.

'He must have always had it in him,' she said, and Liz admitted that Alice had never liked him. She could have added, 'Or anyone else either,' but didn't.

'Very wise of Alice,' said Dot. 'Well, you'll be all right now, Michael will look after you.' She kissed Liz, and would simply have said goodnight to Mike but he seized her first and kissed her roundly. 'Good night Dorothy. Sweet dreams, you deserve them.'

What a very long day it had been, Dot thought, as she made her way upstairs. Long, and very interesting, not at all easy and leaving her with so many things to think about, although tomorrow would be soon enough for that. But it was good that Elizabeth had a practical man like Michael Wainwright to rely on, for on her own, if tonight was anything to go by, there was no telling what she would do next. A romantic, Elizabeth, she needed a man with his feet firmly on the ground.

Downstairs, it had gone very quiet. Exactly as it should be, Dot decided drowsily as her head at last hit the pillow; after the storm, the calm; after the battle, peace, and then sleep overcame her and she knew no more until morning came.

After her stressful weekend away, although on consideration she decided that she had very much enjoyed it in spite of its unexpected postscript, Dot was glad to get back to her native Dorset and her own home. Haymans was a welcoming place to return to, no bitter associations and Leanne there to greet her with a late lunch.

'And did you have a nice weekend, Mrs Nankervis?' Leanne asked, smiling. She found her employer a lot easier these days, without her stuffy friends around to make her show off.

'It was pleasant, but somewhat exhausting,' Dot told her. 'I shall just take my case upstairs, Leanne, and have a quick wash and then I will be down, if you would put everything on a tray. It was good of you to stay on.'

'Well, you've been good to us, too,' Leanne mentioned, and took herself back to the kitchen to check that all was well there.

Dot went upstairs, glowing from that brief appreciation, and carried her case into her bedroom. Laying it on the bed, she went over to the window and took a moment to look out, gloating over her beautiful view. Dartmoor was spectacular, she admitted that, but you really couldn't beat the rolling downland of her native land. She felt a warmth, and a pleasure that was unfamiliar but not, she thought, quite unknown. She had known it once in the distant past, now it was edging back. Perhaps she was a countrywoman at heart. Perhaps she was still Dee inside somewhere.

The field beyond the garden wall was greening over with new grass, it looked a lot cleaner now, she noticed with approval. There were three horses in it that hadn't been there on Friday, Dot looked at them with interest. Presumably they belonged to Francis Chillingworth; she wondered if he would allow Annabel to put her pony in with them, then if Carl and Susan bought a horsebox she could perhaps bring it on holiday and ride it round the farm, again if he would let her. For all Benita's kind offer, made when they discussed it a few days before the visit to Devon, it would be far more convenient than Shortlanesend. Francis was a stranger to Dot, but perhaps Benita would sound him out on the subject? Boats to keep Sebastian happy were, of course, more easily provided, both Susan and Deborah still had many contacts in the sailing world. Dot herself, up until now, had had only a peripheral interest in either pastime since her early Jerry days, and she had no idea that Susan's beautiful *Silver Spirit* now belonged to her own new neighbour.

She must network a bit, find out who did what around here, Valerie Harries would no doubt be happy to help her. She had invited Valerie to lunch tomorrow; it would be good to talk to someone about something other than committees and charity fairs. And then, later on in the afternoon, she had her first session with Andy Worrall, the tennis club professional. She looked forward to that with a lift of the heart that startled her.

Back downstairs again, she found Leanne in the kitchen and enquired about the cats. Debbie's scatty friend Penny should have been in to feed them, Dot hoped that she had remembered. 'I think they missed you,' Leanne told her. 'That girl came and fed them all right, and their appetites was all right too, but they seemed a bit ...' she paused, searching for a word, and came up with '*lonely*, when I come in this morning.'

'I see no sign of them now,' said Dot, looking around.

'They went off when I started with the vacuum,' Leanne told her.

Dot said that she would take her tray into the room that she thought of as her office, since it was there that she worked on her plans for the Dock Inn, and go through her post as she ate it; it wasn't something that she would have dreamed of doing in the past, and Leanne looked a little surprised. Dot was a little surprised herself, but the relaxed attitude of Liz and Mike had maybe begun to rub off on her during her short visit.

'And you must go home, Leanne,' she said, as she picked up the tray. 'I can clear away for myself, and put the things in the dishwasher. This looks very good,' she added, smiling. 'Now, you're already late, so off you go.'

Almost as if she wanted to get rid of me, Leanne thought as she went to her car, and maybe she wasn't so far wrong, either. Not that it was in any way personal; Dot had simply heard enough talk over the past twenty-four hours to make her long for silence. When she heard the door close behind Leanne, a great feeling of peace stole over her.

She enjoyed her informal lunch, and spent a pleasant afternoon checking through her plans for the decoration of the old inn, making sure that they were all ready to show to Mawgan the next time he came. Soon, now, the construction work would be completed and the decorators would move in; then, she would really come into her own. She was looking forward to it. Details of colours and styles in keeping with the period of the place were all in neat cardboard folders, one for each area of the building, and she had sketched out some suggestions for the furnishings, although Mawgan would have his own ideas about that. The fitting out of the kitchen was entirely his department. Tomorrow, before her lesson, she would check on progress; now that Tim had left for Italy it was all in her hands and she must draft a report.

So many interesting things to look forward to. Life had never been like this before, how much she had been missing!

In the evening, Debbie rang. 'Hi Mum! How was your weekend? Did you enjoy yourself?'

Dot gave the answer she had given before. 'It was interesting. I need time to sort out my impressions before I can say more than that.'

'But they were nice to you?' asked Debbie, quickly – sharply, even.

'Very nice, so you needn't jump to my defence. But it was all a bit overwhelming and I need to stand back.'

'But you'll see them again?'

'Isobel has already invited me. Now, is that why you were ringing or can I do something for you?'

'Actually, yes. Mawgan wants to do a check on the inn next week. We wondered if you'd like us to come and stay for a night, I'm longing to see your new house.'

'Both of you, or all three of you?' Dot asked, hardly daring to believe in it.

'All three of us, of course, Danny wants to see his Grandma. We'd come on Sunday, probably get there in the early evening as we can't rush off too early, and then stay until Monday evening. We'd have to leave for Cornwall after tea, we've both got to be back on the job Tuesday morning. Would that be OK?'

'It would be wonderful,' said Dot. They spoke for a few more minutes, and then Debbie said, 'Got to go Mum, things to attend to. But I'll see you in less than a week, and perhaps you'll know by then what you really think.'

'I believe there is every possibility,' said Dot. They said goodnight and she replaced the phone on its rest, carefully as if by being careful she wouldn't quite break the connection. Happiness, she thought, is such a fragile thing. So easily given, so easily wrecked. She would look forward to seeing Debbie and Daniel, it would be a treat, however briefly, to have them under her new roof. She hoped that Debbie would like Haymans, for although Mawgan had seen it on his last flying visit, this would be the first time he had brought her with him. That would be because of Tim, of course, she realised that. Not because he mistrusted Debbie, but because he wanted Tim to be cured of his infatuation, and parading her in front of him before he had something new to distract him would be a backward step; Mawgan was a surprising man. She wondered, fleetingly, if the private detective she had recommended had found any trace of the missing sister. She remembered his mother's face at the christening, and the hopelessness in her voice. They hadn't even been able to hold a funeral, if so be she was dead. If she was, they might never know. If she was alive, the pain of her continuing silence must eat like acid into the pleasure of every family occasion. Dot wasn't given to imagining things, but the recollection of her talk with Cally that day brought a lump into her throat. She turned to Secret Sam, who had strolled in earlier, ignored her completely, and taken up his position in her favourite armchair.

'I'm becoming a silly, sentimental old woman!' she told him. 'Now, you may move over and make room for me. It's time for the News.'

There had been no sign of Catto yet, but then, he had always been the more cautious of the two, in spite of his size. Liz had told her that Tib could sulk for several days after she had been away if he was in the mood, so she wouldn't worry about him, he could get over it on his own. If he had been turning up for meals, there was nothing wrong. She picked up Secret Sam and settled down with him purring on her knee to watch the television.

Catto returned in his own good time. He didn't appear at cat supper time, and Dot went to bed without seeing him and making her peace, but much later, when she got up from her bed to go to the bathroom, she came back to find him curled up on the duvet. She was amazed at how pleased she was to see him.

'I see,' she said. 'I left the kitchen door open and you seized your chance. Well you needn't think you're spending the night *there*, because you're not!' She leaned over to stroke him and lift him up to put him out on the landing, but he rolled over beguilingly, fat paws in the air, and began to purr, and she paused. This room, she thought, must have belonged to one of the boys. Perhaps he was used to sleeping here with his owner, and had been missing him: he certainly hadn't adapted to the new order as swiftly as his companion. Then she reproved herself firmly for allowing herself to be conned by a cat, however beautiful, and made another attempt to shift him. It was like trying to move an elephant. *Not*, said the voice of her *alter ego* Dee, pedantically, *that you have ever tried to shift an elephant.* Cat and woman looked at each other then Dot – or maybe it was Dee – shrugged her shoulders. 'Oh all right, stay then! But you're going to have to shift up, you cannot occupy the very centre of a double bed.' And how dumb was that, talking to an animal?

She set the bedroom door ajar in case her companion wanted to go out before dawn, and slipped back into bed, glad that none of her friends or worse, her children, could see her. She and Catto snuggled up together and very soon they were both fast asleep.

Early in the morning, Dee woke up. She lay for a moment, eyes closed against the growing light of a rosy dawn, thinking, I haven't slept as well as that since I don't know when! She stretched and yawned, and sat up, and her bedfellow made a sleepy protest.

'So you're still here, are you?' She tried not to feel pleased. He was a cat. *Just* a cat. Then she got out of bed and threw back the curtains to greet the misty dawn, before turning to lift the sleepy cat to send him on his way downstairs. But then she hesitated, the cat in her arms, and stood admiring the early morning world outside the window instead.

In the field the horses waded knee deep in swirls of silvery-pink vapour; trees and hedges stood out darkly around it and the downs beyond were almost lost in the light that reflected from low-lying mist. Above, the orange ball of the sun sat low in a golden sky, thin streaks of cloud reflecting the fiery light. It was amazingly beautiful.

'Red sky in the morning, sailor's warning,' Dee said to the cat, stroking his silky back and listening to the rewarding purr. She tucked his furry head under her chin so that his whiskers tickled her cheek and on impulse dipped her head to put a quick kiss between his tufted ears. Then she stood for another few minutes drinking in the scene like a fine wine, content and at peace. This lovely house was hers; she had new friends, family – too much family, indeed, both new and old these days – something rewarding to occupy her time. New experiences to enjoy, new haunts to discover, a reason to look forward to every day. She was going to be on television, however fleetingly, and that she could never have imagined. She was going to play tennis once more, and to crown it all she had two friendly little animals to live with her and share her quiet evenings; she already loved them, and the grandchildren would love them too, they had a kitten of their own.

Below her on the terrace, she could see Secret Sam now, tail held low, slinking across the stones in search of trouble, very much on the prowl, and smiled; it was easy to see how he came by his name.

She was a fortunate woman, more fortunate than she had deserved.

Perhaps she would go on that world cruise, but then again, why bother? She had everything already that she could possibly want.

Dee stayed there for some time, the purring cat in her arms, and the happiness that life had finally handed her rose up in her heart and spread its warmth with the rising sun.